Predators in the Wild

Anacondas

by Anne Welsbacher

Consultants:
The Staff of Black Hills Reptile Gardens
Rapid City, South Dakota

CAPSTONE
HIGH-INTEREST
BOOKS

an imprint of Capstone
Mankato, Minnesc

Capstone High-Interest Books are published by Capstone Press
151 Good Counsel Drive, P.O. Box 669, Mankato, Minnesota 56002
http://www.capstone-press.com

Library of Congress Cataloging-in-Publication Data
Welsbacher, Anne, 1955–
    Anacondas/by Anne Welsbacher.
    p. cm.—(Predators in the wild)
    Includes bibliographical references (p. 31) and index.
    ISBN 0-7368-0785-3
    1. Anaconda—Juvenile literature. [1. Anaconda. 2. Snakes.] I. Title.
II. Series.
QL666.O63 W45 2001
597.96–dc21   00-009932

Summary: Describes anacondas, their habits, where they live, their hunting
methods, and how they exist in the world of people.

Editorial Credits
Blake Hoena, editor; Karen Risch, product planning editor; Timothy Halldin,
    cover designer and illustrator; Katy Kudela, photo researcher

Photo Credits
Allen Blake Sheldon, 17 (bottom left)
Bruce Coleman Inc./Russell A. Mittermeier, 8; Leonard Lee Rue III, 17
    (top left); Joe McDonald 17 (bottom right); Wolfgang Bayer, 20; Erwin
    and Peggy Bauer, 21, 22
Doug Wechsler, cover
Francois Gohier, 16, 29
Joe McDonald, 10, 11, 12
Michael Cardwell/Extreme Wildlife Photography, 6
Robert Winslow/The Viesti Collection, Inc., 14, 15
Sean Fitzgerald, 17 (top right)
Visuals Unlimited/Mary Ann McDonald, 9; Jim Merli, 18; Cheryl A. Ertelt, 24, 27

Table of Contents

Features

Common names: Anaconda; also called water boa because of its ability to swim.

Scientific names: *Eunectes murinus* (green anaconda)
Eunectes notaeus (yellow anaconda)

Length: Most anacondas are 10 to 20 feet (3 to 6.1 meters) long.

Width: Anacondas can be 12 to 14 inches (30 to 36 centimeters) wide.

Weight: In the wild, adult anacondas often weigh more than 200 pounds (90 kilograms). In captivity, they may weigh more than 300 pounds (140 kilograms).

Life span:	Anacondas may live as long as 30 years.
Habitat:	Anacondas live in South America. They are found in marshes, swamps, and near the banks of streams and rivers.
Prey:	Anacondas feed on fish, birds, small mammals, turtles, lizards, deer, and pigs. Some anacondas' diets consist largely of small alligators called caiman.
Eating habits:	Anacondas suffocate their prey through constriction. They then eat their prey whole. Anacondas can live months without eating.

In This Chapter:

* Anacondas are reptiles.

* Anacondas are the world's heaviest snakes.

* Anacondas live in South America.

Chapter 1

Anacondas

Anacondas are among the world's largest and strongest snakes. They can weigh as much as an adult person. Strong neck and body muscles help them catch and kill their prey.

Snake Species

All snakes are reptiles. Other reptiles include lizards, alligators, crocodiles, and turtles.

Snakes are divided into families. These scientific groups separate the different types of snakes. Anacondas are in the Boidae family. Snakes in this group squeeze their prey to death. The Boidae family also includes boa constrictors and pythons.

Anaconda Size

Herpetologist William Lamar reported finding one of the longest anacondas. Herpetologists study amphibians and reptiles. In 1978, Lamar found an anaconda that was 24 feet, 7 inches (7.5 meters) long. He found this snake in Columbia, South America.

Families are further divided into genera. Anacondas are in the *Eunectes* genus. There are three species of anacondas within the *Eunectes* genus. The two most common anaconda species are *Eunectes murinus* and *Eunectes notaeus*. These snakes also are known as the green anaconda and the yellow anaconda.

Size

Green anacondas grow larger than yellow anacondas. Adult green anacondas can weigh more than 200 pounds (90 kilograms) in the wild. They are the world's heaviest snakes. Green anacondas in zoos may weigh more than 300 pounds (140 kilograms). An average yellow anaconda weighs 10 to 20 pounds (4.5 to 9.1 kilograms).

Yellow anacondas are smaller than green anacondas.

Anacondas are among the longest snakes. Only reticulated pythons grow longer. Some green anacondas can grow as long as 20 feet (6.1 meters) or more. Yellow anacondas may grow as long as 10 feet (3 meters) or more. Female anacondas grow larger than males.

Anacondas use the scales on their undersides to move.

Appearances

Green anacondas are olive-green or brown in color. Round black spots line their backs and sides. The spots on their sides have small yellow marks in them. Anacondas' undersides are a light shade of yellow or cream in color.

Anacondas also have dark stripes that run from their eyes to their upper jaws.

Yellow anacondas look similar to green anacondas. But their skin is a shade of yellow.

Scales

Like all snakes, anacondas have scales. Their scales are dry and shiny. Unlike fish scales, snake scales actually are folds of skin.

Anacondas use the scales on their undersides to move. These large scales are called scutes. They are lined up in rows. Scutes grip the ground as an anaconda's strong muscles pull on them. This action moves the anaconda's body forward.

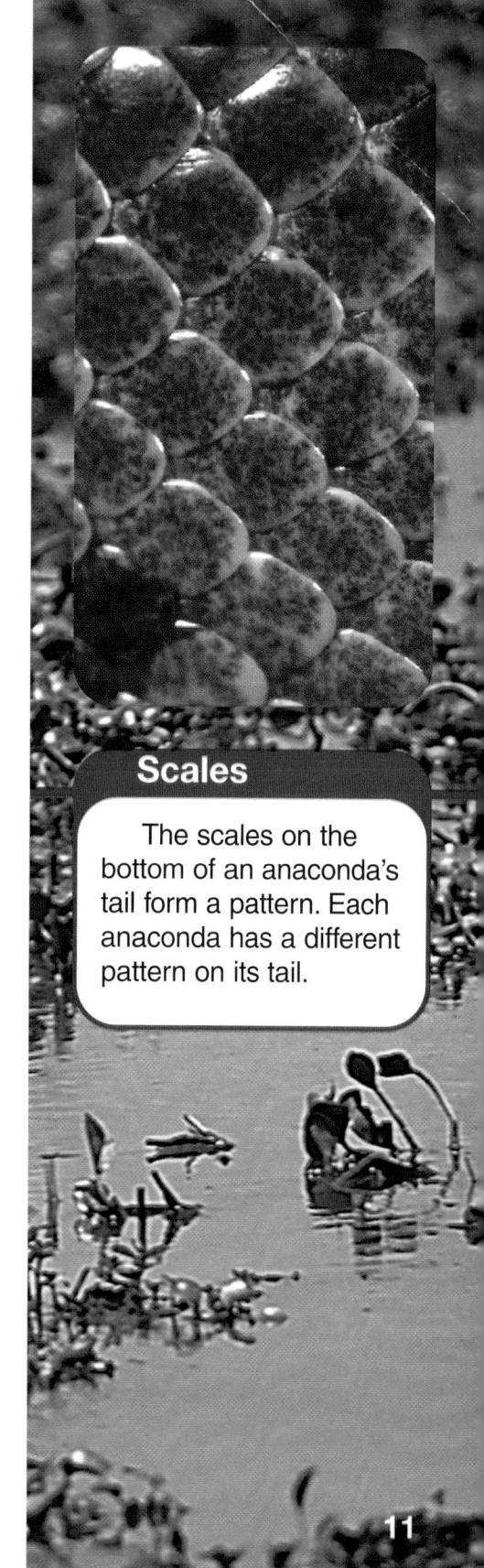

Scales

The scales on the bottom of an anaconda's tail form a pattern. Each anaconda has a different pattern on its tail.

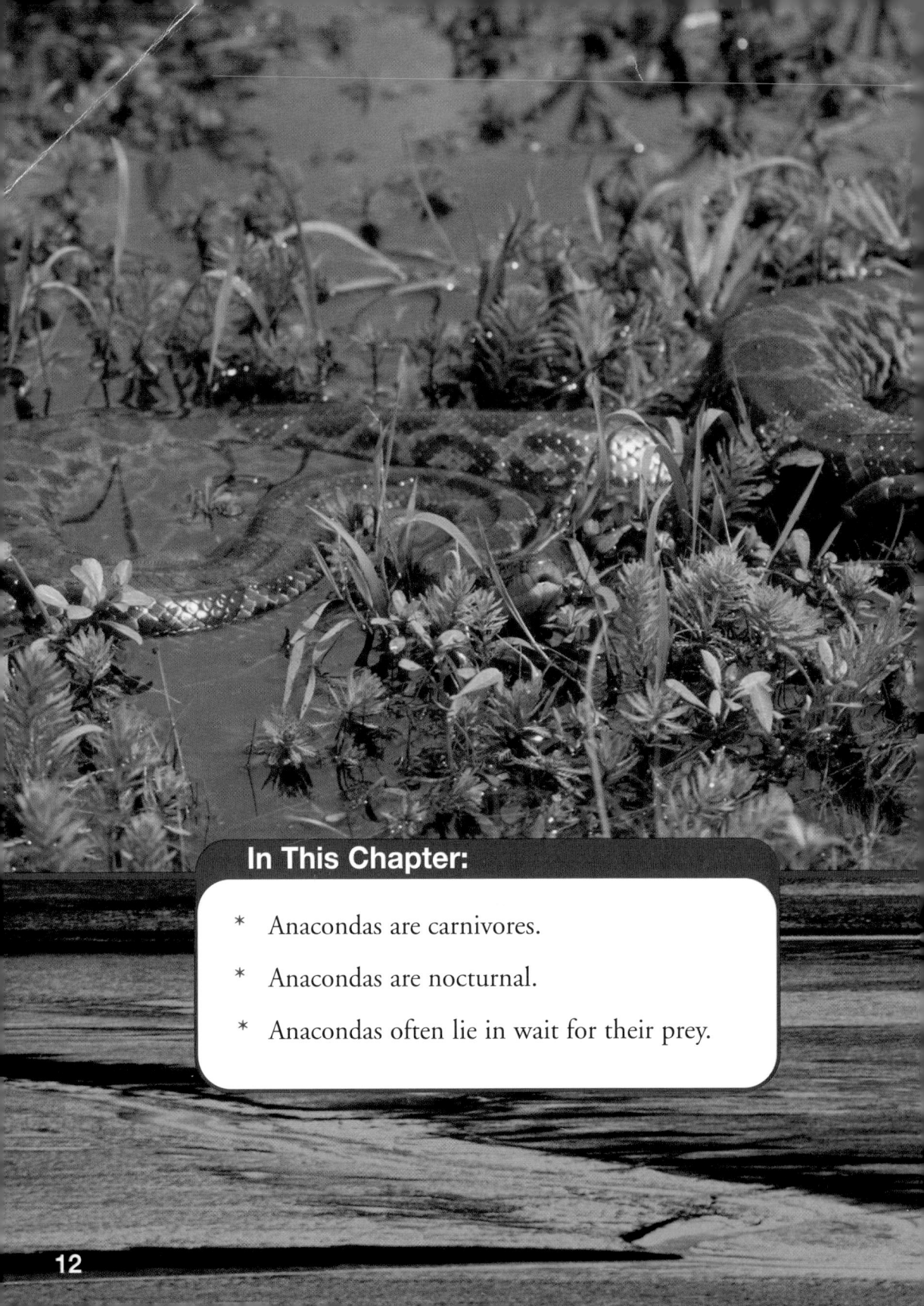

In This Chapter:

* Anacondas are carnivores.

* Anacondas are nocturnal.

* Anacondas often lie in wait for their prey.

Chapter 2

The Hunt

Anacondas are carnivores. They eat meat.
They often eat young caimans. These small
alligators live in South America.

Anacondas eat many types of animals.
They may eat turtles and other reptiles.
Their prey also includes small mammals, fish,
and birds. Anacondas may even eat larger
mammals such as pigs and deer.

Anacondas often sneak up on their prey.

Hunting Habits

Anacondas are nocturnal. They are most active at night. During the day, they often rest in the mud along river banks or in swamps. They also may burrow into holes. Young anacondas sometimes rest in trees.

Anacondas usually stay in slow-moving water. These areas include swamps, marshes, and some rivers. Slow-moving water often is muddy. It is easier for anacondas to hide in muddy water.

Anacondas move slowly. They must sneak up on their prey. Anacondas often wait for prey to come to the water to drink. They wait in shallow water near shore.

Anacondas' coloring and dark spots help camouflage them. Their coloring blends with their surroundings. Animals often do not see anacondas until they strike.

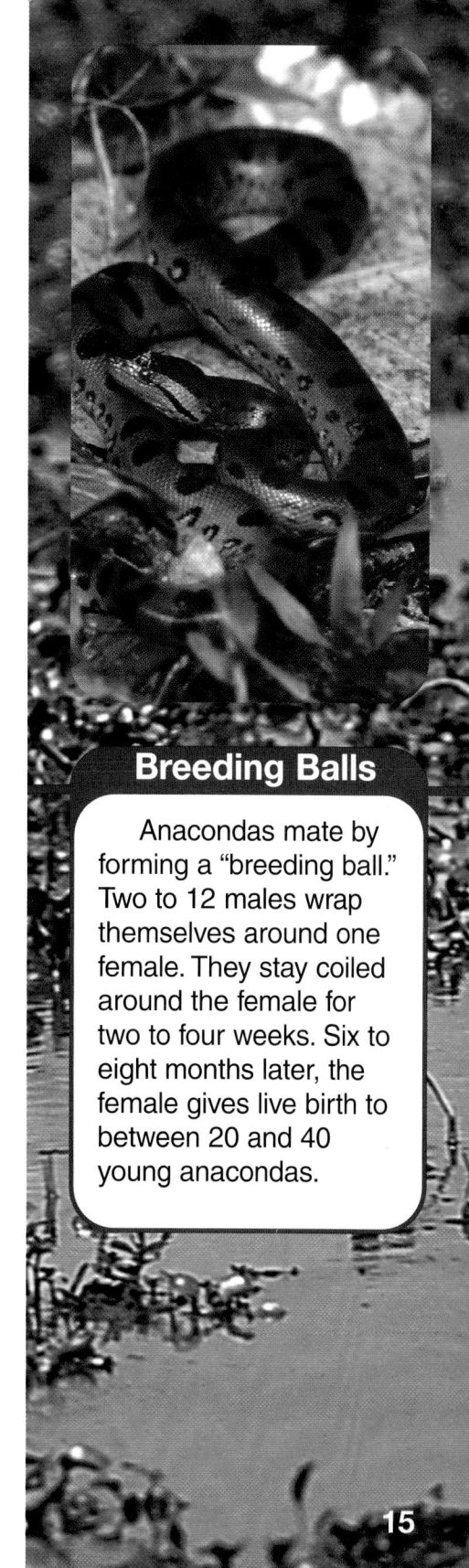

Breeding Balls

Anacondas mate by forming a "breeding ball." Two to 12 males wrap themselves around one female. They stay coiled around the female for two to four weeks. Six to eight months later, the female gives live birth to between 20 and 40 young anacondas.

Anacondas use their Jacobson's organ to smell.

Senses for Hunting

Anacondas cannot see well. But they are able to notice shapes and movement. This ability helps them find prey.

Anacondas cannot hear sounds as people do. Instead, they feel vibrations in the ground, air, or water. These sensations help anacondas know when prey is near.

The Jacobson's organ is located on the roof of an anaconda's mouth. This organ is used to smell. An anaconda flicks out its forked tongue to collect scents in the air and on the ground. The tongue carries the scents to the Jacobson's organ. An anaconda can smell prey with its Jacobson's organ. A male anaconda also can smell females that are ready to mate.

What Anacondas Eat

Birds

Small mammals

Turtles

Caimans

In This Chapter:

*   Anacondas have curved teeth.

*   Anacondas suffocate their prey.

*   Anacondas swallow their prey whole.

Chapter 3

The Kill

Anacondas' teeth are curved toward the back of their throats. This shape helps anacondas hold on to their prey. Anacondas' teeth sink deeper into prey's skin as their prey struggles to escape. Few animals escape once an anaconda bites them.

Constriction

Anacondas wrap their muscular bodies around their prey. They then squeeze the animals that they catch. Anacondas constrict their bodies each time their prey breathes out. This movement prevents their prey from taking another breath. These animals then suffocate and die when they can no longer breathe.

Anacondas often hunt near water. They may drown their prey. Anacondas drag their prey underwater. This action prevents animals from breathing.

Swallowing Prey

Anacondas swallow their prey whole. They also swallow their prey head first. It is easier for anacondas to swallow prey this way. The animal's limbs fold neatly against its body.

An anaconda opens its mouth wide as it begins to swallow its prey. Ligaments connect an anaconda's upper and lower jaws. These stretchy bands of tissue allow an anaconda's jaws to separate. They also allow an anaconda to swallow prey that is much larger than its mouth.

Anacondas wrap themselves around their prey.

Anacondas eat their prey whole.

Muscles in an anaconda's mouth slowly push its prey down its throat. It can take an anaconda several hours to swallow large prey. Anacondas have a windpipe on the bottom of their mouth. This tube allows them to breathe while swallowing prey.

Anacondas rest after swallowing large prey.

Digesting Food

Acids in an anaconda's stomach digest its prey. These chemicals break down food to be used by the anaconda's body. This action may take several days or weeks with large prey. Anacondas rest while digesting food. Anacondas can go several months without eating after a large meal.

The acids in an anaconda's stomach are very strong. Anacondas can digest almost every part of their prey except for hair and teeth. They can even digest bones.

Myth: People have reported finding anacondas 30 feet (9.1 meters) long or longer. In 1948, a 156-foot (48-meter) anaconda was claimed to have knocked over buildings.

Fact: Anacondas usually do not grow longer than 20 feet (6.1 meters). William Lamar recorded finding one of the longest anacondas. It was 24 feet, 7 inches (7.5 meters) long.

Myth: Anacondas hypnotize prey.

Fact: Some small animals freeze when a predator is near. They hope their lack of movement will prevent them from being seen.

Myth: Anacondas' skin is slimy.

Fact: Anacondas' skin actually is dry and shiny.

In This Chapter:

* People kill anacondas for their skin.

* People tell many false stories about anacondas.

* Anacondas do not make good pets.

Chapter 4

n the World of People

Anacondas live in northern and central South America. They often live in swamps and marshes near the Amazon and Orinoco Rivers. These areas include the countries of Brazil, Columbia, and Venezuela.

Anacondas stay near rivers and swamps in the jungle. They avoid people and are good at hiding.

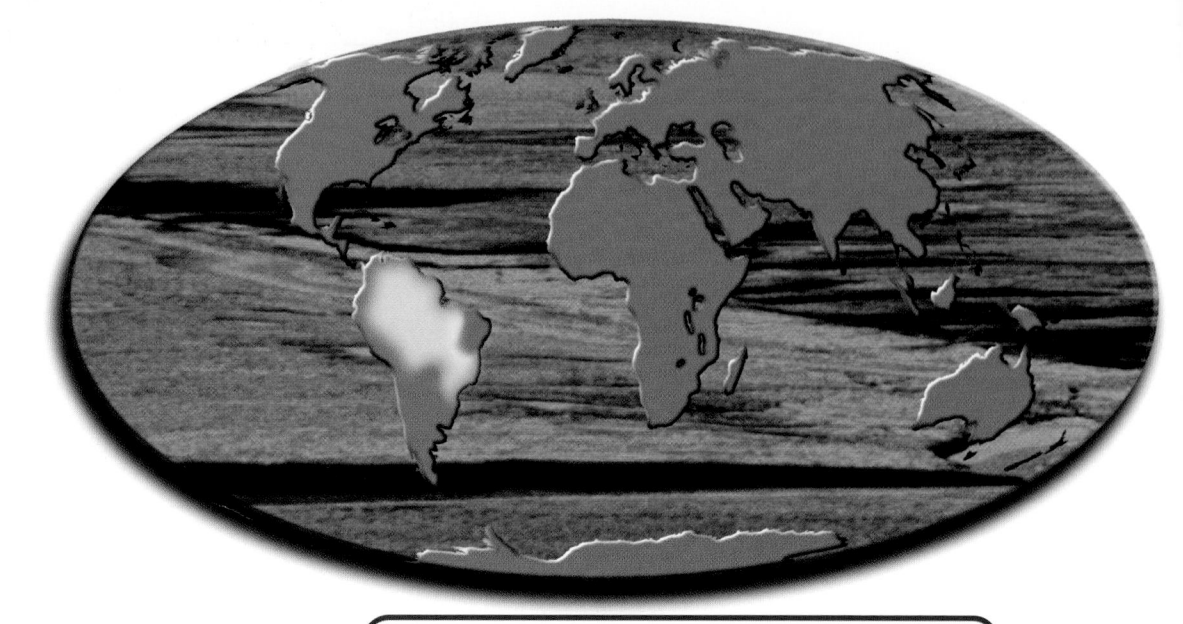

Yellow represents the anaconda's range.

Anacondas' Defenses

Anacondas are large and strong. They have few natural predators. Alligators sometimes catch and eat anacondas. Large birds may eat young anacondas.

Anacondas move slowly on land and cannot easily escape predators. But their coloring helps hide them from predators. They also can swim away from predators. Anacondas hiss or pretend to strike to defend themselves. Anacondas also may bite.

Anaconda Stories

Many people fear anacondas because of myths told about them. Many false stories have been told about anacondas growing to more than 100 feet (30 meters) long. But anacondas seldom grow to be more than 20 feet (6.1 meters) long.

Other stories claim that anacondas attack people. Some people have been attacked by anacondas. But anacondas do not hunt animals that they cannot swallow. Most people are too large for anacondas to eat.

There are many reasons to be careful around anacondas. Most experts believe that anacondas are ill tempered. They often bite people who handle them. Their bites do not kill. But their sharp, curved teeth can seriously injure a person. Scientists who study these snakes often are bitten. Zookeepers never work with large anacondas alone.

Habitat

Anacondas are called water boas because they live in and near water. Anacondas are well suited for living in water. Their eyes and nostrils are on the top of their heads. This positioning helps them see and breathe while they swim. Anacondas swim with their bodies almost completely underwater.

Anacondas and People

Some people hunt snakes for their skins. The skins are used to make shoes, purses, and belts. Thousands of anacondas are killed for their skins each year.

Ranchers in South America may shoot anacondas. These people are afraid anacondas may eat their farm animals.

People sometimes catch wild snakes to sell as pets. Most South American countries do not allow anacondas to be captured and sold as pets. But people smuggle hundreds of anacondas out of these countries. These people then illegally sell anacondas as pets in other countries.

Anaconda Survival

Scientists hope to learn more about anacondas. But little is known about these snakes because they hide themselves so well.

Scientists hope to learn how many anacondas live in the wild. They want to learn whether anacondas are in danger of becoming threatened. But most scientists believe that anacondas are not in danger of disappearing from the wild.

People should not handle large anacondas alone.

acid (ASS-id)—a substance in an animal's stomach that helps it break down food

camouflage (KAM-uh-flahzh)—coloring or covering that makes animals, people, and objects look like their surroundings

carnivore (KAR-nuh-vor)—an animal that eats meat

constrict (kuhn-STRIKT)—to squeeze; anacondas kill their prey by squeezing them until they suffocate.

digest (dye-JEST)—to break down food so that it can be absorbed into the blood and used by the body

herpetologist (hur-pah-TAH-luh-gist)—a scientist who studies reptiles and amphibians

predator (PRED-uh-tur)—an animal that lives by hunting other animals for food

suffocate (SUHF-uh-kate)—to kill by cutting off the supply of air or oxygen; anacondas suffocate their prey.

To Learn More

MacDonald, Mary Ann. *Anacondas.* Chanhassen, Minn.: Child's World, 1999.

Martin, James. *Boa Constrictors.* Animals & the Environment. Mankato, Minn.: Capstone Books, 1996.

Mattison, Christopher. *Snake.* New York: DK Publishing, 1999.

Steele, Christy. *Anacondas.* Animals of the Rain Forest. Austin, Texas: Steadwell Books, 2000.

Useful Addresses

Indianapolis Zoo
1200 West Washington Street
Indianapolis, IN 46222

Black Hills Reptile Gardens
P.O. Box 620
Rapid City, SD 57709

Rainforest Reptile
  Refuge Society
1395 176th Street
Surrey, BC V4P 3H4
Canada

Society for the Study of
  Amphibians and Reptiles
Department of Biology
St. Louis University
3507 Laclede Avenue
St. Louis, MO 63103-2010

Internet Sites

Enchanted Learning: Anacondas
http://www.EnchantedLearning.com/subjects/
reptiles/snakes/Anacondacoloring.shtml

Nashville Zoo: Anaconda
http://www.nashvillezoo.org/anaconda.htm

Reptile Gardens
http://www.reptile-gardens.com

Index

56721578R00425

ALSO BY SUSAN GABRIEL

FICTION

The Wildflower Trilogy:
The Secret Sense of Wildflower
(a Best Book of 2012 – Kirkus Reviews)
Lily's Song
Daisy's Fortune

Trueluck Summer

Temple Secrets Series:
Temple Secrets
Gullah Secrets

Grace, Grits and Ghosts: Southern Short Stories
Seeking Sara Summers
Circle of the Ancestors
Quentin & the Cave Boy

NONFICTION

Fearless Writing for Women:
Extreme Encouragement & Writing Inspiration

Available at all booksellers
in print, ebook and audio formats.

potential heirs must reveal the leaker before the book's secrets tear the sleepy town apart.

Temple Secrets is a hilarious women's fiction novel with a Southern gothic flair. If you like wisecracking humor, headstrong women, and twisty mysteries, then you'll love Susan Gabriel's compelling tale of an unconventional inheritance.

Buy *Temple Secrets* and start unlocking the mysteries today!

Available in paperback, ebook and audiobook.

GULLAH SECRETS: Sequel to Temple Secrets

A family legacy in danger. A stranger in their midst. Do they have the strength to survive the gathering storm of secrets?

For the Temple women, the winds of change are blowing. And if they're not careful, it could sweep them all away…

Gullah Secrets is the sequel to the bestselling novel *Temple Secrets*. If you like Southern gothic literature, characters you won't want to close the cover on, and locations steeped in history, then you'll love this hilarious and warmhearted saga.

TEMPLE SECRETS & GULLAH SECRETS

TWO-BOOK BOX SET ALSO AVAILABLE

TEMPLE SECRETS

A town held together with secrets. A wealthy widow looking for an heir. One choice could shame high society into submission.

Eighty-year-old Southern aristocrat Iris Temple's health may be failing, but her wit is as sharp as ever. Before she joins her ancestral ghosts, she must pick an heir to take over her sprawling estate—and the book of secrets that's kept her family in power for generations. But between her scheming son, her estranged daughter who abandoned Savannah years ago, and her illegitimate half-sister, she's working with slim pickings.

While only her half-sister and cook have put up with her outlandish diet and constant bickering, she can't ignore the powerful hold her late father's 100-year-old mistress has over the two women. When someone leaks embarrassing snippets from the Temple family book, she half suspects the voodoo-practicing centenarian as the elites of Savannah teeter on the edge of revolt. With Iris fading fast, her ragtag bunch of

ABOUT THE AUTHOR

Susan Gabriel is an Amazon and Nook #1 bestselling author who lives in the mountains of North Carolina. Her novel, *The Secret Sense of Wildflower,* earned a starred review ("for books of remarkable merit") from Kirkus Reviews and was selected as one of their Best Books of 2012.

She is also the author of *Temple Secrets, Gullah Secrets, Trueluck Summer, Grace, Grits & Ghosts: Southern Short Stories* and other books. Discover more at SusanGabriel.com.

THE WILDFLOWER TRILOGY

ALSO BY SUSAN GABRIEL

FICTION

The Wildflower Trilogy:

The Secret Sense of Wildflower

(a Best Book of 2012 – Kirkus Reviews)

Lily's Song

Daisy's Fortune

Trueluck Summer

Temple Secrets Series:

Temple Secrets

Gullah Secrets

Grace, Grits and Ghosts: Southern Short Stories

Seeking Sara Summers

Circle of the Ancestors

Quentin & the Cave Boy

NONFICTION

Fearless Writing for Women:

Extreme Encouragement & Writing Inspiration

Available at all booksellers in print, ebook and audio formats.

THE WILDFLOWER TRILOGY

SUSAN GABRIEL

WILD LILY ARTS

ISBN: 978-0-9981050-3- 1

Cover design by Lizzie Gardiner, lizziegardiner.co.uk

Wild Lily Arts

Printed in the United States of America

The Secret Sense
of
Wildflower

A NOVEL BY

SUSAN
GABRIEL

A "Best Book of 2012"

Library of Congress Control Number: 2012936549

ISBN: 978-0-9835882-3-8

Wild Lily Arts

Printed in the United States of America.

For my daughters
Krista and Stacey

Consider the lilies of the field, how they grow:
they neither toil nor spin;
and yet I say to you that even Solomon in all his glory
was not arrayed like one of these.

Matthew 6:28-29

CHAPTER ONE

There are two things I am afraid of. One is dying young. The other is Johnny Monroe. Whenever I see him I get a creepy feeling that crawls up the length of my spine. Daddy used to say that fear is a friend that teaches us life isn't to be played with. Friends like this I can live without.

On my way to the graveyard I run into Johnny standing by the road. His smile shows shreds of chewing tobacco caked around the edges of his teeth. But the scariest thing is the look in his eyes when he sees me or my sisters. He is like a wildcat stalking his next meal. People living in the mountains know that anytime you come across a wildcat you don't look it in the eye or make sudden moves. Every time I see Johnny Monroe I slow down and stare at the tops of my shoes.

"Hey, Louisa May." Johnny drawls out my name. At sixteen, he is nearly four years older than me, and is a good six inches taller, even slouched. He dropped out of school in the sixth grade and spends a lot of time just standing around.

I wish I'd turned back when it first occurred to me. Aunt Sadie, Daddy's sister, calls this my secret sense. The secret sense is a

nudge from somewhere deep inside that keeps you out of harm's way if you listen to it. Aunt Sadie is full of ideas that most people don't cater to. Not to mention that she never married, a fact that makes some people nervous, and sometimes wears a fedora. Sadie collects herbs and roots to make mountain remedies. People come from all over to have her doctor them with red clover blossoms and honey to cure their whooping cough or to get catnip mint to soothe their colicky babies. She also makes the best blackberry wine in three counties.

"What's the matter, girl, you deaf?" Johnny says.

"I'm not talking to you," I hiss behind clinched teeth.

"But you're talking to me right now," he says. He grins.

"Go away," I say. I focus on the worn spot at the end of my shoe and roll my shoulders forward so Johnny will stop staring at my chest, even though there's nothing much to stare at.

"Where's that sister of yours?" Johnny asks.

I know he means Meg. Johnny asks after her every chance he gets.

"I wouldn't mind getting her out behind those bushes. She's not scrawny like you are, Louisa May." Johnny laughs.

An empty tin can sits on the ground next to him and he spits a mouthful of tobacco juice toward the can. It pings against the side. Only Johnny would make a sport of spitting into a can with "cling peaches" written on the side. He could just as well spit on the road, but he appears to take pride in the "ping," like a dart thrower hitting the bright red bull's-eye in the center of the board.

"Maybe I should just settle for scrawny," he says. But it seems he's talking more to himself than to me.

To keep the words from spewing out, I bite my bottom lip hard. I want to call Johnny a low-life and a good-for-nothing, which is exactly what he is. Instead, I shuffle forward and don't look up again until I reach the bend in the road. When I glance back Johnny is still watching me and licks his lips.

Before Johnny, I can't say I ever hated anyone. I've come close a couple of times, with Doc Lester and Preacher Evans, who have the obnoxious habit of acting like they are better than everybody else. They remind me of gnats and I just want to take a newspaper and shoo them away. But Johnny is more like a black widow spider. He stands on that corner every day hoping some unsuspecting girl will fall into his web.

In my weaker moments, I feel sorry for Johnny. Life must be desperate and lonely standing on that road, kicking rocks all day. Not to mention that he doesn't have a mother. Word is she died from tuberculosis when he was nine. Mama said once that his old man hates kids and would just as soon sell them if he could get a decent price.

"Hey, girl," Johnny calls after me. "Come back here and talk." But I know better than to look back.

Johnny has a sister my age named Ruby and another sister named Melody who is probably around ten by now. Ruby doesn't come to school anymore, just stays home to cook and clean for Johnny and the old man. Her younger sister Melody never even started school. I've tried to talk to Ruby a few times, but she won't have any part of people around here. Every time I see her she looks like she's made best friends with misery. She is as slight as a thirteen-year-old girl can be, but she drags herself around like she carries a fifty pound sack of potatoes on her back.

Meanwhile, Johnny stands out on that road like he's waiting for his mother to come back and make his life different than it is. That doesn't make the things he says to me right, or make Meg want to give him the time of day, but in a way I think I understand why Johnny is stuck on that road. He's waiting for a better life to show up since he's been dealt such a crummy one.

If Daddy was here he'd knock Johnny Monroe's rotten teeth right out of his head for looking at me the way Johnny does. But Daddy is one of those markers in the graveyard where if you

subtract the years, you know he was thirty-eight when he died almost a year ago. Every few days I walk up the hill and sit with him and tell him about things in my life so we don't lose touch. That's where I'm headed right now. I won't tell him about Johnny, though, because I wouldn't want him to worry.

Sometimes when I'm at the graveyard I'll hear Daddy talking back to me. Mama would say that's just my imagination working overtime, but Sadie would say it's the secret sense. I'm grateful for it, whatever it is. If we run out of things to catch up on, I'll ask Daddy to talk to God for me. Mainly I have questions, like does a praying mantis really pray? And why does God send lightning to hit old dead trees? And why did Johnny Monroe have to end up here in Katy's Ridge? I've found a favorite sitting spot by Daddy's grave so I can wait for him and God to answer. They haven't so far, but I have time to wait. Time is about the only thing I have plenty of in Katy's Ridge. That, and chigger bites.

With Johnny out of sight, I quit looking at my shoes, pull back my shoulders and approach the shortcut I found to Daddy's final resting place. The old trail meanders up the mountain and to the far corner of the graveyard where they pile all the dead flowers. The path is so overgrown in spots I have to guess which way it points. And it has a footbridge built across the highest point of the stream that has only one sturdy board left. The rest I wouldn't trust to hold a cricket.

A dogwood tree on the shady side of the hill marks the beginning of the trail. That old dogwood is twisted and tangled from fighting its way toward sunlight. But all that struggling has made it beautiful. Thick underbrush hides the trail behind it like a locked gate. As far as I know, nobody else is aware of this old path. With three older sisters, who have already done everything before me, having a secret way through the woods is like finally having something of my own.

I look all around to make sure no one is watching before I enter

the path. Gossip travels the grapevine in Katy's Ridge like Western Union telegrams. If anybody sees me, Mama will know in a matter of minutes. Minding your own business isn't the way of mountain people in Tennessee in 1941, though sometimes I wish it was.

The coast clear, I duck behind the tree and take the secret path. The trail travels a steep hill before it levels out and dips down into the valley again. The footbridge is about halfway between home and the graveyard.

At the bridge, I do my good luck ritual that I've used since I was a little girl. It has three parts. Daddy used to say that threes always happen in fairy tales: three wishes, three ogres, three sisters. Whenever a "three" shows up you can expect some kind of magic to take place. No matter how old I get, I'll use magic, luck, or my own prayer meeting, if it means I get safely across that bridge.

My sister, Meg, gave me a rabbit's foot key chain from Woolworth's last Christmas. I retrieve it from my pocket and squeeze out a dose of good luck. Then I ask Daddy to watch out for me, calling on God and his angels if need be. After that I kiss the dime-sized gold medallion that I have worn around my neck ever since Daddy died. The medallion used to belong to my Grandma McAllister. Engraved on it is a picture of the baby Jesus sitting on his mother's lap. I like looking at the sweet smile on her face on account of my mother hardly ever smiles anymore.

All us girls got something after Grandma McAllister died. Jo got fancy doilies and things, Amy got some of her books and Meg got a set of her dishes. I would have liked to have the books, since I've been a tomboy most of my life and was never much of a jewelry person. But Daddy said, since I got the medallion, that I was the luckiest one because Jesus' mother watches out for people. Standing at the bridge, this seems as good a time as any for her to watch out for me.

Before they moved to the United States, the McAllister's were all Catholic. Sometimes I would see Daddy cross himself the way

the Catholics do. It was usually when nobody else was around. Mama's folks were Lutheran. But after Mama and Daddy moved to Katy's Ridge they joined the Baptists just to keep the peace. At least that's how Daddy put it.

Little Women is Mama's favorite book. A worn copy of it sits on her dresser right next to the King James Bible. I was named after the lady who wrote it, Louisa May Alcott. Destiny must have rewarded Mama for her devotion to the book because she gave Daddy four daughters, just like the March family in the book. My older sisters, Amy, Jo, and Meg, were each named after somebody in the book. Another sister, Beth, died two days after she was born. This explains how I ended up with the name Louisa May, because all the good names were already taken.

I am the youngest McAllister. Jo and Amy, my two older sisters, each got married last spring and live in Katy's Ridge, right down the road from our house. Meg, my closest sister in age, graduated from Rocky Bluff High School last year but still lives at home and works at the Woolworth's store in the town of Rocky Bluff. I like having Meg around because she smoothes things out between Mama and me. Even on our best days, we are like vinegar and soda, always reacting. When Meg isn't there, Mama and I do our level best to avoid each other.

The board of the old footbridge creaks and sways when I step onto it and I have to hold out my arms to steady myself. I shot up like a weed last year, from 4 feet, seven inches to 5 feet 3 and I am still not used to this willowy version of myself.

As far as I can tell, the secret to not falling is to keep your arms out and your feet moving in a straight line, which is probably the one good thing that has come from looking at my shoes so much around Johnny Monroe. While I summon my courage, I am reminded of the pictures I saw once of trapeze artists crossing a wire at a circus. My knees start to shake and I tell them to stop. If I'm not careful I could shake myself right into an early grave. I

bite my lip, which for some odd reason also helps me keep my balance.

Even though I am nearly thirteen years of age, if Mama knew I was crossing this old bridge she'd give me a good talking to, using all three of my given names while she did.

Louisa May McAllister, what were you thinking? Don't you know you could fall in and bust your head against the rocks? You'd be dead in an instant. Then what would I do?

Mama has a way of asking a question that makes my head hurt.

Safe on the other side of the footbridge, I sit cross-legged on the ground and take a few deep breaths. The mountain feels solid underneath me and I thank it for holding me up. I also take time to thank Daddy, my rabbit's foot, and the mother of our good Lord, by way of Grandma McAllister, for helping me get across and not fall into the chasm.

After I begin my trek again, I follow the path that winds up the hill like a snake. At the top of the hill I push open the rusty gate at the back of the graveyard and enter. In the distance stands the willow tree draping its branches above Daddy's final resting place.

The summer before he died, we made fishing poles out of its branches and he told me stories about our people buried here, especially my baby sister Beth. He never failed to mention how old she'd be if she hadn't died, which is always one year older than me at any given moment.

It is still strange to think of Daddy being under the ground in a wooden box, even if his spirit has gone off to live in heaven. It seems like his bones would get to go, too. But Preacher says you throw off your body at the end, just like you throw off an old coat you are tired of wearing. Maybe your bones weigh you down when you get to heaven if you take them with you. I don't know.

I am one month away from my thirteenth birthday and the only girl I know who hangs out in graveyards. But if you don't mind being around dead people, it has a beautiful view over-

looking the Tennessee River. Thick, old maples and oaks grace the hillside and the nearby stream empties into the river at the bottom of the hill. In the distance stands the small Baptist church practically everybody in Katy's Ridge attends. A large weeping willow grows in the center of the graveyard. A willow whose leaves sweep the ground when the wind blows, just like Mama sweeps our porch in the evenings. Last fall it wept down gold, almond-shaped leaves on top of Daddy's grave, and I knew he must be smiling because he always said he'd struck gold when I was born.

"Hi Daddy," I say to his tombstone.

I sit under the willow tree and cross my long legs up under me. With my finger, I trace the dates, 1902-1940, feeling the coldness of the stone. Daddy is the one who nicknamed me "Wildflower" when I was ten-years-old. He said the name fit me perfect since I'd sprung up here in the mountains like a wild trillium. Trillium will take your breath away if you see a patch of them. Daddy had a way with words, like a poet, and not just with me. He could make Mama smile faster than anything. Sometimes he'd get her laughing so hard she'd hold her sides till tears came to her eyes. All us kids stood around with our jaws dropped. To see Mama laugh was as rare as snow in August.

"We miss you, Daddy," I say. "All of us do, especially Mama. But we're doing all right, I guess."

He would want to know that we're doing all right and sometimes I tell him this even when we aren't.

Daddy always put his arms around Mama in the kitchen or laid an extra blanket on the bed because he knew she got cold in the middle of the night when the fire died down. No matter if he was sweating he kept Mama warm. But there aren't enough blankets in the world to make up for Daddy being gone. Sometimes I wonder if she ever gets mad at him for going away. I know I do. After the sadness gnawed me numb, I got pissed as a rattlesnake that he

hadn't been more careful while working at the sawmill, and that he'd left us all alone.

"LOUISA MAY, YOU FELL ASLEEP AGAIN."

The voice hovers over me and I wonder if maybe one of God's angels has come to take me to be with Daddy. Even though I am not a little girl anymore, I like thinking there are angels. When my eyes focus on what I hope will be my first celestial visitor, I see instead my sister, Jo. She is the most beautiful of all us McAllisters. She has golden blond hair the color of the inside of a honey comb, unlike my tangled dirty mop of curls, as Mama likes to call them. Like honey, Jo is also very sweet, but she isn't the angel I hoped for.

"My name is Wildflower," I say half asleep, rolling over on Daddy's grave.

When I was little, Daddy and I used to take naps together on Saturday afternoons like this one. He'd be folded up on one end of the sofa and I'd be on the other, our toes touching, until Mama made us get up to do our chores.

"Mama has dinner ready," Jo says. She taps the bottom of my shoes with hers.

"How's Daniel?" I ask, opening one eye. Her husband is almost as sweet as she is.

"He's fine, and he's waiting on his dinner, too." She reaches down to pull me up.

I brush away the pieces of leaves and dirt that leave spider web patterns on my legs. Jo and I are the same height now, but I haven't filled out like her yet.

"Mama worries about you coming up here all the time," Jo says. "I don't see why you bother. It takes forever to get here."

I don't tell Jo about my secret shortcut. If she knew about the old footbridge she'd probably make me promise not to come that way again.

"Jo, do you ever think about Daddy?"

She pauses, as if my question has surprised her. "All the time," she says softly. She looks down at Daddy's grave like he isn't there at all, but instead lives in her memory. Nobody talks much about him, probably because none of us is fond of crying. I envy Jo sometimes, mainly because she had more time with him. She was eighteen when he died. I had just turned twelve.

"Let's go home," Jo says, sliding her hand into mine. We lock fingers like best girlfriends.

"Goodbye, Daddy," I say, as we walk away.

Goodbye, Wildflower, I imagine him saying.

It takes nearly thirty minutes to get home. My secret way through the woods would have cut that time in half, but I'm not willing to tell anybody about it, not even Jo. Johnny is gone when we reach the crossroads, and my step lightens. I smile at the sky, imagining a world without Johnny Monroe.

Nearer to home the smell of honeysuckle and wild roses walks with us. As the sun dips below the ridge, the crickets warm up their night songs. Jo and I say our goodbyes at the three mailboxes at the bottom of our property. She and Daniel live across the road; Amy and Nathan next door to them. But there are several acres in between. I take the steep dirt path toward home, glad the rainstorm from the day before dampened down the dust from the dirt road.

To announce my arrival, I let the screen door slam. Mama and Meg are in the kitchen.

"Wash up," Mama says, and I do as I'm told.

Then I sit next to Meg who is still in her Woolworth's work clothes. Meg catches a ride to and from work with Cecil Appleby who drives his almost-new 1940 Ford truck into Rocky Bluff to work at the sock factory, an hour away. Not that many people have cars in Katy's Ridge.

"How's Daddy?" Meg asks.

"He's fine," I say. "He asked after you and I told him about your new job."

Meg smiles, but her smile has sadness in it, and I don't know if it's because she misses Daddy or if she's just sad she had to get a job.

Catching rides into Rocky Bluff makes a long day for Meg, because Cecil goes in at seven in the morning and she doesn't start work until nine. For two hours every morning she sits in the diner across from Woolworth's and reads cheap romance novels passed along by one of her customers.

Mama has no idea how much time Meg spends reading trashy novels and she would burn them in the woodstove if she ever found them. I have been sworn to secrecy until the day I die. However, not being one to pass up a business opportunity, I also collect ten cents a month for keeping my mouth shut. While Mama isn't looking, Meg slides me a dime across the table and I put it in my pocket.

A box under our bed is stacked full of books with bare-chested men standing next to women in long, sexy nightgowns. Meg says I can read them if I want to, but I can't get past the first chapter without feeling like heaving my breakfast oatmeal. If what's in those books is romance, I don't want any part of it.

In all my years of schooling, I've never had a boyfriend. I've had plenty of friends who were boys, but beyond that they hold no interest for me. In the country, some girls my age are already thinking about marriage. In the back, back woods, some girls are already having children of their own. But that's the last thing on my mind right now.

The secret sense tells me that Mama wants to say something to me about being at the graveyard again, but she swallows her words. If she wasn't so busy doing chores she might be up on that hill, too, lying next to Daddy's grave like they used to lie in bed together. I've never seen Mama cry, not even the day he died. But

sometimes I hear her through the wall, tossing and turning all over the bed that doesn't have Daddy in it anymore.

"We waited supper on you," Mama says, as if this was a great inconvenience.

"Thank you, Mama," I say. Daddy would want me to be nice to her, even though she hasn't been that nice to me lately.

A large bowl of pinto beans sits on the kitchen table. We eat beans a lot since Daddy died. Mixed in with the beans are pieces of ham, sweet onion, and turnip greens—little surprises that your taste buds stumble upon. Mama places an iron skillet of cornbread just out of the oven on folded dishrags so it won't burn the wood. Next to the cornbread is a big plate of sliced tomatoes that Mama grows in the side yard. I spear three slices with my fork and put them on my plate. Then I remember how Mama always says my eyes are bigger than my stomach and put one back.

"Who came into the store today?" Mama asks Meg.

Meg starts naming names, most of which I recognize. You'd think Woolworth's was the center of our universe as much as they talk about it. The population of Rocky Bluff is roughly six hundred people. Katy's Ridge has all of eighty, five of which are my immediate family, and another dozen or so that are related in one way or another. Some of the markers in the graveyard date back to the 1840s, and there are at least a dozen confederate soldiers there, and two Union soldiers on the far side, a whole graveyard separating them. The 1860s saw a lot of funerals in Katy's Ridge. I can recite nearly every name and date on the tombstones, except the ones that are faded beyond recognition. Meg and Mama like to study the here and now. I like to study the past.

Mama rests her chin in her hand while Meg shares the latest gossip. Tonight's news consists of Marcy Trevor's new dentures that don't fit, even after paying a fancy dentist in Nashville, three hours away. Mama's eyebrows arch, as if hearing about Marcy's troubles gives her a break from her own.

While Mama soaks in the idle chatter, I sneak a third piece of cornbread, missing her speech on gluttony and how I won't always be skinny if I keep eating anything I want. Riled up, Mama can sound just like Preacher.

"Don't you have something to do?" Mama says to me. She doesn't wait for an answer.

I clear the table, a job I inherited after Amy left home. It is a chore I don't mind because I can let my mind wander while standing at the bucket in the kitchen sink. My thoughts travel old paths as well as new ones, depending on what we are studying in school or what I am reading. Pondering comes natural to me. I can sit and be entertained by my thoughts for enormous amounts of time. Mama calls this just being lazy.

I scrape the leftovers into a rusty pie tin to take out back to feed the stray cats that stay under our house. Daddy started this tradition, but Mama doesn't like it. She looks over at me and sighs.

"Your daddy was just too soft hearted with those cats," she says. "He would have attracted every stray cat in the state of Tennessee, if he'd had his way about it."

"Yes, Mama," I say. She says the same thing every night.

"You're lucky I don't drown them all," she says.

This threat is new and she looks at me as if to register the level of my shock. But I don't let my face tell her anything.

Not all the cats decide to stay, but the ones that do, run from Mama every time they see her. Even cats can sense when they're not wanted.

A new one showed up two days before, who is small and orange and doesn't mind being touched. On account of his color, I call him Pumpkin. I go outside and sit on the steps. Pumpkin finishes the little bits of food the other cats let him have and weaves between my ankles. As I rub his whiskers, he soaks up my attention with a raspy purr.

Even though I am full of Mama's cornbread and beans, I have a

deep ache in my stomach when I think about Daddy being in the graveyard instead of sitting on the back porch with me. Evenings are the worst. It's the time of day when we all sat outside together. I lean against the porch post and close my eyes searching my memory for how his voice sounded.

A second later something rustles in the woods and I jump. The cats scatter, taking shelter under the house. Fixing my eyes on the woods, I wait for the next sound. Sometimes wild dogs roam the mountains, or raccoons come to eat what I've put out for the cats. I wrap my sweater closer and get that creepy feeling like when Johnny Monroe watches me.

"Who's out there?" I yell. My voice sounds shaky, so I stand to make up for it.

A million crickets answer my question.

Daddy's shotgun leans next to the back door, but Mama keeps the shells in her dresser drawer, so I'm not sure it would do much good to get it. By the time I got the gun loaded I could be dead and in a grave right next to his.

"Are you all right out here?" Mama says from behind the screen door. I've never been so glad to see her in all my life, but don't tell her that.

Even though I am nearly a woman myself, I am still a little girl in some ways. In the last year, I get scared by things that never used to scare me. It's as if my courage got buried along with Daddy.

"I heard something," I say, looking out into the woods.

Mama stands there for a long time, looking where I point.

"Come on inside," she says finally. The screen door needs grease and squeaks loudly as she opens it. After I pass, she latches it and the regular door, too, something I've never seen her do. Daniel put in the locks after Daddy died, but we've never once used them until now.

"What is it, Mama?" Meg asks. She yawns, as if realizing how long her day has already been.

"Louisa May heard something out back," Mama says.

She closes the short drapes over the kitchen sink, then walks through the living room and latches the front door, too. I like that she is taking me seriously for a change, but it also spooks me.

"Isn't it about time for you to get ready for bed?" Mama asks.

I glance at the clock and it's at least an hour before bed, so I figure she just wants me out of her hair. I leave Mama and Meg in the kitchen and sit in the rocker in the living room near the wood stove Daddy bought from the Sears & Roebuck catalog when I was seven. Daddy's banjo—missing one string he never got to replace —leans against the wall nearby. He used to sing country songs that told stories about people. His voice was deep and rich and it wrapped around you like one of Mama's softest quilts.

In the shadows, I pick up Daddy's old banjo and return to the rocker where he used to sit and play. I wrap his memory around me to try to feel safe. I am quiet, so Meg and Mama won't hear, and pretend to pick at some of the strings while I hum the words of *Down in the valley, valley so low*. At that moment the ache I felt earlier in my stomach moves to my chest. *Hang your head over, hear the wind blow.*

After I finish the song I get up from the rocking chair, being careful not to let it creak on the wooden floor. So Mama won't know I've touched it, I place Daddy's banjo back in its spot where the dust keeps the shape of it. It would be just like her to put it away if she knew I wanted to keep it out.

"What are you doing here in the dark?" Mama asks.

Speak of the devil, I start to say, but then think better of it.

Most of the things Mama says to me are either orders or questions, neither of which ever require an answer. I shrug and shuffle to the bedroom I share with Meg, who has already sunk into a loud snore. I get undressed and put on my nightgown and try not

to think about the noise I heard earlier in the woods behind the house. When I walk down the hall toward Mama's room, I find her sitting on the edge of the bed brushing her hair, which reaches almost to her waist. Her hair is much prettier down, instead of up in the tight bun she wears during the day.

"Can I sleep with you?" I ask her. She looks at me surprised, like when I told her I was changing my name to Wildflower.

For a split second her face softens, but then she says, "Don't be silly, Louisa May. You're grown up now."

Her words sting like a bee stepped on barefooted in a patch of clover, and I want to kick myself for even asking. In my weakness, I imagined Mama opening the covers wide on Daddy's side of the bed while I get in.

Instead, she says, "Let me get at some of those tangles, Louisa May." She motions me over so she can brush my hair.

She starts and I say, "Ouch! Mama, stop!"

"Be still," she tells me, "you're just making my job harder."

While she attacks the tangles in my hair, I refuse to give her the pleasure of knowing how bad she's hurting me. Mama knows I'm tender-headed and I know she knows it. But it's as though I need her to touch me more than I need my pride, so I let her do it. In the meantime, I silently curse the tears that squeeze out of my eyes and promise myself that I'll be tougher once I turn thirteen.

After a while, Mama gives up and declares my tangles a battle she cannot win. Our eyes meet briefly before she turns away, as if the tangled emotions between us are also a losing battle.

I return to the bed I share with Meg. Lying there in the dark, I count backwards from a hundred by threes and try not to think about what's lurking in the woods or the fact that my father will never be coming home. Or my deepest, darkest, secret wish: that Mama had died instead of him.

CHAPTER TWO

The news of Ruby Monroe's death crackles through Katy's Ridge like an unexpected thunderstorm. The next morning, I overhear my sister Amy telling Mama about it in the kitchen. She must have come by early because she is already there when I wake up. Even though I am only days away from my thirteenth birthday, they never include me in their grownup conversations and sometimes I wonder if they ever will.

Squeezed behind the wood box full of kindling in the parlor, I slap at a cobweb that escaped Mama's dust rag. This was one of my many hiding places as a girl that can now barely accommodate me.

It is hot, as August always is, even early in the morning. A slender crack runs the length of the wall between the kitchen and the parlor, and I press my ear close to the wall in order to hear. It takes a few seconds to make out the words, but I tune them in like Daddy used to tune in stations on our old radio.

"Ruby hung herself," Amy says, her voice not much louder than a whisper.

I cover my mouth and swallow a gasp. I've heard of criminals

getting hung, but I've never known anybody to do it to themselves. Especially somebody I just saw at Sweeny's store two days before. Ruby stood in front of the counter barefooted, her feet muddy, counting out pennies to Mr. Sweeny to buy a sack of flour. For all I knew she didn't even own shoes. Her stomach stuck out, like poor people's do, when they don't get enough to eat. I said hello and she nodded before quickly looking away.

After I inhale the dust of weathered oak from the wood box, a sneeze escapes. The muffled voices in the kitchen stop, as if wondering if a *bless you* is called for.

"Where's Louisa May?" Mama asks.

"She's still sleeping," Amy says.

Mama makes a comment about my laziness. At that moment I'm so riled up from being crammed in this hot, tight corner I fantasize about knocking some of Mama's spitefulness out of her.

"They found Ruby swinging in an oak tree," my sister, Amy, continues.

My eyes widen and I lean in closer, not wanting to miss a single detail.

"That poor child," Mama sighs.

"Her daddy came back from one of his hunting trips and found her," Amy says. "That's when he came to get Nathan. Nathan said Mr. Monroe was drunk, too, which didn't help matters. Melody was asleep in the house and Johnny was nowhere around."

Nathan is Amy's husband and one of the calmest human beings alive. He would be a good person to have around in an emergency.

"God rest her soul," Mama says.

"God rest her soul," Amy echoes.

"God rest her soul," I whisper.

Silence overtakes them. Wood dust works its way up my nose and I hold my breath and pinch my nostrils until the urge to sneeze again passes. If Mama catches me eavesdropping, I'll be cleaning the outhouse all afternoon.

"Nathan said it took two of them to cut her down," Amy says finally, her voice breaking.

When I close my eyes I can picture Ruby with her sad eyes and muddy feet, swinging by the neck from a tree she probably played in as a little girl. I feel sick at my stomach and have to remind myself to breathe.

"But I haven't told you the worst of it," Amy says, her words trailing off.

I press my ear into the narrow crack, certain I'll be rubbing out a crease later.

"What could be worse?" Mama asks.

I wonder the same.

"She was . . . in a family way," Amy whispers.

My breathing fills the silence as I imagine the looks they give each other. Mama can say more with her eyes than a whole dictionary full of words.

'In a family way' means Ruby's stomach wasn't just big from being hungry. As I lower my head, sweat drips onto my arm. Tears fill my eyes for Ruby Monroe and for her baby who will never see the light of day. The walls close in. I crawl from behind the wood box and tiptoe out the door, avoiding the floor boards I know will creak and step onto the porch. Fresh, warm air fills my lungs. Air, I am suddenly aware, Ruby will never get to breathe again.

Questions crowd my mind, as if sent to push the feelings away. Why would Ruby do such a thing? How could she possibly be so desperate and scared? And who is the father of her baby? I've never seen any boys around her. If this happened to me I wouldn't have to kill myself; Mama would do it for me.

TWO DAYS LATER, everybody in Katy's Ridge shows up for Ruby's funeral. The whispers are like a fire that refuses to die down and the packed church vibrates with judgment. The people of Katy's

Ridge aren't all that forgiving when it comes to sinning. Meanwhile, Preacher's long face reveals what they already believe: the pearly gates of heaven won't be opening for the likes of Ruby Monroe.

Surely God won't send Ruby to hell just for having a hard life, I think. She didn't even own a pair of shoes and had to tend to a father and a brother who could have cared less about her. Preacher is fond of saying that the first will be last and the last first in God's kingdom. If this is true, then it makes more sense for God to send Ruby and her baby to the head of heaven's line.

Mama and I join Aunt Sadie, Daddy's older sister, and the rest of the family three rows from the front, the pew our family always sits in. The story told to me is that Ruby had an accident. But for the life of me I can't figure out how a rope could, by accident, slide around a person's neck.

I can't seem to take my eyes off of the wooden box that has Ruby in it. It smells of new lumber and hardly seems big enough for a thirteen year old girl and a baby and all the sadness she carried with her. I worry that she still doesn't have on any shoes and close my eyes to ask Daddy to put in a good word to God for Ruby and her baby.

"Have some respect for the dead," Mama whispers to me, as I lean over to get a better view. I want to remind her that I'm the one who spends a fair amount of time in the cemetery, not her, and if anybody has respect for the dead, that would be me.

Arthur Monroe sits on the front row wearing a torn pair of overalls, his dirty hat staying on his head the whole time. I've never seen him in church and he looks about as out of place as a mule in a kitchen. Johnny Monroe sits beside him, staring at the floor, his hair uncombed, with his younger sister, Melody, leaning into his arm. Melody's nose is running and she looks younger than her years. Her hair is tied up with a piece of knotted string.

The church is sweltering. It is three o'clock on an August afternoon with not a hint of breeze. Preacher clutches a worn, black Bible and bellows out the 23rd Psalm like we are all deaf or half-wits. Sweat forms in large half-moon circles under his arms. Droplets dance on his wide forehead as if the fires of hell are nipping at his dusty black shoes. He is bald except for a thin, sagging crescent of hair that reaches from one ear to the other, a temporary dam for the sweat, before it streams down his neck and forehead. To hear Preacher tell it, the whole of Katy's Ridge is doomed to teeth gnashing with the devil because of all the hearty sinning we do.

His face flushes crimson. His voice raised, he speaks of God calling his children home when they least expect it. He shouts "Repent!" several times and warns us to not end up like Ruby. Johnny hasn't looked up once, not even with Preacher standing a foot away from him. If I was a betting person, I'd bet Johnny wishes he had a peach can to sit at Preacher's feet to ping some tobacco spit into.

The top of a whiskey bottle bulges out of Mr. Monroe's pocket and on one of Preacher's *repents* Mr. Monroe snarls and takes out his pocketknife. He opens the blade swiftly with his thumb and scrapes at the dirt caked on the bottom of his boots, letting the dirt fall onto the church floor. Two deacons start to come forward to take Mr. Monroe out of the church but Preacher holds up a hand to stop them, as if even he knows this wouldn't turn out well.

Mr. Monroe doesn't look the least bit sorry for Ruby's death and heat rises to my face. I want to smack the man from here to Christmas, and Preacher, too, whose empty words make no sense. Why would God call Ruby home by way of a rope and an oak tree? A trickle of sweat slides between my shoulder blades and I let out a huff. If God decides to call me home anytime soon, I will refuse to answer.

Arthur Monroe's livelihood is hunting, setting traps and selling the meat. His clothes always stink like a ripe carcass. Though he is an eligible widower, his odor discourages even the most ardent widows and spinsters of Katy's Ridge.

If he manages to corner you anywhere, on the road, or at Sweeny's store, he'll tell you the story of getting gassed in a trench in the big war in Europe, World War I, and the whole time you're getting gassed just standing there. On one of those occasions when I was wishing I had a gas mask, Mr. Monroe told me that once or twice a year he checks into the Veterans Hospital in Nashville with blinding headaches. I got a headache just hearing about it.

A few years ago, during one of those headaches, he came after Johnny at school for forgetting to feed Arthur's old coon dog. The whole school witnessed him bursting through the door and dragging Johnny right out into the schoolyard. While he beat the tar out of him, he kept yelling, "Get behind me, Satan!" A short time after that, Johnny quit coming to school and started hanging out on the road.

Sweat sticks my legs to the wooden bench. I think of Ruby inside that box, her baby inside of her, Ruby's belly being its own little casket. It is entirely possible that I have entered my own version of hell where life is not fair and the wrong people die and for no good reason.

Mama takes my pinkie finger on my right hand and bends it to the point of pain. This is my signal to stop my squirming in church. As I take my hand away, I give her a look that says she will end up like Ruby if she's not careful and she gives me a look back as if daring me to try it. Meanwhile, Preacher is using Ruby's death to put the fear of God in us and further his cause. After Preacher finishes, he looks pleased with himself and wipes the sweat from his face with a starched white handkerchief and looks over at the organ.

In a flourish of wrong notes, Miss Mildred starts playing

Amazing Grace, real slow. This was Daddy's favorite hymn, but I try not to think about that, or about the last time I heard it, which was at his funeral. We all sing along, most of the congregation confident that Ruby Monroe was the wretch that needed saving in the first verse and since she never came to church she was out of luck. Ruby was lost, but nobody even tried to find her.

When the music stops, the four McClure brothers go up front to lift Ruby's pine box to carry it to the gravesite. Buddy, the youngest McClure, grunts as if the box weighs more than he expects. They balance their load and we file out of the church, following the box up the hill. In the distance a pile of fresh red dirt marks Ruby's final resting place, a stone's throw away from Daddy's willow tree.

A fine, misty rain starts to fall and the melody of *Amazing Grace* still plays in my head while we walk up the hill. Aunt Sadie lightly squeezes my hand and I have the secret sense that she knows exactly what I am thinking about. The last time we climbed this hill was nearly a year ago.

"Are you okay, sweetheart?" Aunt Sadie asks, and I say, *yes,* though I'm not the least bit okay. Now I have proof that God doesn't know what he's doing by taking both Daddy and Ruby before their time.

Ruby's box is lowered into the grave with two ropes and Preacher throws a clump of muddy red dirt into the hole. The dirt hits Ruby's coffin with a dull thud and Mama jerks her head like a gun has gone off, and then she glances off into the distance at Daddy's grave. As far as I know, she hasn't visited it once since Daddy died, and I want to take her by the hand and lead her there and show her how beautiful the spot is. But her eyes are as ominous and blue gray as the sky.

"Ashes to ashes, dust to dust," Preacher says and the words sound hollow.

When someone your same age dies, it's like it could have been

you. I hope I never get as desperate and sad as Ruby. Losing my father taught me how deep sadness can go. The rain grows harder and thunder rumbles in the distance. Another summer storm passes through Katy's Ridge as we say our goodbyes to Ruby Monroe.

CHAPTER THREE

When I tell Daniel and Nathan I heard somebody in the woods three nights before, they come by and search the hill behind our house.

"We saw deer tracks," Daniel says, when they return to the back porch. He stomps the mud from his boots on the top step, then uses the side of his boot to sweep the mud away. Daniel looks over at me and shrugs his shoulders in an apology, like he wishes he'd found something.

"It was just Louisa May's imagination getting the best of her," Mama says. "She's been like that since she was a little girl."

Her words make me doubly mad. For one thing she refuses to call me Wildflower, and for another she acts like I don't know the difference between my imagination and something real in the woods. That was no deer that night, I am certain of it. I've been around plenty of deer, and a deer in the woods doesn't make my skin crawl.

Meg comes home from work, fixes herself a glass of tea and joins us.

"What's going on?" Meg asks.

"A wild goose chase, that's what," Mama says.

Daniel puts a hand on my shoulder as if to discourage me from wrestling Mama to the ground.

"You've got a nest of baby possums in the base of that old Hickory," Nathan says, hitching up his pants. He is as lean as the fence rails he put around his field last summer and has to wear both a belt and suspenders. People joke with Amy that she doesn't feed her husband near enough, but I've seen him put away as much food as two regular sized men.

"Are you sure you heard something?" Daniel asks me. He keeps his arm on my shoulder. I am just the right height for Daniel to use as an armrest.

"I'm sure," I say. If anybody else had asked, I'd probably gotten madder still. But Daniel doesn't ask it like he thinks I am somebody who just makes things up.

"Sometimes the wind in the trees makes some weird rustling. It even fools me," he says.

"I know what I heard, Daniel," I say. "It was too heavy-footed for a deer or the wind. It was a person, I'm sure of it. Mama says it was just my imagination but she felt creepy about it, too. She locked up the house tighter than a drum."

Mama looks at me like I've somehow made a liar out of her. I scowl at Meg, leaving space for her to side with me, but she doesn't say a word.

"Who'd be traipsing around in these woods?" Nathan asks.

"I bet I know," I say, regretting the words the moment I speak them. Mama looks at me all curious. This is not a road I want to take. The less information Mama knows the better.

"What did you say?" she asks.

I stick my hands deep into the pockets of my overalls and finger a smooth, round stone I fished out of the streambed the day before. Rocks aren't supposed to interest girls my age, so I hide my treasures now.

"I said I know who it was," I say again, but I sound more timid this time.

Everybody looks at me like I am Moses about to deliver the Ten Commandments. Mama folds her arms into her chest, her lips tight. When I was younger, this could make the truth spill out of me like cornmeal out of a sack. But I am not in the mood to give her what she wants.

"Well, who was it?" Mama asks. "Those baby possums out back have already had time to be weaned and have babies of their own."

Everybody waits while I debate which of my actions will get me in the least amount of trouble. If I tell, Mama will be like a dog given a new bone to chew on. If I don't, Johnny might just walk right into our house someday like he owns the place.

"It was Johnny Monroe, that's who it was," I say finally.

Daniel takes his arm off my shoulder. He places his foot on the porch rail and leans on his knee, as if this information changes things.

"Johnny's a good-for-nothin', that's for sure," Nathan says.

Johnny is Nathan's second cousin, but they aren't close. Practically everybody in their family has given up on Johnny. He is what people around here call a "black sheep."

"It was him," I insist.

Mama presses her fingers into her temples like I am giving her one whopper of a headache.

"I wouldn't put it past him," Daniel says. "Those Monroes know these mountains better than anybody. They might be watching us right now."

"But why would Johnny come up here?" Mama asks. Her eyes narrow like she's just set a trap for me.

I mumble that I don't know and shoot Meg a look that threatens to expose her entire collection of romance novels under our bed. Meg doesn't flinch from my threat and pours herself another glass of tea.

I am not about to tell Mama how many times Johnny has asked after Meg, or the things Johnny has said to me. She'll make too big of a deal about it or no deal at all. But it would be just like Johnny to hike up the ridge and perch on the hillside in the hopes of getting a look at Meg or me in our underwear.

"We could go ask Johnny about it," Daniel says to Mama.

"No, you boys have done enough," Mama says. "I'm sure it's nothing to fuss about." She goes into the pantry and gets them each a jar of homemade applesauce. Mama never lets anybody leave the house without giving them something to take back home. Applesauce, apples, tomatoes, strawberry preserves—-anything she has extra in the pantry. "Tell the girls I said hello," Mama says.

They each kiss Mama on the cheek.

"The best part of having grown daughters is the sons-in-law that come with them," Mama says.

She looks over at Meg and me like she expects us to come up with someone to marry who is just as good. I don't know how to tell her that I have no interest whatsoever. All girls want to do around here when they grow up is get married. But if I can't find somebody as good as Daddy, I'm not going to bother.

Later that night Meg and I are in bed and I give her the silent treatment because I am still fuming that she didn't speak up earlier about what I heard in the woods.

"Johnny gives me the creeps, too," Meg says. She turns a page of her book.

"Really?" I ask, my anger turning to relief.

"Just stay away from him," she says, not looking up.

"I do stay away from him," I say, "except when he's waiting on the road. But what if that was him out back the other night, Meg?"

She puts a finger in the book to mark her place and turns to face me. "Johnny's too lazy to come all the way up here. He hangs out mainly on the road. It was probably a deer or something and you just imagined it was Johnny."

It feels like the hundredth time that day my grasp on reality has been questioned, but I am just too tired to argue.

"I'll turn out the light in a minute," she says. Meg moistens her bottom lip with her tongue like she is reading something delicious, and then turns another page.

According to Preacher, God is real big on forgiveness, especially for us lowly sinners like Meg who has a fondness for romance novels. With that in mind, I decide to forgive Meg, too, though I'm not about to give Preacher credit for it.

I close my eyes and pray for Meg to find someone to love soon so she will quit reading romances and go to bed at a decent hour. She pretends to be happy that Jo and Amy got married last spring, but I know she's jealous and wants someone of her own.

The house is quiet. While she's reading, Meg always keeps one eye on the door in case Mama comes in so she can throw her book under the covers. But Mama has gone to bed early with a headache. A headache she probably blames on me.

I think about Daddy resting in peace on the hillside, the moonlight dancing with the breeze through the weeping willow tree.

"Goodnight, Daddy," I whisper.

Sleep well, Wildflower, he whispers back.

CHAPTER FOUR

On my thirteenth birthday I have cramps so bad I can barely stand. This is my fourth monthly and I am still getting used to the whole thing. Growing up with older sisters has its advantages. It wasn't a mystery for me. When it happened, Mama gave me two cotton pads she had sewn together out of leftover quilt pieces. One I wear inside my underpants. The other I use as a spare when I wash the soiled one out in the evenings. Mama made each of us different colored pads so we could tell them apart. Mine are white, with pieces of light blue running through. With all these girls and Mama, there are times when the back clothesline will have a whole bunch of pads hanging on it, like flags from different countries.

"Come on, Wildflower, open your presents," Daniel says. He motions for me to sit on the porch and everybody else gathers around.

We're all full of Mama's chicken and dumplings she made me for my birthday dinner and are moving kind of slow. Jo baked a cake that we will dig into after presents.

Meg hands me a small package wrapped in paper from the

Sunday funnies and some twine. I open it and find a comb and mirror that all fit together in a little leather pouch from the Woolworth store. I thank her and give her a hug. I love the gifts she's given me since she started working there.

Amy and Nathan's package is much bigger and contains a new dress to wear to church. It is red with a small white daisy pattern. It also has two big pockets on the front because Amy knows I like collecting things.

"Thanks, Amy," I say.

"I know you like red," Amy says, "and daisies are also wildflowers, just like your name."

I appreciate how thoughtful her gift is and tell her so. Amy sews better than anybody in Katy's Ridge and a lot of women pay her to make them things they see in the Sears & Roebuck catalog. The extra money really helps out since Nathan's crops depend on how good the weather is and it isn't always good.

"Here's a little something extra," Nathan says, hitching up his pants for the hundredth time. He hands me a corncob pipe and everybody laughs. "You're old enough now to start up smoking any day," Nathan adds.

I laugh, too, though I'm not feeling that festive.

But then Mama chimes in, "She'd better not ever smoke," and all the laughter stops.

Next to give presents are Daniel and Jo. Daniel hands me a carved wooden box he whittled that has a small wooden cat inside. Both are beautiful and I thank him and Jo for such a perfect gift.

"My turn," Aunt Sadie says. She hands me a present wrapped in fabric with wildflowers stitched on front that is beautiful enough to be the gift itself. Inside is a little book with blank paper in it to write down my pondering thoughts. Only Aunt Sadie would think of something like that. She also brought me some herbs for my cramps, without me even asking; like she had the secret sense that I needed them.

Sadie gives me a big hug and whispers in my ear, "He's looking down on you right now, sweetheart, and he's very proud.

Her words bring tears to my eyes that I brush away as quick as they land on my cheeks.

Aunt Sadie is Daddy's older sister by sixteen years. She took care of him back in Ireland when he was a baby, while their parents worked. She often tells me that I remind her of herself as a girl. She says I have gumption. I'm not sure what 'gumption' is but I take it as a compliment.

Aunt Sadie likes telling the story of how she came to America on her own when she turned twenty-two. Daddy came two years later after Grandpa McAllister died. I asked her once why she decided to settle in Katy's Ridge because it seems to me there would have been much more exciting places to live. She said the Tennessee mountains reminded her of home.

None of my grandparents are still alive, but Aunt Sadie comes closest to being a grandmother to me. She has solid white hair and sometimes uses a walking stick with a tree carved on the side. Not that she is the least bit feeble. It just helps to steady her when she climbs the mountain looking for the plants she needs for her remedies, especially the ginseng, hiding out on damp, shady hillsides. Her dog, Max, always goes with her and carries a leather pouch on his back for collecting the plants and roots Sadie finds. Max and I are friends, too, and whenever I go over to Sadie's house he lets me pick cockleburs out of his fur and brush him.

Today, Max is lying on the end of the porch sleeping. Every now and again he opens his eyes to make sure Sadie is where he left her.

Everybody makes a big deal of my birthday, probably because they know how hard it is to not have Daddy here. Next month marks the one-year-anniversary of his death. Earlier that day at the cemetery, I told God that I'd settle for no presents for the rest of my life if Daddy could just come home one more time. As a

result, I keep glancing down the hill, half-expecting to see him coming home from work, whistling and walking with his familiar gait.

Jo goes inside and in a few seconds brings out the cake she made. We will eat it on the front porch so the crumbs won't get everywhere in the house. Everybody knows how Mama fusses over the house and nobody wants to make her mad.

"Make a wish," Jo says. She lights a single candle in the center of the cake, the same candle we all use for birthdays, kept in the kitchen drawer with the twine and matches.

While everyone watches, I exaggerate a big breath and blow out the candle. Then everybody claps and I glance down the hill to see if my wish has come true. My shoulders drop with the knowledge that I probably won't get my wish of seeing Daddy again until the day I don't have birthdays anymore.

In the meantime, Daniel and Nathan eat big slices of cake with their hands. They make noises like it's the best they've ever tasted. The rest of us have forks and plates, but make the same sounds. It is vanilla cake with vanilla frosting and coconut resting on top like the first snow of winter. The taste is heavenly, which makes me wonder if there is food in heaven. The next time I sit with Daddy in the graveyard I'll have to ask.

After we finish our cake, Mama asks, "So when is Mary Jane coming home, Louisa May?"

I've told her twice already, but it isn't like her to make conversation with me, so I figure, along with the chicken and dumplings, this must be part of my birthday present.

"She won't be home till the first of September," I say.

Mary Jane and I have been inseparable since we were babies and our mother's laid us on a blanket together in Pritchard's Meadow on the 4th of July.

"Oh, that's right," she says. "I think you told me that before."

With a glance, I suggest she ask me something else, since she

had already asked the previous question, but our conversation stops there. If Daddy were here he would joke her out of her grumpiness and have her smiling and hanging on his arm in no time. Wishing for a miracle, I glance down the hill again.

Mary Jane always misses my August birthday because every summer she goes to Little Rock, Arkansas, on a Greyhound bus. If not for Mary Jane I'd be friendless. A year ago, I used to have more friends, but then after Daddy died they acted like they didn't know what to say to me. Mountain people are superstitious, especially about accidents. I think they stay away so they won't get any bad luck on them.

Sometimes Mary Jane goes with me to the graveyard to visit Daddy. She has a couple of uncles there and a grandfather. Whenever we visit she says hello to them, but mostly she just goes to keep me company. Most other girls I know get squeamish about graveyards and tombstones, but not Mary Jane. Dead people don't bother her.

While my family sits on the front porch looking full and content, Amy gets Nathan a second slice of cake. Before the night is over he'll probably get thirds and fourths. Jo and Daniel hold hands in the porch swing that Daddy made. Mama and Aunt Sadie pull out the quilt they've been working on since last Christmas, made out of the scraps of our old clothes. They are good at making something beautiful out of scraps.

As I lean against the porch, I break a stick into knuckle-sized pieces and corral an ant carrying a piece of coconut across the porch rail. The ant keeps hitting against the wall I've created and I feel bad for making its life harder. But in a way it feels like what God has done to me by letting my father die.

Forgetting all about my promise to be tough when I turn thirteen, I start to tear up again. It occurs to me that all this emotion might be from having my monthly, given Jo cries at the sight of a hummingbird when she has hers.

After excusing myself, I meander around back to give Pumpkin some of my cake crumbs. I have to shoo off the other cats. From the ice box, I steal him a tiny bit of cream, hoping mama won't miss it. *Cream is not to be wasted on cats,* she has said more than once.

Pumpkin and I sit on the back porch and watch the last rays of sunlight stream through the trees. It will be dark soon. Lightning bugs blink in the forest like tiny stars come to earth.

My thoughts keep me company as Pumpkin finishes off the last of the cream and begins an extensive cleaning ritual. Thirteen feels old to me. I'll graduate from grade school this year. Not everybody who goes to our grade school goes to high school, too. But Daddy wanted all of us McAllisters to get our high school diplomas so I'll be going to Rocky Bluff High School next year. Meg was the smartest in her class and even gave the commencement speech last June, so it is doubly hard to understand her fascination for tawdry novels.

The grade school in Katy's Ridge had a total of twelve students of various ages. We meet in one big room with a coal stove in the center. A big pile of coal sits out back and we kids take turns going to get a piece to throw in the stove in the winter. Beyond the coal pile we have a field where we play kickball every day after lunch. In contrast, Rocky Bluff High School has nearly a hundred students and more classrooms than I've taken the time to count.

To get to the high school from Katy's Ridge, I will have to walk a mile down the river road to catch an old Rocky Bluff city bus that comes only a little ways into Katy's Ridge. After the weather gets cold, Meg says the buses are freezing and you can see your breath out in front of you. Then you hardly warm up before you have to get back on the cold bus again and head home. On the coldest winter days I plan to wear my overalls under my dress and take them off once I get to school.

From my pocket, I take out Mary Jane's letter that came

yesterday. She will be home next week. I can't wait to show her the things I got for my birthday, and tell her about Ruby Monroe, and about hearing something in the woods behind our house. In her letter she said her grandmother bought her some dresses at the J.C. Penney store in downtown Little Rock. Mary Jane sent me pictures she tore out of the J.C. Penney catalog and I look at them again, thinking they must look like something Shirley Temple wears. I have never owned a store bought dress in my life.

"There you are," Daniel says. He walks around the side of the house and sits next to me on the back porch. "Why'd you leave the party?"

I shrug and Daniel nods like I've given a perfectly good reason. For several seconds the two of us share a duet of silence. Then I notice my pad from yesterday hanging on the clothesline and think, *God in Heaven!* I flush hot from something so private being all exposed. But Daniel doesn't even notice. Or if he does, he doesn't let on.

Pumpkin weaves between our legs. Daniel is the only other human, besides me, he will get close to.

"Thanks for the carving," I say. I pull the wooden cat out of my pocket and admire it for his benefit. I left the wooden box on the porch with my other things.

"I thought you'd like it," he says. "The wood came from the mill. It's oak. It'll last forever." He smiles and looks proud that he's made me happy. Two years before, Daddy got Daniel a job at the sawmill. They used to walk there together every morning.

We sit quietly, watching Pumpkin spear the last piece of coconut on the plate with one claw. He nibbles it down.

"A penny for your thoughts," Daniel finally says.

Maybe my thoughts aren't even worth a penny, I don't know. But I feel like asking for at least a quarter. Grief, I decide, comes at great expense. I shrug again and ponder how the sadness of losing

somebody you love never goes away. It just fades over the years like the pattern on a dress that's been passed down.

"Well, whenever you want to talk about it, I'm here," Daniel says.

I smile, remembering how much Daniel reminds me of Daddy sometimes.

"I can't believe I'm thirteen," I say finally. "It's the oldest I've ever been."

Daniel chuckles, but stops himself when he sees I am being serious.

I spit on my fingers to wipe a streak of mud from my shoes. Truth is I'm not so sure I want to share what I've been thinking. But when I look over at Daniel I know I can trust him to understand.

"Daddy had all these plans for my thirteenth birthday, on account of me becoming a teenager," I say. "He promised to take me on the train to Nashville and visit the state capital."

Daniel pauses. "You still miss him don't you," he says.

"More than anything," I say softly.

"He was a good man," Daniel says, his voice low, matching mine. "I miss him, too."

I tell myself not to cry, that I'm being ridiculous, and the voice in my head sounds a lot like Mama. I choke back the tears that want to pour out over the front of my dress, over Pumpkin, then all the way past the graveyard, and out to the river to the sea.

Daniel puts his arm around me. The scent of sweat and sawdust reminds me even more of what I'm missing. Tears stream from my eyes. I bury my head in the skirt of the dress that Meg handed down to me after it was Amy's before it was Jo's. We McAl-listers usually don't let anybody see us cry, even family, unless something really bad happens.

"It's okay," Daniel says. "There's nobody here to see but God and some crickets."

For the next few minutes I make a friend of my misery imagining how my life could have been different: Daddy here celebrating my 13th birthday with me, playing his banjo on the front porch with everybody dancing and laughing; Daddy looking over at me, smiling, like he's the luckiest man alive to have me as a daughter. Then afterwards we would catch a ride to Rocky Bluff and take the train to Nashville.

These thoughts serve no purpose but to torture me. Meanwhile, Daniel has his arm around me, waiting for the unexpected cloudburst of tears to stop. It feels good to have a man's arm around me, even if he isn't the man I really want.

"Hey you two," Jo says, coming around the corner of the house. She hesitates when she sees me crying, but then keeps coming. Every time I see Jo she gets more beautiful, like those girls in magazines advertising Ivory soap.

"Am I interrupting?" she asks Daniel, resting a hand on his shoulder.

"We've just been reminiscing," he says.

"Do you need more time?" Jo says, stroking my hair.

"No," I say.

I wipe my face on the underside of my dress, and tell myself to snap out of it, that I am not a little girl any more. Again, the voice sounds more like mama's than mine, but it serves its purpose.

"Let's get back to the party," I say, standing up to leave. When I move, Pumpkin runs behind the old washing machine.

Jo hugs me gently, like I am a flower whose blossom might collapse if touched. Jo is my favorite sister, even though I love them all.

"We've got another surprise for you," she says, smiling at Daniel.

"What is it?" I ask. I prefer good news to bad any day.

"We want to tell everybody all at once," Daniel says. He takes

Jo's hand and the three of us follow the path back around the house lined with the rock Daddy and I carried from the river.

Mama is still in her rocking chair with pieces of quilt stretched between her and Aunt Sadie. Nathan balances on the porch rail picking his teeth with a twig he's whittled down, while Amy pours more tea for everybody. Max is asleep at Aunt Sadie's feet. He is the dog version of an old man and doesn't trouble himself with much except watching out for Aunt Sadie.

"It's about time you showed up," Mama says to me. She looks up briefly from her stitching. "What kind of girl disappears from her own party?"

"A beautiful girl," Aunt Sadie says, as if trying to make up for the softness Mama lacks since Daddy died.

I sit on the porch steps and refuse to let Mama ruin my birthday. Torches are lit now that it's getting dark.

"Jo and I have an announcement to make," Daniel says, standing in the middle of the dirt yard.

Amy grins and looks over at Jo like she already knows what it is, and Meg wears that moony look she gets whenever she reads romance stories. Everybody seems to know what Daniel is going to say except me.

"What is it?" I ask, the suspense nudging me from all directions.

"I'm going to have a baby," Jo smiles.

I should have guessed this is what she was going to say. She is more radiant than I've ever seen her.

Everybody converges on Jo and Daniel, laughing and hugging Jo and patting Daniel on the back. Meanwhile, I sit frozen, like somebody has nailed my backside to the porch steps. Unexpected things throw me these days, even if they are good things.

"If it's a boy we're going to name him Joseph, after Daddy," Jo says. "And if it's a girl, we'll call her Penelope."

Mama rises from her rocker, puts the quilt aside and embraces Jo and Daniel. Penelope is Mama's given name, even though

Daddy always called her Nell. Only Sadie calls her Nell now, along with a few people at church. I keep forgetting she has a name besides "Mama."

Aunt Sadie tip-toes into the yard, her arms raised high in the air and starts to dance. Max barks excitedly. Aunt Sadie has been known to dance whenever the spirit moves her. Preacher hates it when the spirit comes over Aunt Sadie in church. Sadie's dancing always sparks a sermon from Preacher about how the "heathens" are taking over the world. To me, it looks like God would want people to dance and celebrate life like that.

The celebration continues around me. I try my best to get excited about Daniel and Jo's news but all I can think about is Daddy missing this moment, and how proud he'd be about having his first grandchild.

"You're going to be an aunt," Daniel says to me, a big grin on his face.

"Congratulations," I say, smiling back. I like the idea of being an aunt, like Aunt Sadie. If Daniel and Jo have a boy, I'll teach him how to use a slingshot and maybe play the banjo. If it is a girl, I'll do my best to teach her how to stay clear of Johnny Monroe.

Jo walks over and gives me another hug. "We thought this would make your thirteenth birthday even more special," she says.

I manage a smile, not wanting to get any of my sadness on the baby. What bothers me most is the thought that life just keeps on going, even when somebody you love dies. Another McAllister is going to be born into the world, one Daddy will never know.

CHAPTER FIVE

"Well, if it isn't my best friend in the whole wide world, Wildflower McAllister," Mary Jane says when she first sees me again. I can tell she's trying to sound more grown up than she was two months ago when I last saw her.

I always forget how red Mary Jane's hair is until she comes home. She is the only person in Katy's Ridge with this distinction. Neither of her parents have red hair, which raises the eyebrows of the old ladies at church when they don't have anything better to gossip about. Not everybody remembers that Mary Jane's grandmother's hair used to be red, before it turned solid gray.

"It's about time you got home," I say. "Katy's Ridge is the most boring place on earth without you."

Mary Jane and I are always trying to outdo each other by talking grand.

"I thought I'd keel over and die without you!" Mary Jane says.

I roll my eyes, calling a halt to the contest.

Mary Jane also has more freckles on her face than all the people in Katy's Ridge combined. One day last year we started counting them during recess and got up to 84 before we had to go back

inside. People expect her to have a fiery temper, too, but in all the years I've known her I've never seen even a hint of one. If anything, I should have red hair instead of her.

We spend the whole morning in Mary Jane's room and she shows me her new school clothes. Preacher says coveting is a sin. Coveting has to do with wanting what other people have, like their land, their wives or mules. I figure this goes for new dresses, too, even though I'd much prefer a new pair of overalls.

Amy makes everything we McAllister's wear and she makes them sturdy—dresses and pants alike. But when it comes to the day-to-day living of life, dresses just aren't practical. Bare legs attract all sorts of annoying things like cuts, scrapes and bug bites. Not to mention that every time I take a notion to swing in grade school, boys try to sneak a peek at my underpants.

Meg says high school boy's eyes wander more to the top part of a girl than the bottom and since I don't have much to show in that department, I should be fine. At least I've had practice with Johnny Monroe.

"Look at this one," Mary Jane says. She takes a dress out of a J.C. Penney box and drapes it across her arm like it is a mink stole.

"That must have cost a fortune," I say.

"How about two fortunes," Mary Jane says.

I lie across Mary Jane's bed, finding it impossible not to covet the J.C. Penney dress before me. It is green plaid and looks like something Katherine Hepburn might wear. I promise myself that the next time I visit the graveyard I will send God, by way of Daddy, my apologies for this latest weakness of mine.

"Grandma also bought me these," Mary Jane says.

I gasp when Mary Jane brings out a brand new box of colored pencils and a pad of drawing paper. I have never in my life owned a box of colored pencils. At best, I've inherited broken crayon stubs, previously used by Jo, Amy, and Meg, kept in an old cigar box. Temptation grows stronger and I feel a sin coming on. Not

coveting Mary Jane's new art supplies is much harder than not coveting her dresses and seems an unfair challenge for God to throw at me.

Thou shalt not covet thy friend's art supplies, may very well be the hardest commandment of all.

Think of all the pictures those colored pencils could make, with their perfectly sharpened tips. This temptation, as Preacher would be happy to point out, puts me right in my very own Garden of Eden talking to the snake. A snake that has every intention of getting me to bite into that apple. Truth be told, I would not hesitate to take a hefty bite out of that wicked fruit if promised art supplies. A fact, of which, I am not particularly proud.

"So what have you been doing all summer?" Mary Jane asks.

"Staying clear of Johnny Monroe, mainly," I say.

"He's disgusting," she says. She uses her hands to smooth some of the creases in the dress.

"Disgusting just about sums it up," I say.

"None of the boys in Katy's Ridge are even worth looking at," she says for about the hundredth time. "However, Little Rock is full of cute boys."

I listen for the next thirty minutes to Mary Jane describe different boys in Little Rock, Arkansas. Her report is so titillating, I start to doze off.

"So have you been to the graveyard lately?" she asks, at the end of her litany.

Her question startles me awake.

"Nearly every day," I say.

Mary Jane is the only person in the world who knows why visiting Daddy is important to me: I'm afraid I'll forget him. The longer he's dead, the more I play moving pictures of him in my mind, anchoring his memory in place.

Just this morning I remembered how when I was a little girl I'd pretend to shave with him. I played that memory over and over in

my mind like I was memorizing a poem for school, except this poem wasn't words but images. I'd use a stick as a razor, imitating him while he stood on the front porch. During the warmer months he always shaved squinting into a tiny mirror tacked up on the house. A basin of soapy water collected the tiny whiskers until he threw it out into the ivy underneath the pine tree beside the porch. He told me that whiskers would grow like pole beans under that pine, and for years I believed him, but they never did.

"I think I'll wear this one the first day back to school," Mary Jane says. She holds up a yellow dress with a green belt. She admires it, her hands on her hips. Unlike me, Mary Jane has filled out instead of up.

"I got a new dress for my birthday," I say. "Amy sewed it."

"Amy's the best seamstress in Katy's Ridge," she says. "Anything she makes is much nicer than these store bought things."

Mary Jane probably knows that if she ever rubs it in about how much more she has than me, we wouldn't be friends. Her grandmother in Little Rock is rich and both my grandmothers are dead. My grandmother on my mother's side died before I was born and the one from my father's side died when I was five. Not to mention that with Daddy gone we barely have any money at all. The government sends Mama a little, but the rest she makes up by selling things in Rocky Bluff like quilts and canned jams and jellies.

Most of the time, I can be happy about Mary Jane's good fortune. But lately, since my birthday, at least, I've felt sorry for myself and thought more about what I don't have instead of what I do.

"Well, hello Louisa May. Did you have a nice summer?" Mary Jane's mother doesn't look at me but admires the dresses spread out across the room.

"Yes, ma'am," I say, wondering why grownups always ask questions instead of talking to you like a normal person.

Even when she's relaxed, Mary Jane's mom stands rigid like she

has a board strapped to her back and looks taller than most women. Mary Jane is so short you'd never think that they were even related. In my family, Meg and Amy look just like Mama and people say I look just like Daddy. Jo doesn't look like anybody, except maybe a movie star. And as far as I can tell, Mary Jane doesn't look like anybody, either, except maybe her grandmother.

"Louisa May, would you like to stay for dinner?" Mary Jane's mother asks.

Mary Jane and I smile at each other like life is good and just got better. "Yes, ma'am," I say. "But I'll need to ask first."

"That's fine," she says. She walks over and smoothes the creases of Mary Jane's new dress with one of her hands. I see the family resemblance in her actions. "Maybe Louisa May would like some of your older dresses, dear," she says to Mary Jane before she leaves, as if it has suddenly occurred to her to have pity on me.

Mary Jane's eyes widen and she looks over at me like I might take a swing at her own mother. She knows I hate being pitied. But instead of reacting, I take a deep breath and sit on my hands. I've faced enough temptation for one day.

According to Preacher, Jesus wants us to turn the other cheek when someone insults us, so I say, "No thank you, ma'am," and bite my lip to keep from smiting Mary Jane's kin.

Given the sheer number of church potlucks we've all attended over the years, it is a well-known fact that Mary Jane's mother can't cook nearly as well as mine. But her family always eats off fancy dishes that have ivy leaves painted all around the edges and were made in China. I also like that Mary Jane has a father sitting at the table, which reminds me of how my family used to be.

Mary Jane and I walk down the road to tell Mama I won't be home for dinner. We are good at moseying and set out to do just that. I already dread the thought of seeing Johnny Monroe on the road and wish we had a telephone so we could just call instead of walk the mile to my house.

Mary Jane's parents own the only telephone in Katy's Ridge. If anybody needs help they go there to call the ambulance in Rocky Bluff. Otherwise, they go to Doc Lester, who isn't really a doctor, but went to veterinary school for a year and still has all the books. Doc Lester smells funny, a sickly combination of rubbing alcohol, hair tonic and cow manure.

It is hot for September and the dirt from the road sticks to our legs as we walk. Mary Jane and I take turns swatting horse flies that love to drink the salty sweat from the creases of our elbows and knees.

We come to the crossroad, about halfway between our two houses, and there stands Johnny Monroe, kicking up the dirt with his scuffed up boots.

"Well, look who's here," Johnny says. "Twiddle Dee and Twiddle Dum." He gives the dirt an extra kick.

Though I am already staring at my shoes, this statement almost prompts me to look up. Not because I am insulted, but because it amazes me that Johnny has ever read a book, especially *Alice in Wonderland*. I decide he must have heard someone else say it.

"What do we do?" Mary Jane whispers to me. She matches my stance, lowering her head and hunching her shoulders since she actually has something to hide.

"Just keep walking and don't say anything," I whisper back.

Since Mary Jane doesn't have to pass this way to go to school, she hasn't had as many dealings with Johnny as I have.

"You girls want to go into the woods and have a little fun?" Johnny laughs.

Something in the way he laughs makes me look up just long enough to see a trickle of brown juice from Johnny's tobacco chew running down his chin. My half-digested lunch quickly rises from my stomach and lodges in my throat. I taste parts of it before swallowing it. Then I grit my teeth and resist the urge to grab a stick and knock the holy crap out of him.

Mary Jane reaches over and grabs my hand. We squeeze courage into each other's palms and walk straight ahead like God has parted the Red Sea and the Promised Land is around the next bend.

"Hey, you all want to see what's in my pocket?" Johnny says.

I can practically hear the smirk he must have on his face. Mary Jane gasps. I keep staring at my shoes, like they are the most fascinating worn-out oxfords on earth. Out of the corner of my eye I see Johnny holding the front of his pants.

"You're disgusting!" I yell, before I can stop myself.

Johnny laughs again and Mary Jane and I start running and don't stop until we get to the mailboxes in front of my house. We collapse on the side of the dirt road in a bed of clover gasping for air amidst the dust we rustled up.

"Did you see what he did?" Mary Jane asks, after she's caught her breath. "He's like some old horny dog." She fans her face that is still flushed from running. When Mary Jane runs, her face turns as red as her hair and her freckles blend into the background. "Do you think we should tell somebody?" she adds.

"I don't know," I say. Even though I'm smart when it comes to school subjects, I feel dumb when it comes to Johnny Monroe.

"If I tell Mama and Daddy they may not let me out of the house again until I'm thirty," Mary Jane says. "What about your mama?"

"She'll think I caused it."

"But you didn't."

"I know," I say. "But Mama thinks I draw trouble the way flowers draw bees."

Mary Jane huffs. "Johnny Monroe is as mean as a rattlesnake, and that has nothing to do with you."

Horseflies catch up with us and we swat them again as I ponder what to do about Johnny Monroe. My life would be a lot simpler if he just dropped off the face of the earth. Next time I'm at the cemetery I think I'll ask God to arrange it.

CHAPTER SIX

W e rest at the mailboxes at the bottom of our hill.

"Johnny Monroe is like a boil on my backside," I say to Mary Jane, which is about as true a statement as I've ever said. Though I've never had one.

Mary Jane laughs and I catch her laughing like a summer cold. Right there in the middle of the road we double over, tears in our eyes. Laughter is the perfect tonic after being so scared and I wonder if Aunt Sadie should try to bottle our giggles instead of her root concoctions that taste like something you shouldn't put in your mouth.

Cecil Appleby, Meg's ride to work, comes around the corner in his truck a little too fast for the curve. To avoid hitting us, he slams on his brakes, leaving tire tracks in the dirt and a shower of dust behind him. We cough from the dust and laugh more.

My sister, Meg, gets out of the truck and thanks Cecil for the ride. Before he drives away, Cecil gives us a quick lecture on the sheer stupidity of playing in the road. While he does, I can't stop looking at the strawberry birthmark that covers one entire side of his face. Cecil is a deacon at the church and a friend of Preachers.

"Aren't you too old to play in the road?" Meg asks. She sounds a little like Mama. I guess because she's tired.

"We weren't playing in the road," I say. "We were resting and laughing. There's a big difference."

Meg asks Mary Jane about her summer in Arkansas and Mary Jane starts telling about all her J.C. Penney dresses. To avoid temptation, I pick at a scab on my knee until it bleeds. When they quit talking Meg rubs the top of my head, like she used to do when I was younger and I yell at her to stop. She smiles as if pleased that she's irritated me and starts up the hill toward the house. A paperback book sticks out of the top of her purse and I yell that she'd better hide it. She stops long enough to push it deep into her bag and thanks me for looking out for her.

"Maybe we should tell Meg," Mary Jane says. She moves to sit on a big rock next to our mailbox. "She's probably the reason Johnny's hanging around so much anyway."

Tiny grains of grit from the road are in my mouth and I try to spit them out. "If we tell anyone it should be Daniel," I say. "He'll know what to do."

"I like Daniel," she says. "He reminds me of Clark Gable in *Gone with the Wind*."

"Everybody likes Daniel," I say. "And he doesn't look anything like Clark Gable."

Ever since Mary Jane saw the movie in Little Rock, she can't quit talking about it.

We cross the street and climb the hill toward Jo and Daniel's house. In Katy's Ridge everything is on a hill. We find Daniel just home from work and watering his vegetable garden at the back of the house. Late tomatoes and green beans are coming in and a few summer squash. Pumpkins are growing, too. Yellow starburst blooms dot the vines.

"Hey, Wildflower. Hey, Mary Jane," he says when he sees us.

I like that he calls me by my chosen name.

"We need to talk to you," I say, real serious.

He turns over the empty bucket and sits on it like a chair. "I'm ready," he says, a hand on each knee.

Mary Jane passes me a look that says she's just appointed me spokesperson. Words stick in my throat like a primed pump that hasn't pulled water yet. Unlike Mama, who would already be off doing something else, Daniel seems content to wait.

Mary Jane nudges me in the ribs and the words rush out fast. "Johnny Monroe said some things to us he shouldn't have said."

"Like what?" Daniel asks.

My stomach feels jittery, like a hive of bees is buzzing around inside. I can't shake the feeling that God might send lightning or a hailstorm to Katy's Ridge if I tell what Johnny said, and that even though we didn't do anything wrong, I'll end up getting punished for it. I remind myself about what Daddy said about fear being a friend and then wonder if this friend and the secret sense are somehow in cahoots.

"He asked us to go into the woods with him," I say finally, "and he wanted to show us what was in his pocket." The words don't sound as bad as Johnny's actions.

"He unbuttoned his overalls and touched himself!" Mary Jane blurts, like this is the part she's been dying to say.

Daniel's eyes widen, like the whole picture has come as crystal clear as Syler's Pond. He says something under his breath and then rises from his bucket. "I'll take care of it," he says, tucking his shirt-tail into his pants.

"Don't tell Mama," I beg Daniel.

"She's your mama, Wildflower, she has a right to know," he says.

"She'll just ask a bunch of her questions and then blame me for it," I say. "And please don't tell Jo, either."

Daniel chews on a piece of straw like he's thinking hard.

"After Daddy died, you said I could come to you and talk about

anything," I remind him. "You said I could trust you." I figure this is just what he needs to be able to keep the secret.

Daniel pauses, like he's giving it some thought. "I guess you don't want your folks to know about it, either," he says to Mary Jane.

"No, sir," she says. "They'll send me to live in Little Rock with my Granny."

Daniel agrees to keep our secret but on the condition that if anything like this happens again, he's telling everybody. Mary Jane and I agree. We even shake on it.

"I'm eating dinner at Mary Jane's," I say, "and we have to walk by Johnny to get back to her house."

"I'll go with you," Daniel offers.

"I have to go tell Mama first, about dinner," I say.

"Come by here when you're ready to go back," Daniel says. "Johnny Monroe won't do anything while I'm around."

For the first time in ages it feels like the boil on my backside might have been lanced. At the house, Mama is busy canning and doesn't catch on that anything has happened. When I tell her I'm eating at Mary Jane's, she looks downright relieved. Before we leave Mama makes us each a big glass of lemonade and asks Mary Jane about her summer in Little Rock, while stirring a big pot of boiling tomatoes. I can't remember the last time Mama showed this much interest in me. I try not to get jealous because I am sure somewhere in the Bible it says, *Thou shalt not be jealous of thy best friend getting attention,* or some such thing. The Bible has a saying for everything, especially for the things you should not do.

After we drain the last little bit of sugar out of the bottom of our glasses, Mary Jane and I walk to Daniel's house again. We enter the kitchen where Jo is frying okra on the stove and fanning herself with a folded up copy of the Rocky Bluff newspaper.

"I'm going to take a walk with the girls," Daniel says to Jo.

"That's fine," she says, looking radiant even while sweating.

Daniel put his arms around Jo, pats her stomach, and then kisses her on the cheek. Mary Jane smiles as though Fred Astaire and Ginger Rogers have just started dancing in the kitchen. I roll my eyes and hope Mary Jane doesn't come down with the swoons like Meg. Then I'll be the only one left with any sense.

We leave the house with Daniel and when we get to the cross-roads, Johnny is nowhere to be seen. For a few seconds I'm disappointed that I won't get to witness a showdown between Daniel and Johnny. It's not like Johnny to have the good sense to leave after saying the things he did.

"Let's pay a visit to his house," Daniel says.

I've never set foot near Johnny's house but Daniel seems to know where it is. We follow the main road another hundred yards and then take a narrow path through the woods littered with trash and broken liquor bottles. Kudzu vines cover the trees making a shroud of shade. We walk deeper and deeper into the woods and I start to remember every fairy tale I've ever read where people get lost in the woods and thrown into ovens or eaten by wolves. When we finally reach the Monroe's house, it isn't even a house, but more like a shack.

As we approach, Daniel calls out, "Is anybody home?"

I can't imagine living anywhere so small and dirty. This house makes ours look like a mansion. A stand of hardwoods surround the shack and make it look even smaller. An oak stands close to the house. One that's young enough that its lower branches can still be climbed. I think of Ruby and imagine the scene I heard Amy and Mama describe in the kitchen a few weeks before. A shudder crawls up my spine.

A crooked porch is attached to the cabin and one of the steps is missing. Wads of yellowed newspaper fill cracks between the boards of the shack. A faded, torn curtain moves from behind the window. Pieces of a face appear: an eye, a cheek. The door opens slowly and catches on a swollen floorboard. The girl peers out.

"Hello, Miss Melody," Daniel says.

"Hello, Mr. Daniel," she says, her words soft. Warily, the girl steps outside, her skin so white it appears to have never seen the sun. Her gaze briefly rests on me and Mary Jane before flitting off like a butterfly lifting from a flower. She brushes a few pieces of stringy hair with her hand, as if her unexpected company warrants a better appearance.

"We're looking for your brother," Daniel says to her.

"Oh," she says. Her eyes shift from left to right and then back to center as if danger could be lurking anywhere.

The look in Melody's eyes reminds me of something I've seen before. The cries of the trapped fox fill my memory, a fox Daddy and I found one time up on the mountain above our house. It was caught in a metal trap. It took forever for Daddy to free it and I covered my ears to try to block out the animal's cries. Finally he covered its head with his flannel coat so it wouldn't bite him and he used his knife to pry the trap open. The fox limped away, its paw nearly severed, leaving a trail of blood behind. Melody's eyes remind me of the fox's eyes.

Rumors around Katy's Ridge have Melody not right in the head. But from what I can tell she'd be perfectly fine if life was gentler with her. I can't imagine what's it like to have a brother like Johnny and I wonder if she misses her sister, Ruby. If I lost one of my sisters, I don't think I would ever recover. I even miss baby Beth, who died when she was two days old, and I never set eyes on her.

Up the hill behind the house, the outhouse door opens with a loud squeak and Johnny steps out. He pulls up his pants and smells his fingers. Just when I thought Johnny Monroe couldn't get more disgusting, he just did. He stops when he sees us, like a crook caught with the goods in his hands. Melody lowers her head and closes the door softly, as if a sleeping baby rests inside.

In the distance, Johnny takes a plug of chewing tobacco from

his pocket and sticks it in his mouth. He shuffles toward us and works the chew with his mouth wide open. Then he grabs a tin can lying in a junk pile among pieces of plows and broken tools along with discarded scraps of wood and pieces of rusted animal traps.

Johnny stops when he sees us. The three of us face him, our own version of David facing Goliath. I wish I'd thought to bring the slingshot Daddy made me. I'd aim right for the center of Johnny's forehead and let it rip.

When Johnny gets close enough that we can read the "cling peaches" on his tin can, he stops and spits a big wad of tobacco juice three inches from Daniel's boot. Johnny smiles, as if impressed with his own skill.

Daniel stays calm, with the exception of one fist that he balls up like he's ready to use it.

We stand under the oak tree and I wonder if Ruby is looking down on us. A vibration starts in my chest and I have the secret sense that Ruby wants me to know what happened to her.

"Johnny, I want you to leave these girls alone," Daniel says. His voice carries like he is God speaking from Mt. Sinai.

"I ain't doing nothin' to those girls," Johnny says. He squirts a mouthful of tobacco juice toward the peach can and misses. He snarls, like it is his first miss in years. The lemonade I had earlier turns sour in my stomach. I've spent so much time looking at my shoes, I haven't taken in the full picture of Johnny. His clothes are covered with a month's worth of dirt. His face is dirty, too. And someone must have used a dull kitchen knife to cut his hair because none of it matches up. When the wind kicks up we smell the stink of sour, dirty clothes and days-old sweat.

"I know you, Johnny," Daniel says. "I'm telling you right now, you leave these girls alone or I'll come after you. You hear me?"

Johnny spits again, but this time off to the side.

Daniel narrows his eyes to make good his threat.

"I hear you," Johnny says finally. His smile reveals two missing teeth, tobacco resting in the crevices.

Mary Jane and I follow Daniel down the path. I glance at the oak tree one last time and the vibration in my chest flutters again, as if Ruby is proud of us for standing up to her brother.

"He won't be any more trouble," Daniel says to us. "That boy's all bark and no bite."

I hope Daniel's right. "Why is he so mean?" I ask. Meanness and goodness are a mystery to me. It seems that everybody has a little of both.

Daniel holds back a large sticker bush from the path so Mary Jane and I can pass.

"It's hard to say what makes a person mean," he says. "For one thing, I don't think anybody's cared for that boy a single day of his life."

We step over piles of garbage thrown on the path. A rustle in the underbrush startles us and Mary Jane grabs my hand. Mr. Monroe approaches, cleaning the barrel of his shotgun with a dirty rag.

"Something I can do for you folks?" Mr. Monroe asks. Arthur Monroe makes Johnny look clean cut.

"It's taken care of," Daniel says.

"What's that boy done now?" he asks. He spits in the vines next to him. Spitting must run in this family, like meanness does. Except that Ruby and Melody don't seem mean at all.

"Johnny's been bothering the girls," Daniel says. "But I think we came to an understanding."

"Johnny does have a way with the girls." Old man Monroe grins and scratches a week's worth of whiskers on his dirty face and then looks over at me. "This one's growing up nice, ain't she," he adds. He gives me a wink.

I snap my head in the other direction and try not to gag. Daniel takes my hand and I take Mary Jane's.

"We'll be going now," Daniel says. "Like I said, your boy and I have come to an understanding. I trust there won't be any more trouble."

"Well if there is, you just let me know, and I'll knock the shit out of him," Mr. Monroe says. "That's all that boy understands, anyway."

Mr. Monroe blows his nose on the same dirty rag he used to clean his gun and shoves it into his back pocket. He walks away and staggers against a pine before righting himself.

We go in the opposite direction, moving quickly through the brush. When we reach the road I breathe deep, relieved to be out of the woods and away from Arthur and Johnny Monroe. But something tells me I may never get away from them.

"I feel sorry for that Melody girl," Mary Jane says, her voice just above a whisper.

"She's got it rough," Daniel says. "Maybe she could help Jo out after the baby comes. We can't pay her much, but at least it would get her out of that house."

I like the idea of getting to know Melody better, as long as her brother isn't anywhere around or her father.

"I couldn't believe she wasn't even wearing shoes," Mary Jane says, like there isn't anything more disgraceful. Whenever I see the part of Mary Jane that is like her mother, I try to ignore it, otherwise I might question why we're friends.

"And poor Ruby," Mary Jane continues. "Accidentally killing herself. Have you ever heard of something so awful?"

"She's in a better place," I say, sounding too much like Preacher. But in the back of my mind I'm thinking that what happened to Ruby was no accident.

"Any place would be a better place than that old shack," Mary Jane says.

Mary Jane doesn't even know the part about Ruby going to have a baby and for some reason I feel protective of Ruby's secret.

We reach the crossroads where Mary Jane and I will turn to go to her house.

"I'd better get back. Jo's probably got the okra ready," Daniel says. "You all promise to tell me if there are any more problems?"

"Promise," I say.

"Promise," Mary Jane echoes.

When Mary Jane and I sit down to dinner at her house we don't mention a word about the Monroes.

"Welcome, Louisa May," Mary Jane's father says and then sets out to say the longest prayer in history. I am certain the mashed potatoes will be as cold as buttermilk by the time he finishes and I am right.

We have roast beef, something we eat rarely at my house, but the meat is tough and by the end of supper my jaws hurt from all the chewing. *What a waste,* I think. Mama could have done a much better job with the meal. The mashed potatoes have huge lumps in them and the peas taste scalded. But the plates we eat off of don't have a single chip.

Mary Jane's father has a wooden leg attached at the knee. He took it off and showed it to me once and I studied it for a long time. His knee looked like the nub of an elbow and hung there like a hunk of sausage in the window of Sweeny's store, which Mary Jane's father owns. He lost his leg in a tractor accident when he was eighteen and then gave up farming to open the store in Katy's Ridge. He told me once that his actual severed leg is buried in his mother's back yard in Arkansas, right next to all their dead pets. For some reason a leg buried among cats, dogs, and rabbits gives me the creeps a lot more than any graveyard.

Mary Jane's brother, Victor, is two years older than me and has all his arms and legs. He works for Mary Jane's father at the grocery store, located on the road to Rocky Bluff. We go there to get bubble gum sometimes and Victor always throws in an extra piece for me. Victor is as close to having a brother as I've ever

come. He respects nature, like Daddy taught me, and won't squash a mosquito unless he has to, figuring they have as much right to be alive as any of us.

We used to catch lightning bugs together—me, Mary Jane and Victor—and we'd fill a Mason jar with holes cut in the top. But Victor always made us let them go after we counted them. Tonight, something's different and Victor avoids looking at me in the eyes like he's all of a sudden become shy. He talks to his father about business and keeps looking over like he's trying to impress me with how much he knows about running a store.

Meanwhile, all through supper, Mary Jane's father scratches his wooden leg like it itches. He'd probably unscrew the thing and use it to serve up the cold, lumpy mashed potatoes if he thought it would get a laugh.

Before dark, Meg and Mama show up at Mary Jane's to walk me home. Even though the Sweeney's have everything they could possibly want or need, Mama brings Mary Jane's mother two jars of her canned tomatoes and a small quilt piece she sewed to put hot things on the dinner table.

Our family has a habit of walking in the evenings when the weather is nice. Daddy always said it helped supper digest. But when we walk these days, there's a big hole where Daddy usually stood and I think we all feel it.

No one stands at the crossroads when we walk by. I think of Melody, living in a shack next to the oak tree where her sister Ruby died. I wouldn't wish that life on anybody.

Daddy would say the Monroes deserve our pity. We don't have much, but we are rich compared to them. We are not to judge people who are going through hard times. He was big on being a good person. But people like Johnny make being a good person much harder than it sounds.

The sun has long gone behind the mountain and the moon is

rising. Shadows of trees blend with the darkness. Crickets sing their chorus, their music surrounding us.

Meg locks her arm in Mama's. Meg is good at getting Mama's attention in a way that Mama doesn't mind. The moonlight serves as a lantern as we walk in silence, our footsteps shuffling in the dirt. We find our way home in total darkness and it's as if our feet have memorized the path.

Back when Daddy used to walk with us he would hold my hand. I'd be on one side while Mama was on the other. He held Mama's hand a lot, too, like they were still courting. Sometimes he would light his pipe and it would be so dark all we could see was the little bowl of fire kept alive by his breath. He knew the path up the hill to our house better than any of us and he would lead the way, guiding our steps to avoid every rock and root.

Jasmine grows along the path and in summer our noses tell us when we are close to home. I imagine Daddy's footsteps joining ours, him leading the way through the darkness, the smell of sweet tobacco mingling with the smell of jasmine.

About halfway up the hill I shiver, even though it isn't the least bit cold, and wrap my arms around myself. I sense someone watching us in the dark. I immediately think of Johnny and I am about to say something to Meg and Mama when I trip and fall to the ground. A hand jerks me up.

"Don't be clumsy, Louisa May," Mama says. Her grasp pinches my skin and I pull away.

"Are you okay?" Meg asks in the darkness.

"I'm fine," I say. My embarrassment chases away any remaining creepy feelings and I brush the dirt from my hands and knees, missing Daddy more than ever.

CHAPTER SEVEN

The next morning, the screen door slaps at my heels as I walk out on the front porch and a knot twists in my stomach. I have had the secret sense more often the last few days. It starts as a vibration in my chest and then extends to my fingertips like a mild charge of electricity. I pause, remembering a similar feeling the day Daddy died.

"Where you headed, Louisa May?" Mama says from behind me. I jump before I can stop myself.

"Why don't you call me by my real name and maybe I'll tell you," I say. The words come out more hateful than I intend.

"Wildflower…" she says. Her patience is as ragged as Daddy's favorite shirt I keep digging out of the rag bin because she keeps throwing it away.

"I'm not a child, Mama. You don't have to know every single place I go." Although I'm convinced she knows exactly where I'm going and that's the whole point of asking me. She just wants me to say it. It is the anniversary of Daddy's accident and I've been thinking about it all morning. Even if everybody else acts like

they've forgotten him, nothing can keep me from going to the graveyard today to pay my respects.

"I'm going to the river," I say, which is a lie. Then I'm down the path before she can stop me.

"Be careful," she yells after me, like she used to say to Daddy every morning he left for the sawmill.

"I will," I yell back, which was always Daddy's answer, too.

Leaves from the poplar trees dot the ground like stars. The poplars are the first to know that fall is coming and the first to drop their leaves. Winter will follow, a hard time in the mountains. Visiting the outhouse with a foot of snow on the ground isn't something anybody looks forward to.

At the crossroads I look out for Johnny, but he isn't around. Daniel's talk must have worked. I take my shortcut, complete with ritual to cross the stream, and minutes later enter the gate in the back of the graveyard. The more I come this way the faster it takes. As I close the gate, my fingers tingle with the electricity of the secret sense. For several seconds I stand without moving, wondering if this means I should turn back.

But it's the anniversary, I say to myself, *Daddy would want me to be with him.* I convince myself to keep going.

When I approach his marker something looks different. The knot in my gut twists tighter, a tingling premonition that something isn't right. Then I see it. A Mason jar, full of clear liquid, lies next to one of the tree roots. The grass is torn up like somebody has stomped around on the grave. I walk closer, feeling like the ground might cave in under me. Daddy's tombstone is streaked with a brown, muddy slash from one end to the other. An empty can is tossed a few feet away on the ground.

I kick the peach can down the hill with all my might. "I hate you, Johnny Monroe!" I yell. A faint echo bounces off a nearby hill.

Tobacco juice spews out in wide, brown arches as the can

thumps end over end down the hill toward the river. My anger comes out in tears, which makes me even madder. I yank a handful of willow leaves from the branch closest to me and scrub the stinking tobacco juice off of my father's name. The leaves are too small to do the job so I run up the hill and get poplar and maple leaves which are bigger. After spitting on the leaves, I frantically rub at the brown juice on Daddy's marker. My knuckles get bruised and bloodied against the stone. I can't believe that even Johnny Monroe would do such a vile thing to the memory of a dead person.

Tears blur my vision as I pick up the Mason jar from the ground and open it. A repulsive stink spreads, worse than any skunk. Moonshine. The same stuff some of the men from the mill passed around behind the church, after Jo and Daniel's wedding. My face grows hot as I imagine Johnny Monroe spitting tobacco juice on Daddy's grave. Careful not to touch where Johnny Monroe's mouth has been, I throw the jar into the woods.

Revenge fills my mind. Revenge I can't act on. Daniel must have made Johnny really mad and he wants me to know it. Telling Daniel again might make Johnny do something even worse, like come after me or Meg or one of my family. If he's willing to defile the final resting place of a good man who was kind to him, I know now that there is nothing so low that Johnny Monroe wouldn't do.

Since it's the anniversary of when everything in my life changed, my tender memories feel all exposed.

"I'm sorry, Daddy," I say. "It's all my fault."

I wrap my arms around his marker, touching my cheek to the rough stone. It smells of crushed leaves mixed with tobacco and it feels cool to my touch, even in the noonday sun. The coolness reminds me of the day he died. His skin kept getting cooler as the warmth left him, like a fire slowly dying away. I force the memory away, wanting only to remember the good things.

In the distance, Miss Mildred practices the organ for Sunday service, the faint tune resembling *The Old Rugged Cross.* Johnny

Monroe knows better than to get anywhere near the church on Sundays, on account of Preacher wanting to snatch his soul from the devil and claim it for the Lord. Preacher would probably get an extra reward in heaven for bagging a big sinner like Johnny. To hear Preacher talk, saving souls is like a baseball game between God and the Devil. Every sinner saved is a home run for the Lord. But Johnny deserves to suffer the fires of hell. If I wasn't convinced of this before, I am now.

The willow tree sways with the breeze and the sun flickers from behind the clouds. A small whirlwind dances on Daddy's grave before skirting down the hillside toward the mound of newly packed earth on top of Ruby Monroe. Her grave remains unmarked, except that somebody has placed a handful of wilted flowers on top of the dirt. Ruby will probably never have a marker because the Monroe's are too poor to get one and it isn't like anybody at the church will take up a collection for it, either, like they did for Daddy.

A twig snaps behind me and I jump. Fear crackles up my spine. Word is there are still mountain lions up in the high hills, though nobody has seen one for over twenty years.

"Well, look who's here," a voice says. In that instant I know that it's a human predator I am dealing with instead of an animal one.

The shock of seeing Johnny Monroe freezes me in my tracks. Goosebumps crawl up my arms. His clothes are covered with dirt and he has a bruise under one eye like somebody beat the fire out of him.

"Hello, Johnny," I say, hiding my fear. If you come across a rattlesnake you're supposed to stop, then slowly back away. But I am still on my knees and backing away isn't an option.

"I thought I'd come visit your daddy," he grins. Whoever blackened his eye, knocked out one of his teeth, too. "Yeah, me and your daddy had a little party up here last night. Did you know he liked moonshine whiskey?"

I clinch my jaw. Anger surges inside me again, but I figure this is just what Johnny wants, an excuse to come after me. I force myself to take a deep breath instead of the short, jagged ones my anger insists on.

"What's wrong? Cat got your tongue?" He pokes me in the shoulder.

"No, I just need to be going, that's all," I say. "Mama's waiting for me."

"No she's not," he says. "I bet she has no idea you're up here."

My insides churn. Johnny is right. He moves closer. His breath stinks of moonshine.

I start to stand, but Johnny pushes me back down. "You ain't goin' no place," he says. He grabs my wrist and squeezes tight. It hurts like blue blazes. When I try to pull away, he holds me fast.

"Okay, maybe I can stay for a while," I say. Even though I act calm, my heart is racing. I decide my best chance of getting out of there is to act like Johnny's friend. "How are you and your Daddy doing, Johnny? I was so sorry about Ruby."

He looks confused and glances over his shoulder at Ruby's grave. For a split second I wonder if he put those flowers there himself. Maybe he misses her. But when he looks back at me I know his rage has left no room for tender heartedness. I wonder if I can outrun him. Maybe if I catch him by surprise. His eyes narrow, as if he has heard my thoughts.

"You don't care about my family," he says.

"It must be hard not having a mother," I say. "Kind of like me not having a father."

I've never seen Johnny Monroe look puzzled. "I've been watching you," he says through gritted teeth.

"So what," I say, trying to act casual. "People watch other people all the time."

Johnny holds my wrist tighter. In the distance, Miss Mildred

and Preacher come out of the church. I yell to them, "Hey, up here! Help!"

Johnny puts his hand over my mouth and squeezes my face. His grip hurts and his hands smell of tobacco. When I scream again, it comes out muffled. Besides, Preacher and Miss Mildred are far enough away that it won't do any good. Preacher locks the door even though there's nothing in there worth stealing—a few hymnals is all, and Miss Mildred's organ, which I can't imagine anyone taking the time to lug down the road.

After they leave, Johnny uncovers my mouth and grabs my wrist again. He looks smug, like he's gotten away with something.

"I really need to go, Johnny. Daniel's going to come looking for me any minute." When I try to jerk free, his grip tightens until my fingers turn white.

"Daniel don't know you're up here. Nobody does. I saw you leave your house," Johnny says.

I knew he'd been watching me and this just confirms it. "Let's just forget all this," I say. "I'll go home and you can get on back to standing on your road and nobody has to know anything about it. I'll even put in a good word about you to Meg."

Johnny leans closer and runs his free hand up and down my arm like he is calming a calf before slitting its throat.

A breeze blows through the willow tree and jiggles the leaves like gold coins. Johnny touches my hair. His hand is awkward, clumsy. "You like that, don't you," he says. His try at tenderness is scarier than his roughness.

I pull away, but the vice of his grip holds firm.

"You're feisty, aren't you?" Johnny says. "I like feisty."

The voice in my head screams out for help, but I am alone. Daddy is gone. I fight back the sadness as hard as I fight back Johnny. It doesn't matter how loud or how long I scream up here, nobody will hear me.

"Johnny you need to let me go," I say again, my voice sweet as molasses. "Your mama wouldn't like you acting like this."

"My mama didn't give a shit about me," he says. He spits and I see in his eyes how much he believes it.

"I'm sure she would be here to help you out if she could, Johnny. Just like my daddy would be here to help me out if he could."

"Your daddy can't do nothin' for you now," he says, "not since he got hisself cut in half."

Johnny's words grip my chest like he's reached in and squeezed my heart with his dirty, bare hands. I aim my fist right at Johnny's nose and swing and hit him as hard as I can. The punch connects. He moans. Blood squirts from his nose onto my face.

"You bitch!" he yells. He grabs his nose and loosens his grip long enough for me to pull away. I run for the shortcut as fast as my legs will go, forcing myself to not look back or it will slow me down. My feet pound the ground with every step, yet it feels like I've sprouted wings. I leap over roots and branches and anything in the path. I've never run this hard. I smile with the thought that I might get away. Then I hear Johnny coming down the hill behind me.

My heart pumps wildly. The footbridge lies over the next rise. If I can make it to the bridge and get across before him, I might have a chance. Johnny weighs more than me. He'll have to slow down to get across. I grip the necklace around my neck while I run and ask Daddy and God and Mary to save me, and anybody else in heaven that will listen.

Through the trees I catch sight of the old footbridge up ahead. Johnny's breathing is heavy and close. Just when I think I'm going to make it, he tackles me to the ground. The fall knocks the breath out of me. I gasp for air. Johnny flips me over hard. He yanks my hair. His nose is red and swollen. Blood streaks across his face like cat's whiskers. His stink smothers me, a foul stench

of moonshine, tobacco and rotten teeth. He pins my shoulders to the ground.

At that moment the thought occurs to me that the two things I fear most are right in front of me: Johnny Monroe and the threat of dying young. If Johnny has his way, he'll put me in the grave right next to Daddy so he can spit tobacco juice on my name, too.

Out of breath, Johnny leans over me and smothers me with his body. His whiskers hurt, brushing my cheeks and neck like a thousand sharp needles. He yanks my hands over my head and holds them there. I pull hard against his grasp but have no strength to move him. Johnny forces his mouth against mine and I taste his rotten spit. I gag and choke. Then he bites my lip and shoves his tongue down my throat. I struggle, jerking my mouth free.

"Johnny, don't!" I cry. He grins at me and I feel like I am looking into the face of the devil himself.

"There's nobody here that can save you," Johnny says, and I believe him.

Then he slaps me so hard my ears ring like the treble notes of Miss Mildred's organ. I taste blood in my mouth and my face is hot and stinging with pain. I turn my head to the side and throw up. This seems to make him even angrier. He slaps me again. The pain is a hundred times worse than anything I've ever felt. When I scream again he covers my mouth with his hand. I bite his hand hard and he slaps me, closed fisted again, so hard this time the pain crescendos into numbness. Urine soaks my underwear and the warmth spreads down my legs.

Seconds later, the pain goes away. I have the odd feeling that I am floating outside of myself, watching the scene. This isn't happening to me at all, but to a stranger, some other foolish thirteen-year-old girl who didn't listen to her secret sense and is powerless to get away.

"What's the matter, Louisa May?"

"My name's Wildflower," I mumble, defiant.

"Wildflower?" he laughs, "Nah . . . people should call you Weed." He grabs my hair again and pulls. "Yeah, I think I'll pull this weed."

As he drags me screaming to a clearing, I search the woods for salvation. But the chance of anyone finding me is about as slim as the chance that Johnny will have a change of heart. Hot tears streak my face and pool in my ears. I tell them to stop so Johnny won't see my weakness but they keep on like the trickle of a stream seeking the river.

"Let's get you comfortable," he says, pulling me over on a bed of leaves. It's as if his motions have nothing to do with me. I could be anybody, or anything—an animal he wrestled to the ground. He pulls a jack knife from his pocket and unfolds it. Then he waves it in front of me, inches from my face. The metal glitters in the patchy sun, as if recently sharpened.

Something moves in the distance and I look past him into the trees. I gasp. Ruby Monroe is hanging by the neck swinging in the breeze. Her eyes, wide open, stare down at me. I watch her until the image fades away.

"What are you looking at?" Johnny says. He throws down his knife, takes my jaw in his hands and holds my head so that I have to look at him.

"Nothing," I say, as if I might get Ruby in trouble.

He rips off my dress; the new one Amy made me for my birthday that I put on this morning in honor of the anniversary of Daddy's death. The seams are tight and not easily torn, but he manages with the help of his knife. The air is cool on my skin. He stares at the yellowing camisole that all my sisters wore before me. Then he takes his knife and cuts it off. His eyes take in my fledgling breasts and he cups a rough hand over each. I dig my heels in the dirt and push away. He pulls me back.

"Well, look at this," he says. He holds Grandma McAllister's medallion in his hand. "Looks like real gold."

"Leave that alone," I say through clenched teeth. He rips the

necklace from my neck. The chain stings my skin and I remember
what Jesus said in the Bible about not throwing your pearls before
swine. But Jesus didn't say what to do if the swine turned out to be
bigger than you and stole your pearls without asking.

Johnny gazes at the necklace. For a moment, his eyes soften.
But then he sees me watching him and his expression changes as
fast as a lightning strike. He touches his nose. A fresh trickle of
blood comes from inside. With new determination, he wraps his
fingers around my neck until I can't breathe. I squirm to get away
and search his face for a sign of mercy. There is none. It occurs to
me that Johnny Monroe's hateful face will be the last thing I see
before I die.

He loosens his grip to whisper in my ear, and I suck much-
needed air into my lungs. "If you tell anybody about this, I'll kill
you," he says. "Y'hear that? You can't hide from me. I'll find you
and kill you dead!"

I nod, thinking it's over, that Johnny's had a change of heart.
He's going to let me go, as long as I promise not to ever tell
anyone. But instead he tightens his grip again and unhooks the
belt on his pants. There is no fight left in me. My heartbeat echoes
in my ears. I pray to God to be rescued and ask him to send Daddy.
I offer wordless prayers to the trees, the river, and the land and
then apologize to Mama for getting myself hurt and to Aunt Sadie
for not paying attention to what she taught me about the secret
sense.

I close my eyes and surrender. Seconds later Daddy comes
toward me. He stands, surrounded by light, and holds out his hand
for me to take. I float toward the treetops to meet him and he takes
me into his arms. When I look back, I see my body still lying on
the ground, Johnny on top of me. I wonder briefly how I can be
two places at once. But it doesn't really matter. All that matters is
that Daddy is here. A year ago he left, but now he's back. He's
come to take me with him.

CHAPTER EIGHT

One Year Earlier

Daniel McBride comes to the schoolhouse during recess. I've seen him around because he works at the Blackstone sawmill with Daddy. Jo has had a secret crush on him ever since he came to our house last Christmas. Daddy always invites anybody that doesn't have family nearby to come to our house on holidays because he says we have enough family and food to share. Daniel used to live up North and he is the only Yankee I've ever seen up close. Since jobs were scarce, he moved to Rocky Bluff to take a position with the railroad. When that didn't work out he took a job at the sawmill, where Daddy is his supervisor. Most people have forgiven him for being a Yankee on account of how nice he is.

Breathless, Daniel's sweat soaks into his shirt. He leans over and whispers something to Mr. Webster, my teacher since first grade, who is sitting in the shade grading papers. Mr. Webster turns and looks over at me on the swing, his face solemn. Mr. Webster is strict, but fair, and always wears a suit coat like being a

school teacher is as important as the President of the United States.

"Louisa May, you need to go home right away," Mr. Webster says.

"Why?" I ask. I've never in six years of schooling been told to go home.

He looks at Daniel and then back at me. "You're needed at home," he repeats, as if this is all the reason I should need.

"But why?" I ask. "What's happened?"

Mr. Webster hardens his face and I remember the last time I had to write *I will not talk back to Mr. Webster* a hundred times on the blackboard.

"Come on, Louisa May," Daniel says. He stands and motions toward the truck.

"What's going on?" Mary Jane asks, walking over from the swing.

"Nobody will say," I tell Mary Jane, "but it can't be good."

"Good luck," Mr. Webster says as I leave.

It feels weird for Mr. Webster to wish me anything, especially good luck. Not to mention how strange it is to go home so early in the day. Sometimes on the last day of school we get to go home early, but never at the first of the year and never before lunch. Even if a big snowstorm hits, we are expected to make it in and stay the full day.

Daniel holds the door open to the sawmill truck while I step inside. He gets in on the drivers side and starts the truck. Flecks of sawdust stick to the sweat on his forehead.

"What's happened?" I ask, still trying to get answers.

He hesitates, as if weighing the consequences of his words, and then says, "There's been an accident. They're taking your daddy home."

"If he's had an accident, why aren't they taking him to the hospital in Rocky Bluff?" I ask.

Daniel pauses again, his arms resting on the steering wheel. When he finally speaks his voice is softer than I expect. "We'll find out when we get you home."

My chest tightens, making it harder to breathe. Something is up, and I am convinced that *something* isn't good. "Does Mama know?" I ask.

"Yes. She's waiting at the house," he says.

We ride in silence the whole way and it is the longest ride home I've ever had. I am afraid to ask any more questions, afraid to know the truth, or maybe I don't want to make Daniel more uncomfortable than he already is. Though he seems nice enough, I hardly know him at all.

Daniel takes it slow over the bluff like everyone does, respecting the sheer drop that accompanies any false turn. After the road levels off, he parks below our house, securing the parking brake despite the level ground. I jump out of the truck and run ahead, realizing halfway up the hill that I forgot to thank him for the ride.

When I get to the house Meg is sitting on the porch sniffing back a steady stream of tears. Her face is red and puffy like it always gets whenever she cries. She stayed home from school to help Mama with some canning. Otherwise she'd be at the high school.

"What happened, Meg?" I ask. Her sobbing commences and I know I won't be getting any answers from her.

Crying is the last thing I feel like doing. I want to know what happened. It doesn't make sense for Daddy to get into an accident at work. It isn't like him to be careless. Once when I went over there he showed me all the machinery and blades not to get close to. If he did get hurt I am certain it can be fixed.

I find Mama in the house sitting at the kitchen table, her face as pale as the bag of White Lily flour on the counter. Daniel comes in behind me and she thanks him for getting me.

"Where's Daddy?" I ask her.

"They're bringing him from the mill," she tells me. Then she looks at Daniel, "Why can't I just go there?" she asks.

"It's best you don't," he says. "They'll bring him by truck until they reach the bottom of the hill."

Daniel puts a hand on Mama's shoulder and I wait for her to slap it away, but she just lets it sit there. In all my twelve years of life, I've never once seen Mama follow orders or sit still. I know at that moment that something is horribly wrong.

"Shouldn't he be here by now?" she asks Daniel.

"Any minute," he answers.

She wrings her hands like they are one of her old mops. Then she gets up and walks through the house to the front porch. We follow. Her eyes are trained down the hill toward the road, watching for Daddy to come home. Sometimes in the evenings she'll watch for him, too, but with a different look on her face, like a schoolgirl waiting for a glimpse of her beau.

We wait, all of us looking down the hill, and I sit on the bottom porch step and kick at dirt clods with my shoe. A fly lights on my knee and walks around, tickling my leg. I catch it in my open fist and let it buzz against the inside of my palm before I set it free. At that moment I feel like that fly. Trapped, and waiting for something bigger to set me free.

We hear them before we see them. A scraping sound first, and then voices growing in volume as they approach. Men are talking to Daddy, encouraging him to hold on.

As they turn the corner we see an old mule pulling a wooden stretcher up the hill. It isn't really a stretcher but something that farmers use to pull firewood or move harvested crops from one end of a field to another. I've never seen it used to pull a person and wonder who came up with the idea. Daddy is wrapped up in blankets like it's the dead of winter, even though it is a warm day in October. Indian Summer, it's called. I don't know why. Next

time I see Horatio Sector I'll have to ask. If anybody knows, he will. The Indians have lived in these mountains longer than anybody.

Nailed to where I stand, I wait for Daddy to lift his head and catch my eye and smile at me to let me know everything is okay. But the bundle that is supposed to be my father doesn't move.

The mule labors up the path, with the stretcher scraping the ground behind it. I've never heard that sound before—wood scraping against rock and dirt—and it strikes me that the men should be carrying him instead of dragging. The hill never seemed that steep to me before. I've run up and down it from the time I was knee high. But the mule struggles with Daddy's weight and one of the men slaps its backside to keep it moving. The men and the stretcher look like they are coming up the hill in slow motion.

Meg cries harder the closer they get and the redness of her face has turned to splotches. Daniel holds onto her while Mama runs down the hill to meet the men. I've never seen Mama run like that. She has a quickness about her like someone younger. She calls Daddy's name and the men part to let her join them. Daddy lies in the center like a king coming to a palace, except it is our house he is being taken to and there aren't any servants except these men from the mill.

I break from my trance and run down the path to meet him, too, but one of the men grabs me before I get too close.

"Easy there," he says. "Your daddy's hurt real bad."

I jerk my shoulder away. When I look down I see a piece of burlap wrapped around Daddy that is soaked dark red. Blood. It is odd to see him lying there not moving. I don't understand how a man that towers over most people can look so small on a stretcher. As far as I'm concerned, Jesus learned how to walk on water from him so it makes no sense that he might be drowning in his own blood. I'm not sure the stain on the cloth is his blood anyway. Somebody could have just put it there. It occurs to me that maybe

this is a joke Daddy is playing on us and any minute he'll hop up and laugh his hearty laugh that he's pulled a prank and we fell for it.

"Daddy, open your eyes. Look at me," I say. "It's Wildflower."

I wish so hard that he would open his eyes that he actually does. But he opens them like they weigh a ton.

"Daddy, what's wrong?" I say.

He turns to look at me, and I see in his eyes more than I want to. He is hurt bad. In an instant his look tells me how sorry he is that he won't get to see me grow up. This truth makes my knees buckle underneath me and one of the men catches me right as I am falling and holds onto me until I can stand upright again. This is the closest I've ever come to fainting and it takes me several steps to get the ground solid underneath me again.

"It's okay, Daddy," I say, walking alongside him up the hill. His eyes open and close every few seconds like he is the sleepiest he has ever been. I want to be strong so he won't feel so bad, and it looks like Mama is doing the same. She holds onto his hand as they make the rest of the way up the hill.

"I love you, Joseph," she keeps saying, strong and solid. "Now, don't you go leaving me. You're the best thing that's ever happened to me."

I feel like I am hearing things I shouldn't be hearing—things that Mama and Daddy don't say in front of anybody else. I am embarrassed that all of Daddy's men heard it, too. To hide my embarrassment, I watch the mule's tail swish back and forth as it hauls the stretcher up the hill. I recognize the mule to be Simon Hatcher's, a man who owns a farm over near the mill.

When the mule stops in front of the porch, Mama says to the men, "Let's get him to the bed."

The four men carefully lift Daddy and carry him up the front porch steps and into their bedroom. He looks the color of the ashes in the wood stove.

Mama leaves to go into the kitchen and comes back with a cloth to wipe Daddy's face. If one of us kids gets sick she always wipes our foreheads with a cold cloth.

Just about the time the men get Daddy situated on the bed, Doc Lester shows up. Every time I see Doc Lester I think of weasels because of the shape of his face. His chin juts out to a point; plus his eyes are beady and too close together. The men step back into the corners of the room, leaving Mama standing at the head of the bed next to Daddy.

Doc Lester places his small black bag on the foot of the bed and peels back the layers of what Daddy is wrapped in. He blocks my view and the only thing I can see is Doc Lester's weasel-like head shake back and forth.

"Poor devil," he mutters. "He's lost a lot of blood." His voice sounds about as grim as a person can sound.

Somebody nudges me on the shoulder and it is Daniel McBride. "Why don't we go outside?" he says, looking out toward the porch.

"But I want to see," I say.

"Best to leave this to the grown-ups," Daniel says. He takes me gently by the arm and leads me toward the front door.

"But I just turned twelve," I say, as if this constitutes being grown up. But I let him lead me out of the room anyway.

As I leave the house, I hear Mama gasp when she sees what is underneath the wrappings. An uneasy feeling settles into the pit of my stomach.

A dazed Meg sits on the porch, her face streaked with tears and crimson, as if the color lost in Mama and Daddy faces has become hers.

"Oh my God, Louisa May, we've lost Daddy!" Meg says. Her voice cracks under the weight of the words. I don't like that she's given up on him so easily.

"Where's Jo and Amy?" I ask.

"When Mama got word they were bringing Daddy home, she sent Jo to pick up Amy at the high school."

"I need to go back," I say to Daniel. "He would want me there." I jerk away from Daniel's grip.

Inside, Doc Lester covers Daddy up and closes his little black bag. "Somebody get Preacher. I've done all I can do here."

"He's on his way," a voice says from the back.

Doc Lester is the only doctor in Katy's Ridge, although it is a stretch of the imagination to call him that. He is also the person who signs the death certificates. Preacher being there is merely a courtesy. I push Doc Lester aside and take my place next to Daddy. His eyes are closed and his mouth, stretched tight in pain, is absent the smile he usually wears.

"Hey, Daddy. It's Louisa May."

He doesn't say anything back. Mama sits on the bed putting a cool rag on his head and I wonder if she realizes that he has more than a fever. Next she'll be breaking out the castor oil and the wooden spoon.

"Daddy?" I whisper, leaning next to him. "It's Wildflower."

"Don't bother him, honey," Mama says, as if I'm trying to ask him a question while he's reading. My face burns. I want to shake some sense into her. Does she not see what is happening?

Daddy's eyes open. They used to be as brown as rich shoe leather, but now are black and dull.

"What happened, Daddy?" I ask.

He looks up at me like he has a lifetime of things to tell me. I know he loves me. But what I see in his eyes is more than love. He is telling me that he will miss me. A lump of sorrow lodges in my throat. I swallow so I won't cry.

"Take care of your mama," he says, his beautiful baritone voice now raspy.

This isn't what I want to hear. I want him to tell me that every-thing is going to be all right, and that he'll be better soon. Instead,

he is letting me know that nothing is ever going to be all right again.

"Promise me," he says.

"I will," I say, not even knowing what I'm promising to do. As far as I'm concerned, it is Mama's job to take care of me, not the other way around. But I will agree to anything at that moment if it will take that look from his eyes. I silently beg God to make him better and promise all sorts of things in return. If God wants me to, I will even stop thinking that Preacher and Doc Lester are idiots every time I see them.

Daddy turns his eyes toward Mama. She strokes his cheek with such tenderness I can't bear to watch. I look out the window at a squirrel burying an acorn under the pine tree and wonder how squirrels remember where they've buried things. Do they make little treasure maps in the tops of trees? When I turn back, Daddy's eyes are closed forever.

Dying seems like such a private thing, even with a dozen people in the room. I want to shield him from the watchers, but it is too late. Doc Lester picks up Daddy's wrist searching for a pulse.

"He's gone," he says, opening his silver pocket watch to note the time.

"Gone where?" I ask.

Doc Lester ignores my question and puts an arm on Mama's shoulder. Mama stares down at Daddy, her eyes vacant, like she's gone, too.

"Somebody tell me what's going on," I say too loud.

Nobody answers. Daddy is the one who always answers my questions, and in the next instant, I realize that I will miss this fiercely. At the same time I keep expecting him to open his eyes and smile and ask, "How's my Wildflower?" Then he'll sit up and say he feels much better now and I'll tell him how he gave us all quite a scare.

Miracles have been known to happen in Katy's Ridge. Little

Wiley Johnson almost drowned last summer. Everybody was crying over him, too, when all of a sudden he spit out a gallon of the lake and choked air back into his lungs. His parents gave Preacher a big offering the next Sunday on account of God giving back their little boy. Afterwards, Preacher said Wiley was destined to do Jesus' work and spread his gospel. Wiley didn't look too thrilled about that. I don't think he has anything against Jesus, but he is still just a kid.

Seconds later, Aunt Sadie arrives breathless at the door. The men part to let her pass. The noise she makes when she sees Daddy is the most lonesome wail I've ever heard and it sends ripples through me because it is the sound of my heart breaking, too.

"Everybody out!" Sadie says, and all the men from the mill obey, until there is just me and Sadie and Mama in the room.

"What's happening, Aunt Sadie? What's going on?" I whisper, like my regular voice might wake Daddy up.

"The world just became a much sadder place," Sadie says.

I step closer and touch Daddy's fingers and wait for them to close around mine and for his lungs to fill deep and wide like whenever he takes in a big breath of fresh mountain air first thing in the mornings.

"Breathe, Daddy," I whisper, praying for a Wiley Johnson sized miracle. I take a big breath myself to show him how it's done.

"It won't do any good, sweetheart," Aunt Sadie says. "It's too late."

I hear the words but refuse to believe them. I tell Mama that Aunt Sadie is wrong. But Mama won't stop staring at Daddy. It's as if somebody yelled "freeze" and she got stuck like a statue.

Just then I remember the little package I received when my grandmother McAllister died. Inside was a small, gold medallion of Jesus as a baby in his mother's lap. People all over the world and especially in Ireland, where our people are from, believe that Mary can grant miracles and they pray to her all the time.

I run into my bedroom and take the medallion out of my dresser drawer. It is still in the box, wrapped in white tissue paper, along with a card with a prayer written on it. I read the words on the card and repeat them over and over again, trying to pray up a miracle. At our church in Katy's Ridge, Jesus' mother isn't talked about much. The only time Preacher mentions her is on Christmas day when we hear the story about her giving birth to Jesus in a stable when there was no room at the inn.

I pray so hard that Mary's face is imprinted on my hand. In the meantime, I wait for the miracle. I bite my bottom lip hard enough that it starts to bleed and taste the salty sweetness of my own blood. As far as I can tell, Mama doesn't even realize I am there. She just keeps rubbing Daddy's forehead with the cool rag. It makes me angry, how useless she is. But I am useless, too. Death makes everybody useless. The pain in my lip takes my mind away from the pain that starts to creep in around my heart. I go outside to continue my praying there.

A bunch of men from the mill stand under the pine trees, smoking cigarettes, with their heads bowed and voices low. Daniel sits on the top step of the porch and I go to sit next to him, still clutching the medallion.

"I'm sorry," Daniel says softly.

"Sorry for what?" I ask. "You didn't do anything."

"I'm sorry that your daddy's passed on," Daniel says.

"Passed on to what?" I ask, genuinely curious what he means. "Is he in heaven now? Just like that? One minute you're here and the next minute you're sitting around with angels?"

Daniel looks over at me like he isn't sure how to answer.

"Well, if anybody gets to sit with the angels, it would be your father," he says.

"But what if there's been a mistake and it isn't his time yet? Does God take it back?" The questions whirl around in my mind so fast they make me feel dizzy.

"I don't think there's been a mistake," Daniel says. "I think it was just a horrible accident."

Seconds later, Jo and Amy run up the hill. "What's happened?" Jo asks, out of breath. The men under the pines are a chorus of muteness.

Daniel stands as if he is going to break the news to her but I blurt it out before he has a chance.

"Daddy's had a horrible accident, Jo. He's dead."

Jo and Amy look at me like I've just said the worst stream of bad words imaginable. Jo doesn't believe me at first and asks Daniel what I am talking about.

"It's true," he says. "I'm so sorry."

Amy's eyes are like full moons. She isn't the type to cry but tears fill her eyes and spill over onto her cheeks. Jo and Amy collapse into each others' arms and then Meg joins them from the porch and then I follow and it is the four of us sisters holding onto each other for dear life like we've just been thrown into a lifeboat together on the Titanic.

Things like this aren't supposed to happen to my family. Daddy is supposed to live to be a hundred, setting a record for Katy's Ridge. Outdoing Cecil Ludlow by one year, who died in his sleep at ninety-nine, after having just rocked one of his great-great granddaughters.

Later that afternoon, Mama breaks from her trance and lays Daddy's hand down like it is a robin's egg she is returning to a nest. Then she goes into the kitchen, puts on her apron and gets busy. From the empty look in her eyes, I know that I have lost Mama, too. In a matter of hours it feels like I have gone from having two, full-fledged parents to being an orphan.

I run out the front door, jumping from the porch to the ground without touching a step like I used to when I was younger. Then I run down the hill, not knowing where I am going, I just have to

run. If I don't I might suffocate from the sadness that threatens to drown me.

I jump over deep ruts made by the stretcher and reach the dirt road at the bottom of the hill in no time at all. Still running, I turn onto the river road. My shoes rub at my heels and I stop my flight long enough to toss them into the bushes. Mama will have a fit if she finds out, but I don't care. I run barefoot toward the river. With each stride I try to forget seeing Daddy being pulled up the hill by Simon Hatcher's mule and all the men he worked with. The same men who visited our house last Christmas and who today carried him so carefully from the stretcher to the bed.

As I run I try to make sense of what has happened, but it is like a horrible dream that I don't know how to wake up from. I want the day to start over. I want my father to be standing in the kitchen filling his thermos and kissing my mother before he goes to work. I want him to come home safe and sound like he always does.

Only old people are supposed to die, and sometimes babies if they are sick. Nobody is supposed to die who is strong and healthy and happy. It goes against the nature of things. A person dying young makes life seem unfair and too scary. It means it could happen to any of us, at any time, when we least expect it.

At the end of the road, I stop and rest my hands on my knees to catch my breath. I haven't run like that since the end of the year races in seventh grade. I came close to winning that year and if Freddie Myers had skipped school that day, like he did most days once planting season commenced, I would have won the ribbon.

The look of the land changes the closer I get to the river, as if the mountains are intent on flattening out to greet it. Making my way through tall grass, I follow the path that Daddy and I must have walked together a thousand times. I smell the water before I see it and emerge from the grasses at a small sandy beach. The sight of the water causes me to sigh. Visiting the riverbank is like

visiting an old friend. I collapse on a mound of earth, still refusing to cry. Crying might make it too real.

I take in a few deep breaths. Then like a summer rain that sneaks up on a sunny day, the tears come. They arrive slowly at first and I wipe each one away as it falls. But pretty soon I am caught in a downpour of tears, at the very place Daddy and I have fished since the time the grasses were taller than me.

When I got older he showed me how to clean the trout we caught, and one Christmas gave me a special knife to use. I never liked cleaning fish, but Daddy was proud that I was more like him instead of my sisters. They scream at the sight of any kind of fish guts, like I'd torn out my very own eyeball for them to see.

Memories flood over me, and then I remember the last time we were together, earlier that morning.

"Have a good day at school," Daddy says, giving me a kiss on the forehead. He's kissed me in that same spot so many times I half expect there to be a worn-out place where his lips touch, like the worn-out place on the kitchen rug where Mama always stands to cook.

"School is so boring," I say, rolling my eyes.

"There's too much to discover for life to be boring," Daddy says back to me. "Study the birds, the trees, the patterns on leaves. There's always something new to see."

It is just like him to say something special like that.

"Waiting on your sister again?" he asks, buttoning the top button of his work shirt.

I nod. Meg always makes us late to school with her prissing.

I hold my stomach and feel a little sick. Not sick-sick, but like a bad storm is coming. "Are you okay?" Daddy asks.

"I guess," I say. "I just feel a little funny."

He feels my forehead where he kissed me to see if I have a fever.

"Daddy, don't treat me like I'm a little girl," I say.

He smiles. "Forgive me, honey, but you'll always be my little girl," he says.

I lean into him, knowing I don't really need to forgive him for anything.

"Do you believe in the secret sense?" I ask him. "Aunt Sadie told me about it yesterday."

"Our grandmother had it," he says. "She could always tell when someone in our village was about to pass on or she would know just when somebody needed something. A kind word. A cup of tea."

"Sadie says I have the gift, too," I say.

"Then you probably do," he says. He smiles like he's just found another reason to be proud of me.

"You two are like two peas in a pod," Mama says from behind the screen door. She startles me, with her way of showing up all unexpected.

"Gotta go to work," he says, winking at me.

"Be careful, Joseph," Mama says.

"You know I will," he says. He throws Mama a kiss and smiles. Mama calls Daddy's smile the "famous McAllister smile." In an old photograph of my grandfather you can see the same smile. Whenever I have private time in front of the mirror in the kitchen, which isn't that often given my three older sisters, I practice that smile. I want to be the first girl in our family to have it.

Daddy grabs his thermos and lunch pail off the top step and starts down the hill. "Take care of that stomach of yours," he says to me.

I'd almost forgotten the feeling in the pit of my stomach and now wonder if this could have anything to do with the secret sense.

He throws his hand up in a goodbye, but doesn't look back. About halfway down the path he begins to whistle like he does every day on his way to work. His whistling often takes over where his banjo can't go. I watch him until he is totally out of sight, with the strange feeling that I might never see him again.

. . .

SITTING beside the deep flowing river, I try to imagine a life where Daddy never whistles or plays the banjo again. A whole new shower of tears begins, and I am glad I am alone with only the river watching me. After a while, I am so worn out with sadness I fall asleep and don't wake up until after the sun has gone behind the ridge. The breeze on the water is cool now and I wish I'd thought to bring a sweater. A maple tree showers down crispy leaves that have started to change colors. The tips of the green leaves are edged in yellow and red. Daddy taught me about trees. He believes that trees are angels, and that a person can pray to trees or the river or the land just like a person can pray to God. We only cut down trees if we absolutely have to, and even then we make sure we make good use of them and thank them for their service. I never thought about how hard that might have made his job at the sawmill. Seeing all those trees come down.

A fish breaks the surface a few feet away, breaking the spell of my memories. I push away the thought that Daddy and I will never stand on this bank together again. After I wipe the last of my tears, I get up to walk back home. Now we are the family with a house of mourning.

I shiver and wrap my arms around myself. The leaves of the maple burn red with the setting sun like the burning bush appearing to Moses. I take this as a sign that on this day my whole life has changed forever.

CHAPTER NINE

A crowd has gathered back at the house. Every light is on and every window open. Neighbors sit on the porch drinking coffee and smoking their hand-rolled cigarettes. It is like a giant party, but nobody is smiling and their voices are low and muffled. Max, Aunt Sadie's dog, is taking a nap and blocks the door into the house. Everybody has to step over him to get inside or out.

A couple of men nod at me when I go by, and I nod back. Their faces say they feel sorry for me. I stick my hands in the pockets of my dress and scoot by people, wishing I could have stayed at the river all night. Even on normal days I don't like being the center of attention. Max thumps his tail twice against the wooden porch as I pass, as if only pretending to be asleep. After I pet him, I go inside looking around for my family. The crowd is as thick as church on Easter Sunday, except without any hope of resurrection.

The first people I see when I go inside are Preacher and his wife sitting in the living room. I have to resist grabbing him by the lapels and tossing him out of Daddy's chair. He takes a neatly folded white handkerchief out of his coat pocket to soak up the

sweat from his forehead. For someone who has a guarantee of going to heaven, he sure does sweat a lot.

Preacher motions for me to come over. "Your Daddy's one of the fortunate to get to go to the Great Beyond so young," he says.

"I wish people would quit saying that," I say. "What exactly is he beyond?"

Preacher's eyes widen like I haven't heard a word he's said every Sunday service since I was a little girl. "Well, he's in heaven, of course. He's in a better place. He's *beyond* this earthly place. "

"What could be better than sitting here amongst all his family and friends?" I ask.

Preachers face turns red and Amy's look tells me I'd better just drop it.

Amy sits squashed between Aunt Chloe and Uncle John, who are both big people. She looks about as miserable as I feel. I walked past their latest new Buick on the road below the house. It looks bigger than the last one, probably to accommodate their size.

Amy nibbles on her fingernails like she does when she's nervous. Every corner of our house has people crammed in it, with no place for the shyest McAllister to hide.

Aunt Chloe is Mama's younger sister and she lives with her husband in Rocky Bluff. My hope is to duck into the kitchen unnoticed, but when Aunt Chloe sees me she hauls herself off the sofa and comes over and hugs me like I am her long lost relative. I let her do it, even though she wears enough perfume to choke a goat. The smell always makes my eyes water and sticks to my skin and clothes. Whenever she comes over for Sunday dinner, her scent lingers in the house well into Tuesday. In the privacy of our bedroom, my sisters and I call it *Ode to Toilet Water.*

"Louisa May, we've been worried about you," Aunt Chloe says. Before I can get away she pulls me into her, and I hold my breath like I am diving into the deep part of the river. After she releases

me I tell her that I am fine, which of course is the lie of the century.

Aunt Chloe's eyes are bloodshot and I wonder if that is from crying over Daddy or from her perfume, which is especially strong tonight. Chloe has had an easier life than Mama. Chloe's husband, my Uncle John, owns a furniture store in Rocky Bluff and makes a good living. They never had any children.

"I just can't think of anything more horrible than what's happened to your daddy," Aunt Chloe continues. She sniffs back tears and plucks a lace handkerchief from her cleavage.

"I'd better check on Mama," I say, stepping away before Aunt Chloe has a chance to hug me again.

In the bedroom, wall to wall people stand around talking about Daddy in whispers. From the look of him, you can't even tell he's been in an accident. All the blood is cleaned up and one of Aunt Sadie's beautiful quilts covers the bed, the one with the humming-birds sewn on each corner. Besides selling mountain remedies and blackberry wine, Aunt Sadie—like Mama—makes quilts to sell to city people, though Sadie is much better than Mama when it comes to making quilts. Mary Jane's grandmother in Little Rock bought one from her when she came to visit two summers ago, and she paid Sadie fifty dollars for it. After that, some of her Little Rock, high-society friends wanted one, too. Sadie manages to make one quilt every winter and has a waiting list seven years long, all the way into 1947.

I try to hide my shock at seeing Daddy laid out on the bed. He is wearing his Sunday shoes and his only suit, the suit he wore to every funeral and wedding in Katy's Ridge, and the suit he always complained about how stiff and uncomfortable it was.

"How dare you make him wear that," I say to Mama over the whispers. "He should be wearing a pair of overalls and his favorite flannel shirt if he has to wear them for all eternity."

I feel bad now for running off to the river and not making sure things were done right.

The voices in the room go silent and a dozen set of eyes look at me like I've just killed Daddy myself.

In a matter of seconds, the look on Mama's face changes from all-consuming grief to fuming anger.

"She's just distraught," somebody says in my defense.

I recognize the voice as Miss Mildred who plays the organ at the church. In the past, I've spent a fair amount of time making fun of Miss Mildred and realize now that I will have to stop, since she spoke up for me.

Not the best organ player, Miss Mildred's hymns are riddled with bad notes that sound like little farts. I have spent my entire childhood swallowing giggles as fast as her little organ farts come out. Some of us learned that you can swallow air and make little farts, too. The boys are really good at this, which guarantees more giggles. If Mama's cold looks don't stop me from rolling all hysterical down the church aisle, I force myself to think of Jesus on the cross.

In the next instant I feel guilty for thinking about farts while Daddy is laying dead. But then I figure that he might find it funny, too. However, the wrath of Mama sobers me quick, as she pulls me through the crowd and outside to a corner of the porch where no one can hear us.

"What do you think you're doing?" Mama says. Her whispered words come out like shouts. "Have you no respect for the dead?"

"*The dead* is Daddy," I say.

She takes a step back like I've just slapped her hard in the face.

Sadie's dog, Max, comes over and sniffs my crotch, as if this is the only comfort he has to offer, given the blessing out I am about to receive.

"Louisa May McAllister, this is how things are done when

someone dies and you *will* respect it or you will be cleaning out the outhouse for the rest of your natural life. Do you hear me?"

I smile, grateful that Mama is taking me down a peg because it makes me not feel so much like an orphan. She narrows her eyes at my smile.

"Yes, ma'am," I say. "I will respect how things are done."

She lifts her head as though proud of winning this battle and I follow her back into the house to pay our respects to Daddy. The crowd parts as Mama makes her way back to the rocking chair next to the bed, the chair where all we babies got rocked, me being the last. This rocker is more like a family member than of a piece of furniture and creaks out a tune on the wooden floors as sweet as any Daddy might have played on the banjo. It will probably be the chair that rocks all the grandbabies, too.

While it is easy to imagine Jo, Amy and Meg having babies and bringing them here to be rocked in the family chair, it is much harder to imagine myself doing it. I've already decided that I'll have babies only after I've finished all the fun things in life, like going on adventures and exploring a world bigger than Katy's Ridge.

Besides all the other things Aunt Sadie does, she also works as a midwife here in Katy's Ridge. I've gone with her a few times on a delivery. Mainly I take care of the younger kids in the family, if there are any. But I've heard enough hollering coming out of bedrooms to wonder if babies are worth all the pain they bring with them.

Contrite as the best Baptist, I make my way back through the crowded room. People nod as if to acknowledge the effort I am making. Even with the window open the room is stuffy. It isn't big enough for this many people. When I reach the bed I touch Daddy's hand and then yank it away. It is cold, like something in the icebox. Before I can stop them, tears rush to my eyes. The last thing I want to do is cry in front of all these

people so I sniff them back so hard I feel a rush of air in my eyeballs.

After I slide in beside her, Mama puts her arm around my waist and anchors me in place as Mr. Blackstone, Daddy's boss at the sawmill, tells her how much Daddy will be missed.

"You're very kind," Mama replies.

"You're very kind," I echo, trying to match Mama's tone.

Mr. Blackstone's daughter, Becky, is four years ahead of me in school. Seeing him this close I now know where Becky gets her big nose because her father has one just like it. Their eyes are alike, too, small and narrow. The only inconsistency being that Mr. Blackstone is practically bald and Becky's hair is long and straight.

"I don't know how we can ever replace him," Mr. Blackstone concludes.

Mama thanks him again for his kindness and squeezes me like I am not to repeat it. If she resents Mr. Blackstone at all for Daddy's accident she doesn't let on, although I heard her say to Daddy more than once that Mr. Blackstone is cheap and hasn't hired enough men for all the logging that needs to get done.

Before he leaves, Mr. Blackstone shakes the tips of my fingers like he is afraid to touch my whole hand, which irritates me to no end. Before I have time to react, Mama shoots me a look that would stop a full grown mountain lion in its tracks. In the meantime, I do my best to ignore the body lying on the bed in the clothes Daddy would have burned if she let him.

"Where are your sisters?" Mama asks.

"I think Jo and Meg are in the kitchen," I say. "And Amy's keeping Aunt Chloe and Uncle John company."

"Why don't you go help Jo and Meg," she says, releasing her arm from my waist.

Mama's answer for everything that ails a person is hard work. For her, life is just one big chore with no end. Daddy always said she was stubborn as an ox, and she plowed to the end of the row of

everything she did. He said we girls would be grateful for that trait someday. Though I don't see how gratitude and working like an ox are related at all.

As I'm leaving, I glance at the old photograph Mama always keeps on her dresser. She never talks about her past. Her parents came over from Germany, but we've not heard one story about them. I've spent some time studying that photograph. The grandparents I never met are standing on a small rug out in a dirt yard, somewhere in Germany, dressed up in front of a Hansel and Gretel house. They look stern, not a bit of happiness on their faces. Aunt Chloe never talks about them either, but sometimes I hear Mama and Chloe talking in German together in the kitchen when they don't think anybody else is listening.

Before leaving the room, I turn and look over at Daddy. I just keep thinking that any minute he will sit up and ask why all these people are in our house. When he hears the story of how we all thought he was dead, he'll probably laugh so loud it can be heard in the next valley. Wishful thinking comes in handy if you want to keep reality from sinking in too fast.

My fantasy fades when I notice my father's arms have been folded neatly across his chest. He could be sleeping except for that. Nobody sleeps that way. Maybe that's why people do it. So mourners won't go poking around on dead people expecting them to wake up.

THE KITCHEN IS CROWDED and busy like Thanksgiving dinner is being made. All sorts of food sits on the kitchen table that people have brought, but Jo and Meg are making more. Every burner on our old stove has something cooking, as well as the oven, and the kitchen is hot as Hades. Jo peels potatoes by the sink and still looks fresh, no matter how hot it is. It doesn't seem fair sometimes that she can be so beautiful and the rest of us are so plain.

What makes it all right is that Jo doesn't seem to know how pretty she is.

"Where have you been?" Jo says to me in the doorway. "We were worried about you."

I can tell she's been crying. "I was down by the river," I say. "I needed some time alone."

"That's what we figured," she says. She dabs a tiny offering of sweat from her forehead onto her sleeve.

In contrast to Jo, Meg looks wilted as she slumps over the kitchen counter cutting dough into biscuits. Her face is still splotched like she has broken out in hives from all the sadness.

"Mama said I should help," I say to Jo.

Sweat trickles down my back, all the way to the elastic in my underwear. I still have on my everyday school dress but nobody seems to care. Luckily, I found my shoes on the way home, so at least I'm not barefooted.

"You could mix the egg salad." Jo points over to the countertop where a bowl waits.

"Why are we cooking so much food?" I ask.

"All these people have to eat something," she says, sounding a little bit like Mama.

"But there's tons of food already here," I say.

"We might run out," Jo says.

Aunt Sadie pulls me in for a hug as she makes tea at the stove. Her eyes look sad and I can tell she's done her fair share of crying, too.

"How are you holding up, sweetheart?" she asks.

I shrug and she pulls me in for another hug. Unlike Aunt Chloe's hugs, I don't mind Sadie's at all. She smells like molasses and I wonder if she's been making one of her tonics because she often adds molasses to disguise the bitter taste of roots and whatnot.

Amy walks into the kitchen, finally free of Aunt Chloe and

Uncle John. She stirs something on the stove and doesn't talk to any of us. You never know what Amy is thinking or feeling because it never makes its way out of her mouth, you just have to guess. My guess is that Amy is as devastated as any of us. It's just all bottled up inside. Amy and Mama are alike in that way. Except Amy isn't as good as Mama at pretending nothing is wrong.

Aunt Sadie fills the pitcher with tea to take back to the living room. She put sprigs of mint in it that float on the top. I want to ask her if Daddy can still see us and hear us, or if he is somewhere in heaven cut off from the rest of us here. I trust Aunt Sadie to tell me the truth. But she is gone before I can ask.

I mash the boiled eggs with a fork and remember how much I hate cooking. I'd rather be doing a hundred other things, most of which are outdoors. I don't mind eating, though. Daddy and I both love to eat. I keep thinking of him lying there in their bed and wonder if Doc Lester even knows how to take a proper pulse. For all we know Daddy just passed out and nobody thought to wake him.

Miss Mildred comes into the kitchen, fanning herself with a piece of music she pulled from her purse.

"I'll play something real pretty for your daddy at the service tomorrow," Miss Mildred says to Jo.

"Thank you, Miss Mildred," Jo says. She glances over at me, her eyes wide. We both know Miss Mildred's best intentions don't always play out.

Daddy's favorite hymn was *Amazing Grace*. It wasn't unusual for him to go around all day on a Saturday singing that song over and over again while he helped Mama. He always liked the church hymns where somebody was lost, then got found. Unlike the people in those hymns, I've never known him to get lost. He knows every nook and cranny of Katy's Ridge and he could tell you the name of every tree, wildflower, bird or animal because he studied them in a book. He probably could have been a professor

at a big college if he wanted to, but Daddy found himself here in Katy's Ridge and made the best of it.

While I mash eggs with a fork, odd thoughts pop into my mind, like I hope Daddy won't have to wait in line in heaven like the one time we went to the picture show in Rocky Bluff. A war is going on overseas and I wonder how God deals with a whole bunch of people showing up at heaven's gate all at once.

"When will they move him to the church?" I ask Miss Mildred, since she seems to be the only one talking about what will happen next.

"Probably first thing in the morning," she whispers, like it is a secret.

I've only been to one other funeral that I remember—old Mr. Williams, who was cranky all the time and walked with a cane. Nobody liked him. He complained about everything under the sun, and if he didn't like something about you he'd tell you right to your face. He called me *Miss Wiggle Worm* when I was a little girl, because I didn't sit still enough in church. On this subject, Mama probably agreed. People paid their respects to Mr. Williams, yet even his widow walked lighter after he was gone.

At his funeral, Preacher said that Mr. Williams had gone on to the *Great Beyond*, this being one of Preacher's favorite sayings, and he kept pointing to a crack in the ceiling of the church like the crack was a pipeline into heaven. This proved God's goodness, as far as I was concerned, if he let crotchety Mr. Williams into heaven.

Daddy's death feels worlds different. People whisper and watch us, as if they secretly wonder what our family did to deserve such bad luck. The whispers stop whenever me or my sisters or Mama come into the room.

"Louisa May, watch what you're doing," Jo says.

Pieces of egg fall on the kitchen table and I apologize and shove the egg back into the bowl.

"Maybe you should go outside for awhile." Jo twists her hair up in the back as if to let in cooler air, and then lets it drop.

I agree and go outside. As the youngest McAllister, I am often treated like the baby of the family. Even though last summer I took on some of Daddy's lankiness and height, this hasn't translated into my family seeing me at all different.

On the porch a different bunch are standing, people from Katy's Ridge I don't see for months at a time. It's hot for October, more like mid-July, but now the breeze is cooler, like the breeze from the river has finally made it up here.

A chill goes through me just thinking about what winter will be like without Daddy here to get us ready for it. He splits and gets in the wood and bundles us up for school and fixes our snowshoes whenever the snow is too deep for regular shoes. To avoid the sadness that comes with it, I shake these thoughts away like snow from a tree branch.

Almost everybody in Katy's Ridge is here in my front yard. Horatio Sector and his wife and their kids stand away from everybody else, in a little huddle. Nobody pays them no mind. The worst you can do to people is to pretend they don't exist. But the Sectors are friends of Daddy's that have come to pay their respects. I let the others stare and walk over to them like Daddy would have done.

"Thanks for coming," I say to Mr. Sector, who holds their youngest boy's hand.

"Your father was a good man, Miss Wildflower," he says.

Mr. Sector is part Cherokee, though he is dark enough to be whole. He and his family live downriver of Katy's Ridge and keep to themselves. People aren't that friendly to him or his family except for Daddy. I walk down with Daddy sometimes to buy honey off of Mr. Sector and they will sit and talk away most of the afternoon. Mr. Sector is married to a white woman named June and they have a bunch of children. None of them come to school,

but even the youngest child can read as well as me. They read Cherokee, too, which I hope to learn someday.

Nobody can figure out why Mr. Sector's cornfield is always about a foot taller than other people's. His bees make a ton more honey, too. Some people say that June Sector is a witch, but I think ignorant people say whatever they think will be the most hurtful. June has blond hair and the children are a mixture of the two of them. Some have blue eyes, some have black, and their skin ranges in tone from golden honey to almost white.

Mr. Sector hands me a small leather pouch with something inside. I pull out a stone the size of a half-dollar that glimmers red from the torches burning in the yard.

"It's beautiful," I say.

"It's a ruby," Mr. Sector says. "I found it myself."

"I'll make sure Mama gets it," I say and thank him.

"No, miss," he hesitates, "it's for you."

I look up at him like he must have made a mistake.

"You and Mister Joseph were very close. This is to help fill the empty space in your heart."

Though it's nearly impossible, I hold back my tears and shake his hand. Some of the men turn to watch, as if touching an Indian's hand is breaking the law and I might get arrested.

"Mister Joseph was very kind to us," June Sector says.

I thank her and shake her hand, as well. Then I excuse myself and go over to sit on the porch steps. The heaviness of the evening makes me tired and I want to cry. The whole community is grieving for Daddy, but I'm not so sure I want to share him this way.

Max moves to the dirt next to Mama's flowerbeds and when I go over to pet him he licks my hand. Kids I know are in the crowd but they look away and step into the shadows, talking amongst themselves. By the light of one of the torches I can see Johnny Monroe and his sisters with big plates of food standing next to

their father, Arthur Monroe. It would be just like the Monroes to come just for the food. They mainly keep to themselves, but in a different way than the Sectors. The people in Katy's Ridge hate the Sectors because Mr. Sector is an Indian and different. But Arthur Monroe doesn't just hate the Sectors, he hates everybody.

Ruby Monroe looks sad tonight, but she always looks sad. Johnny stands between Ruby and his younger sister, Melody. Their clothes are dirty and they look as though they haven't bathed in days.

Moments later Mary Jane and her brother Victor come up the hill with their parents. It feels like a hundred years since I've seen Mary Jane, even though it was earlier that day. Her mother speaks first, telling me how sorry she is about my father. Then her parents walk inside and Mary Jane and Victor stay outside with me. The three of us stand there for a while, like we don't know what to say. Victor draws marks in the dirt with his shoe and keeps his hands in his pockets. His hair looks wet, like he washed it right before he came. Victor is one of Max's favorite people and old Max jumps up on him and pushes at him with his nose.

"He likes you," I say.

"Everybody likes Victor," Mary Jane says.

"It's a curse," Victor says and smiles.

It is good to see a smile amongst all these sad faces, but Victor looks embarrassed by it and stops. He plays some with Max.

"We're going out back, big brother," Mary Jane says.

"Okay," he says, grabbing a stick to throw to Max.

Mary Jane tugs at my dress sleeve and we walk around to the back porch. People have gathered on the back porch, too. Some are standing, some sitting, and not a single stray cat in sight. They probably won't come out from under the house for days after this.

We take one of the lanterns off the end of the porch and go up past the outhouse to sit on a boulder Mary Jane and I used to play on when we were little. I steady the lantern, making sure it won't

fall off and leave us sitting in the dark. When we were younger, we used to pretend this boulder was the broad back of a humped back whale. We sailed out to sea in our imaginations, sailing the waters of oceans far away. I wish I could do that now for real. I want to be a thousand, maybe even a million miles away from what has happened. I need time to think, to get this right in my mind, without a lot of people around.

Below us the house looks spooky. People are like shadows with pipes and cigarettes lighting up the dark hillside like fireflies.

"This is strange, your daddy dying like this," Mary Jane says finally.

"Much more than strange," I say. We let the silence gather around us. I can tell she is uncomfortable. But at the same time I am grateful she is making an effort. Even though we've been friends since we were in diapers, neither one of us have ever gone through anything like this before. If this had happened to Mary Jane's father I wouldn't know what to say to her, either.

"Everybody in Katy's Ridge must be here," she says.

"It looks like it," I say.

Down the hill toward the house I see Jo washing dishes through the kitchen window. I feel guilty for not helping, but I am grateful to be here with my friend.

"Everybody liked him," she says.

"Yeah, I think they did."

Night noises surround us: crickets, toads, lizards and other small critters moving around in the fallen leaves. Do they mourn when one of their own dies?

"He was always helping people out," she says, as if this is something I don't know. "I liked him, too," she says softly.

Mary Jane and I have never been this awkward together for a day in our lives.

"How's your mother taking this?" she asks.

"Pretty good, I guess."

We sit for a long time, not saying much of anything.

"I'm so sorry," Mary Jane says. Then she buries her head in her dress and starts to bawl, complete with snot. I pat her back to comfort her. I have never seen Mary Jane cry like this, and I wish she'd just stop it. My father is laid out in the bedroom and the entire population of Katy's Ridge is at our house, even the Monroes and the Sectors, and it is taking everything I have to hold myself together. The last thing I need is people falling apart right in front of me, especially my best friend.

To my relief, Mary Jane finally stops weeping and wipes a long, slimy trail of snot on the sleeve of her dress. But I guess her crying is better than ignoring me, like the other kids from our school. They act like I have a fatal disease they might catch if they get too close.

Later that night after everybody has eaten and paid their respects to our family, the house starts to empty out. I walk with Mary Jane and Victor to the bottom of the hill. Somebody has put lanterns every few feet along the path so that people can see how to get home. The new moon is no help tonight and the wind blows at the lanterns, trying to put them out. The wind makes the trees creak and moan, as if they miss Daddy, too.

We say our goodbyes, and I walk back up the hill, passing the last of the people going home. When I get to the front porch Mama is standing at the railing looking out into the dark night.

"It was a good crowd," she says.

Since I don't know what else to say, I agree, and feel more tired-out than I've ever been in my life. I leave her standing in the shadows and go inside. The screen door slams shut behind me. Any other day Mama would yell at me for letting the door slam, and I half-wish she'd yell at me now so everything would feel normal, but she doesn't. The truth is I doubt that life will ever feel the same again.

This is about the time of evening Daddy would be picking up

his banjo to pick out his version of a lullaby, while my sisters and I get ready for bed. For once it doesn't bother me that my sisters and I all sleep in one room. After Meg and I came along, Daddy built a small bed in the corner for us next to the big bed in the center that Jo and Amy shared. Because of the small room, we bump elbows when the four of us get on our nightgowns. In spite of the ways they bother me sometimes, I love my sisters. Being the youngest, in one way or another, they all look out for me.

Any other night we'd be talking or laughing before we went to bed, but tonight we are quiet. Meg and I crawl over Jo and Amy to get to our corner of the room like we do every night. In a way it helps to know that I am not the only one left behind.

In the meantime, I haven't given up on a miracle. If Jesus is all that Preacher makes him out to be, I don't see why he can't do for Daddy what he did for Lazarus. Preacher is always bringing Lazarus back to life and it appears to be one of his favorite sermons. He especially likes to point out that Lazarus started to rot before Jesus found him. I force myself not to think about Daddy rotting, even though he and I have always been fascinated with nature's way of decomposing dead things. I get on my knees and pray for a Lazarus-sized miracle instead.

"Jo, where's Mama going to sleep?" I say, suddenly alarmed by the thought of Daddy stretched out on their bed.

"Aunt Sadie made up a bed on the couch," she says.

"Mama probably won't sleep tonight anyway," Meg says.

"I probably won't either," Amy agrees.

"Well, I will," Jo says, turning off the lights. "I'm too sad and exhausted to stay awake."

"Who would have thought people could eat that much?" Meg says from the darkness. "And they brought things, too. Daddy would make some joke that we'll have leftovers for the next two years."

I haven't eaten all day except for breakfast, and I still don't feel

hungry at all. It's as if the sadness from the day filled me up like a full-course meal.

"I think Aunt Chloe filled her plate at least three times," Amy says, giggling. She stops herself and apologizes, but then Meg starts giggling, too. Before long we are all laughing into our pillows or bedcovers or whatever we can find. It feels bad and good at the same time. Laughter gives me hope. Until then, I felt dead like Daddy. We laugh at nothing and everything all at once and decide that if Daddy were here he'd be laughing, too.

We settle back into our beds and I can hear Mama and Aunt Sadie talking softly in the living room. For the first time in our lives, Mama doesn't come in to say goodnight, and she hasn't even scolded us for making noise.

I close my eyes and pretend that nothing has changed. I wait on Daddy to come in and read us part of whatever book he's been reading. Sometimes it is *Robinson Crusoe* or *Moby Dick* or something from the Old Testament where so-and-so begets so-and-so. Those are the nights we fall asleep the fastest.

Everything grows quiet, then. The quietness feels as deep as the deepest part of Sutter's Lake, the part of the lake where I can't see or touch the bottom, no matter how much I hold my breath and dive. I can't stop thinking of Daddy's body in the next room. It wouldn't be like him to haunt a place. He didn't believe in ghosts, no matter how many spooky stories we girls made up to scare him.

After a while Meg starts to cry. I rub her shoulders and back for the longest time, like Daddy always did if we didn't feel well. Afterwards, I close my eyes and think of the river, its waves lapping against the shoreline. In my imagination, a water bug skims on the top. They keep their balance no matter what the water is doing underneath them. I try to be that water bug and let the waves of emotion pass under me without getting capsized.

Meg's crying keeps up until her breathing finally deepens into sleep. In a room filled with sisters, I feel totally alone. In my loneli-

ness, I think of Jesus on the cross when he asked God why he abandoned him. For all I know, I've been praying for miracles from somebody that doesn't even exist. Too tired to question things anymore, the worst day of my life ends when, at last, I fall asleep.

CHAPTER TEN

The morning of the funeral I smell breakfast before I open my eyes. I smile at the thought of Daddy and Mama in the kitchen with their first cup of coffee, then I remember that he won't be there. When I walk by the door to their bedroom it is closed, like he is still sleeping. But the nightmare of the day before is true. The accident really happened. He is really gone.

When I come into the kitchen Aunt Sadie gives me one of her big, strong hugs. She has made a breakfast of eggs, bacon and biscuits.

"I want you to drink this," she says. "It'll keep your strength up."

A glass of something dark green sits on the kitchen counter. All of Aunt Sadie's concoctions taste like tree bark and grass mixed together, but I don't argue with her, I just drink it and hold my nose while I swallow.

We all sit around the kitchen table as if we are in a daze. Jo looks like she's been crying again and Amy is quiet, as usual, and Meg stares into her coffee cup. Even Mama has stopped her busy-ness and is nursing a cup of coffee. Despite all the sadness weighing down the room, the smell of the bacon reminds me of

how hungry I am. Before I know it, I've eaten two eggs, three strips of bacon, and two biscuits with butter and some of Horatio Sector's honey on it.

Just as I finish breakfast a knock comes at the front door and Mama answers it. Men's voices fill the living room. Some of Daddy's friends are here with a pine box in the yard behind them. I smell the wood all the way from the living room.

"I was up all night making it," Silas Magee says. "I think it's the best I've ever done."

Silas is the best carpenter anywhere. He made practically everything we own. Between him and Daddy our family has enough wood and kindling stacked next to the porch to get us through two hard winters.

Mama thanks Silas and the other men but has that faraway look in her eyes again like she might climb in the box with Daddy if given half a chance.

"We need to get him down the hill," Silas says. "Doc Lester has that contraption he bought waiting on the road."

Mama steps aside as the men carry the coffin into the house. Her eyes are fixed on the pine box and when I try to follow the men she holds me back.

"Come on," Jo says from behind me. "Let's go pick flowers for the church." As the oldest, Jo has taken over Mama's job of telling us sisters what to do.

Meg and Amy follow Jo and me out the back door to the path into the woods behind our house. As we walk, I picture Daddy being carried down the hill by the same men who carried him up.

"Will they take him right to the church?" I ask Jo.

"I believe so," she says, locking her arm in mine.

"Will Mama go, too?"

"Probably," she says. "At least for a little while, to make sure everything's set up the way she wants."

We walk to the sunny side of the hill to search for flowers.

Early that summer there were daffodils in bloom, and crocuses, white trillium and crested irises. But now, in early fall, there is only snakeroot, goldenrod, asters and witch hazel. A few crested irises risk a late bloom but they are scrawny compared to weeks before. We gather what we can find, along with fern fronds and take them back to the kitchen and put them in water. Amy will arrange them since she is good at things like that.

The men and Daddy are gone when we get back to the house. For the first time that I can remember, Daddy is on his way to church without us, and something about that makes a lump of grief lodge in my throat.

Every Sunday, rain or shine, freezing cold or summer heat, we walk as a family to the Katy's Ridge Missionary Baptist church, the only church in Katy's Ridge. The cornerstone outside the church kitchen has the date 1911 chiseled into it. Rocky Bluff, the biggest town close to us, has four churches: one Methodist, one Presbyterian, and two more Baptist churches—one being a Baptist church for colored people. Aunt Sadie says the colored people praise Jesus by singing, clapping their hands and dancing in the aisles. That comes closer to my idea of what a church should be. But the coloreds and the whites stay apart in these parts, except for Aunt Sadie who goes to worship with them every now and again, whenever she's invited.

In the past, on days when the temperature fell below freezing, I didn't see why we couldn't skip the freezing walk and just talk to God from in front of our warm wood stove. God made winter in the first place, so why wouldn't he understand? Daddy could have led us in some hymns and Mama could have read from the Bible, some of the good parts that Preacher never got around to, like what love meant to the Corinthians.

Most Sundays, Preacher talks about Satan and the evils of sin and how we have to repent. He says we are all sinners and no matter how hard we try to be good people we can't keep from

sinning. What I never figured out was if people were so horrible already, what was there to aim for? Daddy didn't like it when I questioned Preacher, especially to his face. But I could tell he didn't go along with everything Preacher said, either. Sometimes he would doze off right in the middle of the sermon. When this happened, I was supposed to nudge him awake before Mama noticed.

I am glad it is fall because the church in winter is always too hot or too cold, nothing in between. Preacher's nephew, Gordon, gets a dollar a month to stoke the coal furnace in the basement of the church, and so we either roast like we are already in the fires of hell or freeze like explorers in the Antarctic. But it is warm enough today that maybe some of the windows can be opened and a good breeze let in.

After Mama comes back home, we sit around the kitchen table finishing off an apple pie sharing two forks between us. We are waiting for three o'clock when we are to head to the church. Nobody talks about the empty seat where Daddy usually sits, or how we are supposed to go on with this big empty chair in our lives.

Meg chatters away about nothing and Amy never says a word. Jo and Aunt Sadie stay close to Mama, like she is a daisy whose petals might all fall off at once. Time drags on like a wagon stuck in the mud, a wagon that we're all too sad to get out and push. The red rooster clock over the icebox ticks so loud we can hear it whenever the talking stops. It doesn't seem like we'll ever get to where we are going, not that any of us want to go there anyway.

I excuse myself and go out to the front porch to read in the sun. Two stray cats that have been hanging out at the house since Daddy fed them supper scraps, keep me company. I try to concentrate on a passage in *Oliver Twist* that Daddy and I were reading together two days before, but I read the same paragraph three times without understanding it once.

Aunt Sadie comes to the back door. "It's time to get ready," she says.

I have a thousand questions for Aunt Sadie but my mouth has stopped working just like my mind. I nod and come in the house.

I am the last to take a bath. We take our baths on the back porch in Mama's biggest washtub, except in winter. Right now it is just warm enough for us not to freeze to death, as long as Aunt Sadie keeps the hot water coming that is boiling on the stove. Two kettles of boiling water and a bucket of cold usually get the temperature just right.

We can't afford indoor plumbing yet because we have to hire the men with the things they need to lay the pipes all the way up our hill. But the electric lines were easier, so we've had power for a few years. Mary Jane has indoor plumbing and so does just about everybody else, except for maybe the Monroes, the Sectors and us. The money in the Mason jar just hasn't been enough.

The only fight I ever saw Mama and Daddy have was about Daddy always putting a portion of our jar money into the offering at church. Mama thinks an indoor toilet is more important than Preacher having a new robe to wear at baptisms and she told Daddy so. She said he'd give away our last dime if somebody asked for it, which is probably true.

Aunt Sadie hangs sheets around the bathtub for privacy since my body has started to change. I am going from being a girl to becoming a young woman, and though my sisters and I share a bedroom and have seen each other naked, I still feel shy.

Undressing quickly, I rub the soap over the goose bumps on my arms and legs and then wash my hair and rinse it with a pitcher of water nearby. Aunt Sadie brings out a towel, stiff from hanging on the line, and it softens as I wrap it around my shoulders. I shudder and shake until I put on my underwear, slip and then the dress I will wear to the funeral.

At the kitchen table, Aunt Sadie helps comb the tangles out of

my hair, instead of Mama, and I thank God for small blessings until I remember how angry I am that he hasn't produced any miracles yet.

While everybody else gets ready, I wait in the living room. Daddy's banjo looks lonely just sitting there. Does it miss him? Do the strings hanker to be touched by him again, the frets wait to be turned and tuned? The house seems quiet in a way I can't put my finger on. I study the difference until it hits me that a voice is missing. A baritone voice to balance out all the sopranos. Daddy's voice.

We leave the house going down the path that Daddy's body traveled earlier that morning. Mama, Jo, and Aunt Sadie lead the way, followed by Amy, Meg, and me carrying bunches of wildflowers and ferns. I wear new shoes that scrape against my heels and I can already tell I am going to have a whopper of a blister. Aunt Chloe brought new shoes for all of us that morning and dropped them off when we were picking flowers. In the past, Mama would have refused such charity, even from her sister. But she doesn't seem to have the energy to argue right now.

Aunt Sadie has not left Mama's side. As Daddy's sister, she must have a deep sadness all her own, though other than those first moments when she found out, she hasn't let it show. She just watches out for Mama, because that's what her brother probably would want her to do.

"Daddy will like being the center of attention," Meg says, the first to break the silence.

"Who'd want attention that way?" I say, irked by her dreaminess.

"Remember, we're going to celebrate his life, not his death," Aunt Sadie says.

"It sure doesn't feel like a celebration," I say.

"I know it doesn't," Aunt Sadie says. "It's just what we say so it won't hurt so bad. But I guess nothing could help with that."

She drops back a few steps and puts her arm around me, squeezing my shoulder. I think of Daddy hugging me the day before, when I came into the kitchen for breakfast. If I'd known it would be the last time we hugged, I would have hung on longer, instead of wanting to get to Mama's biscuits.

Sadie moves back to Mama's side and we walk the rest of the way without saying much. Instead of almost twelve, I feel like a little girl again. I kick a rock down the side of the road, something I might have done years ago.

The first thing we see when we near the church is Doc Lester's hearse.

"That is the tackiest contraption I have ever laid eyes on," I say, using the word I heard Silas Magee use earlier.

"He bought it used in Rocky Bluff from the colored people's funeral home," Meg says. She always knows the details of what's going on.

"He must have shined it up special," I say, "because it looks like a brand new copper penny." It sits in front of the church, too fancy for the dinky little building. "Daddy always made fun of that hearse," I continue. "He said if Doc couldn't cure you, he could always drive you away in his hearse. Either way he got paid."

"Louisa May," Mama says, "must you always say exactly what's on your mind." She sighs like I have crawled all over her grief wearing dirty shoes.

What Mama doesn't know, is that the thought of Daddy in Doc Lester's funeral wagon makes me want to cry and hit somebody at the same time, so she's lucky I'm just talking.

The same people from the night before stand around outside the church. Some turn to watch us come down the road. I imagine *Onward Christian Soldiers* playing in the background because we walk like soldiers going to war.

Mama reaches over and takes my hand as we come to the

church, like all is forgiven regarding the earlier hearse comments, and I nearly cry from the unexpected tenderness.

"Don't worry, Louisa May, we're going to be fine," Mama says.

She squeezes my hand.

"I promise to be strong, Mama," I say and squeeze hers back.

At that moment I feel close to her, something I don't feel too often. But as quickly as it comes, it goes, and she drops my hand.

"Right this way, Mrs. McAllister," Preacher says to Mama. He usually calls her Nell, but today he uses her married name.

He leads us to the entrance of the church like we've never been there before. We follow him inside and Jo puts the flowers on the coffin while we take our places on the front row. Miss Mildred starts playing the organ and we are sitting so close we can hear her feet pumping the slats at the bottom that makes the low notes. She hums along, pushing her glasses up on her nose again and again, studying the music intently, as if trying to do an extra special job. She hits sour notes that a week ago would have made me swallow my hysterics, but today I don't feel like laughing.

The pine box with Daddy in it sits at the front of the church. Pots of lilies are placed on either end of Preacher's podium which is moved over to the side. The casket lid is off but we can't see anything. I imagine Daddy sitting up and giving us a wave, a modern-day Lazarus, giving the whole church the shock of a life-time. I wait, sending God the message that this would be the perfect time to prove his greatness. In exchange, I promise not to be mad at him anymore and then cross my fingers, arms, and legs for good luck.

Miss Mildred's solo goes on forever and I pass the time by remembering the only other time I sat on the front row in church. It was the day I got baptized at eight years of age. If you had the unfortunate luck to be nine and still unsaved, people in Katy's Ridge stared at you during altar calls, those times when Preacher invited the unsaved to play on God's team. Once tapped on the

shoulder by Jesus, you were to ask him to come into your heart and be your personal Savior. It seemed a regular Savior would be good enough for me, but as far as I can tell, the Baptist's insist on a *personal* one.

That Sunday I walked down the aisle, trying to make up some tears like Audrey Fisher had the week before, proof that Jesus touched my heart. I liked Jesus just fine, but I hated being stared at, so I tapped Jesus on the shoulder instead of him tapping me just to get the busy-bodies of Katy's Ridge off my back. To make matters worse, when I stood at the altar, Preacher put his hands on my head and prayed for my salvation so long a big drop of sweat fell from his head onto mine. As a result, I bolted upright in complete disgust only to be pushed down again while he kept praying.

The next Sunday Preacher dunked me and Jake Turner—who was two years ahead of me in school and who people had already worried had gone to the Devil—at the place in the river where it is shallow enough to stand in and get dunked from the waist back-wards. As soon as we were up out of the water, Preacher announced Jake and me were full of the Holy Spirit. I kept waiting to feel different, maybe a little lightheaded or something, but mainly I just felt wet.

At the very least I thought an angel should appear and give me a message of some sort. But nothing happened, except I found out why people don't walk around in wet clothes. It is not the least bit comfortable. My dress kept sticking to me and my underwear twisted up so bad I started to get the underwear version of a rope burn. After we dried off, Jake and I sat on the front row of the church and told our testimonies to the whole congregation. This was when I was supposed to say how rotten and lost I was before God shined a light on me and changed my heart forever. These testimonies always made Preacher smile from ear to ear and nod his head and rock back and forth on his dusty black shoes saying "Amen" with every sentence.

Even Jake Turner came up with something good to say about how he would never look at Katy's Ridge the same way again. But I felt like a colossal fake because as far as I could see, nothing had happened to me. I felt the same as I always had, which wasn't good or bad, but just the same. Despite my total lack of revelation, I made up something about how I had suddenly seen the light about how sinful it was to talk back to my mother and pick my nose in public. The last part made Jake Turner laugh. I don't know what made me walk up to the altar in the first place, except to keep from getting stared at.

THE FERNS and flowers we picked look nice and give me something to look at while we wait for Miss Mildred to finish playing the organ. When she finally stops, she smiles over at Mama as Preacher walks up to the podium with his Bible in his hand. Preacher is never without his Bible. He holds onto it like it is glued to his fingers. I wonder sometimes if his wife has to yank it out of his hands at night after he falls asleep.

"Dearly beloved," Preacher starts out, like we are at a wedding instead of a funeral. "We are gathered here today to celebrate the life of Joseph McAllister. . . ."

It never once occurred to me that someday I might be sitting at Daddy's funeral. I never even thought about it happening when he was really old. I just never thought about it. Now I kind of wish I had, so that maybe I could be more ready for what is happening. But nothing could have prepared me for the death of the most important person in my life.

CHAPTER ELEVEN

One Year Later

I wake up with a stabbing pain in my side where Johnny tackled me. Every inch of me hurts. When I try to move, I have no strength to lift myself. My eyesight is blurry and one of my eyes is swollen shut. Because I can't see, I listen, to make sure Johnny is gone.

The wind in the trees sounds like the old widow-women gossiping in the back of the church. I hear the stream, too, rushing down the ridge, full of the autumn rains we had a week before. I cough. Pain fills my chest, and I taste dirt and blood. When I move my tongue over my teeth, I discover the rough edge of a front tooth chipped off. When I try to sit, I scream with pain and wonder if Johnny broke a bunch of my ribs. To my surprise, my scream doesn't sound like me, but more like that fox Daddy and I found in the woods once, its leg caught in a trap.

I yell for Mama, but the call for help sounds like a raspy whisper. I don't expect her to hear me, but more than anything at that

moment I want a mother. Someone to hold me in her arms and tell me everything is going to be all right.

With my good eye I can see the sun is completely behind the mountain. It is getting dark. I must have been knocked out for at least an hour. My family will be looking for me now. Meg and Mama will know something is wrong. But how will they know to look on this side of the mountain?

The footbridge is just ahead. When Johnny caught me, I was halfway home and only a few steps away from getting free. If I can make it to the road somebody will find me. Otherwise I might have to stay here all night, and there will probably be a frost—or worse, Johnny might come back.

I struggle to pull myself up onto my hands and knees. My dress is ripped beyond repair, even by my sister, Amy. I do my best to cover myself but most of me is exposed. Without the sun it is much cooler. Every inch I move causes me yards of pain as I pull myself in the direction of the bridge.

I remember the dream I had where Daddy came to me. Was it really a dream? I call out his name now. But only silence answers me.

"I need your help, Daddy," I say, as I pull myself forward with all my strength.

I stop, hoping to hear his voice or revisit the dream. Tears sting my swollen eye and my nose drips from the tears. Another rush of pain shoots through me when I attempt to wipe my nose with my sleeve.

"My nose must be broken," I say to myself, "and maybe some ribs." Even though my voice is weak it feels good to hear it. It means I am still alive.

After I pull myself onto the first step of the bridge, I stop to rest. The one sturdy board I count on to get me safely across seems more narrow than it ever has. Not to mention that the broken

handrail doesn't look stable enough to hold onto. My only hope is crawling across, with the help of my one good eye.

More than anything, I want to go home. Mama will be mad at me for getting myself in this mess, but it doesn't matter. Nothing she can say or do will be worse than what I've already been through. I drag myself up the two rough steps and steady myself on the board. Then I shuffle my hands and knees forward. With every effort, I cry out in pain. What keeps me going is more than determination. It is anger. I refuse to let Johnny win.

The wind blows through the trees. For a second I think I hear Daddy's voice. I stop to listen. A squirrel chatters on a nearby tree. The bridge sways with my weight. I steady myself again and look up. Since this part of the handrail looks stable, I pull myself up to walk part of the way. I scream and cuss every bad word I know. I take the Lord's name in vain and then dare him to punish me for it. In the meantime, I hug the railing and sweat joins the blood on my face.

Now standing, I feel proud of myself and start to smile, but my busted lip won't let me. While clinging to the rail, I test to see if my feet will move. I take small, shuffling steps across the middle of the bridge. At a certain point I realize there is no turning back. The danger behind is greater than what lies ahead. I call on every ounce of resilience I have and refuse to fall off the bridge into the ravine. I am like Mama. I will plow to the end of this row.

I reach for my medallion and then remember Johnny ripping it from my neck. I look back and think briefly about looking for it. But it is too much to ask myself to do. Instead, I pray for the good Mary's help and also help from the baby Jesus who we learned in Sunday school grew up to be a shepherd of people instead of sheep. Clinging to the rail, I pray to the Lord, who is my shepherd, not to ask me to lie down in green pastures just yet because I am not quite ready to go. I remember how Preacher read the 23rd Psalm at Daddy's funeral and had everybody say it with him. I have

the opposite of still waters here, and my soul could use some help. And I figure I've already walked through the valley of the shadow of death and have seen evil right there in Johnny's eyes. I have trouble right now believing that the Lord is with me. I especially wonder where God was while Johnny was trying to knock my lights out forever.

When I reach into my dress pocket for my rabbit's foot from Woolworth's, I discover it isn't there. I sink my hand deeper into each pocket, thinking it must have fallen out while I ran. Without my medallion or my rabbit's foot I wonder if my luck has run out. I hold my head up and pretend the rabbit's foot is there anyway, as well as my Mary medallion. I give myself three wishes just to round things out. As I inch my way across the footbridge, I wish for courage, sure footing and strength. I thank the trees used to make the lumber to build this old bridge that holds me up. I thank the mountain for holding us all.

The board creaks from my weight and the sound of the stream grows louder. If I don't make it, people in Katy's Ridge will be telling the story forever about that unfortunate girl, Louisa May, who died one year to the day after her poor Daddy died in a horrible sawmill accident.

I take another step. A part of the board snaps. The bridge sways underneath me. A piece of bridge falls away, the size of a small cat, and my body goes rigid. That piece of bridge could have just as easily been me. It crashes on the rocks below. Dizziness sweeps over me as I try to steady myself. I cling to the rail, forcing myself not to look down.

The roaring stream calls out the danger below. After another step I see the end of the bridge and the path beyond. Pain stabs at me, and the tears won't stop. I push them back, thinking they will hinder my survival. My only job is to get back home where it is safe. I can't risk running into Johnny again.

"What did I do to deserve this?" I ask God.

As usual, he doesn't answer. What use is it to have a God who doesn't even help when you need him the most?

People aren't supposed to beat other people up. Johnny used me as a punching bag for all that had ever gone wrong in his life. Then he forced himself on me. That part I have trouble remembering. It's as if my mind wants to protect me from it somehow. But at least I fought back as much as I could. And even though Johnny nearly killed me, and threatened to finish the job if I told, I refuse to let him get away with this.

The handrail now gone, I drop to my knees and begin to crawl again. The board underneath me feels damp. A slippery smooth layer of moss covers the crevices. I grasp the dry edges and shuffle forward, an inchworm in human form. A steady, constant pain stabs at me with every move.

When I finally reach solid ground, I stay on my knees thanking God, Mary, the forest, and every rabbit that ever sacrificed a foot to bring good luck. Exhausted, I roll onto my side, wincing as I do. My cheek rests against the cold, moist earth. I wonder why life has to be so hard. It hurts to move. It hurts not to move. Nothing brings relief. I scream my frustration. My voice echoes faintly against the mountain. I scream again.

My head hurts so much I can barely lift it. Getting across that bridge was one of the hardest things I've ever done; now all I want to do is sleep. But I know how dangerous sleep can be. I need to stay awake, stay warm and yell for help. But when I try to stand the ground rolls and swells underneath me like a stormy ocean, and I begin to fall again. My legs buckle and the ground comes up to meet me. I hit hard. The fall knocks the last bit of fight out of me.

The earth is my bed; the rotting leaves my pillow. I want Daddy back. Preacher says God answers all our questions when we meet him face to face, and I have plenty of those. I want to know why he would let people like Johnny Monroe walk around just to hate and beat up other people.

Darkness is falling. It no longer matters if Johnny wins. All I want is rest. Life doesn't make sense. It doesn't matter if you're good or bad. People die for no reason. People suffer for no reason. I close my eyes and imagine my funeral. Silas Magee will make me a pine box, just like Daddy's but smaller. Miss Mildred will play something off-tune on the organ for me. Preacher will give me the benefit of heaven, since I've been baptized and accepted Jesus into my life. Mama might even cry, when she realizes how little she knew me. And I'll rest forever under the willow tree, right between Daddy and baby Beth, with a little marker paid for out of Aunt Sadie's quilt money reading *Wildflower McAllister, 1928-1941*. Like baby Beth, I will never age. I will always be thirteen. And then, every year on my birthday one of my sisters will wistfully say how old I'd be if Johnny Monroe hadn't killed me with his bare hands.

My body shivers and quakes from the cold. I wait to see what death will be like. Will it hurt? Will my soul throw off my body right in front of me?

In the distance, a light comes toward me. It is the most beautiful light I've ever seen—a combination of sunlight and moonlight, soft and rich, with gold, yellow and white rays coming out of the center. The gold Mary walks toward me with a lamb and a rabbit at her side. I am relieved to see the rabbit still has all his feet and luck with him. The gold Mary smiles at me and glows like the sun. Her rays wash over me, but don't cause pain, only strong, warm, peaceful feelings. The pain leaves me. I become the baby Jesus, resting in her arms.

I will join Daddy soon. We will rest in peace, watching the river flow by Katy's Ridge on its way to the Atlantic Ocean. In spirit, we'll flow with the river, making our way across America and across the wide sea to where my grandparents lived. We'll flow past my ancestors and up into heaven, making our way to God and Mary, where we'll never be alone again.

I close my eyes and let the ocean take me in her arms.

CHAPTER TWELVE

"There she is!" The voice breaks into my dream, sounding far away. I fight to stay where I am, to stay with the golden Mary. I am at peace. I'm not cold anymore.

I hear footsteps. I force one eye open and see a lantern swinging along the path. "Wildflower, is that you?" It sounds like Daniel's voice.

"Oh my God," Mama says in the distance. "What have you gotten yourself into now?" But I hear more fear in her voice than anger. It dawns on me that all her fussing my whole life has been about fear.

I feel regret that I won't be staying with the woman in gold. Her light disappears into the trees and the pain returns. Daniel and Mama arrive at my side. I try to turn in their direction but can't move.

Daniel wraps his jacket around me, covering my exposed skin. My eyes are swollen shut from my beating. The world is fuzzy and dark except for their voices. I listen as they discuss how to get me home.

"Hi Daniel," I say, as if we've just met on the road.

"Everything's going to be fine," he says to me. He sounds like Daddy for a second and tears come quickly to my swollen eyes. Salt water on a wound, the pain stabs fiercely to the point that I can't even scream.

"How bad is she?" Mama asks Daniel.

Daniel doesn't answer.

Mama holds the lantern close to my face. She gasps, as if not expecting what she sees.

"Let's get her home," she says to Daniel, her voice soft and sure. This attitude comes to Mama when a job needs to get done. This is the part of her I can count on. She will get me back home and patch me together again like a broken vase.

Darkness mingles with the lantern light as I sink into Daniel's chest and crawl inside his smell. A dreamy sleep carries me away. Daddy is carrying me now. He is still alive. He has been hiding in the woods. He was lost but now he is found, and he will never leave again.

Every few steps I am jarred awake. I am no longer a little girl and worry that I am too heavy for Daniel to carry. But he doesn't complain. In Daniel's arms, every inch of me cries out in pain. Mama doesn't speak but I hear her breathing next to Daniel's. They are moving as fast as they can without running. Mama pushes away tree branches and vines, clearing the path and telling Daniel the places to look out for, in that same strong voice she used when the men were bringing Daddy up the hill. I wonder if she knows something I don't know. Maybe I have that look that Daddy had, like I am leaving this world and there is nothing anybody can do to stop me.

Daniel's footsteps sound different when they reach the road. The earth has gravel mixed in it. The burden of carrying me runs up through his legs and arms and into me. We turn up the hill, and I know we are almost home. The earth is soft again. Mama's breathing is labored and so is Daniel's. They are racing up the hill

in the dark. With one eye half open, I see stars and lantern light on a swatch of the hill. Daniel's chest heaves underneath my head, his heart and lungs calling on all their strength. I wish I was lighter so he wouldn't have to struggle. Maybe if I were light as a feather I could stay in Daniel's arms forever.

In the blurry, dreamlike darkness, Daniel smells just like Daddy —a mixture of sweat and sawdust, river and earth. I remember Daniel coming up the hill another time, the very first time he came to court Jo. He asked Jo out a few weeks after Daddy died, to go to a movie in Rocky Bluff. Jo had been so shy, which was really not like her, and she had invited him to dinner instead. He sat at the table where Daddy used to sit and Jo blushed more than I've ever seen her blush. Of course we all knew they'd get married after that. It seemed as sure as spring coming after winter, or the dogwood tree blooming down the road.

Preacher married them on a Sunday afternoon six weeks later and they went into Rocky Bluff for the night to have their honeymoon in a room at the Rocky Bluff Inn that Aunt Chloe and Uncle John paid for. It was like a fairy tale how much they loved each other. And now the king and queen are expecting a prince or princess.

Mama's footsteps reach the porch first. I am suddenly home free, as if I've been playing tag and have come to that safe place where no one can touch me. I love this porch. I love the steps, the floorboards, the railings and the porch swing that has hung there all these years.

"You're home, Wildflower," Daniel says, his breath still labored. But I hear relief in his voice, too. With the slam of the screen door the rest of the world goes dark.

CHAPTER THIRTEEN

"She's waking up," Jo says.

Hearing her voice, I wonder if I've fallen asleep on Daddy's grave again, and she's come to find me. Maybe I imagined the whole incident with Johnny Monroe and I still have time to get back to the house before Mama and Meg have time to worry.

I open the one eye that can still see. It is daylight again. Mama and Jo are there, along with Daniel and Amy. My face hurts like it is on fire. I touch my ribs and feel bandages wrapped around my waist, hoping Doc Lester wasn't the one who wrapped them.

I am laid out on Mama's bed like Daddy had been that last day. "Am I dying?" I ask softly.

"You're hurt pretty bad, but you'll mend," Mama says. She sounds confident and I believe her, though I've decided that dying might not be that bad. All your pain goes away and you get to see your loved ones again, not to mention the golden Mary.

"You need to tell us who did this to you," Daniel says, about as serious as I've ever heard him.

Everybody looks at me.

"You need to tell us," Jo repeats.

It isn't that I don't want to tell, I'm just afraid I'll be blamed for what Johnny did.

"You're not in trouble," Mama says to me, like she's been reading my mind.

"Whoever did this won't get away with it," Daniel says.

Amy is stone silent. This isn't that unusual, except she isn't looking at me. Her current silence has secrets in it, like she knows something I don't know. When I try to sit up, pellets of pain shoot through me like buckshot. I can't believe so many different places can hurt at once.

I am afraid to speak. Johnny threatened to kill me if I did. But I'm also too stubborn to let Johnny win.

"Tell us," Daniel says again.

I would do just about anything for Daniel after he carried me home in the dark. The look in his eyes tells me that it's okay to say it, that he'll keep me safe.

"It was Johnny Monroe," I say finally.

"I figured it was him," he says, looking over at Jo. "But we had to be sure. Nathan and his brothers are already out looking for him. His father said he hasn't been around for days."

Jo opens the curtains to let light in. I cover the one eye not swollen shut. I remember the golden Mary, her rays flowing straight through me. I look over at my family, wishing I could tell them about what I've seen. But they don't believe in ghosts or visions. Aunt Sadie is the only one I might tell—someday.

"The sheriff from Rocky Bluff needs to talk to you," Daniel says. "If you don't feel like it today we can put it off till tomorrow, but he needs to make a detailed report."

I can't imagine telling anybody all of what happened to me, especially a stranger. Not to mention that as soon as Johnny catches wind the sheriff is after him, he'll know I told. That's like putting a bulls-eye on my back.

"Maybe we don't need the sheriff," I say.

"Why not?" Daniel asks. It is the first time I've ever seen him even halfway angry.

"Johnny's probably long gone by now," I say, wishing my words could make it true.

"You can't let him get away with this," Amy blurts out. We all turn to look at her, the silent one in our family. "Well, she can't," she says.

I know she knows something. But whatever it is she won't say in front of the rest of the family.

"Did he threaten you?" Daniel asks me.

I don't answer.

"Don't believe it if he did," Daniel says. "He couldn't get to you now if he tried."

I am not so sure.

"Louisa May, you need to say what really happened," Mama says.

I am not so sure of that, either.

"You don't want Johnny doing this to anybody else, do you?" Jo says.

This much is true. I don't want anybody else getting hurt.

"The only place for Johnny Monroe is jail," Daniel says.

I pause. "Okay. I'll tell the sheriff," I say. My words come out mumbled from my busted lip.

"Good girl," Daniel says. "You just get well and we'll take care of it."

"What are you going to do?" Jo asks. She looks concerned. Like she's afraid Johnny might go after Daniel, too.

"Now that we know for sure, I'll go join up with Nathan," Daniel says to Jo.

Before he leaves the room, Daniel kisses me on the forehead and then kisses Jo lightly on the lips.

"How long have I been asleep?" I ask Jo, who is sitting next to me.

"Two days," she says.

"Two days?" I ask in disbelief. "I've never slept two days in my life."

"It's good for you," Mama says. "Doc Lester says you'll probably need to sleep for a week."

"You let that old horse doctor touch me?" I ask.

Mama and Jo smile at each other, like there is still hope if I am complaining about Doc Lester.

"He was the only one around to bandage you up," Mama says to me. "Sadie was out delivering a baby. She's over at the Sector's place now. June's having a rough time with her latest."

I remember the red gemstone Horatio Sector gave me the night Daddy died that is still wrapped in paper inside the leather pouch. I hope June is all right. And I am glad Doc Lester won't get a hold of her.

"Don't worry," Jo says. "Mama watched Doc real close so he wouldn't botch it up." Jo reaches over and holds my hand. "Do you need anything?" she asks.

"Maybe something to drink," I say. "My mouth feels like it's full of cotton."

"How about some sweet tea," Mama asks, as if happy to have something to do.

"Yes, please," I say, and it sounds like "yesh, peas." I touch my swollen jaw. Simply lifting my arm sends a searing reminder of what happened.

Mama leaves and Jo pets my hand while Amy sews. I've never known Amy not to be sewing on something. The world could be ending and she'd have a needle and thread, ready to stitch up a new one. Amy has also never been the type to dwell on bad news. Once things are done, they're done. But she is dwelling on something now because bad news is written all over her face.

Mama returns with the tea and I pull myself up in the bed, nearly screaming. Nothing has ever been this hard for me. All these years, I took feeling good for granted.

"Just try to stay still," Mama says, with the tone of voice she used to use when I was a little girl acting up in church.

Jo shoots her a look like Mama needs to behave. I've never seen Jo defiant, especially to Mama, but even in my pain I enjoy it. "What would make you more comfortable?" Jo asks me.

"Can you help me sit up?" I say.

Jo helps me sit upright against the pillow even as I yelp and moan. I sip the tea slowly, taking in the liquid on the side of my mouth that doesn't hurt.

"Are you hungry?" Mama asks. She doesn't take to sitting still.

"A little bit," I say.

"I have some leftover cornbread," she says. "Would you like that?"

"That sounds good," I say, grateful that there is still something so ordinary and perfect in the world as Mama's cornbread. "Maybe I'll talk to the sheriff tomorrow," I say to Jo. Every word I utter is through gritted teeth, to keep my face from hurting.

"I'll tell Daniel," she says.

Lying there, it's impossible to take in all that has happened. I want my old life back. I want to be an innocent, thirteen-year-old girl again. Too much has changed. I survived the wrath of Johnny Monroe, but just barely. How do I know he won't come looking for me again? Maybe I shouldn't have been so quick to tell who did it.

Mama shows up with a large piece of cornbread on a plate. Jo breaks off tiny pieces and puts it in my mouth like I am a little bird in a nest waiting for its mother to bring a worm. The cornbread, cold and a day old, is still delicious. I yawn, which causes excruciating pain, and I can't believe how sleepy I am even though I've already slept for two days.

With Jo's help I take bird-sized sips of tea and listen to my family talk about normal things. In a way, this is a salve that soothes me most. My family speaks about what needs to be done to get ready for winter and about Jo and Daniel's baby that will be coming next spring. We are awash in normalness, but I can't help noticing that nobody is talking about what happened to me.

I drift off to sleep again and when I wake up the house is dark and quiet. For the longest time I lie motionless in the dark, trying to guess what time it is. Going by the stillness, I decide it must be the middle of the night. I fold my arms across my chest like Daddy when he was laid out in this same spot. I hold my breath, pretending I'm dead, with mourners all around me. I imagine the gold Mary coming to get me, letting me ride in her golden arms to heaven where Daddy waits for me. Then it occurs to me that maybe the gold Mary came for Daddy, too, and that he went to that place that was peaceful and warm. The thought of it makes me want to cry with happiness and sadness all at the same time.

I inhale deeply and my breath catches like barbed wire in my chest. I cuss under my breath, going from heaven to hell in one second. Cussing is a sin, according to Preacher, but it has its place with this level of agony.

Despite the pain, my body wants to function naturally. I need to go to the bathroom. When I notice a figure near the wall, I jump and wince with the pain of moving too fast. My immediate thought is that Johnny has come back to finish the job he started. But then I realize it is Mama, asleep in her rocking chair in the corner. It surprises me that she has stayed so close. "Mama?"

She startles awake. "Joseph?"

"No, Mama, it's me," I answer. "Louisa May." I haven't called myself by my regular name in four years. But it feels like the part of me that was "Wildflower" died in the woods.

"Louisa May, what is it?" she says. She stands in the shadows. With her hair down she could easily be one of my sisters.

"I need to pee," I say.

"I'll go get Bessie," she says, the name for our chamber pot. Daddy was always naming things, like the stand of four red bud trees at the bottom of the hill that Daddy named as sisters, all starting with the letter "S." Sally, Susie, Shirley, and Samantha Red Bud.

"I don't want Bessie," I say. "I need fresh air. I've been in this stuffy old house for days."

Mama doesn't argue. "Do you think you can walk?"

"I don't know, but I might as well find out," I say.

She helps me out of the bed and holds my arm as I shuffle through the living room and into the kitchen. I move at a turtle's pace. With every step it feels like Johnny still has a hold on me, squeezing the breath out of me. My head throbs. I feel sick to my stomach. The pain has worn me out, like a dishrag squeezed dry.

With Mama's help, I slide into a pair of Daddy's boots at the back door that we all use when we go out back in the middle of the night. As a little girl I always liked the feel of my small feet clomping around in his big old boots. At thirteen, they are still roomy, but not nearly as much.

We cross the back porch and Mama lights a lantern to help us make out the steps. With a full bladder, the path to the outhouse seems unending. The October air has turned cold. We arrive at the privy with the half-moon Daddy carved in front. The door creaks open and then slaps closed. The smell of lye and earth and urine hits my nostrils. The half-moon lets in a whisper of fresh air, and I aim my nose in that direction. Mama stands outside with the lantern. My pee lets loose, and I feel instant relief. But the pee burns as it comes out, which doesn't feel right. I've never burned down there before.

"Mama, something's wrong," I say through the door.

"What do you mean?" she asks.

I can hear her shuffling her feet like she is cold.

"My pee burns," I say.

Her silence answers me. I don't know what it means that she isn't saying anything and now I'm sorry I even brought it up. When I come out of the outhouse she has the light pointing down the path toward the house and I can't see her eyes.

"Damn that Johnny Monroe," she says. "I hope he rots in hell."

I've never heard Mama damn anybody before, but then her anger turns toward me. "Louisa May, you don't have the sense God gave you. What were you thinking going out to that graveyard on your own like that?"

Shame crawls up the base of my spine. Did I somehow give Johnny permission to do what he did? My mind flashes on Johnny unbuckling his pants, but I erase the image as quickly as it comes.

"I was just visiting Daddy's grave on the one year anniversary," I say in my defense.

Mama stops mid-stride, as if she's just realized it's been a year.

"There's no use crying over spilt milk," Mama says, the words rough as burlap.

Our breath races toward the moonlight. There is a frost tonight. A hoot owl cries out in the night.

Mama holds the lantern closer to my face, and I cover my eyes to avoid its glare.

"We need to go inside," she says. "It's cold out here."

We walk back to the house in silence. I make the same slow shuffle as when we came out. It irritates me that I want to run and can barely walk. Yet what hurts me more than anything Johnny could do to me is Mama's silence. Her judgment sinks into me like a heavy stone thrown into the river, its ripples extending out from me for maybe years. She blames me for getting hurt. If I had stayed at home that day and forgotten Daddy, just like her, nothing would have happened.

Silent as Daddy's grave, she helps me back into bed.

"Try to get some sleep," she says, pulling the blanket over me.

Before she turns out the light I get a full dose of the disappoint-ment in her eyes. Besides beating me within an inch of my life, Johnny has stolen something from me that I might never get back: Mama's respect.

CHAPTER FOURTEEN

The next morning Sheriff Thompson of Rocky Bluff knocks on the door. When he enters the room I determine that he is the biggest man I've ever seen. The gun strapped around his waist looks small in comparison to the rest of his body. Though he towers over everyone in the room, he stoops his shoulders as if trying not to be so big. In spite of his size he seems kind enough, replying "yes, ma'am" to Mama when she asks him if he wants iced tea. Iced tea runs as free as well water around here. Mama leaves the room to fill his request. Aunt Sadie arrives shortly afterwards with the news of the Sector's new healthy baby boy. She sits on the bed next to me. I don't care how old I am, having Sadie nearby always makes me feel braver.

"Your name is Louisa May McAllister?" the sheriff asks.

"Yes," I answer.

My name had been Wildflower, but I don't feel like Wildflower anymore, not wild or beautiful in any way. Johnny's laughter echoes in my head. *Wildflower? People should call you weed . . . I think I'll pull this weed.*

Sheriff Thompson clumsily juggles a note pad and the glass of

tea Mama hands him and places the glass on a quilt square on her dresser. "I need to know what happened between you and Mister Monroe," he says.

I've never heard anybody call Johnny *Mister Monroe*. It sounds unnatural. Johnny hasn't earned the "Mister" yet. As far as I'm concerned, he never will.

"He came up behind me in the graveyard," I say, my words still coming out in mumbles.

"Graveyard?"

Aunt Sadie sits next to me like a rock, her only job to be solid. She wraps her warm hand around mine and encourages me to go on. I wonder how she and Mama could be so different.

"I was visiting somebody," I say. "It was the anniversary."

"Anniversary?"

I feel irritated. If the sheriff is just going to repeat everything I say this is going to take forever.

"Of when her father died," Sadie says.

The sheriff taps the side of his note pad with his pencil like he is putting something together in his mind. "What time of day was it?" he asks, "when Mister Monroe came up behind you."

"Early afternoon," I say.

I don't tell him that the secret sense told me I shouldn't go and how I ignored it. I haven't told Aunt Sadie, either. I don't think I could bear her being disappointed in me, as well as Mama.

"And what exactly happened when Mister Monroe came across you in the graveyard?" he asks, his pencil poised to take down my answer.

With all this time in bed, I've had a lot of time to think. I figure I've grown up in these last few days. I can't look at the world in the same way anymore. Truth is, things happen that you have no control over and sometimes people act in ways that make no sense. From now on I'll be watching over my shoulder to see who might be coming.

"Like I said, Sheriff, Johnny came up behind me in the graveyard. And when I tried to get away he grabbed my wrist, and I couldn't get free. Then I hit him really hard in the nose and made a run for it. I took the shortcut I found, because I thought that would get me home the fastest, and that maybe Johnny didn't know that back way as good as me."

I sit straighter with Sadie's help. My head has ached for days and all these questions are making it worse. Though the pain has lost its ragged edge, I am still reminded of what happened every time I move.

The sheriff takes a sip of tea and wipes the droplets off the dresser top with his sleeve. "Please go on," he says, sounding more official than he looks. Dark hairs grow out of his nostrils and join up with his mustache. From this angle I also see that his socks don't match, though his shoes are as shiny as Doc Lester's hearse the day of Daddy's funeral.

"Well, Johnny caught up with me," I say. "I bit his hand pretty bad when he tried to cover my mouth."

"Why did he cover your mouth?"

"Because I was screaming bloody murder!"

"Wouldn't you?" Aunt Sadie says to the sheriff, putting a protective arm around me. He gives her a long look, clears his throat and looks at his notes.

"At what point did Mister Monroe leave?" he asks me.

I want the sheriff to quit calling Johnny *Mister* Monroe.

"I don't know," I say. "I passed out and when I woke up Johnny was gone. After that, I knew my family would be looking for me, so I started trying to get home."

The screen door squeaks open, slams, and Daniel walks in. He and the sheriff greet one other. Then the sheriff turns his attention back to me.

"I suppose that wasn't easy," the sheriff says, "hurting as you were."

"No sir, it wasn't," I say.

I can only imagine what the sheriff sees when he looks at me. A thirteen year old girl with two black eyes, a swollen jaw and bruises on her throat and arms that are deep shades of red and purple and yellow, like the fabric Preacher slung over the arms of the cross at church during Easter. I don't see any reason for the sheriff to know everything, at least not now and maybe never, so I stop there.

"Is that all?" the sheriff asks.

I consider for about a half a second telling him about Johnny messing with me. That is the real crime. But with my family all around me, I don't have the guts to say it. Not to mention that Sheriff Thompson is a stranger. Mountain people don't trust strangers, even if they only live over the next hill. "That's all," I say.

"One more question, Louisa May. Do you know the direction Mister Monroe went in after he left you?" he asks.

I pause to remember any clues in those last seconds before Daddy came to get me. I can't think of anything else so I shake my head, no.

"I don't think he would have crossed over that bridge," Daniel says. "I got a look at it the other day. A girl could cross it, but not a man. He must have backtracked to the graveyard or went higher up on the ridge. Those Monroes know these woods pretty good."

"Were you the one who found her?" the sheriff asks Daniel.

"Yes. Me and Nell, Louisa May's mother."

Daniel looks over at me like he's caught himself not using my real name. I don't know how to tell him that it doesn't matter anymore.

"When we found her she was pretty bad off," Daniel adds.

"You're lucky you found her," the sheriff says. "We've had cases that don't turn out that well."

It is hard to imagine anything really bad happening around Rocky Bluff. Maybe a shoplifter gets caught at Woolworth's or

somebody accidentally shoots themselves in the foot while cleaning their shotgun.

Sheriff Thompson closes his note pad. "Well, we'll get men out looking for him," the sheriff says. "Don't worry, Louisa May. If he's still around, we'll get him. But chances are he's long gone."

I like the thought of Johnny being long gone, but I doubt I could be that lucky. Johnny can hide out in the woods for years if he wants to and once he finds out that I told what happened, he'll want revenge.

"So you don't think he'll come back here?" Mama asks.

"No ma'am. I don't think he will," the sheriff says.

"He wouldn't be that stupid," Daniel says.

But Johnny is that stupid, I think. *He'll come back to kill me just like he said he would.*

Daniel leaves with the sheriff, and I hear them talking as they go down the hill. Aunt Sadie opens her cloth bag and puts a gooey yellow salve on my cuts and bruises that smells like beeswax. Her touch is gentle. Mama is in the kitchen again, clanging pots and pans, getting supper ready. Since the night before she's hardly spoken to me. When Sadie finishes, I am sticky and fragrant and wouldn't be surprised if a colony of bees came searching for me, their new queen.

Later in the afternoon Amy comes to sit with me so Aunt Sadie can go back and check on June Sector. This is the first time since Amy's odd behavior the day before that I've had a chance to talk with her. She leans against the back of the bed next to me, a pile of fabric in front of her. Of all my sisters, Amy and I are the most distant. I wouldn't dream of telling her my secrets because she's never told me hers. She also hasn't once mentioned Daddy since he died. It's like her feelings are all sewed up inside her, without an inch of give in the fabric.

I wonder how to get her to open up when she speaks first. "I was in the same year as Johnny in school," she says.

"Yeah, I remember," I say.

She sews a few stitches while I wait for her to go on. When she doesn't continue, I think I'll go crazy from the waiting.

"He used to say mean things to me," she says finally. "At least until Nathan came along."

It never occurred to me that Johnny might have spread his meanness around to Amy before it landed on me.

She keeps sewing like she hasn't said a thing, and I feel the gate she's just opened starting to close. But I am not willing to let it. I prop myself straighter in bed so I can be eye-level with her. "Amy, what did Johnny say to you?"

She pauses, as if she's remembering every single word. "Things I wouldn't want to repeat," she says softly. She stops sewing but doesn't take her eyes from the fabric. "Once he pushed me down on the ground while nobody was looking. You have to understand, Louisa May, I thought it was just me," she adds. A tear falls into the folds of the fabric.

"Why didn't you tell anybody?" I ask, sounding too much like Mama.

She returns to her sewing, making quick, jabbing strokes. "I did tell somebody," she says. "I told Nathan, because Nathan and I were friends. After we started courting he told Johnny if he ever said anything else to me he would kill him. Johnny left me alone after that. It never occurred to me that he would--"

Amy puts her head in her hands and bursts into tears. Since I've only seen her cry once, right after Daddy died, her tears feel like something wild and dangerous that might swallow her up.

"It's okay, Amy," I say. I touch her hand, wanting to release her from whatever she is holding against herself.

"Maybe if I'd said something this wouldn't have happened to you," Amy says, still sobbing. She looks miserable.

"Even if you'd told the whole world it doesn't mean Johnny would have done anything different," I say.

Her gratitude shows in her face. "I'm so sorry, Louisa May." Amy blows her nose on her handkerchief.

"What about Jo and Meg? Do you think he said anything to them?" I ask her.

"I think he left Jo alone. She's older than him, and you know Jo. She's so beautiful. I don't think he had the nerve. But I don't know about Meg."

"Meg told me once to stay away from him," I say. "That he was a no-good. But I didn't ask her what she meant."

For the first time since she arrived, Amy puts down her sewing and looks at me. She looks like Mama, but younger, and without looking cross. "I'm really sorry this happened to you," she says, her eyes red from the tears.

"It's not your fault," I say.

"But it is," she says. "Johnny started saying those things to me right after Daddy passed. I should have told Mama."

"But you didn't want to worry her," I say. "I didn't tell her what Johnny was saying to me on the road because I was afraid she'd think I did something wrong."

"I guess you do understand," Amy says.

"Somehow Daddy dying gave Johnny open season on us McAllister girls," I say.

Amy looks thoughtful. "I think you're right, Louisa May. "He never bothered me before that." She continues her sewing and I am struck by the fact that this is the most we've ever confided in each other.

Later that evening, with Mama and Meg in the kitchen, I quit fighting the memories and let them come. I open my nightgown and study my wounds. The bruises on my body are evidence not only of a beating but that Johnny messed with me, too. The bruises on my inner thighs and breasts look like hand prints. Doc Lester must have seen them when he bandaged me, as well as Mama. Maybe even Jo saw them. But nobody is talking about it.

CHAPTER FIFTEEN

Like a friend who goes away because you never listen to them, my secret sense seems to have left me, too. I sleep uneasily that night. Every time I roll over I am reminded of my bruised ribs. I listen to the house settle into itself, creaking with the slight breeze. I have my ear trained outside, listening to every little sound in the woods, afraid Johnny will come looking for me. Several times a night, I'm convinced I hear someone walking up the path to the house and get out of bed to make sure the doors are locked.

The next day the house is empty except for Mama, who is on the back porch beating the dust out of the rugs with her broom. The wallops echo through the house. She beats them with such force I wonder if she is imagining Johnny Monroe as one of those rugs. Or maybe me.

Holding my bandaged ribs, I shuffle into the living room in my stocking feet, crossing the patches of sunlight making tree shadows across the wooden floors. The metal of Daddy's banjo splinters light across the ceiling. I take the banjo from its place, then sit in the rocker and hold it for a long time, my nose right up

next to the wood. I search for reminders of Daddy's scent, but all I can smell is Mama's lemon oil. I touch the strings he touched, imagining that their tautness helps me hold myself together.

I hug the banjo so hard it starts to dig into me. For a second the pain in my chest takes my mind off the pain in my heart. But then the memories return. They always return. A gentle breeze in the yard reminds me of the sound of the wind in the trees that day. The smell of dust and dirt from Mama's rugs causes tightness in my throat and the feeling of Johnny's hands pressing on my windpipe. Vivid details spring to life. I remember the buttons on Ruby Monroe's dress as she hung in the oak tree watching me. And the look in Johnny's eyes as he crouched on top of me like an animal cornering his prey.

Careful not to nick the wood, I put the banjo back in its place. I haven't told anybody about Daddy appearing to me. It seems too crazy. But he had been there for me, as real as anything. Just like Ruby had been there to witness the scene.

A huge lump of anger wedges in my throat. I resent that Johnny will always be a part of my history now. I can try to forget the beating, but the rest I don't think I can ever forget. He got what he wanted all along. I was just a stupid girl who thought nothing bad would dare touch her again after she lost her father. But I figure bad luck, like good luck, never gets used up.

As for God, I no longer know what to do with him. Since I was *washed in the blood of the lamb* at eight, as Preacher says, it looks like God could have at least warned me, or protected me from Johnny. After Daddy died, I'd pictured them both up in heaven watching out for me. Daddy at God's side, telling him about his Wildflower here on earth. But now, it feels like both have disappeared. Cuts and bruised ribs can heal. But how do you get over heaven turning its back on you?

Becky Blackstone comes over that Saturday to work with me on my schoolwork so I won't get too far behind. I have missed the

beginning of the school year. She is the new teacher at Katy's Ridge grade school. It feels weird to call Becky, *Miss* Blackstone, and obey her every word because she is only four years older than me. She graduated high school early and went to two years of teachers college. When she was a student at the Katy Ridge School, Becky always acted like she was better than everybody else and talked real big about getting out of Katy's Ridge someday. So we were surprised that she came back. Her father owns the sawmill and was Daddy's boss. When we were younger, Becky never let me forget that fact. But she seems different now.

Becky makes herself at home in Mama's rocker, wearing a dress that has a flower print with a lace collar. At that moment, she seems younger than me, chewing on the eraser of her pencil and quizzing me on my history lesson. It makes no sense to study world history when I have my own more recent history to deal with. I've aged in the last few days. I've seen and felt things I hope other girls never have to at thirteen, or at any age.

Mary Jane comes to visit only once, just after the attack. She says her mother doesn't want her to disturb me. But I think her mother is just afraid that some of my bad luck might rub off on Mary Jane. Mary Jane acts like she, too, wonders what I did wrong, and what I could have done to prevent it. For the first time in our long friendship there are silences that I don't know if we can get beyond.

By way of Meg, Victor sends over three packs of peppermint lifesavers from the store. I pocket them to have handy when I can't sleep in the middle of the night. It is just like Victor to do something sweet like that.

That afternoon, after Becky leaves, Preacher's booming voice greets Mama at the door. He comes into the bedroom and walks over next to me. He reeks of mothballs, church hymnals and sweat.

"I trust you're doing well, Louisa May," he says, his Sunday morning voice too loud for the small room.

I sigh, sorry to put down the book I've been reading. Boredom has set in and Preacher isn't helping. He crosses his arms across his chest, Bible still in hand, and looks at me over his glasses. He visits shut-ins and sinners and I'm not sure which camp I fall into.

"Let's see what I can offer you today," he says. He thumbs through the worn leather Bible and reads out loud for several minutes about people being blessed for being meek and lowly. I think "cursed" might have been closer to the truth. Meek and lowly wouldn't have saved me from Johnny. If I'd acted meek and lowly I'd probably be dead.

By the time he finishes reading he has lambs lying down with lions, which doesn't make sense given my life lately, either. I don't have the energy to question him. The quickest way to get rid of him, I decide, is to nod my head every now and again and say, "Amen," until he's convinced his words have sunk straight into my soul. That way, Preacher will think he's delivered God's message loud and clear and I'll be rid of him.

THE NEXT DAY is Sunday and Mama and Meg go about the business of getting ready for church.

. "Jo and Daniel are coming over later to visit while we're gone," Mama says. "Do you need anything?" she adds, tightening the bun of her hair. I like that she is doting on me a little.

I pull myself up in bed. "I'm fine," I say. It's not really true but I know it's what Mama wants to hear.

She takes off her apron and folds it neatly before she puts it on the dresser. Church is about the only place she goes without her apron on, except for maybe a rare trip into Rocky Bluff. She straightens the covers on the bed, pulling the corners so tight I can't move my feet.

"That hair of yours is a mess," she says, taking a closer look at me. "I'm surprised mice haven't made a nest in those tangles."

"I'll comb it later," I say, a lamb to her lion.

I roll over and close my eyes, pretending to sleep. I listen as Mama and Meg chat while they finish getting ready for church. They have an ease with each other I envy.

Jo calls hello from the front porch and the screen door squeaks before slamming in the familiar way. It never occurs to us to grease the hinges. That was Daddy's job.

I hear Daniel's voice, too, and I wonder if he's heard any news from the sheriff. They talk softly in the living room at first, so I scoot out of bed, put a blanket around my shoulders and shuffle toward their voices. I hide behind the door. I can't see but I can hear them pretty well.

"They think he's done this to other girls, too," Daniel says, his voice low. "There's at least two in Rocky Bluff that say somebody attacked them in the woods near there."

"Poor Louisa May," Jo whispers. "I can hardly stand to look at her with all those bruises."

"That's the price you pay for taking shortcuts through the woods," Mama whispers back.

"Oh, Mama," Jo says, "why are you so hard on her?"

Silence answers. I start to wonder if eavesdropping is that smart a practice since a person might accidentally hear something they don't want to hear.

"She's just so much like your father," Mama whispers finally. "It's like being haunted by a ghost."

Mama's voice breaks. She excuses herself and I hear her go into the kitchen. I hobble back toward the bed just as Jo comes in.

"What are you doing out of bed?" Jo asks.

"I'm tired of just laying here," I say, hoping she doesn't realize I heard.

"You must be feeling better, then," Daniel says, entering the room behind her. "I'm not one to lie around either."

"You want to play a game of checkers?" Jo asks. I can't

remember the last time she asked to play checkers. Maybe never, but I pass.

I ask Daniel if he's heard anything from the sheriff and he says no.

"We'll be back soon," Mama calls from the front door. She and Meg leave, and Jo and Daniel and I go out on the porch to sit in the sun. It is chilly, but not cold, and the blanket is warm around my shoulders. In mid-October almost all the leaves are off the trees, but it is still warm in the middle of the day. So warm you can almost trick yourself into thinking that spring waits just around the corner instead of winter.

While I lean against the porch post, Jo rests a hand on her newly bulging stomach. Daniel sits on the step below me, whittling a piece of wood. I remember the cat he made me for my birthday, a day that now feels in the distant past, even though it was just two weeks ago.

"You really do look like you're feeling better," Jo says.

"A little," I say.

"You know, you gave us quite a scare," she says.

"I know." I wrap the blanket closer, thinking about how I haunt Mama just by being alive.

Jo leans toward me and smoothes my hair. I lean into her touch. At that moment, I feel like a little girl and a grown woman at the same time, a frequent occurrence these days.

"I know just what you need," Daniel turns around and says to me. He winks at Jo. "Let's go down by the river."

My body tightens with fear. The river is one of my favorite places, but I don't want to go.

"I don't know if I can walk that far," I say. I've been holed up in the house long enough to see the value in it. Walls keep a person safe. Locked doors do, too.

"I don't think I've ever heard you turn down a trip to the river,"

Daniel says. He glances at Jo, like maybe he's stopped worrying about me too soon.

I think about it for a solid minute and weigh all the things that could go wrong—meaning Johnny—and how wonderful it would feel to visit a place so beautiful. "I guess we could try it," I say finally.

We go inside and Jo goes into my dresser drawer to get a sweater for me to wear and helps me pull it over my head. I make sounds like I'm being tortured. Then she helps me pull on an old pair of pants. My boots, next to the door, are scrubbed clean, as if Mama took her strongest bristle brush to them.

We walk slowly down the hill and I remember the last time I traveled this path in Daniel's arms. My heart beats faster than usual and my eyes dart left and right. I realize I am looking for Johnny behind every tree and rock.

"What's the matter?" Jo asks.

"I'm having a hard time breathing," I say.

Daniel and Jo stop and turn to look at me.

"We're in no rush," Daniel says. "Just take your time."

"But what if he's watching us?" I say to Daniel. My voice sounds small.

"Johnny's probably a hundred miles from here by now," Daniel says. "Sheriff seems to think he's long gone, too. He'd be an idiot to stick around here after what he's done."

I want to believe him, I really do. We start walking again and Daniel and Jo each offer a hand for me to hold onto. After we travel down the road a ways, it starts to feel good to be out of the house. The air is crisp, but not enough to show your breath, and the sun warms my back. I could have done without the sweater, but don't want the pain of taking it off.

We pass the twisted dogwood that hides my shortcut to the graveyard. It isn't a secret anymore, and Daniel takes a long look as we pass as if he's remembering that night, too.

With the baby coming, Jo and Daniel seem happier than ever. They act like newlyweds, giving each other glances that are full of secret meaning. If Meg saw this, she'd be swooning all over the place.

I haven't taken the path to the river since the day of Daddy's accident, afraid it would remind me of all the sadness. But when we get closer I realize how much I've missed it. The path narrows as me and Daniel and Jo walk single file through the reeds. Daddy and I always held our fishing lines over our heads through here, so that our lines wouldn't get tangled. The river gurgles its greeting, ripples expanding outward from the shore.

At the riverbank, Jo spreads a blanket she's brought and we sit; Daniel on one side, Jo on the other. We watch the water for a long time, as if settling into its rhythms. It is a perfect day, blue skies and sunny. I throw a pebble into the water and watch new ripples break the glassy surface.

Daniel weaves two grasses together and places it in my hand like he's offering me a gift. Then his face turns serious, as if he's been waiting for this moment to tell me something.

"Johnny Monroe had no right," he says softly. "You need to know that."

"But Daniel, I shouldn't have gone out that day," I say. "It's my fault."

"You have the right to go anywhere you want, Wildflower," he says.

"You don't have to call me that anymore," I say.

"What do you mean? That's your name," Daniel says.

"It sounds silly, now," I say, ready to be Louisa May the rest of my life.

"But it's the name Daddy gave you," Jo says.

"I know. But nobody has a name like that," I say.

"Don't let Johnny do this to you," Daniel says. "You can't let him

take away your name or your freedom. You're the same person you were."

"No, I'm not," I say. The words feel as true as anything I've ever spoken. "I wish I were the same person, Daniel, but I'm not. That girl, Wildflower, died that day," I add. "She was innocent and naïve and stupid."

"Don't say that," Jo says, looking me squarely in the eyes.

"That's what Mama thinks," I say. "Not to mention, I haunt her because I'm like Daddy."

Jo and Daniel exchange looks.

"Your mama isn't herself these days," Daniel says. "But that's not the point. I don't care what anybody says, you haven't done a damn thing that was wrong."

I pause, grateful for Daniel's words, and hope someday that I believe them.

"I just wish it had never happened," I say finally. "I knew I shouldn't have gone, but I did it anyway."

"We all do things like that," Jo says. "We all have regrets."

I can't imagine Jo regretting anything, but I let it go, like the stick I throw into the river that rides out of sight on the current. After that, we watch the river for a long time. Then a question rises to the surface like one of the trout in the stream. I take this as a good sign since lately I've been more full of fear than questions.

"Why do you think bad things happen to some people but not to others?" I ask. "Mary Jane hasn't had a single bad thing happen to her in her whole life and probably never will."

"Damned if I know," Daniel says. The wisdom of his statement makes me smile, but Jo doesn't seem to see the humor in it.

"We've just got to trust that God knows what he's doing," Jo says.

Without Jo seeing, I roll my eyes toward heaven, which I'm not so sure exists anymore.

Jo takes a good look at the bruises healing on my face. "Does it still hurt?" she asks.

"Sometimes," I say. What I don't tell her is that the memories hurt more than all these physical things combined.

Since yesterday I've been able to see out of my left eye again, and the bruises have changed from red to purple edged in yellow.

The three of us rest on the riverbank letting the sunshine warm us. The church bell rings in the distance, the service over. Coming here feels more like church than Preacher reading from a book and telling us what sinners we are.

"Thanks for bringing me out here," I say. "I'm glad we came."

They each give me a hug and afterwards we retrace our steps back to the house. I didn't lie to Daniel. A part of me did die that night. Despite my belief, I repeat to myself Daniel's words: *You haven't done a damn thing that was wrong.* For the first time in days, I feel myself starting to get better. I also feel something new. I feel mad. Really mad. More than ever, I want Johnny Monroe to pay.

CHAPTER SIXTEEN

For two weeks I slept in Mama and Daddy's bed while Mama slept in mine. This was special for a while, but now it feels good to get back to sharing a room with Meg. We are both in our nightgowns and getting ready to turn out the light.

"Are you really going back to school tomorrow?" Meg asks.

"I've got to go back sometime," I say.

"Things have probably died down by now," she says. "But there will probably be some whispering."

I'd like to think everything could get back to the way things used to be, but that feels like childish wishful thinking. Lately my stomach has been hurting, too, but not enough to tell anybody. Aunt Sadie is away for the day collecting her remedies and I don't want Mama calling Doc Lester. As long as I have feet instead of hooves, I don't want him near me. At least the bruises have faded and I'm sleeping through the night again without waking up and worrying about Johnny hiding in the woods. But I still spend a big part of my day wondering where he is and if he will come after me again.

The next morning I get ready for school like nothing has

changed. Mama makes oatmeal with molasses in it and wraps me up a meatloaf sandwich to take for lunch. Daddy used to say that Mama's meatloaf sandwiches would give a condemned man something to look forward to. That always made Mama smile. But I am not about to mention it now. I don't want to haunt Mama anymore than I have to.

Meg caught her ride with Mr. Appleby earlier that morning, and when I reach the bottom of the hill Jo and Amy are waiting to walk me to school. In the last weeks, my sisters have gathered around me like guards surrounding the British crown jewels that Daddy read us a story about when we were younger.

When I walk through the doors at school, all eyes are on me. Mary Jane is already there and her face lights up like it is Christmas and the 4th of July all at once.

"I'm so glad you're back," Mary Jane says.

I sit at my desk. "I'm glad to be back, too," I say, which is partly true. For some reason, school doesn't seem as important as it did before.

"You act different," Mary Jane says at lunchtime.

"I feel different," I say.

We trade half of her egg salad sandwich for half of my meatloaf one. She is definitely getting the better end of the deal. The Bronson brothers, Kyle and Mark, look at me and whisper. I pull on my dress wondering what they've heard.

I feel sick at my stomach again. While Mary Jane and I eat in silence, she looks at me like I've become a stranger. In a way, I have.

TWO WEEKS PASS and my appetite doesn't return. Mama makes my favorite, chicken and dumplings, convinced I need to get some meat back on my bones. Our chickens are in a pen to the side of the house, near the old shed, so the foxes can't get to them. They

have a coop where Mama collects eggs from the hens. She wrings their necks with one, quick whip. Even though fish guts don't bother me, killing chickens is something I can't bear to do, and luckily she doesn't make me.

Nobody has seen Johnny in weeks and his family has deserted him. According to the Katy's Ridge grapevine, Arthur Monroe has left Katy's Ridge to stay at the Veterans Hospital in Nashville and Melody went to live with an aunt in Louisville, Kentucky, where she has a chance at a better life. Meanwhile, I cling to the belief that Johnny is long gone like Daniel and Sheriff Thompson think.

The next day after school, Daniel meets me to walk over to Aunt Sadie's to get some chamomile tea to settle my stomach. Max runs down the road to meet us. He barks until he recognizes us and then wags his tail in wide circles. Max's eyesight isn't that good anymore so he relies mostly on scent. His hair has turned gray like an old man's. Sadie serves him up one of her potions every night, mixed with supper scraps, which probably keeps him alive longer than most dogs his age.

Aunt Sadie waves when she sees us. She is preparing her garden for the cold weather to come. Winter knocks hard on the door of Katy's Ridge, but today has been warm, inviting people outside to get a few things done. I have not minded winter so much this year. If Johnny is hiding in the mountains, I want him to have every opportunity to freeze to death.

Sadie stands and hugs us both. She studies me, looking deep into my eyes, as if I am a patient of hers that requires a diagnosis.

"I was just going to put on some cider," she says. "Would you like some?"

I say, yes, but Daniel says he has to get back to Jo. He hugs Aunt Sadie and says his goodbyes. "I'll be back for you in an hour or so," he says to me.

I nod, grateful that he is so protective of me.

After Daniel leaves, Sadie gives me another hug like I could use

an extra dose. Then we go into the kitchen where she serves me a mug of cider. She makes apple cider with secret ingredients in it that she promises to pass on to me someday. With mugs in hand, we go back and sit on her porch swing. Then we take sips of the warm brew.

Max claims a worn spot in the flowerbed below us. His panting looks like a wide smile. Sadie doesn't scold him out of her flowerbeds anymore since he's good about staying in the one spot.

I sit quietly, something I do a lot these days. I want to confide in Sadie but ponder the words I might use. Meanwhile, Sadie studies me like I am a storm forming over the mountains. We take turns swinging the porch swing with one foot, letting the squeaking metal serenade us. It sounds like the crows in Nathan's fields calling to each other after the crop is in. Their squawking conversations are loud enough to hurt your ears.

The wind picks up. I pull my frayed coat closer to my neck, buttoning the top button that Mama replaced the night before. I am always losing the top buttons of things, just like Daddy.

"If you're cold we can go inside," Aunt Sadie says.

"I am a little bit, but I like it out here," I say.

The squawking metal hooks announce what I'm about to say.

"Aunt Sadie, if I talk to you about something will you promise not to tell anyone? Especially not Mama."

"Of course, honey," Sadie says. She takes my hand and squeezes her promise into it.

I pause. "My insides don't feel right," I say finally.

"Describe to me what you mean," she says, her face as serious as any doctor's.

"My stomach feels queasy a lot, except for no reason. It's not like I've been sneaking pieces of Mama's pies or anything."

We sip apple cider. Its secret ingredients help settle my stomach. Sadie nods like she's consulting the dictionary of ailments stored in her memory and then stops the swing.

"Are you still having your monthlies?" she asks.

I think back to the last time I washed out the cloth pads Mama made me. It was my birthday, a good six weeks before. "No," I say.

I don't like the expression on her face, which reveals both concern and sadness.

"What is it?" I ask.

"It could just be the trauma," she says.

"The trauma?" I don't even know what a trauma is, but it doesn't sound good. To see Sadie so serious worries me.

"I know we haven't talked very much about that day," Sadie says.

"Nobody has," I say.

"Well, that's not a good thing," she says. "I guess we haven't known what to say. What happened to you was just so horrible, honey." She pats my knee, as if she remembers every bruise. "But still that's no excuse." She pauses. The blue-gray of the sky is mirrored in her eyes. "Country people gossip like blue jays when something happens to somebody else, but when it hits close to home they don't know how to talk about it. I knew that, and I did it myself."

"It's okay," I say. "I haven't known how to talk about it either."

"Honey, I need to ask you a very hard question," Sadie says.

I don't like hard questions and feel queasy again, but I tell her to go ahead and ask.

"Did Johnny do anything to you that you haven't told us?"

"What do you mean?" I ask, but I know exactly what she's referring to.

Max comes up on the porch and puts his paws on my lap.

"Good boy, Max," says Sadie. "He always knows when he might be needed." We pet him and he takes up his new nap place near my feet.

I think the worst: that because Johnny messed with me I'll be

joining Daddy in the graveyard after all because Johnny has given me some disease that kills people.

Sadie stops the swing and turns to face me. "Did Johnny take advantage of you, honey?"

Tears rush like a flash flood down my cheeks, leaving no room to turn back. Aunt Sadie squeezes me tight. The dam in my memory bursts open and I tell her everything. I tell her about how I told Mama I was going to the river but I really went to the graveyard. And how the secret sense told me not to go but I ignored it. Then I tell her about how Johnny was there at the graveyard and how he spit tobacco juice all over Daddy's grave marker. I tell her about running for my life and almost making it to the footbridge but then Johnny catching me instead. I tell her about him beating the living daylights out of me and then taking Grandma McAllister's necklace. Then I tell her about what else he did to me that I swore I would never tell another soul. At this point, Sadie is crying, too. Big tears that slide down her cheeks and collect like raindrops on her shoulders.

"Johnny called me Ruby when he was messing with me," I say. "He cussed at me for killing myself. What he did to me must have been the same things he always did to her. That's why she killed herself, Aunt Sadie. Johnny hurt her, too."

Sadie listens to me as if hearing me out is the most important thing she might ever do.

"And the baby Ruby carried to her grave, Aunt Sadie, it must have been Johnny's. It had to be."

Sadie holds me firm, like an injured bird that might flitter away. She rocks me in her arms while the truth settles in. A bright red and orange horizon settles behind the ridge. I begin to cry like I cried at the river the day Daddy died. I didn't think I'd ever cry like that again. But I do. I cry for Ruby. I cry for the girl I used to be. I cry for all the girls that have ever been made to do things

against their will. And I cry for the baby that possibly rests below my heart.

AFTER I EMPTY myself of tears, I feel almost relieved, like some poison has been released from a wound. Sadie dries my face with a clean handkerchief and gives it to me to blow my nose.

"What am I going to do?" I ask, searching her face for answers.

"We need to wait another month to make sure," Sadie replies. "Then if it's true, we'll just deal with it."

"But what about Mama?" I say. "She'll kill me."

Of all the people that might find out, I dread her the most. But hasn't she suspected it already?

"Your Mama's survived worse, so don't you worry about her," Aunt Sadie says.

Max barks, announcing Daniel coming back to pick me up. He's in his old truck now and I'm glad we don't have to walk home. I blow my nose one last time on Sadie's handkerchief. Daniel won't mind if I cry, but I just can't bear to tell him yet.

"Let me give you something for the nausea," she says. Sadie walks to the opposite end of the porch where her herbs are planted. She takes a handful of leaves and crushes them between her fingers and puts them in a small paper bag. "Chew on these whenever you feel it coming on. I'll bring you more later." Then she goes to her cupboard and pulls out a jar of blackberry wine for me to give to Daniel in exchange for bringing me and picking me up.

Before I leave, Sadie hugs me so tight I can hardly breathe, but it feels good. Daniel waves from the end of the road and waits for me there.

"Don't count your chickens before they're hatched," she says to me. "We've got a few more weeks before we know for sure."

"It's our secret, right? At least for now?" I ask.

"To the grave, if that's how you want it," she says.

I trust Sadie to keep that promise.

When I meet up with Daniel, I pretend that everything is fine. I am getting good at pretending. Max walks with us to the end of the road and then turns back. On the way home, I wonder if Daddy took any secrets to the grave. I guess everybody has them. I picture the graveyard full of secrets, tidy little packages tied onto the limbs of the weeping willow tree.

CHAPTER SEVENTEEN

Whispering in the kitchen wakes me up early. I usually sleep later on Saturdays if Mama will let me. But the air is full of secrets that are as tangible as the smell of coffee. The last time there was whispering in the kitchen was after Ruby Monroe died. I get out of bed and follow the voices to the kitchen. Mama and Aunt Sadie are talking with Daniel and Nathan.

"What's going on?" I ask, wiping sleep from my eyes. It is the first day I can walk without pain or soreness.

"She needs to know," Daniel says to Mama, using his full voice.

Nathan agrees, and then hitches up his pants. Everybody looks at me and the urgency of their looks makes me shiver like someone just walked over my grave.

"Somebody better say something soon," I say.

Mama flashes me an irritated look. "We found a note on the porch this morning," she says.

"From who?" I say, but I've already guessed.

"Johnny," Daniel says, confirming my fears.

The queasiness in my stomach moves up to my throat. "How do you know it was Johnny?" I ask.

"Well, we don't know for sure," Nathan says.

"What did the note say?" I ask. I want to know, but at the same time I don't.

Nathan hands me the note written on a crumpled, dirty piece of brown paper bag. In childlike handwriting it says: YOU TOLD. YOUR DEAD.

Daniel is right. The note has to be from Johnny.

"Where was it?" I say. I take on the manner of a detective and don't let on how terrified I am.

"Under a rock on the front stoop," Nathan says. "I guess he snuck up here in the middle of the night."

The thought of Johnny Monroe only a wall away from where I slept gets my body to shaking. Aunt Sadie puts a protective arm around me. She squeezes my shoulder while Mama sits at the kitchen table. Mama looks tired, like I've made one too many messes that she has to clean up.

My bladder sends an urgent message. "I've got to go up the hill," I say. *Up the hill* means the outhouse. Daniel follows me out and keeps an eye on the woods.

I follow the stone steps, imagining Johnny's invisible footprints are all over the place. A potent morning pee splashes dully into the dirt below the sitting hole, giving me time to think. Like every-body else, I wanted to believe that Johnny was gone and that nothing more would come of him.

When I return to the house the whole family sits around the kitchen table and Mama has biscuits just out of the oven. Her biscuits can cure just about anything, but I still have a gnawing feeling in my stomach that no food is going to help.

"I think Max should stay up here with you all for a while," Aunt Sadie says. "He won't let anybody get within fifty feet of the house without barking."

Mama likes dogs even less than she likes cats, but she puts up with Max because of Sadie.

"Max is a good idea," Daniel says, "but I think we need to do more than that. We've got to find Johnny."

Nathan nods and swallows a mouthful of biscuit. "If Johnny's in these mountains somewhere, he's got to come down before the snows come," he says. "Unless he's in a cave somewhere, but even then he'll need to get his hands on some warm clothes."

"We need to call the sheriff and tell him what's happened," Daniel says, "and then I think we need to go looking for Johnny ourselves."

"Can I go with you to make the phone call?" I ask Daniel. He'll have to make the call from Mary Jane's and I could use a friend right now. But the main reason is I want to stay close to Daniel. I feel safe with him.

"Sure," he says.

"From now on you're not to go anywhere alone," Mama says.

"At least not until Johnny's caught," Daniel agrees.

We walk to Mary Jane's and Daniel calls the sheriff while Nathan waits on the front porch like he is a sentry standing guard. Nathan's grandfather fought in the Civil War for the Confederacy and died at the battle of Vicksburg. Nathan's family still has the sword he carried in the Cavalry.

Even though it has been nearly a hundred years ago, people in Katy's Ridge still talk about the war like it has just been fought. Daddy always said that people in the South have long memories. With this in mind, I wonder how long it will take me to forget Johnny.

"I can't believe he left a note," Mary Jane says. "And right on the front porch."

"It was creepy," I say. We sit on the bed in her bedroom. If feels like a hundred years since we did this last.

"Are you scared?" she asks.

"Sure, I'm scared. I'd be stupid not to be." Even though Mary

Jane is trying to be nice, I realize she has no idea what this is like for me.

"Johnny wouldn't have the nerve to do anything else," she says. She chews on the ends of her hair.

"Yes, he would," I say. "If anybody knows first hand what Johnny Monroe has the nerve to do, it's me."

Mary Jane gets quiet. Ever since Johnny attacked me, she seems different. Or maybe I am the one who is different. Mary Jane still daydreams about boys and about having a fairy tale wedding someday. All I think about is how to stay alive in this moment.

"Are you ready to go?" Daniel says to me after he makes the call. In Mary Jane's bedroom, his head nearly touches the top of the doorframe.

I get up from the bed and take one last look around the room as if I am trying to remember my childhood. Everything has changed. Everything.

"Come over later if you want to do something fun," Mary Jane says.

Playfulness feels like something I lost at the footbridge, along with my medallion, my rabbit's foot and the secret sense.

"It'll probably work better if you come over to my house," I say. "And have Victor walk you so you don't have to go alone."

She frowns, like being my friend isn't any fun anymore and comes at too big of a cost.

Daniel and Nathan and I walk the dirt road back to the house, and I remember all those walks I took in the evenings with Daddy. Back then it never even entered my mind to be scared of anything, or that there were bad people in the world who might be watching.

"One of us should be at the house all the time," Daniel says to Nathan.

Nathan agrees and says he'll take the first shift. Later that night, he sleeps on the sofa while Amy sews in the kitchen. I come in to get a glass of milk and Amy is working on Miss Mildred's latest

dress request, a direct copy from the Sears & Roebuck catalog. Daddy's shotgun sits next to the kitchen table, loaded, a package of shells sitting next to it. She sees me looking at the gun.

"Don't worry, Louisa May, they'll get him," Amy says. Her long hair is in a loose braid.

I always thought me and Amy were as different as night and day. But Johnny threw her to the ground, too, though she never said he did any more than that. Knowing Johnny, he must have tried. But how did Amy escape and not me? My brain is too full of fear to ask.

After drinking the milk, I say my goodnights and go to the bedroom where Meg is already snoring like a lumberjack. She always falls asleep before me. Instead of the porch, where Max usually sleeps, he lies on the floor next to the bed, close enough that I can lean down and pet him.

"Thanks for being here, Max," I whisper, "and don't you worry about Sadie, she'll be just fine." His tail dusts the wooden floor.

It takes forever for me to fall asleep and then when I finally do, a loud gunshot, in the middle of the night, shakes us all awake. Meg and I run in the direction of the shot, following Max who is barking like crazy. Mama, Nathan, Meg and I all arrive in the kitchen at the same time.

The back door stands wide open. Amy has Daddy's shotgun still aimed at the door. Her arms are shaking and the gun rattles with the movement. The acrid smell of gunpowder fills the room. Max runs outside and continues barking on the back porch. Nathan takes the gun from Amy.

"I think I hit him," she says, her voice quivering. "He jimmied the lock and came right on in. I didn't even have time to call out or anything. But he didn't expect I'd be sitting here waiting on him."

Amy buries her head in Nathan's chest, her entire body shaking. "I think I hit him," she says again, her words muffled in Nathan's shirt. She's crying now.

"Go get Daniel," Mama tells Nathan, stepping in to hold Amy.

Nathan does as he is told and goes into the living room to lace up his boots. Within seconds he runs out the door with a lantern. Through the living room window I watch the light he carries fade and then disappear down the hill.

As Meg reloads the shotgun, I pace the house. A kitchen chair is jammed under the doorknob in case Johnny returns. Amy is still shaking like a leaf in a strong wind. But after I tell her about our watchdog, Max, not waking up until the shot, she starts to laugh.

"Max slept through it?" Amy asks. "So much for him not letting anybody get within fifty feet."

"He was curled up in our room," I say.

Amy's laughter calms her and she stops shaking.

"Don't tell Sadie," Mama says. "She thinks that old dog can walk on water."

"Well, at least he's doing a good job, now," I say.

Max hasn't stopped barking on the back porch, no matter how much we try to shush him. Maybe his old man pride is injured and he's trying to make it up to us.

Mama passes Amy to Meg and puts on a pot of coffee while we wait on the men to return. I sit in Daddy's chair in the shadows of the living room, wishing he were here. My hands are shaking now and before I have time to stop it, vomit rises in my throat. I rush outside and heave over the porch rail into the dark night. It is as if my body wants to rid itself of all the fear. The purging feels awful and good at the same time.

I hear Meg's voice behind me. "Are you okay?" she asks.

"Not really," I say truthfully, wiping my mouth on my nightgown.

"We should tell Mama," she says.

"No," I say. "Definitely not."

"Why not? If you're sick she needs to know."

"I'm not sick, I'm just scared," I say. *And maybe in a family way, I*

want to add.

The first hints of daylight outline the mountains in front of us. I turn around. Meg looks worried.

"I'm okay," I say to reassure her.

Seconds later we hear voices. It is Nathan, with Daniel and Jo, coming up the hill. Nathan and Daniel carry shotguns.

As soon as the sun comes up more and they are full of Mama's coffee, Daniel and Nathan go out back to search for clues.

Daniel calls from halfway up the slope that he's found blood.

"Amy must have hit him!" Nathan calls back. He sounds proud.

It never occurred to me that Amy might be a good shot. Daddy taught us all how to shoot, but none of us have ever really practiced. Amy must have a good eye from all that sewing.

The men come back into the house to warm themselves by the stove and plan what to do next. Mama pours them more hot coffee.

"If he's hit we may be able to catch him," Daniel says.

"I agree," Nathan says, "and we need to leave soon if we're going."

Nathan hitches up his pants and tightens his belt while Mama wraps up some ham and biscuits for Daniel to pack in his day bag. They grab their shotguns by the door and are about to set out.

"Wait a minute. I want to go, too," I say. They turn to look at me and I pull myself up to my full height. "If anyone is going to hunt down Johnny Monroe, it's me."

"No you aren't," Mama says.

"I don't see any harm--" I begin.

The look on Mama's face is designed to shut me down.

"I'm not a little girl anymore, Mama," I say. "It's important that I do this. In fact, it may very well be the most important thing I ever do."

My words make me feel strong again, like I may be Wildflower McAllister after all.

"Daddy would understand this," I continue. "You see, Mama, I can't let Johnny Monroe win. If I do, I will forever be looking over my shoulder for him to come back and finish what he started."

"But you're still on the mend," Mama says.

"I feel fine," I say. "Nothing hurts anymore."

Daniel and Nathan stay quiet, as if they know better than to get between Mama and an argument. Mama looks at me for a long time, like she's seeing the ghost of Daddy again and is just now realizing how much she misses him. To my surprise, she nods her okay. Before she has time to change her mind, I give her a quick hug and grab one of her biscuits and wrap it up in a rag.

Within seconds, Nathan leads the way up the hill. It's steep and I'm grateful my soreness is gone. Daniel and Nathan stop to look at something on a cropping of rocks. Daniel motions for me to come look. A blotch of red blood is splattered on the gray stone.

"He's been hit, all right," Daniel says.

"Where do you think he's going?" I ask.

"Probably back to where he's been staying," Daniel says.

For the rest of the morning we wander the mountainside like Indian trackers, searching for which way Johnny might have gone. At the top of the ridge we come to a waterfall that I've only been to once before. Daddy brought me up here a few years ago to show me one of his favorite places. I was still small enough to ride on his shoulders.

The water plunges dramatically over the mountain and down the gorge. The spray from the waterfall chills my face. In the middle of winter icicles edge the rocks. Rosettes are frozen into the mud, paw prints of a big cat, either a wildcat or maybe a cougar. We study them for awhile before continuing on.

Nathan knows this part of woods better than Daniel and I do. He motions for us to follow him as he seeks out the best place to cross. The closer we come to the waterfall the louder it roars. Mist, churned up from the pounding of water, covers our faces. My

teeth chatter from the cold and I pull my wool jacket closer. When I reach to button the top button, it isn't there.

The Farmer's Almanac predicts this winter will be worse than normal. On a normal year we average a foot of snow in December, January, and February. But Thanksgiving is still two weeks away.

We cross several large boulders and come to a place where the water calms. I recognize the place. It is near where Daddy and I found the red fox in the trap.

Nathan points to where we will cross. The sight of the ravine makes my heart pound like the day Johnny chased me.

"Don't worry," Daniel says, putting his arm on my shoulder, his habit with me. "It's not as bad as it looks."

"I hope not," I say. We have to speak loudly to be heard over the waterfall. A thick pine tree leans into the waterfall several feet downstream offering a limb to grab if I need it. The footbridge I cross to get to the graveyard is nothing compared to this.

"Hold onto me," Nathan calls. He hoists up his pants one last time, and I grab his belt. He leads the way with Daniel following me. They put their two shotguns on either side of me like handrails that I can hold onto while we cross. The metal of the guns is ice cold, even through my gloves.

Nathan tests out each step before committing to it and makes his way slowly across the slippery rocks. As soon as his foot leaves a spot I put mine in the same place. The roaring of the waterfall pushes us forward.

I slip and bite my lip and taste my own blood. My vision whirls as the taste of blood brings back the memory of Johnny hitting me in the face. I start to fall and Daniel grabs me from behind.

"Careful there!" he says. He pulls me up by the seat of my pants and places me back on the rock like I weigh no more than a sack of potatoes. My heartbeat echoes in my ears and drowns out the sound of the waterfall. We make our way across boulders as big as a house to get to the other side.

"How are we doing back there?" Nathan asks, not turning around. We are halfway across.

"I'm doing fine," I call over the roar of the water, wondering how I've become such a good liar.

"We're almost there," Daniel says. "We've already done the hardest part."

I remember my words to Mama earlier and wonder where that strong girl went who had the gumption to convince her I could do this. If I had the sense to stay home, I could be sitting in front of the stove having one of Mama's biscuits right now.

When we step on solid ground instead of boulders, I am not the only one relieved. We sit on a dry boulder and Nathan wipes the mist from his forehead. Daniel pats him on the back like he did a good job in leading us. Nathan, always hungry, pulls shelled walnuts out of a pouch for us to eat. They taste good but smell musty, like they have been in that pouch a long time.

"Everything's downhill from here," Daniel says to me.

"Do you really think Johnny came this way?" I ask.

"He might know a better way across," Nathan says. "His daddy had him up here hunting as soon as he could carry a shotgun."

I can't imagine Johnny ever being a little boy. The thought of him rushing to keep up with his father makes him seem too human. I know him as almost a man, and mean.

After we rest we make our way down the other side of the mountain. We don't find much of anything in the way of clues. Squirrels dash to unbury nuts they've stored for winter, making enough noise for us to look to see if it is Johnny.

Our footsteps are loud in the brittle leaves. If Johnny were anywhere around he'd be able to hear us coming, and it makes sense that we could hear him, too. Anytime we stop the forest hushes. Below us, in the distance, is the old footbridge. It looks tiny from this position, a splinter of toothpick, barely in view even with the leaves off the trees.

We descend the mountain and reach the path and the clearing where Johnny caught me. Goose flesh crawls up my arms and I shiver with the feeling that I've just walked over the very spot where I could have died. In my memory the area had grown larger than what I find before me, which is little more than the size of the pitchers mound at school. A fresh blanket of autumn leaves covers the ground. The browns and golds mingle with the forest undergrowth. Dying fern fronds wave at us in the wind. A piece of my dress from that day is hanging from a pale spire of a broken flower. I retrieve the piece of red fabric and put it in my pocket.

"I was hoping we'd catch up with him by now," Nathan says.

"Did you think he doubled back?" Daniel asks, as he leans on the barrel of his shotgun.

"I doubt it," Nathan says.

I leave them talking and sweep the leaves away with my boot looking for my medallion. I've been afraid to see this place again; afraid the memories would chase me back home. But being here, I realize that it is just a place in the woods. It is not the forest that is dangerous. It's Johnny.

In order to stay there longer, I remind myself that I didn't die. Johnny didn't kill me. He wanted to. He meant to. But he didn't. If God and I were still on speaking terms, I'd ask him if he has some special plan for me, like Preacher said about Little Wiley Johnson, who swallowed half the lake, spit it back out and lived.

While Daniel and Nathan stand near the old bridge in a patch of sunlight, I push more leaves aside with my boot and see something white peeking from underneath. It is my rabbit's foot key chain. I hope this means my luck has changed. I pocket the rabbit's foot, wanting to find my medallion, too. I'd worn that medallion around my neck for an entire year. To have Johnny take it added insult to my injury. Especially after I had that vision of the gold Mary walking toward me in the forest.

Before I give up and walk over to Daniel and Nathan, I spend several minutes looking around, turning leaves over with my foot.

"I didn't know this path was here until the other day," Daniel says to Nathan.

"I think it used to be part of an old Indian trail leading to the river," Nathan says. "This old bridge is useless now, though."

I don't mention how many times I've managed to cross that useless bridge to get to the graveyard. I reach into my pocket and squeeze my rabbit's foot thanking it for the good luck it has sent me in the past.

"We should head back," Daniel says. "I'm meeting the sheriff later."

Nathan hitches up his pants. "He needs to get some hounds up here. That's the only way we'll find him."

While I wait, they discuss what to tell the sheriff and I realize how tired and cold I am. Being back at the scene of Johnny's crime reminds me too much of what happened. My determination, so bright before, turns into dull exhaustion. I sit on one of the wooden steps to the bridge and gaze at the distant stream, making its way down the mountain toward the sea.

All of a sudden, something shiny winks at me from the bottom of the ravine. It is a tiny glimmer of light, like the sun reflecting off the silver of Daddy's banjo in the living room. The wind blows and the sunlight makes its way through the trees from directly over-head. I lose sight of the flicker for a moment, but then see it again. Raccoons steal shiny things, but it doesn't look like an area where raccoons would nest. I stand to get a better view and step closer to the edge. I train my eyes to make out familiar shapes. Amid scattered sunlight and shadows, the glimmer of light continues.

"What is it?" Daniel asks.

"There's something down there," I say. "But I can't make it out."

Daniel stares where I point. Then Nathan comes over and does the same. The light flickers again and they both see it this time.

"Let's go down there," Nathan says.

"You think that old bridge can hold us?" Daniel asks. He doesn't look like he's so sure.

Nathan studies it for a while. "If we do it right," he says.

One by one we cross the rickety wooden bridge. I go first and squeeze my rabbit's foot and long for my medallion. Because I still hold a grudge, I don't pray to God and his angels like I would have done before. But I thank the bridge for holding us up and keeping us safe. Halfway across I notice a section of the bridge is missing. I take short, careful steps around the missing section. If there is a baby inside me, I want to keep it safe, even though a part of me hates it for even existing.

Daniel and Nathan follow. They cross, stepping lightly and fast like they are dancing over a hot fire. If they are scared they don't show it. And it is the one time Nathan doesn't stop to hitch up his pants.

Once we are on the other side Daniel leads the way. We leave the path and go down the hillside toward the ravine. The steepness of the rocks makes it slow going. My legs ache from all the walking and climbing we've been doing and I'm still tired and cold. After about 100 yards, Daniel stops and looks over at Nathan. Then he points to something up ahead that I can't see.

"Is that a deer carcass?" Nathan asks Daniel.

"I don't think so," Daniel says. They exchange another look.

"Maybe you should go back and wait for us at home," Daniel says to me.

"I don't want to," I say bluntly. I am tired of being treated like a child.

"I don't want your mama mad at me," Daniel says.

"Not a chance," I say. "She thinks you're the best thing since electricity."

Nathan chuckles.

"Come on, then," Daniel says to me.

I smile, having won a small victory for my independence and follow them into the gully of the ravine. As we walk, I catch glimpses of what is ahead, but I can't clearly see until we stop at the edge of the stream. What Nathan thought was a deer, is a crumpled body in a brown coat. A pool of dark red blood covers the rocks around the body.

Nathan makes his way across several boulders to get a better look. "It's Johnny!" he calls.

I gasp.

"Wait here," Daniel says to me.

I start to follow anyway but he holds out a stiff arm to stop me. His look convinces me I should stay.

Daniel and Nathan turn Johnny over.

Johnny is dead. His skull is cracked open and there is a ragged wound in his thigh from where Amy shot him.

"He probably tried to cross that bridge with the frost still on it," Daniel says.

As if wanting to protect me from the sight, Daniel takes off one of his flannel shirts to put over Johnny's head. Before he covers Johnny's face he leans down and takes something from around Johnny's neck. Then he walks over to me.

"This must have been what you saw from up there," he says.

Daniel hands me my medallion of Mary with Johnny's blood crusted over the baby Jesus. I wash it off in the ice cold water of the stream. The fear and anger I've felt since Johnny attacked me, washes away with the blood. I take a deep breath. For the first time in weeks I feel safe.

I don't know where Johnny will end up for eternity. But in a twinge of mercy, that surprises me, I hope he finally gets to see his mother again and his sister Ruby. I hate Johnny for what he did to me. Like Ruby, it seems he's already lived a life close to what I imagine hell to be. Maybe God will take that into account. If God exists after all.

CHAPTER EIGHTEEN

After the hard winter the Almanac promised, spring shows off in a big way. The first buds are on the trees and the weeping willow has feathery, light green leaves on the tips of its limbs. Sitting in the graveyard, I feel different now. I spent the whole winter holed up in the house. Some days it was so cold we kept our gloves and scarves on all day and didn't venture far from the wood stove. But we survived.

The air still has a hint of coolness to it, like the last little bits of winter are blowing through. Warm breezes promise to follow—breezes filled with the heavy summer sweetness of blossoms and ripe fruit.

Sitting next to Daddy's headstone, I rub my swelling belly that holds Johnny's baby inside. For months I hated this baby, just like I hated its father. But my hatred wore itself out over the long winter and I decided not to blame the baby for being there. Just like me, it had no choice in the matter. But in the middle of the night when doubts creep in, I still blame myself and I think Mama blames me, too.

A week before Christmas, Doc Lester showed up at the house

to talk to me about ways to get rid of it. I knew Mama had put him up to it and I cussed them both to their faces before I made Doc Lester leave. After that, a silence settled between Mama and me that feels permanent.

At least my sisters and Aunt Sadie haven't deserted me. Amy, as quiet as ever, has never spoken again about Johnny. But she comes over and sits with me and sews me new clothes big enough for my swelling belly. She also stitches little outfits for the baby, both pink and blue. Over the winter, Meg took to reading me romance novels out loud. I was so bored, I let her.

Jo is due any day. But I can't help but wonder if some of the joy has been robbed from her because of me. People can't look at her without thinking about me. The two McAllister sisters, both with child, one by good fortune and one by misfortune—the white and the black sheep of Katy's Ridge.

I'm not sure I'll ever get used to the whispers in church. Preacher doesn't come by anymore. Nothing in his big black book instructs him on what to do with an unwed mother whose child was conceived the way mine was. In my own way, I have become Mary Magdalene. It doesn't matter that in the Bible story Jesus was nice to her and considered her a friend in the end. Niceness is too much to ask of the self-righteous of Katy's Ridge.

I don't go to school anymore and do my studies at home. Becky Blackstone comes over every Saturday and ignores the growing lump under my clothes week after week. After about a month, I started calling her Becky again, instead of Miss Blackstone, and she doesn't seem to mind.

Mary Jane's mother won't let her come over anymore. If we see each other at the store or on the road, Mary Jane acts strange, like she doesn't know what to say to me. Her brother, Victor, is the only one who acts like nothing has changed. When I go to the grocery for Mama he always asks how I am and he smoothes his hair down to look nice. This makes no sense given my new role as

outcast. But I appreciate the gesture. Probably more than he will ever know.

Horatio and June Sector invite me over for a picnic in their backyard the first warm day of spring. The kids are all running around barefooted, though there's still a chill in the air. I am beached on a faded old quilt and I don't think I could get up on my own if I had to. Their new baby, about six months old now, is asleep on the edge of the quilt. We fish pickled eggs out of a jar and have honey on fresh baked bread, the pure good-ness of which gives me hope that life might be normal again someday.

Horatio is dark golden and has blue eyes. His wife is just the opposite. June is light skinned and blond headed but with dark eyes that seem to penetrate right into your soul. I show Horatio the ruby he gave me which I have started carrying in the same pocket as my rabbit's foot.

"That's a star ruby, Miss Wildflower, and very rare."

No matter how many times I ask him not to, he always calls me "Wildflower." I thank him again for the ruby.

"I still miss your pa," Horatio says.

"I still miss him, too," I say.

"A spring day as beautiful as this is for the living, not the dead," June says. She is always direct. A trait that is as rare as a star ruby here in the South.

June feels around on my stomach like she's counting fingers and toes through my skin. "It's a girl," she says, "on account of how you're carrying."

Something about hearing that makes having a baby seem more real. Over the winter, I spent a good deal of time pretending it wasn't happening at all, in spite of the fact that it was getting next to impossible to tie my shoes. Now I just wear old sneakers with the laces out of them.

"This baby is going to be good for you," June tells me. "Don't

you listen if people tell you different. She's going to grow up to be very important. A prophet of some kind. Just like you are."

Besides being a mama to four kids, June is also a fortune teller and I wonder if she is reading my future and can see the secret sense there. Maybe I haven't lost it forever after all. Something about the beauty of the day and the possibility of good coming out of the badness of Johnny Monroe makes me smile.

Horatio and June are outcasts, too, and I make up my mind, then and there, that being in exile from all the people on the mountain that make judgments may be a good thing.

THE NEXT WEEK I go spend time with Aunt Sadie. Her house is about the only place I feel at home right now. But even Aunt Sadie is sad these days because Max died on Christmas eve. Daniel and Nathan helped bury him out behind her house. Nothing could console her losing her best friend, so even Christmas was a sad day this year.

I feel like I've lost my best friend, too. Not just Mary Jane, but Daddy. When I sit in the graveyard now, it's like he's finally gone. We don't have conversations anymore, and I can't hear what he's telling me. Under the ground is nothing but a box of bones, a skeleton of memories. The fleshy parts, things I thought I'd never forget, are fading and turning to dust.

"I'm sorry if you're disappointed in me, Daddy," I say, looking at the sky in case he's up there now. The willow tree brushes its leaves against me in the breeze.

I lower my gaze and notice someone walking up the hill toward me. At first I think it might be Johnny and my whole body stiffens and I get ready to run. But then I remember that Johnny is dead and in an unmarked grave next to his sister Ruby.

Once I get the old memories out of the way, I smile when I see who it is.

"I thought you'd be here," Daniel says. He tosses a piece of straw onto the ground that he's been chewing.

I brush the leaves aside so he can sit next to me. "Don't you have anything better to do on a Saturday?" I ask.

"I could ask you the same," he says. "But Jo wanted me to check up on you."

"Mama used to be the one who'd send someone, but I guess she's given up on keeping track of me," I say.

"Give her time," Daniel says.

I feel like I've given her enough time. She's been different ever since Daddy died, and even before that she was not all that patient with me. Now with the baby growing inside me, I've given up hope that we'll ever be close again.

Daniel and I sit together and look at the river in the distance. A whooping crane walks the edge of the reeds. It's one of a pair of cranes who spend spring and summer in Katy's Ridge. I don't see its mate.

"How's Jo?" I ask.

"She's good," he says. "About to bust like an overripe melon," he adds, smiling.

I smile back at him, but then grow serious.

"Daniel, things are so messed up," I say. "You and Jo haven't been able to enjoy your baby coming as much because of me."

"It's not your fault," he says. "We all go through hard times."

"But why do things like this happen?" I ask. This is just the kind of question I would have asked Daddy to ask God for me. But God and I have not been on speaking terms for months now.

"Wildflower, I have no idea," he says.

"Please don't call me that," I say, patting the roundness of my stomach. The girl I used to be has been buried in an unmarked grave, too.

"I like the name Wildflower," he says. "I think it's about time you claimed it back."

"My name is Louisa May," I say. "Plain and simple."

I glance at the newest mound in the graveyard, a lump of red dirt next to Ruby's pile of weeds and dirt. I think of Johnny's crumpled body at the bottom of the ravine, wearing my medallion. As far as I know, he didn't even have a funeral.

"There's nothing plain and simple about you," Daniel says.

We settle into silence. As hard as I wish it never happened, I can't wish this baby away. It would be like trying to wish away the river in front of us. This baby will have a hard enough life without a mother who wished she'd never been born. The gossip in Katy's Ridge will follow her around her whole life. To be a bastard child is just about the worst thing you can be around here, other than colored or Indian.

"What do I do now?" I ask Daniel, resting an arm on my belly.

He pauses like this question requires thought. "No matter what life delivers to us, I think it's important to live with as much honor as possible," Daniel says.

"That sounds just like something Daddy would say," I tell him.

He smiles like I've given him a huge compliment. "Just remember you're not alone. We're all in this together."

"Tell Mama that," I say.

"She'll come around," he says, like he believes it.

"But I'm not so sure I want her to come around," I say. I never told Daniel about Mama bringing Doc Lester to the house to tell me ways to get rid of the baby. If he knew, he probably wouldn't forgive her, either. "I watched a bird once," I continue. "It was pushing its baby from the nest. The little bird fought back, but the mother bird was bigger and pushed it out. The little bird had a bad wing and fell to the ground. It didn't get up again." I pause. "That's Mama, Daniel. I'm on my own, whether I have a bad wing or not."

He nods like he's heard me, but doesn't necessarily agree.

I trace the dates on Daddy's tombstone with my finger,

following a familiar path. "This October will mark two years since he died," I say.

"Has it been that long?" Daniel asks.

"Too long," I say.

Daniel looks out over the river. "I can see why you like to come up here," Daniel says. "It's beautiful."

Ducks honk as they fly overhead and skim the water below in perfect landings. It wasn't the beauty that drew me here in the past, but the feeling that Daddy was here. Now he seems as silent as Mama.

"Are you ready to go home?" he asks.

"I'd like to go to Sadie's instead," I say. "I think she's lonely since Max died."

"I'll walk you there," he says.

The walk is long since I don't take the shortcut anymore. On days like this I wish we had a car. Daniel and Jo have their old truck but it only works half the time. Despite my complaining, it is a lovely day and it feels good to stretch my legs.

When we arrive at Sadie's house she is sitting in a straight-back chair on the porch, a butter churn between her knees. Her face is flushed pink from the churning. I always dread when Mama gets out the old butter churn because the task of churning cream into butter will make your arms ache for days.

"Well hello, you two," she calls from the porch. The absence of Max is impossible to miss.

"Let me take over," Daniel offers.

"Gladly," she says. She wipes beads of sweat from her forehead and stands to hug me. It is a shame that Aunt Sadie never had children because she is a natural at it.

"How are you, honey?" she asks. She spreads her fingers across my belly, as if saying hello to the baby, too.

I tell her I'm fine but she looks over like she doesn't believe me.

"Let me make you some tea," she says. "And a big glass for you, too, Daniel?"

"Yes, please," he says. "Then I need to get back or Jo will come looking for me."

Sadie goes inside, the screen door slamming at her heels. A screen door slamming always irritates Mama, but it doesn't bother Sadie one bit. When she returns we drink tea and talk on the porch until Daniel finishes churning. He wipes his face, finishes his tea in one gulp and gets up to leave.

"I'll let your mama know where you are," Daniel says.

"Not that she cares," I say.

"Talk to her," Daniel says to Sadie.

Aunt Sadie agrees. We finish our tea and Sadie says to me, "Let's take a walk."

We walk past her garden. "The strawberries will be up in a few months," she says. "Right around the time you're due."

"I love your strawberries," I say.

"I love it when you help me pick," she replies.

"I don't know what kind of shape I'll be in this year," I say, patting my belly.

"Having a baby is not an illness," Sadie says. "It's perfectly natural. Women have been doing it for centuries."

I grow quiet, knowing that I will be a mother at thirteen and not through any choice of my own. Something about that doesn't feel so natural.

"Everything is going to work out," Sadie says. She takes my hand as we walk. "And don't you worry; your mama will come around."

"That's what Daniel says."

"Well, Daniel's right." She leans over to look at the young strawberry plants. "I've known Nell for a long time," she continues, "and she can be stubborn, that's for sure. But she's also fiercely loyal and her loyalty will win out in the end. She just needs to

work through her demons, honey, and then she'll be over it. Underneath all that gruffness, your mother has a heart of gold. Joseph recognized that. That's why he married her. So don't lose faith in her. Not yet."

Even though Jesus talked about moving mountains with faith only the size of a mustard seed, I just don't have it where Mama is concerned. But I latch on to Sadie's hope and decide to leave room for a miracle, even though I don't much believe in anything anymore.

CHAPTER NINETEEN

I am almost as ripe as one of Aunt Sadie's strawberries when it comes time to pick them. The first harvest comes early this year because of an unusually hot spring. Jo is past due. We expect news any minute that the baby is coming. Despite Jo's discomfort she remains patient. Meanwhile, I do enough moaning and complaining for both of us. This last month has gone on forever and the baby is kicking up a storm. Fears torture me in the middle of the night—especially that my daughter will be more like Johnny than me and will stand down on the road, spitting into peach cans.

Sadie isn't young anymore but she can handle a whole farm on her own. She manages to get things done that would stretch two people to their limits. Selling her mountain remedies, her blackberry wine and her quilts brings money in. Her house and land she owns outright. My grandfather McAllister left Daddy and Aunt Sadie a little bit of money for land when he died. She has a hundred acres past the field and down the hillside, too steep to plow or put a house on, but it is her drug store, where she collects her ginseng root and herbs.

I crawl on my knees through the rows of strawberry plants; my

belly hanging like an upside-down camel's hump. The rich, sweet earth feels solid underneath me. It is good at growing things and, for now, it looks like I am, too. I pat what I imagine to be the baby's head.

Sadie and I travel down row after row picking the fruit. I fill an old peach basket. Later we'll empty them into the kitchen sink and wash the strawberries before dividing them up and giving them to family. I grow tired quickly these days and stop to rest.

"Strawberries like the heat," Sadie says, as she wipes her face and neck with a red handkerchief. "It gets them excited about blooming."

"Then they must be absolutely thrilled," I say grumpily.

It is unbearably hot. Sweat cuts a pathway down my neck, between the cleavage I've suddenly begun to have, and over my skin stretched tight.

Sadie shoves the red handkerchief into her back pocket. As she makes her way down the rows it sways back and forth like a matador signaling a bull.

The sticky sweetness of the plants covers my hands. Every few feet Sadie scoots forward the empty flour sacks she's sewn together to use as a cushion for her knees. I have a pair, too, that look like giant potholders. Without protection, picking strawberries tears up your knees quicker than anything. The hard clay presses into hairline cuts and scrapes that turns your knees reddish orange and won't come out for days.

Sadie is in a talking mood today. From one row over, I hear about the art of canning okra and the subtle uses of ginger. She also talks about Eleanor Roosevelt, who she simply calls "Eleanor," as if they are best friends. I tune Aunt Sadie in and out like a distant radio station because I have other things on my mind. Becoming a mother worries me day and night. What if I don't know what to do?

The silence between Mama and me has become as thick as a

strong strain of kudzu vine. Kudzu can take over an entire mountain in a summer. It can even swallow up an entire house if left alone. My thoughts eat away at that vine like a goat.

Sadie senses my uneasiness and sits on the ground between the rows. "I think we need a reward for all this hard work," she says.

I sit, too, wondering how I'll ever get up again.

"How about a swim?" she says.

"I'm a whale already," I say. "I'll scare the fish. Besides, I don't have a swimsuit."

"Who needs swimsuits?" she replies.

Sadie's property has private access to the lake.

"Come on," she says, offering me a hand up. My weight nearly pulls us both over and we laugh until we get upright again. Then we take our peach baskets full of strawberries and walk back to the house. On the porch we strip down to what Sadie calls *our birthday suits*. Sadie finds two towels and wraps them around us. My towel barely reaches across my belly, but nobody is around and Sadie could care less.

"Last one in is a big fat toad," she yells. Her skin, as wrinkled as mine is stretched tight, jiggles as she runs down the road, her hand clutching her towel to her chest.

The sun is straight overhead, the temperature stifling hot. The breeze that blows feels more like a heater in my face. But the lake waits about a hundred yards away. Sadie is already halfway there. Her bare, white bottom shines as she runs, as if tossing a greeting in my direction.

"No fair, you got a head start," I yell. I follow her like a waddling duck, with the help of one hand braced underneath my stretched belly. When I reach the lake she is already swimming. I wade in slowly, a cautious convert.

I lower my shoulders into the lake and then my head. The water baptizes me with coolness, dissolving away the sticky strawberry hotness. The bulge in my belly makes it easy for me to float.

The water holds up the baby for a change instead of me. After a few minutes the tiredness leaves me and I feel light again. At this moment, I can almost remember what life was like before Johnny Monroe.

Sadie dives deep into the water, her gray braid plastered down her back. When she comes up to the surface, she is smiling.

"Your mama and I used to do this before you girls were born," Sadie says to me.

"Mama?" I ask. "It's hard to imagine her doing something so playful."

"Your mama's always been serious, even when she was young," she says. "But your daddy had a way of bringing out her carefree side. I've been worried about her since Joseph died."

"Me, too," I say. "It's like her sadness is locked deep inside and she covers it up with all the work she does to keep the family going."

Sadie takes a sideways glance at me. "When did you get to be so wise?" she asks.

Her question makes me smile and gives me a hint of hope that the secret sense may return, since it is supposed to hold wisdom.

After a while, Sadie swims to the shore and gets out of the water. She dries herself off with the towel and I get a glimpse of what it will be like looking in the mirror when I get old.

When Sadie helps me out of the water, I nearly pull her in for her efforts. But as I'm drying off, Sadie says, "The human body is amazing, isn't it? It can grow little people inside." She pats my stomach, a wide smile on her face.

I try to catch her enthusiasm but it slips like a minnow through my fingers.

After I dry off we walk back to the house hand in hand and get dressed again. While Sadie washes the strawberries in the sink, I makes us both some sweet tea. The baby moves and I stop and caress my belly.

"Is she kicking?" she asks.

"Like she's playing a drum," I say.

We both call the baby "she" after I told her about June Sector's prediction.

"It won't be long now," Sadie says. "Maybe another two or three weeks."

"Jo's due any minute," I says. "Daniel's so excited about it."

"Bringing a child into this world is a very exciting thing," she says.

"Not always," I say. I remember all the judging looks I get from the people at church, which is almost as bad as the looks of pity.

"It's a miracle no matter how she gets here," Sadie says. "And don't you for one second think otherwise."

"That sounds like what June Sector said."

"I've always liked June," Sadie says.

We stand side by side washing strawberries at the sink. I love Sadie, but deep down there is a part of me that wishes it was Mama saying and doing these things with me.

"June said this baby will grow up to be a prophet just like me," I say.

"Ooh, I like that," Sadie says, pulling the green tops off the berries.

"What do you think she meant by being a prophet?" I ask.

"That's just another name for the secret sense," Sadie says. "Someone with the secret sense just knows things a little bit before everybody else."

"You know, I haven't felt it since that day," I say.

"Just be patient, sweetheart. It will come back around, just like your mama will."

"I hope you're right," I say. Then Sadie gives me a look that is full of knowing.

"When it's time, you have someone come get me," Sadie says. "I helped your mama with all you girls."

"I'm counting on you being there," I say.

"If I remember right, you came out squalling. You had the healthiest set of lungs I've ever heard."

"Was Mama happy?" I ask.

Sadie pauses. "Yes, I'm certain she was. I seem to recall a smile on her face."

I wonder if Aunt Sadie is making this up.

"Your baby will probably come out squalling, too," she continues. "But I'll do the same with her that I did with you. I'll hold her in my arms and tell her that this world is a fine place to be and that it will hold many lessons, so she might as well quit her crying and enjoy the stay."

We wipe our hands on the same towel. "No matter what happens, Aunt Sadie, don't let Doc Lester get anywhere near me, okay?"

No love is lost between Sadie and Doc Lester. He will tell anyone who will listen that she's a "quack," because her mountain remedies eat into his profits.

"I promise," she says. "Just remember giving birth is one of the most natural things in the world. Think of those kittens being born under your porch all the time. Sometimes the mothers are no more than kittens themselves. But they know what to do when the time comes. Instinct takes over. And Louisa May *Wildflower* McAllister, you have plenty of instinct."

I lean my head into her shoulder. "Thanks, Aunt Sadie."

"You're welcome, honey."

"I guess I'd better get home," I say. "Mama's making fried chicken tonight."

"That would be enough to get me home," Aunt Sadie says. "And remember, don't let Nell get to you. She'll come around."

Before I leave Sadie picks out the best strawberries to send to Mama. It is still daylight as I walk toward home. When I pass the corner where Johnny always stood, it seems like everything that

has happened in the last year has been a dream. I've moved past being so angry I could have killed Johnny myself. But I haven't stopped being angry with God, yet. Preacher is fond of saying that the road to hell is paved with regrets. I refuse to regret having this baby and I will raise her with Mama's help or without it.

CHAPTER TWENTY

A frantic knocking wakes us in the middle of the night. My breathing goes shallow. I bolt upright in bed and wait like a deer getting wind of a hunter. Unexpected noises always make me think of Johnny. Meg stashes the book under the bed she's fallen asleep with. Mama goes to the door and I hear Daniel's voice.

"It's time!" Daniel pants, as if he ran all the way up the hill.

Meg jumps up and I waddle after her.

"Has somebody gone for Sadie?" I ask.

"Nathan's on his way," Daniel says, "and Amy's meeting us at the house."

Meg and I go back to our room and dress as fast as we can. When we return to the porch, Mama has the lantern going and we follow her down the hill and across the road to Jo and Daniel's house. Every light is on inside and the whole house looks wide awake for the event. We go in the kitchen door and Mama gets busy. She gathers towels and puts water on the stove to boil while Meg and I go to the bedroom to check on Jo. Amy is already there.

Jo's face is flushed and she is sweating like it is a hundred degrees, which it might very well be. Every window is up and the

curtains are open wide so more air can come in. Jo grimaces and moans with the latest labor pain, and I reach over and hold her hand. She squeezes it so hard I almost scream myself. I never realized she was so strong. Fear takes hold of me when I realize I'll be doing this same thing soon. I hold on till her pain passes then put Jo's hand in Meg's. Dizzy, I run outside, taking in big gulps of fresh air to keep from passing out.

Jo wails from inside the house as if her insides are being ripped apart. With each wail, my panic rises. I want to run and hide where nobody can find me, not even my baby that seems intent on being born, just like Jo's. I grab a lantern from the kitchen and make my way to Daniel and Jo's barn.

When I open the door, the smell of mellowed wood, dirt, and warm straw comes at me from all directions. In an odd way it reminds me of Daddy's pipe tobacco. The lantern beams out a halo of light. No animals stay in the barn anymore. Yet leather harnesses hang on rusty nails above empty feeding troths like old ghosts. Stalls empty of hay are in one corner. Daniel bought these things from the Tanners, who owned the property before them. Daniel has been saving to get a cow and maybe a goat or two, but having a baby has put that off for the time being.

It is quiet in the old barn and a little cooler. I sink to my knees near the empty horse trough in the center. If I still believed in prayer I would ask God to help me, but since he didn't help me with Johnny, I doubt he would show up for this.

Thoughts rush at me like rain pebbles blowing sideways. *I am too young to have a baby. I don't know how to do this. I don't even know how to be an aunt, much less a mother to some squalling little baby that shouldn't be here in the first place.*

Guilt and shame crash over me in a fresh wave of tears.

"Louisa May?"

I don't hear Mama come into the barn and suck in my breath with surprise. She stands in the doorway, her lantern shining a

swatch of light right toward me. For a second, she reminds me of the gold Mary. Then a tingle begins in my chest and it's as if the secret sense is announcing that something big is coming. Something, that as an old woman, I might think back on when I'm dying. I'm not sure if it's good or bad.

"Is Jo all right?" My voice sounds small again, like it does whenever I've had the wits scared out of me.

"She still has a few more hours," she says. "But Sadie's here."

"Good," I say. Everything seems more manageable whenever Sadie's around.

"What are you doing out here?" Mama asks. She stands a foot away from the door, as if she can't decide whether to come in or not.

I don't feel like lying to her. The truth is, the only time I felt worse was when Johnny beat the living daylights out of me. Except maybe this is worse, because I am beating the living daylights out of myself.

"Louisa May, are you all right?"

"Not really," I say.

She hesitates and then steps farther into the barn. I lower my head to shield my eyes from the light. She can see me all too clearly with the help of her lantern. It threatens to illuminate how scared I am.

I wipe snot on the underside of my dress, stretched taut by the fullness of my belly. No matter how hard I try, the tears won't stop. I keep expecting her to say something about how worthless crying is, but she just stands there.

"Stop looking at me," I say. I lean into my belly and start to rock back and forth, searching for even an ounce of comfort.

She lowers the flame of the lantern, as if to offer me privacy, and walks over to me. The light and shadows make us look like giants against the back of the barn. I hate crying in front of her. I don't want to give her the pleasure of seeing me suffer.

Mama pulls an apple crate next to me and sits, and I have to resist pushing her away. I am tired of thinking of all the ways I've let her down. Not to mention all the ways she's let me down, too.

"Mama, I never should have gone out that day. I should have stayed at home. But it was Daddy's anniversary and I wanted to talk to him because I missed him so much."

I bury my head in my hands. The tears flow. I want her to touch me, to comfort me, but she doesn't. I try to convince myself that I don't care and that I'm better off without her. She is so close I can feel her breath on me.

"Louisa May, I need you to listen to me like you never have," she says. Her words are clear and strong. "Are you listening?"

"Yes, Mama, I'm listening," I say, my words aren't clear and strong at all, only soft.

Her voice softens to match mine. "Louisa May, I'm so sorry that it's taken me so long to tell you this."

She pauses and I wonder if she is about to disown me and throw me and my baby out of the only home I have ever known. She turns my head so that she can look into my eyes.

"Louisa May, you didn't do anything wrong. Do you hear me? You didn't do anything wrong. Johnny had meanness in him. You tried to tell me about him, after you heard something in the woods that night, but I didn't listen . . . Honey, I should have listened."

She starts crying, too. At first, it scares me. I thought she was too strong to cry, or too stubborn. I hug the baby as Mama's crying feels almost unbearable. Like her pain is my pain and my pain is hers. We both miss Daddy. We both have regrets about how life has turned out.

After a while, Mama wipes her tears and takes in a long, deep breath.

"It wasn't your fault that Johnny Monroe came after you," Mama begins again. "None of this was your fault. I'm sorry if I ever made you feel like it was. I just didn't know what to do,

honey. I've never wanted to kill anybody so much in my life as Johnny Monroe. I wanted to take Joseph's shotgun and kill him myself. And as for Doc Lester, I admit I've done some stupid things in my life, but none quite as stupid as that. I guess it was my fear that drove me. I wanted to protect you from what everybody will say and what that precious little child will have to go through just by being born."

In that instant, I understand forgiveness. The kind Preacher said Jesus had for the people that pounded nails into his hands and hung him on the cross. I push myself through the darkness toward Mama's open arms. I fold into her, as if she is the golden Mary come to take me home. My head rests against her shoulder. I close my eyes, soaking in her love.

"We're going to be all right," Mama says. She kisses me on the cheek and rocks me in her arms. "We McAllisters are made of sturdy stock."

We sit in that old barn for a long time. After a while Mama takes another long, deep breath, and releases it, as if she suddenly understands forgiveness, too, and all the breaks between us have mended.

In the moments that follow, I feel the secret sense come alive in me again and I suddenly know that even though life will still be hard, everything is also going to be just fine. I tell Mama that I am going to name the baby Lily because her mother's name is Wildflower. Mama nods and tells me that Lily is a lovely name.

In my memory I hear Daddy playing his banjo in the living room singing an old country song that starts out sad but ends up all right. I can look on the best parts of life now, of having family with me and enough faith in myself that I can find my own way out of just about anything. Maybe someday, God and I will mend the breaks between us, too. Meanwhile, I will raise my daughter, Lily, the best way I know how.

Lily's Song

SUSAN GABRIEL

For my mother

CHAPTER ONE

Lily McAllister

At the kitchen door, I try not to light too long or Granny will give me something to do. Granny doesn't believe in lingering. Lingering makes a soul lazy, she's told me more than once. But it turns out that lingering is what I am especially good at, and my soul doesn't feel lazy at all.

"Where's Mama?" I ask, giving her a quick hug.

"Wildflower's up at the cemetery already," Granny says. "You know how she gets on the anniversary."

Granny takes a baking sheet lined with biscuits out of the oven. My mouth waters from the yeasty smell and the sight of the golden tops. Mama says that Granny's biscuits can make a believer out of anybody. That's because if you add fresh churned butter and a healthy dollop of homemade strawberry preserves, the first words out of your mouth are *Oh, God.* Or *Oh, Lord,* depending on whether you're leaning that day toward the Father or the Son.

"Take those scraps out back for Pumpkin and the others," Granny says.

The biscuits have caused me to linger, and I've been caught doing nothing again. The plate of scraps from breakfast sits next to the sink, and I grab them to do as I'm told. The cats have already gathered, as though possessing secret knowledge that I've been asked to feed them. Pumpkin sits at the center while the others weave around him like kite tails on a windy day.

Pumpkin is a year older than me. Fifteen is old for a cat here in the Tennessee mountains. Most cats are lucky to make it past year one, given hoot owls consider them biscuits right out of the oven. Not to mention the foxes and bobcats who hunt morning and night for their next meal. Pumpkin is good at surviving and has scars to prove it. Half an ear is missing, as well as the tip of his tail, and one paw points to the right like he's hitching a ride into town.

The kite tails mew and stand on their back legs as I lower the plate. Yet they wait until Pumpkin takes the biggest piece of scrambled egg before digging in themselves, as if to show respect to their elder. At least half of the cats assembled are orange tabbies like Pumpkin. He's been a daddy and a granddaddy many times over.

As for me, I've had neither. The mountains are my kin, just as much as the people, my Great Aunt Sadie tells me. So any time I linger on a soft piece of earth, I imagine sitting on my Granddaddy McAllister's lap. I've heard stories about him my entire life. About how he knew all the names for things here in the mountains, read books and played banjo better than anybody in Katy's Ridge. He used to sing, too, and Mama says that's where I got my singing talent.

Every year on the anniversary of the saw mill accident that took his life, Mama spends the day at the cemetery. Today marks fifteen years since it happened, and I think she still misses him.

The longing I feel for a daddy goes beyond missing and is the dull pain that comes from total absence. Sometimes in the middle of the night I can feel the loss at the center of my chest, like old

Pumpkin has fallen asleep there, pressing on my heart. The grief feels as old as he is.

Just this morning I dreamt about a man standing in the shadows of my bedroom watching me. I've had this dream several times in my life, and I can never see his face, but I can hear him breathing and feel his presence. When I wake, I am full of yearning. Mama refuses to tell me who my daddy is, no matter how many times I ask. I know she has her reasons for not telling me, but that doesn't make me not need to know.

"Can I take Mama a biscuit?" I ask, when I come back inside. "She'll be getting hungry about now."

"I reckon," Granny says, tucking a sigh at the end of her words. She and Mama have been tearing down and fixing the same fence their entire lives. Love resides in the center of all the mending. Of this I am certain. But I can't imagine the two of them living together without ending up looking like Pumpkin.

Granny gets a small basket from the cupboard and wraps up two biscuits with melted butter and jam already on them. They ooze their sweetness onto the worn cloth wrapped around them. Granny puts a ball jar full of water in there, too, in case our mouths get gooey.

Before I leave, Granny kisses me on the forehead and says, "Give a kiss to your mama, too."

I tell her I will.

Granny is fond of saying I'm just like Mama, and she smiles when she says it like that's just what she deserves. I'd rather hear how much I am like myself. Or how much I am like my daddy. That would be something different at least. But nobody ever mentions him and me in the same breath. Nobody mentions him at all.

I've lived in Granny's house since the day I was born, so I've had time to figure out ways to stay on Granny's good side, which doesn't have a whole lot of room. Mama says she wasn't always

irritable. She says she changed after Granddaddy died. Sometimes I wish I had known her before.

The anniversary of Granddaddy McAllister's death is treated sacred like Christmas or Easter. If it falls on a weekday, I get to stay out of school so I can go to the cemetery with Mama. Then later this afternoon, all my aunts, uncles and cousins will come over for a special supper and I'll be asked to sing. Usually I sing *Down in the Valley* or *Amazing Grace*, the songs my granddaddy loved most. My family is sometimes my only audience, except for the times I sing at the small Baptist church. At this rate, I'll never reach my dreams.

The first chance I get I'm leaving Katy's Ridge. Although I'm pretty sure it would break Mama's heart if I did. In some ways, I'm all she's got. Yet a voice tells me from somewhere deep inside, I am meant for bigger things. I want to sing in each of the 48 states and then go around the world and sing in every place I've ever read about in books. Cathedrals. Palaces. Concert halls. Nobody knows my dream of becoming a world renowned singer. It is a secret I keep even from Mama.

After leaving the house, I take off down the path that leads to the road. It is 1956 and most of the roads in Katy's Ridge are now paved and a few folks even have paved driveways, but not us. Mama said we didn't have indoor plumbing until after I was born, so I won't be holding my breath for a paved driveway. Unlike me, Granny has never made a friend of change and is fine with her world staying small.

Katy's Ridge is about as small as the world can get. If it were a puppy or a kitten it would be the runt of the litter and in danger of not surviving. Most kids I know have no intention of staying in this area after they graduate high school, and many don't even keep it a secret.

Mama's old Ford truck that she drives to work every day sits at the bottom of the hill, but on the anniversary she walks to the

cemetery. I run my fingers along the truck's passenger side. Although I learned to drive as soon as I was tall enough to reach the brakes, Mama says I can get my driver's license in a year to make it official. Mama's not a big stickler for rules. Never has been, to hear her tell it.

I toss a wave to the four Red Bud sisters, trees that Granddaddy McAllister named back when Mama was a girl: Susie, Samantha, Sally and Shirley Red Bud. More than once I've wished for sisters, at least one, instead of being an only child. It would make it so much easier to leave Katy's Ridge if Mama had someone else to fret over.

After walking down the road a few hundred yards, I take the shortcut beside the old dogwood and follow the path Mama took earlier that morning to the cemetery. Because of my earlier dream, the shadows look thick enough to hide a person and the breeze through the trees sounds like breathing. To take my mind off the creepy things, I pretend I'm Judy Garland walking the yellow brick road. Except I'm actually walking a leaf-covered path that I've taken a million times. I hum *Somewhere Over the Rainbow* and take note of the blue skies, wondering if dreams really do come true.

The Wizard of Oz finally came to the movie theater in Rocky Bluff two summers ago, when I turned twelve. A movie has to be a hundred years old before it makes it to the backwoods of Tennessee. Most Saturday nights the theater runs Gene Autry films and other cowboy westerns that are as dull as old kitchen knives. The women in those pictures work in saloons and are always in need of rescuing. Mama doesn't rely on men for anything, except maybe Uncle Daniel, who keeps the books at the sawmill.

I think of Crow Sector, who I've had a crush on forever. With his black hair and blue eyes, he can ride up on his white horse and rescue me any time he wants. I'll just throw up my arm like in one of those cowboy westerns and let him pull me up in the saddle.

Meanwhile, it is mid-October here in Katy's Ridge and the tree leaves race each other to the ground. They crunch underneath my feet releasing the perfume of fall. On the path in front of me I find a perfect red maple leaf, its color bold in the afternoon sun. I put it in the front pocket of my overalls to give to Mama.

Gusts of wind race over the mountain and my long hair flies wild behind me. I never think to bring a rubber band, and I stop long enough to tuck my hair into the back of my shirt. A whirlwind of leaves dances up the hillside, gathering others to join in. It's the most playful time of year here in the mountains. The leaves and the wind have a last bit of fun before the seasons change. A hint of winter floats on the breeze, a ribbon of cold air mixed in with the warm.

At the footbridge I repeat the ritual Mama taught me when I was younger. A rabbit's foot keychain hangs from a small nail under the top railing of the bridge. I take it off and rub it between my hands before returning it to the nail. Three months ago, on my fourteenth birthday, Mama gave me a necklace that she'd had since she was a girl, a Madonna and Child that my great grandmother gave to her. I kiss the Madonna and ask for her blessing and protection. Then I ask Granddaddy McAllister, and any angels he knows, to help with the crossing, too.

A much older bridge crossed this ravine years ago, but my uncles Daniel and Nathan built a new one the year I was born. It doesn't look so new anymore, but it's as sturdy a footbridge as you'll ever cross. At least that's what my Uncle Daniel says. This doesn't change the fact that I get an uneasy feeling every time I cross it.

At the center of the bridge, the whispers start. I tell myself it's just how the wind sounds when it blows through the trees. But it sounds more like a human voice than the wind. It's like this part of the mountain has a secret story, and it can't help saying: *Once upon a time....* I want to know the rest of the story.

Granny says I'm too curious for my own good, and I should remember what curiosity did to the cat. But this has nothing to do with a cat, I simply want to know things.

The old wood of the bridge creaks when I stop and gaze into the ravine. Goose bumps raise on my arms and the hair prickles at the back of my neck. People say when this happens that you've just walked on top of somebody's grave. I've walked on plenty of dead people in my lifetime, having visited my kinfolk in the graveyard since I was a baby. Something about this old bridge feels just like a graveyard.

Pushed by a sudden gust of wind, I grab my necklace and run the rest of the way across. The whispers call me to come back. They aren't ready for me to leave. Sometimes I wonder if Katy's Ridge will actually let me go when I finally figure out how to leave this place. It's like it has its reasons to keep me here. Reasons I don't begin to understand, but that yank at me whenever I dream of escaping.

At the backside of the cemetery, Mama sits under the biggest weeping willow tree. The sunlight dances off the green and gold almond-shaped leaves. Mama turns and waves to me. On account of her secret sense, it is impossible to sneak up on her. She pats the ground next to where Granddaddy is resting, and I join her. Mama is the one who taught me to linger.

"Granny sent biscuits right out of the oven," I say.

Mama caresses the side of my face like she always does.

I unwrap our treasure and spread out the strawberry stained napkin like it's a fancy tablecloth for our picnic. We each take a bite of biscuit. In a way, it's like we're taking Holy Communion and the biscuits are the wafers. Mama takes a bite and then looks up at the sky like she is seeing a bit of heaven.

"How's Granddaddy today?" I ask.

"He loves getting caught up on how we're all doing," she says,

between bites. "I told him how well you're doing in school, and how you're just like him when it comes to reading big books."

"Did you tell him about my singing?"

"I did. I told him you're the best singer in the Cumberland Mountains."

And someday the world? I want to add. But no one in our family speaks their dreams out loud, as far as I know.

I read the sadness in Mama's eyes that visits her on anniversaries and other days throughout the year. She's even sad on my birthdays sometimes, though she is an expert at hiding it. Once we finish our biscuits, she looks out over the river as though something this beautiful requires witnessing.

"This is the prettiest spot in all of Katy's Ridge," I say, repeating one of Mama's favorite things to say.

"You know, it really is." She smiles, like she's just now noticing.

The wind kicks up and an empty paint can from recent upkeep at the church rattles through the cemetery. Mama sits up with a jolt. Something about the sound turns her eyes dark and narrow, as though she's looking through a portal into the past.

"You okay?" I ask.

She doesn't answer.

Sometimes Mama seems haunted. Haunted by something she never talks about. I wait for her return, pressing bread crumbs into my finger and eating the remains of our host. I begin to hum *Over the Rainbow* again. Sometimes I wish a cyclone would transport me to a world outside of Katy's Ridge. I click my heels together three times, wishing I was anywhere but home.

Before long, the spell Mama has fallen under is broken. She smiles at me again.

"Did I ever tell you how Daddy could make us all laugh until our stomachs hurt?" she asks.

Even though I've heard Mama's stories multiple times, I ask her to tell me again.

"Your Aunt Amy was all grumpy because she'd had a tooth pulled. Doc Lester did the pulling, which is a story I'll save for another time."

A quick grimace turns into a grin.

"Amy's mouth was full of cotton," she begins again, "and we could barely understand her when she talked. When Daddy tried to tease the bad mood out of her she said, 'addy, op it.' 'Who's Addy?' he said. 'I don't know any Addy.' Then he asked every single one of us, including your granny, who this Addy was. He wanted to talk to this Addy, he said, so Amy would feel better. Well, by the time he did that for a while, even Amy had tears in her eyes from laughing."

Mama and I laugh with the telling of the story.

"That was his nickname for Amy. He called her Addy," Mama concludes.

"And he called you Wildflower, right?" Sometimes I ask to hear the story of how she got her nickname just to see Mama's face turn bright.

"Yes, he called me Wildflower," she says. "He said I'd sprung up here in the mountains like a wild trillium, and that trilliums take your breath away if you see a patch of them. I was ten when he gave me that nickname. As you know, some people still call me that. Mostly family."

Mama gets another one of her faraway looks. Sometimes she'll visit the past and stay gone for an entire afternoon. I hope this isn't one of those times. The world gets lonely without Mama in it. Despite my plans to shed Katy's Ridge like a snakeskin, I'm not sure how I'll live without Mama.

Nobody in Katy's Ridge will talk about who my daddy was. I've been told that he died before I was born. But when I ask for his name and what he was like, people tell me to ask Mama. Then when I ask her, she says some things are better left unsaid.

My best friend Pearl thinks my daddy must have been someone

Mama met in Rocky Bluff. Maybe a soldier passing through or a traveling salesman. But Mama isn't the type to take up with someone for just a day or two. She's slow to warm to strangers, although I've heard from her sisters this wasn't always the case. Maybe Granny isn't the only one who changed after Granddaddy McAllister died.

The breeze rattles the leaves on the weeping willow behind us. The branches sway over our heads. The sound reminds me of the electric fan on Mama's dresser that lulls me to sleep on hot nights. I recall the dream again from the night before and wonder if the man in the shadows is my daddy. If I were living in a fairy tale and was granted three wishes, my first wish would be to know who my daddy was. The second wish would be to understand why Mama refuses to tell me. And my third wish would be to live anywhere but Katy's Ridge.

CHAPTER TWO

Wildflower McAllister

Aunt Sadie says Lily's singing talent is repayment for the way she entered this world. She possesses a voice that can make people drop to their knees. I tend to agree that God's hand might be in on it, though God and I have barely spoken for decades now. I also wonder if Daddy might be in on it, too. It would be just like him to make sure things go well for us.

Lily lowers her head into my lap, something she doesn't do that often anymore now that she's fourteen, the age I was when I had her. Her hair is darker than mine, the color of chestnuts. Brown eyes, too, while mine are blue. At times, her features remind me of the one person I most want to forget. Not only in her height—she's taller than me—but also in the way she stands. Like she's waiting at a crossroads for something to happen.

After Daddy died, I sometimes fell asleep on his grave. My sister Jo would come looking for me. Now it is my daughter who sleeps here. Maybe we all sleep on the bones of our ancestors in

one way or another. Each one of us a descendant who eventually becomes the one who came before.

I rest an arm on Lily's shoulder. I've spent fourteen years working to keep her safe. Trying not to hold on so tight that she can feel my grasp. Determined she will never go through what I went through. Determined to keep the secret of how she came into this world. Knowing, too, that the biggest secret I carry has nothing to do with her.

Seconds later, Lily startles awake and looks up at me. Her face flushes, as though caught doing something childlike. More and more I feel her distance, her letting go of me so she can grow up and grab hold of herself. Do daughters ever get fully free from our mamas? It doesn't help that I still live in my mama's house, but I could never afford to live and raise Lily on my own.

Lily sits up, pulls back her long hair and then lets it fall like the tail flick of a chestnut mare. I miss the warmth of her head against my thighs—the closeness that has become rare in the last year.

"I can't tell you how many times I've done the same thing," I say, to soften her embarrassment. "That first year after Daddy died, Mama was sending your Aunt Jo up here to get me all the time." I stare out at the river. A scene that's changed very little since those days.

Over the years, I've grown impatient with cemeteries. More and more I feel the need to have community with the living. I'm twenty-eight-years-old. Daddy was only thirty-eight when he died. Ten years older than I am now. A lump of emotion catches in my throat, the grief revisiting like an unwelcomed guest.

"We'd best head back to help your granny," I say. "Every-body's coming to supper in a couple of hours."

Lily stands first and then offers me a hand. We brush the dirt and leaves off our pants and walk back toward the back gate. At first, we walk hand-in-hand like we used to when Lily was a girl.

Perhaps since this is the anniversary and nobody's looking, she is allowing me this pleasure from her childhood.

"Mama, how old were you when you had your first kiss?" she asks.

Like me as a girl, Lily asks lots of questions. Her curiosity is like her appetite; she's always hungry. I pause, wondering how to answer. For most females, the answer is clear, but does a forced kiss count?

"My first real kiss was with Victor Sweeney," I say, deciding it doesn't. "He was the brother of my best friend, Mary Jane."

"What happened to him?" Lily asks.

"Victor moved away a long time ago," I say.

"Why?"

This was Lily's primary question since the age of three, nearly driving me crazy with its repetition. Mama always thought it humorous.

What goes around, comes around, she'd say, often with a smile.

"A lot of people move away from Katy's Ridge to get better work," I answer.

In truth, this wasn't why Victor left. After Mary Jane moved to Little Rock to go to college and live with her grandmother, Victor took over running his family's store in Katy's Ridge. We had several dates back then—going into Rocky Bluff to see a movie and summer picnics at Sutter's Lake. Lily was only one-year-old. As much as I tried to convince myself that Victor would make a good father for Lily, he felt more like a brother than a potential husband.

It didn't help that people here in Katy's Ridge were slow to let me forget how Lily came into this world. Not that they said a word. It was their looks that spoke their condemnation, as if I was to blame. Victor began to lose business just by dating me. In the end, it was no surprise he closed the store and moved away. Last I heard, he's married now with three small children, and sells insur-

ance in Memphis. How would life be different if I was the wife of an insurance salesman?

Mary Jane and I stopped being friends that summer after Lily was born. Sometimes I still miss her. Aunt Sadie says my life simply took a different road than Mary Jane's did, leaving us nothing left to do except wish each other a safe journey.

"What are you thinking about?" Lily asks, as we continue to walk.

"Victor," I say.

"You've told me about him," she says. "He's the one you swear isn't my daddy."

"Still true," I say, wishing Lily would drop it. I don't want to deal with all her questions today.

We take the path down the mountain that has grown over in places and lift our clasped hands to avoid the briars and vines that take over the trail and grab at our ankles.

"Have you ever thought of leaving Katy's Ridge?" she asks, letting go of my hand.

We stop on the path. A flicker of fear passes through me. I wonder briefly if her question about kissing was simply a warmup to this one. "I did think of leaving right after you were born," I say, surprising myself with my candor.

"Why didn't you?" she asks.

"It's a long story," I say.

"I like long stories," she says.

Lily can be relentless when searching out the truth of things.

"The McAllisters have been here since the 1840s," I say, as if this is reason enough to stay. "Besides, I run the saw mill that your granddaddy used to run. If I left, it would probably shut down."

A woman in backwoods Tennessee running a sawmill is unusual, but I needed to make money doing something. Not to mention, Mr. Blackstone—the owner of the mill—had sufficient guilt over what happened to Daddy to agree to take me on.

Lily eyes me like I'm a puzzle she's trying to solve, and it reminds me of how I used to look at Mama.

"In case you're wondering, I haven't kissed any boys yet," she tells me.

I hide my relief.

"Do you think there's something wrong with me?" she asks. "That I haven't been kissed?"

I put a hand on her shoulder, pretending I have the wisdom of Aunt Sadie.

"Lily, coming to love someone is a long, slow process. It'll happen, but you're still young."

"I'm not that young," she says, as if I've insulted her.

"Makes no sense to push the river," I say.

My own love life is more complicated than anyone can imagine, not that Lily knows a thing about it.

"Have you ever been in love?" she asks.

Her question gets me walking again, and she has to run a bit to catch up.

"My love life is none of your business, Lily McAllister."

"So you did have one at some point?" she asks, hiding a grin.

I stop long enough to point a finger at her. "Where did you learn to be so sneaky?" I say with a smile. "You're like a fox stealing eggs from Mama's hen house."

"I know you don't have anybody now," she says with conviction.

You'd be surprised, I want to say, but tighten my lips instead. *Loose lips sink ships,* Daniel likes to say, ever since he came back from World War II.

We approach the section of the path where my life changed forever. Somber now, I slow my gait. It is the anniversary of another death that feels just as real. In a way, it is the death of my childhood, or at the very least my innocence.

"It's so beautiful here," Lily says, not knowing the history of this

place. She doesn't ask why we always linger here. Beauty gives us reason enough.

Over a decade ago, I planted thousands of seeds of wildflowers in this spot. Today the last of the autumn flowers are in bloom. Several river rocks tower among them like monuments built to honor past wars. Fourteen years ago, I could have easily died here. In the early spring the tiger lilies I planted remind me of the gold Mary, the vision that visited me that day.

Nobody knows what really happened here. I told parts of it to Daniel and Mama and the sheriff from Rocky Bluff who came to the house that day. I told them just enough to quiet them. My heartbeat quickens, and I take a deep breath to calm the nerves that want to come. I've done what I can to make peace with this place, and most days I'm fine. But something about today has awakened my secret sense. However, what I am to be watchful about is still unclear.

Aunt Sadie says the secret sense is the wisest part of us. It knows when something's not right and steers us clear of what's bad for us. It also guides us toward what is right, and sometimes it's hard to tell which is which. That day, fourteen years ago, I didn't listen when it told me not to go to the cemetery. But, over the years, I've become better at listening. At least I hope I have.

Opening Daddy's pocket watch, I check the time. It is nearly 3 o'clock and the sun sits atop the tallest ridge. Supper is at 4:30.

"We'd best get home," I say.

We continue walking, kicking leaves as we go. I didn't anticipate staying at the cemetery this long, or the length of Lily's nap. I didn't anticipate what happened fourteen years ago, either. A lot of what happens to us is unexpected.

"Tell me a story you've never told me before," Lily says. "Like if you could only tell me one more story in my entire life, what would it be?"

"It would be about the gold Mary," I say, before I have time to talk myself out of it.

"The gold Mary?" she repeats.

I pause, wondering what compelled me to talk about this now. But it is a good story. At least it is if I leave all the bad parts out.

"I saw her right about here," I begin. "The sun had already dropped low behind the mountain and it was getting dark."

A shiver comes, and I shake it away like a chill. I leave out why she came to me. Details I hope Lily never knows.

"She was like a vision except she seemed real as anything," I continue. "Just like you and me. But I could see through her to the trees behind."

Lily is as quiet as I've ever known her. The fallen leaves are so dry under our feet they sound like short bouts of applause.

"Do you think the gold Mary has anything to do with the whispers?" Lily asks.

"The whispers?"

"You know, the whispers that happen at the footbridge."

I stop and look at her. "I don't hear whispers when I cross the footbridge."

"You don't?"

Lily looks surprised. I am about to ask her more questions when she insists that I continue the story. She promises to tell me about the whispers another time.

"When did you see the gold Mary? Was it on the anniversary?" She looks around as if hopeful we might see her again.

"Yes it was," I say, "and Daddy was with her. He had died the year before. He seemed real, too. I remember thinking at the time that he had brought the gold Mary to me."

Her eyes widen. "How come you've never told me about this?" she asks, all serious.

I wonder why she hasn't told me about the whispers.

"I haven't told anyone about her," I say. "Only you."

Despite her seriousness, she looks pleased.

"But why did the gold Mary come to you? What happened?"

I tell her I don't know, all the while hoping a lightning bolt doesn't get tossed at me for the lie I just told. I'm not sure why I am telling Lily about the gold Mary at all, except that whenever we pass this place I think of her.

Lily stares at the gold medallion around her neck that I gave her for her last birthday, as if all of a sudden realizing its meaning.

"I only saw her that once, but what's strange is I have moments when I miss her terribly," I begin again. "Plenty of times I've wondered if I just imagined her."

Lily's gaze shifts from the necklace to me. I didn't plan to tell Lily this much, and wonder if I've overdone it.

"I wish you'd just tell me who my daddy is," Lily says, as if taking advantage of a small opening. "I don't understand why it has to be such a big secret."

My attention darts down the path like an animal looking for a place to hide. I do not deny my daughter anything, except this.

"Just tell me, Mama. I don't understand why you won't."

I know she deserves to know, but as many times as I've thought of different ways to tell her, I never have the courage to say the words. What if she blames me for what happened?

"Lily, I can't do this right now." I feel more sad than angry. The anniversary always weakens me.

The McAllister women are known for being strong. Sometimes, too strong. Strong enough to scare away tears that are better off shed. My face warms with a familiar shame. Does Lily not see the way the old women at the church look at me? Or how they look at her when they think nobody else is watching? In those moments, my sisters literally surround Lily, to protect her from the judgment. Christians can be some of the worst people there are for judgment.

Why can't I just tell her? I ask myself.

Aunt Sadie and I have talked numerous times about this. But the truth always lodges in my throat, making me mute. If I tell Lily, she will never see herself the same way again. I can't risk that.

We continue walking, this time faster. Anger sweeps down the mountain with the shame. Lily offers an apology, as if she knows she's caused me to flee.

"Why can't you leave well enough alone?" I ask, although I know if our positions were reversed I'd be asking the same questions.

The only sound is the thundering water in the deepest part of the ravine.

"I have no one to visit in the cemetery, Mama," Lily begins, her words soft. "You've told me he's dead, but I don't know where he's buried. I don't even know how he died. Can you at least tell me that much?"

"Not now, Lily," I say. "Not now."

Chased by the past, I approach the footbridge. Fourteen years ago today, I was too injured to cross this bridge. Today, I barely slow down and walk straight across without doing any of the rituals I've practiced since I was a girl.

Without meaning to, I have fallen into the depths of my history. The history that lies at the bottom of the ravine. I think of Lily hearing whispers here and wonder if she's inherited an aspect of the secret sense after all.

A nagging from somewhere deep inside informs me that this story isn't over yet, and that what's coming may be just as dangerous as what came before.

CHAPTER THREE

Lily

The rest of the way home, Mama is quiet, as though carrying something weighty up the hill to our house. I wonder if Mama's secrets are heavy like a ten-pound bag of flour or sugar that make your arms ache. I'm glad she told me about the gold Mary, though. It makes me not feel so strange about the whispers that seemed louder than ever as we crossed the footbridge.

Mama and I go into the kitchen where Granny is basting a chicken in the oven. She's made cornbread stuffing, too, like she does at Thanksgiving. Green beans cook on the top of the stove, and I give them a stir anticipating what will be asked of me. A piece of lard the size of a hen's egg bubbles on the top with the beans. Baked sweet potatoes, their skins puckered and dark, rest in between the stove eyes to keep them warm. The smells make my mouth water.

Mama tells me to go ahead and set the table, and Granny hands me her grandmother's tablecloth from the top shelf of the cabinet. Brought over from the old country by Granny, this tablecloth

marks every special occasion that involves a meal, and she has promised to pass it on to me after she dies. Will this change when I move away?

"How is he?" Granny asks Mama, and I know she's talking about Granddaddy.

"He sends his regards," Mama says.

Granny scoffs at Mama's silliness, but her eyes get misty.

"Be sure and use the good dishes," Granny tells me, and grins from behind the mist. There are no 'good' dishes, only the dishes we use every day. The extra leaf is already in the table and the smaller card table is set up in the living room just like on other holidays that have a big meal that go with them. While the younger cousins are doomed to sit in the living room, the grownups gather around the big kitchen table.

Since I turned fourteen last summer, this is my first time at the grownups table.

With anticipation, I set ten places in the kitchen and five at the card table, all the while imagining the secrets I might hear while in the company of adults. Maybe Mama or one of the others will let a clue slip about the mystery I am intent on solving.

"Stop daydreaming," Granny tells me, giving a soft nudge with her elbow. "This meal won't get on the table by itself."

"Yes, Granny," I say and lower my eyes to show my remorse. Granny loves repentance as much as Preacher Evans.

"You and your mama are the most daydreaming bunch I've ever seen," Granny says, more to herself than to me.

Mama gives Granny a look that says *go easy on her*. She is protective, even when I don't want her to be.

"Lily, you need to change your clothes to get ready," she says.

"Why do we have to get dressed up for a meal in the kitchen?" I ask.

Mama answers with a look she inherited from Granny.

In the bedroom Mama and I share, I change into a skirt and

blouse and shine my saddle shoes with spit and a tissue. With the help of the mirror over the dresser, I run a quick brush through my hair and gather it in a rubber band.

A rap at the window causes me to jump, and my best friend Pearl laughs at me through the glass. Pearl is part Cherokee and part white, which makes her a shade or two darker than me. She motions for me to come outside. When I do, Pearl is all grins and giggles, to the point that it's irritating.

"What is it?" I ask. "We're about to have supper."

"Crow's home," she says.

"Crow?" My knees hint at weakness until I pull myself tall again. Crow looks like Elvis Presley, who is new to the radio this year. My Aunt Meg showed me Elvis' picture in one of her movie magazines. Crow is four years older than me and has been away for a solid year, stationed in Korea with the Army. It took me a long time to find Korea on the map. The war ended three years ago, but they still have troops there to keep the peace.

Pearl is all grins again. "Mama wants to know if you can have supper at our house."

Pearl's mama, June Sector, is one of my mama's best friends. She gets messages from dead people, and I've been after her for years to get a message to my daddy that I want him to contact me. But June says it doesn't always work out the way we hope. I wonder if anything works out the way we want it to.

"What's wrong with you?" Pearl asks. "Your face just went all white."

"I'm getting that feeling again, Pearl, like I'm a mermaid living in a tiny pond. I want to swim in bigger seas."

"What brought this on?" she asks.

"It's the anniversary, remember?" I say to Pearl. "That's why I wasn't at school today."

Pearl goes from goofy grin to frown in record time.

"How long is your brother staying?" I ask.

"Just through the weekend," Pearl says. "Then he gets shipped back to Korea."

"Ask your mama if I can come tomorrow instead," I say. "Or any night except this one. Mama would never forgive me if I missed the anniversary."

"Are you going to come back every year, even after we move away?" she whispers.

"If people are still talking to me," I whisper back. "That's a secret, remember?"

Pearl slouches. Everybody in Katy's Ridge knows she can't keep a secret to save her life. Perhaps I was foolish to confide in her how much I want to leave.

Neither of us has ever traveled any further than Rocky Bluff. In our fantasies, I marry Crow so Pearl can be an aunt to all the kids Crow and I have. Since I am an only child, I want bunches of babies, at least four, maybe seven. But what Pearl doesn't know is that I also want to travel the world singing, so I'm not sure how that will work if I have babies hanging all over me.

"Tell Crow I said 'hello,' okay? Tell him I'll come visit as soon as I can."

She agrees and we say our goodbyes. When I go back into the kitchen it's time to crimp the edges of Granny's apple pie that's about to go into the oven now that the chicken is out.

"Where you been?" Granny asks, wiping the sweat from her forehead with a dishtowel. She gives me a look like she's caught me lingering again.

"Pearl came over," I say.

With the oven on and all the burners going, the kitchen feels like a summer heat wave. We're lucky that it's still warm enough to keep the house open to let the heat disperse. But that will change soon enough.

Mama comes in from outside with a worried look.

"You okay?" I ask.

"Why does everybody keep asking me that?" She sounds irritated.

"Because you've got that pale look you get when you're about to get sick," Granny says to Mama.

"I feel fine," she says. "Maybe it's just my secret sense."

Granny gives Mama a look that says, *don't start with that nonsense.*

Minutes later, I hear my cousins racing up the hill to see who can touch the porch first and go outside to see who wins. If I'm racing, I usually win. Otherwise, it's a tie between Bolt and Danny. Bolt is Jo and Daniel's oldest son and Danny is the youngest. They are a year apart but look almost like twins. Bolt's real name is Joseph, after Granddaddy. He got the nickname when he was four years old and swallowed a small tractor bolt. Luckily, it didn't cause any damage. Bolt is a few months older than me. He sat at the grownups table for the first time last Easter and has rubbed it in for months.

Aunt Amy and Uncle Nathan's kids come in third and fourth. Lizzy, ten, is a total brat and Nat, twelve, is the opposite. They're wearing new outfits that Aunt Amy sewed for them. Aunt Amy owns a seamstress shop in Rocky Bluff where she makes dresses and also does alterations. Out front she also sells threads and fabrics. Uncle Nathan died in World War II. A photograph of him hangs on the living room wall. He is in uniform and has a hand on his hip like he's hitching up his pants. Another photograph sits on Mama's bureau of him holding me as a baby.

Uncle Daniel comes into view walking with his usual limp. He was in the same Army troop as Nathan and got injured in the same battle that cost Uncle Nathan his life. Aunt Jo and Aunt Amy walk next to him carrying casserole dishes propped on thick potholders. When she gets to the yard, my cousin Lizzy snarls at me like she's already bored and it's my fault. I have to resist pulling one of her pigtails.

"I'm starving," she says, as though she might swoon on the spot.

"Ask Granny for something," I say.

Lizzy runs into the house.

"Thanks for getting rid of her," Nat says.

"Anytime," I say, and we exchange a grin. Nat and I have spent entire summers making it a sport to avoid Lizzy.

A copy of *Robinson Crusoe* is tucked under his arm. Mama says Nat prefers books to people, and it's true that he spends most of his time reading. But I think it's because he doesn't have a daddy, either. It does something to a person.

"Aunt Meg called Mama and said that she and Cecil are running late," Nat says.

With all the *Mama's* in the house at the same time, it can get confusing. At more than one family get-together, I've yelled 'Mama?' and had four women answer back.

Uncle Daniel greets me in the front yard with a hug. After he looks around to make sure nobody is looking, he passes me a roll of cherry Lifesavers like we're passing secrets to the allies. I know he does this with all the cousins, pretending each of us is his favorite, but I play along.

"Where's your mama?" he asks.

"In the kitchen with Granny," I say.

It takes effort for Uncle Daniel to get up the porch steps on account of the shrapnel that's still in his leg. He never complains, though. The cane he uses has the etchings of an oak tree on the side. He's the best whittler in Katy's Ridge.

Mama must hear him coming because she opens the screen door for him to enter.

"Good to see you, Wildflower," he says to Mama.

"Are you ever going to stop calling me that?" she asks, but she smiles at him like she counts on him not to forget.

"Can I get your help inside?" Mama says to me. "Granny wants

you to put everything into serving bowls," she says. "She trusts you with her food more than me."

When I come into the kitchen, Granny tosses me her spare apron. Without saying a word, she hands me several large bowls. I know what to do. It is no secret that Mama never learned to cook. She swears good cooks skip generations in a family. She can make oatmeal and toast and that's about it. Granny has taught me everything she knows, even how to make a meringue for her lemon pies. I get busy, trying not to think of how much I'll miss these gatherings once I become a world-renowned singer.

A baked chicken fits onto her white platter that has a chip on one of the handles. I carry it to the table, surprised by how heavy it is. I place the chicken at the center of the lace tablecloth. Green beans fill the second smaller bowl, and Granny's cornbread dressing fills the third. I take the bowl of churned butter from the refrigerator and put it next to a plate of plain cornbread. Aunt Jo places her sweet potato pudding on the table, too, and Aunt Amy's macaroni and cheese.

Upon seeing the spread, my dreams of leaving Katy's Ridge dim. The kitchen hums with the voices of my family as they gather at their places. When I think of living someplace different, I can't imagine what it will be like without my family around. At moments like this, it's as though Katy's Ridge pulls me back just as I'm about to get away.

Sweat dots Daniel's brow, as well as Bolt's. So far, the adult table isn't that much different from the kids, except the adult table is hotter. But maybe all those family secrets will come to a boil, and the truth will burst open.

My cousin Lizzy weaves in and out of the adults, picking up bits of macaroni and cheese with her fingers. Aunt Amy tells her to stop, but Lizzy never listens. We'd be eating already if we weren't waiting for Aunt Meg and Uncle Cecil to arrive. As if on cue, the screen door slams announcing their arrival, and they make their

way through the house full of apologies. Uncle Cecil's daughter, Janie, age 10—a whisper of a girl—skulks at their heels.

Aunt Meg used to ride to Rocky Bluff with Uncle Cecil when she worked at the Woolworths, a job she quit after they got married last year. Now she stays home and takes care of Janie who is Uncle Cecil's child by his first wife. She died ten years ago giving birth to Janie at the small hospital in Rocky Bluff. Janie almost didn't make it either, on account of she didn't breathe right away after she was born, so she always looks like she's gasping for air.

Pearl says Janie's not the sharpest crayon in the box. Truth is, if she were a crayon—sharp or not—she'd probably be the color beige. Aunt Amy makes Janie colorful clothes so people won't notice how bland she is, but it's hard to miss.

Uncle Cecil has the opposite problem. A strawberry birthmark takes up the entire right side of his face. A birthmark I've spent a great deal of time trying not to stare at. Shaped like a map of Russia, the birthmark has a mole right where Moscow would be.

Until Aunt Meg and Uncle Cecil got married, she was the oldest old maid in Katy's Ridge. Now it's Miss Blackstone who teaches at the school. Mama would be next in line for old maid status, but I'm not sure it counts if you've never been married but have a daughter. There may be another name for that.

The back door is open, as well as the window, to help the kitchen cool down. Pumpkin and two of his offspring look in through the screen door, as though plotting a way to overtake the chicken platter while nobody's looking. Granny calls for everyone to take their seats. My feelings act like a yo-yo going around the world. One second I'm ready to leave, the next I'm ready to stay. It's no wonder I feel a little nauseous.

Great Aunt Sadie comes in from the back porch and puts a hand on my shoulder and kisses me on the cheek. Her eyes are gray/blue and her white hair is pulled up in a bun on the top of her head. When she smiles it looks like her wrinkles smile, too. Great

Aunt Sadie attends all family functions, but she also keeps to herself more and more these days. A fact that worries Mama.

"You set a beautiful table," she tells me, leaning in so I can hear over everybody talking. "You're going to join us at the big table, right?"

I tell her I'm looking forward to it.

"It's a rite of passage in the McAllister family," she says, squeezing my shoulder like she's proud of me. "After today, you will never again be exiled to the living room."

She touches a finger to the tip of my nose like she did when I was younger, and then embraces Mama before sitting at the table. I wonder which spot will be mine until Mama pats the chair next to hers. I sit between her and Great Aunt Sadie, with Uncle Daniel on the other side of Mama, then Aunt Jo, Bolt, Aunt Amy, Uncle Cecil and Aunt Meg. Bolt looks over and gives me a wink, as though to welcome me to the grownup table. I'm not sure what we'll do when the other kids get old enough to join us because we already sit elbow to elbow. I imagine it may be good that I plan to leave Katy's Ridge after all.

Lizzy's obnoxiousness can be heard from the next room, the others complaining that she's drinking out of their cups. I imagine my other cousin, Janie, blending in with the beige walls, and Danny and Nat talking about cars. I sit straighter with the knowledge that the kids' table isn't where I belong anymore. This is my next step to being free.

Mama wears pants and a flowered blouse, the closest she gets to dressing up. She glances at Granddaddy's watch like she has somewhere to go, and I wonder if she and Miss Blackstone have a Scrabble game planned for later.

When Granny takes off her apron and sits at the table, the room grows quiet enough for pins to drop while angels dance on the heads. But it is Mama who speaks instead of Granny.

"We're here to remember Daddy today," Mama says, a slight

quiver in her voice. "We need to remember Nathan, too, who we lost in the war. These were two great men who we sorely miss."

Aunt Amy's lips tighten with the emotion she rarely shows.

Nobody in our family is real big on feelings, except maybe Great Aunt Sadie. Granny will tell anyone who'll listen, that feelings should be saved for death beds, so it isn't surprising when she announces that the food is getting cold.

We've come to expect Granny's interruptions, and everyone laughs.

Uncle Daniel says a quick grace before passing the green beans. My aunts fill plates for the younger kids and take them into the living room before filling their own. Meanwhile, a flurry of serving dishes are passed at the big table and plates are filled. I wait to feel different, yet it's like everything has changed and nothing at all.

"So what's it like to sit at the grownups' table?" Aunt Jo asks, passing me the gravy.

When I look at her, I realize again how beautiful my Aunt Jo is. She's as pretty as Sandra Dee, who appears in the Hollywood magazines, and is about the same age.

Several people turn to look, expecting me to say something thoughtful. Instead, I shrug, something Mama has asked me to never do again.

Everyone eats. Uncle Daniel and Bolt fill their plates twice, while Mama and Uncle Daniel talk about the mill. At the same time, Granny complains to no one in particular about the price of electricity and that it is President Eisenhower's fault. Every now and again I hear talking and laughing from the kids' table and wonder if being a grownup isn't all it's cracked up to be.

Every now and again, Mama squeezes my hand to let me know she hasn't forgotten me, but mainly I am left to my own thoughts. Thoughts that even when I'm full of good food, challenge me about where I fit in the world. My last name is McAllister, just like

my Mama's. She didn't take my daddy's name, which means they weren't married. In the third grade, Davy Jenkins called me a *bastard*. I didn't even know what it meant back then, but I do now.

My father's side of the family is totally unknown. I wonder what it would be like to have supper with them, but it's like a blank slate in my imagination. My insides feel jumpy. Is this the secret sense Mama keeps talking about? Until now, I thought that skipped generations like cooking talents.

Bolt looks at me. He knows I am quieter than usual. In the past, at the kids' table, I challenged Lizzy to count her green beans as she ate them, or umpired Nat and Danny's thumb-wrestling contests, or tried to get Janie to say even a few words. For years, I thought I must be missing the best part of family gatherings by being stuck in the living room. I never dreamed that sitting at the grownups' table was more than a little boring. No secrets. No confessions. No big deal.

Why do I always I crave a bigger life than the one I have? I wonder.

Pearl and I have spent entire afternoons imagining glamorous lives where we live in big cities, far away from tiny Katy's Ridge. Cities where we go to parties and I sing while she works at a swanky job.

Near the end of the meal, Mama rests her hand on mine. "You're awfully quiet," she says. The worry from earlier hasn't left her. "Something you want to tell me?"

I shrug again, and then try to erase it, but it's hard to take back a shrug. How do I tell her that every day I wish I was anywhere but here?

"Please answer with words, Lily," she says.

"She doesn't have to tell you everything," Granny says to Mama. For someone who is hard of hearing, she often chimes in like she's heard every word. "Lily, why don't you get the apple pie ready," Granny adds.

Mama gives me a look that says *we'll talk later.*

When I fetch the pie, Pumpkin stretches against the back screen door as though to remind me he's waiting for his special holiday scraps. His old claws get stuck in the screen, and I hope Granny doesn't see him or he'll get a swift slap with her broom. Two pies sit on the kitchen counter. I slice enough pieces so that everyone has a slice, and then pass them around. Once everybody has dessert, the room gets quiet again except for the occasional noise of pure satisfaction. It occurs to me that the world could avoid wars if there was enough pie to go around.

Meanwhile, discomfort is wedged in my stomach that is either indigestion or my fledgling secret sense. Great Aunt Sadie looks at me, as though picking up on the message I'm receiving. She sends a message to Mama with her eyes, like we're all hooked up to the same telephone party-line. Until now, it never occurred to me that we could have an entire conversation using only our eyes.

Nothing ever happens in Katy's Ridge. Especially nothing big. Yet something is up. Something that has the smell of secrets all around it. Something that could change everything.

CHAPTER FOUR

Wildflower

After supper, our family congregates on the front porch. With the sun behind the ridge, it is chillier, but still warm enough to wear only a sweater. Lily sits on the porch swing between me and Aunt Sadie. She acted strange all through supper. It was Aunt Sadie who tapped my shoe under the table and drew my attention to it. Sometimes I'm so close to Lily, I don't realize the subtle things. But Aunt Sadie does. She knows whenever something big is going on with Lily and when Lily's thoughts are playing out like a thunderstorm behind her eyes.

A long time ago I learned not to ignore my secret sense. I check the sky to see if a storm is moving in, but there are no clouds in sight. I want to believe this premonition is nothing. Yet something has been pestering me all afternoon.

Behind us, Bolt, Danny and Lizzy toss a ball against the side of the house and take turns catching it while Janie looks on. Poor Janie. I want to pull her up onto my lap and make up for the first ten years of her life when she didn't have a mama.

On the other end of the porch, my nephew Nat sits reading a book. Does he suffer from similar losses? I think of his father, Nathan, all the time. About how he won over Mama early on, about how he helped us track down Johnny that day and how he made Amy much happier than she is now and more agreeable. Grief does surprising things to people. It breaks us down and makes us stronger, sometimes all at once. I've seen it in Mama, too.

"Will you sing us something?" I ask Lily.

If anything can be a healing salve it is Lily's singing. Even Mama calls her a natural. I imagine her musical talent comes from Daddy, the only other musician in the McAllister family. Daniel claps to encourage her, and the others tell her how nice it would be to hear a tune. No family gathering takes place these days without Lily singing a song.

"Sing Amazing Grace," Jo says. "It was Daddy's favorite. He'd love that."

Lily agrees and her mood appears to lighten. She stands and leans against the porch rail facing the house. It is a small stage. Too small. I can't help thinking she is destined for bigger things. Not that I've ever said this out loud.

Lily closes her eyes like she's gathering the song in her memory. She hums the tune first to warm her voice, like Daddy used to do before he sang. I've always wondered how she knew to do that. I like to think it's a part of him coming through her.

Amazing Grace, how sweet the sound, she begins. The words are soft at first, but then build.

Every time Lily sings, a lump of thankfulness catches in my throat. How can the ugliest moment of my life result in something so beautiful and pure? People say Lily's voice is as good as Kate Smith's, who sings *God Bless America* on the radio. Preacher used to say that pride comes before a fall. But there's nothing wrong with this kind of pride. The pride that comes from hearing something beautiful and being proud of humanity.

My sisters, brothers-in-law, nieces and nephews, are spell-bound, as are Mama and Aunt Sadie. Whenever Lily sings everyone goes quiet, like they're walking around inside a church. She goes on to another verse and then another. The melody soars and my chest expands. For nine months she lived inside of me, and even though she's her own person now, her songs will be stored forever in my heart.

Earlier that day, Lily asked the one question I never know how to answer. Someday soon I will have to tell her the truth. It's amazing she hasn't found out already, given the *loose lips* in these parts. But at the same time, mountain people will keep a secret forever if their own shame is attached to it somehow. Everybody knew Johnny was trouble. Everybody. Yet nobody did anything. Guilt has kept that secret sealed, as surely as if it were in a bank vault.

Oddly enough, as we were walking home, Lily asked if I'd ever felt like moving away. Earlier today, at the cemetery, I was thinking about that very thing. I wondered if a place existed where I could go and totally be myself without anyone judging me. If so, I'd be tempted to pack all our bags this evening. However, I doubt such a place exists.

After Lily finishes her song, everyone stays quiet for several seconds like the song is somehow healing all the lonely places inside each of us. Finally, Daniel and the boys begin to whistle and all of us clap.

"Daddy would have loved that," I say, giving Lily a hug.

"You should sing on the radio," Jo says, and everyone agrees.

Lily's face colors and she lowers her head. Whenever she sings at church, all of us come to hear her—even me—even though it's a guarantee that Preacher will sermonize about heathens turning their back on the Lord. But, as far as I'm concerned, it was the Lord and the Church who turned their backs on me.

Moments after finishing her song, Lily sits on the porch steps

while Aunt Sadie and I claim the porch swing again. The others talk. Yet I am not hearing most of it and rub the center of my chest.

"What is it?" Aunt Sadie asks.

"Do you remember those dreams I had after Lily was born?"

"They were more like nightmares," she says. "You were terrified for days afterward."

In the dreams, Lily fell down a ravine and died crashing against the rocks like Johnny did. Sometimes, I'd wake up screaming. But I haven't had them for years. Not since she was an infant.

We are all protective of Lily. Me. Aunt Sadie. Mama. Daniel. My sisters, too, but not as much, now that they have their own broods to watch out for.

"Are you having a premonition?" Aunt Sadie asks.

According to her, premonitions are just a fancy name for the secret sense. Along the same lines, June says I can foretell the future as good as she can if I take the time to pay attention.

"It may be nothing," I say.

Mama comes out of the house, her apron finally off for the day. She looks impatient with me, even though I haven't said a word to her.

"What are you brooding about now?" she asks me.

My irritation flares. The look we exchange has our history in it. A history neither of us has forgotten. Fourteen years ago, Mama and I made our amends in Daniel and Jo's barn. It was the closest I ever felt to her. Even though I know she would walk into a burning house to rescue me, as I would her, that doesn't mean we're close. If she had to choose, I still think she would rather have Daddy sitting here on the porch than me. It probably doesn't help that I've always looked like him, especially as I've aged. I sit before her, a constant reminder of what she's lost.

"Have a seat, Nell," Aunt Sadie says. "You're just ornery because you're tired."

Mama sits in the rocker reserved for her. I wish I didn't take her moods so personally. In the next second my secret sense twists my gut. I turn to Aunt Sadie, finally clear on what it's telling me.

"A stranger is coming," I whisper.

"A stranger?" Aunt Sadie turns to look down the path that leads to the house, as if someone might appear at any moment.

I think of all the hours I've sat on this front porch, looking down this hill waiting on Daddy to come home, and he never did.

"Whatever it is, we'll get through it," Aunt Sadie says to me.

Daniel turns away from Cecil and looks at me as if he might be needed. I smile so he'll think everything is fine. He sits in the rocker on the other side of the door, a toothpick stuck between his lips. His leg must be bothering him because he winces as he helps it bend. Bolt runs to the porch steps to ask if Daniel wants to shoot basketballs into the wooden hoop nailed into one of the oak trees by the house. Daniel declines. The valley on his forehead deepens, like he's thinking a father should play ball with his sons.

Lizzy yells for Bolt to return, but it sounds more like a whine. Amy has confided in me that she can't wait until Lizzy outgrows her childishness, but I'm not so sure she will. Meanwhile, Jo looks through a McCall's magazine, while Lily and Nat talk about books and Meg goes inside and brings out the transistor radio from the kitchen and sets it on the porch rail. She turns the knob to tune in the one station we can get here in the mountains that comes in from Nashville. Jim Reeves is singing his latest hit. From the look of things, it is a normal afternoon in the life of the McAllister family, but something doesn't feel normal about it at all.

A hint of winter blows in from the west, and I pull my sweater closer. Before long, we'll gather around the wood stove in the living room instead of the front porch. If a stranger is coming, they'd best arrive soon. Winter is a difficult time here. It's hard to imagine someone new coming to Katy's Ridge at any time of year. It's not the type of place that collects newcomers.

My secret sense vibrates at the center of my chest and causes me to stand. I look down the hill with anticipation. A woman wearing a white dress approaches. A white purse hangs over one arm and she has a red ribbon in her hair. Something about her seems familiar. As she gets closer I can see that her hair needs a good washing and her dress is faded and worn. The pattern on it is almost completely washed off.

When I finally recognize who she is, I gasp. I don't want the woman to come any closer. She is pale like a ghost, an apparition from the graveyard of my past. My bottom lip quivers like it knows something the rest of me doesn't. Lily looks at me, her expression alive with another of her unending questions.

The woman stops a few feet away from the porch.

"Can we help you?" I say. I search the past for the name of someone I haven't thought about for over a decade.

"Oh my heavens," Aunt Sadie says softly, before covering her mouth.

Mud is caked around the woman's white shoes like she's traipsed through every mud hole in Katy's Ridge to get here. She presses the stub of her cigarette into the soil with her dirty shoe. I step to the end of the porch, telling Lily to stay where she is. The woman looks at me like she's daring me to recognize her. The look in her eyes makes me shiver. A deep sadness has made a home there.

"Wildflower, do you remember me?" the woman asks.

It is odd to hear a stranger call me Wildflower. A name only used by close family when I was a girl. Most people call me Louisa May now, except for Daniel, and occasionally Mama, and my best friend, Bee Blackstone, who calls me Lou.

The surprise has turned me into one of the icicles that clings to the rocks behind our house in winter. I am frozen. Lily stands next to me. Is she being protective or just curious? Nobody else moves, except for Amy who nibbles on her

fingernails. Even Daniel appears at a loss as to what to do next.

"Who is this, Mama?" Lily whispers. She takes my sweaty palm. I'm not sure how to answer.

"I'm Melody Monroe," the stranger says. "I used to live here in Katy's Ridge. You may remember my brother, Johnny."

Melody Monroe trains her eyes on Lily, taking a long look. It reminds me of how her brother used to look at me when I walked down the road toward school or to the cemetery or to see Mary Jane. My heartbeat accelerates and a memory chases after me. I am running from the cemetery down the mountain path to get away from Johnny, my arms pumping wild. For years I've run away from these memories. Now a ghost of that long ago terror stands in our front yard.

CHAPTER FIVE

Lily

Great Aunt Sadie steps to the other side of Mama like we're all about to sing the hymn *A Mighty Fortress is Our God*. We are all steeped in hymns, even though none of us attend church anymore unless I'm singing. The last time we attended, Mama swore if she heard Preacher Evans say *Repent* one more time, while looking straight at her, she'd throw up her morning oatmeal on his suit. Even Granny misses most Sundays and has taken to saying her prayers on the back porch while she peels potatoes into a bucket.

"Can we help you with something?" Great Aunt Sadie asks the stranger.

"What's going on?" I ask. The look on Mama's face is one I've never seen before.

Uncle Daniel stands now, his bad leg collapsing until he rights himself again. My family has been turned into pillars of salt like Lot's wife when she looked back on Sodom, a story I heard in a rare trip to Sunday School.

I ask the question again, this time louder. Bolt, Danny and Lizzy have stopped playing ball and have turned into statues, too.

"Are you going to tell her, or am I?" the stranger says to Mama.

Mama snaps awake, as if a mountain lion has come down from the higher mountains and is threatening us.

"You're not welcome here. Go back where you came from." She points down the hill toward the road.

The woman doesn't move. "I'm only here for a visit," she says.

Whoever this woman is, she isn't welcome. My family is usually friendly to strangers. But not this one. Mama squeezes sweat into my palm again, and Great Aunt Sadie places a heavy hand on my shoulder as though I might get kidnapped.

In the westerns I've seen at the Rocky Bluff Theater, there's always a standoff between the good guys and the bad guys. If this were one of those movies, Mama would be in the role of Gene Autry, and the villain in this scene would be a woman who needs to clean her shoes.

Granny is the first family statue to come alive. She gets up from her rocker and walks into the house letting the screen door slam behind her. A few seconds later she returns with the shotgun she keeps next to the back door to scare away the foxes and bobcats from her hen house. Evidently this stranger is someone she sees as a threat.

"You've been asked to leave," Granny says. She raises the shotgun and points it straight at the woman.

I gasp. Mama taught me to never point a shotgun at a person or an animal unless I intend to kill them.

The woman lowers her head and takes two steps back, holding up an arm to prevent Granny from coming any closer.

All the McAllisters know how to load and shoot a shotgun, even me. Mama taught me around the same time I learned to drive the truck.

"No need to get upset, Mrs. McAllister."

"Why are you here?" Great Aunt Sadie asks.

"I'm only back for a visit," the stranger says. "We've still got land here."

"What's your real reason for being here?" Mama asks.

The woman hesitates and glances at me.

"I've been hearing things, and I wanted to check it out for myself," the woman says. She doesn't take her eyes from me.

"Hearing things?" Mama asks. "Like what?"

"Maybe now's not the proper time," the stranger says, glancing over at Granny who hasn't moved.

Uncle Daniel steps to the porch rail. "Whatever you're peddling, we're not interested," he says.

She offers Daniel a slight smile, as though recognizing him.

"I don't want any trouble, Mister Daniel," she says. "The only thing I'm peddling is the truth."

I doubt Aunt Amy has a fingernail left, and I've never seen Aunt Meg's eyes so big. Not even when she's telling a big piece of juicy gossip. Aunt Jo is now in the yard with the kids making sure none of them get any closer.

"Like I said," Uncle Daniel begins again. "We're not interested."

"Somebody, please tell me what's going on?" I say. This time I practically shout. If there's anything I hate, it's being the last to know something.

For the first time since the stranger arrived, Mama looks over at me. "It's something that happened before you were born," she says, as if this should be enough for me to drop it.

"What is it? What happened?" I ask.

My questions are met with silence.

"Y'all are acting like a bunch of cowards," I say, my frustration growing.

Mama shoots me a look that isn't the least bit cowardly.

From behind me the shotgun cocks. I can't believe the stranger

is still within a mile of here. If Granny had a gun aimed at me, I'd be halfway to Rocky Bluff by now.

"If you want to talk, I'm staying at my family's place until Friday," she says directly to me.

"Why would I want to talk?" I ask, confused that she has spoken to me.

"'Cause it looks like you're not getting any answers from your family." Her lips form a straight line and nearly disappear.

Granny cocks the other barrel, and the stranger announces she's leaving. With a swift turn she walks down the hill, kicking up dirt and pebbles on the path. After she passes the Red Bud sisters, the stranger disappears out of sight. Everyone on the porch exhales at once and the statues come alive. Chatter begins.

"Are you all right?" I ask Mama. Her face is pale and her hands are trembling.

"I've been better." She offers a faint smile.

Mama is the bravest person I know and to see her scared makes me feel jittery inside. Great Aunt Sadie is taking care of her, though, and takes both Mama's hands, like she's giving her something solid to hold onto. Mama's eyes have that look she gets when she disappears into the past. Aunt Sadie makes Mama sit on the porch swing.

"You're safe, sweetheart," she says. "You're safe."

Safe from what? I want to ask. What does Mama need to be safe from?

My hands find their way to my hips. "Somebody needs to tell me what this is about," I say. My entire family turns toward me, even my cousins.

Mama looks straight at me, but doesn't speak.

My face grows hot. In that instant, I hate my entire family with their statue ways and how nobody talks. I fortify my hatred by telling myself this is one of the reasons I am perfectly fine leaving Katy's Ridge forever.

"Tell me," I say, my voice raising, giving them one more chance.

It's hard to believe that minutes ago I was singing a song about grace and everything felt right. But now, everything feels wrong. What hurts the most is that I'm being lied to by the one person in the world I thought I could count on—Mama.

A secret needs to be told. A secret that involves me. A secret, it appears, that Mama has no intention of telling.

CHAPTER SIX

Wildflower

A tremor runs through my body like a bird coming back to life that a cat has left for dead. My teeth chatter. It feels like it is twenty degrees outside and I am without a coat. It's been years since I've had a spell like this, probably since the night Lily was born.

"Have Daniel take Lily," I tell Aunt Sadie through chattering teeth.

Aunt Sadie pulls Daniel aside to speak to him and everyone leaves shortly afterward. Daniel and Jo take Lily to their house.

"Sit over here," Aunt Sadie says to me.

The memories come close together like labor pains, forcing me to remember what I've spent years trying to forget. The sound of Johnny running close behind me, and then finally catching up. The helplessness of being thrown to the ground, the breath forced out of me. The smell of the liquor on his breath.

"Wildflower, you're going to be all right," Aunt Sadie says. "Breathe deeply for me."

Aunt Sadie sounds like she's midwifing one of her expectant mothers. I remember the night she helped Lily come into the world. Giving birth teaches a woman how to surrender and just let life do to you what it insists on doing. However, I don't get the reward of a newborn at the end of this. What I'm giving birth to feels like something old that shouldn't still be alive.

Lily out of sight, I curl into a ball on the porch. Mama brings a quilt and Aunt Sadie wraps it over me. The wood feels cool on the side of my face, and I can smell the aging pine. Mama asks Aunt Sadie what she should do. The last time I heard that worry in her voice was when she and Daniel carried me home after Johnny left me for dead.

"Don't worry, Nell," Aunt Sadie says. "She needs to do this to get free of the ghosts. It won't last long. Maybe you could make her a glass of tea."

With that, Mama goes into the house, and I'm glad she's gone. Now it's just Aunt Sadie and me.

"What's happening?" My voice shakes to match the chattering of my teeth.

"You stored up all that hurt from years ago. It's good that it's coming out," she says. "Best thing you can do is not be afraid of it."

Aunt Sadie reminds me to take deep breaths of mountain air to soothe myself. The trembling scares me. I want to believe it won't last long. Mama arrives with tea and puts it on the porch next to me. Aunt Sadie asks her if we can be alone, and Mama goes into the house again, this time taking the shotgun sitting next to the screen door. I remember Johnny breaking into the house and Amy wounding him with the same gun. The next morning, Daniel, Nathan and I followed the blood trail and found Johnny dead at the bottom of the ravine. Dead from the fall, not the gunshot wound.

A breeze comes up that rushes below the floorboards. It carries the dank smell of the dirt that lives under the porch. I shiver like

I'm shaking off a fever. At the same time, sounds and pictures of the past come without my bidding. Aunt Sadie sits next to me on the porch, running a gentle hand through my hair like she did when I was a girl. Waves of panic rise and then fall. I count them. Ten. Eleven. Twelve. I wait for more, but the shaking stops.

"Good girl," Aunt Sadie says.

Though I'm not a girl anymore, I feel like I'm thirteen again, the age of the memories. Aunt Sadie rubs my back, offering me every bit of comfort she can. I remember how solid she was after it happened. I'm not sure what I would do without Aunt Sadie. Then and now.

Time slows. My breath deepens. Minutes later, I make my way to sitting, the quilt falling from my shoulders.

"I feel better," I say.

"Good." Her face relaxes into a smile.

"What happened?" I ask her, taking a sip of tea.

"It must have been Melody Monroe showing up," she says. "It woke up all those memories that had been sleeping."

"I haven't felt that way since—" I can't say the words.

"I know," she says.

"It felt awful. Like it was happening again."

"You needed to release it," Aunt Sadie says. "You needed to rid yourself of that pain that got buried."

Mama comes back outside asking if I need anything. Though I am calm, she looks worried. I reach for her hand and squeeze it. I wonder if she ever gets jealous of the closeness between Aunt Sadie and me—her dead husband's sister.

Aunt Sadie and Mama help me to stand, and I feel almost normal again.

Mama goes back inside, and Aunt Sadie and I sit on the porch swing.

"Lily is upset with me," I say. "I don't blame her. She deserves to know the truth."

"You can't protect her forever," Aunt Sadie says.

"I just want to know why Melody Monroe is back in Katy's Ridge," I say.

"Maybe she's trying to rid herself of painful memories, too," Aunt Sadie says.

"You don't think she's come back just to stir up trouble?" I ask.

"If she has, it's worked. But it could also be for the best," she says. "Gifts come in surprising packages sometimes."

"I wish you wouldn't speak in riddles," I say.

"But you've always been good at riddles," she says to me with a wink.

I pause, unable to fully take in all that the day has brought. We slowly rock the porch swing and look down the hill.

"Did you know that Lily is almost the same age I was when it happened?" I say to Aunt Sadie.

She lets out a moan, followed by a sigh. "Oh my, I never thought of that."

"I was so young," I say.

Aunt Sadie takes a deep breath. "Nobody should have to go through what happened to you," she says, her words soft.

"Should I tell Lily the truth?" My question is in earnest now.

Aunt Sadie pauses for what feels like several minutes, but what might have been seconds instead.

"I honestly don't know," she says. "I wish I did. I imagine there will be tradeoffs with either choice you make."

"But what if Lily gets angry with me? What if she doesn't understand?"

"There isn't a child alive who doesn't hate their parents at one time or another."

I wonder how Aunt Sadie got so wise about children when she never had any.

"I don't remember hating Daddy," I say.

"If he had lived longer, you might have," she says. "Joseph wasn't perfect. He could be as stubborn as an ox sometimes."

To my surprise, I remember the mule that carried Daddy home on the stretcher that last time. Memories have come unbidden all day.

"Isn't it odd that Melody would show up fourteen years later? To the day?" I ask.

Aunt Sadie nods. "There's an invisible world out there that we barely take into account," she says. "A world full of mystery and coincidences."

However, it's the visible world I'm worried about. "What if Melody tells Lily what happened?" I ask.

"How would she even know?" Aunt Sadie says. "She was living in Kentucky with her aunt by then."

"Someone from Katy's Ridge must have told her about Lily," I say.

"I'm not sure who she's in touch with," Aunt Sadie says. "There wasn't a soul at Johnny's funeral."

Surprised, I turn to look at her. "You went to Johnny's funeral?"

She folds her arms, as if feeling a sudden chill. "It was just me and Preacher and a bunch of crows in the trees."

The hairs prickle on the back of my neck.

"Help me understand why you would go to the funeral of someone who nearly beat me to death," I say, trying not to feel betrayed.

After a lifetime of knowing her, I can't remember a single time I've been upset with Aunt Sadie. Until now.

"I felt sorry for him," she says, offering no apology.

"And you didn't feel sorry for me?"

"Of course I did," she says. Her eyes don't release me. "And if you recall, I was there for you the entire time." She pauses and looks at me. "Maybe all that hurt you stored up had anger in it, too."

At that moment, I am not willing to tell her she could be right.

"I believe that everybody should have at least one additional person present at their birth and at their funeral," she says. "I don't care what unforgiveable sin they've committed."

It is the midwife in her that sees it this way, and perhaps it is the little girl in me that is hurt that she could go to Johnny's funeral while I was in bed, unable to move, covered with cuts and bruises.

"I know you've been very loyal to me, Aunt Sadie." My voice is softer now. "It's just a surprise, I guess. A surprise on top of the shock of Melody showing up. I had forgotten she even existed. It never occurred to me that she might know about Lily and show up some day to see her and talk to her. It never occurred to me once."

"We'd like to think life is predictable, but it isn't," Aunt Sadie says, staring off into the distance.

All of a sudden I am tired of Aunt Sadie's wisdom and tired of a past that won't seem to rest.

"I need to go to work," I say to her, which is the only thing I can think of to say.

The day has contained too much history, and I need to get away. But I also need to talk to Bee and the mill is somewhere we can have privacy. I pretend I'm not angry at her, and give Aunt Sadie a hug. Then I follow the path that Melody Monroe took down the hill.

TWENTY MINUTES LATER, Bee enters the small office at the back of the sawmill where I sit at Daddy's old desk. Sometimes I can still smell him here, as though he never left. One of his old flannel shirts hangs on a nail on the back of the door. I refuse to move it, even this many years later. On a rustic bookcase in the corner are several books and a collection of things my sisters and I made him when we were girls: clay ashtrays shaped like hand prints with his

initials in the palms, acorn paperweights heavy with school glue, boxes made of sticks meant to hold letters, and brittle dried wildflowers filling ball jars.

Bee sits on the edge of the desk. Her father used to own the sawmill, but over the years he let me buy him out with a portion of the money that came in. Now, it is mostly mine. The mill is the first thing I've ever attempted to own, besides my truck. Bee's parents live in Rocky Bluff now, but Bee still lives in their house in Katy's Ridge near the elementary school where she teaches.

"What's happened?" she asks. "You look awful."

Bee is an expert worrier, and I try not to give her anything to concern herself over. But I need a friend to listen to me. Someone I'm not related to, and who didn't go to Johnny's funeral. My hurt feelings return. For some reason it feels like everything has changed in the last few hours.

"Two things happened today," I begin. "One is that I had a horrible fight with Aunt Sadie."

Bee smiles like she thinks I'm joking. When she figures out I'm not, she repositions herself on a chair near the desk, her posture arrow straight.

"She told me she went to Johnny's funeral," I say.

Bee grimaces. "Why did she do that?"

"It doesn't matter why," I say. "It's the fact that she did it at all."

Bee touches my arm. "Calm down," she says. "I'm sure she had her reasons. Aunt Sadie wouldn't do anything to hurt you on purpose. You know that."

"I do know that," I say. "That's why I was so shocked."

Bee nods her understanding.

"But that's not the biggest shock, Bee. There's more."

She looks at me with renewed worry.

"A stranger showed up at the house a little while ago. At least I thought it was a stranger at first."

"Out of the blue?" asks Bee.

I nod.

"Well, don't keep me in suspense. Who was it?" She adjusts her sweater, and I notice the latest bumblebee she's stitched onto one of her blouses.

"It was Melody Monroe," I say.

Bee lets out a soft gasp, "Melody Monroe?" She pauses. "What is she doing back in Katy's Ridge?" she asks.

"I'm not sure, but she showed up on our doorstep right after supper. She mentioned Johnny."

The look on Bee's face confirms that I'm not overreacting.

"Are you okay?" Bee asks again, reaching her hand toward mine.

"Not really," I say. "It was like seeing a ghost, and I had this strange reaction afterward. I couldn't stop trembling."

Bee scoots to the edge of her chair. "What did Melody want?"

"She spent a lot of time looking at Lily, and then mentioned Johnny's name like she was threatening to tell." A brief quiver returns.

"You look flushed," Bee says. "Are you sure you're okay?"

I tell her about my reaction after Melody left and how Aunt Sadie said it was a way to release old hurts. I tell her Aunt Sadie said it was a good thing, but she looks doubtful.

"How did Lily react?" she asks. "Did she say anything after Melody left?"

"She was full of questions about who Melody was, of course, and didn't want to let it go."

"Sounds like her." Bee taught Lily in school, back when she still called herself Becky Blackstone instead of Bee.

"Can you blame her for wanting to know who her father is?" Bee twists a strand of thin long hair and then pushes it behind her ear.

I walk to the window and back again, something I do when I'm at a loss.

"Pacing won't help," Bee says, like she is an expert on going back and forth.

She wears one of her navy blue skirts with a white blouse and a yellow sweater that perfectly matches the yellow of the quarter-sized bumblebee stitched onto her collar. Bee has offered to stitch a wildflower onto the bib of my overalls to honor my nickname, but I've declined.

"You were sweet to come over," I say, but Bee is distracted, as if visiting a part of her past, as well.

"I taught Melody before she moved away," she says. "It was the year her sister Ruby died. They were such a sad pair, those girls. Melody didn't talk to anybody but Ruby at school, and then after Ruby died she quit talking altogether."

"I was in Ruby's grade, remember?" I say.

At first, she looks at me as if this can't possibly be true, but then nods as she remembers.

Bee is six years older than me and she was just out of teacher's college when she came to teach at the small elementary school in Katy's Ridge. I was in eighth grade and she taught me for one year before I went off to Rocky Bluff High School. She was *Miss Blackstone* then.

"Ruby's funeral was so sad," Bee says.

I flash on the oak tree where Ruby hung herself and shudder. I was always afraid of dying young back then. Not because of Ruby. But because two years earlier I overheard Mama tell Preacher during a home visit that she had given birth to a baby named Beth who died right before I was born. After that, death felt too close. It could have been me that died instead of Beth.

"I went to the Monroe house once," I say to Bee. "It was easy to feel sorry for them. Good luck just couldn't find them."

"The father showed up at school one time when I was alone," Bee says, her voice low. "He didn't do anything, but I had a feeling

that he wanted to. It was probably good Melody moved away," she continues. "I just hope wherever she went was better."

"Given the way she was dressed today, I'm not so sure."

Bee frowns.

"Maybe I should tell Lily about Johnny before Melody does," I say.

"Do you really think Melody would have that much nerve?" Bee asks.

"It looked like it today."

We pause, and I lean against Daddy's desk.

"Maybe you should just play it by ear," Bee says. "Maybe that *secret sense* you're always talking about will tell you if it's the right time or not."

We say our goodbyes. I'm not convinced I need to rush out and tell Lily about her father. I'm also not convinced I need to keep the secret.

When I go home, I find Lily at the kitchen table playing rummy with Mama. Rummy is Mama's favorite game and she can play for hours, causing her opponents to drop out from sheer fatigue.

"Who's winning?" I ask.

Lily's lips are tight and she doesn't look at me. Over the years, we've had a few spats that provoked a pout or a snarl at most, but she's never refused to look at me. She's not the type to punish with silence. That would mean she couldn't ask questions.

Mama gives me a look that says: *She's just like you. See what I've had to put up with?*

I pour myself a glass of tea and think of the willow tree up at the cemetery. I want Daddy to help me make sense of what I should do. Losing him was horrible. But losing Lily, even for an evening, feels like more than I can bear.

CHAPTER SEVEN

Lily

Refusing to look at Mama, I fume in silence. Between my huffing and sighs of exasperation, I play cards with Granny, who isn't in the mood for niceness, either. We don't talk, and each take turns slapping down our cards on the kitchen table like we're pissed as rattlesnakes over the hand life has dealt us. Mama finally leaves, tossing a sigh into the discard pile.

"You finished punishing her yet?" Granny asks me.

It's unlike Granny to take Mama's side. "Who's punishing who?" I say. "I have a right to know, and you know it."

If I had any nerve at all I would go over to that Melody woman's house and ask her what in the hell she has to tell me. *I'm a big girl,* I tell myself. *I can handle it.* At the same time, I wonder if I can.

"I wish we had a telephone so I could call Pearl," I say to Granny, who lifts an eyebrow as if she's studying me. "We're practically the only family in Katy's Ridge that doesn't have one." *It's*

1956, for God's sake, I want to add, but Granny will not tolerate cussing in her kitchen.

"Once you can pay for it, we'll get one," Granny says.

"We live in the Dark Ages," I say, after discarding a jack of hearts.

I fume in silence for Granny's benefit, too.

"Most families have telephones and television sets by now," I continue. "I've watched Ed Sullivan at Pearl's house and can't believe all the good things we're missing."

"If you don't like it here, feel free to leave," Granny says, studying her cards.

Picking a fight with Granny is never a good idea, so I let it drop.

When the crickets tune up for the evening to sing their songs, I want to tell them to shut up. For the rest of the evening, I avoid the living room where Mama is reading and take an extra-long bath hoping she's waiting to get into the bathroom.

When I dry off, I put on my pajamas and then go into our bedroom. Mama follows me in.

"Can I brush your hair?" she asks.

I stand in our bedroom with my hands on my hips, wondering how long I can stay mad at her if she insists on being nice. She pats the bed.

I sit with a huff and bounce on the worn out springs just to irritate her, but she isn't the least bit irritated. My hair is long enough that I can sit on it if I'm not careful. Mama said she used to have hair as long as mine, too, but now she wears it short to avoid accidents at the sawmill.

Hair brushing is something we rarely miss. I take my place at the foot of the bed and Mama sits behind me. With slow, gentle strokes, she brushes my hair as if it is made of birds' nests that will fly apart if touched too roughly. Over and over, she sweeps my hair back and gathers it and then lets it drop. I close my eyes. This

rhythm is like a lullaby. My breathing deepens, and I expel the last of my anger with a sigh.

How is it that even without a daddy, I feel completely loved?

"I'm sorry, Mama."

"I'm sorry, too," she says.

Mama puts the brush on the bed, and I turn to see her head bowed like she's praying.

"Does this mean that you and God are on speaking terms again?" I ask.

She lifts her head and looks at me, her eyes shiny with unshed tears.

"Maybe someday we will be again," she says, like it's a secret wish she's not sure will get fulfilled. "I don't want you to hate me," she adds, her voice soft.

"I don't hate you, Mama," I say, although twenty minutes before I would have sworn on a Bible I did.

She leans over and rests her head on my shoulder.

"We need to not have secrets from one another," I say.

She raises her head and her eyes find mine.

"I'm not so sure I agree," she says.

I start to ask why, and she answers as if she's already heard my question.

"It's my job to protect you, Lily, in the best way I know how. When you're a parent, that's what you do."

"Remember when you used to read me fairy tales at night from Granddaddy's book?" I ask.

She nods. "It was a book he used to read to me and my sisters at night," she says.

"Well, if there's a kingdom where secrets are kept, you're the queen," I say to her. "And the castle where you keep those secrets has a deep moat with alligators in it."

She laughs. "That's probably true," she says. "But you've kept secrets from me, too, haven't you?"

I pause, remembering my plans to leave Katy's Ridge as soon as I am out of high school.

"I take that as a 'yes,'" she says, her smile brief.

She looks at me in that way she always does, like she's recognizing somebody she used to know.

"My secrets are nothing bad," I say, thinking, *at least nothing bad to me.*

"Listen, sweetheart, you're as entitled to your confidences as I am to mine."

She says this like she's closing a loop on a sweater she's knitting to keep it from ever unraveling. "A mother never knows everything about her daughter, and a daughter never knows everything about her mother. It's just the way it is."

In my imagination, I hear a snap, the jaws of the alligator in the moat.

"But what if your secrets involve someone else who has a right to know?" I ask.

"Oh, Lily," she says, as though I'm intent on making her life harder than it already is. But I detect a little give in the fabric of her protection of me.

I pick up the hairbrush and motion for Mama to turn so I can brush her hair, too. Her hair is short, but thick, and she's tender-headed, so I am as gentle with her as she was with me.

"Telling secrets has consequences," she says, as though the matter isn't entirely closed.

"But not telling them has consequences, too, doesn't it?" I ask.

She turns and looks at me.

"You have to decide whether telling the secret is going to hurt anybody or not," she says. "If telling it gives you relief, then you just pass that hurt onto other people. In that case, it was probably selfish to tell."

"So you don't want to tell me about my daddy because it might hurt me?" I ask.

Mama sighs.

"Lily, it's been a really long day. I just can't do this right now."

Mama stands and takes the brush from my hand and places it on top of the old bureau that she and her sisters used to share. Before I have time to crawl under the covers, she turns out the light.

Through the thin walls, I can hear Granny getting ready for bed. The rocking chair in her room begins its faint crackling against the wooden floors. Sometimes Granny rocks deep into the night. Tonight, I wonder if she's thinking of Granddaddy, who died fifteen years ago today. Or maybe she's wishing she'd pulled the trigger of that shotgun.

As I ready for sleep, I think of the stranger with the muddy shoes and the look on Mama's face at the time, like a ghost had appeared right in front of her.

My cousin, Bolt, told me years ago that the Monroe land was haunted. It lies beyond the crossroads over near Sutter's Lake. A girl hung herself in an oak tree on that property.

Tomorrow after school, I want to find the stranger's cabin. She may know something about my daddy.

Mama reaches over and touches my arm in the darkness. "Are you still awake?" she whispers.

"Yeah," I whisper back. I'm glad I'm not angry at her any-more. I've never been able to stay mad at her for long.

"I love you, Lily," she says.

"Your secret sense knew the stranger was coming, didn't it?" I ask.

"It did," she answers.

"Do you think I'll get the secret sense someday?"

"Even if you don't, you have other very special gifts, Lily McAllister."

"Like what?" I say, but I know she's talking about my singing.

"Go to sleep," she says, turning to face the wall.

I close my eyes, but I can't quit thinking about the stranger. I'm convinced she holds pieces of the puzzle I've been trying to solve my entire life.

"If you don't tell me, I'll ask her," I whisper. It sounds like a threat, though I don't mean it to. Or maybe I do.

The mattress squeaks as Mama turns to face me again. I imagine her raised brow along with that don't-even-think-about-it look.

"I'm serious, Lily, don't go looking for trouble," Mama's voice breaks out of a whisper.

In the next room, Granny's rocker stops. Has she heard us? The wooden floors announce her movement across the room, followed by the metallic moan of the iron bed that receives her.

"I just want the truth," I whisper back. "When you're ready," I add, knowing it's best not to force things. If Mama feels pushed into a corner she fights back like a bobcat.

"I'll think about it," she says, as though too tired to fight.

I smile. A tiny victory.

According to Mama, everything in nature has a timing to it, and she taught me to respect the timing of things. You can't open a cocoon before its ready, or the butterfly will die. You can't force a flower to bloom by pulling it apart. You can't force the river to flow faster than it does. You can't force people to move faster than they want to, either. If Mama says she'll think about it, she will. But that doesn't mean I'll get what I want. At least I know now who to go to for answers if Mama denies my request—the stranger named Melody Monroe.

CHAPTER EIGHT

Wildflower

After a fitful night's sleep, I go into the kitchen the next morning to find Mama already at the table. Four quilt squares sit next to her as well as a needle with thread marking where she stopped the night before.

"I made it strong," she says, holding up her coffee cup. Did she have trouble sleeping, too?

My dreams were full of chase scenes. Lily running through the forest, fleeing from an unseen assailant. Sometimes I wonder if dreams are my secret sense just coming out in a different way.

"You're up early," Mama says. "You got a meeting I don't know about?"

I pause long enough to wonder if I should tell her the truth. The truth wins out. "Actually, I'm going to go by the Monroe place and talk to Melody."

Her voice starts off loud and then goes to a disapproving whisper: "You're going to do what? Why would you do that?"

Mama is protective of all her children and until I had Lily, I took her way of caring as an insult.

"It may be the stupidest thing I ever do, Mama, but I can't just sit around and wait for the shoe to drop."

Mama looks at the kitchen door as if to make sure she won't be overheard. Her words come out in a whisper again: "Do you think Melody Monroe knows that Johnny is Lily's daddy?"

"That's what I need to find out," I say. "I don't know what she knows. But when she was here yesterday, she couldn't take her eyes off Lily and that concerns me."

"You want me to go with you?" Mama asks, glancing over at the shotgun by the door.

"I don't want to scare her," I say. "I want to have a calm conversation."

"I don't know if that's possible with that woman," Mama says with a scoff. "My guess is she's here to make a mess of things."

"Maybe she is," I say. "That's what I want to find out."

"You be careful," Mama says.

I grab a biscuit left over from yesterday and fold two pieces of bacon into the center of it and wrap it into a napkin.

At the front door, I yell a quick goodbye to Lily, who is getting ready for school. She yells back the same. At least she's still speaking to me. I remember how Mama and I barely spoke for weeks after Johnny attacked me. Back then, I thought Mama's silence might kill me. Even the simplest people are complicated, and I don't know that I'll ever understand most folks. I'm not sure I even understand myself.

At the bottom of the hill I slide into my pickup and let it warm up while I eat my biscuit. I toss the crumbs outside for the birds. I drive in the opposite direction of the sawmill toward the Monroe place. The paved road changes to dirt and gravel and then to just dirt. No matter how slow I go, the shocks on my old truck squeak and moan. With the ruts and potholes, it's like riding a wild horse

who refuses to be tamed. I pull over and park where the road becomes impassable. A few yards away, I find the remnants of an even narrower dirt road that leads into the forest.

The last time I was here I was Lily's age, or maybe a little younger. On a post to the left of the road is a rusty white sign that once had *No Trespassing* painted on it. Now it reads *o espassin*. The road is grown over and looks like a mud farm at best. Standing water sits in deep craters, and it takes some doing to avoid the puddles. It reminds me of jumping hopscotch squares in elementary school. I think of Bee. I could never spend an entire day with a bunch of kids like she does.

I walk deeper into the woods. Even with the leaves halfway off the trees, it is still dark. I shudder and think of the dream I had the night before of Lily being chased. My stomach rumbles with the strong coffee and biscuit. I shouldn't be here. I have work to do at the mill. But I need to ask Melody about her intentions.

Nothing much has changed about the Monroe place except that, with no one cutting trees for firewood, the forest is denser. Wisteria vines have captured the front porch and threaten to overtake the rest of the house. Even from a distance the old wood smells rotten. The floor boards of the porch visibly buckle in places with green vines reaching for sunlight between the boards. A three-legged stool sits next to an old washing machine with rollers. A stack of firewood is covered with a white fungus that stretches its fingers in every direction and looks almost as rotten as the porch. At the bottom step I stomp the mud off my boots to announce my arrival, and call out Melody's name. On the step next to me is a graveyard of cigarettes twisted into the dark, damp wood. The cabin reeks of sour cigarettes and rot.

Several long seconds later, the door opens just enough for Melody to peek outside. Even though it's after 9 o'clock, she looks like she's just woken up. I remember the first time I came to this cabin, when Melody and I were both girls. Daniel was with me and

my best friend, Mary Jane. Daniel had asked Melody where Johnny was, so he could tell him to leave us alone.

"You wanted to talk with me?" She wipes her eyes.

"I do," I say. I pause long enough to wish I'd pondered a strategy on the way over. "I'd like to know your plans."

"My plans?" she says with a short laugh, like she's never had a plan in her life. Even though there's a chill in the air she opens the door wide. "You drink tea?" she asks. She disappears into the cabin.

"Sure," I say, even though I just had coffee.

I test the porch steps before I climb them, grateful my feet don't break through the boards long overdue for being replaced.

A shiver splits my ribcage when I step inside the house. I've never been in the Monroe cabin and the smallness of it feels like what I imagine a prison cell is like. I wonder how an entire family could have lived in it. In the next second it occurs to me that four of this family of five are dead, leaving only Melody behind.

Melody stands at a small wood stove with a pan of water on top heating to a boil. A small table with two chairs is in front of a cracked window that offers the only light in the room. Mama's kitchen looks fit for royalty compared to this.

"I guess I gave you quite a jolt yesterday," Melody says, inviting me to sit at the table.

I thank her and take a seat in an uncomfortable chair whose woven seat has almost busted through. With the door open, the dampness of the forest permeates the room. I half expect mold to climb up my ankles if I sit still long enough.

"You gave us all a shock," I say.

"I bet I did," she says with a grin that quickly fades.

If history had been gentler with both of us, perhaps we would have been friends. Yet right now she feels more like an enemy than anything, and I need to determine what weapons she has.

A bed takes up a corner of the small room, the old mattress

torn and spitting out its stuffing in different places. A threadbare
blanket lays across the bed to serve as a sheet and a faded quilt
covers the top. A smaller bed, without a mattress, is on the opposite side of the room. I wonder where Johnny and the girls used to
sleep. This cabin is barely big enough for Melody and me.

In the last decade, I've reached the beginnings of forgiveness
for what Johnny did to me. I've even begun to forgive myself, the
hardest task of all. But seeing Melody again makes me feel like the
ground I've fought for all these years is crumbling underneath me.

"Why are you back here?" I ask, sounding harsher than I intend.
"I mean, if you don't mind my asking."

She takes a sideways glance at me, as if to determine whether
she should answer. Then she lights a cigarette with a match from a
box of kitchen matches kept in a small metal box. The fingers on
her right hand are yellow and tough from holding cigarettes.

"After my aunt died, I found an old letter addressed to her from
Doc Lester," she begins. "My aunt lived in Katy's Ridge when she
was younger and they used to be friends."

It is hard to imagine that Doc Lester has friends, even old ones,
given I typically think of vermin whenever his name is mentioned.
I'm not the only person in Katy's Ridge who feels this way.

"Doc wrote my aunt after Johnny died." She takes a seat at the
table and unfolds a letter from her dress pocket as if to offer proof.

A wave of nausea hits, and I hold my stomach to calm the wave.

"You okay?" Melody asks.

"I've been better," I say. I remember the tremors that shook
through me yesterday like an earthquake, an unexpected reaction
to Melody showing up at our door.

"The tea should be ready," she says, getting up from the table.
"I'm afraid I don't have cream and sugar."

"That's all right," I say. I never drink hot tea anyway. But it gives
me a reason to sit a while.

After putting a pinch of leaves into a small cloth bag, she steeps

it in the water that has just boiled. Melody gathers cups and saucers to put on the table. One cup is chipped. The other is missing a handle. Their flower design is just as faded as her dress. Yet both hint at beauty and better times. Then she returns to the stove and waits for the leaves to finish steeping. Melody doesn't speak, but stares out the window like I do sometimes when I'm remembering something from a long time ago.

A ragged potholder hangs from a nail near the stove. She grasps the pot with it and pours the tea into each of our cups. Then she sits at the table to join me. The chair beneath me has a hole in the weaving, and I hope I don't bust right through it and end up on the floor.

The tea tastes bitter and stale like it's been sitting in a tin for a long time.

"Lots of ghosts in these parts," she says, looking around the room.

I nod. We sit in silence for several seconds, as if paying our respects to the spirits of the dead who are everywhere. If I didn't feel the need to protect Lily, I would have already left.

"My aunt didn't tell me that Johnny died," she begins again. "I had to find out from the letters. All this time, I imagined he was still living in this cabin, up to no good."

I wonder if she's come to Katy's Ridge for answers.

"Do you remember when it happened?" she asks me.

"It was a long time ago," I say, thinking it was more like a lifetime.

"You know what's odd?" she asks, without waiting for an answer. "It's odd to me that Johnny died by falling down a mountain. Johnny knew these hills up, down and sideways. He would never have been that reckless."

Her eyes don't leave mine, as though she's challenging me to a game of truth or dare.

"From what I heard, it was winter," I say. "The footbridge was

icy." These are the facts. But what I don't tell her, is that I would have killed Johnny myself if he hadn't fallen.

Her eyes narrow. "How do you know this?" she asks.

"I know because Daniel and Nathan found him," I say, which sounds innocent enough.

She sits straighter in her chair, as though curious. "They must have been looking for him to find him at the bottom of the ravine. It's not like there's a clear view."

Melody is clever, and I search the past for the truth. I was the one who spotted Johnny at first. I saw something shiny at the bottom of the gorge. Johnny was wearing the gold medallion he had stolen from me. Later, I thought that Johnny taking the necklace was his way of getting his mama back. Lily wears it now, unaware of its history. I wanted to give her a piece of the gold Mary. But I wonder now if I was also giving her a bit of her father.

I force myself out of the past. "Why did you come back, Melody?"

She squints from the cigarette smoke. Then drops the butt in an empty jelly jar with an inch of water in the bottom. It gives a short hiss.

"Like I said yesterday, I came back to sell the place. Not that anyone would have it."

Melody glances around as if calculating the cabin's worth.

"In his last letter to my aunt, Doc Lester said she might want to come and meet Lily. He said she was a very special girl. Imagine my surprise to learn I had a niece."

I exhale, hearing the imaginary other shoe drop. Melody looks at me like a cat waiting for an apology from a mouse.

You'll get an apology when hell freezes over, I want to tell her.

The only sunlight in the room is hidden by a cloud and her face falls in shadow.

"Listen, I can't imagine that you actually wanted to have John-

ny's child," she says. "He forced himself on my sister, Ruby, too." She glances out the window toward the oak tree.

At the time of Ruby's death, news of her unborn child flew through Katy's Ridge like a flock of sparrows going from tree to tree. I remember seeing Ruby in that small coffin, knowing she had a tiny unborn baby still in her belly. Over a decade later, I still shiver with the thought.

Secrets get buried all the time. I'll keep mine buried, too, especially if they might cause Lily to suffer. I clinch my jaw. I've spent the last fourteen years making sure that my shame didn't touch my daughter, and Melody could erase all that in a day.

My thoughts capture me, and I'm startled when Melody begins speaking again.

"Did it ever occur to you that we might like to know that Johnny had a child?" she asks.

"I didn't think you'd care," I say, though in truth, it never occurred to me that Johnny's family had any rights to my child.

"My aunt is near death and would like to see her," Melody says.

"I thought you said your aunt was dead."

Melody's eyes dart toward the door, as if looking for a way out of her lie.

"I meant to say she's dying," Melody says.

"She even sent money for the bus, so I can bring Lily home." She pulls a few bills from her tattered dress pocket. I'm not sure which story to believe.

The sun returns but offers little comfort. "Lily's home is here," I say.

It never occurred to me that a member of Johnny's family might get curious and come looking for Lily. Or that the news would ever go beyond Katy's Ridge.

However, if there is anyone who might want to bring trouble to the McAllister family, it is Doc Lester. He hates Aunt Sadie, and was less than useless after Daddy's accident. Not to mention his

suggestion to get rid of Lily before she was born. I'm not sure what he had in mind, but if she were a kitten he probably would have drowned her in a bucket. His treatment of us since then hasn't been much better.

I always thought it would be Preacher who would condemn me to eternal damnation and treat me accordingly. But even he has managed to swallow whatever judgments he has about me and Lily, which I imagine are considerable. Perhaps it helps that Lily sings so beautifully in his struggling choir and often sings solos that bring the old widows of Katy's Ridge to tears. Tears that guarantee to up the totals in his collection plate.

"So you haven't told her who her father is?"

Melody's eyebrows arch toward the sagging ceiling that has a greenish tint. If Mama were here she'd take a scrub brush and a bucket of bleach to it.

"I don't blame you," she quickly adds. "I'd make up a story myself before I'd say Johnny was the father. Hell, that's like admitting you had a thing for Hitler."

Her giggle sounds childlike, as though all these years she's never left this cabin. Even today, she's barefoot, like the last time I saw her when she was a girl. At least we have one thing in common. It appears she hates Johnny as much as I do. I can't imagine hating one of my sisters as much as she hates her only brother.

Melody puts the wad of dollar bills on the table as though offering to buy her. My scalp tingles and my secret sense gives me a nudge to get out of there. But I can't go just yet. I need to get what I came for.

"Are you going to tell her?" I ask.

She smiles and I remember Johnny's crooked teeth.

"I might," she says. "Don't you think she deserves to know?"

Lily has said similar things.

All of a sudden the dark cabin feels like it might swallow me.

"I guess I'll leave it up to Lily," I say. "But if you really care about her—" The words tighten my throat. Melody doesn't even know Lily. There's been no time for caring to grow.

Silence fills the room. It is Melody who studies me now, as if disappointed my fear doesn't give her more pleasure.

"I'll leave it up to Lily, too," she says finally, and folds the money into her pocket. "If she asks, I'll tell her what I know. If she doesn't, I'll leave it alone."

A lone cicada sings, trapped in this cabin for so long it has no idea whether it's day or night, summer or fall.

"But what about your dying aunt?" I ask. "I thought she wanted to see Lily."

She hesitates. A smile comes and goes so quickly I question whether I've imagined it.

"I can always keep the money and tell her Lily changed her mind after I'd already bought the bus ticket," she says.

The deep breath I take makes her smile again, as if she realizes how she's held me hostage.

"Lily is a great kid," Melody says, and I wonder how she would know that after only laying eyes on her for the first time yesterday. "No doubt that's your influence. Though Johnny wasn't all bad, either."

Her generosity surprises me.

"From what Ruby told me, he was actually a sweet boy before Mama died. He was my older brother, by about six years, so we weren't really close. By the time I knew him he wasn't that nice."

She looks around like her family's history is recorded on the walls like ancient cave paintings. A history she would rather not revisit, either.

"Do you mind if I ask you something?" she begins again.

"No," I say, though the opposite is true.

"Does it bother you that she looks so much like Johnny?" she asks.

Though everyone must think it, no one has ever spoken these words. Lily is Johnny's child, if only in looks. She is tall, thin and has his intense eyes. Eyes that won't let you get away with anything. Eyes that penetrate and see the things you wish they didn't see.

I stand. "To me, Lily looks like Lily," I say.

What I will never tell Melody, is that it did bother me at first. Immensely. Even when she was small, I could see Johnny in her bone structure, her way of standing. If Johnny was still alive, all Lily would have to do to confirm paternity would be to look at him. But Johnny isn't living, and nobody—until now—has even brought it up.

"I've got to get to work," I say. I stop at the door and turn before leaving. "So you promise you won't tell Lily anything unless she asks you?"

"That's right," Melody says.

Something causes me to linger. I want to give her something more so she might keep her promise. "I hope life has been okay for you, Melody. You know, in recent years."

She stares into the teacup resting between her hands like June Sector does when she reads tea leaves. I imagine her tea is cold now, yet she holds it as though it warms her hands.

"It could have been better, I guess," she says.

We end our conversation with the pleasantries that often begin one. But something tells me that the trouble is far from over.

CHAPTER NINE

Lily

T he morning is crisp and the dew makes the path down the
hill slippery in places. When I reach the bottom, Mama's
truck is gone, and I wonder why she felt the need to leave the
house so early. At the road I hesitate, wondering what I'll miss at
school today, and then turn toward the old Monroe place. I have
never skipped school before. Not once. But today I have a higher
quest. I need to find out the truth.

With every step my guilt rises with the oatmeal in my stomach.
I stop at the crossroads where one road leads to the elementary
school and the other leads to the mill, and rethink my decision.
Even though I've missed the bus, I could still go to the mill and
make up a story. I could tell Mama I wasn't feeling well at first, but
that now I would like to go to school. Then either she or Uncle
Daniel could drive me into Rocky Bluff.

Going to the high school is the only break I get from the smallness of Katy's Ridge. While the population here hovers around

fifty, Rocky Bluff has almost 1500 residents, and is a metropolis in comparison. Still, it's not like me to break the rules.

A truck drives around the bend, and I'm relieved it's not Mama. The driver slows when he sees me. It's my Uncle Cecil. Not my favorite person. The truck idles as he rolls down his window. From the passenger side, Janie looks at me with her flat expression. Uncle Cecil's birthmark reminds me of my geography teacher saying the Soviet leader, Khrushchev, was a scary man.

"You miss the bus?" Uncle Cecil says.

I pause long enough for a fresh wave of guilt to crest. "I'm helping out at the elementary school today," I say.

Janie turns her beige face toward me like my 'helping out' is news to her.

"Hop in. That's where we're going." He leans over Janie and opens the door so I can get inside.

"Actually, I'm enjoying the walk this morning. Mama says walking is good for me." I give him a smile, surprised by how easy it is to lie.

Uncle Cecil shrugs and closes the door before giving me a short wave and driving away. He is new to the family, but is nice enough, and I can't believe I've just lied to him. It's not like I can get away with it, either. If Janie doesn't tell, it will come out when he tells Aunt Meg that he saw me on the road this morning. There is no way I won't get in trouble for this, but I can't seem to stop myself.

For the longest time I stand at the crossroads kicking rocks from one side to the other. A feeling comes over me that I've had more than once. A feeling that someone is watching me, even though nobody is around. A gust of wind brings down a flurry of leaves that scoot along the road and gather in a dusty whirlwind before dancing away. I pull my sweater close and remember the stranger from the day before with her mud-caked shoes. The thought of her gathers me up in her whirlwind, and I turn in the

direction of the Monroe property. Since I'm probably already in trouble, I might as well do what I set out to do.

Around the bend in the road, I hide my lunch pail behind a boulder, planning to pick it up again on my way home. A few steps later I take off my heavy sweater and tie it around my waist. The sun, having risen above the ridge, is now warming up the day. When I get to the dirt road off the main road, Mama's truck is pulled off on the side.

What's Mama doing here? Her empty coffee cup sits on the seat of her truck. Is this why she tossed and turned all night? Was she dreaming up a plan to visit the stranger? I take off down a narrow dirt road that is pocked with mud puddles.

One summer, Bolt and Nat and I went in search of the empty Monroe cabin. We'd heard for years that it was haunted and wanted to check it out. Back then we were in the midst of a dry spell so it wasn't this muddy.

In no time, mud cakes around my good shoes Mama bought me for my birthday last July. My feet get heavy, and I wonder how the stranger managed to keep her shoes as clean as they were. At this rate, I'll be scrubbing mine for hours, removing the evidence of where I've been. To avoid the deepest mud holes, I perch on mounds of grass when possible, leaping to the next clump of grass. Several leaps later, I come upon the small cabin. When I see Mama standing in the doorway talking to the stranger, I duck behind a large sycamore tree. I am too far away to make out any of their words.

A circle of oak trees guards the house, and I remember the story of the girl who hung herself. The place would feel creepy even without knowing the story. The dark forest makes this place look like a Hansel and Gretel fairy tale. I half expect to see bread-crumbs in the mud, leading the way out of the forest. If I were smart, I would probably follow them.

The wind pushes the cabin's bitter smell in my direction. This

old house has been in the process of falling down for years. Patches of light green moss grow on the roof and vines as thick as three fingers hold the house hostage. I wonder if I can get close enough to hear what Mama and the lady are talking about. I hide behind trees and underbrush, inching my way closer to the cabin. I crouch at the right side of the porch behind an old rusty washing machine. I listen to Mama's lower voice and the stranger's higher one. A duet in a minor key. Although I can't make out any words, I can tell from the way Mama's holding her body that she's not happy.

When Mama walks out the front door, I drop to my knees to stay hidden. She takes the path back to her truck, and the look on her face is one I've never seen before. Regret? Sadness? Cold mud soaks into my bottom of my dress. Now I've ruined my dress, as well as my shoes. Trouble piles on top of trouble.

Seconds later the stranger steps out on the porch without shoes, wearing the same dress from yesterday. She mumbles something under her breath about teaching Mama a lesson, and then goes back into the house. I can't tell if she's disappointed or angry or just acting normal.

I keep an eye on Mama, just in case she comes back, prepared to dive into the dark recesses under the porch. I don't move until her truck starts up and the gravel spews as she drives away. Then I stand and look down at the red Tennessee clay pressed into my knees, as well as the mud damage to my shoes.

I sit on an old log next to the house and lean against the rotting wood to decide what to do next. Not only have I skipped school, but I've ruined my things. The woman inside the cabin begins to sweep. I contemplate whether I should just walk away or knock on the door.

Warmth comes to my face. I decide to make the best of all the stuff I've ruined, and stand and brush myself off. Then I make a

wide circle back through the woods so I can approach the house as though I'm just now showing up.

When I get to the porch steps I call out 'hello.'

The stranger comes to the door, broom in hand.

"Does she know you're here?" She looks out into the forest, the way Mama left.

"No," I say.

"So you were hiding out here the whole time?"

"Not the whole time," I say.

She gives a slight grin like I remind her of somebody.

"I wondered if you'd have the guts to show up," she says.

When her grin grows into a smile she looks younger and not nearly as scary. She is pale, like her life has seen very little sunlight. "Come inside," she says. "Leave your shoes at the door."

"You have something to tell me?" I ask, not moving. I don't even want to think about what Mama would do if she knew I was here.

"You willing to listen?" she says back.

"Depends on what you have to say," I answer.

"Come inside," she says. She goes into the house leaving the door open.

I can't move. It's like my feet are anchored to the earth with mud, and I've been made a prisoner.

"Come on," the stranger says, from inside the house.

I think of Hansel and Gretel again. Is there a big stove in there that she'll throw me into?

You read too many fairy tales, I tell myself.

I wish I had Mama's secret sense. It would tell me what to do. But the secret sense is a language I've never learned to speak. At least not yet.

The rickety steps lead to an unstable porch. It helps that I just saw Mama leave here alive and well. I approach the door not knowing what I might find inside. The stranger sits at a small table

in the corner. A chair is pulled out where I imagine Mama sat. I take a seat and glance around the small, dark room.

"Could you tell me your name again?" I ask, feeling bold. "I don't remember from yesterday."

"Melody," she says, in a sing-song voice, like she recognizes the irony of someone so sad having such a beautiful name.

Her feet are dirty but the floor is clean from the sweeping.

"Where are you from?" I ask. This is not a question I ever get to ask in Katy's Ridge since few people visit here.

"I was born here in this cabin," she says. "But when I was a girl, I was sent to live with my aunt in Louisville, Kentucky."

In my mind, I put Louisville on my list of places to visit some-day. I would travel there now if the opportunity presented itself.

"Why'd you come back?" I ask.

"You ask a lot of questions," she says. "Anybody ever tell you that?"

"Just about everybody tells me that," I say, looking away from her grin.

"It's okay. I'm not mad at you or anything," she says. "You skip-ping school?" she asks, like it's her turn to find out things.

I nod, and lower my head. Skipping school is nothing to be proud of.

"We can keep it a secret if you want," she says. "I'm good at keeping secrets."

I wonder if this is true.

Two teacups sit on the table. I hope she doesn't offer me anything to drink.

"When you came to the house yesterday, you said to come see you if I wanted to talk."

She nods.

"Why would I talk to you? What do you want to tell me?" I ask, looking up at her again.

"There's two more," she says, as if catching me at something.

"Two more?"

"Questions," she says.

"Listen, I can go if you want," I say, standing.

"No, no," she says. "I want to get to know you." She motions for me to sit again.

"Why?" I say, before I can catch myself. But we both smile this time.

"You can call me Melody if you want," she says.

I nod, but I'm not ready to call her anything.

"You may be related to someone I used to know," she says.

"I take it you don't mean Mama," I say.

"No," she answers. "I think I knew your daddy."

My breathing goes shallow. All these years I've wanted this question answered and now that it's as close as the cracked teacup sitting in front of me, I'm not so sure I want to know. If I listen to what she has to say, it feels like it might change everything. And maybe not in a good way.

Dozens of questions rush forward wanting answers, but I don't speak.

"Would you like to know more?" she asks, like she sees my predicament.

I say I do, but I'm not so sure. All of a sudden, my heart beats like it has a race to run.

She walks over to the door like she's making sure Mama isn't coming back. Then she turns to face me again. She isn't wearing a slip, and her dress—backlit by the sun—reveals her scrawny legs.

"I think your daddy was my brother, Johnny Monroe." She grins like she takes pleasure from saying it. "He was a couple of years older than your mama and they went to the same school. At least before Johnny dropped out in sixth grade."

Over the years, I'd imagined that my daddy was smart like Granddaddy. Maybe he even had a college education, which would

be a first in my family. It never occurred to me that he might be a sixth grade dropout.

"That was the year our mama died," she says, as if feeling the need to give a reason. "She died of TB when I was six."

Melody glances at the bed like that's the last place she saw her mother alive.

Tuberculosis is feared here in the mountains. Several people have died from it. I wonder if the tuberculosis germs are still living in that bed. Or maybe they are circulating in the air. I hold my breath for a few seconds until I realize I've probably already breathed them in anyway.

A part of me wants to run out of the cabin and keep on running until I make it back to Granny's kitchen. Another part of me feels bolted to the floor. The two parts battle it out in silence.

What if she's just making this up? Great Aunt Sadie says you can tell from someone's eyes whether they're telling the truth or not. If they're lying, their eyes dart like hummingbirds drinking from flower to flower.

"What are you thinking about?" she asks me. Her voice sounds caring, but her expression reveals something else. If I had to guess, I'd say she's getting pleasure from somebody else suffering for a change.

"What was he like?" My voice sounds shaky at first, but I smooth it out.

"The truth?" she asks.

I nod to avoid the words shaking again.

"Your daddy was mean as a snake," she says, her eyes holding steady.

After a short gasp, I have the beginnings of a coughing fit. Melody brings me a glass of water that is slightly brown. The father I imagined was kind, never mean. She reaches over and pats my hand as though life disappoints all of us, so I might as well get used to it. I challenge myself not to pull my hand away, even

though her touch is as cold and clammy as a fish out of the Tennessee River.

"How do you know for sure he's my daddy?"

"I don't know for sure," she says. "On account of he's not here to ask. He died right before you were born."

"What killed him?" I ask, as another of my fantasies dies. This one being that my daddy isn't dead at all, but is living somewhere around here and will show up any day to apologize for not being better in touch.

"He fell down a mountain," she says. "At least that's what your mama told me."

"Mama told you that?"

"She sure did. Right before you got here."

I want to know why Mama kept this from me for all these years and then tells Melody the first day she sees her.

"But how do you know he's even my daddy?" I ask again, my voice getting stronger.

She pauses. "You know Doc Lester?"

I nod. My family hates Doc Lester, especially Mama. She won't let him get near me with his doctoring. If Aunt Sadie can't find a remedy for whatever ails me, Mama says she'll take me to see the doctor in Rocky Bluff, even though he charges two dollars for an office visit.

"Doc wrote a letter to my aunt in Louisville saying that Johnny had a daughter. He said her name was Lily. That's your name, right?"

I start to stand, and the chair I'm sitting in crashes to the floor with me in it. I'm lucky the old floor is half rotten or I might have knocked myself out.

"You all right?" Melody leans over me on one knee.

Flat on my back, I take in this person, with bad breath to accompany her bad teeth, who is quite possibly my aunt. The

thought occurs to me that I've got plenty of aunts already, what do I need with one more?

"You're wrong," I say. "Doc Lester lied to you." I scramble from the floor, my head throbbing. Once upright, the dizziness sets in followed by the tears that threaten to come.

Within seconds, I bolt out of the cabin, hearing Melody call out my name. The mud slows me down as I run through the woods and toward the road. Even though I heard her drive away ages ago, I want Mama's truck to still be there. By the time I reach the crossroads, it feels like my lungs might burst from my chest. I stop running and lean over to slow my breathing. Once I can stand up straight again, I try to decide what to do next. I take off walking in the direction of the mill where Mama works. She has some major explaining to do.

CHAPTER TEN

Wildflower

My hands are still trembling when I park my truck outside the sawmill. I will do anything to keep Lily safe, yet I'm not sure how to protect her from the truth. I leave my muddy boots at the side door and walk into the office in my socks. Daniel sits at the desk we share, working on the ledger where we keep track of all our orders. Orders that promise to grow leaner as we head into the winter months. Silas—who made Daddy's coffin and is an old family friend—only works two or three days a week. He cuts the lumber, and with the help of his son, delivers it to wherever it's needed.

The day before, Daniel assured me that Melody wasn't up to anything and would be gone soon. But he wasn't in that cabin with her. Nor did he catch her in the lie about her dead or not-so-dead aunt.

When Daniel starts to get up, I motion for him to stay seated and pull another chair next to the desk.

"I need to talk to you," I say. "It's serious."

He puts down the pencil and turns to look at me, his face showing immediate concern. Ever since Daddy died, I've relied on Daniel to help me figure things out.

"I've just come from the Monroe place," I say. "I talked to Melody, and if Lily asks, she plans to tell her who her daddy is."

"Good lord," Daniel says, his voice soft. He closes the ledger and takes off his glasses that he uses to see the small numbers.

"I don't trust her, Daniel. Melody Monroe is up to something. I am certain of it."

"Sounds like you may be right," he says.

We pause, as if taking this in.

"The timing is uncanny, isn't it?" I begin again. "She shows up on the anniversary of Daddy's death, which is also the anniversary of—" I don't want to say the words. But Daniel knows as well as I do what happened on that first anniversary because he and Mama found me in the woods and carried me all the way home.

I flash on the feeling of being carried in his arms and Mama's voice calm and steady saying not to give up, that we'd be home soon. Then I wonder how something that happened so long ago can still be so fresh in my memory.

"Uncanny is a good word for it," Daniel says, his forehead creased.

We exchange looks, unprepared to fight old battles. Daniel studies the eagle tattoo on his arm, as if remembering the war from which Amy's husband, Nathan, didn't return. The shrapnel in his leg causes him pain, although most of the time he tries to pretend it doesn't. On the days it's hurting him, he chews aspirin like they were peppermints.

"There are ghosts out at that place, Daniel. It's creepy. Bad things have happened in that cabin. You can just feel it. Like it's seeping out of the walls or something."

Daniel looks thoughtful, like he's trying to make sense of things. "From what I can tell, broken families are everywhere," he

says. "The Monroes are one of those broken families. Whatever good was there at one time died away. In some ways, they never had a chance."

"I think you're right," I say.

"Tell me what you two talked about," Daniel says.

"She wanted to know how Johnny died," I tell him. "I didn't mention that he may not have died in the first place if we hadn't been chasing him."

"Johnny brought this on himself," Daniel says. "He threatened you. Then he broke into the house. There was a reason he was being chased. We were trying to keep you safe."

"I'm not sure Melody would see it that way," I tell him.

"It was his choosing," Daniel says. "If he hadn't come after you, he would still be alive."

I remember the Monroe cabin and wonder if choosing has anything to do with all that happened there. Sometimes life has nothing to do with choice.

"Daniel, why did I lie to Lily all these years? I should have told her the truth the first time she asked me." An unexpected sob catches in my throat.

"You didn't lie to her," he says, leaning closer to pat my hand.

"Not saying is the same as lying," I say. "She's asked me for years who her daddy is, and I've refused to tell her. Nothing kindles a fire like the flames of silence."

"You're being too hard on yourself," Daniel says. "You were just trying to protect her. Anybody in your position would have done the same thing."

"Anybody?"

"Anybody," he says. He acts certain, but Daniel is loyal to a fault. I'm not sure I can trust him to tell me when I'm truly in the wrong.

"I should have made up a story. Anything to throw her off track. It was the secretiveness that was wrong. It just made things too enticing."

"Tell me exactly what Melody said when you talked to her," Daniel says, repositioning his hurt leg.

"She said Lily has a right to know, and that if Lily asks her, she will tell her."

"Maybe Lily won't ask."

We exchange a look.

"Right. When has Lily ever not asked?" he says.

"Lily not asking is like laying odds that the sun won't come up tomorrow morning," I say.

"Not very good odds," Daniel says, looking thoughtful again. "Well, she's at school now, so at least it won't happen anytime soon. You'll have a little time to prepare."

I glance at the ledger that documents all the revenue and expenses of the sawmill.

"Do you think I should offer Melody money not to tell Lily?"

"Trust me," Daniel says, "you don't have any money to offer her."

"Maybe I should have reasoned with her more," I say, biting my bottom lip.

"It's easy for parents to think they didn't do enough," Daniel says. "But when is anything ever enough? More love could always be given. That goes for compassion and kindness, too."

"It's clear I messed up, Daniel."

He pauses, "If you really feel that way, then maybe telling Lily makes sense."

"It's going to hurt her," I say.

"Life hurts us all," he says.

"For years, Lily's built up these fantasies about who her daddy was," I begin again. "You know what a big dreamer she is. Always has been. She expects life to turn out okay no matter what. I was that way, too, remember? Until that day—"

"Bad things happen to everybody," he says, patting his leg.

"When are you going to get it into that thick skull of yours that you didn't do anything wrong?"

"I may never get it," I say, lowering my eyes.

Daniel stands, grabs his cane that is hooked on the handle of the desk drawer and puts a hand on my shoulder.

Tears come.

"If Daddy had been alive, he would have protected me from Johnny," I begin. "But then Lily wouldn't exist, and I'm not sure who I'd be without Lily. How can the worst thing to happen in my life, give me the best thing to ever happen? I just don't get it."

"I don't get it, either," he says. "Life is a mystery to all of us."

Daniel goes back to the ledger. I need to tell Lily the truth before Melody does, but this thought scares me almost as much as the other secret of my life coming to light. I just don't want Lily to have to grow up as fast as I did. But I have to prepare Lily for the world. Otherwise, what kind of parent am I?

The telephone rings and gives us both a start. The voice on the line is the secretary from the high school. I listen and then thank her, telling her that I'll handle it. I hang up the phone.

"I may be too late in wanting to do the right thing," I say to Daniel. "Looks like Lily skipped school today. For all I know, Lily is already at Melody's learning the truth about who her father was."

Daniel stands and cusses. I wonder if he's cussing because of what I just told him or if his leg is hurting him.

"I don't want to lose her, Daniel. There for a while, Mama almost lost me. If I lost Lily, it would break my heart."

"It would break both your hearts," he says, handing me my coat.

I put on my muddy boots and run outside to my truck, retracing the way I came thirty minutes before. After the truck jolts to life, I shift the gears from first to third, pushing the old truck as fast as it can go toward the Monroe cabin, wondering if my relationship with Lily is strong enough to bear the truth.

CHAPTER ELEVEN

Lily

When I arrive at the sawmill, Mama's truck isn't in front but Uncle Daniel's is. I can't quit thinking about what Melody told me. I find Uncle Daniel sitting in the office doing the books.

"Where's Mama?" I ask.

He stands, a grimace crossing his face from the pain in his leg. "She just left. She's out looking for you. I'm surprised you didn't see her."

"Why is she looking for me?" I ask.

"The school called," he says. "She knows you didn't go today."

I moan. Who gets caught the one time they skip? *You do*, I say to myself. You with the mean daddy who dropped out of school in sixth grade.

"Can you take me over to Great Aunt Sadie's?" I ask him. I'm not sure why I want to go there, except I need to talk to someone. Great Aunt Sadie is who Mama goes to when something is bothering her, either her or Uncle Daniel.

"Wouldn't you rather stay here and wait on your mama?" he asks.

I cross my arms, trying to keep my anger from spilling out all over Uncle Daniel. "Can you take me to Great Aunt Sadie's or not?" I ask. "I need to talk to her. It's important."

"Why don't you tell me about it? Maybe I can help," he says.

"No thank you," I say.

I love my Uncle Daniel, but he's not the one I need to talk to. I need to talk to Mama. But if she's not around then I need to ask Great Aunt Sadie why Mama lied to me all these years. Although, if what Melody said is true, maybe she was too embarrassed to tell.

Uncle Daniel limps out to his truck with me following close behind. His truck is newer than Mama's but is still old, and a Chevrolet instead of a Ford. On the dashboard are photographs of my Aunt Jo and my cousins, Bolt and Nat. Uncle Daniel starts the engine and puts it into gear. He drives slow, and I wonder if he's stalling for time, hoping we will meet Mama on the road.

"I'll tell your mother you're at your Great Aunt Sadie's," he says.

"Don't tell her anything," I say.

He glances at me while he drives. "You know I can't do that, Lily. I never keep secrets from your mother."

I huff, and Uncle Daniel rubs his bad leg like I'm making it worse. We ride along in silence until he tries to make conversation again, but I'm not in the mood. Great Aunt Sadie is the one person in my family I can count on to tell me the truth. If this Johnny Monroe character is my father, I want to hear it from her lips.

"Did you know that woman who showed up yesterday?" I ask, thinking Uncle Daniel probably knows everything, but he's under Mama's spell and sworn to secrecy.

He stops on the side of the road, letting the truck idle. Then he turns and looks at me like he's weighing the checks and balances on one of his ledgers.

"Melody grew up here," he says. "I knew her family for years."

"Tell me about them," I say.

Uncle Daniel taps the steering wheel, like he's drumming up the past.

"Arthur Monroe, Melody's father, served in World War I and got gassed and supposedly was never the same," he begins. "Arthur couldn't get work, and they were really struggling. I used to take them vegetables from our garden every now and again, and your grandfather used to take them eggs and whatever he thought would help."

I wonder if this Arthur Monroe is my other grandfather.

"The mother died pretty young, and there were three children," he continues. "An older boy, Johnny, and then two girls, Ruby and Melody. Melody was the youngest. I hadn't seen her since she was a little girl. Skinny little thing. Really quiet. The other sister, Ruby, died young, and then Melody was sent off to live with relatives. She's had a rough life, that's for sure," Uncle Daniel concludes.

"What was the brother like?" I ask, not telling him why I want to know.

Uncle Daniel pauses again, and winces as though his leg is bothering him, but he hasn't even used the clutch. "Johnny was a sad case," he begins again, "especially since his daddy used to slap him around."

"How did he die?" I ask. It is a simple question, except I may be talking about my daddy.

"Accident," Uncle Daniel says. "He fell."

I wait for more. "If that's the long answer, I'd hate to hear the short version," I say. I try to be funny, like Mama is sometimes, but Uncle Daniel isn't amused. He rubs his other leg like that one is suddenly hurting, too. I wonder how far to go with my questions, but then he starts the truck again like he's finished. We are quiet for the rest of the ride.

When we turn to go down the road to Great Aunt Sadie's

house, Uncle Daniel tells me he's not going to lie to Mama about where I am.

"Tell her I'll talk to her when she gets home after work," I say.

He says he will.

"Give me a call if you need a ride home," he says.

I say I will and get out of the truck.

As I approach the house, Great Aunt Sadie comes out of the barn carrying a baby goat. For an old lady, she is still strong. She smiles when she sees me like I am a friend she hasn't seen for a while. A hawk feather sticks out her brown fedora, her long, white hair captured under the hat.

At the end of the driveway, Uncle Daniel gives the truck horn a quick toot and waves to Great Aunt Sadie. I hadn't realized he was watching.

"To what do I owe this pleasure?" she says.

She delivers the baby goat to my arms. "Isn't she a beauty?" she asks, before I have time to answer. "I'm taking her to the side yard so she can hang out with the other kids for a while and give her mama a rest."

The faint smell of mama's milk is on the kid's breath, and I can feel its beating heart against my chest.

"Baby animals make the world softer somehow," Great Aunt Sadie says. "Birth of any kind is a miracle when you think about it."

For the first time that day I think of Crow and wonder if I'll have a family someday.

When Great Aunt Sadie opens the wooden gate to the side field, I put the goat down and she wobbles off to meet her siblings and cousins. My great aunt hasn't asked why I'm not in school or why I might want to visit a day after I just saw her.

"You need to talk?" She has a way of knowing things even if you don't speak them. "Let's go inside," she adds, with a nod.

Unlike Uncle Daniel, whose allegiances are clearly drawn, Great Aunt Sadie is as loyal to me as she is to Mama. She brought

us both into the world. We make our way into the kitchen and wash the goat smell off our hands.

In contrast to the Monroe cabin, the room is full of light and living things. Different herbs line the window sills and English ivy crawls from pots toward the light. She likes to bring outside things inside, and on warmer days she practically lives outside.

An abandoned wasp's nest is on the top of the tall kitchen cabinet and a small robin's nest with two broken blue shells sits at the center of the table. I take note to see if there's anything new and spy a fragile snakeskin resting on the ledge near the door. Several smooth white stones are stacked nearby.

"Thirsty?" she asks.

I nod.

She gives me a glass of pure well water from a white pitcher. I drink it all at once.

"You had lunch?"

"Not yet," I say, knowing it won't be long before I have a feast before me.

As expected, she cuts up potatoes and onions and fries them in butter on the stove and tosses in herbs from the windowsill. Then she takes four eggs sitting in a basket and breaks them in the middle of the potatoes and onions. She slices two big pieces of bread from the loaf sitting on the counter and places them in the oven to brown. Then she sets the strawberry preserves that Granny made on the table. Her food always tastes different than Granny's, with different flavors that taste like surprises.

Plates in front of us, she tosses her hat on a nearby chair, and her hair falls to her shoulders.

"Bless this food we are about to receive," she says, with a wink toward the ceiling like she and God share the kitchen.

I hadn't realized how hungry I was until the food was before me. Somehow finding out secrets steals an appetite away, at least until enticed by a lunch like this one.

"Okay, out with it," she says, after a few bites. "I know you've got questions or you wouldn't be here."

I pause long enough to form the words. "Does it count as a lie if someone knows something you should know but they don't tell you?"

"Is this a riddle?" she asks, dead serious.

I pause again to figure out how to make it clear.

"Like if someone has a secret that involves you, but they don't tell you about it, is that still a lie?"

"I guess it's a lie of omission," Great Aunt Sadie says. "Why?"

"I went to see Melody Monroe," I say, my confession unplanned.

Sadie stops mid-chew.

"What did she say?" she asks, her voice veering towards what could be mistaken as a low growl.

"She said that her brother, Johnny, is my father."

Her fork falls on the plate with a sharp clang, making us both jump. Then her eyes grow serious. "Does your mother know you talked to her?"

"Not yet."

Great Aunt Sadie wrings her hands long enough for her food to grow cold, and the wrinkles on her forehead have multiplied. I don't like seeing her worried. It makes me wonder if I am wrong for seeking out the truth.

"Keep in mind, Lily, that nothing is as it seems," she says, finally. "You may think you know the story and it can turn out to be something else entirely."

"Did all of you know?" I ask.

"Did all of us know what?" she says.

"Did all of you know who my father was? Did all of you keep it from me?"

She pushes aside her plate, the eggs and potatoes of little interest to her now. "You need to talk to your mother," she says.

"But she's the one who lied to me." I tell myself to stay calm.

Her look has kindness in it. "First of all, you need to hear the whole story before you make up your mind about things," she says. "You know your mama wouldn't knowingly do anything to hurt you. You know that, Lily, don't you?"

I don't answer and push my plate away, too. It's true that Melody may be lying, but that doesn't change the fact that my entire family has been lying to me by omission for the last fourteen years. Mama being the one who omitted the most.

"Melody said her brother, Johnny, dropped out of sixth grade and was meaner than a snake. Is that who my father was? A lowlife who didn't even finish elementary school? Why was Mama with him? Was she that hard up?"

Great Aunt Sadie rises, placing her fists on the wooden table. "Don't you ever talk about your mama like that." Her eyes don't waver from mine.

I swallow. It's the first time she's raised her voice to me.

"Your mama is one of the bravest souls I've ever met on this earth," she says. "And she does not deserve one moment of your criticism."

I lower my head and agree.

"I've said too much already," she continues. "You need to talk to her, and not make harsh conclusions until you hear the whole story."

Her lips form a stern line and her eyes appear darker than their usual gray.

"I guarantee you that Melody Monroe wants something out of this," she begins again. "I could see that look in her eyes when she showed up at your house yesterday. That girl has had a hard life. Her daddy wasn't right in the head, and her sister was one of the saddest souls I've ever seen. You be careful, Lily," she continues. "You be careful who you trust and who you don't trust. Your mama

has stood by you every day of your life. You need to hear her side of the story before you go jumping to conclusions."

Two robin's eggs shells sit on the windowsill. More than ever, I want to fly away from Katy's Ridge and never return. For the first time, I don't care how much my leaving will hurt Mama. Even after Great Aunt Sadie told me not trust Melody's words, I somehow know it is true that Johnny Monroe is my daddy. And no matter how much people defend Mama, she should have told me these things a long time ago.

CHAPTER TWELVE

Wildflower

After arriving back at the mill, I find Daniel still sitting at Daddy's desk. "Lily knows about Johnny," he says.

I close my eyes and shake my head, not knowing whether to cry or cuss. "Where is she?"

"Sadie's," he says.

"What should I do, Daniel? Should I go to her?"

"I don't think so," he says. "I think she needs time to get used to it. Sadie will help with that."

It's hard for me not to rush over to Aunt Sadie's house, but I need to think about what to do next. I don't know how much she knows, or what Melody told her. That will have a lot to do with how I respond.

Unable to get anything done at the mill, I drive to June Sector's house. I need a friend to talk to and Bee is still in school. All morning I've been thinking about how to tell Lily the truth, but Melody has beat me to it. I hate to think of Lily in that broken-down cabin, and I am relieved to know she's now over at Aunt

Sadie's.

I park in the grass near the house, next to the Sector's old Buick, and walk toward the door. When I reach the porch, Horatio, June's husband, greets me—his tall, thin frame towering over me. Horatio is full Cherokee and his wife, June, is white. Until I gave birth to Lily, they were the primary outcasts in Katy's Ridge.

"Still got that good luck charm I gave you?" Horatio asks the same question every time he sees me.

From my pocket, I pull out the small leather pouch with the star ruby inside to show him that I still carry it everywhere I go. The ruby was a gift from Horatio after Daddy died. For years now I've felt that Lily was my good luck charm, a gemstone in the midst of a sea of ordinary rocks.

"June around?" I ask.

"Out back," he says.

A moment later, Crow comes out of the house to greet me.

"I didn't know you were home," I say.

"I'm on military leave," he says.

I remember when Crow was a toddler running around the yard. Now he's taller than his daddy and handsome—dark hair, blue eyes—blessed by the best parts of his parents.

"Does Lily know you're home?" I ask. It's no secret she's had a crush on him since she was in third grade and he was in seventh.

"Pearl asked her over for supper." He smiles, like it's something he's looking forward to.

Since Daniel said Lily wants to talk tonight, I'm wondering how she plans to do both.

"I'm here to see your mom," I say to Crow.

"She's out back," he says, sounding like his daddy.

When I walk around the side of the house, I find June hanging laundry on the line. A breeze blows the clothes like sails on giant sailboats I've seen pictures of in Daddy's books.

"You got time to talk?" I ask.

"Sure," she says, as if she's been expecting me.

June continues hanging the line, and I grab a wet blouse from the top of the clothes basket. I shake the water and wrinkles out and hang the blouse on the line.

"What's up?" she says.

"All hell is breaking loose," I say.

She glances over at me. "What do you mean?"

June has always been easy to talk to, easier than anyone in my family, and maybe even easier than Bee.

"Melody Monroe came back to Katy's Ridge yesterday," I say.

June's eyes widen, confirmation that I'm not imagining how bad this is.

"Why in the world would she come back?" June asks.

"Doc Lester wrote a letter telling her she had a niece."

"He sticks his nose into everything," June says, hanging several pairs of white socks on the clothesline.

I agree.

Doc Lester has called June a witch on more than one occasion because she reads palms and tea leaves. He's said similar things about Aunt Sadie.

"How do you know she's back?"

"She showed up at the house yesterday."

"On the anniversary?" June's eyes widen again.

I nod. "There's more," I say. "I went to see her this morning and told her that if she cared about Lily she wouldn't tell her anything about Johnny. But I just heard from Daniel that she already did."

June snaps the wrinkles out of one of Crow's uniform shirts and finishes the last of the laundry. She offers me one of the chairs Horatio made for the backyard. Then she joins me. The spot over-looks a valley with the soft mountains circling like ancestors. I take a deep breath.

"I've always loved it here." I tell her.

June looks out over the mountains, as if she hasn't seen them thousands of times before. "Does Melody know what happened?"

"I'm not sure," I say. "She knows Johnny is Lily's father because she asked me what it was like that Lily looked so much like him."

"She said that? Oh, honey, I'm so sorry." She pats my hand. "Should have known Doc Lester would be at the center of this mess."

"To be honest, I'm surprised it has stayed a secret for as long as it did," I say.

"Mountain people can be loyal even when they shun you." June grins, but then gets serious again.

"Isn't it strange that Lily hasn't found out before now?" I say. "Looks like somebody would have told her."

"That child's been protected her whole life," June begins, "and not just by you. Sometimes I think your daddy is watching out for her, too."

Tears threaten to come and June takes my hand.

"Don't worry, you'll get through this," she says. "You've been through much harder things."

"But, June, what if this leads to that other secret coming out?"

She looks at me. She knows exactly what secret I'm referring to. "Then we'll deal with that, too," she says, her tone resolute.

"Have you thought about confronting Doc Lester?" she asks.

"And say what?" I ask. "He's basically told a secret that everybody in Katy's Ridge already knows."

"Except Lily," June reminds me.

"Except Lily," I repeat. "I'm beginning to see the unfairness in not telling her." I can tell June things I've never told anyone. Not even Bee. For some reason, I feel totally safe with her.

"What else did Melody tell you?" June asks.

"She wants to take Lily to Kentucky to visit an old dying aunt who wants to meet her. But something doesn't feel right."

"Then don't let her go," June says.

"Don't worry," I say. "I have no intention of letting her go."

"Does Nell know Melody is back?

"Mama pulled a shotgun on her yesterday and had it cocked before Melody finally got the message to leave."

June laughs. "She protects her own, your mother."

I nod. "I wonder what Daddy would do about Melody," I say to June.

"He'd probably try to reason with her," she says.

I pause. "Actually, I think Daddy probably would have told Lily the truth a long time ago, when she first asked," I say. "But I didn't have the courage for that, evidently."

We look at the mountains, as if they might hold answers to my current situation.

"By the way, Lily didn't go to school today," I begin again. "She went over to the Monroe cabin and now she's at Aunt Sadie's."

"Well, if anybody can talk sense into her, it will be Sadie," June says.

I agree.

"You need to talk to Lily, too," June says. "It's time."

"I know," I say, "but that doesn't mean I want to do it."

"I know," she echoes.

"Why did I think I could keep this secret indefinitely?" I ask her.

She glances back at the house. "A time comes when we can't protect our children from the world anymore."

"That's exactly what Daniel said," I say.

"Well, Daniel's right," she begins again. "We can't prevent them being hurt. The best we can do is be around to help pick up the pieces if they fall."

I thank June for being here for me.

"When does Crow leave?" I ask.

"Tomorrow, late," she says, with a quick inhale. "Pearl invited Lily over for supper. That okay with you?"

"Sure," I say. "Though she hasn't said a word to me about it yet, and she told Daniel she wanted to talk to me tonight."

"She's got other things on her mind, I guess," she says. "We'll have plenty, regardless. You're welcome to come, too," she adds.

I thank her again, not knowing what my evening may bring. "June, what if Lily hates me after this? If Mama kept a secret from me for fourteen years, I'd be furious."

She stands, looking over at the laundry on the line. "She won't stay angry for long," June says. "She knows how much you love her. Hell, everybody in Katy's Ridge knows how much you love her."

"Do they?"

"That's another reason they've probably kept quiet all these years," she says. "They've been struck speechless by how much you love that girl. Don't underestimate the power of love when it comes to healing things."

We walk together to the front of the house where Horatio and Crow sit on the porch. In the distance, Pearl walks down the road with two of her siblings. School is out.

"You stay safe," I say, and give Crow a hug.

He promises he will.

Pearl walks up to the porch and smiles at her brother, happy he's still here.

"You see Lily today?" I ask her.

She looks away.

"I know she skipped school," I say. "They called."

"I haven't talked to her since yesterday afternoon when I came over to your house," Pearl says.

I realize that was before Melody made her appearance. "She may need to talk to you later," I say. "Something big has happened."

Pearl grins like she's itching to know what happened. Sometimes I wonder why Pearl and Lily are friends. Pearl seems younger, somehow. Lily is quieter. She might even be called shy, if

not for her singing. When she sings, she changes. She fills with life. She's happy when she sings, and her constant questioning stops. It's as if the answers flow from her then, and she is totally herself. The feeling visits me again that whatever is going on is far from over, and that no secret is safe.

CHAPTER THIRTEEN

Lily

After talking to Great Aunt Sadie, I decide to go to the mill to talk to Mama. When I walk I usually sing something, or at the very least I hum a tune, but today I don't feel like singing. I can't remember another time when this was true.

As I come to the crossroads, I stop long enough to grab my school books and the lunch Granny packed for me that morning from behind the boulder. I take a bite out of the apple from my lunch and glance down the road that leads back to the Monroe place. I wonder if the woman, who could be my aunt, is still sitting in that dark cabin.

In the span of one day, I am in more trouble than I've ever been. I skipped school. I went to a stranger's cabin without telling anybody where I was going, and I lied to Uncle Cecil. According to Daniel, the school called so Mama already knows about the skipping. Right now, I don't even care if I have to do extra chores for an entire year. I deserve punishment.

Whenever I act like Mama, Granny likes to say that the apple

doesn't fall far from the tree. Maybe getting in all this trouble is me being like my daddy. I toss what's left of the apple as far as I can into the woods, wishing I'd never gone to Melody Monroe's.

I need to ask Mama flat out: *Is Johnny Monroe my daddy?* And if he is, she needs to tell me her side of the story, like Great Aunt Sadie said.

When I get to the mill, it is late afternoon and Miss Blackstone's car is parked out front. Uncle Daniel and Silas—who help out—are gone. Miss Blackstone was my elementary school teacher for years, since all of the grades are in one room. For as long as I can remember, she's been Mama's best friend. Like Pearl and me, they spend a lot of time together talking. It suddenly occurs to me that I haven't given Pearl an answer about coming to supper. Crow is only home for two more days, and I almost forgot because of everything else that's going on. But first, I need to deal with Mama.

Miss Blackstone's Ford sedan is a newer model, black with white trim. Her family has enough money for newer cars. She wears store bought dresses and always buttons the top button of her blouses. She is tall and lean and doesn't have much of a figure. Whenever I was bored at school, I would study her, like you study someone you admire. If becoming a world renowned singer doesn't work out, I might teach school when I grow up. Miss Blackstone said I was smart enough.

Besides the older widows at church, Mama and Miss Blackstone are the only unmarried women in Katy's Ridge. As far as I know, Miss Blackstone has never dated, and appears about as interested in the possibility as Mama.

I think of Melody Monroe. I didn't see a ring on her hand, either, making her a maiden aunt if she's anything at all.

Please, God, don't let me be related to her, I say to myself.

With no saws running, the double doors in front are closed and the mill is quiet. I walk around to the side door, a short cut to Mama's office. A small window is on the outside wall, about six

feet from the ground. I want to see what kind of mood Mama is in before I talk to her, so I stand on a large log to see inside. A twinge of guilt causes me to pause, as I add spying to the list of bad things I've done today. If Johnny Monroe was kin, I'm collecting my inheritance awfully fast.

Through the window, I see Mama in her office talking to Miss Blackstone. They are both smiling, a good sign that this may be the time to talk. Mama is never this happy at home. I lean closer to hear, but their voices are muffled. Seeing them together invites a prickle of goosebumps onto my arms. It reminds me of the time I accidentally saw Granny stepping out of the bath tub. Seeing all that flesh that was usually hidden under a dress and apron was shocking to me. Her breasts sagged like flour sacks, and I remember the light brown V of hair between her legs.

Mama and Miss Blackstone are different together. Miss Blackstone, who was serious at school, is smiling, too, like there's no place she'd rather be than talking to Mama. I think of my friendship with Pearl, and how we're never this happy. Pearl irritates me when she goes on and on about boys, and she has the patience of a flea on a dog when it comes to listening to me. Pearl is probably looking for me right now. I remind myself I need to see Crow before he leaves, but I can't pull myself away from watching Mama be so happy.

I feel like Pumpkin waiting at the door for scraps. But every time I start to step away from the window, I get pulled back to the scene. Their movements tell a story. They touch each other occasionally. A hand on an arm. A finger pointing that the other one grabs. It is Mama's playfulness that surprises me most. Though I've known her playful, it's mainly been with me, not other grownups.

If anything, Mama can be way too serious. Yet when she puts the worry down—like now—she looks like a totally different person. A beautiful person. I like that Miss Blackstone brings this

out in her, and surprise myself with the wish that I could someday make her this happy, too. The closest I get is when I sing.

Captured by the scene, I forget why I'm here. As much as I know it isn't respectful to spy on people, I can't seem to walk away. Something is about to happen, and if I turn away I'll miss it. The whole day has felt like this. I wonder again if this is the secret sense Mama's talked about. My life feels like one of those radio series Granny loves to listen to. A mystery is about to be solved, and somehow Mama and Miss Blackstone are part of the mystery, too.

The desk is the biggest thing in the small room. A couple of wooden chairs sit along one wall. Chairs I used to build a fort when I was a little girl and spent time in Mama's office. Now Mama and Miss Blackstone laugh, and I try to remember the last time I saw Miss Blackstone even chuckle. Maybe it was the time Crow stuck a piece of chalk up his nose and pretended it was an elephant tusk. Crow was four grades ahead of me and sat at the other end of the room, and was always trying to make us laugh.

Every now and again I realize how pretty Mama is. Not the way Aunt Jo is pretty, in that movie star way, but Mama has her own beauty that's hard to describe. It's like she fits perfectly in her skin, and possesses an ease I hope I have someday, instead of always feeling so awkward. It's hard to see how I'm like her when I look in the mirror. For the first time I wonder if she's been looking at me my entire life and remembering someone *as mean as a snake.*

Mama would be upset if she knew I was spying on her. She's cautioned me more than once that I might regret overhearing things. I imagine those regrets go for seeing things, too.

Mama moves closer to Miss Blackstone, her hand touching her arm. For a long time, they just look at each other, and then Mama touches her face. Gripping the window ledge, I lean closer to the glass to make sure it's not a distortion. Through the dirty panes, I see Mama lean forward and kiss Miss Blackstone on the lips. Not a

quick peck between friends, but a kiss I imagined I'd have with Crow someday after we got married. I remember the romance novels I found hidden in the closet that belonged to Aunt Meg. Books I sneaked and read on the flat boulder back behind the house. Books whose stories seem mild compared to what I'm seeing now.

My breath fogs up the window, and I lean back to erase my presence. In my awkwardness, I jerk back and lose my footing, unable to right myself. When I fall, I knock over a wheelbarrow nearby that clunks to the ground. I land on sawdust so I'm not hurt, but I'm certain I've been heard.

Within seconds, the door opens and Mama looks down at me, her face as red as mine feels.

Mama's expression spells out bad news like a headline on the Rocky Bluff newspaper. Miss Blackstone stands behind Mama, almost a head taller. Their kiss replays in my mind. I didn't know women kissed each other like that.

"Lily McAllister, how long have you been spying on us?" Mama says. Upon hearing my full name, I know I am in trouble with a capital T.

"Not long," I say, but the truth is, I've been standing there long enough for my whole life to change. From now on, I will always look at the two of them differently.

Brushing sawdust from my clothes, I get to my feet. For the second time that day I get the urge to run. This time I do.

CHAPTER FOURTEEN

Wildflower

Lily takes off running, and I know better than to take off after her. She can easily outrun her boy cousins, as well as me.

"Oh my God, what have we done?" I say to Bee.

Bee covers her mouth, as though to keep herself from screaming.

I pick up the wheelbarrow, giving it a kick as I do.

"Should I go after her? Should I try to explain?" I ask.

Bee sends a frantic look in my direction. "I don't know what we should do," she says.

We exchange desperate looks.

"I was afraid this would happen," I say to her. "I was afraid someone might see us. But I didn't think anyone would be around."

"Let's just stay calm," Bee says. She rests a hand on her neck like she does when she's thinking and stares at the floor. "Do you think Lily will tell anybody?" She looks at me.

"I don't think so, but how would I know? This has never happened before."

We go back to my office. I sit at Daddy's desk while Bee paces the room. I search for solutions written on the wooden floors.

"We've been so careful," she says. "Spacing out our visits. Not spending too much time at either of our houses. Early curfews."

"What if Lily never speaks to me again, Bee? What if she hates me now?" I bury my head in my hands.

"That doesn't sound like Lily," Bee says, her voice softer now.

"This is my fault," I say, looking up at her. "I told Daniel to tell Lily to come by and see me. Then I forgot about it. When you're around I forget about everything." I glance at Bee and my face colors again.

"You'll talk to her," Bee says. "You'll tell her how important it is that nobody know."

People finding out is Bee's biggest fear. Mine is having the people I love turn their back on me.

"We're not criminals," I say.

"It's the mountain laws of Katy's Ridge we've got to worry about," she says. "The people here are frightened of anything they don't understand. They surely won't understand this."

We pause in our panic. We are as far away from each other as we can get in the small room. Her at the window. Me now standing by the door. My face has not cooled down. I remember reading *The Scarlet Letter* and wonder what initial I will have to sew onto my clothes for this transgression. I walk over and sit at Daddy's desk. It is the desk version of trying to fill someone's shoes. It is too big for me. For the first time I'm glad he isn't alive to see my possible downfall.

"What is wrong with us?" I say, the tears starting now. "Why can't we be normal?"

"Hush, Wildflower," she says, her voice softer still. She rarely

calls me Wildflower anymore, and I am surprised by how much comfort the name offers.

We've had this conversation many times before. I've spent hours wishing I was different. Wishing I didn't love Bee the way I do. I've fallen to my knees many times, not a soul to comfort me, except for the woman I can't help loving. Somehow, I don't think Daddy would condemn me. He would love me regardless. It would never occur to him not to. Though I doubt Mama would ever understand. This is the kind of thing that might finally break us apart forever. As for Aunt Sadie, I feel safe from judgment, but she may feel hurt that she didn't know. I haven't had the courage to speak to her about it. Not yet.

When it occurs to me how many people could be hurt, I lower my head and a tear drops into my lap. "Maybe we should end this, Bee. End it before anybody else finds out."

She stops her pacing and walks over to the desk. "Is that what you want to do?" she asks.

When I finally look up, tears glisten in her brown eyes. "No," I say, even though I'm not so sure. "All I know is I can't bring any more shame to my family, Bee. Remember Lily's birth? The whispers in church?"

"That was Johnny's shame, not yours," she says, her voice raised. "You fought back as hard as you could and you still nearly died."

Bee can get like this. Protective. Supportive. Refusing to let ignorance win. Even my own. "I haven't forgotten," she begins again. "I came to see you after it happened. Remember? He beat you up so badly you couldn't move. You have not brought shame on your family, Wildflower McAllister. You have not!"

She takes my chin and raises it so our eyes meet. Her bottom lip quivers and a tear slides down her cheek. I look away. It feels unbearable to see her in pain, a mirror of my own.

"As for us, we try to be honorable people," she continues, her

knuckles rapping on the desk. "We go out of our way to be helpful. We love our families—"

Bee's tears flow now. I hand her one of Daddy's handkerchiefs from my pocket. To see someone experiencing so much sorrow feels almost unbearable to me. She blows her nose and wipes the tears away, but they keep coming. I can't help but think that I'm the cause of her unhappiness. I apologize and she tells me to stop. Then I hold her, feeling her body quake, until her tears finally stop. It doesn't seem fair that so much pain could come from loving another person. But it does.

Minutes later, I remember the look in Lily's eyes. She is hurting now, too. The hurt of not understanding what she saw. Shame threatens to overpower me again. I push it away. Life can be such a mess sometimes. Daddy always said that people will do the right thing if challenged, that goodness will win out. But I'm not so sure I believe that anymore. From my experience, people choose meanness at about the same rate as they choose goodness. It's the conflicts in life that test us to see which side we'll choose.

"What do we do now?" Bee asks, pulling me from my thoughts. She looks beaten and afraid.

"First, I need to find Lily and talk to her," I say.

"What will you tell her?" Bee asks.

"I'm not sure." I grab the keys to my truck off the desk and kiss Bee lightly on the lips, glancing up at the window where Lily watched us. I'm surprised I didn't see her.

"Let me know what happens," she says.

"I will if I can," I say. "But I may not come back here today." The only place I can use the telephone to call Bee is from the sawmill. It's too big a risk to call her from one of my sisters' houses. I wonder if Mama will ever give in to having a telephone installed at the house. She was slow to see the benefits of indoor plumbing. It was Daddy who could talk her into the 20th century. But I have much bigger problems at this moment than telephones.

"Were you serious about breaking up with me?" Bee's eyes are rimmed with red.

"I didn't mean it," I say. "It was just a reaction to the day. It's just sometimes I think it would be easier."

She turns away, and I apologize again. However, if it came to having to choose whether to have Lily in my life or Bee, chances are Bee wouldn't like my answer.

CHAPTER FIFTEEN

Lily

I can't remember the last time I ran like this. Away from the one person I thought I could count on. A part of me wants to run all the way to Rocky Bluff and then to the first city I can find. Chattanooga or Nashville or maybe even Knoxville. Then I will finally be rid of Katy's Ridge forever. What I didn't anticipate is that I want to rid myself of Mama, too.

Is Mama in love with Miss Blackstone? I ask myself.

The thought tastes bitter in my mouth, like the goldenseal or dandelion that Great Aunt Sadie uses in her strong tonics when one of us is sick.

My hair flies wherever it wants to go. I wish I had on my old shoes instead of the new ones that aren't fully broken in. They would be easier to run in. But these will do. I slow down long enough to take the dirt road to Pearl's house. I have so much to tell her. Too much. But I can't tell her about Mama. I can't run the risk of everybody in Katy's Ridge finding out. But I can tell her what I found out from Melody Monroe. Al-though that feels like old

news now. News I found out a hundred years ago instead of this morning.

Shame pumps through me as I run. Followed by hatred. I have never hated Mama before, not for one second. But I do now. I hate her for not telling me about Johnny Monroe. I hate her for kissing Miss Blackstone. I hate her for not being like everybody else.

At school, most people my age have mothers who stay at home. Or they work as school teachers or nurses. They certainly don't work at sawmills or run their own businesses. And they certainly don't kiss another woman.

"I hate you!" I yell as loud as I can on the way to Pearl's house.

Spit mixes with my fly-away hair. The road is not muddy like on the way to the Monroe place, but I slow my pace. I feel tired from the day. Tired from running like a colt out of a barn into an unfenced pasture. My heartbeat echoes in my ears. My day was already spoiled with the visit to Melody's. And now this. I flash on Mama looking into Miss Blackstone's eyes and touching her face and then shake my head to wipe away the pictures. In the next instant, I decide I hate Miss Blackstone, too. Up until twenty minutes ago, she was probably one of the five people I most admired in the world, along with Mama. But now, I never want to see either of them again.

My lungs burning, I slow to a walk. When I reach Pearl's house, I knock on the door, winded and close to tears.

June Sector opens the screen door, an old diaper slung over her shoulder like she's been cleaning.

"Lily, are you okay?" she says when she gets a look at me.

"I'm fine, ma'am," I say, thinking that I'm getting good at being a liar, which is probably a Monroe family trait.

"You don't look fine," she says.

"Is Crow still here?" I ask.

Seeing Crow again may be the only thing that can redeem one of the worst days of my life. The only thing that comes close to

competing is when I got my period in eighth grade on a day I wore a white dress to school. Miss Blackstone went with me to the bathroom and helped me wash out my dress, and then loaned me a Kotex pad and a sanitary belt and one of her big sweaters to wear over the dress. Thankfully, Miss Blackstone is tall so the sweater was almost as long as my dress. I tremble with the thought. Then I remember Mama kissing Miss Blackstone and shudder.

"Crow is out hunting with his daddy," June Sector says. "Does your mama know you're here?"

I tell her no.

The Sectors are friends of Mama's. I've played with Pearl and her brothers and sisters since I was in diapers. No wonder Mama is friends with every outcast in Katy's Ridge. She's one, too. I guess I didn't want to see it, because that makes me the daughter of an outcast, and one of them. I'm not sure why this never occurred to me. I guess I didn't want to see it. After all, the reason Mama is an outsider is because she had me.

June Sector hasn't moved from the door and looks at me like she's trying to get a reading.

"I'm actually here for Pearl," I say, standing straighter, doing my level best to act normal.

She calls for Pearl.

Rumors have spread for years that June Sector is a witch. But I've known her for as long as I can remember, and I've never seen her do anything witch-like. No brooms or caldrons or black clothes are in sight. Although to some people even having the secret sense is suspect, so telling fortunes is even worse. Backward ways, Mama calls them. Everybody has backward ways, she says, even people in big cities. But I don't trust what Mama says anymore. My list of reasons to leave Katy's Ridge is growing.

When I look up from my thoughts, June Sector is still at the door. "Are you staying for supper, Lily?"

It's only then I remember I'm supposed to come to supper

tonight. I can't believe I forgot about this in the midst of all the other trouble. Any other time I would have been dreamy all day with anticipation.

"I haven't asked permission yet, but I guess so," I say. At that moment, I don't care if Mama gets mad at me. I wish I could leave with Crow tomorrow and go to Korea, or anywhere far away.

If Granny finds out Mama has been kissing Miss Blackstone, I doubt Mama will be welcome to live at the house anymore. Will I have to go, too? What will we do then? Mama always tells me there are consequences to our behavior.

Well, Mama, what are the consequences of this? I want to ask her. My confusion deepens.

Even though I've seen Mama and Miss Blackstone together hundreds of times, I've never seen them smile at each other the way they did at the mill. I've never seen them hold hands or even touch. For them to be so different behind closed doors means it's a secret what they're doing, and maybe it's a dangerous secret at that.

When Pearl arrives, her hair is wet from a bath. She pulls me to the side porch where we can't be overheard.

"Lily, what's wrong? You look horrible. Have you been crying?"

I'm not sure what to say, or where to start.

"Talk to me," she says in a half-whisper. "Where were you today? You didn't come to school."

"Long story," I say, finding my voice again.

It really is a long story. I haven't even told her about the stranger who visited yesterday. A stranger named Melody, who could very well be my aunt, the sister of my daddy. My daddy being a stupid snake, as it turns out. It also turns out that Mama may be something even worse.

All of a sudden, I don't want to call him 'daddy' any more. It's like he hasn't earned it. A daddy is what Bolt and Nat have in

Uncle Daniel. A daddy is what Pearl has with Mr. Sector. It's someone who has been around and helped you with things.

My thoughts are still running even though I'm standing still. If it's okay for two women to kiss, then why have I never seen anyone doing it before? And why would Mama hang around with someone snake-like? Questions overwhelm me. Questions I may never find out the answers to since Mama—who I plan to never speak to again—is my main source for answers. I'm not even sure what Great Aunt Sadie would have to say about this.

"Talk to me," Pearl says. "You're acting like you've seen a ghost or something."

"Not a ghost," I say, thinking the apparition that's shown itself is actually a side of mama I never knew existed.

"Tell me what's happened." She grabs both of my shoulders and gives me a shake. I have to resist knocking her to the ground.

"Are you mad at me?" she asks. Her lips form a pout.

"No," I say. "I've just had a really bad day."

"I wish you'd tell me what happened," she says. "We're best friends."

I pause. I can't tell Pearl. Pearl's loose lips could sink a fleet of battleships, and no matter how angry I am at Mama and Miss Blackstone, I don't want them to get in trouble.

Seconds later, Crow and Mr. Sector come out of the forest each carrying a rifle and two rabbits. Rabbit stew is probably on the menu for supper. Crow smiles when he sees me and it reminds me of how Mama smiled at Miss Blackstone. I wonder if I'll ever be able to get that picture out of my mind.

Crow seems older than when he left to join the Army a year ago. His eyes linger on mine, as though he's noticing how much I've grown up, too. I even have a bit of a figure now. Though, honestly, not that much of one. I couldn't be Lana Turner if I tried.

Pearl gives me a poke in the ribs that nearly knocks me off the porch, and Crow grins at me again.

"See, I told you he likes you," she whispers.

I imagine Cupid's arrow aimed at my heart, but I don't have time to fall in love right now. My whole life is collapsing in a heap on the floor like a steamer trunk emptying itself of secrets. Not to mention that I'm about to disown Mama.

CHAPTER SIXTEEN

Wildflower

Running up a hill reminds you real quick how old you are, but I need to find Lily. It will be dark in an hour. When I arrive, instead of Lily, I find Mama sweeping the front porch. A ritual she does every evening for three seasons of the year. Out of breath, I stop at the bottom of the steps and lean over.

"What is it?" she asks. Her frantic voice and the alarm in her eyes give me a snapshot of history—the day they brought Daddy up this hill for the last time. The day that changed all of our lives in an instant. My biggest fear is that *this* day will change all our lives, too. Especially mine and Lily's, and maybe Bee's.

My breath still labored, Mama snaps her broom to attention. "Louisa May, if you don't tell me this instant what's going on I'm going to swat you with this broom."

"Is Lily here?" I ask.

"No she isn't," Mama says. "What's wrong?"

"I just need to talk to her." A stitch grabs my side. I lean over again to give myself relief.

"You don't run all the way up that steep hill just because you need to talk to somebody. What's happened?" she asks again.

I make sure I'm not within swatting distance. Mama is almost as dangerous with a broom as she is with a shotgun.

"You two have a falling out?" she asks, a hand on one hip.

"Yes, Mama, you could say that we've had a falling out."

I wait for her to look pleased, but she doesn't.

"Sometimes I think you spoil that girl," she says instead.

Now that my breath has returned, I feel riled. "The only thing I've spoiled Lily with is love," I say.

We exchange a stare like old times.

Mama begins to sweep again, with a fierceness that was absent before. But then she stops, like she's thought better of it. After Daddy died, she gritted her teeth and kept going, determined to plow through to the end of the row. Yet, as she ages, I've noticed her jaw loosen, as if she's given up some of her fight.

"She'll be home directly. It's almost supper time," Mama says. "That girl doesn't miss a meal."

My shoulders relax. I'm glad we're not going to fight. I don't think I could take two members of my immediate family angry at me. Not today, anyway.

I remember what June said earlier about inviting Lily over to supper. "She may be eating at Pearl's tonight," I say, to the sound of the broom hitting the wooden floor.

The swish stops. "Well, I wish somebody had told me that," Mama says. "I've cooked enough for three people."

Truth is, Mama always cooks for six, as if Daddy and all my sisters still lived at home.

"Of course, you two never think of me," she adds.

"You know that's not true," I say to her.

My anger kicks up dust again that no broom can touch. But it's not Mama that I'm angry with. It's the world. A world that says Bee and me loving each other is wrong and needs hiding. A world

where women aren't always given a choice. A world where mothers and daughters don't talk about things and misunderstand each other.

"I don't want to fight, Mama, I'm just worried about Lily."

"What did you two get in a tiff about?" Mama leans her broom against the house and sits in her porch rocker like she's all of a sudden tired. I forget sometimes that she'll soon be fifty years old.

Before answering her question, I play with the idea of being honest. What would life be like if every single one of us just told the truth? My bravery rises and falls with the swiftness of a chimney sweep.

"It's nothing really," I say. "Just a misunderstanding. If she shows up here at the house, just tell her I'm looking for her."

Mama rocks, and I catch a glimpse of her in her old age. Frail. Tired. Ready to meet up with Daddy again. Sometimes it feels like I will always be the girl I was at thirteen, and Mama will always be the same age she was back then. But time keeps rocking on. All of us in the rhythm of growing older.

My thoughts swing from Mama to Lily. For the first time I realize that—unlike me—Lily probably won't stay in Katy's Ridge her whole life. She doesn't talk about it, but I know from the books she reads that she wants to travel. She can name every state capital in the U.S., learned from a map tacked inside the bedroom closet we share. The same closet I shared with my sisters when I was growing up. Pretty soon it will be me sitting on this porch, rocking into my old age, finally getting a bedroom to myself and waiting for Lily to find time in her busy life to visit me. I don't want anything to push her away before she's ready, and this thing with Bee might give her a reason to leave too soon.

Meanwhile, Mama looks at me like I'm a place she'll never get to visit, the distance between us too great. I wish I could send her an imaginary postcard that says *I love you* and *wish you were here*.

"Don't wait supper on me, Mama. I need to find Lily, and then she and I need to talk."

"Well, don't talk her ear off," Mama says. "Not everybody thinks that talking is the cure for whatever ails a person."

"Yes, Mama," I say. I walk up on the porch and give her a kiss on the cheek.

She shoos me away like I'm a gnat circling her head, but then her mood changes, as if I'm not the only one thinking of a time when she won't be here anymore. She takes my hand and looks at me. I can't remember the last time she did such a tender, simple thing. Her touch is cool, her skin rough. She has the hands of someone who has scrubbed floors her entire life, as well as labored at a thousand other things.

"I know you haven't spoiled that child," she says.

Her words are soft, forgiving and unexpected.

"Lily is the luckiest girl in the world to have you as her mother," she begins again. She strokes my hand like she's rubbing a cool lotion into all the dry, cracked places of my soul.

My eyes water. "Thank you, Mama. That means a lot to me. It truly does."

The look she gives me is full of tenderness. I soak it in, remembering the night in the barn so many years ago, the first time I saw the love at the center of her fierceness.

"Now, go find your daughter and bring her home," she says. She pats my hand and the door to her softness closes. Yet, in a day that has shown no mercy, her tenderness feels like a moment of grace.

As the sun drops behind the mountain, I say goodbye to Mama and head back down the hill. Sometimes, we feel about as different as two people can be. Yet, over the years, we've worked at finding a path to each other, if only for moments at a time. Sometimes you don't even have to leave home to travel great distances.

CHAPTER SEVENTEEN

Lily

Mama's truck travels up the dirt road to the Sector's house and pulls up into the worn spot in the yard where people park. The driver's side door opens with a loud squeak. Worry dances across Mama's face. As only Mama can do, she strides up the walk. Proud and determined.

In the late afternoon sun, I stand on the porch and fortify myself for what's to come, making an effort to not look scared.

"I've been looking all over for you," she says to me.

Compared to Crow and Mister Sector who have just returned from hunting, Mama is tiny, though she comes across as someone who is six feet tall. She greets all the Sectors and then shoots her worried look toward June before it settles on me again. I shoot her back a look that bypasses worry and goes straight to sheer meanness.

I am not speaking to you, my look says. *I may never speak to you again.*

My expression stops her at the steps.

"We need to talk," she says to me.

"No we don't," I say, realizing I just broke my vow to never speak to her again.

Looking at her now, I see more than my mama, I see a stranger. Someone who hides things from people like the names of fathers and the people she's in love with.

"What's going on?" June asks her.

"You wouldn't believe me if I told you," Mama says.

However, the look they exchange tells me that maybe June knows. If that's true, she doesn't seem the least bit shocked or surprised.

I have never been so confused in my life, and if I weren't so worn out from running here I'd take off again.

"We need to talk, Lily," Mama says again. "Get in the truck. I'll take you home."

"I'm having supper here," I say.

"You are?" Pearl says, like it's news to her.

Meanwhile, it bothers me that Crow is a witness to all this. For someone who doesn't know what happened, I could come across as hateful. Then it dawns on me that given who my daddy is, hatefulness may be another family trait, just like lying. I ball up a fist ready to scream, or better yet, punch someone. Preferably Mama.

"We can do supper another time," June Sector says to me.

"We can't do it another time. Crow will be leaving tomorrow," Pearl says, her tone approaching a whine.

My face turns hot all over again, as though my private undergarments are hanging on the Sector's clothesline for Crow to see. Mama tells me with a look that this isn't the time or place to air our laundry, dirty or clean, and that I'd best be getting in the truck.

I cross my arms, refusing to go anywhere, and increasing the amount of trouble I'm in.

Pearl is wide-eyed, like she's wondering what's got into me. Meanwhile, Crow and Mr. Sector stand holding the dead rabbits,

and Crow is staring down at his Army boots like they could use a polish.

"Lily McAllister, I want you in that truck this instant." Mama's finger points like an arrow toward the beat up Ford she bought third-hand. Her eyes tell me that I don't want to know what will happen if I defy her. As much as I am ready to leave Katy's Ridge forever, I'd like to leave with Mama's blessing, not a curse.

Silent, heart racing, I saunter over and get in Mama's truck. I slam the door, putting so much anger into the slam that the truck rocks, the shock absorbers singing in the choir with the squeaking door.

Mama and I have never had a fight this big, much less in front of people. She gets in the driver's side of the truck and starts it. The truck sputters and clunks to life like it always does. Uncle Cecil is the only mechanic this old truck has ever seen, and he isn't even a real mechanic.

As she puts the gears in reverse and backs out, I wish I could put the day in reverse and start it all over again. This time I'd go to school like I'm supposed to, and not go anywhere near Melody Monroe. If I'd done that to begin with, I'd be about to spend the entire evening with Crow.

Sometimes one decision can set your life on a totally different path. Mama's told me this before, but it's the first time I've ever understood it. If I had inherited Mama's secret sense, I probably would have known today would turn out this way. Instead, I've been ignorant and embarrassed myself in front of Crow and his family.

Even though the day is cooling, I feel hot and roll down the window. I shake my head in disbelief that this much trouble could happen in the 24 hours since that woman showed up in Katy's Ridge. She's like a bad luck charm, if there is such a thing. Yet at this moment, Melody Monroe seems the least of my worries.

Mama wants to talk. And I'm guessing it's about what I saw at the mill, not what Melody Monroe told me.

Instead of going home, Mama pulls off on the side of the road near the river. It's a place she's never taken me before, and I thought I knew every inch of Katy's Ridge. I wonder if Granny is waiting supper for us, and figure both of us will be in plenty of trouble if she is. Then I think about all the complaining I've done over nothing ever happening in Katy's Ridge. Turns out I didn't know how lucky I was.

CHAPTER EIGHTEEN

Wildflower

Talking to Lily at home isn't an option since Mama is an expert at overhearing things. And the sawmill is definitely out, given what just happened there. I pull off at a place by the river where Daddy taught me to fish. The first fish I caught was a catfish. It was ugly as sin, as Mama would say, but was a delicacy once it was fried in cornmeal. My stomach growls just thinking about it, but my hunger will have to wait.

"Why are we stopping here?" Lily asks.

"We need to talk and we need privacy to do it," I say.

"But it's almost dark and it's getting cold," she says, as if these are things I haven't noticed.

I'm hungry and tired and have no idea what I'm going to say to my daughter. From behind the seat, I pull out one of my old jackets and hand it to her. She puts it on.

"It smells like you," she says, like she's forgotten for a moment how much she hates me.

Lily pulls the smell close. She used to crawl into my lap when

she was a little girl to smell the back of my hands and my hair, as if memorizing my scent. She is a creature of smells and songs.

What I forget sometimes is that it hasn't been that long ago that Lily was a little girl and a person in need of a mother. At fourteen, she's already practicing to be a woman. The same age I was when I had just given birth to her. If anything, seeing Lily now helps me see how young I was to have a baby. Too young. Mama had Jo when she was eighteen, but there are plenty of girls in the mountains having kids at fifteen and sixteen and dropping out of high school to raise them. Mama made sure I finished. She refused to let me be one of those girls. She kept Lily during the day so I could. She said it was what Daddy would have wanted. But she must have wanted it, too.

The day has wrung me out like a dishrag. I feel too tired to clean up the mess I made at the sawmill by not being discreet. No matter how hard it is, it's important that Lily and I talk. That last morning I saw Daddy alive, my secret sense told me to run after him and tell him how much I loved him. Unfortunately, I talked myself right out of it. I told myself I'd have plenty of time to tell him later. Well, life doesn't always give us a *later*. You have to make time to say things that need to be said.

I ran away the day Daddy died, just like Lily ran away from the sawmill. Sometimes running is the only thing we know to do. It was here that I ran, to this place by the river. A place I haven't returned to in years. Somehow, Daddy's death seems to have set everything in motion that has happened since. Not only what transpired with Johnny, but also all that's happened today. It reminds me of all those begets in the Bible that Daddy used to read to me and my sisters when we were trying to get to sleep at night. So-and-so begat so-and-so. Everything and everybody connected to what came before.

"It's getting dark, so we'll need a few things," I say to Lily. "Hand me those matches in the glove box."

Lily opens the compartment and digs out the matches. When she tries to shut it the latch doesn't grab and she slams it four times until I put my hand on hers. I latch it easily, knowing how to finesse it closed. Lily's angry look returns.

We get out of the truck and I grab the flashlight I keep in the back.

"Stay close," I say.

Lily huffs.

Who can blame her for being upset? To protect her, I've deliberately kept things from her for years. Or maybe it was more to protect me.

As we take the skinny path to the river, the flashlight offers circles of light for us to follow. Crickets voice their surprise at seeing us. The sun has dropped further behind the hillside and the river holds the last of the light. A sliver of a new moon has risen and it promises to be as dark a night as it gets in these parts.

"Gather sticks and branches for a fire," I tell her.

Thankfully, she doesn't sass me.

We rummage around the trees along the riverbank for dropped branches that we break against our knees and throw in a pile. After arranging them, I light a match and place the flame at the bottom.

"Would you like to sit?" I ask Lily. My nerves feel as jumbled as the mound of sticks I've just laid.

She shrugs and then sits near the fire, positioning the coat to sit on instead of the cold ground.

In the dim light, Lily pulls something out of her pocket. It is a sandwich wrapped in waxed paper, a toothpick piercing the thin covering like a safety pin to hold it all together. It looks like it's been in her pocket for a long time. She tears the sandwich down the middle and hands me half. It is one of Mama's leftover chicken sandwiches, with a generous helping of mayonnaise. The bread is soggy, but at that moment I've never tasted anything better. I thank

Lily for sharing. When we finish, we lick our fingers and dry them on our coats, then we sit in silence as the river gently laps the shore.

"I wish you hadn't run away," I say.

Lily doesn't answer. The only other time she was this quiet was last spring when I told her about the birds and bees, as it is commonly called. She finally confessed to reading Meg's romance novels hidden in the bedroom closet, and figuring it out on her own. Compared to the awkwardness we are experiencing now, that talk feels like nothing.

A fish jumps near the riverbank, a flash of silver in the dark water that echoes the silver of the moon. Water continues to lap gently at the shore. I am ready for this day to end, but I have things to say if Lily will listen. At least I don't have to worry about her running away this time. It is too dark to go anywhere.

The ground is cold underneath me and the fire warms my face. I throw another stick on the flame and an owl hoots in the distance, as if to ask what we're doing in his territory. I imagine him swooping down with silent wings to capture my words before I have time to speak them.

The last time I sat at this spot was the day Daddy died. My heart was breaking. At least nobody is dead this time. I take a deep breath, knowing I can't put off talking to Lily any longer. It is too cold to take the time to grow the courage I need or choose perfect words.

Still I hesitate.

Lily looks at me, her face a mixture of shadow and firelight. She wants this to be over, too. At least that's what I tell myself.

"Bee and I—Miss Blackstone and I—love each other," I begin, surprising myself with my honesty. "We've loved each other for a long time. Almost ten years now." My voice falters. "Nobody knows. We're afraid people won't understand. Not that it's any of their business, anyway. But we love each other, Lily. We truly do.

And I don't see how that's anything different from what your Aunt Jo and Uncle Daniel have."

"Except they aren't ashamed," Lily says. "That's the biggest difference, isn't it?"

I turn to look at her, wondering how she became so wise. She's right, of course. It isn't the same. Like dew on a foggy morning, shame covers every aspect of my life with Bee.

"The world is a complicated place," I say. "At your age, you're not meant to understand everything."

"Do you understand it?" she asks.

I pause. "Actually, I don't. I wish I did."

"You need to stop this," Lily says. "You need to never see her again."

Her words surprise me. They sound hard, like Mama's get sometimes. But I don't blame her for saying them. I've said the same thing to myself.

"I wish I could," I say. "Bee and I have tried to break it off many times."

"Try harder," Lily says. She pokes the fire.

"It's not as easy as it sounds," I say.

"That makes no sense at all," Lily says with another huff. I can't believe how much she sounds like Mama.

"All I know is that I'm a better person when Bee's around. A happier person," I say, determined to hold my ground.

The fire in Lily's eyes grows wilder. It is obvious she is confused and doesn't understand. I'm not sure I understand, either. In fact, I feel exhausted from all the years I've spent trying to be normal.

My shoulders drop. Emotion chokes out my words. I tell myself not to weep, but I am too tired to resist. The tears come. Not of someone grieving, but of someone defeated.

The crossness leaves Lily's face. She apologizes. I seldom let

Lily see the side of me that isn't strong. The side that is just as lost as everybody else about how to love and be loved.

"It's not your fault," I tell her, my tears slowing. I use the handkerchief Bee used earlier to dry my face, and then sit straighter. "The funny thing is, it all feels so natural. Like I've loved Bee my whole life."

My confession brings her into my arms. Our reunion brings more tears. I think of times I've held Lily while she cried. The result of scraped knees, hurtful friends and the rejections life brings, either real or imagined. I got fighting mad at whoever hurt her, and at this moment I feel fighting mad at myself. I wish I could be different.

"You shouldn't have to deal with anything like this," I say to her. "I've spent fourteen years trying to protect you from hard things."

Lily releases our embrace and sits back to stare at the fire.

"I'm not sure if I can get used to seeing you and Miss Blackstone together," she says thoughtfully. "But I think it would be the same if you fell in love with a man."

I exhale, not even realizing that I'd been holding my breath.

"I don't want to share you," she continues. "But I don't want you to be alone, either. Nobody should be alone."

She looks off into the darkness, her thoughts taking her far away.

Meanwhile, a ripple of gratitude washes over me, and the crickets turn up their volume to remind us they are here. It has been unusually warm this fall and the cricket season has been extended. I imagine this concert offers one of their last songs before winter.

For the first time this evening, I think about Melody Monroe. Daniel said Lily went over there this morning, which means we have more to talk about. It is perhaps the most important conversation we will ever have. But it seems neither of us have the strength for that one. At least not now.

"Nobody else knows about you and Miss Blackstone?" Lily asks.

"The Sectors know," I say. "Sometimes Bee and I go over for lunch on a Saturday so we can have time together where we don't have to worry about people seeing us."

"You mean Pearl knows?" Lily asks.

I nod.

"But Pearl never said a word to me, and she's never, *ever* been able to keep a secret."

"Well, she's kept this one," I say.

"Crow knows, too?" she asks.

I nod again.

"Then why didn't you tell *me*?" She looks hurt again.

"Because of what happened today," I say. "I was afraid it would scare you or make you hate me."

A possum sticks her long nose out of the brush to investigate the fire, a welcome distraction. Her beady eyes take us in, and she sniffs in our direction. She hisses at us before turning away and disappearing into the underbrush.

Bee was one of the few people in Katy's Ridge who didn't turn away from me when I was carrying Lily. My best friend Mary Jane wouldn't have anything to do with me after that. Or maybe her parents wouldn't allow it. But it was hard losing a best friend. It helps to have a big family. But we are meant to have friends, too. So it was a lonely time. People just stopped talking to me. Or did their best to avoid me.

For months after Lily was born, Bee came over every Saturday morning to help me with her. She'd bring a loaf of banana bread that her mother made. Then we'd talk about books and about different things that were happening in the world. We could talk about anything. We became really good friends. It was years later before we admitted our feelings had grown into something more than a friendship. I remember how hard those days were. Both of

us feeling crazy and bad. Feeling drawn together one minute and denying it the next.

Lily wraps her coat closer, and we stare into the crackling fire. Her confusion hasn't left her face, but it would be impossible—at least before we have our other talk—to explain how it was when I was pregnant with her.

"For a while, I didn't think I'd ever see Bee again," I say, reaching toward the fire to warm my hands. "She moved to Nashville to teach," I say. "I was heartbroken, but I understood."

"How old was I?"

"It was the summer of your third birthday."

Sticks collapse into the fire and sparks fly. I toss on more branches realizing how cold we'd be without the flames.

"I remember when she came back," Lily says. "It was such a relief not to have Mr. Collins anymore."

Lily had Mr. Collins for first and second grade. He was unmerciful in how he disciplined the boys, and Lily feared him. I don't think there was a single student or parent who wasn't relieved when Bee returned.

"She told me she couldn't stand living without me," I begin again. "Truth is, I was having a hard time living without her, too. To find somebody you truly love is a rare thing, Lily, and isn't to be taken for granted."

She turns away, and I wonder if she's thinking about Crow, her crush of many years.

A nearby bullfrog begins a throaty, vibrating call.

"Can we go home now?" Lily stands. "Granny might be worried about us."

"Do you have any more questions?" I ask.

"No," she says.

"Well, whenever you do, I'd be happy to answer them," I say.

"Okay," she says back.

She has listened. That's all that I could ask for. If she is stunned

or hurt by the news, she doesn't let on, and her anger seems to have died away like the fire. I trust her not to tell anyone what we've talked about. I imagine she wants to keep it a secret as much as I do.

With my boot, I sweep a layer of sandy soil over what's left of the embers. The world slowly becomes dark again. The moon winks at us. I turn on my flashlight and lead us back to the truck. Cold air nips at my cheeks, reminding me that winter will be arriving soon. The sounds of the river fade, and Lily is quiet. Too quiet, I decide, as we get into the truck. But I honor her need for silence.

Within a couple of minutes, we arrive back home and get out of the truck to climb the dark hill to our house, the flashlight growing dimmer with every few steps. Our footsteps join the sounds of our breathing, mine heavier than Lily's. As we walk the familiar path, I think of Bee. We will have plenty to talk about the next time we get together. I squeeze the buckeye I always carry with me. Bee and I found them on a walk together one day over at Sutter's Lake. We each carry one. Buckeyes are good luck when carried in a pocket and are even known for curing headaches.

We ascend the steepest part of the path and see our house, the single bulb on the porch calling to us like a beacon. Mama will be upset with us for coming home so late. But she will have also saved us supper in the oven, a plate covering it to hold in the heat and moisture. Some things I can count on with Mama.

Walking up the porch steps, I am reminded of the year the country fair came to Rocky Bluff. It was the first time I ever rode a roller coaster. Today has felt just as harrowing.

CHAPTER NINETEEN

Lily

Mama falls asleep fast, her breathing deepening into her usual light snore. After what happened at the mill today, we didn't even have a chance to talk about my visit to see Melody and what I found out there. In some ways it feels like an entire week has been crammed into this one day. All that's happened weighs heavy on me like Great Aunt Sadie's quilt that Mama put on the bed tonight. No matter how much I wish for it, sleep refuses to come.

I try to imagine loving someone and having to keep it a secret. I think of Crow. Not everyone in Katy's Ridge is accepting of the Sectors. If I married Crow, people might look at me the same way. Not to mention any children we have.

It dawns on me how difficult the world can be if you're the least bit different. Who is it, exactly, that decided that white people rule the world, and everybody else is out of luck? Or maybe it's that men rule the world and women don't get to rule anything, except maybe the kitchen and the babies.

My frustration pushes me out of bed.

Mama startles awake. "You okay, sweetheart?" she asks sleepily.

"Can't sleep. Going into the living room to read," I whisper.

"Make yourself warm milk," she whispers back, and then mumbles like she's talking to someone in her dreams.

The bedroom dark, I've long since memorized every inch of it. I know the floorboards that creak and the way to turn the closet doorknob so that it doesn't stick. I slide on a pair of corduroy pants Aunt Amy made for me to go with a wool sweater that was a gift from Great Aunt Sadie. I grab my shoes and socks to put on in the kitchen. Once I make it to the hallway, I find my way through the house with the help of the light in the bathroom that Granny leaves on with the door cracked. I am good at being quiet. As the resident night owl, it's required.

In the kitchen, I open the refrigerator and drink milk right out of the bottle. I take the last slice of apple pie left over from the anniversary. The clock on the wall reaches its hands toward midnight. After putting on my socks and shoes, I slip on Granddaddy's old coat that Granny puts on to go feed the chickens. Then I step out onto the back porch.

The chilly night air prickles my face, but otherwise I feel warm in the coat that used to swamp me with its size. To the right of the back door is the small bench where Granny keeps a big flashlight. I test it to make sure the batteries are good. A warm glow lights the way ahead. For a moment, I shine the artificial light under the porch and see Pumpkin and his kin curled next to each other, unmoving, only mildly curious about why I'm not curled up in my own bed.

The moon is of no help tonight as I walk around the side of the house where the two bedroom windows are. I step as lightly as I can, not wanting to wake up Granny and her shotgun. It is only when I get to the Red Bud Sisters that I let myself make my usual walking noises. Meanwhile, the crickets throb in the forest, their

voices weak with autumn. Like my bedroom, I know every inch of the path down the hill. Yet it looks different at night and things scurry away out of sight.

The night shift, Mama calls them. Those animals that do their hunting and visiting at night.

When I get to Mama's truck, I touch the hood, as though it might still hold warmth from hours before. However, it is as cold as the night.

The sound of my footsteps on the pavement keeps me company as I walk. I note the distinctive sound of the soles of my shoes, mixed with my stride. Just like no two fingerprints are ever alike, that probably goes for footsteps, too. I skip a few steps just to break up the rhythm and think of a song I heard on the radio by a new singer named Elvis Presley. Music is what keeps me company best, yet no sound comes. Any songs I might sing seem to have been stolen by the events of the day.

As I pass Aunt Jo and Uncle Daniel's place, a single light outside the barn produces a whitish yellow glow. Dew moistens my face and the flashlight illuminates the fog that gathers along the river. The world is completely quiet, and it feels like a dream I might be having if I was sleeping right now.

I begin to hear other footsteps echoing in the night and pause mid-step, searching for sounds in the darkness. Nothing. I tell myself I imagined it. Besides, who in the world would be out here walking in the middle of the night except me? The whispers start again as I pass the old trail that leads to the cemetery. It seems odd that Mama didn't hear the whispers, too. Usually she's the one that notices things like that. She tried to convince me it was the wind in the trees at the bottom of the ravine, or the shape of the hillside that made the whispers, but I didn't believe that for a second. The flashlight falters, and I refuse to get scared. I shake it to renew its strength. It flickers twice, then a third time, but continues to light the way. In the distance, at

about eye level, a tiny red glow is suspended in the woods. It looks like a lightning bug that's on fire, with a red glow instead of gold.

The whispers get louder and the red glow grows more intense. I stop walking, my heart looking for a way to escape my chest.

"You hear it, too?" a voice says. I jump like someone's goosed me.

I recognize the voice and shine my light toward the woods and see Melody Monroe. She is smoking a cigarette at the entrance to the path to the cemetery.

"Hear what?" I say.

She sits in the pitch black of night without a flashlight or anything.

"Turn off that light," she says. "It's hurting my eyes."

Reluctantly I do, and the darkness gets darker.

"You hear that?" she says, from inside the darkness.

"Hear what?" I repeat, my frustration growing.

"The whispers," she says, herself whispering.

A sudden chill passes through me.

She inhales and the red tip of her cigarette glows brighter like a monster with a single red eye.

"Yeah, I hear it," I say.

"Who do you think that is?" she says.

"Who?" I say.

Our two voices reach toward the night. I wonder if this is what it's like to be a ghost and not have a body that's yours anymore.

Whenever Melody inhales her cigarette, the faint glow outlines her face. Underneath the smell of cigarettes, I smell something sour, like moonshine.

"Who do you think is whispering to us?" she asks again, her words slurring.

I don't answer and wonder if I should continue on to the Sectors or turn around and go back home.

"I think the whispers are your daddy," she says. "I think it's Johnny."

I gasp, before I can stop myself.

"Your mama told me today that he slipped on icy rocks and fell down the mountain," she begins again. "It would be around here where they found him. Near that old footbridge. You know the one?"

"I know it," I say.

"Maybe we should get closer so we can hear him better," she says.

A shiver of cold caresses my neck, and I reach for the gold medallion Mama gave me and find it missing. I search my pockets and then shine the light on the ground. Melody whines for me to turn it off. Mama is going to kill me for losing it, but I'll have to search for it another time. I'm not going anywhere near that footbridge, not in the middle of the night, and not without my necklace to protect me and certainly not with Melody Monroe who smells like a giant jar of moonshine mixed with stale cigarettes.

"What do you think Johnny's trying to tell us?" Her words continue to slur. "Do you think he's trying to tell us who his murderer was?"

"Murderer?" I ask.

Melody laughs.

"Oh, that's right, your mama said he fell."

She is silent now, as though letting her words have time to sink in.

"So, what are you doing out here in the middle of the night?" she asks.

I could ask her the same. "I couldn't sleep," I say. "I was just taking a walk."

She lights another cigarette off the one that's almost finished. Then she flips one of the tiny red glows to the ground.

She stands and then stumbles toward me. I take a step back and feel her reaching toward my arm.

"What are you doing?" I say into the blackness.

"I'm going to introduce you to your daddy."

She lunges forward and this time grabs my arm instead of air. "Hey, stop it!" I say. Her grip is strong for someone who has been drinking all night.

"Johnny would like you," she says. "Probably like he liked my sister."

The laugh that follows doesn't have any humor in it. Melody seemed much nicer in the light of day.

"Come on, girl," she says, trying to drag me.

"Let me go!" I jerk away and she loses her grip. I turn on the flashlight and shine it right into her eyes. She winces and puts her hands up as protection from the light. It's then that I realize how weak she is, and the fear I felt moments ago drifts away on the cold breeze.

"Well, if you're not going with me to hear what Johnny has to say, I guess I'll go by myself," she says. "Knowing Johnny, he'll probably give me an earful about how your mama was the one that killed him. But knowing Johnny, he probably deserved to get killed."

"Mama would never kill somebody," I say.

"You'd be surprised what people will do," she says, as though she's had experience in being surprised. "You be careful," she adds. "All sorts of ghosts out here."

But she is the one stumbling around. She is the one that needs to be careful. I think of the footbridge she will have to cross to make it to the cemetery and wonder if she can stay upright long enough to cross it. She goes in that direction, and I call out for her to be careful. She trips and cusses and then pulls herself up again.

When her footsteps finally fade, I turn on the flashlight again, grateful to have the way illuminated. At the boulder where Melody

sat are the butts of several cigarettes, as though she'd been sitting there a long time.

How dare she say that Mama killed someone. Mama would never resort to violence to solve anything. Granny might, but not Mama. I tell myself to forget about running into Melody Monroe and try to shake the creepiness away, but it sticks to me like the falling dew.

Halfway between both places, I wonder whether to go back home or to the Sectors. In the next second the wind picks up, and the whispers return, this time louder. I listen for a message on the wind that will solve this mystery once and for all.

CHAPTER TWENTY

Wildflower

In the dream, Lily is about to fall into the ravine. Over the years, I've had this dream a dozen times and was reminded of it yesterday before Melody Monroe arrived. It always gets my heart racing. Awake, I tell myself it isn't real. That everything is all right. But something feels terribly wrong. To reassure myself, I reach a hand over to Lily's side of the bed. I roll over and touch the other side of the mattress. I sit up in bed.

"Lily?" I call, not caring if I wake up Mama. "Lily?" I call louder.

I get up and turn on the light, stepping into my slippers and then putting on my robe. I open the door and find Mama in the hallway.

"What's wrong?" she says, shotgun in hand. Her long gray hair drapes down her back. I hadn't realized Mama's hair had grown so long.

"Are you sleeping with that thing now?" I ask, pointing to the shotgun.

She doesn't answer.

"Do you know where Lily is?" I ask.

"No idea," she says. "Maybe she's reading in the kitchen."

I follow Mama into the empty kitchen. A plate sits by the sink, evidence that Lily has had a snack. Mama never leaves even one plate or cup unwashed before bed.

I turn on the back porch light and step outside. Winter is close. I can feel it in the breeze. "Lily?" I call again.

Mama steps outside, too. "My flashlight's gone," she says. "And Joseph's coat."

"Where would she go on a night like this?" I ask, more to myself than Mama.

"You two have a fight?" Mama says.

She sits the shotgun next to the door, perhaps ruling out foul play unless I've caused it.

I pause to think, rubbing warmth into my arms. "I brushed her hair before bedtime. I thought we were back on good terms."

"It's hard to know with Lily," Mama says. "She's much quieter than you are about things."

We go back into the house. "I wish we had a telephone," I say to her. "Now I've got to wake up Daniel and Jo."

"Who would you call?" she asks.

"Pearl, I guess."

"June would have sent word already if Lily was over there. She wouldn't want you to worry."

Mama's right. June would have sent Horatio over here in the middle of the night just to set my mind at ease.

"Where is she, Mama?" I ask.

With no answers, she looks as worried as I feel.

To make sure we haven't missed her, Mama and I search in every room. Our house is small enough that it doesn't take long. There are no real hiding places in this house. The closets are small and have too many things inside to hide a person. Quilts are stored under the bed. I go to the front door and turn on the porch light

and go outside. I call Lily again. Then I remember Melody Monroe standing in the yard. Could she be at Melody's?

I run into the house and throw on my clothes from the day before. Mama studies my every move, telling me not to panic, but she doesn't look that calm, either.

"I'm going to drive over to the Monroe place and see if she went over there," I say.

"Surely she wouldn't have," Mama says.

Lily's whole life has turned upside down in these last two days. I'm not sure what she will do anymore. I take the flashlight I used the night before and go into the kitchen to find new batteries. Luckily Mama has one package left.

"Do you want me to come?" Mama says, looking around for her shotgun.

"It's on the back porch," I tell her, "but no, I don't want you to come."

She looks relieved.

"Maybe you should go get Daniel," she says.

"No need to wake everybody up, at least not yet," I say. "Let me go over to Melody's and just make sure she's not there."

It's the fastest I've gone down the hill in a long time. The truck complains when I start it, like an old man not wanting to turn over and get out of bed. I don't give it time to warm up before I pull out and drive down the road toward the crossroads. I park where I did the day before and head into the woods with the flashlight. I can't imagine what Melody might have told Lily. We never got to talk about that yesterday. Melody has no way of knowing the whole story, anyway. Though from what she said to me, she has guessed some of it.

After a day of sunshine, the mud is less sloppy in places but it is still slow going. The cabin door is open and the light is on. It looks like somebody might have just stepped out to get a piece of fire-wood for the wood stove. I call Melody's name. Then Lily's.

"You in there?" I ask, stepping onto the front porch. My heartbeat quickens. I wonder if Melody has a shotgun she keeps close like Mama does.

An empty jar of moonshine sits on the table, as well as the same faded china cup with the chip on the handle. There's a letter beside the cup, and I step close enough to read it. It's addressed to someone I don't recognize, probably Melody's aunt, and it is signed Lester, short for Doc Lester. I pick it up and hurriedly try to make out his messy scrawl.

Doc Lester writes Melody's aunt that she might want to meet Lily. That she is a special young lady. He tells her that she sings at the church, and then he says something about me. I shine the light closer. *Her mama doesn't deserve her. She's a bad influence,* he writes. *As her next of kin, you should come and take her back with you.*

His words frighten me. There's never been any love lost between us, but I never thought he hated me enough to think me unfit.

I search the room to see if Melody's things are gone. Could she have taken Lily back to Kentucky on the bus tonight? My body tenses. But her open purse is still on the bed, revealing the wadded dollar bills she offered me earlier. She hasn't gone far without any money. But where has she gone on this dark night? I go outside again and up the slight rise to the outhouse. I pass the huge oak tree where Melody's sister Ruby hung herself when I was twelve. A branch, as big as I am, has broken off and fallen to the ground. I shine a flashlight into the top of the tree and remember Ruby's funeral—easily the saddest I've ever attended, aside from Daddy's. A shiver climbs the back of my neck.

At the outhouse, I call Melody's name again. Something scurries away, and I catch the tail of a raccoon in the beam of my flashlight.

If Melody and Lily are together, where would they go? My secret sense answers me and I stop cold. Half running, half trying

not to trip, I make my way back to the truck. I drive past our house and driveway and stop on the road at the beginning of the path to the cemetery. Cigarette butts are tossed next to the boulder in front of the gnarled dogwood tree that marks the beginning of the path. I remember the dream that woke me earlier. Lily falling. Lily falling into the ravine. Forcing myself awake before she landed.

Aiming the flashlight up the path, I begin to run. Every few yards I call out Lily's name. When I get to the footbridge, I stop to catch a jagged breath. I shine the light down into the ravine, but its beam doesn't reach the bottom. I call for both Melody and Lily, my shout edging toward a scream. But the forest is quiet. Dead quiet. I remember how Lily said she heard whispers here, and I wonder what the ravine would have to say if it could speak. Would it tell the story of Johnny's death? Johnny lying dead at the bottom. My gold medallion around his neck? Sadness reaches for me in the darkness, as if tapping me on the shoulder to get my attention. It is an old sadness. One I haven't felt in a long time.

The wind shifts in the trees, and the sound of the rushing water drifts from below. I remind myself that a forest at night isn't a scary thing for me. Daddy would take me fishing in the middle of the night or he'd take me and my sisters to a dark meadow to count lightning bugs. Daddy made nighttime seem magical instead of scary. Yet the darkness tonight feels different. The night is hiding something from me.

Searching for relief from my panic, I shine the flashlight into the forest. It feels like someone is watching me, but I see no one. I call out Lily's name. I wait, listening for an answer. When none comes, I turn around and retrace my steps, pleading with the angels and demons of the past to not let history repeat itself.

CHAPTER TWENTY-ONE

Lily

A fter walking down the middle of the dirt road that leads to the Sector's house, I question what I'm doing here. Not being able to sleep was part of it, and then running into Melody Monroe. But also, I want to see Crow before he leaves.

One light is on in the kitchen window of the small farmhouse. It occurs to me how easy it would be to spy on people if a person wanted to. I turn off my flashlight and let the kitchen light guide me in. It could be anybody in that kitchen. Horatio or June, or any of their four kids, Crow being the oldest.

Please, God, let it be Crow, I say out loud.

Mama says she and God aren't on speaking terms anymore. But how can you see a gold Mary and be mad at God at the same time? Aren't they related? I step closer, grateful that the curtains were left open. A lone figure sits at the kitchen table reading a book, his back to the window.

Thank you, I say, looking up into the starless night.

I tap on the window and shine the flashlight to light up my face. Crow smiles. He opens the kitchen door.

"What are you doing here?" he whispers.

"I couldn't sleep," I whisper back.

"I couldn't either," he says. His smile feels as bright as the flashlight I've just turned off.

He invites me to sit at the kitchen table. I've never seen Crow in his pajamas. He asks if I want a cup of coffee, and I say yes even though I never drink it. He asks if I want cream and sugar, and I say yes to that, too. Truth is I'd probably say *yes* to anything Crow suggested. I pretend I know what I'm doing and add cream and sugar until the liquid turns the color of Crow's skin. I take a sip and then turn away to make a face, unsure how anyone could drink something so bitter.

Before Crow joined the Army, his black hair dropped down into his eyes and he had this habit of tossing his hair to the side so he could see. Now his head is completely shaved, and I miss the long hair that made him so much of who he is.

"I'm glad you came," he says, as we continue our conversation in whispers.

His grin reveals the dimple he was famous for at Rocky Bluff High School. Despite his mixed race, he played on the football team and was quite popular. The number of touchdowns he got on Friday nights mattered more to the townspeople than who his daddy was. Although, that didn't mean girls were allowed to date him. At least that's what Pearl told me. I find myself hoping she doesn't wake up and find me here or this time will become all about her.

"Don't tell Pearl I was here," I say.

"I won't," he says, showing off his dimple again. "Best not to tell anybody."

I nod, thinking about what Granny would do if she found out I

was sitting with Crow while he was wearing his flannel pajamas. Not that Mama would like it one bit, either.

"Hey, you want to go out by the creek?" he asks. "There's a couple of chairs out there and we won't have to whisper."

I think of the voices near the footbridge, and wonder if there's any truth to my daddy trying to get messages to me.

"It's cold outside," I say. "You probably wouldn't want to wear just your pajamas."

He goes to change. While he's gone I get familiar with the kitchen clock shaped like a rooster whose tail clicks back and forth with every second that goes by. I try another sip of coffee and rush over to spit it out in the sink. I pour the whole cup down the drain and wash out the cup and dry it and put it back in the cabinet so no one will know I was here. Listening to all those detective radio shows with Granny has taught me a few things about hiding evidence.

After Crow returns in regular clothes and a coat, we go out the kitchen door. Once we're outside, I turn on my flashlight again. Crow takes my hand and leads me to the creek. He's never held my hand before and despite the growing coldness of the night my body feels warm. The sound of the creek gets louder with each step and we stop at two wooden chairs sitting on a little rise. When I've visited Pearl, I've seen her parents sit out here in the evenings. We sit and the dew on the arms of the chairs soaks into my palms. I pull Granddaddy's coat closer and turn off the flashlight to save the batteries so I can get home.

In the daylight, this is a beautiful spot and even now the sound is beautiful, a trickling melody flowing between river rock. We don't have to whisper any longer, but the words have escaped us.

Finally, it is Crow who speaks first. "I don't want to go back," he says, as though the darkness has invited honesty.

"What?" I say, unable to hide my surprise. "I thought you liked the Army."

"I like getting paid," he says. His words have a smile in them, even though I can't see it.

"Don't you like going to new places?" I ask, thinking I would sign up this minute if I could.

"Not really," he says. "I'd rather be right here in Katy's Ridge. That's why I couldn't sleep. I don't look forward to leaving tomorrow."

The dream Pearl and I have had forever is that Crow comes with us to live in a big city where we would all live together. A dream from which I now feel rudely awakened. How are Crow and I going to end up together if he never wants to leave Katy's Ridge? All of a sudden I wish I was home and in my bed. This day has gone on too long. But at the same time, I like sitting with him here in the dark.

"How long do you have left?" I ask.

"Another year," he says, like a year is a long time away from home. "Why couldn't *you* sleep?" he asks.

I pause, feeling protective of Mama, but then remember that all the Sectors know.

"I just found out about Mama and Miss Blackstone," I say. "Actually, I found out accidentally. I was spying on them and saw them kiss."

Something about the near total darkness of the new moon invites confessions, and I wonder what he would confess to me if he had a chance. But perhaps he already has, about wanting to stay in Katy's Ridge forever.

"Are you okay?" he asks.

"Well, not okay enough to sleep," I say, with a short laugh.

The darkness is like wearing a blindfold, and I wish I could see his face to see his reaction to my words. Instead, I can only feel the nearness of him—the warmth of our arms sitting close to each other on the chairs.

"Your mama and Bee are good people," he says. "I don't see any harm in them loving each other."

"But what will people say?" I ask.

He pauses, and I wonder if he's upset with me. "Do you know how many people like me there are in the Army?" he asks. "Half-Cherokee and half-white? If I cared what people said, I'd be miserable."

He moves his arm, and I feel his warmth go away. "But how do you not care?" I ask, my question genuine. "I care if people like my singing. I care if people might judge Mama and treat her badly. Aren't those normal things to care about?"

His warmth returns and, even wearing a coat, the hairs on my arms reach toward his.

"I don't pretend to have any answers, Lily." His voice softens. "I just don't want you to get hurt, is all. People can be mean, so you got to at least pretend that you don't care. Otherwise, it lets the mean people win."

I wonder if it's true that my father was famous for his meanness. At least his sister thinks so. I won't confess any of this new information to Crow tonight. What he might think is another thing I care about. Not that he would judge me for it. At least I don't think so. I also won't tell him about the whispers near the footbridge. This seems too crazy to confess to anyone, much less someone I want to like me.

In the cool darkness, his fingers reach toward mine. We clasp hands with intertwining fingers, and I can hear the blood rushing in my ears. Not that I'm scared. It's more like I'm too excited to sit still, and at the same time don't want to move. We listen to the sound of a mountain stream singing its song in the middle of the night. Crow is eighteen and feels a world older than me. While I have only been as far as Rocky Bluff, he's left Katy's Ridge. He's been on a plane. He's flown to other countries. Even Melody Monroe went to Louisville, Kentucky to live with her aunt. It's

hard to imagine that all Crow wants to do after seeing the world is come home to boring Katy's Ridge.

The new moon peeks through the trees. My face is cold compared to the warmth of Crow's hand. I've waited for years for him to realize he loves me. But none of that matters if it means I have to live in Katy's Ridge forever. A thought that causes my throat to tighten.

I hope Mama doesn't wake up to find me gone. I should have left a note just in case. I wouldn't want to worry her. But she was exhausted when she went to bed, so I doubt she'll wake up before morning.

"I'd better get back," I say.

He releases my hand so quickly I have to resist reaching for it.

"Try not to give your mama a hard time," he says, as though finishing all he meant to say. "Bee's a good person."

He stands, his shape towering over me like a mountain.

"I do want Mama to have someone in her life who loves her," I say. "I just don't want her to get hurt."

"We all get hurt," he says. "No way to avoid it."

Crow acts more mature since he went away, and I wonder if that's what happens when you enlist in the Army.

"Let me walk you to the road," he says.

The flashlight stays in my coat pocket. We've made peace with the darkness, and I can make out the shapes of things now. In the span of an hour, I've become a nocturnal animal.

After hearing my footsteps alone on the way here, it is intriguing to get in step with another person. At the paved road, we stop. Given he's going to leave for Korea tomorrow, we have goodbyes to say. However, we both appear too awkward to say them. Crow pats me on the shoulder and says he'll see me later, and I repeat the same thing back to him. It's the best we can do and it will have to be enough.

As I walk toward the house, the night feels colder. I pull Grand-

daddy's jacket close, and wish for about the hundredth time that I had known him. I turn on the flashlight again, letting it lead me home. In the quietness, I remember the feeling of Crow's hand in mine. I've never held hands with a boy. A boy who is almost a man.

When I pass the boulder, the whispers call for me again. If my father has something to say to me, he will have to wait. All I can think about is sleep.

As I climb the hill to our house, I notice every light is on. Mama is standing on the porch looking frantic, a flashlight in her hand. It is only then that I realize how much trouble I am in.

CHAPTER TWENTY-TWO

Wildflower

The light from the other flashlight bounces up the hill. It is Lily. My relief comes out as anger.

"You scared the life out of me," I say, when Lily reaches the porch. "Where have you been?" I clutch the top of my robe, suddenly feeling the cold air again. "Were you at Melody's?"

"I was at Pearl's," Lily says, avoiding looking at me, which means there's more to the story than she's saying. "Why would you think I was at Melody's?" she asks.

I pause. I don't have an answer, except that my worst fear was that Lily was already in Kentucky.

She steps inside the house and leaves her shoes at the door. Inside, she tosses Daddy's coat onto the back of the sofa. I resist yelling at her to put away her things.

"By my watch, it's three in the morning," I say, following her into the kitchen. "What were you doing at Pearl's? I woke up at 1 o'clock and couldn't find you."

Mama stands at the kitchen table, where she's been holding a prayer meeting all by herself.

"I made coffee," she says to me. Then she stands and gives Lily a look like she's glad she's not her. It is unlike Mama to stay out of things, but I'm glad she is. "I'm going back to bed," she adds, and closes the door so Lily and I can talk.

"Was Pearl up in the middle of the night?" I ask.

Without answering, Lily gets a glass of milk from the refrigerator, drinks it down and then places the glass in the sink. She seems tired, but also distracted. Not to mention, silent.

"I don't care how angry you are," I begin again. "That gives you no excuse for taking off in the middle of the night without leaving a note."

"I'm not angry at you," she says.

"Then why would you go to Pearl's?" I ask.

Lily hesitates. Her shoulders drop. "Don't get mad," she says.

I wait. Anytime a conversation is prefaced with *don't get mad*, I know it's something guaranteed to anger me.

"I was actually talking to Crow," she says.

"In the middle of the night?" My voice reaches toward a shriek, and I sound like Mama.

Lily turns to face me. "I couldn't sleep after all that happened yesterday, so I went to see Pearl but she was sleeping." Lily's words race to explain. "But then I saw Crow was in the kitchen so I knocked on the window, and he invited me in. He was having trouble sleeping, too."

"What did you two do?" I forget how much I like Crow, and that I've known him since he was a baby. He is a man now. Eighteen years old while Lily is fourteen.

"We just talked." Lily's cheeks flush.

I tell myself not to overreact, and my worry returns about history repeating itself. Until now, it never occurred to me how much I fear Lily finding herself with a baby at fourteen. I stand

and go to the sink, washing her glass, not knowing what else to do.

"What did you talk about?" I ask, trying to stay calm.

"We talked about how lucky you are to have Bee," Lily says. "And about how it doesn't matter what people say. And how everybody gets hurt, whether we want to or not."

"You talked about all that?" I ask.

"That, and about how he can't wait to get back to Katy's Ridge." Lily sits at the table. She seems to have matured overnight. For a few seconds, I get a secret sense that somehow life will be kind to her.

"I was selfish for wanting things different," Lily says, looking at me.

"Selfish?" I ask.

"You should get to love whoever you want to," she says, as though convinced.

Lily stands, and I wonder if I imagined what she just said. She tells me she has to go to bed, and kisses me on the cheek before leaving the kitchen. I pour myself a cup of coffee and sit back at the kitchen table. I feel grateful to Crow, and really all of the Sectors. I allow myself to fantasize about it being a different world, where Bee and I don't have to pretend we're only friends.

For years, I've feared what might happen if Lily found out. By the time I went to bed last night I had decided that she would warm to Bee eventually, if we were patient and lucky. It never occurred to me that her acceptance might come so fast, though it sounds like Crow's response helped. Of course, her understanding could also be short-lived.

While searching for Lily, I questioned whether I should break it off with Bee. That seemed the safest thing to do. I have a business here, and if anybody else finds out, I could lose it. I know these people. It took them nearly a decade to grant me eye contact after Lily was born. Then I remember my next set of worries: Melody

Monroe. I want her to leave. Sooner rather than later. And if she comes near Lily again, Mama won't be the only one looking for the shotgun.

After the sun comes up, Mama comes into the kitchen where I remain sitting.

"Louisa May, did you not go back to bed?"

"Couldn't sleep," I say.

Mama puts on her apron, as she does first thing every morning, and sits in her place at the table. I pour her a cup of warmed over coffee and place it in front of her. A cat scratches at the kitchen door, as if noting that the McAllister Diner is now open.

"Will you let Pumpkin in?" she asks.

"I thought you hated cats," I say, remembering a time when she threatened to drown them all.

"I do," she says. "But this old boy and I have become friends."

Secrets everywhere, I say to myself, including my own.

Mama drinks her coffee without speaking as Pumpkin sits in her lap. When you've spent your whole life with someone, surprises are rare.

"You're awfully quiet this morning," Mama says.

It isn't like her to notice my quietness.

The cat arches his boney backside and lifts his rump to enjoy the last benefits of Mama stroking him. Pumpkin and I exchange a look, and I can almost hear him bragging about how he won her over.

"How did your talk go last night? Before Lily pulled her disappearing act."

Directness is not like Mama.

"It went okay," I say.

She knows better than to ask me details. We McAllisters aren't big talkers.

"Where was she last night?" she asks.

"She was with Pearl," I say, deciding a half-lie is better than the truth in this instance.

"Growing pains?" To Mama, no matter what age you are, every problem in life has something to do with growing pains.

"In a way," I say, thinking that Lily has certainly grown in knowledge about me and Bee.

Mama lowers her voice. "Is it about that Melody woman?"

I pause. "I went to see her yesterday morning."

Mama stands, dumping Pumpkin off her lap. He lands on his feet, but looks up at her like he should have known not to trust her. She opens the kitchen door and shoos him outside. He turns and looks at her with what I take as disgust.

"You went to visit that woman?" Mama says, now standing over me.

Mama is not an overly large woman, but the force of her question causes me to scoot back in my chair.

"This isn't the day to test me, Mama."

Our eyes lock, like our horns have plenty of times. But neither of us wants to fight.

She backs off and sits in her chair.

"I went to ask Melody what she was going to tell Lily."

"What did she say?" Mama asks.

"She said she wouldn't tell Lily anything unless Lily asks."

"And you think Lily won't ask?"

I sigh.

Despite Mama's grumbling, I don't have the energy to tell her that Lily skipped school yesterday and that she's already talked to Melody. Nor will I tell her what Lily saw at the mill.

"I don't understand why Melody Monroe would show up in the first place," Mama says. "Is that place of hers even livable?"

"Barely," I say. "You should see it, Mama. It's so small and sad. I can't believe a whole family used to live there."

Mama nods. "Mabel Monroe used to take in people's laundry,

and they sold practically everything they had just to get by. Your Daddy would drop things by to help out. He even gave them two good laying hens," she continues. "Arthur worked for a while at the mill, but he only came half the time, so Joseph had to let him go."

This is the most I've ever heard Mama say about the Monroe family.

"What else did Melody say?" she asks.

I hesitate, wondering how much to tell her. "She wants Lily to visit Kentucky. Evidently her aunt sent money so Melody and Lily could go back on the bus."

"Over my dead body," Mama says. "Don't you dare let that child go anywhere near those people."

I nod. For once in my life, Mama and I are in full agreement.

A knock on the front door breaks the growing tension. Mama stays in the kitchen, tidying up, and I go to see who it is. When I open the door, Bee is standing on the porch.

"What are you doing here?" I say, surprised to see her.

"I brought banana bread." She holds up the basket that looks like her mother packed it. Like me, Bee is not much of a cook, but her mother is. "I was worried," she adds in a whisper.

Bee is dressed in her Sunday best, even though it's only Saturday. I forgot how concerned she must have been, not hearing from me last night, but I was certain she would already be in bed by the time Lily and I got back to the house. I was also too tired to go back to the mill or to Daniel and Jo's to use the phone.

"I'm not sure this is a good idea," I say to her.

"Are we okay?" Her eyes don't leave mine.

Mama steps up behind me and Bee beams a smile at her.

"Anybody in the mood for banana bread?" Her eyebrows raise with the question.

Mama invites her inside and tells me to go get dressed. Greeting guests in a housecoat and slippers is never encouraged. Granny leads Bee into the warm kitchen, and I go into the

bedroom to change. Lily is sleeping, her head covered to shield her from the morning sun making its way into the room.

I get dressed, run a brush through my hair and pull it back with a rubber band. When I glance into the small round mirror on the wall by the door, I practice a smile, even though I don't feel like smiling.

When I go back to the kitchen, Mama has put on a fresh pot of coffee and is just unwrapping the basket with the banana bread inside. She makes the noises she only makes for company, telling Bee how sweet she is to bring banana bread by. Mama can be practically friendly sometimes, and not just at church. Perhaps Bee has encouraged her by wearing church clothes to the house.

After filling coffee cups, Mama returns to the table where Bee and I sit. I feel jittery after all the coffee I've had, not to mention the secret sitting here in the kitchen between us.

"Banana bread is my favorite," I say to Bee, as if this is something she doesn't know.

"I remembered that," Bee answers.

At that moment, we act like acquaintances instead of what we really are. At least Lily knows now, and is reaching toward acceptance, thanks to Crow. When I try to imagine Mama's reaction if she knew our secret, all I can see is a shotgun pointing toward Bee. I shut down my imagination before she has time to pull the trigger. Whatever the scenario, I can't imagine it would be good.

"Did Louisa May tell you about the stranger who came to visit us two days ago?" Mama asks Bee. Whenever Mama calls me by my given name, I wonder if I'm in trouble. When I was younger, I wished sometimes that *Jane Eyre* had been her favorite book, instead of *Little Women,* since Charlotte is a much more glamorous name than Louisa May. At least to me.

"Lou—isa did tell me," Bee says, with an awkward glance in my direction. When we are alone together, Bee calls me Lou, and it isn't like her to slip and call me that in front of someone.

"That Melody woman stood there in the front yard as brazen as a hussy," Mama says. Calling someone *hussy* is as mean as Mama gets in front of company.

"I remember her brother Johnny. I went to school with him," Bee says. "We were in the same grade."

I turn to look at her. "I'd forgotten about that," I say, which is true. Somehow, I always think of Bee teaching school, not being taught.

Mama mumbles something under her breath about Johnny that I decide to let drop.

Bee glances at me periodically to determine if we are okay, and I try to reassure her with a glance that everything is fine. Though I'm convinced nothing will be fine until Melody Monroe leaves Katy's Ridge for good.

A railroad of secrets chugs along underneath all the polite conversation, while the three of us enjoy the banana bread. We are only one secret away from Mama throwing Bee out of her house, and probably me along with her. If I liked drama, this might be exciting. But as it is, I'm trying not to choke on the banana bread.

CHAPTER TWENTY-THREE

Lily

Voices wake me, and I try to decipher who is here. The smell of banana bread propels me to get dressed. When I enter the kitchen, I expect to see Great Aunt Sadie, who often brings over whatever she's made that day, but instead I find Miss Blackstone sitting at our kitchen table.

Seeing her reminds me of the kiss and a grumpiness descends like the fog that is just now rising along the river valley. Talking to Crow last night helped with the situation, but I didn't anticipate how I would feel seeing the two of them together again.

I greet Miss Blackstone, sounding less than thrilled, and Granny sends me a look that reminds me to respect my elders. I offer a 'sorry' as I sit at the table. This is more than I wanted to face this morning, especially after so little sleep.

While I take a piece of banana bread, I push away the scene that replays of Mama and Miss Blackstone in the mill office. I wonder if a person can wash out their eyes with soap to clean away something they've seen. Mama looks like she's seeing inside my

thoughts and isn't pleased. I try to remember how happy she looked when she and Miss Blackstone were together, but this does little to soften my mood.

Mama and Miss Blackstone exchange cautious looks, like they're afraid I'll tell Granny their secret. But I have no desire to see World War III erupt right in the middle of the kitchen.

The conversation steers toward safe things. Mama and Miss Blackstone glance at me like they've known me my whole life, but I've all of a sudden become a stranger. While I've seen them together hundreds of times, I've never given it a thought. But now I'm remembering everything. Sometimes on Sunday afternoons they'd read together in the living room. Other times they'd go into Rocky Bluff together on a Saturday to see a movie or to run errands. Mama would often be invited over to Miss Blackstone's house for supper, and she wouldn't get home until after I'd fallen asleep. Later she'd say they'd played a long game of Scrabble that Mama won. She'd even throw in the words she won with like zenith or cosmos. Maybe if I'd had Mama's secret sense, I would have known about them a long time ago.

After finishing her coffee, Miss Blackstone announces that she'd best be getting home. Mama stands, almost too eager to walk her to the door.

I need to talk to Pearl and wish for the thousandth time we had a telephone. I want to tell her I know about Mama and Miss Blackstone and ask her how she managed to keep it a secret.

After they leave, Granny wipes her hands on a dishtowel and then stands staring at me, her hands on her hips. She's caught me lingering again, and I wonder if it's too late to make a quick exit.

"You've been different since that Melody woman showed up," she says.

"Have I?" I say, surprised she noticed.

"You'd best stay away from her, Lily. That whole family is bad

news. The Lord would be smart to smite the whole bunch of them."

"But I've already talked to her," I say.

"You what?" Granny's voice gets as big as her eyes. "Why in God's name did you do that?"

"Because I wanted answers," I say.

"Damn it, Lily McAllister, why do you and your mama always go looking for trouble?"

Until this moment, I had never heard my grandmother say a cuss word. Not once. And for some reason it gives me permission to say what I really want to say.

"Is it true?" I ask. "Is Johnny Monroe my father?" My question surprises even me. It's the one I'd intended to ask Mama yesterday, before I saw what I wasn't supposed to see.

Granny's lips form a thin line in the sand, daring me to cross.

"Is it true?" I ask again, knowing I'm crossing the line.

She takes a wooden spoon from beside the stove and uses it to point at me. I get a sense of what it must have been like for Melody to stare down Granny's shotgun. Then Granny's eyes get watery like she might cry and the answer suddenly scares me even though I haven't heard it yet.

"He hurt your mama," she begins. I expect her loud voice, but the words come out soft. Somehow this feels even more dangerous. "Johnny Monroe doesn't deserve to be your daddy."

I swallow hard. When I look up, Mama is standing in the kitchen doorway.

"What's going on in here?" she asks.

"Lily and I were just talking," Granny says.

Mama looks at me like she's wondering if I told Granny about Miss Blackstone.

I shake my head, no.

Granny puts her wooden spoon back on the stove and then

goes over and starts to scrub the sink like she's trying to scrub her memories clean.

Granny's words soak into me: *He didn't deserve to be my daddy. He hurt Mama.* More clues to the mystery of who my father was. The blank chalkboard of my past is filling up with words. Words I never expected to see written there: *Mean as a snake. Dropped out of school. Hurt Mama bad.*

Meanwhile, in fourteen years of life, I've never felt so lost. I cross my arms in front of my chest and think about how Mama is all of a sudden a stranger to me. Is anybody as they seem? Maybe everybody in Katy's Ridge is just walking around pretending they are somebody they're not. All these years I've imagined my father was a good man. But it seems I was wrong. Dead wrong.

Another knock on the door causes everyone to jump.

"This place is becoming busy as a beehive," Granny announces, not hiding her irritation. "Lily, see who that is," she says. "Maybe somebody's brought sausages to go with the banana bread." She looks toward the ceiling as though God is getting special pleasure in irritating her, and then she starts to make more coffee. I go to the front door and open it.

At first I think it's a stranger, but then realize it is Crow wearing his uniform. It's the first time in my life I feel like swooning from the beauty of someone. But then I remember he has no ambition other than to live in Katy's Ridge after he does his time in the military.

"What are you doing here?" I say.

"I wanted to make sure you got home all right," Crow says.

Crow isn't like his nickname, except for the blackness of his hair. Real crows are mischief makers and hang out in groups. Their squawks and calls get the attention of anybody around. Crow, however, is soft-spoken, and the tone of his voice is low, like Johnny Cash, who debuted on the Grand Ole Opry last

summer right around my birthday. Granny and I listened to him on the radio.

"I made it home just fine," I say, not mentioning how hell broke loose when I did.

"I'm glad," he says, with a smile that adds to the potential swooning. "I just passed Bee on the road," he adds.

"She brought banana bread," I say. "Would you like a slice?"

He says he would and then follows me inside.

As we walk together, I catch a whiff of Old Spice aftershave. I know the smell because Pearl bought a bottle at the drugstore in Rocky Bluff for her dad at Christmas with the money she'd saved from babysitting. That same trip she bought herself a lipstick called Cherries in the Snow, even though her mother doesn't let her wear lipstick, and it stays hidden in the bottom of her dresser drawer.

In the kitchen, Mama and Granny greet Crow, and Granny goes on and on about how handsome he looks in his uniform. She pours him a cup of coffee and then gets him a plate to put his banana bread on. When he joins us at the table, Mama asks him questions about the Army.

Every now and again, Crow glances at me like he's remembering us sitting alone in the dark next to the mountain stream just a few hours before. At the same time, I pretend I'm not disappointed that he'll never leave Katy's Ridge. Maybe Granny is right about Melody Monroe being bad news. Trouble started as soon as she came back to Katy's Ridge. I remember her staggering off into the darkness last night, and hope she made it home all right, too.

While Crow eats his second piece of banana bread, Granny excuses herself and goes into the living room. She brings back a gold picture frame Aunt Meg gave Granny from Woolworths, with a photograph inside of my Uncle Nathan holding me while wearing his Army uniform.

"Our Nathan didn't come back," Granny says, her voice shaking a little. "But I want you to promise me that you will."

Crow promises, and looks over at me like I'm one of the reasons he might make such a promise. A lump of new emotion catches in my throat. He glances at his watch and apologizes that he has to leave. He thanks Granny for the banana bread and coffee, and I walk him to the door just like Mama did Miss Blackstone.

"I enjoyed spending time with you last night," he says on the front porch, looking about as sleepy as I feel.

"I enjoyed it, too," I say.

"Is it okay if I write to you?" he asks. "I mean if you don't want me to, that's fine, too." He looks at his shoes, something he seems to do when at a loss.

"I'd like that," I say, and wonder if I might be persuaded to stay in Katy's Ridge after all.

He hesitates again.

"Can I kiss you?" he asks.

"That would be nice," I say, feeling about as awkward as a mule on roller skates.

When Crow leans in, I have to resist backing up. But then I follow his lead. He closes his eyes, and I do, too. His lips feel soft and warm at the same time. A tingle shoots through my body like a small electrical charge that's looking for a place to ground itself.

The kiss ends, and I thank him like he's just given me a gift. He thanks me back, and then we laugh. It seems I'm not the only one wearing roller skates. Then the events from the day before push their way into my thoughts and I almost scream my frustration at remembering Mama and Miss Blackstone's kiss, too.

"I guess I'd better go," he says. "My dad is waiting at the bottom of the hill to take me to the bus station."

We look at each other, and I feel like I'm in one of Aunt Meg's romance novels, where the two main characters are trying to memorize each other's faces before they part.

"Stay safe," I say, not wanting him to go.

He smiles again and gives me a little salute before taking off down the hill. After I lose sight of him, I touch my lips, remembering our kiss. But before I have time to go back into the house, a third visitor walks up the path.

CHAPTER TWENTY-FOUR

Wildflower

L ily calls me from the front door, her voice sounding desperate. I rush to the porch to see Melody Monroe weaving in the yard, sipping a familiar clear liquid from a ball jar. The past flares my nostrils as I remember the smell of corn liquor, and Melody's brother, Johnny, drinking from a similar jar.

After the morning I've had, I'm not sure I can take much more drama. It doesn't help that I've barely slept and have drunk enough coffee to keep a coal miner awake.

"She's drunk," Lily whispers, as if I haven't noticed.

Melody nods her head in an exaggerated way to confirm the situation. She can barely stand.

"I thought you were going to come visit me today," Melody says to Lily, her speech slurring.

I step to the front edge of the porch to discourage Melody from coming any closer.

"Were you supposed to visit her?" I ask Lily.

"I don't think so," Lily says.

Melody's shoes and clothes are still muddy, and I wonder if she has soap up at that old cabin.

"Why are you lying like that, girl?" Melody yells to Lily. "Of course you said you'd visit. You said it last night when we heard the whispers."

"Last night?" I say, looking at Lily.

"She was standing by the road," Lily says to me. "At the start of the path that goes to the cemetery. I didn't say anything about visiting her today."

"Chip off the old block," Melody says to Lily. "Your daddy was quite the liar, too."

My hackles raise. "I have a mind to slap you from here to Sunday," I call out to Melody.

She laughs as though that's been tried before. Yesterday, she was friendly. I don't understand why she's being so different now, except that the liquor has changed her.

Melody's hair hasn't been combed today, and even from twenty paces I can smell the alcohol. She is wearing a different dress, her arms and legs exposed on this late October day. Her thinness reminds me of the photographs in the newspapers when the Americans liberated the concentration camps in the last war. It is easy to imagine the skeleton underneath. The mother in me wonders if she's had anything to eat today. Should I offer her some of Bee's banana bread?

The screen door slams behind me, and Mama joins us with Daddy's shotgun again.

"What's with you people and shotguns?" Melody asks, attempting to focus on the current danger.

"You best be getting home," I say to Melody.

"You best be watching yourself," Melody says.

"Why are you here?" I ask.

"I came to help you," she says. "The rumor mill has started up and the story isn't good." Melody's words slip and slide like a car

on icy mountain roads.

"I'm not worried about rumor mills," I say.

"Well, you should be," she says, with a drunken wink.

Mama and her gun take a step closer. "What's she saying, Louisa May? I can't hear."

"It's nothing, Mama," I call to her.

"That's probably smart," Melody says, keeping her voice low. "You wouldn't want your mama to hear about this. It would probably break her heart."

I narrow my eyes at her, wondering what she thinks she's protecting me from. "I'm not interested in the gossip on the party lines, Melody."

"Oh, you'll be interested in this," she says with a grin. "It's about your fondness for a certain teacher who lives here in Katy's Ridge."

I take a step back and glance at Mama on the porch, who asks again what's being said.

"You want me to speak up, Mrs. McAllister?" Melody raises her voice. "I was just telling your daughter here about—"

I charge toward Melody like a bull after a red cape. When I stop inches from her face, she looks surprised, like I've performed a magic trick and appeared out of thin air. Instead of being scared, she smiles at me.

"You will *not* destroy my family like your brother nearly did," I say through gritted teeth.

The smell of corn liquor makes my gut tighten. I want to run like Lily did the day before.

"Looks like you and that teacher have already destroyed your family without any help from me," she says, sounding almost lucid. "You think the dear people of Katy's Ridge will have anything to do with you when they find this out?" She pauses. The look in her eye is one of wickedness. "I never would have taken you for one of the devil's own," she whispers. "No wonder my brother couldn't keep his hands off you."

"Go home," I say, my jaw clenched nearly shut.

Not that I would want to go home either, considering where she's living right now. Not even corn liquor could help that place feel like a home.

"Does your girlfriend know how tough you are?" Melody smiles again. "Or maybe she likes you tough."

Her words knock the wind out of me, like when her brother tackled me to the ground. I try to get my bearings, and hope Mama's hearing doesn't all of a sudden get better.

I point a finger in her face. "How dare you come here and says these things."

She slaps at my fingers but misses. "You've got a lot of nerve acting all holier than thou." Her retort has a sneer in it and reminds me of Johnny. "That girl of yours looks just like her daddy. Now, who could that be?"

Lily takes a step forward like she's going to defend me, but I put up a hand to stop her. My secret sense tells me that Lily should get the hell away from Melody.

"Lily, I don't want you having anything to do with this woman," I say.

"We need to talk about what she told me yesterday," Lily says.

"I promise we will," I say.

I pivot back to Melody. "You need to leave," I tell her.

She takes another sip from the ball jar. "You know where I am if you have more questions," she says to Lily. "We can talk about you coming to Kentucky, too."

"She won't be going anywhere near Kentucky," I say.

She narrows her eyes at me. "I'd take those rumor mills seriously if I were you," she says, before turning to walk away.

Melody takes off down the hill again with an unsteady gait.

Meanwhile, Mama goes back in the house like she's had enough company for one day. I trust she hasn't heard what Melody said or she would be yelling at me about finding another place to live.

At the cemetery two days before, I felt that life was somehow on track, like a railway car with a clear destination. Safe. Secure. With no possibility of derailing. Yet does anything ever go according to human plans? Fourteen years after my life was forever changed, trouble has come looking for me again, and found me.

CHAPTER TWENTY-FIVE

Lily

"We need to talk, Lily, and I'm not taking no for an answer," Mama says, all solemn.

"Where we going this time?" I ask her. We both know that no serious talking can happen while Granny's around.

"The sawmill," she says. "Unless you've got a better idea."

I tell her I don't.

We've had a year's worth of big talks in less than a day. It turns out Mama isn't who I thought she was. Turns out I barely know her at all.

We follow the steady stream of visitors that have headed down the hill this morning. At the bottom, we get into Mama's pickup and pull into the road. In the opposite direction, Melody weaves down the middle of the road toward her house.

While driving, Mama doesn't speak. Instead, she chews her bottom lip, her forehead creased. I feel like I'm being punished for something, but as far as I can tell I'm not the one who did anything

wrong. Once we get to the mill, Mama unlocks the front door and we go inside. The smell of lumber meets us at the doorway as it always does, and the floor is littered with sawdust that feels like a carpet of moss. Silas, who saws the trees into lumber, doesn't work on Saturdays so we have the place to ourselves.

We stand in the main room where all the lumber is cut. The giant rough-toothed saw stands in the center like a silent witness. I wonder if Mama is avoiding her office because of what I saw happen in there.

"What do you want to know?" she asks.

Something about her willingness to finally speak about it makes me quiet.

"Talk to me," she says, and rests a hand on the long table next to the saw.

I imagine she is alarmed about Melody's threats, but can only deal with one thing at a time.

"Were you ever going to tell me about Miss Blackstone?" I ask.

"We went over that last night," she says. "But if you need to talk about it again—"

"No," I say, remembering how emotional Mama got telling me about it. I don't think I could take her tears right now.

"What did Melody tell you?" she asks.

I pause long enough for her to ask me again.

"She told me that her brother, Johnny, was my father," I begin, "and that he was as mean as a snake."

Calling someone a snake is about as insulting as you can get in these parts. I've never had anything against snakes. They serve an earthly purpose just like everything else. They keep the rat population down and that's a good thing. But church people tie them to temptation and blame them for Eve eating apples in the Garden of Eden.

Meanwhile, Mama is silent and stares at the sawdust like any

words she might speak have spilled out of her mouth and landed at her feet.

"Mama, are you okay?"

"What else did she say?" she asks, looking up at me.

"She said I looked just like him," I say.

"What else?"

"That's about it," I say. "But then Granny told me that Johnny Monroe hurt you bad and that you didn't have a choice."

Mama lowers herself to a nearby stool and the color leaves her face.

"Is it true?" I ask. "I don't want to hurt you, but I have to know.
"

"It's not as simple as all that," she says, her voice soft, almost weak.

"What I want to know, is why you didn't think you could tell me?" I ask.

Mama doesn't look up.

"Didn't you think I deserved to know?" I ask.

She hesitates before lifting her head and looking me directly in the eyes. "Sometimes knowing the truth does more harm than good, Lily. Sometimes knowing the truth changes everything."

I remember seeing her and Miss Blackstone kiss, and agree that the truth can change everything.

"How come Granny knows?" I ask.

"About Johnny?"

I nod.

"Because she and Daniel found me that night," Mama says, her voice heavy with history.

"What about Aunt Jo?"

"Everybody in Katy's Ridge knows," she says, sadness in her voice.

"Everybody except me, you mean?"

If I could turn into an insect at this moment, I'd choose a bee. I want to sting her, even if it means I die as a result.

Mama takes a deep breath.

"If it matters, I was going to tell you once you got older," she says.

I scoff. "I'm trying not to hate you right now," I say, feeling snake-like.

She looks disappointed, but then softens like she doesn't blame me for hating her.

"I know what it's like to hate people," she says. "I can't say that it does much good. But sometimes it's what you need to do."

Her understanding ignites my frustration. I would hurt her, if she wasn't already doing such a good job of hurting herself.

"You lied to me," I say, but it comes out half-hearted. "You've lied to me for fourteen years."

"I kept the truth from you," she says, as though this is different. "But I had my reasons," she adds.

"Just like you have your reasons for kissing Miss Blackstone?"

She narrows her eyes at me, and I sip pleasure from the moment.

"So you're going to threaten me, like Melody?" she asks.

"What if I am?" I sound like a puffed up bully, but I don't even care. My whole life has been a lie.

"Do what you want," Mama says, as if she's tired of worrying about it. "Just remember that everything has a cost, and not always the cost you think."

I put a hand on my hip, daring myself to stand up to her.

"What did he do to you?" I ask Mama. But I'm not so sure I want to know anymore. Maybe Mama's right. Maybe the truth is best left buried sometimes.

She pauses for a long time, like she's considering the cost of this one thing. She stands and reaches for the large push broom nearby.

"I need to sweep," she says.

Like Granny, Mama sweeps when she needs to think. Sometimes she'll sweep the entire house when she's got something bothering her. Granny says we have the cleanest floors in Katy's Ridge, on account of all the thinking she and Mama do.

She begins to sweep the sawdust, creating small piles of powder that were once trees. I tap my foot, wishing I felt like singing or humming so I'd have something to do while I wait. Mama sweeps the piles of sawdust out the door, and then stops and looks over at me.

"To answer your question, Lily, sometimes a woman doesn't have a choice in life."

She sounds like Great Aunt Sadie. "What do you mean?" I ask, tapping my foot again.

"I was younger than you are now when I had you," she begins. "I imagine you've figured that out already, subtracting our ages. But I wasn't a woman at all. I was still a girl. A girl forced into being a woman way too soon."

Even though part of me wants to run, my shoes feel nailed to the floor. Does every family have these kinds of secrets? Or is it just mine?

"The crazy thing is, for the longest time I thought I deserved it," Mama begins again. "That day, my secret sense warned me that something bad was going to happen, but I didn't listen."

Mama has preached to me my whole life about how important it is to listen to your intuition. Great Aunt Sadie has said the same thing. Now I know why.

"When I was thirteen," she continues, "Johnny started bothering me and saying things to me that he shouldn't have said. He was older than me. Daddy had died by then, so I told your Uncle Daniel about it. He went to talk to Johnny and Johnny's father, who didn't seem to care."

Mama puts away the push broom and sits on the stool again.

"Melody Monroe was still living at the cabin then," she says, her eyes thoughtful. "She was a sad little thing. Her sister Ruby had just died who was the same age as me in school."

She pauses, like the story is a river that could meander off course if she isn't careful.

"I was up at the cemetery for the one-year anniversary of your Granddaddy's death, and Johnny followed me up there."

She stops and looks over at me. "Do you want me to keep going?"

I nod and stand straighter. Bravery is called for when it comes to hearing the truth. But I need to know where I come from. I need to know who my people are, and not just the McAllister side of the family.

"On the way back from the cemetery, Johnny attacked me," she says.

Even though I'd guessed what was coming, the words shock me. "He attacked you?" I ask.

"He chased me and then tackled me to the ground," she says.

Tears come to her eyes again, and I fight the guilt of needing to know.

"I fought back as hard as I could, but he was just too strong," she continues. "Then at some point I passed out."

Mama looks at me as though the war she's been fighting for years has been lost, and she has finally raised the white flag. I turn away, not wanting to see her surrender.

Secrets are like genies in bottles, I decide. Once they come out, you can't get them back in again. No matter how hard you try. Words can't be unspoken. Nor can I ever undo seeing Mama and Miss Blackstone kiss. But maybe learning a painful truth is a necessary thing, too. When I look back at Mama the surrender has passed and she seems lighter, like she's finally set down something heavy she was dragging around.

"When did you know you were carrying me?" I ask.

"Right away," she says. "I just kind of knew, deep down, that something good was going to come out of it."

Mama stands. When she opens her arms, it's like a magnet turns on and pulls me toward her, into her embrace.

CHAPTER TWENTY-SIX

Wildflower

As Lily and I release our embrace, Daniel opens the door to the mill.

"You two okay in here?" he asks. "Nell got worried. She came to the house. Said you just disappeared and she didn't know where you'd gone."

It is just like Mama to send Daniel looking for us. He takes off his hat and steps inside, pulling his bum leg over the threshold. He waits at the door until I motion him in.

"I just told Lily what happened with Johnny," I say to him.

He walks over to where we're standing, and puts an arm around Lily, asking how she is.

"Why didn't anybody tell me?" she asks us.

"We were trying to protect you," I say. "But maybe we were wrong to do that. If we were, I'm sorry."

"Now I wish I'd just left well enough alone," Lily says, although that wouldn't be like her at all.

"Anyone would have been curious," Daniel tells her.

My gratitude for Daniel at that moment is no surprise. If he hadn't found me in the forest that night, I might have frozen to death, and Lily and I wouldn't be here at all.

"Does everybody know except me?" she asks. "Do the kids at school know?"

"Probably not," Daniel says. "It's ancient history now."

But it wasn't ancient history after it happened. I remember how people looked at me and how many friends I lost. It was like I had a contagious disease that everybody was afraid to catch. Bee was the only non-family member to stay by my side. None of us were equipped to handle it.

The three of us stand in a small circle in the large room.

"Tell me about what happened when you found Mama that night," Lily says to Daniel.

Daniel and I exchange looks, as though questioning the wisdom of telling more. My instinct is to pull Lily close and cover her ears, shielding her from the rest of the story. But Daniel takes a seat on the stool next to the biggest saw, and we pull up two more. I take a deep breath, readying myself.

"When your granny and I found your mother she was beaten so badly we thought she was dead," Daniel says to Lily. He studies his hands like they hold his memories. "Nell and I exchanged a look that night that I'll never forget. We both thought we'd lost your mother." Daniel looks over at me, his eyes soft.

Hearing the story reminds me of the gold Mary. I didn't want to leave her that day. She was going to take me to Daddy. But it wasn't my time to go. I know that now.

"It took her weeks to recover," Daniel begins again. "Then at some point she discovered she was going to have you." He pauses, studying his hands again. "After you were born, Wildflower never looked back. We all helped the best we could, but your mama raised you with an astonishing amount of love and care." His voice cracks with emotion.

For a long time, we are silent. I can't imagine what it is like for Lily to hear some of the events surrounding the beginning of her life. At least she hasn't run away.

"We agreed as a family to keep what happened from you as long as we could," Daniel begins again. "Or at least until you wanted to know. If we failed you in that way, I'm very sorry. But your mother is a brave woman, Lily, and trust me when I say you are lucky to have her."

Again, it occurs to me how lucky we are to have Daniel here. He's like the footbridge helping us get across this rough part of the path.

"Lily, I know you've wanted to know for a long time now who your father was," I say. "But I just didn't know how to tell you." I apologize again and she lowers her head. "Wounds heal," I tell her. "And sometimes in the middle of a curse is a blessing. I got you out of it, after all, and you've been the brightest and best gift of my life." My voice wavers, and I bite my bottom lip to keep from crying again.

Lily's brow is furrowed in that way she gets when she's thinking hard about something, I can almost see her effort to make peace with it. Although, I know from personal experience, that peace takes a long time to come with things like this.

Outside, the wind picks up, as if announcing a new direction. The boards of the old sawmill creak.

"How do you not think of him when you see me?" Lily says finally.

Her question causes me to pause, and I choose my words carefully. "The night you were born I knew you were mine and mine alone," I begin. "I named you Lily because lilies are resurrection flowers. You see them on Easter because they promise to bring new life. Aunt Sadie says they are the flower most associated with Mary, Jesus' mother. She holds them in those paintings of the Annunciation from a long time ago."

For the first time I realize Lily isn't wearing the necklace I gave her. It was my way of giving her a piece of her story. But now isn't the time to ask her about it. She gets quiet again, and Daniel and I exchange another look. I'm not convinced that knowing the reality of the situation is the best thing.

I think about what Melody said in her drunken state. That people know about me and Bee.

What people? I wanted to ask her.

With the exception of yesterday, Bee and I had been so careful. It is hard to imagine how Melody might have found out.

"How did my father die?" Lily asks, as though one question remains unanswered.

Daniel looks at me, and I motion that I will tell her.

"A couple of weeks after it happened, Johnny tried to break into the house and your Aunt Amy shot him," I say.

"Aunt Amy shot him?" A disbelieving look crosses her face.

"He was wounded," I begin again, "but not badly. That day, your Uncle Daniel and Uncle Nathan and I went out looking for Johnny. We found him at the bottom of the ravine. He had evidently fallen off the old footbridge trying to get away."

"So he really did die before I was born?" Lily asks.

"He really did," I say. "He's buried up in the cemetery. I can show you where, if you want me to."

Lily pauses, as though trying to take everything in.

"All this time, I imagined my father was someone totally different than who he was," Lily says. "I made up this whole story about a stranger who came to Katy's Ridge and swept you off your feet. A soldier maybe, who went off to war, never to return." She looks at me, her expression wistful. "I imagined the tragedy was so great when you lost this amazing man that no one could bear to talk about it. Especially not you, Mama, because your heart was broken."

Lily's wistfulness falls to the floor like sawdust.

"I would have preferred that story, too," I say. "But life isn't a romance novel, Lily, no matter how much we wish it were. The truth is, life is really hard sometimes."

"I know that," she says lowering her eyes again.

The secret finally out, I expect us all to look different somehow, but everyone looks the same. But then a relief comes, after finally releasing what I've kept a tight grip on for so many years. I'm not sure whether to laugh or cry. What quickly follows is fear. Fear that my secret about Bee may yet cause the most damage to our lives.

CHAPTER TWENTY-SEVEN

Lily

With Granny feeding the chickens, I am finishing up the breakfast dishes at the kitchen sink when Mama comes in. It has been a week since she and Uncle Daniel told me about my father, and I am still getting used to not having a fantasy to rely on anymore. In addition, after a week of rain and gray days, a grouchiness has descended on me that I can't seem to shake. A grouchiness that seems to be aimed at Mama.

"Want to go to a movie in Rocky Bluff this afternoon?" she asks. "Your Aunt Jo and Aunt Meg want to see *The King and I.*"

The Rocky Bluff Theater only shows movies on Saturdays, and it doesn't usually get a movie so recently released. Not to mention it's a musical, which is rarer, still. But I haven't sung for over a week now, and I wonder if I'll ever feel like singing again. Besides, my current state of misery won't allow for anything that could be fun.

"No, thank you," I say. Is it my imagination or does my response make the room feel colder?

Other things feel more urgent. I need to talk to Melody again, who as far as I know is still in Katy's Ridge. The story of how my life started is like a nightmare crossing over into the daytime. My father was a monster. Yet, as Great Aunt Sadie says, even monsters aren't only one thing, so I need to know more.

At least with Mama at the movies, I won't have to sneak around.

"Oh, come on, sweetheart. Come into town with us." It's not like Mama to plead. "You know how much fun you have with Meg and Jo. We can stop at the Woolworth's after the show."

"No, thank you," I repeat, this time louder in case she's suddenly gone deaf.

I glimpse the disappointment in her eyes. It's not right to blame Mama for any of this, but that's exactly what I'm doing. If Johnny Monroe was so mean, she should have stayed away from him. She should have fought harder. Surely there was something she could have done to stop him.

I wish Crow were here to talk me out of my bad mood. I can't believe I used to complain about nothing ever happening in Katy's Ridge. Now I just want to get back to my boring, uneventful life.

I'm not the only one who has been moping around. Ever since Melody Monroe told Mama she knew about Bee, Mama has, too. As far as I know, she hasn't told Bee about it, probably because she doesn't want to upset her.

With Mama getting dressed to go to Rocky Bluff, I go over to telephone Pearl from Uncle Daniel's and she agrees to go talk to Melody with me. After I get back home, I wait on the porch for Pearl and see Aunt Jo and Aunt Meg traipsing up the hill smiling. It is a cool day and requires a sweater, but the sun is out and hits the south facing porch.

"You coming with us?" Aunt Meg calls to me.

"Not today," I say.

"But it's *The King and I*," Aunt Jo says. "Deborah Kerr and Yul Brynner."

She looks at me like Preacher does whenever he's rounding up sinners, full of hope and expectation.

"The singing is supposed to be incredible," Aunt Meg says. "All the Hollywood magazines say so."

I'm not sure I can bear to hear singing when a song hasn't graced my lips for days. It's like they've dried up after I found out about my father.

"I can't believe you're passing up a chance to see a musical," Aunt Jo says, her smile fading. "Are you not feeling well?"

"Save your breath," Mama says, coming out of the house. "I've already tried to convince her."

Mama joins them in the yard. At that moment, they look like the Red Bud sisters standing there, their relatedness unmistakable. All three women are about the same size and height, their hair and eye color in harmony, their features offering the only variety. Mama looks like a photograph I've seen of Granddaddy McAllister. Aunt Jo looks like a beautiful version of Granny and Aunt Meg looks like a mixture of both. Aunt Amy was the unluckiest in the family, getting the big version of Granny's nose, and the tiny version of Granddaddy's eyes.

Aunt Amy isn't the type to go to movies and is probably sewing today, getting dress orders ready for Thanksgiving and Christmas. She disappears every fall, which is her busiest season.

"Last chance?" Mama says.

I tell them to go on and hide my regrets. The truth is, I don't feel like I deserve to go to the movies right now. Bad blood flows through my veins. Blood, that until recently, I thought was perfectly fine and maybe even superior to everybody else in Katy's Ridge. Bigger places called me. I thought I was special. But it turns out I'm half-hoodlum. Destined to be unremarkable.

Shortly after Mama and her sisters leave, Granny comes out of the house carrying a basket of quilt pieces.

"If you need me, I'll be at Sadie's," she says, and takes off following the others.

I go inside. It is rare to have the house to myself. The only sound is the crackling of wood in the wood stove in the living room. While I wait for Pearl to arrive, I go into the bedroom Mama and I share and open the bottom dresser drawer. This is Mama's private space, where she keeps all her special things. Out of respect, I've never looked inside, but I wonder now if there's any information about my father in there.

I pull out a large cigar box and sit on the bed debating whether to open it. I imagine my father would have done more than open it, maybe even stealing it or tossing away the contents. I give myself permission to look inside. On top are a pair of booties I used to wear and a faded bib, hand-stitched, folded in a small square. A handful of photographs are scattered within. One is of Miss Blackstone in a small golden frame. Others are loose in the box. A man is in one. The name Victor is written on the back, with the date 1946. Another one is of a girl and Mama standing arm-in-arm. The name Mary Jane is written on the back of that one, and the date 1941.

Mama would never go through my things. She would be too honorable. But it turns out I'm not as decent as she is, especially when I want information. A small white Bible is tucked in the corner the box. Inside, the date she got baptized is written in the faded blue ink of a fountain pen. I thumb through its thin pages and find two yellowing newspaper clippings. One is the obituary of Joseph McAllister, my grandfather. It tells of an unfortunate accident at the local sawmill. It then lists the names of his wife and daughters left behind. *Louisa May, age 12,* is listed last.

In that moment, the poignancy of Mama's loss becomes real to me. I imagine it is much different to know who your father is for

twelve years before losing him, instead of never knowing who he was in the first place.

The second clipping is also an obituary from the Rocky Bluff newspaper and is much smaller. It reads:

JOHNNY M. MONROE, *age 17, fell to his death in Katy's Ridge. He is preceded in death by his mother, Mabel; his father, Arthur, as well as his sister Ruby Monroe, who died at age 12. He leaves behind one surviving sister, Melody, age 10, who resides in Louisville, Kentucky.*

I STARE at the words and hold the clipping for a long time. Long enough for my hand to begin to shake.

At least somebody put it in the newspaper, I tell myself, even if it is a tiny announcement. There is no photograph, and I wonder if one even exists. Mama told me once that when she was a girl, a man with a big camera would come to Katy's Ridge every year or two to take photographs for anybody who had the money to pay for them. From the looks of that cabin, I doubt the Monroes had any spare money hanging around for such a thing. I try to imagine someone who looks like me, but who is taller and almost a man.

"Hey! What are you doing?"

Pearl startles me so bad I let out a short scream.

"You scared me to death," I say. I put a hand to my racing heart, as though it might otherwise jump right out of my chest.

She mumbles an apology. "Are you going through your mama's private things?" She tilts her head like the truth, and nothing but the truth, is required.

"I found out who my father was," I say, as if this gives me permission to snoop.

"Just now?"

"No, last Saturday."

Pearl looks hurt. "Why am I just now finding out about it?"

It is a good question. Truth is, I don't feel as close to Pearl as I used to. It's like life has forced me to grow up, but she gets to stay a kid.

"A lot's been going on," I say, which is an understatement.

"Well, who is it?" Pearl asks.

"Not who I'd hoped," I say.

"You mean it's not Cary Grant?" She giggles.

"Not even close," I say.

At least she is one other person who didn't already know like almost everybody else. She sits on the bed next to me, giving it a bounce. Pearl knows I've been wanting to know his identity my entire life. "Tell me," she says.

Despite Pearl's admirable secret-keeping about Mama and Miss Blackstone, I don't want to risk anybody else finding out that Johnny Monroe is my father. Pearl waits for me to answer, exhibiting a patience that is unusual for her. I put Mama's secret box back in the bottom drawer and close it.

"You can't tell a soul," I say, not knowing a way to back out.

Pearl licks her lips as though secrets are a delicious treat she doesn't get that often. I make her do a double pinkie swear, and then tell her the one thing that causes my cheeks to burn with shame. Johnny Monroe is my father. Johnny Monroe forced himself on her and didn't give Mama a choice. That means I was never meant to exist.

CHAPTER TWENTY-EIGHT

Wildflower

Two of my three sisters are in my truck, our hips touching in the front seat. We are on our way to see a movie in Rocky Bluff. Initially, it was planned as a special treat for Lily, but she refused to come along. My heart isn't exactly in it now, but Jo and Meg are so excited I decide to go anyway.

Earlier that morning when I went over to Jo's to see if she was up for a movie, I telephoned Meg and Amy from Jo's house, and also Bee. I invited her to join us and make it look like a coincidence. For the last few days, I've avoided Bee, not having the heart to tell her what Melody said. Maybe it's nothing. A wild threat. But something tells me it isn't. Someone is feeding Melody information, and I can't put off much longer talking to Bee about it.

"How is Lily taking the news that Johnny's her father?" Meg asks.

Daniel must have told Jo and Jo told Meg and Amy about the talk we had at the mill. I imagine they've all formed an opinion

about it. I crack my window suddenly needing air, and Jo holds her long hair with one hand to keep it from blowing in the wind.

"She's been very quiet about it all," I say. "She had this huge fantasy built up about who her father was."

"I wish she hadn't turned down going to see the musical," Meg says. "Musicals make anybody feel better."

"I think she's had about all she can stand of me for a while," I say. "I'm trying not to worry."

"I would be worried, too," Jo says. "When Daniel gets quiet like that I know he's remembering the war. And when he's remembering the war, he shuts himself in our bedroom and doesn't come out for a while. I hate it when he does that."

I've experienced the part of Daniel that gets quiet, too, but not that often.

"You know, I haven't heard Lily sing for days," I tell them. "It used to be I couldn't walk into the house without hearing her singing something."

Both sisters turn to look at me.

"That's not good," Meg says.

"I know," I say.

"It's hard to imagine Lily not singing," Jo says.

We ride a few miles in somber silence—the shocks squeaking with every bump in the road—as if the thought of Lily not singing is reason enough to be gloomy.

"Maybe she just needs time," Meg says. "Things will get back to normal soon enough."

"Lily's good enough to sing in a musical herself," Jo says. "She should go to Nashville or someplace where they pay people to sing like that."

"Or New York City," Meg says. "The King and I was a Broadway play before it was a movie. Yul Brynner starred in that one, too."

Meg reads movie magazines and is the dreamiest of my sisters.

I doubt there's a practical bone in her body, except that she married Cecil.

"Yul Brynner is bald," Jo says. "I like a man with hair."

The mood lightens and the three of us laugh.

"Daniel has a nice head of hair," Meg says.

"I've threatened to leave him if he goes bald," Jo says with a smile, though I can't imagine her ever leaving Daniel for any reason.

"Well, it's too late for Cecil," Meg says, with a sigh.

I'm not sure what Meg sees in Cecil. I imagine she was just tired of being unmarried. At least I don't have to worry about Bee going bald, but I'm not about to say this to my sisters. Although sometimes I wish I could.

"We need to find Wildflower a man with a good head of hair," Jo says. "It's about time you settled down with someone, little sister."

They look at me as if their matchmaking project requires a response.

"You haven't called me Wildflower in years," I say to Jo. "Nobody has, except Daniel."

"Perhaps it's time we started calling you that again," she says.

In the pause that follows, I play around with the notion of telling my sisters about Bee. It's hard to imagine their reactions, other than pure shock.

"What about Crow Sector?" Meg says finally, as if she's been making a list in her mind of all the eligible men in Katy's Ridge.

"He's Lily's age," I say. "I used to babysit him."

"Yeah, too young," Jo says.

"Besides, Lily is the one with the crush on him," I say.

"Really?" Jo says.

"I thought you knew that," Meg says to Jo.

"I guess I didn't," Jo says.

We bounce along the main road out of Katy's Ridge. I know this road so well I could practically drive it without looking.

Outings with my older sisters are rare these days. Jo stays busy with the house and farm while Daniel works at the mill. And most of the time Meg is distracted with Cecil and her step-daughter, Janie, who—at best—is a strange girl.

"I can't imagine what it's like for Lily to find out about Johnny," Jo says.

"How do you make peace with Johnny Monroe being your father?" Meg says, her voice somber.

Meg and Jo both sat with me in the days that followed Johnny's attack. They know full well what he was capable of.

"When I went to see her, Melody promised she wouldn't tell Lily unless she asked."

"I guess Lily asked," Meg says. "She's always been full of questions."

"Reminds me of somebody else I know," Jo says.

Meg and Jo exchange a look that tells me I wasn't always the easiest of siblings.

"But why on earth would Melody show up now?" Jo says.

Evidently she found some old letters written to her aunt," I say. "They were about Johnny dying and also about Lily."

"Melody didn't even know Johnny was dead?" Jo asks.

"Not until recently," I say.

"How awful," Jo says, looking out her window.

"Who wrote the letters?" Meg asks.

"Doc Lester," I say.

She grimaces.

"It's a shame Lily knows," Jo says. "She's obviously hurt."

"I probably would have kept the secret forever if Lily had left it alone," I say. "But I was totally naïve to think I could keep it from her."

I wonder what else I've been immature about. I'm almost thirty

years old and sometimes I feel like I haven't learned a thing. I remember Melody's threat to expose me and Bee and wonder if 'normal' is too much to ask for. This saga isn't over. And if I tell Bee, I fear she may leave Katy's Ridge again.

We go along the narrowest part of the road that hugs up against the mountain, and I grip the steering wheel tighter. We always stop talking along this stretch and hold our breath. On the other side is a sheer drop down to the river, the reason this section is called the bluff. Tree roots dangle where the road was cut into the mountain. Suspended like flailing legs reaching, to no avail, for solid ground.

I can relate to exposed roots. It feels like my private life is being cut away and revealed. Things I've preferred to keep buried.

"Time heals all wounds," Meg says, with a sigh.

I wonder if she's talking about Lily or if she's heard my private thoughts.

Fifteen years after Daddy's death I still think of him every day. Not in the painful longing way that it was at first. But at certain milestones, I miss him. Like when Lily was born and when she first sang at the church. Actually, every time she sings I wish he could hear her. I imagine he would be so proud. Like I am proud.

The road widens, and we all start talking again. The bluff is one of the reasons Katy's Ridge stays small. Not that many people want to make such a hazardous drive to get in and out of the area.

We park in front of the small theater in Rocky Bluff, and I look around for Bee's car. As planned, Bee stands in the small lobby holding a bag of popcorn, pretending not to wait for anyone. I let Jo and Meg go in ahead of me to discover her first and hear their greetings. It feels special to run into people we know in Rocky Bluff, even though this incidence is prearranged.

I greet Bee, dulling my smile so as not to appear too glad to see her. "Are you here alone?" I ask, like an actress playing a small part in a play.

"Join us," Meg says, grabbing her arm. Bee puts up a tiny fight just for show.

Melody's threat follows me into the darkened theater. I wonder if anybody knows. I give myself permission to not think about it while the movie is playing, and let the others go in first so I can sit next to Bee.

Our shoes touch as Deborah Kerr and Yul Brynner go from adversaries to two people who respect each other. When they sing *Shall We Dance?* our hands reach into the bag of popcorn in a move as orchestrated as the score that plays in the background. Our hands touch. Stolen moments. Stolen in dark places where prying eyes can't see. Yet eyes have seen. At least according to Melody Monroe.

Only once do we let our hands touch between our chairs. Skin against skin. The tingle of recognition that this is the hand of the person I love, even if our hands can never touch in public. For years I tried to see Victor as more than a friend. He didn't deserve to be strung along. But the more I wanted to love him, to commit to a life with him, the more it didn't happen.

If God and I were still on speaking terms, I would ask why life is so hard sometimes, for the God-fearing and heathen alike. As far as I can tell, no one escapes difficulties and some suffer more than most. Yet there are everyday miracles, too. I can't imagine a life without Lily or Bee or my family. Or June and Horatio, who welcome us into their home. In terms of work, after years of struggle, the sawmill finally has enough customers to sustain us. I never thought the mill would be part mine someday, and eventually all mine.

In the movie, the King and Anna are ending their dance. It is nice to get a respite from all that is going on. But then, a foreboding shivers through me that is so strong I gasp. Lily is in danger. I have to get home.

Bee looks at me, her eyes questioning. "I need you to give Jo

and Meg a ride back to Katy's Ridge," I whisper to her. "Something isn't right."

"Are you sure?" she whispers back.

Actually, I'm not sure, but I can't take the chance. Not while Melody Monroe is still around. I rush out of the theater and back to Katy's Ridge, unsure of what I might find.

CHAPTER TWENTY-NINE

Lily

With the last few sunny days, the mud has hardened, making it easier to get to the Monroe cabin. This doesn't stop Pearl from complaining every few steps.

"Why are we doing this again?" she asks.

"Because I want to find out more about my father," I say.

"Don't you know enough?" she asks. "Sounds like he's not much to write home about."

"Nobody is all one thing," I say, repeating what Great Aunt Sadie said. "Even monsters have a bit of goodness inside, just like saints have a bit of badness."

"You say the strangest things," Pearl says. She leans over to wipe dirt from her shoes, before complaining again.

As much as I wish it weren't true, Melody Monroe is kin. I figure I owe her an explanation as to why I'm never going to see her again. But before that, I want to learn more about my ne'er-do-well father, Johnny Monroe. Mama wouldn't like that I'm coming

here. Something about it feels dangerous, even to me. I reach for the gold Mary around my neck for added protection and realize again that I've lost her. As far as I can figure, it must have been the night I walked to Crow's house in the dark.

When we get there, the door to the cabin is wide open.

"This place is creepy," Pearl says.

I don't tell her about the girl who died here, or I'll be seeing Pearl's backside as she hightails it home. I step up to the door and call out Melody's name. When she doesn't answer, I take a step inside and find her sleeping on an old mattress in the corner. A mason jar sits on the small kitchen table with clear liquid inside, along with a loaf of bread and a hunk of cheese. I remember the banana bread Miss Blackstone brought last Saturday morning and how elegant it was in comparison.

Melody snorts awake and jumps when she sees me standing there. "You know I could shoot you for trespassing, don't you?" She sits up and holds her head like it weighs a thousand pounds. "That is, if I had a gun," she adds.

Pearl's eyes widen like she's asking what I got us into.

"I need you to tell me more about my father," I say to her.

"Oh, so you believe me now?" she asks.

"Mama told me the story," I say.

"Did she?" Melody makes her way to the kitchen table. "What would that story be?" she asks. She spies the leftover liquor and puts it up in the cabinet, as though not willing to share.

"She was attacked and left for dead," I say, not naming any names.

Pearl looks at me. I can tell she's never heard this part of the story.

"That sounds like something Johnny would do," Melody says, matter-of-fact. "But Doc Lester said she asked for it."

"Well, Doc Lester is a liar and a horse's ass," I say.

Pearl giggles, and then stops herself when Melody turns to look at her. Pearl's been known to laugh at inappropriate times when she's nervous.

"Your daddy's that Indian, isn't he?" she says to Pearl.

Pearl nods.

"His name is Horatio Sector," I say.

"And your mama's white?"

Pearl nods again.

Melody gives Pearl the once-over, like she's trying to see the Indian in her.

"Something tells me you have something to ask me, little-miss-full-of-questions." Melody turns her heavy head toward me.

"I want to hear more about what he was like," I say.

"You mean Johnny?" She plops down in the chair and it wobbles even though she doesn't weigh much at all. "Well, like I said, he was mean as a snake."

A stray piece of sunlight breaks through the small window and touches the top of the table.

"What was he like besides being mean?" I ask.

Melody scoffs and puts her hand on the piece of sunlight, as if to claim it as her own. She pushes the spare chair out with her bare foot so I can join her, and then rubs her eyes to clear the sleep out of them. Pearl is left standing, but she doesn't seem to care. My guess is she's happy to stand if it means she will get a head start running if we need to get out of here.

The cabin smells sour from cigarettes and rotting wood.

"I want to know what he was like besides being a monster," I say.

Melody grunts a short laugh. Then she looks up at the ceiling, as if her memories are all stored in the single light bulb that lights the room. She sits long enough without speaking that I wonder if she's fallen back to sleep with her eyes open. But then she leans forward.

"Before our mother died, Johnny was a different boy," she begins. "Our life was a lot better then. But after our mother died, our father started drinking more and more. He was a horrible drunk," she says. "It was our mother who kept him civilized, and without her he didn't stand a chance."

I've seen Melody do a lot of drinking in the short time she's been here and wonder if it's a family trait. She pulls off a chunk of bread and offers some to me and Pearl. We decline.

"Johnny was older than me by four years, and my sister, Ruby, was two years older."

She stops long enough to cut a slice of cheese with a rusty knife and eats it with the bread. She doesn't offer us any cheese. The cups from our tea the week before still sit on the end of the table. The one I used overflows with the stubbed out ends of cigarettes. I try not to gag.

"I still miss Ruby," she begins again. "Hung herself out in that old oak out there."

Melody points with the knife to a tree in the distance.

Pearl's eyes get about as wide as the silver dollar she gets in her Christmas stocking every year. I hope she doesn't take off running and leave me here.

"How old was your sister?" I ask.

"Almost thirteen," Melody says. "But I could understand why she did it. If I'd had the nerve, I would have joined her."

Melody's eyes grow dark, as though visiting the past requires dim lighting.

"But why would she do such a thing?" I ask.

"When you're being messed with, it's hard not to feel trapped," she says. It sounds like she's given this some thought.

Melody stands and goes to the cupboard to get the liquor she put away earlier. Instead of drinking out of the jar, she pours some in one of the teacups and drinks it.

Pearl inches toward the door. I make a motion with my hand to

stay put. It's obvious she doesn't want to be here, but I may never get this chance again.

Melody stares at the old bed in the middle of the room like it's a crystal ball showing her the past. "I think Daddy knew about Johnny, and that's why he sent me to Aunt Reenie's." She pauses and takes another sip. "I guess there was enough decency left in him that he didn't want what happened to Ruby to happen to me."

"Why did you come back to Katy's Ridge if it holds so many bad memories?" I ask.

Melody takes another sip and sits straighter, as though the liquid is giving her courage.

"I found out a couple of years ago that I can't have children," she says. "So when I read Doc Lester's letters to my aunt, it gave me hope that the family wouldn't die out." She finishes off what's in the teacup.

I haven't given a whole lot of thought to family bloodlines and didn't realize it was so important to some people.

"You have Monroe blood in you," Melody begins again, confirming my thought. "My parents came over from northern Scotland," she continues, staring into the empty teacup. "They headed south because the land was cheaper. They ran into somebody in Virginia who told them about this little place called Katy's Ridge that was a gem. Hard to think of this place as a gem," she says, looking around the room.

I'd heard others who'd settled in Katy's Ridge tell similar stories. Granddaddy and Great Aunt Sadie came over from Ireland, too, and Granny came over from Germany with her sister. Everybody's family is from somewhere else, except maybe Horatio Sector. Pearl told me the Cherokee are from North Carolina and Tennessee, and that her father's grandparents went to Oklahoma by way of something called the Trail of Tears.

"What were your parents like?" I ask, wanting to fill in the missing picture of my unknown grandparents.

"Would you believe my mother laughed all the time?" Melody says, looking straight at me. "That's what I remember about her most. Her laughter. And then after she died it was like all laughter died with her."

Melody's smile fades and sadness takes its place. Her sorrow appears as tangible as the design on the teacup. The design and the sorrow weathered, but not really gone.

"We were all devastated," Melody continues. "But it hurt Johnny the most. As the oldest, he never got over it. He was a mama's boy before he got mean. 'Sweetest little boy in the world,' Mama used to call him."

It's a long journey from *sweetest little boy in the world* to *mean as a snake.* I imagine it's a sad journey, too. Mama likes to say that everybody's got reasons for being the way they are. Even Mama and Miss Blackstone have their reasons for loving each other. It doesn't matter whether I understand it or not. I want to ask Melody how she knows about them, but don't want to distract her from talking about her family. *Our* family.

"After our mother died, Johnny couldn't even get to school on time anymore, and Daddy took switches to him," Melody continues. "Of course, that just made matters worse."

Melody looks at Pearl standing near the door and asks if she'd like to sit down, as though all of a sudden remembering her manners. Pearl declines. It is the quietest I've ever known her. I don't think either of us expected Melody to tell all this. Most grownups won't even talk to people our age. But she seems younger than most adults.

"Before our mother died, Johnny won the third grade spelling bee," Melody begins again. "He was also a good reader. Way better than Ruby and me. And he was good with numbers, too. But none of that seemed to matter to him anymore after our mother died."

Melody walks over to the door and Pearl steps aside. Melody stares out into the forest, the sun sprinkled through the trees and

smiles. Then she twirls once, as though hearing a distant tune and dancing with a ghost. A ghost she's missed.

"Lily won the spelling bee in third grade, too," Pearl says to Melody.

"She did? You did?" She turns to me. "That's Johnny's influence, I bet." She looks almost pleased.

A sadness visits me that feels older than this cabin. I remember the whispers again. If I could ask my father a question, I would ask him how someone who used to be so smart could drop out in the sixth grade and turn mean. But I already know the answer. If Mama died, I would be heartbroken, too, and I'm not sure I'd ever get over it. At this moment, I'm not sure how I'll ever leave Katy's Ridge without her.

"Johnny really changed," Melody says, as though intent on finishing her story. "He took out every bit of anger he had about Mama dying and tormented me and Ruby. I remember asking him once where that sweet little boy went, and he slapped me hard in the face like he was slapping that memory right out of my head. I think that little boy died when Mama died."

I stand next to my chair, feeling almost dizzy from all I've heard. Pearl's eyes plead with me to go.

"We've got to get home," I tell Melody. "Thanks for telling me all this."

"Wait," she says. "You've got to come with me to Kentucky. It's just a few hours by bus."

"Now?" I say.

"Good a time as any," she answers. "You don't belong here," she whispers, and I think of the whispers at the footbridge. "Louisville is a big city. There's a lot more going on."

A Greyhound bus stops at the Texaco station every day in Rocky Bluff. More than once, I've fantasized about hopping onboard and going anywhere north of here or south or east or west.

"I doubt Mama would go for that," I say.

"Don't tell her," Melody says. "Just come with me." She extends a hand like she might offer me a poison apple.

"We need to go," Pearl says to me.

"We can leave for Louisville right after I pay my respects to Ruby and Johnny," Melody says. "This place gets under my skin. I can't stomach it for much longer."

I wonder if this is why the moonshine is never far away from her.

"So what do you say?" she asks, as if not willing to let it go.

"I can't do that to Mama," I say.

"Sure you can," she says. "We could be in Louisville by tomorrow morning." She reaches for me again.

"Lily, we need to go," Pearl says, her voice strong.

"Sorry," I say to Melody.

She lets out a long sigh, as though Mama's just won at a game they've been playing.

"Suit yourself," she says. "Come give your Aunt Melody a hug." She stands and opens her skinny arms.

Pearl gives me a wary look, but I decide that one hug can't hurt anything. Melody's embrace is weak, though the smell of alcohol and cigarettes is much stronger. Melody must not have had much practice. She holds me longer than I expect, and I have to push her away, which isn't hard because she's so thin. She finally takes a step back.

"Doc Lester says you can sing. Is that true?" she asks me.

"She sings like an angel," Pearl says. "She's the best singer in Tennessee."

Despite the sudden chill in the cabin, I feel my face warm.

"Well, just so you know, Johnny couldn't sing a lick," she says to me. "So you must have gotten that from the McAllister side of the family."

Pearl stands at the door, tapping her foot. Mama would be glad

she's trying to get me out of there. But it appears Melody has more to say. In a way, it's as though this might be the last time she sees me, and she wants to make sure she says certain things.

"I hope you can forgive Johnny for what he did to your mother," she begins again. "I wish that it hadn't happened, but life is just full of things we all wish had never happened."

Melody is smarter than I thought she was at first. Just because someone has a hard life doesn't mean they're stupid. Everybody is unlucky in one way or another. Johnny being my father wasn't the luckiest thing, but having Mama as a mother has made up for it.

All of a sudden a creepiness descends, and I want to be home. At fourteen, I'd like to think I'm past needing a mother, but right now I do. Something about the way Melody is acting scares me. I head for the door again, but Melody grabs my arm.

"If you won't go to Kentucky with me, come to the cemetery. I want to introduce you to your grandparents and Ruby and Johnny."

The last place I want to go with Melody Monroe is the cemetery. The moment feels so ominous, I almost expect to hear the organ music they play on the radio mysteries that Granny listens to in the kitchen.

"I need to get home," I say, looking down at her hand on my arm.

"If we go to the cemetery, I bet we'll hear the whispers again," she continues, her fingers digging in a little more. "Don't you want to know what they're saying?"

A shudder climbs my spine. My fledgling secret sense tells me to get out of there, but I'm so surprised it finally showed up, I forget to take action.

"Let's go," Pearl says, grabbing my other arm. Melody finally releases her grip and we rush down the porch steps and run through the forest, as though Melody is chasing us.

When we finally stop at the road, we lean over to catch our breath. As I straighten up, I get that creepy feeling again like I've just walked over somebody's grave. The whispers voice their agreement.

CHAPTER THIRTY

Wildflower

I t was Lily who noticed the body at the bottom of the ravine, similar to where I had seen Johnny's body that day many years ago. She had been inconsolable at first, never having seen a dead body. Who wouldn't be? Melody Monroe was dressed in the same clothes she'd worn when she arrived. She'd likely been drinking, the authorities said, and had somehow fallen from the footbridge trying to see the ravine below. But I wondered if she had chosen to jump.

Lily went on and on about how Melody had wanted her to come with her to the cemetery that day, and also about the whispers. About how Melody had heard them, too, and thought they were Johnny trying to talk to Lily from the grave. Perhaps the whispers called Melody home with the rest of the family. For whatever reason, Lily says she hasn't heard them since Melody's body was retrieved.

Three days later Lily, Aunt Sadie and Bee and I attend Melody's

service. Mama refuses to go after hearing about Melody trying to get Lily to go to Louisville. The only other person there, besides Preacher Evans, is Doc Lester. It is a small gathering for a funeral. Perhaps only Johnny's was smaller.

I wonder how many will attend my burial rites when the time comes. Daddy's funeral filled the church to overflowing, and I get teary just thinking about it. Sitting in the usual McAllister pew, waiting for the service to begin, I finally understand Aunt Sadie's reasoning. Everybody should have someone to witness the end of their life. No matter how many devils or angels sat on their shoulders during their lifetime.

The ceremony begins and Preacher says his usual things about heavenly rewards and pearly gates. He does little to hide his dislike of Aunt Sadie and me, for not being regular churchgoers, or his continuing desire to get Lily to sing in order to fill his offering plate. I keep thinking about the time Bee saw him in downtown Nashville picking up a lady of the evening, and wonder if anybody is what they seem.

Doc Lester, in the pew opposite us, keeps an eye on me. His letters to Melody's aunt are why we're all here. The ceremony begins and Preacher asks if anyone wants to say something. I doubt he remembers much about Melody Monroe. All of us are quiet. Somehow, there is too much tragedy to make room for words.

Any other time I would expect Lily to sing. Perhaps *Amazing Grace,* the song Miss Mildred played at Ruby's funeral, fifteen years before. The song Lily sang two weeks ago for the anniversary, minutes before Melody Monroe walked up the hill to our house. Had it only been two weeks ago? Somehow it seems longer. I nudge Lily and whisper the suggestion that she sing something, but her lips form a tight line and she refuses.

. . .

IT IS ALREADY DARK when Bee puts two plates and silverware on her small white kitchen table for us, supper still cooking on the stove.

"It's so tragic about Melody," she says. "I wish I'd said something at the funeral."

"We were all struck speechless," I say. "Some things just don't make sense."

Melody died in the same manner Johnny had, landing only a foot or two away. So close they could have held hands if they'd been there together. I still haven't told Bee about Melody's threat, and hope that Melody's knowledge of the two of us died with her. Yet something tells me it isn't over, and that Bee needs to know.

We stand in Bee's small kitchen, the curtains pulled closed even though there aren't any neighbors for miles. We are used to this. We are used to hiding.

"I need to tell you something," I say.

"Okay," she says, not looking up.

I always fear that Bee will take off again. She can get a job teaching practically anywhere, and has made it clear that the only reason she's still in Katy's Ridge is me.

I hesitate, and Bee turns to look at me. "Before she died, Melody visited the house again and said some things that concern me," I begin. I don't tell her that it was actually several days before that, before we went to the movie. The day I rushed home from the theater and found Lily and Pearl in the bedroom talking. At first I thought I'd rushed home for nothing, until I later learned that Lily and Pearl had been with Melody the same time I got my premonition. In fact, Melody had tried to make Lily go to the cemetery with her that afternoon. The next morning Melody was found dead.

"What did Melody say?" Bee asks.

I pause. Bee touches my hand. "Just spit it out, Lou," she says.

This nickname is only ours, though I call her *Bee,* as does the

rest of the world, except for her parents who still call her Becky. What I'm about to tell her won't go over well, but she needs to know. No matter how much my bravery wanes.

Bee leans against the counter. I forget how beautiful she is sometimes. At least beautiful to me. I wonder if there are other women like me and Bee. Just because I've never seen any, doesn't mean they don't exist. Planets exist that I've never seen. Millions of them. Yet, when I look up at the sky, it's hard not to feel alone.

"You're driving me crazy," she says. "Tell me what Melody said that has you all riled." Bee folds her arms at her chest, waiting. I stare at the hands of the gold wristwatch her parents bought her last Christmas, the hands pointing straight up and down to 6 o'clock.

"Melody asked if anybody else knew about me and you," I say.

Bee releases her arms, her eyes flashing a sudden terror, "She asked what? Tell me exactly what she said."

A timer goes off on top of the stove, as if to add further alarm. She turns off a burner, all the while shaking her head like she can't believe what she's just heard. I am too far in to stop now. She turns around again to face me. I wonder briefly if I should hide her suitcase.

"Melody said she knew about us," I begin again, "and that everybody else might find out if she had anything to do with it. Something about the rumor mill starting up."

Worry digs a trench along Bee's brow. "But how would Melody know these things?" She sits at the kitchen table. I sit across from her, and reach for a hand that she doesn't offer. From the smell of supper cooking, I also have other concerns. Bee isn't that great a cook.

"Maybe she was just guessing." Bee looks up at me, a hopeful tone to her voice.

"That's a pretty accurate guess," I say.

She frowns again. "We've been so careful," she says. "Well, except with Lily."

"That was an accident," I say. "Lily never comes to the mill that time of day. She was upset. She had been over at Melody's."

"I can't believe all the trouble that woman has caused," Bee says.

Perhaps it is a good thing that the last of the Monroe family is dead, except for the part that lives in Lily. After Melody was found and I tried to get in touch with her aunt in Kentucky, I learned that the old woman had been dead for years. Melody evidently lived over a bar she worked at until she was fired a few months before for drinking away their profits. No one I talked to was surprised about her death.

"You don't think Lily told her, do you?" Bee's cheeks redden.

"I honestly don't," I say. Not that I haven't given it a thought myself. More than one teenager has complained about their parents to the outside world. "The timing doesn't match up anyway," I continue. "She hadn't seen us yet. Lily saw Melody the morning before she saw us."

Bee stirs another pot on the stove, as if stirring up her concern. My stomach growls, reminding me how hungry I am. At the same time, I don't feel like eating. I'm not sure I can take much more trouble.

"Maybe everything will go back to normal now that Melody is gone," I say. "Let's hope all this trouble died with her." But Bee doesn't look convinced.

"What if people find out?" Bee says. "Lou, I could lose my job. You could lose your customers."

She pours me a glass of tea without ice and no lemon.

"Could be nothing," I say. "Could be she just wanted to scare us."

"Could be she wanted to ruin us, too," Bee says. "Where was she getting this? That's what I want to know."

"I'm just so tired of hiding," I say, taking a sip of tea that could

use sugar. "Every time I visit you it's like something out of a radio mystery," I continue. "I stop at the end of your road to make sure nobody's looking and then accelerate to get out of sight quickly, and then duck into your driveway. Not that anyone is even around. If Katy's Ridge had sidewalks, they'd be rolled up by 5 o'clock at night."

I want to laugh at the situation, but can't even muster a smile.

"I'm tired of hiding, too," Bee says. "I've forgotten what normal is like. If I ever knew. I guess if we were normal, we would have married someone years ago and never looked back. At least you had an offer."

When Victor and I dated, it never occurred to me to keep it a secret. In fact, I wanted everyone to see me. It was my proof that I didn't have feelings for Bee. Of course, this wasn't at all fair to Victor.

"Maybe you should have married him," Bee says, as if she's read my thoughts. "Then I would have stayed in Nashville and never would have come back to Katy's Ridge."

"We're not criminals," I say.

"Aren't we?" She motions for me to sit and goes back into the kitchen with our plates, serving us from the stove.

The meatloaf is burned and the color of tire rubber. The mashed potatoes, piled high on the side, have visible lumps. The peas, from a can, have a tiny dab of margarine on the top. While I adore Bee, I am not that fond of her cooking.

She joins me at the table and unfolds a napkin, placing it across her lap. Her family lives in Rocky Bluff and even has a house-keeper. In this way, she is much more sophisticated than me.

When I make a bold cut into the meatloaf, the burnt crust crackles and steam escapes. I move the margarine with the tip of my knife to encourage it to melt. It isn't encouraged. I hide it underneath the peas to avoid eating it. I make sounds like I enjoy the food, even though it is the worst meatloaf I've ever tasted.

She chews the meatloaf and makes a face. "Oh my, this is awful," she says, offering an apologetic look. She retrieves a bottle of ketchup from the refrigerator. We both pour on an ample amount. I chew a lump of mashed potato and wish Bee had a dog. A hungry dog, under the table. I pour on more ketchup.

"Do you think the Sectors told?" Bee asks.

"Never," I say.

"Then who told Melody?" she asks.

"That's the big mystery," I say.

We sit in silence for several seconds.

"Sorry about supper," Bee says.

"It's delicious," I say, convinced a lie isn't always a sin. According to firsts and lasts, if all the cooks were lined up in heaven, Bee would be at the head of the line.

In spite of my need for levity, my secret sense stops me mid-chew.

"What is it?" Bee says.

"I think somebody's here," I whisper.

Bee starts to stand, but I motion for her to stay seated. Butter knife in hand, I creep toward the front door. The porch light is on, and I pull back the curtains to get a look. Another face looks back at me. I scream, and then fling the door open.

"What are you doing here?" I ask.

On his knees, Doc Lester looks up and his weasel eyes accuse me. He is in a perfect position to see through the tiny opening in the front door curtain. He smells like someone who hasn't bathed for a while, his graying hair dirty and slicked back. I can understand now why he's always lived alone. With the two doctors in Rocky Bluff who actually have medical degrees, his kind of quack doctoring is no longer needed.

"I should be asking what *you* are doing here," he says. It takes him a while to stand, as if he's been on his knees for a long time.

He is a head taller than me, yet I am not intimidated. He's aged significantly in the last few years.

Bee enters the hallway.

"He was spying on us," I tell her.

"You two are going to burn in the fires of hell," Doc Lester tells us, his eyes wide.

"For eating supper together?" I say, to cool the hellfire.

"That's not all you're doing," he says. His look is sour, as if he's taken a bite of Bee's meatloaf.

"You need to leave," I tell him.

He takes a step back to unleash more hatefulness.

"God will smite you down for this, Wildflower McAllister. I've known you were no-good for years now."

"Keep your smites to yourself," I say, grateful that he isn't a physical danger.

"You won't be saying that when everybody in Katy's Ridge knows about you two." He raises an eyebrow, as if excited by the exchange.

Bee appears frozen in place. Up until a few minutes ago, the biggest problem of the evening was getting supper down.

"You're trespassing," Bee says, finding her voice. "This is my property. You're breaking the law."

"Didn't see no *No Trespassing* signs up anywhere." He sticks his tongue in the side of his cheek like he's pleased to get the better of her.

"What do you want?" I say to him.

The other eyebrow raises, a drop of saliva dots the edge of his lip.

My throat tightens. I always thought Doc Lester was lazy, so it makes no sense that he would go to all this trouble to spy on us out in the middle of nowhere unless he wanted something.

"You want to know what I want?" He pauses. "Let me watch," he says finally, lowering his voice, a crooked smile on his face.

Bee steps forward and shoves him off her steps. "You're disgusting," she says. "Get out of here!" I've never heard such fury in her voice.

Doc Lester laughs and his voice fades when I close the door and bolt it. It is only then that Bee sinks to her knees and begins to cry in deep, gulping sobs.

CHAPTER THIRTY-ONE

Lily

The whispers vanished after I found Melody at the bottom of the ravine that morning. I wondered if my father was somehow satisfied to have his sister finally with him. Or if he'd simply given up on getting through to me. After it happened, Mama barely left my side for three days and took off time from work to talk whenever I needed to talk. I'm not sure how a person makes peace with where they come from. It's not like we have any say in the matter.

While one mystery is finally solved, another has sprung in its place. I have no idea who I am anymore. It's like all my dreams died away with the whispers. I haven't felt like singing for days, and for the first time I've begun to question if leaving Katy's Ridge is my fate. Maybe I am meant to stay right here and marry Crow and have babies and sing in the small choir at the Baptist church. Maybe I've been fooling myself all this time that I'm meant for bigger things.

As a result of the ice storm, school has been called off for the

day. Granny has a big fire going in the old wood stove in the living room, and I'm catching up on school work I missed while I attended Melody's funeral. Tiny ice pellets hit the tin roof with a ping that sounds like notes on Granddaddy's banjo that sits in the living room in the same place it was sitting the day he died. Mama dusts it every now and again, and I try to tune it when I have the patience, but it's like all the banjo's songs have dried up like mine.

A light knock on the door startles me. Uncle Daniel takes a wobbly step inside. Tiny ice pellets stick to his hat and coat and he takes them off and hangs them on the pegs next to the door.

"What is it?" I ask. "Is Mama okay?"

Against Granny's better judgment, Mama went into work this morning to do a few things, since she'd spent so much time watching out for me.

"She's okay," he says, "but she sent me to tell you something."

"Why didn't she come and tell me herself?" I ask him.

"She's fielding telephone calls at the sawmill," he says. He looks around like he's looking for Granny. I point to the kitchen. Granny spends most of her time in there with the oven door open to keep things toasty warm.

"Is there a place we can talk in private?" Daniel whispers, keeping an eye on the kitchen.

I lead him to the bedroom I share with Mama and then close the door. Uncle Daniel and I haven't really talked since I ran to get him when I found Melody that morning. I was on my way up to the cemetery to try to find my father's grave when I found an empty jar of moonshine sitting on the railing of the footbridge and cigarette butts twisted into the wood. It was Uncle Daniel who called the sheriff in Rocky Bluff to report Melody's death.

"Tell me what's going on," I say, all of a sudden scared that Mama is in danger.

He sits on the bed next to me, one hand on the cane he always uses.

"Word's got out about her and Bee," he says. "She wanted me to warn you."

His words jolt me to standing. "But who told?" I can only imagine how Mama might feel about this. At Melody's funeral two days ago she looked weary and older than I've ever seen her.

"She thinks it was Doc Lester," Daniel says, rubbing his bad leg like it's acting up on him. "A bunch of people are calling and canceling their accounts. We're losing customers like an artery has burst," he continues. "Wildflower's trying to talk them out of taking their business elsewhere. She's offering discounts and all sorts of bargains, but they're just hanging up on her. Not to mention the names they're calling her. My God, Lily, it's like another war." He rubs his leg again.

"Is she okay?" I ask.

"Not really," he says. "This will probably be the end of the sawmill. Your mama will lose all the money she's put into it. She'll lose her livelihood."

Uncle Daniel drops his head as if a prayer is called for, but maybe he's thinking about wringing necks, too.

"What about you?" I ask, knowing Mama pays him for keeping the books and that he and Jo count on that money.

"We'll be fine," he says. "We've got the farm, and I can always pick up something in Rocky Bluff if I have to. It's your mama I'm worried about, and Bee," he continues. "Mack Avery turned Bee away at the door when she went in to get papers to grade. Told her to pack her bags. To get out of town if she knew what was good for her."

"This all happened this morning?" I ask.

He nods.

"How can people be so mean?" I say.

"Honest to God, Lily, I have no idea. These are supposedly Christian people. At least most of them."

I wonder if I'll ever be asked to sing at the church again, and

then feel selfish to think of myself. Truth is, my singing career may be over before it got started.

"Did you know about Mama and Miss Blackstone?" I ask.

"I didn't," he says. "But in a way, I wasn't surprised. Your mama has a lot of love to give, and she would need someone special."

I should have known Uncle Daniel would never abandon Mama, even about something he may not understand.

"Jo's having a hard time with it," he says. "So are Meg and Amy."

I wonder if all my cousins are overhearing what has happened. We made a game sometimes of snooping to hear what the grownups were talking about, and I imagine this is no exception.

"It's more about it being such a surprise," Daniel continues. "Your mother kept this huge secret from her entire family. I hate that she felt like she couldn't confide in anybody."

I remember the talk Mama and I had at the river where she was so honest about her feelings. "I think it's because she's ashamed, Uncle Daniel."

He looks at me like this idea never occurred to him. "Your mama shouldn't be ashamed of anything," he says. "She's the bravest person I've ever known."

"I don't think she feels brave about this," I say.

We exchange looks, and I can see how much he loves her and also how he's scared for her.

"Downright shame," he says.

"What can I do?" I ask. "Should I go over there, Uncle Daniel?"

"Actually, she said she needs you here. She wants you to make sure your granny doesn't hear about it before she can make it home and tell her herself," he says.

"Granny's not going to take this well," I say.

"I don't imagine she will," he says. "But Nell has surprised me before."

He turns and looks at me like he's wondering if it's okay to talk about my no-good father.

"It's okay," I say to him. "I'm getting used to knowing."

"You were brave to want to know the truth," he says. "You're just like your mama in the courage department."

"I don't think I could ever do what she's doing now, Uncle Daniel. How do you talk people into not hating you?"

Until recently, I never realized how strong Mama is. But now I'm realizing how much she's been through, and how she's always been there for me no matter what.

"How long have you known?" Uncle Daniel asks.

"Not long," I say, not mentioning the kiss.

"Did anybody else know before all this happened?"

"The Sectors know," I say. "Mama and Miss Blackstone go over there sometimes."

"Should have known the Sectors would lead the way on how to be decent human beings," he says.

I remember how Crow wants to stay in Katy's Ridge forever. Would he still be interested in me if I didn't sing anymore? He's always said how much he loves my singing.

"Your mama will come home as soon as the phone stops ringing," Uncle Daniel says, pulling me back into the current crisis. "There can't be that many customers left." He rubs his eyes like he's feeling weary, too.

"Maybe you should go get Great Aunt Sadie and bring her over here," I say. "Tell her what's going on. She'll want to support Mama. Granny will listen to her faster than she listens to anybody else. If she's speaking reason, it may go over better."

"Good idea," he says, and stands. "If your mama gets back here before I do, tell her to hold off on telling Nell. Tell her Sadie's on her way."

"I will," I say. "Until then, I'll go spend time with Granny and try to soften her up."

"Good luck," he says, and we walk to the door. "We need to

keep an eye on this weather, too," he adds. "Looks like this storm may be a big one."

Before he leaves, he gives me a hug. Because of his height, a hug with Uncle Daniel means a big stretch, even when he meets me halfway.

"Who was that? I heard voices," Granny says, coming out of the kitchen.

"It was Uncle Daniel. He says bad weather might be coming in."

"I wondered about that," she says. "My arthritis is acting up."

I follow her back into the kitchen and offer to help with supper. I imagine Granny as the Thanksgiving turkey that I am supposed to butter up. She can be hard on Mama sometimes, and I can't imagine how this latest news will be taken any different.

THIRTY MINUTES LATER, Great Aunt Sadie calls from the front porch needing help with getting off her boots. I find her sitting on the porch swing waiting for me to give them a pull. Yesterday the weather was sunny and almost warm. Yet today, the cold wind hits us from every direction.

"How's it going in there?" she asks, as I pull the first boot off revealing a red wool sock.

Great Aunt Sadie is wearing her old fedora and a scarf around her neck and her big coat. Sticking out of one pocket is a bottle of her blackberry spirits. She looks worried, which isn't like her.

"You thinking about Mama?" I ask.

She nods. "Some people get more than their fair share of suffering, and your mama hasn't done one thing to deserve a lick of it."

"I'm glad you're here," I say, tugging at the other boot. After it slides free, I wrap my arms around myself to capture warmth.

"I didn't see your mama's truck. She isn't home yet?"

"Not yet," I say.

"And Nell has no idea?"

"She's too calm to know anything," I say. "Right now she's mainly worried about Mama making it home safe."

"It's not quite freezing yet, but it will be soon. If she comes home within the next thirty minutes or so, I think she'll be okay."

She leaves her winter things just inside the door and we go into the kitchen. Like old friends sometimes do, Granny and Great Aunt Sadie forego greetings, and Granny serves her a cup of coffee she's heated up on the stove.

"How's the weather?" Granny asks.

"It's gearing up for something big," she tells her. Then she pours blackberry spirits in her coffee and offers the same to Granny.

"What's the occasion?" Granny asks her.

"No occasion at all," she says, glancing in my direction.

The three of us sit in the kitchen, the clock over the stove clicking off the seconds as the storm brews and we wait for Mama's return.

CHAPTER THIRTY-TWO

Wildflower

A slushy ice has accumulated on my windshield by the time I leave the mill. The temperature is hovering around freezing. Now if I can just make it home and up the hill before it freezes. It is already dusk. Our hill is almost impossible to climb in ice. Winter has caught me by surprise.

My business is ruined. The only accounts that weren't closed are the Sectors and Sweeney's store. Sweeney's does little business now that the big grocery store in Rocky Bluff opened, and the Sectors use even less lumber. When I anticipated the worst of what might happen if news of Bee and I got out, it wasn't this bad. The biggest surprise was the coldness with which people closed their accounts. They told me that I should be ashamed and that I was going to hell, and that was before the name-calling started. This from people I'd grown up with. People my family had helped through hard times. People who practiced the golden rule, at least on Sundays.

Tears blur into the mess of old windshield wipers brushing

away slushy ice. I feel tired down to my bones, but promised Bee I would come by. I pull in front of her house, momentarily grateful that I no longer have to hide my truck behind the biggest hedge. A handmade *No Trespassing* sign is sitting by the front door.

"I was worried about you," she says, meeting me at the door.

To my surprise, Bee appears almost calm. Instead of her usual school clothes, she wears a pair of denim pants and a blouse with a bumblebee stitched onto the collar. It has been a day of surprises. A winter storm is coming, not even predicted in the Farmer's Almanac. I've lost the sawmill. And now Bee, at a time when I imagined she'd be sobbing, is unruffled.

"I'm exhausted," I say.

"How bad is it?" she asks.

"I'm officially out of business."

"Well, I'm officially out of a job," she counters. "It only took Mack Avery until noon to bring all my things from the school. He stood here in the doorway until I gave him the key to the building. I'm not to talk to any students or parents and never step foot on the school grounds again or he's threatened to have me arrested."

"Why don't you look upset?" I ask.

"I cried a river after Mack left here, but now I'm angry."

"I haven't reached anger yet," I say.

We move from the doorway and she takes my coat and hangs it on the coat rack. Bee leads us into the living room, not even closing the drapes. I never realized how much it bothered me that whenever we were alone we were concealing ourselves. The thought of not hiding behind thick curtains feels liberating, but also exposed, like two deer in a large meadow with hunters nearby.

"I've still got to go home and tell Mama," I say. "It's one of the few times I've been glad we don't have a telephone. She won't know yet, unless someone's come to the house. Lily's waiting there for me, and Daniel called the mill to tell me he went to pick up

Aunt Sadie and took her to the house. At least I'll have rein-forcements."

"How do you think she'll react?" she asks.

"I don't even want to think about it, Bee. But the first thing I'm doing when I get home is hiding her shotgun."

I attempt a laugh. We sit on the couch, and Bee holds my hand in hers. "What do we do now?" she asks.

A mixture of rain and ice begins to hit the picture window.

"I'm not sure," I say. "But I can't stay long. I've got to get home. If it's all right with you, I'll come by as soon as I can get down the hill again and we'll talk it through."

I squeeze her hand to reassure her.

"It must have been Doc Lester who told," she says.

"Who else?" I say.

My legs feel heavy as I go to the door and put on my coat again, so soon after I took it off.

"Good luck telling your mother," Bee says, buttoning the top button of my coat.

"She won't understand this," I say. "Next time you see me I may be looking for a place to live."

"You can always stay here," she says.

"And risk someone burning the place down?" I ask. My mood doesn't allow for a happy ending.

We say our goodbyes and a blast of cold air cuts through my coat as I make my way to the truck. A misty sleet has begun to fall. Chains still in the bed of the truck, I drive slow and pull off onto the side of the road instead of on the slight incline where I usually park. The slush is hardening to a light crunch. Two sets of foot-prints go up the hill before me, probably Daniel and Aunt Sadie. I hate to think how Daniel's leg must have hurt him as he helped her up the hill. The wind rips across the mountain and the ice is in solid pellets now. I'm glad I thought to put Daddy's old rain slicker over my winter coat. The ice hits it with dull pops.

I make my way home holding onto the branches of trees and bushes to keep me from sliding back down. The last fifteen years have, in some ways, felt like an uphill climb. Lily has helped me have no regrets, the reward of having her in my life has been so great. On my way up the steepest part of the hill, I wonder if telling Mama about Bee will break us apart forever.

When I get in sight of the house, every light is on. I remember the night when people came to pay their respects after Daddy died. The whole community of Katy's Ridge showed up. Some of the same loving and caring people who called me today and told me they were never doing business with me again because I was now loathsome and disgusting.

On the front porch, I stomp the caked ice from my boots and call on whatever courage I have left for the next obstacle. I leave my boots next to Aunt Sadie's, relieved that she will be with me as I face Mama.

Warm air greets me as I open the door. I am lucky to make it home. Aunt Sadie will probably be spending the night until this storm moves through.

Voices come from the kitchen and then laughter. The laughter is probably Lily's doing. She knows how to tame Mama's lion side. I go into the bedroom and change out of my work clothes. When I catch a quick glance in the mirror, dark circles are underneath my eyes. How is it possible that I look ten years older than I did this morning?

I sigh, wishing I could run away instead of tell Mama the truth. Then I go to her bedroom and take the shotgun from behind her door and slide it under my bed. Not that Mama would actually use it, but why take chances. I take a deep breath, wishing Daddy were here.

It's twice as warm in the kitchen as it is in the rest of the house. Three people I love sit at the kitchen table, dirty supper dishes

pushed to the side. Mama stands as I enter, as if her relief at seeing me safe and sound has pulled her tall.

"You made it," she says.

"I made it," I repeat.

"I've got your supper warming in the oven," she says.

Of all the suppers we've had together in this kitchen, I wonder if this will be the last one.

"I'm actually not hungry, Mama," I say.

"Since when are you not hungry?" Mama asks. She hands me a plate full of food anyway.

"Did you have trouble getting up the hill?" Aunt Sadie says. She beams courage in my direction. Tears threaten to come.

Lily stands and puts her arms around my neck. I want to thank her for not hating me and make every effort not to weep. Not every child would be so accepting. It occurs to me that as long as my family doesn't desert me, I can take whatever the rest of the world says.

"Sit down," Mama says. "You want a cup of coffee?"

I nod. It's late, but I am tired enough to sleep tonight even after a dozen cups of coffee.

"Tell us about your day," Mama says.

At that moment, I want to keep her unaware. I can't bear her being disappointed in me like everybody else in Katy's Ridge.

"I have something I need to tell you," I say to her, wishing the strong coffee could give me more backbone.

Mama's face turns from sunlight to dark clouds. "What is it?"

I take a bite of the pork chop on my plate to fortify me, followed by a bite each of mashed potatoes and collard greens. Mama's country cooking could strengthen anyone.

"Something's happened that you need to know about," I say.

"Something bad?" she asks, her eyebrows raised.

"Something bad," I repeat, thinking the only worse news I might deliver would be another death in the family. Al-though, it's

entirely possible that I will be dead to Mama after this, which is kind of the same thing.

Mama's lips tighten. She does not cater to bad news.

Aunt Sadie offers her more blackberry spirits, and Mama brushes the offer away, all the while keeping her eyes on me.

"Nell, it's important to remember that nobody's hurt and nobody's dead," Aunt Sadie says, like she's been reading my thoughts.

"You know what's coming then?" she asks Aunt Sadie, her voice low.

"I do," Aunt Sadie says.

"You know what's coming, too?" Mama turns to Lily.

Lily nods.

"It seems a conspiracy's afoot," Mama says, her look the opposite of pleased. She turns back to me. "Best to pull the bandage off real quick then," she tells me.

I hesitate. The speech I'd practiced on the way up the hill disappears like the dove of a county fair magician.

"Mama—" I falter again.

"You'd best be saying something quick, Louisa May." Her voice is louder and her eyes don't leave mine.

I start talking, unrehearsed, and tell her everything: that Bee and I have been more than friends for years now and that we've been keeping it a secret all this time.

Mama's expression doesn't change.

"Trouble is, the word's got out and everybody in Katy's Ridge knows," I say. "And today Bee got fired from teaching and nearly everybody we had business with at the sawmill has canceled their accounts."

I pause long enough to hope the shotgun isn't loaded that's under my bed that Mama might find if she takes a notion to. "I'm very sorry if you're ashamed of me," I continue, "but I didn't set out to hurt you or anybody else. Not at all."

The clock over the stove is the only sound in the room, as if clicking down the seconds before Mama hits the roof.

Outside, the wind soars down the mountain behind the house and rattles the door and windows. Ice pierces the tin roof. Mama's expression still hasn't changed. Aunt Sadie and Lily seem as puzzled as I am by her silence.

"Are you okay, Nell?" Aunt Sadie asks.

Mama doesn't answer and looks like she's giving serious thought to how to react. Either that or she's having a stroke and unable to tell us.

Lily looks at me, one brow raised with an unasked question.

I give a slight, one shoulder shrug. I expected yelling, maybe even weeping, not silence.

"Mama, did you hear me?" I ask.

Her gray eyes fill with tears. My shoulders drop with the knowledge I've broken my mother's heart.

I tell her how sorry I am, and lower my head.

"It's not the end of the world," Aunt Sadie says to her. "Wild-flower's just being the person God meant her to be."

"That's right, Granny," Lily says. "We want Mama to be happy, don't we?"

Tears cling to my eyelids like the ice clinging to the trees outside.

Mama wipes her tears and turns to me with the same fierce, loving look she wore in Daniel and Jo's barn before Lily was born. A look I've wondered if I'd ever see again.

"Louisa May, I knew you two were in love as soon as she came back from Nashville and started teaching in Katy's Ridge again."

I exhale, wondering if I heard her right. Aunt Sadie and I exchange a look that reminds me of when I was in labor with Lily. I remember that last push Aunt Sadie encouraged me to make after the long, twenty-hour ordeal. At the end of all that pain, Lily came into the world with a sudden ease.

"You knew all along?" I ask Mama.

She nods. "Of course it worried me at first. Worried me a lot. I prayed about it every day here in this kitchen, petting that boney cat until I thought his hair might fall out. But I couldn't throw you out, not after all you'd been through. I'm more loyal to my kin than that," she continues. "Then over the years as I watched the two of you together, I didn't see what harm happiness could do. Not to you or to anybody else."

"Why didn't you tell me?" I ask, thinking of all the grief this might have saved me.

"Well, it wasn't really any of my business until you decided to tell me about it," she says. "That day Bee brought over the banana bread, I thought you two might finally tell me then. But off you go, sneaking around and kissing each other at the front door. I know I'm going a little deaf, but do you think I'm blind, too?"

She laughs a short laugh before her expression turns serious again.

"As for you losing all your business, and Bee getting fired from being a school teacher, that disappoints me. I wish you'd been more careful. But country people despise anybody or anything different. When we moved here, your daddy said we'd best be careful who we trusted, that they could turn on a dime. He was right about a lot of things, my Joseph."

"But what will I do to make a living?" I ask her. "What will Bee do?"

"You are smart girls. You'll do what you have to do," Mama says. "Maybe you'll leave Katy's Ridge and find someplace new."

"But won't it be the same everywhere?" Lily asks.

Until now, I haven't realized how quiet she's been.

"What you're always looking for are the pockets of good people," Aunt Sadie says. "There are good people everywhere. There are good people here, too, just not enough to keep the mill open."

Mama swipes a wayward tear and straightens her apron. "This isn't something that can be solved in an evening," she says to me. "Do you want me to heat up your supper again?"

All of a sudden, I am ravenous and tell her so. Mama gets up to warm the food again. I am relieved and exhausted at the same time and unsure of what to do next. Rest is required.

As Mama readies the food, I walk over to the stove where she stands. "I underestimated you," I tell her. She laughs a short laugh.

"About time you realized who you're dealing with," she says.

We embrace for several seconds, longer that we've ever hugged each other before. Mama smells of wood smoke and supper cooking and Jergen's lotion. She smells like herself. Like Mama. If forced to move away, I will miss this smell. I will miss living so close to my family—to my sisters and Daniel and my nieces and nephews. I will miss Aunt Sadie most of all, and the memories here that have Daddy in them. I will even miss visiting that old grave-yard. What I won't miss is how frightened people are with their small ways. I won't miss that at all.

It dawns on me, am I really considering leaving Katy's Ridge?

CHAPTER THIRTY-THREE

Lily

The ice storm keeps us at home for two days until it feels like I might go crazy with boredom. Pearl shows up at the house with a message from June to Mama that the roads are mostly clear. Granny makes us hot chocolate and we sit in the living room and talk in whispers. Pearl tells me about the latest boy she's decided she has a crush on—which feels almost as boring as being stuck in the house for two days—and I tell her about Granny surprising us all by not throwing a fit about Mama and Bee.

Mama has been quiet during our time at home, as though doing major thinking. No more has been said about what she might do after the sawmill closes for good.

Right as Pearl leaves, Uncle Daniel comes up the hill to take Great Aunt Sadie back to her house now that the roads are clear. Mama and Uncle Daniel talk in hushed tones before he leaves.

"I need to talk to Bee," Mama says, a few minutes later. "You want to come?"

Thrilled by the thought of getting out of the house, I agree.

Patches of ice remain in the shade and on the north sides of hills, but the path and the road are clear. At the road, we see several cars over at Uncle Daniel's.

"Looks like somebody's called a meeting I don't know about," Mama says.

It is unusual for her sisters to get together without inviting Mama, but part of the reason may be that they all have telephones and Granny doesn't.

"We need to go over there," Mama says to me. "I haven't talked to them since all hell broke loose. You okay with that?"

I tell her I am.

When we go over to Aunt Jo's, we find Aunt Meg and Aunt Amy there, too, along with all of my cousins. You'd think Aunt Jo was having Thanksgiving at her house this year. The room falls silent when we come through the back door. Within seconds, the cousins and me are shooed out of the house, but I refuse to go. Luckily, nobody forces me to.

Nat is ushered out by Bolt and gives me a look that asks what's going on. Meanwhile, Lizzy takes a second to make sure she smirks at me. It is only Janie who appears to know what's going on and for once the dull sheen on her face has color to it.

I realize how little I've seen my cousins in the last few weeks. The last time being at the anniversary of Granddaddy's death. That was the day Melody Monroe showed up and my whole life changed. All of a sudden, I had an aunt I never knew existed, and a mama with a secret she hoped no one ever found out about. Like country folks, who Granny says can turn on a dime, my life turned on a dime. One day it was nothing new, the next it was full of unexpected trouble. The biggest surprise, however, is playing out in front of me as my aunts and uncles gang up on Mama.

"You disgraced us," Uncle Cecil says to Mama, his voice raised. "Now we're all in danger of losing our jobs."

I can't imagine how Mama could disgrace anybody.

"Did you not think about how this might affect us?" he says.

In Jo and Daniel's living room, Mama stands in the middle of all of them, while I stand next to the wall that leads to the kitchen. She looks tiny compared to everyone else, like the runt of a litter. I wonder why I never noticed that before. Uncle Cecil, especially, towers over her. He's never been one of my favorite people, and now he's proving why.

"I can understand why you might be upset," Mama says. "But I didn't plan for any of this."

"Well, you must have known it might get out," Aunt Amy says, the first of her sisters to speak. The others chime in their agreement.

Aunt Jo isn't looking at Mama and has her arms folded across her chest like she's trying to hold herself together and not say anything. Uncle Daniel isn't back from taking Great Aunt Sadie home, or I imagine he would step up in defense of Mama. Perhaps that's why they've started without him.

Aunt Meg looks away, as though she's feeling guilty. Uncle Cecil is leading the dissension and the angrier he gets, the redder his strawberry birth mark. Then everybody starts talking at once with Mama just standing there watching them like she's having a bad dream. A minute or so later Uncle Daniel walks into the living room and asks what's going on. He steps in next to Mama and tells everybody to quiet down.

"Is this how you treat family?" Uncle Daniel asks the others, raising his voice, too.

"What about how she's treated us?" Aunt Jo says.

Uncle Daniel shoots her a look I've never seen him give her, like she should be ashamed. "Wildflower is family," he begins again. "And I, for one, don't turn on my family. If our family turns on us, who do we have?"

I think of what Granny said, along the same lines, when she found out about Mama and Miss Blackstone.

Uncle Cecil scoffs. "This is ridiculous," he says.

"What if we all disagreed with something you did, Cecil?" Uncle Daniel says.

"Well, I'd never do anything to put this family in danger," he says.

At that moment, I want to slap Russia right off his face.

"Just so you know," Daniel continues, "Nell has known all along and she sees nothing wrong with it."

The reaction is of stirring bees in a hive. It takes a few minutes for everybody to settle down again. Meanwhile, Mama stands in the middle of the living room like the wary queen, though I don't think anybody recognizes her nobility besides me.

"It's just caught us all unawares," Aunt Jo says to Mama. "It's hard to stand by somebody when you're the last to know something. Makes me feel like I've been shut out. I can't believe you told Mama before you told us."

I wonder how Aunt Jo knows this and then realize Pearl must have gone straight across the road to tell everybody what I shared with her this morning.

Everybody looks at Mama, including me, waiting on her to defend herself about telling Granny. Pearl's going to need to defend herself, too, next time I see her. Her secret-telling is a part of this hornet's nest.

"If the Sectors knew all along, why not tell us, too?" Aunt Meg asks.

The hive gets stirred again.

"Settle down," Uncle Daniel yells over the buzz.

Everybody does.

"Wildflower needs to think about what loyalty means," Aunt Jo says. "She let us get blindsided by all this."

"Everybody in Katy's Ridge knew before I did," Aunt Amy says. "One of my customers in Rocky Bluff asked me if the rumors were true and I had to say 'What rumors?'" She looks straight at Mama.

They have never been the closest of siblings and at that moment the gap widens. "I've never been so embarrassed in my life," Aunt Amy concludes.

Meanwhile, Lizzy spies through the front window and gives me a look of total glee that Mama is in trouble. When I turn back to look, the color has left Mama's face. She needs rescuing fast, and even Uncle Daniel has been unable to control how everyone is acting. Maybe if I sang one of Granddaddy's favorite songs, like *Down in the Valley*, that would get everyone's attention. Mama says my singing calms anyone who listens, and calmness is what is needed. But when I open my mouth there's no song there. I momentarily panic. I've never had music abandon me like this, and somehow this feels more alarming than what's happening between Mama and our family.

"We can talk about this later, whenever you want," Mama announces. "But right now I have somewhere I need to be." Then she motions for me to follow her and we leave Uncle Daniel's house. She has a speed to her step that she seldom has. I even have to run to catch up. I don't have to ask where we're going.

Within minutes, Mama knocks on Miss Blackstone's door. She opens it with a cautious smile. I imagine we are unexpected, in an expected kind of way, in that we were bound to show up eventually. We take off our coats and Miss Blackstone leads us into the living room where packing boxes are stacked.

"You going somewhere?" Mama asks her.

"Got to find work," she says, in a matter-of-fact way.

"Were you going to tell me?" Mama asks, her eyes wild and full of instant tears.

They sit on a light green sofa together, and I sit in an armchair to the side with soft cushions that are the same light green. Though I'm sitting still, Mama's tears make me want to squirm out the door. She tells Miss Blackstone what just happened at Uncle Daniel and Aunt Jo's. When she hears the story, the tenderness on

Miss Blackstone's face makes me look away. But I am relieved that Mama has someone to rely on besides me.

A clock ticks on the fireplace mantle. A table with a lamp sits nearby with a few neatly stacked books. For some reason, I imagined Miss Blackstone read textbooks, not poetry and novels. Sometimes, I wish Miss Blackstone was still my teacher. It's because of her that I graduated elementary school a year early. My high school English teacher doesn't take an interest in me the way she did. But now I wonder if Miss Blackstone's interest was because of Mama and not me.

The north facing road that stretches between Katy's Ridge and Rocky Bluff stays icy longer than the main roads, so I won't be expected to return to school for another day or two. I am a sophomore this year and wonder if the gossip will reach the high school by the time I return.

"We'll figure this out," Miss Blackstone tells Mama, when her tears finally slow to a stop.

"Lily, can you give us a minute?" Miss Blackstone asks.

I stand and look around. I have no idea where to go or what to do to give them a minute.

"Maybe you could put the kettle on the stove so we can have some hot tea," she says. "You can close the kitchen door if you want."

When I call her Miss Blackstone, she says to call her Bee, but I don't see that happening any time soon, if at all. I walk into the kitchen and find the empty tea kettle already sitting on the stove. I fill it with water and turn on the electric stove eye with a simple click. Granny's old one uses gas and we have to light it with matches. I wish Granny could see this one. It looks brand new. Not that she sees any use in new things when the old ones still work.

The voices from the living room are muffled, but Mama still sounds upset. I busy myself with looking through the cabinets for

teacups and saucers and set out three sets. I remember Melody Monroe offering me tea in the tiny cabin. A civilized thing to do in such poor surroundings. I find a box of Lipton tea bags and drop a tea bag into each cup.

After a while the tea kettle rattles and then sings and I turn it off, realizing the voices in the living room are now quiet. Moments later, the kitchen door opens and Mama and Miss Blackstone come inside.

"We need to talk to you," Mama says. Her tears have passed, but her eyes are still red.

Miss Blackstone pours hot water in the teacups and cov-ers each with a saucer. She tells me I did a good job putting the kettle on, and I am surprised by how much this means to me. It is strange to touch her things and see her and Mama together now that I know about them. But it is a strangeness that I am willing to get used to. Miss Blackstone brings a chair from her bedroom to put at the end of the table that only seats two people.

"Join us," she says.

We doctor our tea with sugar and milk, me imitating Miss Blackstone's motions. Then it is Mama who starts talking.

"How would you feel about moving to Nashville?" she asks me.

I stop stirring my tea. Have I misheard? I look at them and wonder if this is what it's like to be thunderstruck. How is it that just when I decide to stay in Katy's Ridge and possibly settle down with Crow, I am presented with the one thing I've dreamed about for years?

When I don't answer, Mama repeats her question, and I wonder if I've lost my speaking voice, as well as my singing. Nash-ville is an hour and a half away, almost in the center of the state. It's the capital of Tennessee. Compared to the tiny hamlet of Katy's Ridge, it's the entire Roman Empire.

"I lived in Nashville for a couple of years and already know some people there," Miss Blackstone says.

"That's where the Grand Ole Opry is, too," Mama says, in case I've lost my mind and don't remember.

Granny listens to the Opry every Saturday night. I listen, too, whenever there are female singers on like Kitty Wells or Mother Maybelle Carter and the Carter Sisters. Granny says I sing as well as they do, but grandmothers are supposed to say things like that.

"Lily, are you okay?" Mama asks, her expression serious.

"I don't know what to say," I answer, which is the truth.

A look passes between Mama and Miss Blackstone. "I thought you'd be overjoyed," Mama says. "I've known you wanted to leave Katy's Ridge ever since you started keeping a road atlas under the mattress."

Miss Blackstone laughs and asks, "Is that true?"

Mama says it is. But I don't feel like joining in their laughter. How do I tell Mama that all my dreams have died and been buried along with the knowledge that I am the daughter of a snake? Someone who didn't give her a choice. How do I tell her that if the world were a better place, I wouldn't even be here? No wonder I haven't felt like singing for weeks. For all I know I may have lost my voice forever. Someone like me doesn't belong in front of an audience, singing all over the world. I deserve much smaller things. I deserve to stay here with all the ghosts.

Mama tries to act excited about the possible move, but I can tell this is hard for her. She probably thought she'd be staying in Katy's Ridge the rest of her life. I was the one who was going to fly the nest as soon as I figured out how to grow wings.

"Can I think about it?" I say. It surprises me that I've not already packed my suitcase. It evidently surprises Mama, too.

"Of course," Mama says.

They exchange another look. Miss Blackstone's forehead crinkles like it does whenever she gets worried. I wonder if Mama's told her that she won't go anywhere unless I agree.

"There's a university in Nashville, too," she says to me. "You are

more than smart enough to attend Vanderbilt. You could major in music there."

Just hearing the word *music* is like hearing the name of someone I used to love who has now died. It would make more sense to wear black and sit in the cemetery. Maybe I will start having an anniversary this time every year, too. I think of Granny and Great Aunt Sadie and all the aunts and uncles and cousins we would leave behind if we moved to Nashville. But after what happened today, where my aunts and Uncle Cecil ganged up on Mama, I'm not so sure I'd miss them.

CHAPTER THIRTY-FOUR

Wildflower
Six Months Later

We stand outside a large church in downtown Nashville. Desperate to find a soloist when their usual one got the flu, Lily has been asked to sing. A woman Bee works with lined it up for her, taking Bee's word for it that Lily was an amazing singer. It is a fancy church. Rumor has it that people in the music industry go here. It is across town from where we're living, in a rich area. My old truck looks out of place in the parking lot, and I hope they don't tow it off.

"Are you nervous?" I ask Lily, feeling my own butterflies bumping against each other in my stomach.

"More nervous than I've ever been in my life," Lily says. "This isn't Katy's Ridge," she adds with a swallow.

"No it isn't," I say. "But this is good, Lil. This is meant to be."

She looks at me like I'm about to throw her into a lion's den. She hasn't sung in front of anyone in over six months. Bee and I have worried over this for at least that long. Our hope is that this

solo will help Lily remember who she is and what she has to offer the world. It is a huge risk to take, but we fear that the longer she goes without singing, the easier it will be for her to forget.

We enter the immense foyer. Worshipers straighten themselves and tidy their children before walking into the sanctuary and finding seats. Being Easter, the church is packed with people. Family after family—the men and boys in suits and ties on this hot spring day, and the girls and women in store-bought dresses, hats and gloves—file past us. I look down at my simple dress, no hat or gloves. Although Bee did go out behind our small apartment building this morning and find a wildflower that she pinned to my dress.

Lily is to enter with the minister and the choir who create a procession down the center aisle. I've never been in a church building this big in my entire life. Our church in Katy's Ridge could practically fit inside this single entryway.

"What if nothing comes out?" she says, her eyes wide.

This is our fear, of course. The thing Bee and I have discussed many times. We've agreed that if we need to, we'll simply walk up front to wherever Lily is standing and each take her by the hand and walk out of the church, heads high.

"You'll be fine," I say, reassuring her. "You've done this hundreds of times. Just pretend you're standing on the front porch of Mama's house, singing to your family."

I straighten the small bow on the front of her dress. A dress Amy made special for the occasion, now that we're finally speaking to each other again. The fabric matches Lily's rosy cheeks and she looks grown up, a proper young woman. She's wearing the gold medallion I gave her that she found one afternoon while we were packing. A side pocket on her dress reveals a letter tucked inside.

"Is that from Crow?" I ask.

She forgets her nerves and smiles. "He gets military leave again

in a few months and he wants to stop in Nashville before going home." Her pleasure contains hints of sadness.

All of us have been homesick to one degree or another. I, for one, never dreamed how difficult it might be to leave Katy's Ridge. For months now I've missed everything about it. Not only Mama and Aunt Sadie and my sisters and Daniel, but also the way the mountains burst with spring every year. The light green of new leaves and blossoms walking up the hillside like an old woman sowing seeds. I miss the quietness there, the bustle of squirrels instead of traffic. I miss visiting Daddy's grave and sitting underneath the old willow tree and telling him about my life. I miss how the wind sounds when it plays in the trees. I even miss old Pumpkin, who Mama told us in her last letter, is of failing health. I don't know what she'll do when Pumpkin dies, now that she's living in that old house alone. Yet Aunt Sadie has been sticking close and they are working on a new quilt.

Crow's letters to Lily arrive faithfully once a week, and I'm convinced they've helped Lily with the move. Pearl sends letters, too, but infrequent ones. Their friendship has waned, and I wonder if the people we grow up with ever stay best friends for life.

"Where's Bee?" Lily asks.

"She's saving me a seat near the front," I say.

Lily and Bee have become good friends over the last six months. Bee got a job at the high school Lily attends and they ride in together. My job is quite different from the sawmill and has taken some time to get used to. As a secretary in the admissions office at Vanderbilt University, I have to dress up every day. No more boots and overalls. It took weeks to get used to wearing even short heels. But at least it's close enough that I can walk to work when the weather is good.

I have not made peace with churches. Even ones as large and beautiful as this. Nor have I made peace with God or God's people.

It has been hard to forget the names I was called when people found out about me and Bee, evidence of their less than Christ-like natures.

The choir gathers wearing purple choir robes—thirty people at least—along with a choir director and a young organist who proceeds down the side aisle alone so he can play as the choir enters. Lily is singing during the offertory, when the collection plates are passed.

Why do all churches smell alike? Is it the hymnals? A universal cleaning product only sold to churches, mixed in with old lady perfume dabbed on a little too freely?

Lily grabs my arm, her fear renewed. "Mama, I can't do this," she whispers.

Her grip makes me wince. I take Lily's hands in mine and look into her eyes. "Remember that first time you sang in church in Katy's Ridge when you were nine years old?"

She nods.

"Remember how easy it was to sing nearly every Sunday after that?"

She nods again.

"Well, you're on the same path, just a little farther along. Some day, *this* place will feel small."

"Are you trying to scare me more?" she asks.

"You're going to be fine," I tell her.

She pauses, like she wants to believe me, but isn't quite sure. "I miss it, you know. I miss Katy's Ridge. I never thought I would." Her eyes mist.

"I miss it, too, honey," I say. "You can't live somewhere your whole life and not miss it."

"I'm so glad Granny and Great Aunt Sadie are coming for Easter supper," Lily says. "I wish the others could come, too."

"They'll visit another time," I say.

Daniel and Jo are to bring Aunt Sadie and Mama up from

Katy's Ridge this afternoon. They will see our small two-bedroom apartment for the first time. Evidently Meg and Amy weren't up for the trip, though they were invited. There's still mending to do with my sisters. Amy made Lily's dress, but things have been strained for months. Meg has been distant, too, which isn't like her. She says it is Cecil who is having a hard time with me and Bee and that he doesn't want Janie exposed to the likes of us. To me, odd Janie could only benefit from knowing that people can be different.

"I wish they were all coming to hear me sing," Lily says. "Like they used to at home." She bites her lip.

"I wish they were, too," I say, "but Mama wanted to go to Easter service in Katy's Ridge, so she could stare down the people who said hateful things to me."

Lily smiles. Mama writes as faithfully as Crow and her letters are full of her advice. A small price to pay after she surprised me with her acceptance of Bee and me. Aunt Sadie told me once that Daddy would have never married Mama if he hadn't seen something special in her. It has taken me years to see that specialness.

The organist begins playing the introduction to the first hymn and the congregation stands. Lily shoots me a look of sheer terror. My butterflies lurch on her behalf. She looks toward the door and I wonder for a second if she's going to take off running. But then she looks at me with a determination I haven't seen from her in a while.

"I'll be fine," she tells me. She stands straighter and clears her throat. She hums a few notes, the first I've heard out of her mouth in months.

"I guess I'd better go to my seat," I say. "You okay?"

She nods, and I believe her.

As the first stanza is sung, I walk down the side aisle looking for Bee's familiar yellow hat, a bumble bee stitched on the side. I find her on the second row and scoot in next to her, taking my half

of the hymnal. She points to the verse, but I have no interest in singing. She leans close to my ear.

"Lily okay?"

I give a hopeful shrug.

It is hot for April and all the windows in the church are open to let in the breeze. Programs are used as paper fans and are already going limp. Strangers surround us. Other women note what we're wearing. I imagine they think Bee and I are two single friends going to church together, trying to attract the eyes of a man. People see what they want to see.

After we finish the hymn, there are several scripture readings and then the sermon begins. My mind wanders. The lesson rambles like a stream down a mountain, gravity pulling it toward a certain conclusion. From an open window, I view a squirrel playing in a pruned dogwood tree in the courtyard, along with a male and female cardinal, the red vivid against the white dogwood blossoms. Tennessee is the most beautiful place on earth when the dogwoods bloom in April. I remember the gnarled dogwood—wild, instead of tamed like this one—that marks the beginning of the trail to the old cemetery.

As the warm breeze scoots through the window next to me, I close my eyes and picture the weeping willow in the graveyard dropping leaves onto Daddy's grave. I send him greetings—Air Mail—floating on my thoughts. I imagine the church service going on down the hill from his final resting place. So much history is there. My history.

In my imagination, Mama sits in her usual pew, wearing one of her better old dresses, with the hat she wears on special Sundays. A purple ribbon around the brim in honor of Easter. No matter how many times Amy has offered to make Mama brand new dresses for holidays, she insists on wearing the old ones. I remember the faded dress Melody wore the day she showed up in Katy's Ridge. She was wearing the same dress the

day she died. I imagine her at peace in the old cemetery, talking with her family, maybe even conversing with Daddy from time to time.

I picture Daniel and Jo sitting next to Mama, Bolt and Nat in the pew behind, along with Lizzy looking grumpy as usual, and Janie blending into the beige wood of the pew. Next to Jo will be Amy, and then Meg and Cecil, and then the rest of the pew will be empty, where Lily and I might normally sit. An ache rises from deep inside my chest. A broken place that hasn't healed, from having to leave the mountain home I know and love.

I want to squeeze Bee's hand and get her support, but we would never risk it in public. In proper society, even friends don't touch unless there is good reason. I don't understand this world we live in, or the suffering that goes on in the midst of family, friends and strangers alike, with no one acknowledging the pain. It seems we are beasts of burden with blinders on, urged ahead by an unseen driver. I refuse to believe that God is the one who is driving us. This wouldn't make any sense.

During the prayer following the sermon, I take a deep breath and Bee glances at me, her eyes asking if I'm okay. I don't know how to tell her that at that moment I am so homesick I might burst into tears that flood the sanctuary. Her shoe touches mine, a secret signal that she's here for me. It is Easter, and I am in need of a resurrection. A coming back to life in this new place. Perhaps God can spare one not only for Jesus but for me, too. For all of us who are tired of having blinders on.

The sermon has ended and the offering begins, Lily's time to sing. I am so nervous for her, I have to remind myself to breathe. She rises from her seat next to the choir and steps up to the front. A piano begins to play, and I think of Miss Mildred at the Katy's Ridge Church, approaching eighty and still playing. Her bad notes have increased over the years and now she is losing her eyesight, so sometimes the congregation can't even recognize the hymn. But

that is not the case in this church. It sounds like an angel is playing, each note perfect.

Lily wipes her hands on her dress. She will be fifteen this summer. It is hard to believe I have a child this old. Sometimes I still feel fifteen myself, instead of twenty-eight, and sometimes I feel fifty.

When she was hours old, I held Lily in my arms and fell in love with this helpless creature that had come through me. Now that she is in front of this crowd, without knowing if her voice will betray her or not, I feel like I might faint from fear. The hardest thing any parent does is watch their child step out into life, not knowing if they will experience painful stumbles or great accomplishments. I don't know how she'll react if she does poorly. The move from Katy's Ridge has made her more cautious. Occasionally she asks a question about Johnny, and I realize that she's still grappling with the knowledge of how she came into this world.

The intro plays, and I wonder if my heart can take it. Will her voice be there? Will the song insist on being sung? It is a song I haven't heard her sing before. It is a gospel song. *His Eye is on the Sparrow.*

When Lily begins to sing her voice is soft at first and shakes as if announcing her nerves. *Why should I be discouraged?* the song begins, but she quickly gains control. By the refrain of the first verse, her voice is steady and strong and soars toward the rafters. More than one person gasps.

Bee and I exchange smiles. Our gamble, of whether or not to let Lily sing, has worked. As the melody builds, Lily's tone becomes as clear as a mountain stream that flows through the Appalachians. Her nervousness falls away and she looks out over the congregation as if to sing the song to every single person.

Goosebumps rise on my arms and Bee pulls a handkerchief from her purse and wipes her eyes. We've been through a lot together in the last few months. It started last fall with the

anniversary of Daddy's death and the arrival of Melody Monroe. Up until then, I never dreamed I'd leave Katy's Ridge or that the sawmill would be boarded up and closed once and for all. Easter is about Jesus lying in the tomb, waiting for three days, before being restored to life. In a way, this transition has been about waiting. Waiting to feel at home again.

All of a sudden, the sun pours through the window, making the walls look gilded. I wonder if the gold Mary has decided to join us. Tears blur the scene. Fourteen years ago she came to me. A gold woman in the trees, surrounded by light, reaching to take my hand, Daddy standing next to her. That day, I thought I was going to die and that she and Daddy had come to take me to where they were. I felt at peace to be going, and then sad when I realized it wasn't my time.

As Lily continues to sing, I become aware of how motionless everyone is. Enraptured. They haven't taken their eyes from her. Even their makeshift fans have stopped beating the breeze. Lily comes to the last verse leading to the final chorus. Whatever nerves she had before, are completely gone. I have never heard her sing better. I imagine Daddy in the graveyard, listening to his granddaughter on this Easter morning.

The song soars to its conclusion:

I sing because I'm happy, the song says. *I sing because I'm free. His eye is on the sparrow....*

In a moment of what I can only call grace, my heartache releases. I take my first deep breath in years. Maybe ever. A cool breeze makes its way into the warm church, as though arriving special delivery from Katy's Ridge. My chest expands, and I clasp Bee's hand.

At that moment, I feel free. Free to release Lily into her own life where her music will always be with her. Free from the past that has often kept me prisoner. Free to start over somewhere fresh. A new life delivered on the wings of Lily's song.

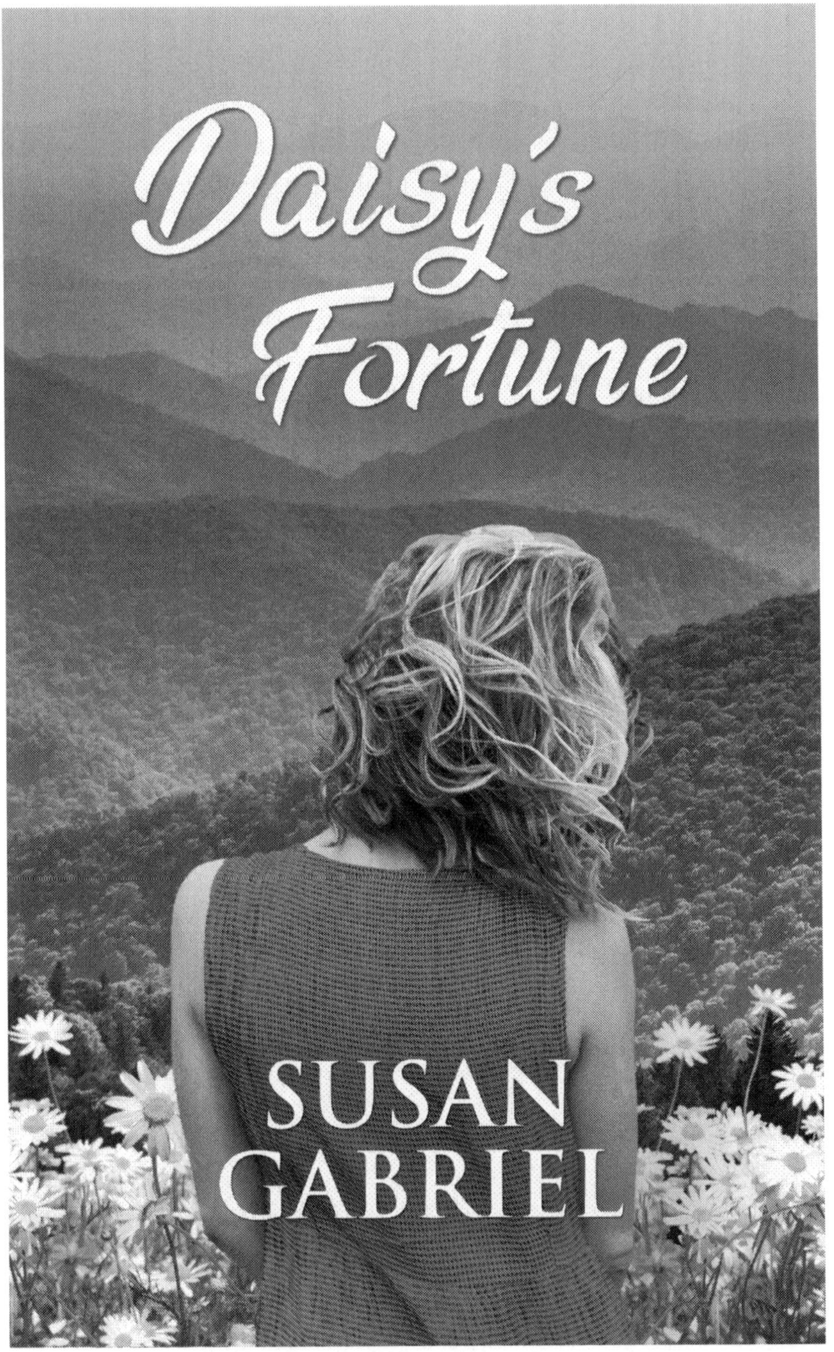
Daisy's
Fortune
SUSAN
GABRIEL

ISBN: 978-0-9981050-2-4

Cover design by Lizzie Gardiner, lizziegardiner.co.uk

Wild Lily Arts

Printed in the United States of America

For seven generations

CHAPTER ONE

Wildflower

The smell of honeysuckle fills the mountain path. I am a girl again in Katy's Ridge. Thirteen. A time when everything changed. The sun has fallen below the mountain, and shadows creep along the forest floor. Three crows sit atop the gate at the back of the cemetery. We exchange looks. One of the crows points her beak toward the ground, drawing my attention to something shiny on the path. It is the gold medallion I used to wear for protection, covered in Johnny Monroe's blood. Yet in the dream, it now belongs to Daisy.

The telephone rings. I gasp awake. For weeks now, I have been dreaming of Katy's Ridge.

"Wildflower?"

Is Aunt Sadie part of the dream?

No, I decide. Does this have something to do with the nudges I've been getting from my secret sense? Nudges I keep ignoring? Nudges that tell me I need to go back to Katy's Ridge?

"It's your mama," Aunt Sadie says.

A beat of silence follows. Then another. Unspoken words communicate a lifetime of history between us.

"I'll be there by lunchtime," I tell her.

We end our call.

In the early-morning light, I put on the coffee and stand at the kitchen window overlooking a small courtyard behind my apartment building. A lonely red maple stands in the center surrounded by boxwoods, a feeble attempt by the management to add a hint of nature amid all the brick and concrete.

The small wooden cat Daniel carved for my thirteenth birthday sits on the windowsill. After Daddy died, Daniel—my sister Jo's husband—was like a father to me. A wave of homesickness catches me by surprise. It is 1982, twenty-five years since I left Katy's Ridge, and even now the thought of it causes a physical ache deep inside me. A lingering longing. Longing that nudges me in the middle of the night when I can't sleep and sends messages in my dreams. The landscape is what I miss the most. The hills and valleys of my childhood. Mountain streams so sparkling clear they reflect a person's soul. My soul.

After pouring my first cup of coffee, I telephone Bee, who is in Baltimore for a teacher's convention. Her big presentation is today. The one about at-risk children in Appalachia. The one she worked on for almost a year and practiced in front of me a dozen times while trying not to look at her notecards. The operator at the Holiday Inn stifles a yawn before connecting me to Bee's room.

"What's wrong, Lou?" she says before I have time to identify myself.

"It's Mama. I have to go to Katy's Ridge."

Silence. She knows what this means. We were friends for years before we became more, and she knows how difficult my relationship with Mama has been at times.

"You okay?" she asks. Just hearing her voice soothes me.

"Not really." Anchoring the portable phone between my shoulder and ear, I pour the rest of the hot coffee into my work thermos, though I won't be working today. It is a telephone that Lily bought and had installed. Not only for our weekly telephone calls, but for her long calls with Daisy whenever Lily travels.

"I wish I could go with you," Bee says, and I wonder if this is true.

"I'll call you tonight and let you know how Mama is," I say.

I imagine Bee in bed, her book and reading glasses a placeholder for where I used to be. On the bedside table, her pink windup travel alarm is probably set to go off soon.

"Good luck with your speech," I tell her.

She thanks me, confessing how nervous she is. At this moment, it feels like we are still together.

After we left Katy's Ridge, a hairline of distance opened between us. A tiny fissure that grew over the years until it felt like a chasm. A chasm that neither of us quite knew how to cross. A memory comes of Daniel and Nathan, my brothers-in-law, rebuilding the footbridge on the way to the cemetery. The same path as in my dream. Bee and I needed to build a bridge between us, too. For a while, that bridge was my daughter, Lily, but after Lily left home, there wasn't much to hold us together as a couple. For years I wondered what happened to us, tracing back every thread of disagreement to find where the weave loosened. Unfortunately, endings don't always make sense.

In the stack of mail on the table by the front door, I find the itinerary Lily gave me before she left on her latest singing tour. She is in Scotland for the next two days. When I can't reach her business manager, I call Jerry, her ex-husband, who is also her record producer, and leave a message on his answering machine:

Hi, Jerry. This is Wildflower McAllister. Could you please give Lily the message that Aunt Sadie called, and I have to go to Katy's Ridge

today? We were supposed to talk on the phone later, and I want her to know why I won't be here.

I thank him, though I have never liked Jerry. Something about him has never sat right with me.

Daisy, my only grandchild, turned thirteen yesterday. We went out to dinner at a local restaurant, where I discovered that trying to get Daisy to talk is like lowering a heavy bucket into a deep well and not knowing if you will come up with anything after all the effort.

While Lily is on tour this summer, Daisy asked to stay with me instead of her father—a change that surprised everyone concerned, including me. Touring is a big part of Lily's singing career. She performed in small venues for fifteen years before her fourth album became a gold record and her music found a wider audience.

Lily admits her success is a blessing on the best days and a curse on the worst. She has told me how much she misses Daisy when she is away. She telephones whenever she can and sends concert T-shirts and coffee mugs with *Lily McAllister* on them. Yesterday a box arrived for Daisy's birthday containing a leather-bound diary and a fountain pen, and they talked on the telephone for over an hour. I tried not to worry about how much the long-distance charges would cost Lily. Evidently, she can afford it.

After getting dressed, I gather a few clothes in a suitcase, thinking of Mama. Aunt Sadie wouldn't call unless things were bad. I walk into the small second bedroom full of houseplants where I set up a twin bed for Daisy to sleep. A sheet covers her head, her hair a mess of blond curls. When calling her name doesn't work, I give her shoulder a gentle shake. She sits straight up, as though breaking through the water's surface after a deep dive.

Daisy's wide eyes blink at me, their blue-green color reminding

me of Sutter's Lake in Katy's Ridge on a cloudless day. She looks around the room as if to determine where she is.

"What is it?" she asks, vigilant.

Except for the curls, Daisy looks like Lily at that age, but their temperaments are oceans apart. While Lily was inquisitive and outgoing at thirteen, Daisy is quiet. Too quiet, in my view. Even as a young child, she was challenging to get to know, her play more solitary than communal. If we played hide-and-seek, she preferred to stay hidden.

"I have to go to Katy's Ridge," I say.

Daisy falls back onto the bed and covers her head with the sheet.

"You have to come with me."

Daisy sits up again, her wide eyes narrowing. "Why?"

"Your great-grandmother isn't well," I say, probably an understatement given Aunt Sadie's call.

Daisy looks at me as though the name has no meaning to her.

"Your great-grandmother," I repeat. "Granny McAllister." I remind her that she has an extended family, even if she rarely sees them.

While Lily was also an only child, she had plenty of cousins to keep her company. I doubt Daisy could even name all her cousins. Not to mention the aunts and uncles that are practically strangers to her.

"I hate it there," Daisy says, her sullenness waking up for the day.

It occurs to me that Mama's prolonged grief after Daddy died may have skipped two generations and has now taken up residence in my granddaughter. But Daisy's pain seems a different animal. I remember the dream, the blood-covered gold medallion that had somehow become Daisy's. A slow shiver walks up my spine.

The truth is, neither of us knows the other that well. Age

doesn't help. While I cling to the outer edges of middle age, Daisy is making her slow, painful-to-those-around-her journey through early adolescence.

"It doesn't matter whether you love it or hate it," I say to her. "We're going." My voice leaves no options.

Daisy huffs and tosses off the covers, mumbling something about unfairness. At the same time, she seems relieved to have someone else in charge.

In the kitchen, I call the plant nursery where I work and tell them I have a family emergency. I have enough sick and vacation days saved up to leave for a good six months. It never occurs to me to go on a vacation. Mama and Daddy never took a vacation in their lives. Nor has Aunt Sadie, my role model for all life's essential things. Not that going home to be with Mama is a vacation.

Since a hungry teenager might worsen matters, I scramble Daisy two eggs and make toast. I am not the greatest of cooks, but eggs and toast I can manage. Lily is the cook in the family. She learned from Mama. After we moved to Nashville, it was Lily who cooked most of our meals, with an ease I always envied.

Moments later, my granddaughter slumps onto a kitchen chair as I place her food and a glass of orange juice in front of her. She eats without commentary. My thoughts travel again to Mama. Every morning of my childhood, I woke to the comforting sounds and smells of Mama cooking breakfast. A pot of coffee was always on the stove and biscuits in the oven. Eggs gathered from her chickens were scrambled or fried, depending on Mama's mood, and served in a bowl on the kitchen table, covered with a plate to keep in the heat. The memory makes my mouth water as I take a bite of bland toast.

After Daisy finishes breakfast, she washes her plate, silverware, and juice glass in the sink and puts them in the drainer. I credit Lily for teaching her this thoughtfulness. At my request, she

gathers a few clothes to take with her, along with the diary and pen Lily sent her for her birthday.

Minutes later, we get into my small pickup and head to Interstate 40, which will take us east toward Knoxville. My thoughts merge with different trips I've made from Nashville to Katy's Ridge over the last twenty-five years. Most of my visits home these days have been quick visits on Thanksgiving and Christmas. Trips where the family gathers and time is spent catching up, without in-depth conversation. Trips that feel like crumbs when what I need to satiate my hunger is an entire loaf of Mama's homemade bread.

Staying connected to the family from a hundred miles away isn't easy, and in truth, I have made little effort except for occasionally answering Mama's letters. I think I blame Katy's Ridge for my exile, something I wouldn't have done if people had treated me better. Perhaps that is something that can begin to heal while I am home this time. Forgiveness is needed. Forgiveness of place and people.

An 18-wheeler passes in the left lane of the interstate, and the entire pickup shudders in its wake. The thought of Mama not doing well shakes the ground underneath me. Ground that usually feels solid. Daisy looks over at me as though aware of my unsettledness. With one hand, she holds her shoulder-length hair to keep it from flying in the wind from the open window. The distance between us feels like miles instead of inches. She reminds me of an abandoned barn I saw out in the country once, totally overtaken with wisteria vines and aflame with purple blooms. Beautiful, solitary, and somehow secretive.

Another truck passes, this one carrying new cars strategically balanced. Even while in a rush, I am slower than most. A result, perhaps, of growing up in Katy's Ridge. In those days, time passed at an inchworm's pace. I became an expert at moseying, a southern art form I would like to become good at again. After moving to

Nashville, time raced by like those calendars in old black-and-white movies. Months flying by, ripped off by an urgent wind. Lately, I've begun to long for a simpler time.

"Why are we going here again?" Daisy asks, not looking at me.

"My mama is sick," I say. "Your great-grandmother."

Could Daisy fill out even a short limb on her family tree?

"Mama has always been a strong woman, so it's hard to think about her being sick and weak." *Maybe even dying,* I want to say. But I am not about to try to explain my complicated relationship with Mama to a teenager, and a new teen at that.

Daisy's disinterest peaks with a sigh.

On the ancestral airwaves, I send Mama a message to not go dying on me before I can get there.

In my imagination, I hear her say back to me: *That is just like you, Louisa May. Only thinking of yourself and wanting me to hold off on resting in peace so that it will be more convenient for you.*

My relationship with Mama is not something I get homesick for. We are too different to appreciate each other. Although the older I get, the more I wonder if we may be more alike than I realize. I can be stubborn like Mama. A dog with a bone. A trait that can be helpful at times when things need to get done, and not the least bit helpful when letting go is required.

To go from Nashville to Katy's Ridge—doorstep to doorstep—takes two hours. My pickup rattles its need for a tune-up. If Daniel's son Danny is available, I'll have him look at it while I'm home. He owns a gas station in Rocky Bluff.

The warm June wind rushes through the windows of the pickup. I have never owned a car with an air conditioner, and on days like this, I wish I did. The radio is on a Nashville country station when one of Lily's songs comes on. I turn it up.

"Turn that off!" Daisy says, coming to life.

When I protest, the look she gives stops me mid-sentence. I turn off the radio.

"Does it make you miss your mama?" I ask.

Without answering, Daisy pulls her diary from her backpack and opens it. A furious flurry of sentences follows. The fountain pen scratches the page like a flock of angry chickens pecking the ground. In ten minutes of writing, she expresses more words than I've heard her say in her lifetime. I smile, imagining all those pent-up sentences finally free from Daisy's mind.

"Do you like the diary?" I ask, looking over at her, determined to make conversation with my only grandchild.

Daisy offers only a quick shrug, not looking up. Her writing slows and then pauses. She flips to the front and rereads the inscription Lily wrote in the book, wishing her a happy birthday and telling her how much she loves her. Then Daisy closes her diary and pulls a paperback novel out of her backpack. It is the same book she was reading yesterday. Dog-eared, with loose pages. A girl on the cover holds a spear and stands on a cliff at the edge of the sea. Blue dolphins jump out of the water below her.

"Did I ever tell you about the first time I heard one of your mama's songs on the radio?" I ask.

Daisy turns her head away to look out the window, her curls parting from the wind like the Red Sea.

"I pulled over on the side of the highway to listen to her," I continue, not one to be deterred. "An old farmer and his wife thought I had car trouble and stopped to see if I needed any help. I told them that my daughter was singing on the radio. I can still remember how excited they were."

Daisy turns toward me. "You sound so country."

"Is that a bad thing?" I ask.

She rolls her eyes. I used to be fluent in eye rolls myself back when I was Daisy's age.

"They were coming from church," I begin again, refusing to let go of that bone. "They wrote Lily's name in the back of their Bible

with a yellow Putt-Putt golf course pencil so they could remember her name and get one of her records."

Daisy stares out the side window, as though considering jumping from a moving vehicle. When I was Daisy's age, Daddy had been dead for almost a year, and Johnny Monroe was standing at that crossroads, ready to pounce.

"Why are you so unhappy these days?" I ask her. Directness is not a trait practiced south of the Mason-Dixon line, but at this rate, I'll be dead and buried before Daisy gets around to telling me anything.

She doesn't answer.

"Is it Lily being on tour? Or did something happen at school?"

She twists a curl.

Unlike Daisy, Lily talked practically nonstop and asked endless questions. I was the one keeping secrets. It took months of Lily asking who her father was before she finally found out. She still wouldn't know if she hadn't persisted.

Daisy's parents split up before she was old enough to remember them together. She has always had two bedrooms, one at each parent's house. Always been one of the few children in school whose parents were divorced. Despite this, she is well-adjusted. Yet something has ahold of her right now. Something that feels deeper, dark, and somehow familiar.

I lean over and touch her leg.

She jumps as though I've slapped my open palm across her face.

"Sweetheart, what's going on?" I ask.

Lips stern, she returns to her book, as if the act of opening the pages will close the issue. Gripping the wheel tighter, I steer clear of the hopelessness I feel. At this rate, this is going to be a long summer. Even though Daisy stares at her book for the next several miles, no pages turn to advance the story.

I think of Mama again, hoping Aunt Sadie told her I am on my way. We were like mixing vinegar and soda, Mama used to say, and

we are running out of time to understand each other. When Sadie called, I was so focused on the dream that I didn't think to ask more questions. The truth is, it may be time to say goodbye to the woman who carried me into this world. A woman who could be difficult even on her better days. A woman who was not only my biggest challenge but my greatest champion.

CHAPTER TWO

Daisy

My book is my protective shield, cover for whenever I don't want to talk, which is often. I have already read *Island of the Blue Dolphins* six times. I have the pages practically memorized. I want to be like Karana, the main character. I want to need nobody and live on a deserted island.

Sometimes I hear voices in my head. They don't talk to me; I just listen to them, like a television playing in the next room with the volume turned up. I only hear the voices at certain times. Sometimes I wish they would leave me alone.

I am also good at overhearing actual conversations. It is unreal what grown-ups say when they think a kid is reading and not listening. Last weekend I heard my father tell my second stepmother that my mom should be paying him child support instead of the other way around and that he should take her back to court now that she has made it big.

It is hard to imagine my parents married, much less happy together. My father likes to push people around, and sometimes

my mom lets him do that. He doesn't have talent like she has. Not many people do. Any skill I have is hidden. Unless hearing voices counts.

As far as grandmothers go, my mom's mom—Gran—is okay. People call her Wildflower, which I think is weird. The McAllister side of my family is funny about names. Gran's nickname is Wildflower. My mom's name is Lily, and mine is Daisy. What's with all these flower names? I guess I'm lucky I wasn't called Tulip or Daffodil. But Daisy is easily the most boring name on the planet.

Thankfully, Gran doesn't require a lot from me when I stay with her. We usually keep to ourselves. But not today. Today we are driving out to the *sticks* to see my great-grandmother. My mom hates going back to the place she grew up. As a result, I have only visited a couple of times, and I was not the least bit impressed.

"You sure you don't want to talk?" Gran asks me.

I press my lips tighter, not willing to give her what she wants.

The first time I heard my mom singing on the radio, it was no big deal. By the time I was five years old, I had listened to all of my mom's songs a million times. When I was a little girl, she took me to her concerts. As the family story goes, after she left my father, I slept backstage in car seats and strollers. To this day, I can sleep just about anywhere, even with loud music playing.

Even though my mom was up for a Grammy last year, I don't tell people that I am Lily McAllister's daughter. As far as I can tell, the best way to get by in life is to not draw attention to myself, especially when I am staying with my father. Thankfully, I don't stay with him that often unless Mom is touring. She used to travel only in this country, but now she tours in Europe, too. This summer I asked to stay with Gran.

"Here's the exit." Gran puts on the turn signal of the old truck she drives. Grandmothers aren't supposed to drive old pickups that have dents and chipping paint. They are supposed to drive

shiny Buicks or Chryslers or something respectable. My father drives a Mercedes because he wants people to think he's hot shit. Evidently, Gran doesn't care what people think.

When we reach the interstate exit for Rocky Bluff, the sign looks like someone has used the *O* in *Rocky* for target practice. A spattering of holes bleeds rust. Whoever did this was a good shot.

"Rocky Bluff is practically New York City compared to how it was when I was a girl," Gran says.

You've got to be kidding, I think.

Gran pulls her silver pocket watch from her jeans and checks the time. It makes a soft click when it closes. Grandmothers are not supposed to carry men's pocket watches, either, or wear faded blue jeans for that matter. But Gran isn't like most grandmothers. I still haven't decided if this is a good thing.

Fast-food joints litter the main road, alongside gas stations servicing travelers coming off the interstate. A huge billboard, next to the sign for the city limits, announces that the Rocky Bluff High School Bobcats were the 1979 State Football Champions—three years ago. A circle of stadium lights towers over the ball field and the blue-and-gold bleachers. Looming behind it is a metal water tank that could use a coat of white paint.

"I attended a lot of football games there," Gran says. "Your mama had a big crush on one of the players on the team. His name was Crow Sector."

Crow? What is it with these country people and names? Can't they call people Jill or Jack or something?

Gran taps the steering wheel of the old truck.

"What was he like?" I ask, knowing this is what Gran wants. She wants me to talk to her. Show an interest. Not hide. However, hiding is what I do best. If gifted superpowers, I would choose invisibility every time.

"Crow was charming," she begins. "His hair was jet black. Still is, I imagine. That's why his nickname is Crow." She pauses.

"Come to think of it, I don't know his real name." She smiles. "His mother, June, is a good friend of mine. She helped me through a really rough period in my life, and she was the only friend who knew about Bee."

Gran's smile fades. I wonder if she misses Bee as much as I do. When I was younger, I was closer to Bee. Bee taught school and was off every summer and took me to museums and art galleries. If we walked in a park, she taught me about photosynthesis and the water cycle. Bee was cool that way and didn't mind if I was quiet. She told me I was always wearing my thinking cap. Once we spent an entire afternoon making thinking caps with construction paper and magic markers. Mine still sits on the desk in my bedroom at Mom's house. I miss my bedroom when Mom's away. I have a bedroom at my father's house, too, but it's all frilly and pink from my first stepmother decorating it. I hate that room. It's like being trapped inside a cotton candy machine.

Bedrooms aside, Gran is different from Bee. If Bee is like an open door, Gran is a closed one. Gran has secrets. Secrets that nobody, including a granddaughter, is allowed to know. I have secrets, too.

"It's ugly here," I say, matter-of-fact.

She smiles. "It was the center of the universe when I was a kid."

We drive past empty buildings, signs of a small town worn out.

"Rocky Bluff is experiencing a slow demise," Gran says.

"It doesn't seem that slow to me," I say.

She smiles again.

The two times I came to Katy's Ridge, I didn't even notice this town. It seems sad in a way, and lonely.

Gran slows down and points. "One of my sisters has a seamstress shop on that corner, next to that run-down Revco."

She never talks about her sisters, and I wonder if they are close. I would give anything to have a sister. Or a little brother like Karana has on the island at first. Being an only child isn't horrible,

but it's intense to only be around grown-ups all the time. It's like you forget you're a kid, and your parents do, too.

Gran drives through the small town at a turtle's pace. Even though no one is behind us, I pretend to jam my sneaker on the gas and get us out of here. I remind myself that in only three years, I will have my driver's license. This fantasy rescues me with growing frequency.

Gran stops at a long red light, and when it turns green she presses down the clutch and coaxes the pickup into first gear. I study the moves. Could I drive a stick shift if I had to? First gear looks like the gearshift is standing at attention. With second gear, you press in the clutch and pull the stick straight down. Third gear goes up and to the right to find the sweet spot, which evidently isn't always easy to find in Gran's truck. Sometimes it takes her two tries. With fourth gear, you move the stick straight down again. My father's Mercedes is automatic, which seems dull in comparison.

Looking into the side mirror, I catch myself frowning. Stepmother number one always told me that I was unattractive when I frowned. She also said that I should start saving money for a boob job.

Meanwhile, Gran is my tour guide for the most dilapidated main street I've ever seen.

"That furniture store over there used to belong to my Aunt Chloe and my Uncle John," Gran says. "They both died in the early seventies."

A yellowed SALE sign stretches across the big front window. In some ways, it feels like I am in the middle of a ghost town, held captive by a nostalgic grandmother. I imagine there are worse things. And as long as she keeps talking, I don't have to.

"That old theater closed several years ago," Gran says. "I saw *The King and I* there with my sisters and Bee." She takes a long,

slow look, craning her neck as we pass. The sign out front announces the Masons' Christmas party in 1967.

I wonder what kids my age do for fun in this town—not that I see anyone my age.

Gran looks at her watch again. "Why am I wasting time?"

Sometimes Gran says her thoughts aloud, not requiring an answer. She speeds up, but not by much.

"Tell me something you dread." She looks over to me.

Gran is always asking dorky questions that are not even questions.

Sheer boredom pushes me to respond.

"For starters, I dread going to the boonies to see a bunch of people I don't even know."

She laughs a short laugh. "Fair enough."

To my surprise, I say more. I tell Gran about how I dread going back to school in September, and how I dread tests, and Monday mornings, and seeing Mom pack before a trip, and spending the night at my father's house. I stop. I didn't plan to say that last one.

"That's a lot of dread," she says, tapping the steering wheel again.

My awkward smile leads to my ugly frown, and I wonder if she thinks I need a boob job. But why would I need a "job" for something that barely exists?

"What do you dread?" I ask her.

"Death." She grins, as though she's caught herself saying something she didn't intend to, either.

For a few seconds, the heaviness in my chest lightens. At least Gran is trying to get to know me. Most people don't even try.

We leave downtown and turn onto a county road. Potholes provide an immediate obstacle course, and the truck squeaks with every bump. Gran talks about bucking broncos and how the road needs taming. She swerves to miss a pothole and cusses. "Shit" is

her favorite cuss word. Grandmothers aren't supposed to cuss, either.

"This morning, when the phone rang, I was dreaming that I was walking an old trail in Katy's Ridge that I used to walk when I was a girl. And now here we are," Gran says.

I don't tell her that I was dreaming about being stalked by killer sharks when she woke me up. It might spark another conversation.

"Did you like growing up here?" I ask. The question sounds lame. But I'm grateful Gran has agreed to let me stay with her this summer.

She pauses before answering. "It was my home, you know. I didn't think anything of it. But looking back on it now, I feel like I grew up in the arms of mountains."

I imagine Karana held in the arms of her island.

"Why did you leave?" I ask, surprised by my interest.

She shifts into a lower gear to get up the hill we're climbing. "Well, I thought I'd be living in Katy's Ridge my entire life. But then, people found out about your Grandmother Bee and me."

Growing up around Gran and Bee meant I never gave their relationship a thought. I didn't realize it was different until I went places with them and saw the disapproving looks they got sometimes. It made me angry. A line in one of the songs Mom wrote says that finding love is a miracle and that you can't make love wrong. I always wondered if she wrote that song for Gran and Bee.

"I can't imagine how my sisters are taking Mama going downhill," Gran says, more to herself than to me.

I begin to wonder what *downhill* looks like, and if this is something I want to watch. The only thing I remember about my great-grandmother is that we had a staring contest, and I lost. She kind of scared me. I was around seven at the time. That was the last time I was here, and I suddenly wonder why, if Katy's Ridge is only

two hours away. The only reason I remember that particular trip is because Mom took pictures that are in the photo album in the den.

"My family and I haven't been that close since I moved to Nashville," Gran says.

I nod, watching the scenery out the window.

For the next few minutes, Gran is silent. We go deeper and deeper into the country. Traveling the mountain roads feels like being rocked as a baby, and I try to imagine being held by these mountains like Gran was.

Every now and again, I glimpse the river below. Sunlight sparkles off the water's surface. We drive through pockets of shade that cool the car in an instant before the warm sun returns. It is an ordinary day, yet it somehow also feels extraordinary. When I look over, Gran wipes away a tear. I hear her unspoken words: *I'm home.*

CHAPTER THREE

Wildflower

Memories rush to greet me at the faded welcome sign to Katy's Ridge: Daddy teaching me to read long before I went to elementary school. Mama combing my tangles with a less-than-gentle touch. My sister Jo coming to look for me at the cemetery after Daddy died. Then my mouth waters with the memory of Mama's chicken and dumplings the first time Jo brought Daniel, her future husband, to the house. When the memories darken, I think of Daniel carrying me home in his arms after Johnny Monroe attacked me. A time that feels like a thousand years ago, and also only yesterday.

Sunlight winks through the trees, reminding me of the gold Mary—the angel that appeared to me as a girl, bright as the noonday sun. It has been years since I thought of her. Years since I realized how much I missed her. More than I've even missed Mama.

Mama never believed in ghosts or visions. Spirits went against her practical nature. They were nonsense that got in the way of the

hard work of life. If asked, I imagine she might say that seeing spirits was pure laziness, just like anything else that caused a person to ponder life.

Meanwhile, driving into Katy's Ridge is like going back in time fifty years. People aren't the only ones to mosey. Progress does, too. Especially here. Living in a city is different from living in the country. They are complex in different ways. Instead of high-rises worshipping commerce, the forest adores the mountains. Instead of avenues crisscrossing, running in straight lines, a river meanders south as it has for millions of years. Mountain streams swell with rain and push their way to the sea as they have for centuries.

Daisy stares out the window, her book now in her backpack. It is cooler here. Thick trees are in competition as they reach for the sun. Day after day, I rode the school bus to and from the high school in Rocky Bluff, watching the familiar scenery pass by. The same scenery that Daisy appears to be taking in for the first time.

After I moved away, nostalgia accompanied me everywhere I went for months, if not years. Perhaps that's because Bee and I had no choice about leaving. Not when our livelihoods ended. A mob with pitchforks chased us out of town. Imaginary pitchforks, but ones dipped in the poison of judgment and fear.

A new stretch of road stops my reminiscing. It bypasses the high bluff and travels alongside the river, elevated just enough to avoid flooding. Remnants of the harrowing old road along the cliff appear periodically. A reminder of the old way of entering and leaving Katy's Ridge.

To my surprise, I miss the thrill of driving the narrow and dangerous old road. Undivided attention was required to avoid a fatal swerve off the cliff into the rocky riverbed below. I still miss my first pickup, which I learned how to drive on these curves. A vehicle I drove until the engine fell out one day while I was waiting at a red light on Church Street in Nashville.

The road tames, and we enter the valley where little has changed.

"Down that dirt road is the sawmill that I used to run."

Daisy glances. Weeds have grown up and hidden the sign.

"You ran a sawmill?" she asks.

"Me and your Great-Uncle Daniel," I say.

Katy's Ridge is like a tea bag steeped in history. My history. By a miracle of grace, the tea has not turned bitter.

Daisy observes, her eyes wide as if swallowing Katy's Ridge whole.

We pass the dirt road that goes to the Sectors. Though the house isn't in view, I beep my horn in greeting. I will visit with June when I can. I imagine she knows what is going on with Mama. All of Katy's Ridge probably knows. The grapevine has never been more vibrant, according to Mama's letters.

Moments later, I pull over and leave the truck idling.

"This is where Bee used to live," I tell Daisy.

At the end of a short gravel road sits a small house that Bee still owns and rents out to a young family from Chattanooga.

A colorful mess of big-wheeled trikes covers the yard. A clothesline stretches from a maple tree to the front porch, the line full of clean clothes blowing in the mountain breeze.

"Bee used to sit under that maple and read in the summer," I say.

I look at Daisy, and she nods as though imagining it. She is a deep thinker like me.

I pull out my watch again. In an hour, Bee will give her speech in front of several hundred teachers at a conference in Boston. I imagine her nervousness is kicking in about now. She has never spoken in front of that many people. But she couldn't pass up the opportunity to bring attention to the small schools here in the mountains. Schools with outdated textbooks and no community resources for the most impoverished children.

"I miss Bee," Daisy says.

"I do, too," I say, more wistfully than I intend.

Sometimes I forget how close Daisy and Bee are. Bee has always treated Daisy like a favored grandchild. Bee and Lily are close, too, and sometimes I think Lily was more devastated than I was when Bee and I parted.

At the main crossroads, street signs now give the names of the roads. When I was growing up, they were unmarked. Everyone knew the names already. I brake at a shiny new stop sign at the intersection where Johnny used to throw rocks from one side of the road to the other while spitting tobacco juice into a peach can. I wonder how many days Johnny stood at this crossroads waiting for his life to change, and how many times I have wished I never walked by that day. Probably more than I can count.

All of a sudden, I turn, taking the road to the right, away from Mama's house. I can't bear the thought of seeing her lying in bed, possibly saying goodbye to this life. I want to run like I did the day Daddy died. I want to run to the river and pretend that endings don't exist.

New gravel covers the road leading to the elementary school where I spent eight years of my life. It is summer vacation, and two men clear brush from around the playground. Why is it that the places we grew up always seem smaller than we remember them?

"The school has two buildings now, but it used to have only one," I say to Daisy.

She narrows her eyes, as though trying to imagine it. "Mom went here?"

"She was top of her class," I say.

"I wish I had inherited her intelligence."

"You're plenty smart," I say. "You just haven't found your passion yet."

A wry smile crosses her face, as though she has spotted my affinity for self-help books.

"Lily's passion was to get out of Katy's Ridge and travel the world."

"Well, she got her wish. She's never home." Daisy's moodiness returns for an encore.

"Singing is her job, honey. You know she loves you more than anything."

Daisy crosses her arms as if a drawbridge has suddenly closed. I question again if she is somehow in trouble. Trouble that she refuses to discuss. At least for now. She will be staying with me for the rest of the summer. A summer that feels suddenly momentous.

"Bee was just out of teachers college when she taught me in that one little building," I begin again, sticking to more comfortable subjects. "There were twelve of us, ranging in ages from first to eighth grade. My best friend, Mary Jane, and I were the only two students in our grade. Everybody else was either younger or older. Years later, she taught Lily, too."

"What happened to your best friend?" she asks.

"I have no idea," I say. "Last I heard, Mary Jane had moved to downtown Little Rock."

My pickup idles, and I suggest we go. Mary Jane is a part of the past. A past that I don't care to remember.

As I drive toward Mama's house, the smell of honeysuckle and wild roses fills the car—the aroma of summertime in the mountains. I come to the three mailboxes next to the big boulder at the bottom of the driveway. Mama's is in the center. Jo and Daniel live across the street, and theirs is to the right. Amy's mailbox is on the left. After her husband, Nathan, died, my sister moved to a small house next door to Jo and Daniel. Meg lives farther down the road past the church.

I pull up Mama's gravel driveway, which now extends halfway up the hill and ends at a clearing just below the four redbud trees that Daddy called the Redbud Sisters. Daddy could be silly about naming things, but as girls, my sisters and I loved it. While

working at the nursery, I continued his tradition, although mine is a secret naming.

The engine off, I take a deep breath. My childhood home sits atop the rise, barely visible behind the trees. A couple of years ago, Lily had Mama's house renovated with money she made from her gold record. Around the same time, she offered to build me a new home in Nashville. My refusal created a sore spot between us that hasn't quite healed. The truth is, if given a choice, I wouldn't want to stay in Nashville forever, though I'm not sure where I belong anymore.

Our old house is now a much grander version of its original self. The front porch, no longer rickety, stretches around the house. A small barn is in the side yard, next to a new chicken coop. New windows and doors smile into the forest. The best in indoor plumbing replaced aging pipes throughout, along with new kitchen appliances, and a room built onto the back of the house for the new washer and dryer. In the old days, the washer and dryer lived on the back porch.

For months, Mama's letters were full of the news about all the changes, as well as her complaints of workers underfoot. I wish Daddy could see the transformation of the old place. But maybe he has.

"Why are we just sitting here?" Daisy asks.

With all the memories rushing toward me, I forgot she was even there.

"It's always strange to come home again," I say.

She sighs.

The thought crosses my mind again that this could be a long summer.

"It's going to be a long summer for me, too," she says.

My eyes widen as I turn to look at her. How does she know what I just thought?

However, there is no time to solve this current mystery. Mama

is waiting. After getting out of the pickup, I toss my keys onto the front seat, something I would never do outside my apartment in Nashville. Here in the country, I have no worries about anything getting stolen. Not that my pickup is anything of great value.

The sun directly overhead, Daisy and I begin our trek up the hill. In the distance, Aunt Sadie stands on the porch. With the simple sight of her, tears spring to my eyes.

Years ago, after Lily and Bee and I moved away from Katy's Ridge, it was Aunt Sadie I missed the most, along with Daniel. Not Mama, or my sisters. A fact that surprised me at the time. I brush away tears and return a quick wave. Meanwhile, Daisy drags herself up the hill as though sentenced to an unfair prison sentence nowhere near completion.

"Give these mountains a chance," I say to her.

She doesn't question what I mean, her quota of words possibly fulfilled for the day.

Meanwhile, I wonder what I will find at the top of the hill. It seems I have been approaching this moment my entire life. A moment where I must give Mama a final goodbye, just like I did with Daddy forty years ago.

In my memory, I hear the stretcher dragging as Simon Hatcher's mule pulls Daddy up the hill after his sawmill accident, the life pouring out of him. Death makes everybody useless. Useless as the day we were born. The only thing those left behind can do is to witness it.

After Daddy died, I ran like a wild animal down the river road to forget seeing him take his last breath. In some ways, it feels like I am still running. And now, here I come again, donning my running shoes for Mama.

Daddy's memory kisses me in the same place he always kissed me, my forehead a monument to his love. My scalp tingles. I never feel alone here in the mountains as I do in Nashville. The spirits of the dead are everywhere, like the negatives of old photographs.

Imprinted forever on my mind. Ready to be restored to full color with a sound, a smell, the sight of home.

I think of the last words Daddy said to me on his deathbed: *Take care of your mama. Promise me.*

At that moment, I would have promised him anything. But did I keep my promise? Mama has always been prickly and not the easiest to take care of without getting pricked.

Sorry, Daddy, I think. *I wish I'd done better.*

Whistling travels on a summer breeze, a faraway memory. Daddy always whistled when he walked this path, and I suddenly wonder if he has come to greet me. Seconds later, I smell the aftershave he used to wear to church. My sisters and I saved our pennies and nickels for an entire year to get him a bottle one Christmas, and he wore it in abundance as if to show his love for us.

"Daddy?" I stop on the trail and look around.

Daisy turns to me, a question in her eyes.

I tell her it is nothing and wonder if it is.

The first time Daddy appeared to me in spirit form was when he came to get me that day that Johnny hurt me. It seemed crazy then, and it feels crazy now. But he felt as real as anything those many years ago, just like he feels as real as anything today.

In the distance, Aunt Sadie holds up a hand to shade her eyes from the sun. She smiles. Not everyone coming up this hill is welcome. I think of Johnny's sister, Melody Monroe, staggering up this same hill to find Lily, her brother's child. I've thought before about how life can turn on a dime. If Melody hadn't traveled to Katy's Ridge that day, I might still be living here, and Bee and I might even be together, though living a secret life. The older I get, the more I realize how one incident can alter a life forever. A road you thought you would travel forever becomes the road left behind.

Daddy's aftershave fades, and the smell of lavender take its

place. He planted lavender to keep the deer away from Mama's flowers. Daisy lingers in the yard while I approach Aunt Sadie, whose hair has been solid white for as long as I have known her. Her eyes crease into little branches like one of the ancient oaks behind the house. Sadie is Daddy's sister and was my age when he died. She is ninety-six years old now, but when I step into her arms, her embrace is strong. After Daddy died, I relied on Aunt Sadie to love me no matter what, because Mama was no longer available.

Our embrace ends, and I miss her closeness instantly. I ask her about Mama.

"I'm glad you're here," she says.

Sadie looks behind me and smiles at Daisy, who hasn't come within hugging distance. Instead she stares at the laces of her tennis shoes.

"Let her be," Aunt Sadie says, her words soft. "She can stay out here while you say your hellos."

And goodbyes, I can almost hear her say. She takes my hand and squeezes courage into my palm as we cross the threshold into the house. A threshold that leads to a lifetime of memories.

CHAPTER FOUR

Daisy

An old woman stands on the porch waiting for us, easily the oldest woman I have ever seen. I may have met her before, but it has been six years since my mom brought me here. When the old lady looks at me, I turn away. It feels as though she can see right through me to every thought and feeling I have ever had.

Moments ago, when Gran called out for her father, a chill rushed up my spine, and all sorts of conversations from the past rushed at me. This place is alive with stories. Voices I don't recognize and can't put faces to except for Gran, who sounds young but still like herself.

An old black dog sits at the old woman's feet. His muzzle is gray, and he makes no effort to bark when we approach. A dollop of drool drips from his mouth onto the porch as he pants and smiles. The old woman gives Gran a big hug, and I hear Gran sigh. I usually complain about Gran's hugs and try to duck away. But in truth, I don't mind them.

When the old lady greets me, my face flushes hot, and I lower my eyes.

"I'm Sadie," she says. "You don't have to do anything here that you don't want to do. Is that clear?"

When I look into her eyes, I find softness there. My shoulders relax, a wild thing suddenly tamed.

"Why don't you wait out here on the front porch while Wildflower visits with her mama," she says. "Or you're welcome to come inside, too. You get to decide."

I look at Gran, who has her hand on the door.

"I'll stay out here," I say.

"Don't you want some iced tea or a bathroom?" Grans asks.

I tell her I don't.

After Gran and the old woman go into the house, I sit on the white porch swing and push off with my legs. The swing squeaks to life. It is old but newly painted, just like the house. What a strange place this is. I don't think I've ever seen so many trees. Surrounded by forest, I breathe deeper. A moment's peace leads to something unsettled. Whenever Gran asks me what's wrong, I tell her I'm fine. The truth is, nothing is okay. Nothing at school. Nothing at home. Nothing.

I twist a strand of hair and put it into my mouth, tasting a bitter remnant of my apricot shampoo. My mother grew up here, and she never talks about this place. When I try to imagine her as a girl playing on this porch or out in the yard, I can't. All the photographs of her start when she was my age and lived in Nashville with Gran and Bee, not here.

Alone on the porch, I continue to play with my hair. If Mom were here, she would ask me to stop, but playing with my curls gives me something to do while I think about the mess my life is in.

The house smells old and new at the same time. The outside is

painted white. No designer colors like stepmom number two insists on in their big home in Nashville. This house is much simpler. The old black dog smiles at me. I pat my leg to call him over. With great effort, he pulls himself to standing and comes. Fur flies as I pet him. I am usually scared of dogs, but not this one.

A voice startles me. When I look up, a girl about my age stands at the bottom of the porch steps looking up at me.

"Where did you come from?" I ask.

"I was out back gathering eggs," she says. "I'm Nellie."

I look at her blankly.

"My mom is Jo," she says. "Wildflower's older sister."

I translate Wildflower to be Gran.

"I live across the street. My daddy is Daniel. I'm a change-of-life baby," she continues. "Mama and Daddy call me their 'sweet little surprise.'" Nellie laughs. "Isn't that tacky?"

I agree that it is tacky.

She waits for me to say more, and maybe give the conversation a spark. But I have never been good at sparking talks.

"You're Lily's girl, right?"

I imagine this is something she already knows, but I play along and answer in the affirmative. She cocks her head as though I may require studying.

"It won't be long now," Nellie says, her curiosity turning serious.

My confusion is genuine.

"You know." She motions her head toward the door. "It's almost Granny McAllister's time," she whispers.

"You mean, Gran's mother is going to die?" I say, forgetting to whisper.

Nellie puts a finger over her lips to shush me.

"Does she not know she's dying?" I whisper back.

Nellie comes up on the porch and plops herself into the

rocking chair next to the swing where I sit. She wears cutoff over-alls and sneakers without socks. She has an abundance of freckles, and her legs are tan even though it is only June.

"Do you sing like your mama?" Nellie's hair is longer and much straighter than mine and is pulled back into a red hair ribbon, though her shirt is pink.

"No, I don't sing," I say. It has never occurred to me to call my mother Mama instead of Mom.

"What's it like to live in Nashville?" she asks, her southern accent turned up on high. Kids at my school would make fun of Nellie if given a chance.

"Busy," I say. "And loud." I take note of how quiet the mountains are at this moment. No car noises. No machines running. Only birds giving a chirp every now and again and the sound of clucking chickens in the backyard.

"Can you tell me what that sweet smell is coming from the woods?" I ask her.

She sniffs and smiles, not hiding her surprise. "It's honeysuckle, silly," she says. "Don't they have honeysuckle in Nashville?"

My face momentarily warms, but to Nellie's credit, I don't feel judged. Her look is of a botanist with a new specimen.

"I've always wanted to go to Opryland." Her expression lightens.

"It's nice," I say, not mentioning that I have been to Opryland so many times I could puke. "What's she sick with?" I motion toward the house as Nellie did.

"Old age."

"Old age?"

"It's her time. That's all." Nellie sounds like the old lady with the old dog. "It's almost Rufus's time, too." Nellie pets the dog who has left my side to be closer to her.

"His name is Rufus?" I ask.

She nods. "Rufus is over a hundred years old in dog years. He's been with Aunt Sadie forever."

In the distance, a man comes into view, ambling up the hill with a cane. He waves a greeting when he sees us. A short, high salute.

"That's my daddy," Nellie says. "He's coming to see Wildflower and check in on Granny."

I wonder if I will get used to Gran being called Wildflower.

When Nellie's father stands on the porch, he towers over me, but not in a threatening way.

"We've met before, but you were tiny," he says, extending his hand. "I'm Daniel. Jo's husband. How's your mama doing?"

"She's fine," I say, though I have no idea how she is. I got a phone call on the morning of my birthday, and she was getting ready for a performance and couldn't talk for long. She sounded tired. But these days she always seems tired.

"Isn't she over in Europe right now?" His face is wrinkled by the sun, though he looks younger up close than he did walking up the hill. I wonder what happened to his leg.

I tell him that yes, my mother is in Europe, but I'm not sure where. I leave out how tired she is.

When he kisses Nellie on the forehead, she smiles up at him—a daughter's love unhindered. It would never occur to me to smile at my father that way.

"Is Wildflower inside?" Daniel asks.

I nod.

He leans down to kiss my forehead, too, but I lean away. His thoughtful look hints at bewilderment. He bows his apology, his eyes closing as he bows. He reminds me of a prince in a storybook. A weathered prince, perhaps, but one who has fought many battles and grown in wisdom. I wish now I hadn't ducked.

In the meantime, Nellie looks at me as though I am a thousand-

piece puzzle that may take more time than she realized to figure out. I can't say that I have come anywhere near to solving it myself. But being here feels important, as if the mountains are somehow magical and a lifetime of mysteries might be resolved in a single afternoon. In agreement, Rufus looks at me and wags his tail.

CHAPTER FIVE

Wildflower

A quilt with hummingbirds graces the top of Mama's bed. A quilt that Mama and Aunt Sadie made together in the evenings when I was growing up. It is a replica of another quilt that was in the family for ages, one that my Grandma McAllister brought over from the old country. The first hummingbird quilt was wrapped around Daddy and went with him to his grave. The McAllister family doesn't have family heirlooms. No gold jewelry or silver or china plates. But according to Sadie, this hummingbird quilt will pass to me someday, and then to Lily, and then to Daisy. I'm not sure how she and Mama decided this, given I have three sisters, but I am grateful that it will.

Mama looks small, lying on the bed. Why is it that people who are dying always look smaller than when they were alive and well? A formidable woman, Mama could evoke fear in me with a single look. A look that could convey her instant disappointment in me, and her secret wish that I was different. Quieter. More controlled. Less emotional.

As I approach, I remember Daddy lying on this same bed when he left this world for the next one. A leave-taking that at the tender age of twelve woke me up to the randomness of life and death. It didn't matter if you were kind or how much you were needed, you could still be taken away in an instant, never to be seen again. Carried away by a God who supposedly kept good people for himself. This consolation never made sense. The world needs all the good people here, not in heaven.

When I look down at Mama in her bed, I realize how strange it is to see her without her apron. As long as I have known her, she took turns wearing three aprons that lived on wooden pegs on the back of the kitchen door. All were too faded and nondescript to be such a critical uniform in her life. Mama seems somehow naked with only a nightgown showing beneath the quilt, her pale chest covered in wrinkled age spots. Her hair is now white with streaks of gray running through it, and it still reaches to her waist. It is down instead of up in her usual bun. This, too, adds to the strangeness.

Aunt Sadie looks over at me as if to give me strength. After Daddy died, she stepped in to help fill the space her brother left behind. She showed up on anniversaries, birthdays, and holidays and insisted we take her homemade tonics to avoid colds every winter. Sadie was loyal to all of us, not just Mama. Mama and Sadie have lived together these last few years. More like sisters than in-laws sharing meals and companionship. Playing cards, working on quilts, and watching a television show or two.

For the longest time, we stand at her bedside and watch Mama sleep. For years I tried to get her to go to a regular doctor and have tests run so we could get some formal kind of diagnosis and know what we're dealing with, but she refused. If Aunt Sadie couldn't fix it with her herbal remedies, Mama didn't want it fixed. Perhaps there is wisdom in this choice. Maybe not. Mama can be more

stubborn than the most stubborn mule. At the same time, Aunt Sadie, at ninety-six years of age, has been an expert in mountain plant cures for over half a century.

"Will you be okay staying here if I go and get lunch started?" Aunt Sadie asks, her voice just above a whisper.

"Of course," I whisper back. When I hold Mama's hand, I notice that she has clear nail polish on her fingers. I imagine Meg painted them, since she won't even walk to the mailbox without a fresh coat of polish, and I anticipate seeing my sisters later for lunch.

"Our job is just to try to make her transition as smooth as possible," Sadie says, patting my shoulder.

"Smooth as possible," I repeat, not having a clue what that means.

The room smells of Aunt Sadie's blackberry spirits, mixed in with other elixirs in nature's medicine cabinet. Remedies used to make Mama more comfortable in this grandest of transitions.

"I'll check on Daisy on my way to the kitchen," Aunt Sadie says.

I thank her as she leaves the room, quietly latching the door behind her. I feel suddenly claustrophobic in the closed room and take a couple of deep breaths, willing myself to stay calm and be here for Mama.

Then I think of Daddy and how I could feel him on the path up to the house. Being back in Katy's Ridge is like having a family reunion with those who have gone on before, and those who are going soon.

Mama stirs. She lets out a soft moan before opening her eyes. She appears to focus, and then she smiles her delight at seeing me. I have experienced her irritation many times, but I can't say I have ever experienced her joy. My heart opens to the miracle of finally being seen by the woman who gave birth to me. A girlish giggle escapes my lips. Mama's eyes fill with tears before she sweeps them away. The McAllisters have never liked to be seen crying.

She takes my hand.

"I didn't think I'd ever see you again."

"I got here as fast as I could," I say. I move closer, squeezing Mama's veined hand, her skin tinted gray rather than flesh tone. Her hands are callused as someone who has worked hard her entire life. They are cool to the touch, almost cold.

Most importantly, her smile, through tears, hasn't waned. I soak in the sunshine of her approval. A gift I have waited my entire life to receive. I have always thought that I was too much for Mama to handle. Too talkative. Too imaginative. Too *everything*. However, at this moment, I feel I am exactly who she needs.

Mama looks at me, gathering her strength to speak. "I've missed you so much, Joseph,"

A slight gasp escapes my lips, as Mama's approval feels suddenly snatched away. She always said that I looked just like Daddy, that we were two peas in a pod.

Mama's cheeks blush a dull pink like a young woman awaiting her beau. Her smile makes her look decades younger. It seems that Mama—like Aunt Sadie—has been old forever, but when I left Katy's Ridge with Bee and Lily, Mama was younger than I am now.

"I knew you'd come," she says, her gaze unwavering.

A shiver tickles my spine as I remember the smell of aftershave on the trail and the whistling I heard on the wind.

"Come closer." Mama takes my hands, squeezing them weakly to test their realness. I am the ghost of my father. This belief animates her.

"It's not like me to take to my bed," she says to her long-dead husband. "I only did this on the days our babies were coming. Remember?"

I nod and smile, an unwitting stand-in for my father.

"All our girls came quickly once the pains started," she begins again. "Even Jo was shorter than the usual first labor. Then eighteen months later, Meg came. Then Amy. Then—"

Mama's voice grows softer. "A month doesn't pass that I don't think of our baby Beth." Her eyes glisten with new tears.

I squeeze her hand again, wishing I knew what to say. Beth was the baby whose tiny grave is right next to Daddy's in the cemetery.

"I remember," I say, wanting to give her something—anything—to comfort her.

Her voice changes again, from soft to stern.

"A year later, Louisa May came. She whooshed out of me like she was late for supper. A meal that child has never been late for a day in her life, I might add."

The last girl, I was to be named Louisa May because all the character names in *Little Women* were taken. But instead of being honored to be named after the author, Louisa May Alcott, I felt like I had missed out on being one of the sisters. Years later, it was Daddy who nicknamed me Wildflower for my wildness and supposed beauty. Daddy was the one who always saw me as I was.

"The hardest part to having Louisa May came later," Mama continues, "whenever I tried to keep that strong will of hers in check." She looks as though she's tasted something bitter. "You were the one who always knew how to handle her. How dare you leave me just when I needed you the most." She shoots a scolding look in my direction.

"I'm sorry, Nell," I say, pretending to be my father. "It wasn't my choice to leave. And you did the best you could."

Mama's fury softens into a faint smile. "I did do my best, Joseph." She closes her eyes again, as though exhausted by the memories, and begins a light snore.

A knock on the door pulls my attention away from Mama. Daniel steps inside, and we embrace. I will never forget the night he rescued me in the woods and carried me home. I crawled inside his smell that night. A scent that reminded me of Daddy. A mixture of sweat and sawdust, river and earth. Years later, Daniel

would work with me at the sawmill and help me keep the business going. Until people found out about Bee and me.

"I'm glad you're here, Wildflower." His low voice resonates through me, soothing everything that ails.

"She doesn't recognize me, Daniel. She thinks I'm Daddy."

He looks at Mama sleeping. "She comes and goes right now. It's just the way these things are." Aunt Sadie said something similar, and I realize that they have been dealing with this a lot longer than I have.

Mama fidgets, restless. Life and death play tug-of-war. She opens her eyes again. Daniel steps forward.

"You need anything, Nell?" he asks.

She narrows her eyes as though trying to decipher who he is. Memory wins. "I'm fine, Daniel."

"Spoken like a true southern woman," he says. "Everything's fine, even on her deathbed."

A slight smile crosses her lips. She has always said that she can trust Daniel to tell her the truth. Mama knows it's her time.

"Joseph was here, Daniel. We had a nice chat."

Daniel and I exchange a quick look.

"Wildflower is here, too, Nell." Daniel steps aside to reveal me standing near the end of her bed.

A flash of irritation crosses Mama's face. "It's about time."

I was always the one to catch Mama's wrath. A fact that is hard not to take personally, especially now. She looks at me only briefly before returning to Daniel.

"I wouldn't let Sadie call her until the last minute," Mama says to Daniel. "Louisa May moped around here for a solid year after Joseph died, reminding us all how life had dealt her the worst of blows. But life had dealt the same blow to me," she continues. "Of course, it never dawned on her what Joseph's death was like for me. Or how hard I worked to keep from collapsing in a heap on the floor and never getting up again."

Her bitterness surprises me.

"I was twelve, Mama," I say. "It wasn't my job to understand. I couldn't have if I'd tried. I was a child."

She doesn't appear to hear.

One minute Mama sounds lucid and in the present day, and the next minute it is 1941, and she is grieving her newly dead husband.

"Wildflower came as soon as she heard," Daniel says in my defense.

"Louisa May always wore that big heart of hers on her sleeve," Mama says, as if this is the worst of sins.

Daniel starts to correct her, but even weakened, Mama will have none of it. His look tells me that she isn't herself, she doesn't know what she's saying.

Now that I am Louisa May and not Daddy, Mama hasn't looked at me once. I can't tell if she knows I am in the room or not. I hang on to the thin rope of knowledge that she loves me and would move mountains for me if she could. Yet her words tell me a different story. A story of grievances held on to for years.

But then Mama's words soften again. "Truth be told, I let her down, Daniel. I need to apologize for that before I go. That's why I need to wait until she gets here."

"Wildflower is here, Nell." Daniel motions for me to join him at the bed, and Mama appears to see me for the first time.

"Is Lily here, too?"

"She's on tour, Mama. But Daisy is here."

"Daisy?"

"Lily's daughter," I say. "Your great-granddaughter."

Mama nods. "Next time I see Joseph, I want to tell him about Lily being famous."

"Were you dreaming earlier?" I ask. "You looked so happy."

"Joseph came to me," she says. "He says I get to go with him soon." Mama closes her eyes as if practicing her leave-taking. I

wonder if she has fallen asleep again, but then she mumbles something about having things she needs to tell Wildflower.

Daniel and I exchange another look. Mama's confusion fades in and out like an old-timey radio station.

"Mama, I'm here," I say, holding her hand.

"I'm glad she's on her way," Mama says, not opening her eyes. "I need to tell Joseph that Lily is famous," she repeats.

Mama has been one of the most dependable people to ever walk this earth, and for her to be this confused is hard to witness.

"Would you like me to bring you some of Aunt Sadie's special tea?" Daniel says to Mama.

"I hate that 'special tea.'" Mama spits out the words as though spitting out the tea. "But it does make my memories come alive."

Daniel leaves to get Sadie, and Mama appears to be sleeping again. I suddenly realize how tired I am. It has already been a long day, and it's barely lunchtime. It is Sadie who returns, not Daniel, carrying a cup and saucer.

"What do you put in that special tea of yours?" I ask Aunt Sadie.

"Just things to help her rest," she says.

The smell of blackberry spirits fills the room again, and Mama opens her eyes.

Sadie places the cup to Mama's lips, and Mama takes small sips in what I can only guess is a rare act of obedience.

"I don't know what I'd do without you," Mama says to Sadie.

"I don't know what I'd do without you, either." Aunt Sadie caresses Mama's hair like a mother touching the head of a sick child.

For the longest time, the three of us listen to the clock on the nightstand click the moments of Mama's life away.

Then Mama tells Sadie about seeing Joseph. I sometimes forget that Daddy was Sadie's younger brother. She asks how he looked.

Mama pauses, as though picturing him. "He looked the same as the day he left and never came back."

Sadie looks out the window as though remembering that day, too. "When he first told me about you, he couldn't stop smiling," Sadie says. "He was so smitten."

"I was smitten, too," Mama says. "I can't believe I was ever that young and that in love."

"That young woman is still in there somewhere," Sadie says to Mama, and then looks over at me and winks.

"I doubt it." Mama offers a gruff chuckle.

Growing up, whenever Daddy made Mama laugh—that was the only time I saw the young part of her. Now she looks tired. Worn down. A pencil that has been sharpened to the nub with only a tiny bit of eraser left.

Mama's face relaxes as Aunt Sadie's tea takes effect. She closes her eyes, as if this helps her see Daddy more clearly. "His eyes were gray with a hint of blue sky mixed in," she says. "I could lose myself in those eyes and that famous McAllister smile." She sighs. "I could forgive him for almost anything, Sadie, though he didn't do much that required forgiving."

While Mama's eyes remain closed, Aunt Sadie rubs lotion into her hands. Her familiarity touches me. I always thought that Aunt Sadie would go first since she is at least fifteen years older than Mama. But I have no doubt Mama would do the same thing for her.

Minutes later, Mama is sleeping again, and Sadie motions for me to come with her. We go into the living room to talk, our voices lowered.

"It's hard to see her like this," I say.

"I know," she says to me. "The dying have work to do. It's their job to remember the past and see the span of their lives. I've sat at enough deathbeds to know this process."

"I'm sorry I wasn't here sooner," I say. "But it doesn't seem to matter anyway."

"You mustn't take Nell's bitterness personally, sweetheart," she

tells me. "You're just the closest hook for her to hang her grief coat on. That coat is ragged by now."

"You could have been a poet," I say.

She smiles. "I could have been a lot of things."

For the first time I wonder if Aunt Sadie has regrets. She was never married. Never had children. Her career was making mountain remedies, being a midwife, and stitching quilts. Not to mention making her famous blackberry spirits. She always seemed to have enough of what she needed. Did she want more? But it is Mama who holds her full attention now. Any regrets will have to wait.

"Nell's life hasn't been easy," Aunt Sadie begins again. "She did the best she could, and I know you wish she'd been different. I think she wishes she'd been different, too, but her stubbornness is what has kept her going all these years."

"I wish I understood her as you do," I say.

"It's easier for friends to see than daughters," she says. "But it's good you're here. It's never too late for some final mending."

I nod. "Do you think it will be soon?" I ask.

"I think so," she says. "Every creature knows when it's their time. Cats will go off deep in the forest to be by themselves, seeking out a spot on the rich forest floor to dig their claws into before nuzzling down."

I think of Pumpkin, who one day wandered off and just disappeared. I was outside calling him deep into the night.

"Nell wants to die where she lived her life. In this house and in this bed that she and Joseph shared. I want to honor her wishes."

The bed Mama refuses to leave is the same one where Daddy died. It is also the bed where my Grandma McAllister passed when I was five years old. This house was hers before it was Mama's. I forget that, sometimes. A homestead has deep layers of history if it has been around a while.

Today the past feels more alive than ever. While Mama lays her burdens down, I want to believe what Aunt Sadie says about Mama's bitterness not being personal. What would a final mending look like between Mama and me? With that thought, I lean toward forgiveness.

CHAPTER SIX

Daisy

Gran opens the screen door and asks me to sit in Granny McAllister's room while she talks to Daniel and Sadie.

"What if she dies while I'm sitting there?" I ask.

"Then come get me," Gran says. "But I doubt that will happen. She's been talking a blue streak, and nothing can shut Mama up if she has something to say."

"What if she starts talking to me?" I ask.

"Then listen," Gran says. "Sometimes listening is the biggest gift you can give a person."

I follow Gran into the house and enter a room filled with the smell of blackberries and my father's liquor cabinet. Until today I have spent very little time with old people. Now they seem to be everywhere.

With Gran's encouragement, I sit in an old rocker in the corner of the smelly room. The rocker creaks against the wooden floor every time I move, so I don't move. The old lady in the bed is

sleeping. She is Gran's mother, but Gran doesn't look anything like her.

"Come get me if you need me," Gran says at the door before leaving.

I need her now, but don't say it.

As soon as Gran is gone, I quietly open the window a couple of inches to let out some of the smell. For the second time today I want my mom. Everything is strange here. Everybody acts like they know me. I am Lily's girl. But the truth is, nobody knows the real me. Or the secrets I carry that haunt me.

The rocker crackles against the wooden floor, and I accidentally wake the almost-dead. The old lady opens her eyes and looks straight at me.

Startled, I look away. Should I run to get someone?

When I glance again, she holds me with her gaze. "Who are you?"

"I'm Lily's girl, Daisy."

Narrowing her eyes, she looks at me as though searching for the family resemblance. I turn so she can see my profile. She nods, content with my proof.

"What are you doing here?" She sounds like a blues singer—her voice raspy.

"I'm staying with Gran this summer while my mom travels."

"Who's your mother again?"

I start to answer, and she says, "Just kidding. I know who your mother is."

"I didn't realize dying people made jokes," I say.

A chuckle catches in her throat, followed by a cough, and the world turns serious again.

"Should I go get somebody?"

"No," she says. "I'm fine with choking to death."

I offer her a glass of water sitting on the nightstand. She takes a

sip and thanks me. Veins stretch like purple snakes up the backs of her hands, and her skin is paper-thin. Brown spots cover the surface like large freckles. I remember what Gran told me before she left, about how listening can be a gift. I turn toward the old woman with renewed purpose.

"I'll listen if you feel like talking," I say.

Her gaze softens, followed by a long pause.

"My husband died a long time ago," she begins, "but today I've remembered the day we met. We talked for hours, and by that evening, I knew I would become Mrs. Joseph McAllister." She smiles and turns toward the window, as though it has opened into the past.

"He proposed over at Sadie's place," she begins again. "We were having a picnic under a giant oak." She lifts her chin as though feeling the sunlight on her face. "Are you married?" she asks me.

"No, I'm thirteen."

"Oh," she says. "Well, before I met Sadie, I didn't realize women didn't have to marry and have a mess of children if they didn't want to. Sadie lived alone, managed a piece of farmland, and learned everything she could about mountain medicine. It turns out there were all sorts of elders here in the mountains who knew about such things. Some had learned them from the Cherokee."

She closes her eyes, as if that helps her remember. When she opens them again, she asks if I'd like to hear more. I tell her yes. At this point, I am not only giving her the gift of listening, I actually want to hear more. It occurs to me that I should move closer, but I am not ready for that yet.

"The first time Joseph kissed me, my knees went wobbly," she says with a grin.

Goosebumps tingle up my arms. Do wobbly knees come before falling in love?

"When Joseph asked if I would marry him, my voice was calm

when I answered yes, but my insides were shooting off fireworks like the Fourth of July."

She looks suddenly younger, as though old age is a mask she's been wearing.

"After that, Sadie and Joseph and I danced in the open field behind Sadie's house."

I smile picturing it—people I've only seen old, dancing in their youth.

"Later, Sadie told me that she knew all along that Joseph and I would be together. Sadie has a way of knowing things."

I wonder if I have this "knowing," too, but it is more like a hearing. Hearing voices from the past.

In the seconds that follow, we exchange a look, as though both aware that I will carry this family story with me for the rest of my life. A story that will remind me of who I am: the great-granddaughter of Joseph and Granny McAllister.

A black bird lands on the windowsill outside as if bearing another gift. I never notice birds in Nashville, and I suddenly wonder why. The crow looks in on us, slowly rocking its head from side to side. It flies to the back of the porch swing and perches there.

"Crows know when someone is dying," she says.

"They do?" I shiver.

"I'm ready to go," she says. "I've got one foot in the grave already." She shakes her left foot under the quilt as if pulling my leg.

"Are you afraid?" I ask.

"No," she says. "It's my reward."

"Reward?"

"Haven't you ever heard of heaven? What's your mama been teaching you?"

I shrug.

"Use words, girl. Nobody knows what those shrugs mean."

For someone who is dying, she sure is speaking her mind. At this moment, the woman everyone calls Granny McAllister seems too ornery to die. For the longest time, we sit in silence. The crow on the porch calls out before flying away.

"How many times did it call out?" she asks.

"Three times."

She appears to ponder this. "That means I only have three hours or three days before I'm dead."

I shiver again.

Then she looks toward the door. Her cheeks turn a light shade of pink. A slight smile graces her lips, and her eyes widen as though someone has just walked into the room.

"Do you see him, Daisy?" she whispers.

"See who?" My whisper matches hers.

I turn toward where she is looking. An old housecoat hangs on the back of the door, blue with small white flowers. Other than that, I see nothing.

"He's here," she whispers again, sounding like a young bride. "You see him, don't you?"

I nod, wanting to see him.

"Joseph, this is Daisy," she says.

Her eyes follow him across the small room until he is standing by her bed. Whatever she sees is real to her. Tears pool around the edges of her eyes.

Then the voices start. Overlapping snatches of conversations of their life together here in this house. They are happy here. A girl laughs. A girl Joseph calls Wildflower. When I look over at Granny McAllister, her eyes are closed, and she is smiling. Her left foot, the one foot in the grave, moves to the slow rhythm of a banjo playing.

The tune sounds familiar. Then I remember where I've heard it. It was a lullaby my mom sang to me before bed when I was

younger. Now she sings it at the end of her shows as an encore. My great-grandfather, Joseph, has a bright, steady voice and sings along with his banjo, the same song I've heard my mom sing many times:

Goodnight, Irene. Goodnight, Irene. I'll see you in my dreams.

CHAPTER SEVEN

Wildflower

When I return to check on Mama and Daisy, Mama is sleeping, and Daisy has her eyes closed. She is humming something.

"What's going on?" I ask.

She stops humming and opens her eyes. "Nothing," she says, but her *nothing* is full of *something*.

"Has Mama been sleeping this whole time?"

"Not the whole time."

I wait for her to say more, but instead she hums again. I have never known Daisy to hum. It reminds me of Daddy. The rocking chair creaks on the old wooden floor, an accompaniment to the melody. The sound sparks a memory of when I found Mama sleeping in that chair after Johnny attacked me. For weeks I slept in her bed. It was the first time I realized Mama's devotion to me. I look over at her, seeking forgiveness. Both hers and mine.

This old house contains layer upon layer of McAllister history. Stories fill the place. Those told and untold. Daniel reminded me

recently of how Mama spoke fluent German and hid this fact from everyone in Katy's Ridge. Especially after Hitler rose to power. She lived in fear that she might be accused of being a Nazi sympathizer. She burned any proof of her German heritage. I hadn't remembered that at all. I look at Mama now and wonder what else I have forgotten. Probably thousands of things.

"You sure you're okay?" I ask Daisy.

She nods, and I believe her.

Meanwhile, Mama moves slightly and moans.

"Is that you, Wildflower?" she asks, her eyes closed.

I am surprised she doesn't call me *Louisa May*.

Mama never took to calling me the nickname Daddy gave me. A name I reclaimed four years ago when I turned fifty. A milestone birthday required a proclamation of some kind. So, with the help of the great State of Tennessee, I legally became Wildflower McAllister in hopes of claiming back some of the confidence I used to possess.

"Have you heard from Lily?" Mama asks, her voice sounding weaker than it was when I first arrived.

Of all her grandchildren and great-grandchildren, Lily is the one she asks after the most.

"She's on tour again, Mama."

"Where this time?"

"Scotland," I say.

"You know, your Daddy's people are from there," Mama says.

I sit on the bed and hold her hand. "Lily found some McAllisters in a cemetery near Glasgow," I tell her.

"Did you hear that, Joseph?" Mama says, looking to her left. "Lily found some McAllisters in Glasgow." I always think of Daddy living at the cemetery, not hanging out in Mama's bedroom. But perhaps he has come home to retrieve her.

I wish Bee were here. The old Bee. The not-so-busy Bee. The woman who used to stitch needlepoint bumblebees to the collars

of her blouses and whose face brightened whenever she saw me. Right about now, I could use her reassurance that everything is going to be all right.

"Your daddy misses you," Mama says to me.

Being home has primed the pump for tears. If I'm not careful, I'll start gushing.

When I was a girl, Aunt Sadie told me that spirits were all over these mountains. Not just wood sprites and fairies like in the old country that Daddy used to talk about, but the souls of people who walked the land before us. Not only my family but Horatio's people, the Cherokee, who were here before any of us. Horatio was a friend of Daddy's and is married to my friend June. I remember the dream I had this morning of walking the hidden path to the cemetery. A way that was my secret as a girl. What are my secrets now? And why would Daisy be in my dream?

Mama squints toward the rocking chair as if spying a stranger in the room.

"That's Daisy, Mama. Lily's girl."

The McAllister family tree has three generations of daughters. No sons. I think of the magic threes Daddy used to talk about that were always in fairy tales. He said that whenever a three shows up, you can expect magic just around the corner. I want to believe that this dull, complicated world can have magic in it.

"Lily's girl?" Mama says, as though forgetting that Lily is grown now.

Sometimes I forget Lily is grown, too. Grown and living a life vastly different from my own. A life so busy she barely has time to see Daisy, much less her extended family and me. At best her trips back to Katy's Ridge have been infrequent. But Lily outgrew Katy's Ridge in the womb. Spirits haunted her, too.

Not that I've been much different. After we left, it was too painful to spend any amount of time here. Too painful to remember the scandal and the shame that came from people

judging Bee and me. People said hurtful things. Called us names. Without any livelihood, we didn't have a choice about whether to stay or leave. Our secret pushed us out into the bigger world.

However, Mama never wavered in her support. More than once, I underestimated her. Mama pats the bed for Daisy to sit next to her. Daisy and I trade places, me taking the rocker.

"You're Lily's girl?" Mama pats her hand.

"Yes, ma'am," Daisy says.

Her level of politeness surprises me. She never says, "ma'am." Has Katy's Ridge changed her this quickly?

"Why isn't Lily here?" Mama asks her.

"She's on tour," Daisy says.

"That's right," Mama says, closing her eyes. "Lily is visiting Joseph's family."

Within seconds, Mama is sleeping again. We leave her resting, and Daisy follows me out into the living room.

"Is she okay to be left alone?" Daisy asks.

"I think so, but we'll check on her soon," I tell her. "My sisters are coming over, too. Get ready for a lot of people."

Daisy's momentary concern fades, and she begins to hum again.

"That song sounds familiar, what is it?" I ask her.

"'Goodnight, Irene.'"

"That's right," I say, suddenly remembering the tune. "Growing up, Daddy used to sing that song at the end of the day to Mama and all us girls. Mama told me once that she wished her name had been Irene instead of Penelope."

"Her name is Penelope?"

"Well, everyone calls her Nell except for her kids, who call her 'Mama,' and her grandchildren and great-grandchildren, who call her 'Granny McAllister.'"

Daisy nods, as though filing this away in her memory.

"Mom sings that song as an encore," Daisy says.

"How did I not know that?"

"Maybe because you've never been to one of her concerts," Daisy says.

"I haven't? Yes, I have. Haven't I?"

Hundreds of times, I have watched Lily sing, but Daisy is right that I haven't been to one of her full concerts. When she sang at the Grand Ole Opry that first time, I did wait backstage. I was so nervous I thought I might lose my supper the whole time. It worried me that she might mess up in front of millions of people on television. I hate big crowds, too, and most of her concerts these days could hold the entire population of Katy's Ridge several times over. But I remind myself to apologize for the oversight next time I see her.

"Do you mind if I get my book from the car?" Daisy asks.

"Of course not," I say.

She leaves to retrieve it, her dark mood a tad lighter. Perhaps being around family—even family she doesn't know—will be right for her. Maybe being home will be good for me, too. My family is like Mama's hummingbird quilt, and I am one of the fabric squares stitched into the quilt. In Nashville, I have never quite felt a part of anything, but here in Mama's house, I seem to remember who I am.

For a few seconds, the clock on the bedside table and Daddy's pocket watch are in sync before they wander off on different paths again. I think of Mama and her life winding down like a watch. We are all watches in the process of winding down. Since I turned fifty, four years ago, I think about this fact more and more.

For years after Daddy died, Mama kept his pocket watch nearby, winding it every evening before bed like he used to. Somehow that old watch kept him alive for her. When I moved to Nashville, Mama gave me Daddy's watch, telling me that he would have wanted me to have it. Of all my possessions, Daddy's watch is one of the things I cherish the most. Out of habit, I tap the

pocket of my blue jeans, feeling the watch's heartbeat against my skin.

In the kitchen, I join Sadie and Daniel. They catch me up on the mundane happenings of Katy's Ridge before Sadie excuses herself to go check on Mama.

The round table in Mama's kitchen looks smaller. A table that has graced the McAllister kitchen for as long as I can remember. It is practically a member of the family, always there to hold us together. With the renovations, the room now extends beyond where the porch used to be. Growing up, six of us sat around this same table. The two youngest, Meg and I, sat on stools that Daddy made, while my two older sisters and Mama and Daddy used the four chairs that came with the table.

Celebrations involving extended family required an extra leaf put in the table that was so heavy it took two people to lift and place it. A card table was set up in the living room for the kids. Graduating from the kid's table was a rite of passage in the McAllister family. In some ways, it still feels like an honor to sit here, even four decades later.

An orange tabby named Oscar weaves around my ankles, a distant descendant of Pumpkin, who was our cat when I was a girl. Mama's letters over the last few years always contained Oscar's latest escapades. She named him after the character on *The Odd Couple* who made messes. I imagine he doesn't know what to do without Mama fawning over him. For years she gave Daddy a hard time for feeding whatever cats showed up on the back porch, but it turns out she was the cat lover in the family.

Sadie returns and reports that Mama is still sleeping. Then Daisy sits beside me, a worn paperback in her hand.

"Iced tea?" Aunt Sadie asks. "All these life-and-death matters make a person thirsty."

We thank her, and she fills four glasses with ice cubes that she empties from the metal trays in the freezer. With the weight of the

tea pitcher, her hand trembles, and I rush to help her. All this time, I haven't given a thought to what it must be like for Aunt Sadie—a woman in her nineties—to care for Mama full time. Nor have I given a thought that a glass tea pitcher might be cumbersome for her. I vow to do better.

Thankfully, Mama's decline has been quick. Just last week she was still walking around feeding her chickens and hadn't yet taken to her bed. This thought eases my guilt.

Aunt Sadie takes a boxed apple pie from the top of the refrigerator and cuts us each a slice, as though our coming grief requires food. Her hand trembles cutting it, too, and I suddenly realize that not only am I losing Mama, but someday I will also lose Aunt Sadie. At this moment, life feels not only unfair but also full of loss. Loss I'm not even sure a piece of pie can cure.

In the meantime, I never thought I'd see a store-bought pie in Mama's kitchen. As long as I can remember, she made all her pies herself and taught Lily to do the same. I was often assigned to peel the apples, since I wasn't much good for anything else.

"Do you still have Daddy's old knife?" I ask Daniel.

He pulls it from his pocket, a gift I gave him when we worked at the sawmill together twenty-five years ago.

"Your daddy could peel an entire apple in one long peel," Daniel says. "Do you remember that?"

I tell him I do, and my memory produces a dangling roll of unbroken peel almost reaching the floor, along with the smell of sliced apple.

"It took me years to finally be able to do that myself," I say. "Mama used to hate it when I practiced, leaving peels everywhere."

They laugh, but the mention of Mama causes us to go quiet. Daisy pretends to read. No pages turn. I imagine she is listening. Always. She is so much more mature than I was at thirteen. Maybe that's from being an only child and watching the grown-ups. Her

childhood will be gone soon enough as it is. I wish she didn't feel the need to be so watchful.

"I can't imagine Nell not being here anymore," Aunt Sadie says.

"I can't, either," I say.

"It's going to be hard," Daniel says. He stares at his hands as though helpless to stop what is happening. Mama and Daniel have been close since Daddy died. She relied on him to do the things she couldn't do herself and repaid him with friendship.

"Nell's tired," Sadie says. "She's ready to go. Not everybody is. So that's a blessing, at least."

I think of Daddy, who was not ready to go. His life shortened by an accident. A pang of familiar guilt visits me. Guilt that if I'd listened to my secret sense and convinced him not to go, he might be sitting with us at this table. If Mama were here, she would accuse me of beating a dead horse and tell me to get over it. Guilt serves no purpose in Mama's world. Not when work needs doing.

Our conversation pauses again. Death requires pauses. Especially death that lingers in the hallway, allowing for longer goodbyes.

"How long has Mama been talking to Daddy?" I ask Sadie.

"I've sensed his presence since last night," she says. "That's why I called you this morning."

Daisy looks up from her book.

"What is it?" I ask her.

The shake of her head says *nothing*, but I know it is more than nothing. Does she sense that Daddy is here, too?

Unlike Lily and me, Daisy didn't grow up in these mountains where long-forgotten voices whisper in the wind. Daisy is a city girl, with no reason to believe in invisible things and long-silent voices with stories to tell. In all the years I've lived in Nashville, I never once heard anyone talk about death. Not to mention ghosts or spirits. Not once.

However, now I wonder if Daisy is more versed in spirits than I

give her credit for. Maybe it doesn't matter where you live, but whether or not you are paying attention.

"Last night Nell started talking to her sister, too," Aunt Sadie says. "In German."

I nod. "Sometimes when I was a girl, I would overhear Mama and Aunt Chloe whispering in German here in the kitchen," I say. "It was weird to hear her speak a foreign language, but that doesn't freak me out as much as her talking to Daddy in English like he's sitting right there in the room. I got goosebumps."

"Goosebumps tell us when spirits are close," Aunt Sadie says.

She told me this when I was younger, except now it has more meaning.

Daisy rubs her arms, as though she has goosebumps, too. Aunt Sadie and I exchange a look, both of us wondering if the secret sense has passed to the latest generation.

CHAPTER EIGHT

Daisy

I turn a page of my book, not reading a word. In a roomful of people, I am good at becoming invisible.

"I've never known Nell to talk so much," my great-great Aunt Sadie says. "She's turned into a chatterbox."

You have no idea, I want to say. Nobody knows that I heard her story about meeting and marrying her beloved Joseph.

Gran agrees with Sadie. "For a woman of few words, Mama has a lot to say."

I am a person of few words, too. I wonder if I got this trait from Granny McAllister.

"Maybe Nell felt talking was a luxury she didn't have time for," Daniel says.

He catches me studying him, but he doesn't give me away.

"I'm still having a hard time believing Mama isn't going to live forever," Gran says.

Sadie agrees and pats Gran's hand. Sometimes she acts like Gran's mom.

It feels strange that the person they already miss is still a stranger to me.

"As a girl, I didn't think Mama even slept," Gran says. "She was always up before me and was the last to go to bed."

"She's making up for that now," Sadie says, tapping the kitchen table three times with her index finger as though adding exclamation points to her words.

"The blackberry spirits help," Daniel says.

Sadie lets out a brief chuckle. "Blackberry spirits could never hurt."

The laugh opens into a silence that lasts for over a minute, but it isn't an uncomfortable silence like at the dinner table with my father. At his house, I feel like Karana in *Island of the Blue Dolphins* —all alone and fending for myself, but without a wild dog to talk to like Karana.

"When are the others coming?" Gran asks.

She must be talking about her sisters. Siblings are hard for me to imagine.

Sadie looks at the kitchen clock.

"An hour from now," she says. "I think I'll go rest for a while if it's okay."

Gran and Daniel encourage her to rest.

"I'll check on Nell," Daniel says.

Sadie nods and places a hand on my shoulder as she's leaving the kitchen.

"I'm glad you're here, Daisy."

I look up at her wrinkled face and thank her.

"If Daniel's sitting with Mama, I may take Daisy to the cemetery," Gran says. "I need to get out of the house for a while."

Is going to a cemetery Gran's idea of a joke?

"Say hello to Joseph for me," Daniel says. "Unless, of course, he's in the bedroom with Nell. In that case, I'll say hello myself."

Despite their sadness, they laugh. I've never heard anybody talk about ghosts, and I'm not sure I want to visit a graveyard.

Sadie leaves, followed by Daniel, leaving Gran and me alone in the kitchen. Gran washes the tea glasses and pie plates and leaves them to dry on a towel.

"Isn't going to the cemetery putting the cart before the horse?" I ask, repeating a phrase my cousin Nellie used earlier.

She smiles. "You have more of a sense of humor than I realized."

I stand, pleased that she has underestimated me. I return my book to my backpack before zipping it closed.

"I've been hanging out in cemeteries since I was a girl," Gran says. "You'd be surprised how peaceful it is."

As Gran gathers herself, I go out to the front porch, thinking of the crow that looked in Granny McAllister's window. Sadie's dog, Rufus, lifts his eyes at me but not his head. I sit beside him, and he moves his head to my lap. As I pet him, he softly moans his pleasure. He is not a wild dog on Karana's island, but he will do.

When Gran comes outside, Rufus gathers himself and stands at attention, though he is a bit wobbly.

"I used to walk to the cemetery from here," Gran says, "but today we'll drive since we only have an hour."

In the pickup again, we travel the roads of Gran's childhood. She tells me about the different places we pass.

"When I was a girl, I never thought anything of the distances I traveled on foot," she says. "I easily walked a mile or two to see Mary Jane. It was even farther to school, and June and Horatio's house."

She looks over at me as though I should be impressed.

"Sweeney's store was my farthest jaunt." She points to an old building boarded up on a corner with vines covering it. A white sign with faded red letters is above the door. "Sweeney's was far

enough to warrant a rest, and I'd sit out front and enjoy the penny candy that Victor always gave me."

"Victor?" I ask.

"An old friend," she says. "His father owned the store."

We continue along the river, and Gran shifts down before pulling into the parking lot beside a small white church.

"We're going to church?" I ask.

"Not exactly," Gran says. "This is where my family went to church when I was a girl. We were here every Sunday until I was your age. The cemetery is behind it."

"Why did you stop going to church?" I ask.

"It's a long story," she says with a sigh.

I wait. I have plenty of time for long stories.

Gran looks over again. "You really want to hear this?"

I nod.

Her forehead creases. "Well, the long and short of it is that Preacher said I was the one in the wrong for what Johnny Monroe did to me, and that I should pray for forgiveness. I never forgave him for that. Nor did Mama. The whole family went less and less."

"Who is Johnny?"

"A boy I used to go to school with."

"What did he do?"

Gran turns off the engine and gets out of the pickup as if typing THE END on the final page of her story. The sound of hammering comes from inside the church, and she suggests we go inside. The doors are open wide, and I follow Gran. The old windows are open, too. A dull breeze blows. Heavy and warm. Honeysuckle blooms somewhere nearby.

Gran walks down the aisle like a hesitant bride. Then the voices start that she can't hear. Voices from the past. Voices all speaking at once. I cover my ears to block out the desperate prayers haunting the church, and I suddenly realize that Gran is

also talking and asking if I'm okay. I uncover my ears and tell her I am, though this is far from the truth.

Thankfully, the voices stop.

Meanwhile, Gran takes a long, slow look around. "Daddy preferred an unroofed church," she says, and I ask her what she means by that.

"A place in nature," she says, "like a mountain stream or an oak grove. God was everywhere to him. Not just in a building."

I don't tell Gran that I've seldom thought about God at all.

She stops at the third row from the front of the church and looks at the long bench as though it holds a lifetime of stories. "This is the family pew," she says. "Mama, Daddy, me, and all my sisters sat in this row. Aunt Sadie always sat on the end near the aisle in case Preacher said something that made her angry and she needed to make a quick exit."

For the longest time, I stare at the bench and imagine having a big family. A family that includes a mother, father, sisters, and aunts.

"I wish I knew what goes on in that head of yours," she says.

I open my mouth, tempted to tell her about the voices, but then close it. Hammering begins again on what Gran calls the new addition.

"Miss Mildred would have loved that shiny new pipe organ," she says as she walks past it.

I don't ask who Miss Mildred is, except that I'm pretty sure she is one of the voices that haunts this place.

The hammering continues. Gran goes to investigate, with me close behind. A young man with black hair, maybe eighteen, hammers a board on the floor. When he sees us, he puts his hammer on a ladder and approaches.

"How's your daddy?" Gran asks him.

"Good," he says with a smile.

"Daisy, this is Adam Sector. Your mom used to date his dad, Crow."

Adam wipes a hand on his overalls before shaking mine. My face grows momentarily hot.

"This is Lily's daughter," Gran says.

I study my shoes.

"Grandma June told me this morning you two were coming," he says, giving me a brief smile.

"Should have known she'd be looking for me," Gran says. "June has always had a way of seeing things before they happen."

Adam agrees. "Sorry about your mama," he says.

She thanks him.

While I soak in shyness, they talk until Gran looks at her pocket watch and says we have to go. We say our goodbyes and leave the church. When the hammering begins again, I think of the blueness of Adam's eyes and how the color goes perfectly with his black hair. Meanwhile, the graveyard stretches across a hillside above us. I wait for the voices, but it is quiet.

CHAPTER NINE

Wildflower

The church grounds are newly mown, and the smell of fresh-cut grass lightens my mood. Sometimes I wish I'd kept track of how many times I have visited this cemetery. I don't feel Daddy's presence here at all. It's like only his bones are here. His spirit seems to have more flexibility.

As usual, Daisy is quiet, the deepest of still waters. However, the blush of femininity that rose when meeting Adam has not faded. I skipped that level when I was her age. The step that contains the infatuation with boys and the sweet and harmless flir-tations of youth. Johnny took that away from me.

Daisy and I walk up the hill toward the weeping willow.

"Let's go barefoot," I suggest, slipping off my sandals.

Daisy glances back at the church. The hammering continues. She slides off her shoes. The grass is soft, a plush carpet of green. Plastic flowers—faded in the sun—stick out of the dirt around a few tombstones. Otherwise, most of the gravesites are bare. I stop halfway up the hill to rest. It is steeper than the path at Mama's

house. When I was younger, I could run up this hill and not think anything of it. But at fifty-four just walking up it takes more energy than I want to admit.

Daisy waits up ahead. I take note of a tombstone with the name Floyd "Doc" Lester on the front. Mama wrote to me a few years ago that he had died. Surprising myself, I spit on his grave. Nothing ever happened to him for spying on Bee and me. Or for presenting himself as a real doctor when he had no training with human beings. Sometimes spitting is the only justice a person gets.

Daisy doesn't appear interested in the scenic river below, nor in the thick oaks and maples creating ample shade or the majestic weeping willow in the center of the knoll. Perhaps graveyards are an acquired taste.

In the distance, handpicked flowers rest on the graves where the Monroes are buried. The mother was the first to go. Then the older daughter, Ruby. I attended Ruby's funeral. Her death was shocking because she was a girl my age. Ruby Monroe has been dead almost as long as Daddy, as has Ruby's brother, Johnny. Johnny is a part of my history that I don't have the luxury to forget, given he is Lily's father. His younger sister, Melody, died a decade later. At the final resting places of the Monroe clan, there are new headstones where none existed before, giving the dates of birth and death. As far as I know, the Monroe lineage has died out, so it is a mystery who might be leaving flowers or paying for engraved markers.

Up ahead, Daisy has pulled her book out of her backpack and sits against a maple tree reading.

My scalp tingles. Johnny's words from forty years ago force their way into my mind: *Wildflower? People should call you weed. I think I'll pull this weed.* After the attack, I spent decades being that weed.

Daisy looks up from her book, giving me a piercing look, as though she has somehow heard Johnny's words. I tell Johnny to

leave her alone. Leave us both in peace. But fear cuts through me. Fear that has lived inside me for decades. I try to remember a time when it never entered my mind to be scared. Or a time when I didn't worry that bad people might be watching. Daisy walks over to me. I stand taller for her, trying to shake off the fright. For her, if not for me.

"What's happened?" Daisy asks. "You look like you've seen a ghost." She seems to know more than she's saying.

"Nothing's happened," I say, when "everything" is closer to the truth.

"I heard—" She stops there.

"It's nothing," I say again.

To distract myself, I lead her up the hill to the willow tree. At Nathan's grave, I introduce Daisy to Amy's husband, who died in World War II. Amy has been a widow for three decades. Perhaps that's why she has become so disagreeable over the years. I tell Daisy that Nathan always hitched up his pants. A man so skinny his hips were practically nonexistent. A small American flag graces the soil in front of his grave. Perhaps in preparation for the Fourth of July in a few days.

Nearby, I pay my respects to Baby Beth, the sister who died the year before I was born. Leaning over, I pull several weeds that have grown up around her baby lamb marker and toss them in a pile next to the tree. I think of my job at the nursery. Planting and weeding is such a solitary job, and one of the reasons I chose it in the first place.

When we approach Daddy's grave, I smell tobacco juice and moonshine, remembering the day Johnny defiled his tombstone. Glancing back at Johnny's new marker, I wish him the opposite of resting in peace. But this trip home isn't about Johnny. It's about saying goodbye to Mama, and maybe more. I can't shake the feeling that being here is about Daisy, too.

Standing in front of Daddy's marker, I greet him like I always

do, giving him time to answer. "I brought Daisy with me," I say. "Lily's girl, your great-granddaughter."

A soft breeze rises and rustles in the willow. All of a sudden, I feel Daddy close. Aunt Sadie once promised me that the dead never leave us. Moments like these help me believe it.

However, the message that comes to me is unexpected.

Protect Daisy, Daddy says. *Keep her safe.*

The breeze drops, as if Daddy is rushing off to be with Mama again. I ponder his message, wondering if this has something to do with the sadness she carries.

Daisy's eyes find mine. "You look like him," she says.

"How do you know?" I ask. "You've never met him."

Only a handful of photographs of Daddy exist. Pictures Mama tucked away somewhere, so she wouldn't be reminded of the life she lost.

Daisy lowers her eyes and stares at the tombstone. "He was young when he died."

"Thirty-eight," I say, "younger than Lily is now."

Daisy's expression doesn't change. I doubt she thinks about death as much as I did at her age. After Daddy died, I was convinced I would die young. Taken away in an instant like him.

For the first time I notice the moss-covered area next to Daddy's grave that is reserved for Mama. All these years, I have hidden from myself that she would join him under this same willow tree.

"Did something bad happen here?" Daisy asks.

"What makes you say that?" I ask.

She doesn't answer, and I think of Daddy's message to protect her and keep her safe. As always, I question if I've imagined it. It's not like Daddy to give me messages from the grave. In fact, this is the first one I've received in forty years. But it seems an odd thing for me to imagine, too.

"How did he die?" Daisy asks.

"Lily never told you?"

"No," she says.

"That surprises me." I sit on the ground and invite Daisy to join me. "How can you know who you are without hearing the family stories?"

Daisy shrugs, a gesture that is already tiring the second day of our summer together.

"I don't know my father's family stories, either."

"I find that very sad," I say. "To answer your question, Daddy died from a sawmill accident. The men he worked with brought him home. He lived just long enough to say goodbye. Everybody in Katy's Ridge came to the funeral. I wish you could have known him."

Daisy looks toward the river. "In a way, I feel like I do."

Before I have time to ask her what she means, the gate squeaks open behind us. I jump, thinking of Johnny. My heart beats faster, remembering the past. My legs twitch, ready to run. I remind myself that Johnny has been dead for decades. His grave is just down the hill.

A tall stranger steps into the cemetery carrying a handful of wildflowers. He appears not to see us and walks in the direction of the Monroe graves.

Daisy looks at me, an eyebrow raised to ask who he is.

"No idea," I whisper.

The stranger wears blue jeans and a blue T-shirt and hiking boots. He is midforties, physically fit. Something about him feels familiar, like an actor you've seen on television before, but you can't place the face with the program.

Katy's Ridge has never collected newcomers. The stranger adds wildflowers to the Monroe graves. I wonder if he picked them down the trail at the memorial I created to mark what happened that day.

Hammering starts up again at the church and breaks the spell. I

look at my pocket watch, aware that my sisters will be arriving soon. I stand, telling Daisy that we had better get back. I say goodbye to Daddy, but it feels like he's already at the house waiting.

As we walk down the hill, the man spots us. His surprise elicits a hand wave that I return. The familiarity nags at me again. He is tall and lean like the Monroes. The tilt of the head while walking seems familiar, too. Then I realize he looks like an older version of Johnny. Although this is not someone who had a hard life and stood at a crossroads spitting tobacco juice into an old peach can. This is someone who stood at a crossroads and chose a direction to go in and took it. However, my secret sense is not convinced I should trust him. There is unfinished business there. Somehow, it seems, our fates are connected.

CHAPTER TEN

Daisy

The hammering continues inside the church. Adam is much more handsome than the boys at my school with their picked-at acne and their tendency to make fun of girls. I can't believe my mom dated his father. A man named after a bird. I don't think of my mom dating anyone except my father. She should have gone with Crow.

Gran stops to wave at the stranger in the cemetery. She looks like she's seen a ghost again and gets really still. I've never seen this side of Gran. A woman with a history.

I am ready to leave this place. I nudge Gran, and she suggests we go. My relief comes out in a shrug. Then I remember what Granny McAllister said about using words instead of shrugs.

We get in Gran's pickup, and I slam the door so that it will stay shut. My father calls her truck a "bucket of bolts." He and Gran don't get along.

Gran looks over at me as if I am a bank safe she wants to crack

open but doesn't know the combination. I want to tell her things, but I don't know how.

In the meantime, Katy's Ridge is starting to grow on me. Compared to Nashville, it feels simple here. In three months, I start a new middle school, which is the opposite of simple. The school is huge. Just finding my classes will be a nightmare. It's supposed to be a decent school, but I don't know anybody there, and it means spending more time at my father's house because the new school is closer to where he lives than my mom's house. I chew on my bottom lip. I hate my dad.

"Would you like me to teach you how to drive while we're here?" Gran asks.

"Are you serious?" I ask, sitting taller in the seat.

"Dead serious," she says. "It's safer to learn on these old country roads."

"I'd like that," I say, taking a deep breath of mountain air.

"First, though, we need to get back and check on Mama," she says, "and have lunch with my sisters, but maybe afterward."

Having never been the type to jump up and down and show excitement, I hug my book to my chest, pushing my sneakers against the floorboard, braking and accelerating in my imagination. Driving means I am almost an adult. Driving means freedom.

As Gran starts the pickup, I look over as though seeing her for the first time. She isn't as affectionate as Bee is—I miss Bee—but she tries, and she has a room in her apartment for me to live when Mom is touring, so I don't have to stay at my father's house. Now she has agreed to teach me how to drive a stick shift. More than anyone, she seems to want to know me. I have plenty to tell her, but I'm not ready for that yet.

I ponder how a person might start a conversation to show their interest. I hug my book again, thinking how much I am like Karana. Even though I live in a big city, sometimes I feel like I live

on a deserted island like her, and I'm doing everything I can to survive without getting killed.

"What is it like to have sisters?" I ask.

Gran looks at me as if my question has opened a little door where she can see inside. I look away and hug my book tighter.

"Well, we don't get to pick our siblings or our lack of siblings," Gran says. "My sisters could be irritating when I was a kid, but they could also be lifesavers. We're not as close now," she continues, "and I regret that. If I still lived here that might be different." Gran pauses and taps the steering wheel.

For the second time in an hour, I try to imagine having family around. My father's family lives in California, and I haven't met most of them. Now it turns out that my mom has been keeping her family a secret. Not on purpose. I think she has just been intent on not coming back here.

"Are you close to your father?" Gran asks.

My throat tightens. Here we were wading into a sweet talk, and now we're at the deep end of the pool.

"Not really," I say, resisting my inclination to shrug.

She nods, as if she can understand why.

"You've never really liked him, have you?" I ask.

"No," she says simply.

"Not many people do," I say. "He's bossy and conceited. But mom says he can also be charming sometimes."

We turn into Granny McAllister's gravel driveway leading up the hill. Gran parks and turns off the pickup and then turns toward me.

"There's no love lost between your father and me, and I won't pretend differently," she says. "What matters is that you have a good relationship with him. I want that for you."

I lower my head, not knowing what a "good" relationship is. Whatever my father and I have, it sure doesn't feel right.

Gran looks up the hill toward the house. I wonder if her hesitation is about seeing Granny McAllister or her sisters. Or maybe both.

"If you ever need to talk about anything, I'm here," she says. Gran squeezes my hand, and to both our surprise, I squeeze back.

CHAPTER ELEVEN

Wildflower

At the house, Meg sits with Daniel on the porch swing, and Nellie sits on the step. Meg is my sister closest in age, with me being the youngest. Her hair is dyed black. She is wearing bright red nail polish with matching lipstick and looks like the Katy's Ridge version of Elizabeth Taylor. Meg used to read Holly-wood magazines when she worked at Woolworths, and as a teenager, she hid romance novels in our closet and underneath our bed. Meg always knows the gossip of the rich and famous, as well as the poor and forgotten here in Katy's Ridge.

We embrace, and she tells me how much I haven't changed. I am never sure if this is a compliment.

It is hard to forget Meg's reaction to finding out about Bee and me. It was a disappointment at best. But at least she was better about it than my sister Amy, whose judgment blindsided me. Of my three sisters, Jo handled it with the most acceptance. Although part of the deal was that we never speak of it again.

Meg smells of White Shoulders. A perfume meant to attract,

but that I find repelling. She greets Daisy, introducing herself as Aunt Meg. Though they have met before, it has been a while. Daisy says hello to her cousin Nellie and then leans down to pet Rufus, who drools his happiness.

"Mama still sleeping?" I ask.

Daniel says she is. It seems a luxury to see Daniel twice in one day. It reminds me of the times when we spent entire days working together at the sawmill.

Aunt Sadie steps onto the porch, closing the screen door with a delicate touch. She invites us to come inside for lunch.

Sometimes it shocks me that I am fifty-four and that Mama and Aunt Sadie are as old as they are. If we're lucky, time moves us along at a rapid pace. Lucky, that is, if we are granted longevity. Plenty of people in the graveyard weren't fortunate that way. Daddy included.

If I get to be seventy-eight, Mama's age, will Lily be the one sitting by my bedside? If so, I wonder if I will mistake her for Johnny, as Mama mistook me for Daddy. Lily looks like Johnny if the light catches her just right. I think of the stranger tending to the Monroe graves. A stranger who felt more like a ghost than a man. A stranger who earned my mistrust and dislike by merely being a Monroe.

A plate piled high with pimento cheese sandwiches cut into triangles sits on the table. The pimento cheese is Sadie's own recipe, but she is using store-bought bread. I'm not sure why these changes surprise me, except that they are parts of the past that I want to stay the same.

A guest now, I am not allowed to help, though I spent years helping prepare meals in this room. Jo and Daniel's youngest daughter, Nellie, pours glasses of iced tea. She is a different kind of beautiful than Jo was as a teenager. A wholesome beauty instead of the movie-star variety. She is competent in the kitchen, as

someone might be who helps in the kitchen often. I wonder where Jo is.

I always felt more confident in Aunt Sadie's kitchen than in Mama's. I felt free to help and unjudged by my lack of skill. Mama's kitchen is more functional, and minus the bird's nests, houseplants, and river rocks of Aunt Sadie's. With the renovations, shiny new appliances are everywhere, and a large gas stove and central heating now replace the wood stove that used to live in the corner. No wood chopping is needed anymore. No need for anyone to run out to the back porch on the frostiest of mornings to grab pieces of wood.

Daisy takes a chair at the back of the round table next to me, while Meg and I talk about the new church addition and Adam Sector and how much he's grown. The latest news from the Katy's Ridge grapevine is about little Wiley Johnson—now an extra-large man in his thirties—who as a child almost drowned in Sutter's Lake and who Preacher deemed destined to do God's work. It seems Wiley is now in prison drowning in bank fraud.

Amy enters the kitchen with hellos. It is incredible how much she looks like Mama now. Amy is carrying a large Tupperware container protecting her strawberry shortcake. Her way of showing disapproval is to not look at me, and from the look of things, she definitely disapproves.

Jo enters next, as beautiful as ever, apologizing for being late, though she is right on time. Jo is approaching sixty now. My favorite sister, Jo is the one who took the most time with me when I was younger. She places a big salad and two large bags of potato chips on the table. My family could always throw together a decent meal at a moment's notice, and today is no exception.

I think of Daisy's question again, asking what it was like to have sisters. We may disagree, but the bond is there regardless. Three sisters are bounty indeed, compared to being an only child,

and I think I've taken this for granted for every single one of my fifty-four years.

Everyone talks at once, exchanging news. Being with the family has always been the salve that soothed my broken places, and I realize now how much I've missed it. When Bee and I parted, I got used to living alone, but something about it never felt right.

The look on Daisy's face is of someone caught in a sudden rainstorm after a drought, not knowing whether to be delighted or angry about getting drenched. I know better than to pull her into the conversation; that will have her seeking refuge somewhere else. The tone grows quieter when sharing news about Mama, who is sleeping in her room. That Mama is not part of the kitchen gathering is well noted—the missing captain of the McAllister ship.

I remember what it was like to lose Daddy so suddenly. The hole he left in the family was a gaping wound for years. We would have gone aground if not for Mama, Aunt Sadie, and Daniel. It is hard to imagine Mama being a widow for forty years—most of my life really. I don't think it occurred to any of us that she might remarry. It might have never occurred to her, either. Daddy was her one great love. We all knew that. How could she possibly move on to someone else?

I think of Bee and hope her talk went well. While I have somewhat moved on from what caused us to leave Katy's Ridge, Bee has not. Over the years, she has refused to even speak of it.

As for my sisters, Meg has been a widow now for five years. Cecil died of a heart attack in his chair while watching *The Waltons* on television. Cecil's daughter, Janie, Meg's stepdaughter, still lives with Meg and never married. She works at the hospital in Rocky Bluff as a secretary. Amy still sews and has a shop in Harriman now, too, as well as in Rocky Bluff. She never remarried after Nathan died, perhaps following Mama's example.

Of all my sisters, I am the least settled. While Bee moved from teaching to be an administrator, I have had a series of jobs, none of

which appealed to me. Working at the nursery has been the best fit so far. At least I get to spend my time outside. But even though I am in good shape for my age, it is getting harder to dig, lift, and plant.

My family gathers, and I ask about the stranger at the cemetery who was at the Monroe graves.

My sisters exchange looks, but it is Sadie who finally speaks.

"Nell didn't want you to know," she says.

Mama used to tell me everything in her letters, once even sharing her pride in her regular bowel movements, so it's hard to believe she didn't mention a newcomer to Katy's Ridge.

"Why didn't she want me to know?"

An uneasy silence settles over the kitchen, broken only by the sounds of familial chewing. It might be humorous if not so unnerving. Daisy tosses an unspoken question in my direction, and I throw her back a reassuring look. I imagine the bigness of the McAllister clan has her a bit unnerved, and these are only the elders. First, second, and third cousins are absent. That gathering would genuinely blow her mind, as the kids say these days.

"Okay, someone needs to tell me what's going on," I say. "Or at least tell me why you don't want to talk about it."

Uneasiness passes around the table like an empty butter dish.

It is Daniel who finally speaks. "That stranger you saw is Melody's son."

After turning fifty, I thought nothing would shock me anymore, but at this moment I am indeed shocked. "Melody Monroe had a son?"

"Evidently," Meg says. She and Amy look at each other as if they have talked at length about this issue.

I pause to put the latest puzzle pieces together.

"He's been here for a little over a year now," Aunt Sadie begins. "He showed up out of the blue just like Melody did that day looking for Lily. It seems he inherited the old Monroe place."

A shudder passes through my body. Melody Monroe set in motion the events that exiled me from Katy's Ridge.

"Melody never mentioned having a son when she came back that time," I say. "She acted like Lily was the last of the Monroe line."

"My mom is part of the Monroe line?" Daisy asks.

We turn in her direction. I imagine cats rushing out of bags. Has Lily never told Daisy who Lily's father was? Has Lily been so busy she hasn't given Daisy even a basic family history?

"Melody Monroe wasn't in her right mind when she came here," Aunt Sadie begins again. "She'd been drinking heavily for years. The boy was living with his father at the time."

I sit with this new information, creating a rough road map in my mind where there wasn't even a path before.

"What is he doing here?" I ask.

"Nobody knows," Meg says. "But he seems harmless enough."

"Harmless or not, why are you just now telling me?" I look around the family table.

Daniel looks at his hands. "We were being protective."

I suddenly feel tired. It seems like days since Daisy and I arrived in Katy's Ridge, and it has only been a few hours. Meanwhile, secrets are already bubbling to the surface like hot springs.

"What do you know about him?" I ask.

"He may be wealthy," Meg says. "He tore down the Monroe cabin and started over. Built a nice house in its place."

A wealthy Monroe is hard to imagine. I remember Johnny's tattered clothes and smelly breath before shaking the image away. Until this morning, I hadn't dreamed about him for years. I thought I had finally erased him.

"People rarely move to Katy's Ridge," Jo says. "It gives us something to talk about at least." She smiles at Daniel. Nellie, who has been leaning against the counter all this time, walks over to her mother and begins to braid her hair. I wonder how my life

may have been different if Mama had let me touch her in this way.

"Who knows, maybe someday you'll come back to Katy's Ridge, too, Wildflower." Meg winks.

I tell her it will never happen, but somehow, even my resistance feels tired.

For one thing, Bee is my family, too, and she would never move back to Katy's Ridge. Even Nashville seems too small for her now. If not for Lily and Daisy and me, she might be living in Atlanta or Boston. A place with museums and symphonies instead of the birthplace of country music.

"How's Lily?" Meg asks me.

Lily has done things none of us imagined a McAllister would ever do—traveled the world, had a gold record, won a Grammy Award. All this in the last three years.

I glance at Daisy. "We heard from her briefly yesterday since it was Daisy's birthday."

Birthday wishes spread around the table, making Daisy blush and duck her head back into her book. It strikes me as sad that none of them knew.

I think again of Melody Monroe having a son and my family still trying to protect me from the past. I wonder at what point the past isn't an issue anymore.

"I think I'll go check on Mama," I say. Rising from the table, I rest a hand on Daisy's shoulder, telling her I'll return shortly. I need a break from my well-meaning family. I need a break from my granddaughter, too, and her unrelenting, silent intensity.

When I open the door, Mama is still sleeping. I hope she is dreaming of Daddy. Her breathing is shallow, and more color has left her face. I keep thinking that any minute she will get out of bed, put her apron on, and get busy. But it appears Mama's busyness has finally stopped. The last floor has been swept. The last of the firewood stacked. The final meal cooked.

"I love you, Mama," I whisper.

She takes a deep, raspy breath, as though she has heard me but doesn't want to come back from wherever she is.

Aunt Sadie comes in and puts an arm around my waist.

"Do you think it's okay if I get out of here for a while?" I say to her. "I need some fresh air."

She says she understands.

I have no idea where I need to go, but I make my apologies in the kitchen and tell everyone that I will be back soon. The look on Daisy's face causes me to motion for her to come along. She puts her book in her backpack, tossing it over her shoulder. We will escape together.

CHAPTER TWELVE

Daisy

Leaving the house, the mountain air smells sweet with honeysuckle. Something else is blooming that I don't know the name of.

"We're going to run the roads some," Gran says. "You okay with that?"

I nod. Not many people get to run country roads with their grandmother in a beat-up pickup that she is also going to teach me to drive. For several sweet seconds, my life feels good, and I wonder what it would be like to feel this way all the time.

"We're going to the old sawmill," Gran says.

I wonder if this is the same sawmill where my great-grandfather, Joseph McAllister, had his accident. I envision bloody saw blades and faded pools of blood still on the floor from long ago. Although I doubt Gran would take me there if it were gruesome.

The road is grown over in parts. Gran drives slow. Huge potholes, half-filled with water, dot the bumpy dirt road. When we come to a field of wildflowers, Gran calls them by their names.

Crested irises. Tiger lilies. I add these to my list of things I never knew existed. I do, however, recognize the daisies. Millions of them it seems. I always thought they were such ordinary flowers. But seeing them out like this, covering the landscape, they don't seem the least bit ordinary.

"Aren't the daisies beautiful?" Gran says. "Just like you." My face grows hot, and she tells me that she didn't mean to embarrass me. Mom tells me I'm beautiful all the time, but moms are supposed to say things like that.

"Why did you leave Katy's Ridge if it's so beautiful to you?" I ask.

"Didn't Lily ever tell you?"

"Mom never talks about this place," I say.

Gran's surprise makes me wonder why I never questioned my mom about her childhood or the place she grew up. Somehow, I got the message that she wouldn't like that. Or maybe I thought everybody had hidden family tucked away in the hills somewhere that they never saw.

Gran slows the truck to drive through a deep pothole that covers the entire road and looks like the beginning of a small lake.

"To answer your question, we left Katy's Ridge because people found out about Bee and me."

I always thought Bee and Gran just decided to move someplace bigger. Nobody could blame them for that. It never occurred to me they might have left because of a problem.

"What did they do?" I ask.

"People stopped doing business at the mill, and Bee lost her job teaching. With both livelihoods gone, we had to leave, and Nashville made the most sense."

A single tear falls down her cheek.

"I'm sorry," I say. "No wonder Mom doesn't like coming back."

"Lily was fine with getting the hell out of Dodge," Gran says.

"Do you ever wish you'd stayed?" I ask.

Gran puts the pickup in a lower gear to get ready for the next potholes. "Leaving here was a little like leaving the best part of me behind."

"I've never felt that way about a place," I say. "But sometimes I wish I could live at my mom's and not at my father's. I'd like to have just one bedroom for a change."

Gran looks at me. "Have you told Lily that?"

"No," I say.

"I think you should tell her," she says. "To want to only live in one place doesn't sound unreasonable to me."

I don't tell Gran that I would be okay with never going back to my father's house again.

We stop in front of the sawmill.

A NO TRESPASSING sign is tacked onto the door of what looks like a large barn.

"The mill still belongs to Bee's parents," Gran says. "Several years ago, they moved to Florida and never took the time to sell it. It will belong to Bee eventually."

A rusty chain and padlock are wrapped around the door handles. I follow Gran around to a side door. A bench sits below the window.

Gran tries the door, and she acts surprised when it opens. We walk inside. She flips a light switch, but nothing happens.

"What's that smell?" I ask.

"Rotting wood," she says.

I think of Granny McAllister and try to picture her Joseph here.

A conversation from the past begins: *We need to finish this order as soon as possible,* a man says. I wonder if this is Joseph.

Another man says that his wife just went into labor and that he told her he'd be home an hour ago. After a pause, Joseph tells the man to go home, that he'll do the order himself. He isn't angry. It is an act of kindness.

The voices from the past fade.

When I look up, Gran is watching me.

"Where did you go?" she asks.

I resort to another shrug.

It is too soon to tell Gran about what I overheard. Too early to tell anyone, if I ever do.

We walk among the saws and long tables. Sunlight filters through the high windows. Thankfully, I don't hear any voices from this room concerning the accident.

"I couldn't have held this place together without Daniel," Gran says.

She looks around as if overcome with memories. I leave her and go outside and eventually end up back in the truck.

Gran returns. "Tell you what," she says. "I'll let you start the engine, and you can practice putting it into first gear."

She tosses me the keys. They jingle their importance. Meanwhile, Gran looks back at the crumbling sawmill as if she is now the one hearing conversations from the past.

CHAPTER THIRTEEN

Wildflower

When we return to the house, everyone has left, and Aunt Sadie confirms that Mama is slipping away from us. I sit next to her bed, already missing her, and longing for what could have been, instead of what was.

After Mama goes, Sadie is next in line, then my sisters and me. Heartbreak is woven into every life. All of us in the process of slipping away.

Later that evening Bee calls and Daisy and I go into the kitchen to talk to her. A lone telephone hangs on the far wall next to the pantry—evidence that the McAllisters have finally entered the current century. The phone is red and doesn't quite match the red of the old rooster clock that hangs over the new gas stove. The clock ticks as noisily as ever, keeping steady time with the day, reminding us with every moment that life is ticking away.

The long cord twists like a jump rope. Daisy talks first and tells Bee about her driving lesson. They have a closeness that I sometimes envy. When Daisy hands me the telephone, my eyes tear up

from hearing Bee's voice. Even though we are no longer together, she is my dearest friend. A person who feels as much like family as Daisy does.

"How did the speech go?" I ask her.

She hesitates. "I was so nervous my voice shook, Lou. That's the part I hated. But the shaking stopped after a minute or two. And a bunch of people told me it went really well."

I tell her how proud I am of her.

"How's your mama?" she asks, concern in her voice.

Bee and Mama always got along. But with Bee's refusal to set foot in Katy's Ridge again and Mama's refusal to leave all the chores she must attend to, they haven't seen each other for years. However, in my letters to Mama, Bee always wrote a paragraph or two at the end. I often thought Mama appreciated those paragraphs more than she did the rest of the letter.

"Mama's sleeping a lot," I say. "Sadie says that's perfectly normal for—"

Seconds pass. Though hundreds of miles separate us, I can feel her presence. She knows the struggles I've had with Mama. She also knows how much I love her despite our struggles.

"She thought I was Daddy, Bee. She just kept talking to me like I was him."

"Sounds like you've had a rough day," she says, in that way that makes me feel not only heard but loved.

"I wish you were here," I say.

"I do, too," she answers, though I know this isn't true. Bee will never forgive Katy's Ridge for turning on her. On us.

I glance at Daisy sitting at the kitchen table. Even as a baby, she appeared to be listening, as though the heavens were speaking, and she didn't want to miss a word.

My secret sense twangs like a string on Daddy's old banjo. I look at Daisy. What is my intuition trying to tell me? Is it my turn to listen? But how do you listen to someone so reluctant to speak?

In the next second I wonder what happened to Daddy's banjo. I can't remember when it stopped being in the living room, where it always sat next to the woodstove.

I tell Bee that I should go. I hate that she's paying for long-distance when she doesn't make that much even as a school administrator. "I'm so glad your speech went well," I tell her.

"Take care of yourself," she tells me. "Give that mind of yours a rest."

Bee knows how much I lose sleep thinking about things. My thoughts are like a wheel stuck in the mud that keeps turning and digging itself deeper. Bee never loses sleep over anything. She is the type to close her eyes and wake eight hours later feeling refreshed. Something I'm not sure I've ever done.

We skip the *I love you* at the end of the call, though I know love is still there. After I hang up the phone, I untwist the long cord, and Daisy and I join Aunt Sadie outside on the front porch where she sits petting Rufus.

"That was Bee," I say.

Aunt Sadie nods. "How is she?"

I tell her about Bee's talk, and Sadie says how lucky the schoolchildren are to have Bee on their side. I agree and glance through Mama's bedroom window, which overlooks the porch. Daniel and Jo are with her now. The family will take turns sitting with Mama until there's no need to anymore. When Mama passes, the world will keep going like it did before. No one will even notice, except for those close to her.

When the sun drops below the highest ridge, the cicadas warm up their melodies. Nighttime ambles across the mountains. With every passing minute, the heat of the day cools. I think again of my secret sense, wondering what it sees coming that I don't.

On the porch swing, Daisy turns her head as though hearing something. Her uneasiness passes to me. Within seconds, a figure comes into view, walking up the hill. At first I think of Daddy.

Then I flash on Melody Monroe, who showed up drunk in 1956, wanting to find Lily. Rufus stands. Half-blind and half-deaf, he barks, an echo of his former self.

We wait for the figure to come into view.

"It's Melody's son," Aunt Sadie says.

Even at ninety-six, she has better eyesight than most.

"What's he doing here?" I recognize the man I watched in the cemetery put fresh wildflowers on the Monroe graves. A man who looks more and more like Johnny. He carries more flowers in a mason jar. But like Rufus, I am not willing to relax just yet. This stranger is a Monroe, after all, and I have learned through experience to never trust a Monroe. In the mountains, a poison and its antidote often grow near each other, like poison ivy and witch hazel. I wonder what the cure is for this particular Monroe.

Aunt Sadie quiets old Rufus, and the stranger addresses her as the elder. He glances at me with a disarming smile. "I heard Mrs. McAllister is ailing and wanted to pay my respects," he says. After climbing the hill at a faster pace than most, he is hardly winded.

Sadie nods, motioning for me to take the flowers he holds, which are equally disarming. The two of us meet in the middle of the porch steps.

"Wildflower McAllister," I say, by way of introduction.

"Matt Monroe."

Johnny peers at me from behind Matt Monroe's brown eyes. I flash on Johnny tossing me to the ground. A splinter of a memory. Was it only this morning that I dreamed of Johnny's blood on the gold medallion? Matt Monroe is Johnny's blood relative. Yet Lily told me years ago that Melody told her she couldn't have children, and that Lily was her only remaining relative. If so, then how does Melody have a son?

However, the look of a Monroe is unmistakable, and like Lily, Matt Monroe has had better luck with the gene pool.

"So, you're Wildflower McAllister," he says, as though he's

heard stories. But what kind of stories has he heard? My forced exile from Katy's Ridge? He couldn't possibly know about what happened with Johnny, the uncle he never met, could he? I suddenly wonder how long it takes for stories to wither on the Katy's Ridge grapevine.

"How is she doing?" he asks Sadie, motioning toward the house.

"Won't be long now," Sadie says.

He lowers his head and looks at his shoes as though an actor on a stage conveying remorse. My resentment flares. Who is he to ask after Mama? And since when does a Monroe show up at our door without a motive? The Monroes have always been takers. Takers of anything or anyone they want. Johnny took me that day, and I barely survived.

"I'll put these in Nell's room," Aunt Sadie says, taking the flowers and thanking Matt Monroe for his thoughtfulness. This seems overly generous to me. She excuses herself to go in to check on Mama, leaving Daisy and me to deal with Matt Monroe.

Seconds later, Daisy excuses herself and goes inside, too.

"Something I said?" Matt Monroe offers a brief smile.

The day has been too long for me to return the smile.

"Mind if I sit for a minute?" he asks.

Southern manners win out over my skepticism, and I motion for him to sit on the porch. For several seconds, we sit in awkward silence.

"Did you know my mother?" Matt asks, studying the knuckles on his hands.

"I did."

He waits for me to say more. I don't.

"She died here in Katy's Ridge." His eyes find mine.

My resistance collides with my resentment. More silence is the result. There are many things I won't tell Matt Monroe. For instance, Melody's body was found in almost the exact spot as

her brother, Johnny's. It was ruled an accident by the sheriff in Rocky Bluff, just like Johnny's death, an odd coincidence at best. Melody had been staggering drunk the night she died, and the last time I saw her, she was following the whispers she heard in the woods. The real cause of death might just as well be those whispers.

Our family in the old country believed in fairies and tree spirits, but they would never hurt anyone like those whispers hurt Melody when she followed them that night.

"We didn't know about you," I say to Matt Monroe. "Melody never mentioned having a son. She seemed more interested in finding Lily than anything."

"Lily?"

"My daughter." He doesn't ask the next logical question, which is why his mother might look for my daughter. But maybe he already knows the answer.

"I grew up in Louisville with my great-aunt," he says instead. "I barely knew my mother. Then when I was eleven, we got a telegram that said she had died. It said she'd fallen off a mountain or something."

"I saw her that night," I say.

"I know," he says.

I aim my distrust in his direction.

"After I moved here, I went in search of the sheriff's report, and your name was listed as the last person to see her. That's usually the prime suspect in a murder investigation, you know." I hesitate, imagining Johnny laughing from the grave.

"You think I murdered your mother?"

He grins. "Of course not." His eyes dart toward his shoes again. "It was clearly an accident."

"Did you know your mother had a drinking problem?" I ask.

"Everybody knew my mother had a drinking problem," he says.

"I was surprised she could still walk around that night," I say. "I

tried to get her to turn around, but she was determined to go down that trail."

It is dusk now, and Matt Monroe shows no signs of leaving. I wish Aunt Sadie or Daisy would return.

"What brought you here?" I ask, deciding a change of subject might help.

"I inherited a hundred acres here."

"The Monroes had a hundred acres?" I think of how poor they were and that horrible little cabin and wonder why they didn't sell off some of that land and live decently.

"By the time I got here, the cabin had collapsed," he says, "but the land it was sitting on was quite beautiful."

"You don't look old enough to be retired," I say.

"Inheritance from my father. He owned property in downtown Louisville. I would have thought you already knew this. Gossip is like kudzu around here."

"Gives people something to do," I say.

He grins again.

Mama keeps a shotgun by the back door for the foxes that might threaten her henhouse. Is there another fox in our midst? Then I remember Mama pointing that shotgun at Melody. She never trusted the Monroes, either.

"Do you live here in Katy's Ridge?" he asks me.

"Not anymore," I say, feeling like we are playing a game where we ask each other questions we already know the answers to. "I live in Nashville now."

"That's quite different, I imagine."

I laugh a short laugh. "For sure."

"Do you ever miss this place?"

I pause, wondering how much truth to share with a possible fox.

"I do," I say.

"What do you miss?"

I hesitate again, questioning whether to answer him. "I miss nights like this," I begin.

"Nights where the only noise is the sound of the mountains vibrating with life. Coyotes. Owls. Foxes out and about." I narrow my eyes before offering a grin. I can be disarming, too.

Aunt Sadie steps up to the screen door and startles me, but seeing her also brings relief. "Time for you to come," she says.

The game Matt Monroe and I are playing ends in a tie.

He offers his condolences and walks back down the hill.

Aunt Sadie waits on me at the door. "I've called Meg and Amy. You ready?" she asks.

Emotion catches in my throat, a lump impossible to swallow. "Is anybody ever ready?"

"No," Sadie says, lowering her eyes, and we walk into Mama's room to say our final goodbyes.

CHAPTER FOURTEEN

Daisy

Gran sits by her mother's bedside. Gran's sisters are here, too, along with Daniel. Periodically different neighbors and people from the church walk up the hill and squeeze into the room and then leave again. It feels like a small, crowded airport where Granny McAllister's flight has been called, and the plane is ready for takeoff. Destination unknown.

I stand by the window, waiting like everyone else. After a few moments, the radio frequencies of the past align, and I hear two voices. The voices are a much younger Granny McAllister and her beloved Joseph. It must be a time early in their marriage. The conversation fades in and out, then suddenly becomes clear as though happening now.

You need to promise me something, Joseph says, sounding serious.

What do you mean? She sounds young, almost playful.

Exactly what I said, Nell.

Why do you do this, Joseph? Why do you always make a big deal out of everything?

Because it is a big deal. I need you to tell me that you understand what I'm about to say to you.

The voices pause, and I imagine a young Granny McAllister rolling her eyes.

Okay, out with it, she says, but she isn't angry.

If anything ever happens to me—

She stops him, telling him not to be silly. But her voice finally grows serious, too. She is the one asking for promises now. Promises that nothing will ever happen to him.

You must hear what I am about to say. I imagine Joseph making her sit as they look into each other's eyes.

In front of the boulder in the back, I buried a metal box.

Why would you bury something in the backyard?

Because I want to keep it safe. There are people in Katy's Ridge that I don't trust.

You're scaring me, Joseph.

I'm not trying to scare you, he says. *I'm trying to tell you something important.*

She grows silent.

The metal box I buried contains everything my daddy left us. If anything ever happens to me—

Nothing is ever going to happen to you, Joseph McAllister. I won't allow it!

The voices fade.

But I wonder if Granny McAllister kept that promise. I overheard my mom tell my father once that she grew up poor. If Granny McAllister had dug up the metal box, wouldn't that have changed things?

Later that night I am told to go to bed, but I can't sleep thinking of buried treasure by the big boulder in the backyard, as well as Granny McAllister dying in the next room.

CHAPTER FIFTEEN

Wildflower

The house is quiet without Mama in it. It has been three days since she died. During a passing thunderstorm in the middle of the night, the house moaned with the wind as though grieving her loss, too. For decades she cleaned and dusted every inch of this place, and I imagine she knew where every cobweb was known to hide. This old house was used to her touch, both gentle and harsh.

In the waiting time before the funeral, Daisy has been reading Daddy's books: Shakespeare sonnets, the Bible, Mark Twain, and others. She is also working on a project in the back of the house requiring a shovel. I have no idea what she is up to, but I hope she buries the melancholy that has descended on her in the last few months.

After Mama died, I was able to reach Lily by telephone to tell her the news. When she mentioned postponing her concert dates, I told her Mama wouldn't mind her not coming home for her

funeral on account of Mama being so proud. She wouldn't want Lily to miss a moment of her success.

I find Aunt Sadie sitting on the porch, staring out into the forest and seeming to remember every conversation she and Mama had while sitting in this same spot. They were sisters-in-law and best friends for all these many years. I can't imagine her loss. Nor, I guess, can she imagine mine.

Gravel crunches in the driveway, and Jo blows the horn of her Buick to tell us it is time to go to the church. Aunt Sadie sits in front with Jo, while Daisy sits with Nellie in the back seat. Daniel and I ride over in my pickup. It is altogether strange to be going to church without Mama with us. Who will complain about how hot the church is? Who will straighten our clothes, even though we are past middle age? Who will caution us about the dangers in the world? Mama was Mama. She was not perfect. Not even close. But her presence will be missed.

Walking from the parking lot, I approach the small, white Baptist church that I attended throughout my childhood. The doors are wide open on this warm summer day. Because of the renovations, the church smells of old and new lumber. People wait out front before going inside, where it is guaranteed to be at least ten degrees hotter.

People turn, their eyes following me as I approach the church. Then their eyes turn to someone standing near the door. When I see Bee, tears come, but I refuse to let them fall and water the grapevine any more than I already have.

"I didn't know you were coming." I lower my voice, as well as my eyes, not wanting to tempt the tears.

"I didn't want to," she confesses, "but how could I not? It's your mother, Lou."

I want to squeeze her hand but don't. She wouldn't want me to. She wouldn't want me to do anything to create a wave in this tiny pond. Instead I thank her for coming.

Within seconds, Daisy arrives with Aunt Sadie, Jo, and Daniel. When Daisy sees Bee, she offers a rare smile and hugs her.

"I didn't know you were coming," Daisy says.

"I didn't think I was until the last minute." Bee looks nervous, the way I feel.

"Daggers from every direction," Daniel says, looking around. "I'd like to withdraw my membership from the human race, please." I have always appreciated Daniel's loyalty.

"Shall we do this?" I ask.

We turn and walk inside. Do all these people want to pay their respects, or are they here for the sideshow? While I love Katy's Ridge, and my family is here, I would prefer not to deal with the small-mindedness of a few people. One of them, my sister Amy, our harshest critic, refuses to look at Bee. At least Meg greeted her with a nod.

Bee takes a seat in the back row. I want to insist she join us, but then think better of it. We walk up front where the family is to sit. The packed church inhales to receive us. I think of other funerals I've attended here: Ruby Monroe. Daddy. Nathan. Melody Monroe. Now Mama.

I study the people around me—country people in their Sunday clothes. They speak in whispers, as though not wanting to disturb the person in the open casket. The lump in my throat returns.

Please, God, let my tears hold off until after the service.

A few people, bearing no daggers, shake my hand and offer condolences.

After everyone has taken their seats, Daisy leans in to my shoulder. "You look beautiful," she whispers as though a dollop of sweetness might help the sourness in life.

I tell her she does, too, which is true. Amy made her a dress for the occasion in two days, and it is lovely. While Amy's views can be ugly, she sure makes pretty clothes.

Soft organ music begins to play. An older preacher with gray

Elvis sideburns steps up in front of Mama. Mama wrote about Preacher Bill in her letters. He is still the "new" preacher even though he has been here a decade. Thin and wrinkled, Preacher Bill looks like he would be more at home on a tractor than in a pulpit. The congregation quiets, and I pull a tissue from the pocket of my dress to have handy in case of what Mama always called my waterworks. The preacher welcomes everyone and then announces the first hymn, which has me fumbling for a hymnal that Daisy and I share. "Shall We Gather at the River" was always one of Mama's favorite hymns. We can actually see the Tennessee River from here, and after a hard rain, we can even smell it.

Aunt Sadie and I exchange a look while singing about God's celestial shore. It occurs to me that we are singing at Mama's funeral. Can a person become an orphan at fifty-four years of age? Yet, in a way, I felt orphaned after Daddy died, Mama's grief seemingly separating us forever.

We sing another verse, and another, always coming back to the refrain and to the river. The beautiful, the beautiful river. A picture of how life continues to flow along even after the people we love pass away.

With Lily McAllister as her mother, people often ask if Daisy can sing, too. If she has any talents, they are not visible. She pretends to sing, emitting no sound. I hope Daisy doesn't have regrets someday like I do. Regrets that her relationship with Lily wasn't more. Something deeper. Richer. Closer. The hymn ends.

Outside, a car skids to a stop on the gravel. Heads turn toward the high windows that face the parking lot. Heels click on the concrete sidewalk. Someone is late. Even Preacher Bill pauses to see who it is since all heads have now turned toward the back of the room. A woman steps into view, followed by a collective gasp.

"Sorry, everyone."

Lily stands in the back of the small church. She seems to sparkle against the gray backdrop of the foyer, grandly different

from anyone else attending. *Worldly* is the word that comes to me. Her dangling silver earrings match the silver bangles around her wrists. She wears a long, flowing black skirt, black heels, and a gray blouse. Her long brown hair is touched with blond tints. She is not one of us, but at the same time, she is.

Everyone on the family bench scoots down to allow room for the sparkling woman walking down the aisle. I stand. Lily gives me a kiss on the cheek and then steps past me. She does the same with Daisy and then sits between us, putting her sizeable glittery purse under the pew.

All this time Preacher Bill has waited, his thin lips revealing a slight smile despite the gravitas of Mama's funeral. It is not every day that an international singing sensation attends the small Katy's Ridge Baptist Church. The full church flutters like a flock of birds about to take off from an open field. It takes several minutes for the deceased to regain the full attention of the crowd.

Lily, Daisy, and I hold hands. A united force. Three generations of McAllister women, saying goodbye to a fourth. I imagine the entire maternal line. Unbroken. All the generations holding hands, today back to ancient times.

Preacher Bill reads a Bible verse from the book of Matthew that he says Mama picked out for the occasion: "Consider the lilies of the field, how they grow: they neither toil nor spin; and yet I say to you that even Solomon in all his glory was not arrayed like one of these."

This was actually Daddy's favorite verse. He told me once that it was one of the reasons he nicknamed me Wildflower. That same verse is why I named my daughter Lily. Hearing it again causes an ache in my chest, as though Mama has sent me a love letter from the grave.

Tears rush down my cheek, and I quickly wipe them away. Meanwhile, Mama is in the wooden box in front of the altar. This reality keeps hitting me like the clang of a church bell. Preacher

Bill invites people up to the pulpit to tell stories about Mama. They come up one by one, occasionally glancing down at Mama in repose in her simple white coffin, and often over at Lily, the McAllisters' shining star. I can't imagine what it is like to carry the weight of all that admiration. I wonder if this is why she always looks so tired.

The stories tell of how generous Mama was with whatever she had, and what a good cook she was. Whenever the church had potlucks, her food always ran out first, someone says, and there was often a line. People laugh. Several mention her banana pudding. I also hear about how stubborn she could be as if it was an endearing trait. Several older folks say how hard it was on her after her husband died, and how she raised four daughters on her own.

All four of those daughters and their families sit in the first two pews on the right side of the church, facing Mama. After a steady stream of people shares memories, the preacher asks the family to say a few words.

Taking a deep breath, I stand. It was decided earlier that I would speak for the family, and I question now why I agreed to do this. I gently touch Mama's casket on the way to the lectern. I glance inside the box at the woman made-up at the funeral home. She looks nothing like herself. Mama never wore lipstick or eyeshadow. Looking out at the full church, tears threaten again. A river of tears as we gather to say goodbye to Mama.

My hands tremble, and I fold them in front of me. "Mama would love that you all are here," I begin. "She'd be embarrassed by the attention, that's for sure. I know I would—"

Tension fills the room like a hive of bees starting to stir. Tension buzzing with judgment. Some of those gathered give me an eyeful of evil. Defiance straightens my backbone. I search for friendly faces.

"Mama would be very grateful for the honor you pay her by being here." I challenge myself to stay strong.

"I like to think Mama is with Daddy now," I begin again. "A few days ago, when I first arrived back in Katy's Ridge, Mama saw me and thought I was Daddy coming to take her home. I don't think I've ever seen her so happy."

Emotion cracks open my words, and my voice shakes. I apologize to the friendly faces. The tissue I hold is in a tight white ball and would be useless if any tears began to fall. Through the open doors of the church, I glimpse Daddy's willow tree in the distance. I imagine Mama and Daddy standing together under that tree, reunited. I let out a soft gasp, pulling in tears at the same time.

"Family meant everything to Mama," I begin again. "She was very proud of her children, grandchildren, and great-grandchildren, as well as her son-in-law." I glance at Daniel.

I pause, wondering what else I should say. From the back row, Bee beams me courage.

"The McAllister clan is grieving today," I say. Then I thank Aunt Sadie for being so kind to Mama for all these years and for taking care of her at the end. Sadie lowers her head, and her body quakes with silent tears. Daisy, sitting closest, puts an arm around her, and then Lily puts an arm around Daisy.

Finally I send Lily a questioning look, inviting her to sing. She nods her okay and then stands and walks to the front, where we hug. She whispers, "Good job," before I return to the pew and sit next to Daisy.

While I have seen Lily sing hundreds of times, somehow this time feels different. We are saying goodbye to the matriarch of the McAllister clan. A woman some of us feared. A woman all of us respected.

Lily steps out from behind the lectern and closer to the crowd. She clears her throat and then closes her eyes, as though flipping

through a songbook in her mind. Then the tiredness and jetlag Lily wore into the church appear to fade away. Without opening her eyes, she lifts her head and begins to sing a song I've heard before. A song that typically is sung fast, but she is singing it slow. The slowness of the fast tune makes the words seem more meaningful. Lily's rich voice fills the church, which is hear-a-pin-drop silent. Goosebumps climb my arms, and my resistant tears begin to flow.

"Some bright morning when this life is over, I'll fly away," Lily sings. "To that home on God's celestial shore, I'll fly away." When she begins the chorus, her voice reaches for the rafters, and the congregation has more tear-filled eyes than dry ones. I hope Mama can hear Lily's song. It would mean so much to her.

"I'll fly away, oh glory, I'll fly away, in the morning. When I die, Hallelujah by and by, I'll fly away."

Boxes of tissues pass down the pews like offering plates. By the time Lily finishes, I am ready to fly away, too.

CHAPTER SIXTEEN

Daisy

As Gran is speaking in the church, I notice how beautiful she is. Not in a glamorous way like my mom or my great-aunt Jo, but in a down-to-earth way. Her black dress is plain on her thin frame, and she wears a sprig of wildflowers in her long hair. I turn to look at Bee in the back row. She winks at me and puts a tissue to her eyes.

Scanning the crowd, I narrow my eyes at the people who refuse to look at Gran.

Some people are just stupid, I decide. If they really knew Gran, they wouldn't act this way.

At the other end of the long bench sits Nellie, who gives me a grieved smile. We have spent more time together in the last few days, whenever I am not in the backyard digging. I never even knew I had a second cousin. Her father is my great-uncle. He told me I could call him Daniel. He and Gran are like best friends. He uses a cane because of an injury he got in World War II. I also had a great-uncle named Nathan, who died in the same war. His wife is my great-aunt,

Amy. It isn't easy to keep all the sisters and husbands and kids straight. But after a while, it starts to make sense and fit together.

My great-aunt Amy made the dress I'm wearing. I've never actually known anyone who made a dress from scratch. She looked at a teen magazine and found one to recreate. It has layers to it that make the top look flowy. I borrowed a pair of Nellie's church shoes to wear with it since we wear the same size.

It seems incredible that all these relatives resulted from two people getting married and having children. For the first time in my life I feel like I am part of something bigger. Something I never even knew existed. A week ago, I had no idea that two hours east of Nashville, I had a huge extended family.

After my mom starts to sing, everything changes. The sneers and judgments fade into the background. This happens a lot with her singing, especially her slow songs, and I like how she's singing this one unhurried. To have a famous mom isn't always easy. The hardest part is sharing her with her fans. Sometimes I would just like to have her to myself.

Tissues pass down the row. When Mom finishes singing, the room is silent, as if everyone is holding their breath. This is followed by a giant exhale. Then Mom's high heels click on the wooden floors as she comes back to the bench. Gran pats Mom's arm and thanks her.

The old minister talks more about how Granny McAllister is in a better place. When Mom holds my hand, I realize how much I have missed her. This year has been her busiest touring year yet. She looks tired, and not just from jetlag.

With the service finally over, people file out of the church. Several people come to tell my mom how much they liked her song and how much Granny McAllister would have liked it, too. Gran takes my hand, and we leave Mom with the crowd outside the church and find a shady spot under a tree near the parking lot.

In the distance, Mom signs the front of several funeral service programs as people ask for her autograph.

"What happens next?" I ask Gran.

"Most of these people will leave," she begins. "Then Mama's casket will be driven to the back of the cemetery and carried to where she will be buried. After that, there's another little ceremony at the gravesite, mostly family."

I decide that funerals are exhausting.

"You okay? I know this was your first." Gran turns toward the graveyard as though remembering her first, too.

I nod.

"It's harder because she was a close relative of yours," Gran says.

Close? I want to say. I feel like I just met her.

Mom breaks away from the crowd and finds us under the tree. "Sorry about that," she says, giving me a hug. "How are you holding up, Mama?" she asks Gran.

"I've been better," Gran says.

"How was the song?" Mom asks.

"Gorgeous," Gran says. "You outdid yourself, honey, and that's saying something."

Mom smiles. Every now and again, I realize how close they are, as well as how much I've missed her.

"How long can you stay?" Gran asks her as if she has missed her, too.

"I'm not sure, Mama. I'll make a phone call when we get back to the house."

Gran tosses me a glance. Neither of us has much hope that Mom will stick around. I'm surprised she even came to the funeral. Gran excuses herself to check on how things are going with the next phase of the funeral, as if realizing I might need time alone with Mom.

"Sorry your summer vacation got upended," Mom says to me. "I imagine Katy's Ridge is the last place you'd like to be."

"I don't mind it," I say. "It's simpler here."

She looks at me as though I've surprised her. "Has your gran told you how long you'll stay?"

"Not yet," I say.

"Well, hopefully it won't be much longer." She looks around like she has already been here long enough, and it has only been an hour.

"Were you close to Granny McAllister?" I ask.

Mom looks at me all curious. "Of course I was. She was my grandmother."

I nod, wondering why she didn't bring me here more often if she was so close to her grandmother.

"People grieve in different ways," she says, looking toward the cemetery. Then she sighs, seeming to realize how tired she is. "Granny was very good to me," she begins again, her voice softer. "She taught me how to cook and watched out for me. And after we moved to Nashville, she sent me letters every week asking me how I was, how school was going, and later how my singing career was going. I now regret that I didn't write her back more often."

My feet shuffle like they are ready to go. I hate to see my mom sad.

"How are you, sweetheart?" she asks, putting an arm around me.

I want to duck away, but at the same time, I enjoy her touch. Sometimes I do this when she calls me when she is away, too. I pretend I am totally uninterested in what she has to say, while at the same time, I am hungry to hear her voice.

I pause to answer her question. I don't know how I am. I am here. That's about all I know. Then I shrug.

"You're such an enigma," she says.

My feet go quiet.

"A what?"

"A great mystery."

She smiles, and I catch myself smiling back. I guess I like thinking of myself as a mystery.

Looking at my hands, I notice dirt under a couple of my fingernails. Everyone has been so distracted by Granny McAllister's death, nobody has seen me digging for buried treasure in the backyard. I know there is probably no real treasure there, but the mystery of what might be hidden has given me something to do.

"Do you think there's a heaven?" I ask, surprising myself with the question.

Mom looks surprised, too.

"I'd like to think so," she says.

"Do you think Gran believes in heaven?"

"You need to ask her, Daisy, but I imagine so."

She smiles at me as though I have become even more mysterious.

"Do you have to go back?" I ask, already knowing the answer.

She hugs me and sighs. "I wish I could stay, but I have people counting on me," she says, as though even she knows how lame this answer is, when I count on her, too.

Gran returns and says that everyone will be walking to the gravesite now. Mom takes my hand, and we enter the old cemetery that contains a whole slew of the family I never knew I had. All of a sudden, this feels like a buried treasure of a different kind.

CHAPTER SEVENTEEN

Wildflower

Mourners walk up the hill to the gravesite. It is a much smaller group than there was inside. Bee is talking to someone in the church. I wonder if she is making herself scarce on purpose. Aunt Sadie rides up with Mama's casket in a truck that belongs to Silas, an old friend of Daddy's. He and Daddy were the same age, and I try to imagine what Daddy would look like if he hadn't died forty years ago in a sawmill accident. He'd be an old man now. Seventy-eight years of age. My thoughts progress, and I wonder how life would be different if Daddy hadn't gone to work that day, or if the saw blade hadn't cut so deep. Would Lily even exist? Or Daisy? I forget who told me life could turn on a dime. Probably Aunt Sadie. In some ways, I feel like that dime hasn't stopped spinning for forty years.

Lily and Daisy walk behind me, holding hands. When I glance at Daisy, hints of her teenage glumness remain, but not nearly as much as when she rode in my pickup to Katy's Ridge three days

ago. I still want to talk to Lily. Surely she has noticed the change, too.

The solemn procession advances up the hill while Lily and Daisy join me. Bee is somewhere behind us. I hate that she doesn't want to walk with us. It was ridiculous not to hug her when I saw her at the church. Everyone hugs at funerals. All of us happy to be among the living. But I knew she wouldn't want us to. She has spent a lifetime trying to not draw attention to herself; that's why speaking at that conference was so hard for her.

At this moment, grief feels like an old friend. A friend I met when Daddy died, and that stuck around for years. Leaving Katy's Ridge was a different kind of grief. It wasn't the loss of a person, but the loss of a place that was my home. I hate to admit how tender the scar still is. I glance back to find Bee. I am braver than her. If left up to me, I would have held her hand through the entire service. To hell with small-minded people. But I wasn't about to disrespect her wishes. I will invite her to come to Mama's house after the service and spend some time with Lily and Daisy and me, but I don't know if she will even do that.

We catch up with Daniel, cane in hand, walking up the hill. Until a few years ago, he had shrapnel in his leg from the war and chewed aspirin like they were peppermints. But then he had an operation at the Veterans Affairs hospital in Nashville and now only has a faint limp with the help of his cane.

June Sector waits at the top of the hill. I didn't see her in the church. As with Mama and me, June and I have not missed a month of exchanging letters. She checked in on Mama for me and looks after Aunt Sadie, too. Although neither of them would admit to needing to be looked after.

June holds a handful of lilies from her yard to put on Mama's grave. If anyone knows firsthand what it is like to be an outsider in Katy's Ridge, it is June and her husband, Horatio. Even in this day and age, marriage between a white woman and a Cherokee man

invites all sorts of disapproval. June helped me survive as a young mother, and I relied on her friendship. Lily and I take turns hugging her. Before her attention turns to me, her gaze lingers on Daisy as if seeing something unexpected.

"I just couldn't deal with the crowd," she says to me, offering an apology.

I tell her that I understand.

As we approach the gravesite, I notice the hole dug into the earth under the willow tree, right next to Daddy. I swallow a sob. My sister Jo and I exchange a look, as though remembering when she came to retrieve me after Daddy died. Losing him seemed unbearable that first year and evolved into something I could survive. I turn and look at the river. A scene that has changed very little except for trees that have grown taller.

In the distance, Matt Monroe stands close to his family's graves. A surge of resentment surprises me, as though he is the latest Monroe to spit on Daddy's grave. I don't want a Monroe anywhere near my parents' graves. If an apple doesn't fall far from the tree, I suspect Matt Monroe may very well be worm-infested.

Preacher Bill begins to speak again, words I don't even hear. Grief blurs the rest of the ceremony. While losing Mama is something I always knew would happen, I still can't believe she is gone. June lays the lilies on top of Mama's grave, and Bee adds a bouquet of wildflowers, something I wish I'd thought to do as well. Lily takes one of my hands, and Daisy the other. In the distance, I hear the faint sounds of Daddy's banjo riding in on the summer breeze. He plays the same soulful tune Lily sang in the church. *When I die, Hallelujah by and by, I'll fly away.*

CHAPTER EIGHTEEN

Daisy

We stand beside Bee's car in the church parking lot saying our goodbyes. Everyone has left except us. Aunt Sadie went back with Daniel and Jo, and Mom left earlier in her rental car to go back to Granny McAllister's and get a little rest.

"Can you come by the house?" Gran asks Bee.

"I'd better get back," she says. "I'm worn out from all those looks."

Gran and Bee have not touched once, and I wonder if it is hard for them to act like they don't care for each other. Bee puts a soft hand on my cheek. "Good seeing you, sweetheart."

"Good seeing you, too." We embrace.

"How about I take you out to dinner when you get back to Nashville?" she asks. "It can be a late birthday celebration."

I tell her I'd like that, and then she turns to Gran.

"Sorry about your mama, Lou." Her words are soft.

"I hope you know how much she loved you," Gran says to her.

The edges of Bee's eyes turn red, and she nods.

"Call me later?" Bee says to her.

Gran nods.

Before leaving, Bee whispers in my ear, "Take care of your Gran, okay?"

I tell her I will, though I have no idea what that might look like. Gran doesn't seem to need taking care of, but maybe she needs people more than she lets on.

Bee gets into her car and waves before driving away. Gran's shoulders drop as if a sad day just got more miserable.

"Shall we go home?" she asks me.

For a moment I wonder if she is talking about Nashville, but I have never known Gran to call Nashville home.

We are silent on the short ride, and I even forget to pay attention to her shifting gears. For days now, there have been no driving lessons. When Gran enters the driveway, Mom's rental car sits in the other parking space. We find Mom napping on the couch, and Aunt Sadie having a cup of tea in the kitchen. Gran and Sadie talk about the service while my eye wanders to the boulder outside that is taller than the chicken coop. Having never dug a hole with a shovel before, I had no idea how hard it was. My thoughts drift to things dead and buried.

Mom comes into the kitchen, and before I have time to talk myself out of it, I hug her.

"What's gotten into you?" she says, giving me a squeeze.

My face warms, and I wonder the same.

"Sadie says I can stay over at her house tonight," Mom says to me. "You want to go over and help me air the place out? She says it's been sitting empty for months."

"You're not going straight back?" I ask.

"Not planning to," she says, "but I've got to make some calls." She asks Sadie if the phone line is still hooked up, and Sadie says it is.

I try to imagine my mom growing up in this kitchen and can't.

She seems too big to be contained within these walls. While Mom and Gran talk, I put my things in my backpack. Within minutes, we get in Mom's rental car and drive over to Sadie's farm. I am learning my way around Katy's Ridge now, and we drive out past the elementary school and beyond to a road that leads to a lake.

Sadie's place is called a farm, but it doesn't look like one. There are no animals anymore, but it does have a barn and a big white farmhouse. A considerable porch is attached, and there is a big welcoming front door. Mom looks at the place like she remembers a lifetime of visits and has missed this place.

"Can you believe Sadie never locks her door out here?" she says, not waiting for an answer.

She steps inside and starts opening doors and windows and inviting in the fresh air. I never realized before that air could have different smells. Fresh air smells like trees and light and is totally different from the air in Nashville.

"I've always loved this house," Mom says. She checks the cabinets to see what food might be there. I like that she seems to be settling in and catch myself daydreaming about what it might be like to have her around for a while.

Mom tosses me a rag and asks me to dust the countertops, and then she finds a box of Lipton tea bags to make iced tea. When I finish dusting, I fill two glasses with ice from the freezer. With drinks in hand, we go outside on the porch. The day is heating up, as Gran likes to say, but there is a promise of a breeze once the sun goes behind the mountain in an hour or so. I am getting to know the rhythms here, too, the rhythms of the simple mountain days.

As I sit in the swing, Mom lounges in a chair nearby. Porch swings are as plentiful as honeysuckle here in the mountains. This swing has a lonesome melody all its own.

Mom asks me how I'm doing, and I say I'm fine. She lets it go at that.

"Do you think the song at the funeral went over okay?" she asks.

I'm always surprised when she asks questions like this. It's like she's just starting out instead of someone who has sung all over the world. "It was smart to sing it slow," I say.

She smiles. "Emmylou does that sometimes, to surprise folks. I think it's very effective."

"It was," I say, thinking about the time I met Emmylou Harris, who was not only beautiful but incredibly nice.

"How have you been getting along with Mama?" she asks. "This is the most time you've spent with her when she wasn't working, right?"

"I like her," I say.

She laughs. "Well, you should. She's your gran."

"She said I could call her Wildflower if I ever get tired of calling her Gran," I say.

"Did she?" She yawns.

"Were you two close when you were my age?"

She looks at me as though I've asked something peculiar.

"We were very close," she says. "I guess that was part of the problem."

I ask her what she means.

She cocks her head, as though the motion helps her think. "Well, I was just a different person than Mama," she begins. "I needed an adventure. She would have been fine living in these mountains her whole life, but I was suffocating here." She looks around as if the wide-open space of Sadie's valley is not nearly wide enough.

"Why do you never talk about your father?" I ask.

Her face registers surprise. "I never knew him," she says. "Did Mama bring him up?"

"No," I say. "It's just that—"

I pause, aware that this is already more than Mom and I usually

talk. By now, she is often busy with something. Something that involves work, not me. But it seems Katy's Ridge has slowed her down, too. If she's not careful, she may start to relax.

"It doesn't matter," I say.

Mom nods, and then takes a big breath as though relieved I have dropped the subject. We sit in silence for several seconds while the porch swing moans a lonely tune. How is it that I can miss my mom even when we're sitting across from each other?

"What have you been doing while you're here?" she asks.

"Different things," I say.

"Yeah?" She yawns again.

"Gran says she's going to teach me how to mosey while I'm here." I don't mention she has also promised to teach me how to drive.

Mom smiles. "You'll probably be good at moseying," she says. "It's in your blood, after all."

I wonder if it is in my mom's blood, too, but maybe she's had a transfusion.

"I still can't believe Granny is gone," she says, more to herself than to me.

"When she was dying, she told me the story of how she met Joseph," I say.

"She did? I thought she was out of it there at the end."

"She was that, too," I say. "But one time she woke up when it was only me in the room, and she told me this long story about how they met."

"I don't think I've heard that story," she says.

"Gran says that family stories are really important," I say.

"Does she?" She raises an eyebrow.

I stop the porch swing, and the world gets quiet. "Can you tell me about your father?" I ask, my curiosity returning.

Her shoulders drop, as if she has already climbed one mountain

today and I am asking her to climb another. "Is this something you need to know right this second?"

I shrug and then challenge myself to use words. "Since I've been here I've realized that I have all this family I never knew I had."

She sighs and finishes her iced tea. "Fair enough. What do you want to know?"

"Now that I know a little about Joseph, my great-grandfather on the McAllister side, I'd like to know about my great-grandfather on the other side. Like what was his name?"

"His name was Arthur Monroe, and your grandfather was Johnny Monroe," she says. "Trust me. He wasn't a nice guy."

"What do you mean?" I say, pushing off the porch swing with my toes.

Her eyes narrow, and she looks over at me like she is creating a list of reasons why this is a bad idea. How bad a guy was my grandfather? Did he murder people? Rob banks?

I am aware that at any moment, my mom might wander into the kitchen to find the coffeepot. Instead she finally says the words she's been debating:

"Johnny Monroe forced himself on Mama, and I was the result."

I gasp and let this news settle in. "Did he go to jail for it?"

"No. He died a week later from a fall down a mountain."

I gasp a second time.

"Why didn't you tell me?" I ask.

"It's not something I usually tell people," she says. "Your father doesn't even know."

It occurs to me that I now know what the word dumbfounded means.

"It took me years to get the truth out of Mama," she begins again. "Now I wish I'd left it alone."

The porch swing sings its sad song. A song that somehow feels appropriate given what I've just heard.

"When I was your age, Johnny's sister came to visit, and I talked

to her a few times," she begins. "Her name was Melody. She told me that my father, Johnny, wasn't all bad. Nobody is, I guess."

She pauses and takes a long sip of air while I contemplate another family member I never knew I had.

"You said *was*. What happened to her?"

"Well, she fell down the same mountain. Died in almost the very spot as her brother. It was eerie. Before that, she had heard these whispers coming from the bottom of that ravine, and it was almost like her brother—my daddy—was calling her to join him."

I gasp for the third time in my life, and she nods as if she understands.

"Welcome to Katy's Ridge," she says, as if this is what I get for being curious about the mysterious ways of mountain people.

"A guy came to the house before the funeral and introduced himself as a Monroe. Gran turned as white as a sheet," I say.

"A Monroe came to the house?" she says, sounding slightly alarmed. "Do you remember his name?"

"No, but I think he said he was Melody's son."

Mom sits straighter. "Melody's son?" Her brow wrinkles the way it does when she's thinking. "Was he just visiting?"

"No, I think he lives here."

"Your gran must be having conniptions," she says.

I wonder what conniptions are.

"Granny McAllister died right after that," I say, "and Gran hasn't brought it up again."

We sit in silence, as though collecting these revelations in a folder marked, FAMILY SECRETS. I think of my own secret that I don't want her to ever find out about.

The telephone rings in the kitchen.

"I'd better get that," she says. "I gave my agent this number."

Seconds later, I hear her talking to someone but can't tell what she's saying. I realize how fast my heart is beating at the thought of my mom leaving again so soon. When it comes to her career, she

can't seem to say no to anything. I take a deep breath to calm it while the porch swing sings along.

After Mom gets off the phone, she comes back outside and tells me that she has to give a radio interview over the telephone in an hour. I follow her into the kitchen while she finds the coffeepot and coffee grounds and puts it on.

"Fortification," she says, suddenly looking tired again.

Then she asks if I'm hungry and says she can fix me something if I want. I tell her I'm fine. In the meantime, the smell of coffee fills the room. Mom pours some in a cup with yellow flowers along the edge. She always drinks her coffee black and strong.

The telephone rings again, and Mom is what she calls *on*. As she talks, she is more animated and smiles nonstop, as if the people on the radio can see her as well as hear her. I listen to her talk about her music and her fans and realize again how different she is from most moms. People think her life is all golden records and glowing fans, but there is a downside, too. She is always working. Always composing, practicing, or talking about her job to radio stations and for magazine articles. I wonder if this is the price of being someone different. I think of one of the songs she wrote, about wearing golden handcuffs. The lyrics talk about how beautiful they are, and how she's looked all over but can't seem to find the key to unlock them. I imagine she is wearing those golden handcuffs now.

CHAPTER NINETEEN

Wildflower

The next morning I drive to Sadie's to pick up Daisy. I am taking her to June's house, something we arranged last night at dinner.

"Mom's got another telephone interview," Daisy says, meeting me at the door. We go to the kitchen, where Lily is on the phone telling someone about her first appearance at the Grand Ole Opry. She winks at me. Bee and I were there that night. We were in charge of keeping four-year-old Daisy occupied. Daisy wore a yellow dress that Amy made, and Bee embroidered a white daisy etched in green on the collar. It is hard to see that little girl now. Though she has always been quiet, her seriousness seems more recent. I leave Lily a note on the kitchen counter telling her that she is welcome to join us later if she wants.

When I open the door to the pickup, I toss my keys to Daisy. She gives an uncharacteristic squeal. I laugh, despite my grief. We buried Mama yesterday. Yet throwing a set of car keys to a thir-

teen-year-old elicits unhindered joy. Further proof that life goes on.

Daisy goes to the driver's side and slides in while I settle into the passenger side. With the keys in the ignition, Daisy places her hands on the steering wheel in the two o'clock and ten o'clock positions. She pauses, as though pulling from her brain the things I taught her the other day.

I glance toward the house. "Maybe don't tell your mom yet about the driving lessons," I say.

Daisy agrees. She puts her foot on the clutch, makes sure it is in park, and then turns on the engine. The pickup sputters its consent.

As taught, Daisy checks the rearview and side mirrors and slowly lets up on the clutch while pressing the gas. We jerk forward. The engine dies.

She huffs. Her face colors.

"Everybody does that when they're learning," I say. "You'll get the hang of it."

Daisy starts the truck again. We jerk forward. It dies again as soon as she puts on the gas. She glances toward the house. I coach her on how to find the spot between letting off on the clutch and pressing on the gas pedal. Letting go and moving on. Letting go and moving on. A task I am not so good at myself. Eventually, she finds it. We cruise along at the breakneck speed of fifteen miles per hour. I encourage her to speed up a bit and put it into third gear. She does. I then encourage her to relax her hands. Color returns to her white knuckles.

"June is Adam's grandmother," I say. "The Adam you met at the church the other day?"

"He'll be there?" She looks at me, and we swerve toward the ditch. I urge her to pay better attention. She brakes, the truck dies, we start over. Being a grandmother requires more patience than I realized.

The pickup strains forward in first gear until it screams for relief.

"Put it in second now," I say, trying to remain calm.

She does as told, and then grinds my old truck into third. I offer a silent apology to the pickup. It strains with Daisy's indecision about whether to go into fourth.

"You're doing great," I say, deciding to err on the side of encouragement. "Since we're going to turn soon, just slow down a little and keep it in third."

The decision makes Daisy's foot, and the pickup, relax. I wish I could do the same. She slows at the turn onto the road and the pickup heaves and jerks until I feel like my teeth might rattle out of my head. I direct Daisy to shift down, but we haven't had that lesson yet, and the pickup dies again on the dirt road. A road we luckily have to ourselves.

"Sorry," she says, lowering her head.

"No big deal," I say. "When Daddy was teaching me to drive his old truck, I jerked us all over these mountain roads. I'm surprised we didn't get whiplash."

"Really?" she says.

"At some point, it will be easy, Daisy. I promise."

I was twelve when Daddy first taught me. Unlike Daisy, whose legs are already longer than mine, I could barely reach the pedals. But I started begging him to teach me when I was eleven. Perhaps I somehow knew that he wasn't going to be around when I was older. Or maybe I just wanted to be like Meg, who Daddy had been teaching that year, too. Daisy starts the truck and begins again. So much of life is about stalling out and beginning again.

"That's June's house at the end of the road," I say. "Just park in front."

Daisy does as I tell her, ending in another abrupt stop. We exchange a look that might have us laughing if Mama wasn't with Daddy under the willow tree. Two other pickups are out front. We

approach the house, a log cabin with a big porch and wooden rockers lining the front. It overlooks a valley with the mountains rising in the distance.

"I've always loved this spot," I say to Daisy. "When I was pregnant, I would come up here, and we'd have picnics. June's husband, Horatio, is Cherokee. He and June are two of the nicest people you'll ever meet. She'll read your fortune if you want her to."

"She tells fortunes?"

"For as long as I've known her," I say. "She predicted your mama being a famous singer even before Lily had sung a note."

June also knew that Crow and Lily wouldn't end up together, just like she knew that her daughter Pearl, Lily's best friend growing up, would end up living someplace far away. She is in California now, living in San Diego. I wonder what she might predict for Daisy.

June steps outside onto the porch, her gray hair in a long braid. She wears an apron over her clothes like Mama always did. Next to her stands Horatio, his long hair in a twist, too. When I step onto the porch, they hug me like I am their long-lost relative finally come home.

"Good to see you, Miss Wildflower," Horatio says. "So sorry about your mama."

Horatio has called me Wildflower since Daddy first gave me the nickname. He must be in his seventies now, but his hair is black as a piece of coal.

"June said it was a lovely service," he says.

I agree. Was that only yesterday? Horatio has never stepped foot inside the church in Katy's Ridge, and I didn't expect him to start with Mama.

"Still got that good luck charm I gave you?" he asks.

Knowing I would probably see him, I brought the star ruby with me, though it usually stays in my jewelry box these days. I take the small pouch from my pocket to show him.

Daisy stands in the yard, watching our reunion. I introduce her.

"Apple cider is in the kitchen," June says, motioning for her to join us. "There's catching up to do." She smiles back at Daisy and adds, "Catching up and getting acquainted."

We follow June into the spotless small house. It hasn't changed since the last time I was here. Small wood carvings grace the mantel above the chimney: birds, foxes, and little black bears—a mama and two cubs. Colorful blankets cover the furniture in the living room, and the scent of cinnamon and apples makes the place smell heavenly. I think of Lily and wonder if she is finally off the telephone. I hope she joins us.

When we walk into the kitchen, Adam is there, as well as Crow, who, unlike his father, has a few streaks of gray in his black hair. He must be forty now. I introduce him to Daisy.

"I used to be in love with your mama," Crow says to her.

June gives her son a playful slap. "Since when are you so forward," she says to him.

"You remember Adam," I say to Daisy.

She lowers her eyes, giving away what I deem a seedling crush.

"Crow and Adam came by for lunch," June says. "They're on a break from working at the church."

She offers to fix us lunch, too, but I tell her that we're fine.

Crow stands and takes his dishes to the sink. Adam follows his father's lead, but not before aiming a dimpled smile in Daisy's direction.

"Well, we need to get back to work," Crow says. "Nice to meet you," he says to Daisy.

I imagine what it would have been like for Daisy to have had Crow as a father instead of Jerry. But that would have required Lily to stay in Katy's Ridge, and she had bigger plans.

June hugs her son and grandson, and Horatio walks them outside. Daisy's expression borders on a frown. This is confusing

to me. Is it hard for her to see such a close-knit family when hers has been in tatters most of her life?

We go out back and sit at a picnic table that Horatio made. June brings apple cider and homemade gingersnaps. Daisy and I help carry the glasses, napkins, and small plates. Birds chirp and flit between bird feeders made from various-sized gourds hanging in trees or on poles. White beehives line one side of the property. If I lived here, I would want to eat outside all the time. I taste a ginger-snap and sip cider, and my taste buds become wide awake.

"How are you doing since your mama passed?" June asks me.

I tell her I've been better, and it strikes me anew that Mama isn't at the house waiting for me to come home. Only June would ask me how I'm doing and really want to know. In Nashville, I haven't found a best friend or even the beginnings of one, unless you count Bee.

Looking out over the mountains, unexpected contentment falls over me. I question why I ever left this place. My mind wanders to how my life might have been different if I hadn't moved. From somewhere deep inside, a sudden longing rises in search of what could have been. But then, my heart heavy, I remember exactly why I left.

"I told Daisy about you telling fortunes," I say to June.

"I do," June says. "You want me to read yours, Daisy?"

Daisy hesitates, her look admonishing me for putting her on the spot.

"You can do mine first," I say to June. "Then, Daisy will know what to expect." I wink at Daisy, who doesn't smile back.

June goes back into the house to retrieve her fortune-telling cards.

"Don't you worry that she's putting ideas into your head?" Daisy asks.

"June's not like that," I say. "She doesn't tell me I'm going to meet a tall, dark stranger or anything."

Daisy looks away. "I wish Mom had come with us."

"I do, too." I can only imagine what it's like for Daisy to have Lily gone all the time. "Maybe she'll surprise us and stay for a while," I add.

"She's been like this forever, though," Daisy says. "I'm not sure she could change if she wanted to."

"She hasn't always been like this, Daisy."

Her look says she disagrees.

June returns to the picnic table with an old deck of tarot cards. Well worn, the pictures are dull and the edges ragged. My fortune involves significant changes. Unexpected twists and turns. I thank June and tell Daisy it is her turn.

After shuffling the cards again, June puts them on the table, letting Daisy cut the deck. Daisy watches with noted curiosity as June places four cards faceup on the table. June pauses and stares at the spread for several seconds.

"What is it?" I ask.

She looks at me. Her eyes apologize. "Family darkness," she says.

"Mama's death?" I ask.

"Further back." She doesn't look up from the cards. "A ghost from the past."

"A ghost?" Daisy looks intently at the cards as though trying to see what June sees.

"An old pattern," June begins. "Something unresolved that needs to be dealt with in this generation." She looks at Daisy and then at me as if making a secret connection. Her eyes widen.

"What does it mean?" I ask, looking from June to Daisy.

June pauses as if debating how much to say. "A darkness needs to be confronted and witnessed. Once you do, it will lift."

June's lips tighten, as if unwilling to let more words pass. Horatio steps out on the back porch, as though summoned. She looks at him, and a silent message passes.

"June, can you help me a minute?" he asks.

June swoops up the cards, returning them to the deck. She excuses herself and goes with Horatio into the house, taking the cards with her and putting them in the pocket of her apron.

Daisy and I exchange a confused look.

"That was weird," I say. "I've never seen June act like that."

"What are we supposed to do?" Daisy asks.

"I have no idea," I say.

When June returns, her apron is off, and she apologizes for being in the house for so long. "Horatio was trying to fix our old furnace and needed a hand," she says.

But something doesn't feel right. June never lies to me, but right now, she is hiding something.

As though starting over, she asks Daisy about her school, her interests. She asks me how Aunt Sadie is taking the loss of Mama. We don't talk about the cards again, yet they are ever-present in my mind. Something strange has happened, and I have no idea what it is.

On the drive back, Daisy and I are quiet. I wish now that I hadn't suggested she have her fortune read. I saw it as something fun to do, but it turned into something serious. When we arrive at Aunt Sadie's house, we find Lily folding clothes and putting them in her suitcase on the bed. Daisy's gloominess intensifies.

"Where are you going?" she asks Lily.

"They've rescheduled the concerts I missed," Lily says.

"I thought you were going to stay awhile." Daisy's voice weakens.

"Sorry, honey. It can't be helped." Lily tucks a white slip into the suitcase, along with several pairs of pantyhose.

"Can I talk to you?" I ask Lily, who at the moment seems more like a stranger than kin.

Lily momentarily looks up. "Sure, Mama."

I give Daisy a reassuring look before she leaves the room.

The smell of a cedar haunts Aunt Sadie's bedroom. A closet she added sometime in the late sixties.

"How was June?" Lily arranges the clothes in her suitcase with the precision of someone who has packed a thousand times.

"Fine," I say, not going into the fiasco of the fortune-telling.

"What do you want to talk to me about?" She counts underwear and socks.

I look at the child I carried inside me for the hardest nine months of my life. A child who is now approaching middle age. My love for her was instantaneous. A saving grace for a terrifying circumstance. I have often thought that our love for each other saved us both. However, at this moment, I feel disappointed in her. I bite my lip to silence the part of me that speaks her mind. The part that received Mama's wrath more than once. The part that may have even driven Bee away. Despite knowing better, nothing stops the words that want to come.

"I can't believe you used to love to linger," I say to her.

"Mama, don't start." Her voice is low.

I think of patterns passing. Family darkness. My silence causes Lily to finally look up. Does she know how unusual it is for me to keep silent? I close the door to ensure Daisy won't overhear. If I don't tell Lily, no one will.

"What is it?" she asks, now concerned more than irritated. "Are you okay?"

"Honey, I'm worried about Daisy," I say. "I think she may be in trouble."

"What kind of trouble?" Her sudden attention reminds me of how much she loves Daisy.

"I'm not sure."

My answer causes her to frown as though she was looking for a reason to stay behind, but my uncertainty is too vague. Lily returns to her suitcase and folds her nightgown into a small square of fabric. I see the girl she used to be, focused on moving

on. Going to the next city, the next country, the next pin on the map.

"Please stop and listen to me for a minute," I say, my voice giving away my frustration. Frustration not only at Lily for not taking this seriously, but also for my inability to figure out what the actual problem is. June's cards confirm something is going on. Something serious enough that June couldn't bring herself to say more.

Lily sighs before sitting on the end of the bed.

"Sorry, Mama. I'm listening."

I hesitate, my thoughts like chickens in the yard that refuse to gather. "When Daisy arrived, she seemed different. Withdrawn. Closed."

"She's always been that way," Lily says.

"No, she hasn't," I say. "She's always been quiet, but not sullen and sad."

"She's a teenager," Lily says. "Teenagers are always sullen."

"You weren't," I say.

"I would have been if I'd known it was an option." When I look at her, I see a woman possessing more than a little bit of Mama's stubbornness.

"It's more than being a teenager," I say. "She listens to everything and everybody as if her life depends on it. She's always studying people, and disappears into every crowd, and hides behind a book."

"Maybe it's because she's an only child," Lily says. "They're always more grown-up than people with lots of siblings. They relate more to their parents and other grown-ups than their peers."

Lily sounds like she has read up on this.

"Well, that makes sense, but I swear it's something deeper." *Something darker,* I want to say.

"Oh, Mama. You see shadows where there's nothing but light. Why are you bringing this up right before I'm leaving?"

"What other option do I have? You're always leaving. If Mama hadn't died, I wouldn't even have the opportunity now."

"Don't start," she repeats with a sigh.

"I'm not trying to start anything, sweetheart, I'm trying to protect Daisy."

"Protect her from what?" Lily raises her head, and our eyes meet.

I pause and lower my voice. "I don't even know."

Lily stands and goes back to her suitcase and the pile of neatly folded clothes on the bed. Is it my imagination, or does she tend to run away from hard things? Her first inclination after she found out about Bee and me was to run away, too.

"Well, when you figure it out, let me know," she says. For an instant, Lily looks like Johnny. I almost expect her to spit tobacco juice at me.

"What's her relationship like with her father?" I ask.

Lily stops again. "Why would you ask that?"

"I don't know," I say. "Daisy sure doesn't like to go over there."

"What did she say?" Lily stands straighter, a doe alerted to something in the forest.

I search my memory. "I get the impression that Daisy hates his new wife."

"Well, I do, too, but that doesn't make me sullen."

"I never liked him," I say, regretting my words the second they leave my mouth.

"That's not news, Mama," Lily snaps. "Tell me something I don't know."

We exchange another look. It isn't like Lily to snap at me. And it isn't like me to channel Mama, either, sharing my judgments with whoever will listen.

"You've been pushing the river your entire life," I say, my voice softening. "Don't you ever get tired from all that pushing?"

Lily walks over to me. She has Johnny's intense eyes. Eyes that

penetrate and won't let you escape. But I am convinced that she is the one that isn't seeing right now. She places a hand on each of my shoulders. I have to resist brushing them away. "Feel free to talk to Daisy and ask her what's going on."

"Why don't you?" I ask, my frustration growing again.

"I can, but I don't have much time. I have a flight out of Nashville tonight."

Since when are you an absent mother? I want to say.

Instead I close my lips, so the words don't escape. More than once, I've said something I regretted. Something that I couldn't go back and retrieve before it did its damage.

On the way outside, I pass Aunt Sadie's old walking stick and fedora hanging on a hook by the door. The past is everywhere. When I was Daisy's age, Aunt Sadie and I sat on this very swing as I confessed what Johnny did to me. Her words were like a healing balm on a raw wound. She told me I didn't do anything wrong, and she was the first person to know I might be carrying Johnny's child. I realized recently that Sadie was only fifty when I had Lily, two years younger than I am now, and I already thought she was old.

I join Daisy on the porch swing. The swing squeaks loudly, crying out for grease. Greasing things was always Daddy's job. After he died, there seemed to be crying hinges everywhere. Daisy chews on a fingernail, pretending to read. What Lily and I talked about, she isn't ready to hear.

"I thought that maybe we could stay in Katy's Ridge for the rest of the summer," I say. "I've got all sorts of vacation time saved up, and it might do both of us good to get out of Nashville for a while."

Daisy looks up at me as though I've extended her driving lessons indefinitely.

"So it's okay with you?" I ask.

She nods, and her shoulders relax. A burden somehow lifted.

CHAPTER TWENTY

Daisy

Gran and I sit on Sadie's front porch overlooking the valley surrounded by mountains. A bed of wildflowers waves in the breeze below the porch. Small birds hover among the blossoms, a light hum accompanying their flight. They dip and dive at one another and hover over the flowers.

"Those are hummingbirds," Gran says.

"Hummingbirds," I repeat. Another thing I never knew existed, like honeysuckle, lavender, and tree frogs the size of quarters that come out after a rainstorm.

The screen door opens, and Mom rolls her sizeable black suitcase onto the porch. When I was younger, seeing this suitcase made me automatically cry, and though I don't weep anymore, a familiar heaviness sweeps in on the breeze.

"Well, if it isn't my two favorite people in the whole world," Mom says with a smile.

I imagine Gran and I both know she means it, but somehow it isn't enough. Spending time with people is how you know you

matter to them. Spending time and listening. I'm not sure Mom has ever been good at either. Like the hummingbirds, she flits from flower to flower, her songs the nectar for strangers.

"Will you let us know you arrived safely?" Gran asks my mom.

"Of course," she says. "I'll call you sometime tomorrow."

Mom will do as she says. She will call the house and say something sweet to me like how great it was to spend time together, which will make her absence hurt even more. I get up from the swing and roll her cumbersome suitcase down the steps and along the rocky walkway toward the rental car. In a way, I wish I could go with her, not that she has ever asked me along.

Mom hugs Gran on the front porch and then walks down the stone path behind me. Together we lift her suitcase into the trunk. I want to beg her to stay, but I know it won't do any good. It will just make her feel worse for leaving when she feels she has to.

A makeshift valet, I open the car door for her. Gran joins me, and we stand at the end of the walkway and wave as Mom drives away. As the dirt rises and falls, Gran squeezes me, as though she knows what it's like to be left behind.

Shortly after, we close up Aunt Sadie's house and return to Granny McAllister's. When we arrive, we find boxes stacked by the front door full of Sadie's things. We find her in the kitchen packing up herbs and tinctures in small bottles. Her eyes are red. A small pile of tissues graces the kitchen counter.

"I thought I'd go back home, so you and Daisy can have more room," she says, as though she already knows that we are spending the rest of the summer.

"There's no need for that," Gran says. "This is your home, too."

Aunt Sadie pauses. "Truth is, Wildflower, I came to help Nell. I've missed my place. Rufus has, too."

She pats her dog, whose panting smile confirms he would be happy anywhere, as long as Sadie is there. Rufus and I have

become friends. He won't chase a ball anymore, but if I throw a stick, he wanders over and sniffs it as if humoring me.

Gran thanks Sadie again for her excellent job of taking care of Mama. Sadie pulls another tissue from the box on the kitchen table, wiping away fresh tears. I have never been around so much crying as I have since Granny McAllister died. At first it bothered me, but now it reminds me of one of those fast-moving summer thunderstorms that come almost every afternoon. They are scary at the time, but nobody gets hurt, and the air smells cleaner afterward.

"I still can't believe Mama is gone," Gran says to Sadie.

Aunt Sadie agrees, and her eyes redden again.

"You sure you'll be okay all alone?" Gran asks.

"Of course," she says. "I've lived alone most of my life. It's people that challenge me." She offers a brief smile.

Gran and I help Sadie finish packing, and then we load her things into the back of the pickup before the three of us, and Rufus, return to Sadie's and help her unpack.

IN THE MIDDLE of the night, I call out, a dream pushing me awake. Gran rushes into the room, asking if I'm all right. My summer nightgown is drenched with sweat. I am sleeping in what was Gran's bedroom when she was a girl. The same bedroom Aunt Sadie stayed in while she nursed Granny McAllister.

"I had nightmares when I was your age, too," Gran says. "Do you want to talk about it?"

I sit up in bed to shake away the dream.

"A man was in the house creeping around in the shadows," I begin. "Except it wasn't this house. It was in Nashville. My father's house." Gran hands me the small glass of water on the nightstand. I take a sip.

"You're safe here," Gran says. "I'm here, and Daniel is just across the road. Only a phone call away."

"Tell me about Johnny Monroe," I say, an odd request given it's the middle of the night.

Gran hesitates. "Did Lily say something?"

I nod, remembering what Mom told me.

Gran sighs. "Why don't we talk on the porch in the morning."

I agree, and she stays a little longer before suggesting that I try to get more sleep.

When I wake the next morning, Gran has breakfast made. Within an hour, we are sitting in two rockers on the porch. Gran's coffee sits on the table between us, steam rising. The smell makes me miss my mom. The mountains are still foggy, and the morning sun is only beginning to break through the trees.

Gran angles her rocker so that we face each other. I question if I really want to know what she has to say.

"This is a family story I never thought I'd tell you." Her words are clear, as though she has been practicing what she is going to say. "Daddy had died the year before. I had just turned thirteen. I was on my way to the cemetery because it was the anniversary of his death."

I try to imagine Gran at thirteen. My age. I think of the dream again—the man in the shadows.

"Johnny was always crass with girls, even my sisters," she continues. "One day, he was up at the cemetery and had been drinking. He was more brazen than usual. I told him to leave me alone. But he chased me down the path behind the cemetery, and finally caught me."

Gran pauses. My imagination fills in the rest.

"Daniel and Mama found me in the woods later that night and brought me home."

We sit in silence, my thoughts traveling the hills. I don't know

whether to feel angry or sad. Right now, I feel both. "I'm sorry," I say finally.

"I am, too," Gran says. "For years I thought it was my fault. But what I've learned from my fifty years of living is that sometimes bad things happen, and you didn't do a single thing to deserve it or bring it on."

Gran's words sink in deep.

Something catches in my throat, making it difficult to swallow.

"You know you can tell me anything, right?" Her words are soft.

Not this, I want to say.

"Anything," she repeats.

A tear slides down my cheek. I stand. "I'm supposed to meet Nellie at the bottom of the hill. We're taking a walk by the river."

"Anything," she says a third time.

I wipe the tears as quickly as they come.

Gran lowers her eyes as if to offer me privacy. "We McAllisters have never liked to be seen crying, but sometimes it's the best thing you can do," she says.

"I've got to go." I leave the porch and walk down the hill. Before I know it, I am running. Running from the man in the shadows. Running like Gran down the path in the back of the cemetery. Running to escape. All the while, running to embrace the words I desperately needed to hear: *Sometimes bad things happen, and you didn't do a single thing to deserve it or bring it on.*

CHAPTER TWENTY-ONE

Wildflower

A broom sits in the corner of the front porch where Mama left it. Suddenly her absence makes my chest ache. With Daisy gone, and the house empty, I move from Mama's rocker to the top porch step where I used to sit as a girl waiting for Daddy to come home. In a way, that girl is still waiting.

Telling Daisy about Johnny reminds me of the shame I carried after it happened and still do. Shame that feels perfectly preserved, like taking off the lid to a jar of Mama's strawberry jam. Even years later, it is as fresh as the day it was sealed.

Pushing down feelings is the McAllister way. Yet Mama's death has invited new grief. With the thought of returning to Nashville, my homesickness returns, an echo of the feelings I had when we first moved away. In those days, I doubled over aching for the mountains where I was born. Not only for the people I left behind, but for the land spread out before me now. The forest. The contour of the land. The ease of the river. The birds. Chipmunks and squirrels. The deer grazing in the valley. Everything.

Endings are a part of life as often as beginnings. Mama is gone to be with Daddy. I am home again. But only for a brief time.

A car pulls up the gravel driveway, unseen but not unheard. The last thing I want to deal with right now is another person. It is probably someone paying their condolences. Doing what they think is right instead of what a person might need. From the sound of the gravel, it is a heavier car. I blow my nose with a used tissue in my pocket. I stand but then sit again, fantasizing about hiding in the house, locking the doors. But the notion of southern hospitality has been bred into me like the McAllisters' blue eyes.

A woman comes into view, laboring up the hill. A woman with some heft to her. I squint to make out her features, searching for recognition.

"Is that you, Wildflower?" the woman calls from below.

I recognize the voice of Mary Jane, my childhood friend, but don't recognize her.

Our friendship didn't last after Lily was born, her mother seemingly afraid that my bad luck might rub off on her daughter. At least that's the story I heard.

Mary Jane labors up the path in front of her. As she approaches, I stand again, feeling my past catch up with me. She stops a few feet from the steps.

Despite her breathlessness, a smile erupts. "Wildflower?"

I return the smile.

As the most agile between us, I approach, and we embrace. I didn't realize how short Mary Jane was when we were kids. Now, more than fully grown, she is all of five feet. Though her body has changed, her voice has remained youthful.

"What are you doing here?" I ask.

"I heard about your mama." Her expression drifts from buoyant to sad.

"You came all the way from Arkansas to give your condolences?" I ask.

"Well, no, I'm also visiting Victor."

"Victor's here?"

Victor is Mary Jane's older brother. How have I not thought about him for all these years? Victor, who for weeks after the attack sent me peppermint lifesavers by way of Meg, calling them courage pills, prescribing them three times a day. Victor, who would have gladly been Lily's stepfather if I had only been willing to marry him. A man everyone liked. Every dog in the county seemed to like him, too.

"You don't know?" Mary Jane asks.

"Know what?" I imagine Victor dead and gone, Mary Jane visiting his grave somewhere in the cemetery, and me not even knowing about it. Dead from some mysterious disease that only takes the kindest of people. Renewed sadness comes, mixed with a sudden regret that I never thanked him properly.

"Victor lives in Katy's Ridge now," Mary Jane says.

"He does?" My words come out in a whoosh of relief. Relief that I don't have to add one more person to the list of all I grieve. Then I wonder why Mama never mentioned Victor's return in her letters. That would be big news. Nor did she mention Matt Monroe. I always thought she told me everything, but it turns out she was selective.

Mary Jane lowers her purse to the ground, as if no longer willing to carry it. "Victor built a big house over where we used to live," she begins. "Well, it's a second home, really, or actually it's his third."

Mary Jane never could resist bragging.

Meanwhile, I can't imagine even one home, having lived in apartments for so many years. I invite her inside for a glass of tea, but she doesn't budge. Nor does she seem to want to sit for a while on the porch. I decide to sit again on the top step. We are eye level.

"How are your parents?" I ask.

She rests a hand on a generous hip.

"Mama's still around, living in Little Rock, but Daddy died two summers ago."

I tell her how sorry I am. "I liked your father," I add.

"He was such a cutup," she says. "Do you know what his final wish was?"

"No idea," I say.

"For us to go to granddaddy's yard and dig up that leg he lost in the first world war—the one buried with all the family pets? He wanted us to put it in his coffin."

Mary Jane giggles like the girl she used to be, and I catch the giggles like a summer cold. The laughter, after so many tears, lightens my grief.

"We found two cat skeletons right beside his leg bone," Mary Jane continues, "so we threw them into his casket, too. Daddy always did like cats."

We laugh like we used to as girls. At this moment, I forgive her for abandoning me when I needed her most, but then I wonder if I am too generous. Friends who betray friends are nearly impossible to trust again unless they fess up to their betrayal.

"Remember that time Cecil Appleby nearly ran over us when we were rolling in laughter down by the mailboxes?" she says.

"Do you remember what we were laughing at?" I ask.

She says she doesn't. We think for a while.

"Oh, I think it was something about Johnny being a boil on my backside," I say, "and me wanting to lance it."

I start to laugh again, but with the mention of Johnny, Mary Jane goes quiet, as though I have broken an unspoken rule by mentioning this part of the past.

She clears her throat, and I feel a sudden chill.

"I'm staying with Victor while I'm here," she says. "I'll tell him you asked after him."

I thank her, perplexed by her sudden change. "Tell Victor I appreciated all those peppermint lifesavers," I say.

Her eyes dart her discomfort. She picks up her purse, ready to leave, but then pauses.

"Why don't you come up and have dinner with Victor and me tonight?" Mary Jane says.

I hesitate, not knowing if I can get through an entire dinner with Mary Jane's moods. But I'd love to see Victor.

"Do you mind if I bring my granddaughter, Daisy?" I ask. "She's staying with me this summer."

"Sure, bring her along," she says. "It will be like old times, the three of us. Plus Daisy." She turns to leave and then stops again.

"By the way, Victor never married," she says. "Never found anyone good enough, I guess."

For a moment, she seems to be playing matchmaker. Has Mary Jane forgotten about Bee? Or maybe she never knew. Her family moved to Little Rock after Mary Jane graduated from high school. I'm not sure the Katy's Ridge grapevine extends that far west.

The sun directly overhead, sweat forms on Mary Jane's forehead. She gives me directions to Victor's house that I don't need, and we say our goodbyes. After she leaves, the thought of seeing Victor again causes me to smile. Here in the mountains, it is said that if you don't like the weather, wait five minutes and it will change. Minutes ago, I was engulfed in sadness. Now, a reunion is planned. A reunion with what is, and what could have been.

CHAPTER TWENTY-TWO

Daisy

Tall grasses lead to a small sandy beach by the river. Nellie leads the way. Something about this place feels familiar, though I've never been here. Voices fade in and out from an earlier time. My mom and Gran are talking. Gran is telling her about Bee. Are they why this place feels familiar? I push their voices away, determined to spend the time with Nellie. The river current pulses gently against the land. The water looks more brown than blue and smells fishy.

"How did you know about this path?" I ask Nellie.

"From exploring," she says.

"Exploring?"

"Don't you ever explore?" Nellie looks at me as though I am not from around here and am altogether strange. An inhabitant from another planet, perhaps. Someone unfamiliar with human ways.

"Sometimes Bee and I go to museums and things," I say.

She nods, her expression softening. "That counts."

Nellie is easy. Uncomplicated. I don't have to worry that she only likes me because of who my mother is.

"I wish my hair were curly like yours," she says.

"Your hair is beautiful," I say.

"Don't be silly." Nellie tosses a stick into the water, watching the current take it away.

"Do you like living here?" I ask.

"Don't know anyplace else," she says. "I've been to Nashville. It's exciting and all, but I'm not sure I could live there."

She tosses another stick in the river. I imagine she could do this all day. Sending sticks downriver on a journey that she sees no need in making herself.

"What do you do if you want to see a movie?" I ask.

"We go to Harriman. It's not that far. They've got a mall with a movie duplex." She pauses to toss another stick. "I have all sorts of cousins who drive. It's easy to catch a ride. Or sometimes Mama and Daddy will go, too. We saw *E.T.* recently."

We sit together on the small beach, the sun behind us, while I try to imagine Daniel, Jo, and Nellie seated in a dark movie theater watching E.T. phone home. It isn't easy.

"It's just a different way of life out here," I say, imitating Nellie's southern accent. Trying it on to see how it fits. I quickly decide it doesn't. "I'm not saying it's bad," I add in my usual voice, a much watered-down version of the southern dialect.

"A lot of kids can hardly wait to get out of Katy's Ridge," she says. "I'm not blaming them. This place can be boring as dirt sometimes. It just works for me."

"What will you do after you graduate?" I ask.

Personally, I hate that question because I have no idea. I'm not like Mom, who has undeniable talent. Unless reading lots of books counts for anything.

"I want to get married." Nellie says this with a dreamy smile before tossing another stick in the river.

Getting married is not something I aspire to. But if I do, I will keep the McAllister name like Mom did. She refused to be a Rooney like my dad. She said Lily Rooney sounded like something you would order at an Italian restaurant. After I was born, she insisted that my last name be McAllister on my birth certificate, too, and thankfully, my father went along with it.

"You have a boyfriend yet?" Nellie asks.

"No," I say. "You?"

She blushes.

"You know Adam Sector?"

We are sitting side by side; otherwise, Nellie might notice my surprise. "I met him the other day," I say, trying to sound indifferent.

"We've been eyeing each other since we were kids." Nellie nudges me with her shoulder and then smiles. I wonder if she has written *Mrs. Adam Sector* a zillion times. The only things I write into the night are secrets and cuss words in my diary.

Nellie and I sit in silence, the ample shade adding a hint of coolness to the summer day. Nellie's ease is about as foreign to me as her life here in Katy's Ridge. Could I be content staying in one place the rest of my life? Content with marrying the boy I went to school with who will build me a house one day while we create children together? I think I would always question if there was something better out there for me, more exciting or more adventurous.

Something rustles in the underbrush, and Nellie touches my arm, pointing toward the tall grasses a few yards away. At first I don't see anything, but finally I notice the fox inching up to a small rabbit on a rock. My eyes widen when I realize that the rabbit is about to become the fox's lunch. In the next instant Nellie claps her hands and scares the fox, who darts away as the rabbit hops into the tall brush.

"You don't see stuff like that in the city," I say, smiling my relief.

"Well, we've got foxes, rabbits, possums, bobcats, and bears, among other things."

"We had mice in our kitchen once," I say.

Nellie laughs.

"Have you had your first kiss yet?"

Though we're the same age, she seems much younger. I shrug, darting away from the question like the fox.

"Have you?" I ask.

"Not yet," she says, blushing again.

I imagine her thinking of handsome Adam and their kid-filled house that he built himself. With renewed awareness, I decide my life is totally screwed up.

"Your father seems nice," I say, changing the subject.

"He's a war hero, but he doesn't tell anybody about that," she says. "He even has a medal the Army gave him for saving a bunch of people. He was trying to save my Uncle Nathan, too, who was in the same outfit, but he couldn't . . ." Her voice trails off.

"Gran showed me Nathan's grave in the cemetery," I say.

Nellie nods. "What's your father like?"

"Nothing like yours," I say, thinking my father wouldn't get a medal for anything unless making money and random creepiness qualified.

Nellie turns to me as though I am a dark cloud sitting next to her, and a silver lining is called for. "Well, it must be exciting to have a mother in the country music business." Her smile practically glows.

"It has its moments," I say.

Nellie's glow dulls as she looks at me. "Daisy, I don't think you are very happy."

"Sure, I'm happy," I say, working up a snarl.

She stands, tossing a final stick into the river that bobs along with the current.

"Well, I'd better go help Mama with supper." She brushes the sand off her hands.

We walk back to the mailboxes in silence. I want to apologize for being me but say nothing. In Nellie's generous way, she smiles and tells me it was nice to get to know me a little better.

As she crosses the road, I wonder why I am so different and see dark clouds instead of rainbows, as the poster in my third-grade classroom admonished. I begin my trek up the hill. Next to Gran's pickup is a large, light yellow Cadillac with fins on the back. It is odd to see such a big car in such a small driveway. A short, roundish woman is coming down the path as I am going up. She stops and smiles at me.

"You must be Daisy," she says, slightly out of breath. "I'm an old friend of your grandmother's."

Offering a moist, wimpy handshake, she tells me that she will see me later tonight. She waves as gravity aids her descent.

As I approach the house, Gran sits on the steps of the porch. She looks tired, or maybe sad, or perhaps both. She stands and hugs me.

"You okay?" she asks.

I choose words instead of a shrug. "I've been better."

She nods as though she knows the feeling.

"Let's go inside, and I'll fix you a snack," she says. "We've been invited out to dinner, and it's going to be later than usual."

"Who was that?" I ask.

"A friend who deserted me a long time ago."

"And we're having dinner with her?"

"Her and her brother, Victor. He's the one I want to see," Gran says. "He didn't desert me at all."

"Good to know," I say.

We walk into the house, the screen door slamming at my heels, and I imagine all those sticks Nellie threw into the river, slowly making their way to the sea.

CHAPTER TWENTY-THREE

Wildflower

Thunder rumbles.

The sun hides behind the growing dark clouds. The wind dashes through the trees, announcing what is to come. During the summer months, afternoon thunderstorms are frequent here in the Tennessee mountains.

Daisy and I sit on the porch as the skies open. The deluge of rain hammers out a staccato melody on the tin roof. We are protected by the porch, yet part of the storm.

"I found some things in Mama's closet that she saved for me," I say, raising my voice to be heard over the storm.

I take from my pocket my rabbit's foot keychain and hand it to her. "I thought I'd lost this forever. It's supposed to be good luck."

Daisy studies the rabbit's foot, holding it as if she could use some luck. She then closes her eyes and squeezes it for maybe an extra dose.

Thunder rumbles again, and the storm intensifies. A gully washer, Mama would call it. The rain will run off the mountain,

cutting into the land, making new streams. Daisy watches while holding on to the rabbit's foot.

"You can keep that," I say.

She thanks me.

"There's a secret path that leads to the back of the cemetery," I say. "I'll show it to you while you're here if you want me to."

"A secret path?"

I nod.

"There used to be an old rickety footbridge that stretched across a ravine. I carried that rabbit's foot for good luck to get safely across."

"You did?"

I nod. "Mountain people often use charms for luck," I begin again. "Daddy had a lucky silver dollar that he always carried in his pocket. Horatio gave me the star ruby, and Daniel still carries a buckeye."

She studies the rabbit's foot before tucking it into her shorts pocket.

"Mama had saved this for me, too." I hand Daisy a photograph of Lily and me when Lily was a baby.

"Is that Mom?" she asks, studying the image.

I nod. I look awkward holding Lily, and young enough to still play with dolls instead of hold a baby of my own.

"I didn't realize you were so young when you had Mom," Daisy says, looking at me.

"I was your age."

A thunderclap makes us jump in unison, as if God himself is making a comment. The rain surges and then begins to slow.

"What was Mom like when she was growing up?" Daisy asks.

I welcome her question. "Incredibly curious and always hungry." I laugh. "Mama took care of the hunger part, but it was a full-time job answering her questions."

"I'm different from her," Daisy says.

"Yes, you are," I say, "and that's not a bad thing."

Within ten minutes the rain has stopped, but with the trees dripping, it sounds like it is still raining. Checking Daddy's watch, I tell Daisy that we need to get ready for our dinner out. "You may want to wash under your fingernails," I say.

Daisy closes her hands as if hiding the evidence of her digging.

"We're walking, by the way."

"Walking?" she asks, probably disappointed that the pickup keys will not be tossed in her direction.

"It will be dark by the time we head home. I'll grab a couple of Mama's flashlights off the back porch. Walking at night is really peaceful," I continue. "It will be good for us."

Daisy doesn't look convinced.

An hour later, we leave the house without locking the door. As far as I know, the only time this house was locked was after Johnny broke in and my sister Amy shot him. Shortly before, Johnny had left a note threatening me for telling what he did. We figured he would come back to make good on his threat. Sure enough, he did. Thankfully, Amy is a better shot than Mama and my other sisters.

Life, it seems, is divided into two parts. The years before Johnny and the years after. The *before* years were when my life felt open and safe. The *after* years, closed and locked. But I am ready to be free again.

When we reach the road, we take a left. When I was a girl, I could have walked blindfolded to find Mary Jane's house. I look forward to seeing what Victor has done with the old place. In the twilight, Daisy and I are silent. The day has already held too many words. The cicadas are in full voice, and the tree frogs add bass notes to their song. The forest is dense with humidity from the earlier rain.

When we approach, we see Mary Jane's Cadillac in the driveway, alongside a new Jeep. Victor has done well for himself. The brand-new house is almost too fancy for Katy's Ridge. When I was

a girl, the Sweeney house was the biggest in our small mountain community. For a while, it was the only house with a telephone. Sweeney's Country Store was a cornerstone in the community. We saved our pennies to buy candy there when we picked up flour and sugar for Mama. After his father retired, Victor ran the store for years before moving to Arkansas and evidently making his fortune.

When Victor opens the door, I am surprised to see a gray-headed man. He is only two years older, but I seem to have come face-to-face with my own aging process. However, he has the same caring eyes of his youth, and I find myself hoping that life has been kind to him.

Pleasantries abound. I introduce Daisy. Victor offers me a glass of white wine, Daisy lemonade. Mary Jane announces that Victor has prepared the entire meal, then tells the story of how the only person allowed in her kitchen is Roberta, her black cook. Mary Jane can be counted on to embellish things. Somehow, Victor was never like his sister and never flaunted the Sweeney wealth.

We sit at the large dining room table, and I think back to the meals I had with Mary Jane's family when we were girls. My thoughts jump to Mary Jane's father, who is now—in death—reunited with the leg he lost in the war, as well as several house cats.

Around Mama's table, everyone talked at once, and not a single plate was without a chip. But the food was always delicious. At Mary Jane's, it was the opposite. The food tasted like cardboard covered with tasteless gravy but was served on perfect china plates. Tonight, the décor is no exception. The table contains matching china in an oriental pattern, polished silver, and crystal goblets for iced tea. Unlike his mother, however, Victor is a surprisingly good cook.

Daisy glances in my direction. The only time she seems

halfway comfortable is when she has dirt under her fingernails or when she is reading. I give her a reassuring look in return.

"I'm sorry I didn't make it to your mother's funeral," Victor says to me. "I was out of town until late yesterday."

I tell him no apologies are needed and that it was a beautiful service.

"Everybody's talking about Lily singing. That must have been very special." He smiles at Daisy, who focuses her interest on a crystal saltshaker. But at least her fingernails are free of dirt.

"Yes, it was exceptional," I say.

Mary Jane finishes her wine in one gulp; light sparkles off her many rings as she pours herself another glass.

"Do you miss Nashville?" Victor asks Daisy.

"Not at all," Daisy says, the answer so decisive it makes him chuckle.

"A woman who knows her mind." He lifts his wineglass in a salute.

Daisy offers her first smile of the evening, so brief I question if I imagined it.

Victor seems intent on making her feel welcome, and I appreciate his efforts.

"What's it like to be staying in your mother's house again?" he asks me.

"It's strange," I say. "Especially now, without Mama there." Tears threaten to come, and I take a sip of wine instead. I don't usually drink, and I never have wine with a meal. In fact, I could write my complete knowledge of different wines on the top of a cork.

"I imagine it is strange." Victor touches my hand on the table, an action that doesn't escape Daisy's observation.

When I talk to Bee later, I will tell her about seeing Victor again. Bee always liked Victor. He was her prize student. She always believed he would do great things.

Mary Jane finishes a second glass of wine and becomes more animated, telling stories of the past. Stories about her clothes and different birthday parties that "everyone" attended. Parties I clearly wasn't invited to, like her Sweet Sixteen. My exclusion may have had something to do with me having a three-year-old at the time.

Meanwhile, Daisy hides a yawn behind her napkin.

Not all childhood friends make sense as adults. Victor is the exception. If I had married him when he asked, my life would have played out in a totally different way. How rare it is for a man to be willing to take on a young mother with a small child? I find myself grateful all over again, and also convinced that it would have never worked, no matter how kind a man he was.

Victor and I wash dishes by hand in his massive kitchen with floor-to-ceiling windows facing into the forest. Daisy watches us while pretending to read a book pulled from Victor's oak book-shelves in the living room. A book by C. S. Lewis about different types of love.

Minutes later, we say our goodbyes, promising to get together again soon.

"Are you sure I can't drive you home?" he asks at the door. "Happy to."

Daisy looks at me with pleading eyes. Not only does she want a ride, but I imagine she also wants me to convince our host to let her drive.

"It's such a beautiful evening to walk," I say. "It's not something I get to do living in Nashville."

With a smile, he says he understands, and I am sure he does.

Daisy and I walk down the road, our footsteps echoing into the night. Daisy is quiet, which doesn't alarm me. I imagine she is thinking about the evening. Our flashlights steady, we illuminate the way ahead of us like headlights of the car she hopes to drive someday.

As before, night noises surround us. Something scurries by the side of the road. Maybe a possum or a raccoon. I wonder how many times I've walked this same road in darkness. When I was a girl, it was with Daddy. Other times, with Mama and my sisters in different combinations. As a girl, I never would have imagined that on an evening in the future, I would be walking with my granddaughter along this familiar road. That I have a granddaughter at all is sometimes startling.

"I need to tell you something." Daisy's words come out of the darkness like a car from out of nowhere.

My secret sense drops into my gut, as though it already knows what's coming. "I'm listening," I say.

We keep walking, and I wonder if we should stop. But somehow it seems that the walking and the darkness are necessary components to any confession.

"Promise you won't hate me?"

"I could never hate you, Daisy. Never."

"Promise me?"

"I promise."

With my left hand, since my right is holding the flashlight, I cross my heart and hope to die, but this promise won't require a death. It will be easy to keep.

We continue another hundred yards, maybe more. Long enough for me to wonder if Daisy has said all she needs to say. It reminds me of the few times I confessed to friends about Bee. It was agonizing, not knowing if I would lose the friendship for being honest. Telling myself that if I did lose it, I didn't need that person in my life anyway. Not if they couldn't accept this part of me. But it was hard. To trust someone with our secrets is the biggest of big deals.

"I promise, Daisy," I say again, wanting to prime the pump, wanting the secret to spill out of her, because then she won't be alone.

We continue walking. When Daisy finally speaks, her words are softer than I expect.

"My father comes into my room at night when I stay with him."

"What?" I say, my voice a screaming whisper.

My flashlight drops on the road, the light bouncing into the trees before becoming still again. I take Daisy into my arms. At first she stiffens, but then she slowly allows the embrace. I imagine ice melting. A princess locked in a castle tower. A secret keeping her prisoner. My tower is forty years older than Daisy's, but it is a fortress I know well. Not because my father climbed into bed with me, but because Johnny Monroe didn't give me a choice. Different, yet the same.

Darkness embraces us.

In the moments that follow, I hold Daisy the way I wish Mama had held me after it happened. I hold her the way Aunt Sadie did. All we need is one person willing to hold us. One person who will see our shame and love us anyway. Perhaps even love us more.

Daisy in my arms, I tell her everything will be all right, not knowing if it will. I tell her that she is safe. I tell her that she is loved. It is only then that the tower walls gently tumble and Daisy begins to weep.

CHAPTER TWENTY-FOUR

Daisy

Gran's strong embrace protects me as I empty myself of tears.

"Did I say that, or just think it?" I say into the darkness.

"You said it," she says. "And I'm glad you did."

"You believe me?" I ask.

"Of course I believe you," she says.

I think of the river, the ripples gently lapping against the bank. New tears come in on the next wave.

She believes me.

My father told me no one would.

Blowing my nose into Gran's bandana, which appears magically from her pocket, I feel somehow lighter.

"Shall we go back to the house and talk?" She leans over to retrieve her flashlight.

I agree, feeling like my life has forever changed with the telling of one secret. Is it too late to take it back?

While I had no intention of telling Gran, something about walking through the darkness invited it. Voices walked with us. Voices of family. Ancestors. A chorus of footsteps marching through time. Footsteps of a clan named McAllister.

Not quite full, the moon watches us as we walk up the hill toward the house. I smell what I now know is jasmine, thanks to Gran educating me. Last week, I couldn't have told you three names of trees. Or even two names of birds. But after a few days in the mountains, I now know what honeysuckle is, as well as hummingbirds and chickadees. Cardinals and blue jays. Trees called redbuds and maples. Weeping willows, dogwoods, and oaks. Thanks to Nellie, I also know the subtle difference between mountain laurel and rhododendron. The smaller leaves and blossoms are mountain laurel. The bigger leaves and flowers are rhododendron. They bloom at different times in the spring. Mountain laurels are always first.

The porch light up ahead, I think of my mom somewhere on tour in another country. Far away. Unreachable. More than ever, I wish she were here. At the same time, I vowed to never tell her. My father told me it would hurt her. Break her heart. He also said she would never believe me. I wonder if this is true.

Now that the secret is out, I feel empty and light at the same time. Until I spoke it, I never realized how heavy it was to carry around, like my purple backpack filled with unneeded textbooks.

Gran turns on lights in the house. I follow her into the kitchen, the informal meeting room of all things McAllister.

"Hot cocoa?" she asks.

I nod, feeling suddenly naked in front of her. Exposed. Something keeps me anchored to the floor, even though I want to run away. Ever since I arrived this summer, I have pushed Gran away, but what I now realize is that I need her to stay close.

Gran mixes the milk and cocoa on the stove, adding a spoonful

of sugar. I think of Mary Poppins helping the medicine go down. But Gran is not magical, only an ordinary grandmother. Although I have underestimated her gentleness and her love for me.

We sit at the table with our hot cocoa. I stir and blow the top to cool it.

"You did the right thing," Gran says, putting her hand on mine. "Now that it's out in the open, we need to figure out what to do about it."

Out in the open. The words feel dangerous.

"We're going to do something about it?" I ask, not realizing action was an option.

"Of course," she says. "Your father doesn't get to get away with this."

"But . . ."

She waits for more, but I don't have words, only a thousand regrets.

"He's my father," I say.

"Yes, he is," Gran says. "But he has committed a crime against you."

"A crime?" I ask, my voice soft. "I don't want him to get in trouble," I add, even softer.

The confusion on Gran's face mirrors how I feel.

"Daisy, we have to tell the authorities."

"No, I don't want that," I say.

Words flow out of me that I never intended to tell anyone. I tell her I don't want my father to get into trouble, and I don't want Mom to have to come home from her tour again. I tell Gran that I'll be okay. That he hasn't really done anything yet. That he just lays there and whispers to me. That he only touches my arms and face. That he probably won't do more.

Gran's eyes reveal deep sadness. My confession may be the most I've ever said to her at one time.

"Daisy," she says, her voice full of tenderness, "we've got to tell someone so that he will stop."

"If we tell someone he will stop?" For some reason, this never occurred to me.

"Yes, of course," Gran says, her eyes softening to match her voice.

"I didn't tell you to get him in trouble," I say again.

Gran holds her head as though a puzzle just got harder to solve. "It's almost midnight," she says. "We should try to get some sleep and talk about this tomorrow. Is that okay with you?"

I nod.

We get ready for bed. I wonder how Gran can sleep in the bed her mother died in a few nights ago, even with clean sheets.

Before I turn out the light, Gran comes into my room and sits on my side of the bed. She asks me to look into her eyes.

"I'm glad you told me, Daisy. This secret is way too much for you to carry all on your own. At thirteen, your only job in life is to be a kid."

Weariness settles around her eyes, replacing the sadness. I realize this isn't easy for her, either.

"The most important thing," she begins again, "is knowing that you didn't do anything wrong. Hear me?"

I wonder if this is true. Gran looks at me as if waiting for an answer. "I hear you," I say, though I'm not sure I believe it.

"Now, get some sleep," Gran says. "Rest assured that you did the right thing."

I've never seen this side of Gran. The part that is more like Bee. Forceful and loving.

She tucks me in as though I am three instead of thirteen. Then she kisses me on the forehead.

"I love you, Daisy."

I tell her I love her, too, and I realize that I mean it. She turns

out the light. The darkness is immediate and substantial. I imagine my father in jail, and my mom so heartbroken she can't sing.

What have I done? I say to myself, as regrets crawl under the covers with me.

CHAPTER TWENTY-FIVE

Wildflower

E arly the next morning I put on Mama's housecoat and go
into the kitchen to call Daniel. I know he has been up for at
least an hour. I have barely slept, thinking through the options of
how to keep Daisy safe.

He answers the phone in the kitchen. I can hear Jo making his
breakfast. He's wearing his I-haven't-had-my-coffee-yet voice.

"Something's happened, Daniel. I need your help."

He clears his throat. "Just tell me what you want me to do."

"Meet me at the mailboxes to talk in thirty minutes?"

He says he will.

Daisy is still sleeping. Thankfully, she did not swear me to
secrecy about what she told me, although keeping someone safe is
more important than any secret.

When I make it to the mailboxes, Daniel is already waiting. I
tell him what Daisy told me, and his shock comes out in anger. He
offers to kill the bastard. I entertain the idea of Jerry's demise
before telling him my plan.

"We need him to know that Daisy isn't alone," I say. "That she has people looking after her. That he has to stop."

His brow crumpled, Daniel nods in agreement. I remember the time Mary Jane and I went to him and told him that Johnny was scaring us. Within minutes we were on our way to the Monroe cabin to confront Johnny. Daniel didn't hesitate then, and he doesn't hesitate now. I tell him I'm not sure what I'll do next but that I'll keep him posted.

Then I go back to the house and call June and ask her if I can come over. I tell her it's important, and that I need to talk to Horatio, too. She says she will put the coffee on.

My final call of the morning is to Bee. Hearing her answer the telephone calms me. I picture her sitting at the kitchen table in the small house we used to live in together. Then I tell her what Daisy told me. Her reaction is swift. She asks what we should do, and I hear her searching for tissues. Whenever Bee gets angry, tears always follow.

"She doesn't want Jerry to get in trouble," I say.

"But we have to tell the authorities," Bee says. "She's just a child. She doesn't get to decide."

"I think she's already starting to regret she told me," I say.

"Well, I'm so glad she did," Bee says. "How long has it been going on?"

"Sounds like months," I say. "I keep thinking that it's good that nothing's happened yet, but the fact that Jerry is even going into her room—"

"I know," Bee says. "Bad stuff has happened, just not the worst."

Bee sighs, and for several seconds, we are silent on the phone, trying to think of what to do, thinking of Daisy.

My hands begin to shake holding the phone. Until now, I hadn't realized how absolutely furious I am.

"I never liked Jerry," I say between gritted teeth, not that she needs reminding. "What do you do when your granddaughter

confides that someone is hurting her, and then insists that they not get into trouble?"

"You protect her," Bee says. "You do what's right, and hope she forgives you. Let me check around and find out what the protocol is for things like this."

We agree to talk later. Before we end our call, Bee asks if I am okay.

"Not really," I say, "but I'm going over to June's as soon as we get off the phone." I don't tell Bee of my plan. It isn't really fully formed yet, and I imagine she wouldn't go along with it anyway.

"I'm so glad Daisy is with you this summer," Bee says. "I like how far away you are from Jerry."

I agree.

After we say our goodbyes, I leave a note for Daisy on the kitchen table with June's telephone number, telling her to call when she gets up. Knowing her usual sleeping patterns, I will probably be home before that happens. I go back to Mama's room to get dressed. Not only am I dealing with Mama's death, but now, I must face a genuine threat to Daisy. The only thing I know for sure is that I can't drop this bombshell on Lily when she's so far away. For now, it is my dilemma to deal with, and action is required.

Thirty minutes later, I am sitting in June's kitchen. We wait for Horatio to return from working with the beehives. In the meantime, June pours me a cup of coffee and gives me a biscuit with butter and honey. The biscuits aren't as good as Mama's but close to it, and the honey is marvelous. Until that moment, I hadn't realized I was hungry.

"You sounded so worried over the phone," June says. "What's happened?"

"Should we wait for Horatio?"

She looks out the back window. "He might be busy for a while."

I hesitate. The words are hard to even contemplate, much less

say. "Daisy told me something when we were walking home last night," I say.

June's expression darkens, as though she already knows what I might say.

"I saw something in the cards," she says.

"What did you see?" I remember how June suddenly stopped reading Daisy's fortune.

"It was something dark," June says. "A pattern from the past."

I lower my voice. "Her father is coming into her room at night."

June winces and damns Jerry to hell. I repeat her sentiments.

"Do you know what I realized last night?" I ask. "That Daisy is the same age I was when Johnny attacked me."

Our eyes meet. "Is this coincidence or fate?" I ask her.

"It's like an echo of what happened before," June says.

"So history is repeating itself, but with a different twist?"

June nods. We look at each other as though we have just figured out that two plus two equals four.

"But maybe it's also an opportunity to set it right," June says. "So that it never happens again."

"How?" I am genuinely curious. If I had known how to set things right so that this wouldn't happen to Daisy, I would have done it a long time ago.

"It's like putting a stick in the bike spokes," she says. "You do everything you can to stop the pattern."

I wish I understood.

Horatio walks into the kitchen. "Good morning, Miss Wildflower."

I return his good morning, even though I'm not so sure it is. While he makes himself a cup of coffee, I think about what June said. How do you break a pattern you didn't even know existed?

When Horatio joins us at the table, June tells him what has happened. His dark eyes appear to become even darker.

"Round up three men, Miss Wildflower. I can be one of them. A

predator needs to know he is being watched. He needs to be sent a message."

"I was thinking the same thing, Horatio. Jerry needs to know that Daisy isn't alone. There's strength in numbers, right?"

Horatio nods.

"I've already talked to Daniel," I say. "He's willing to do anything we need."

But who will be the third? I think of Victor. Victor stood up for me even after Mary Jane abandoned me. But would he be willing to confront Jerry? It is a lot to ask of anyone.

"Daisy won't like this plan," I say.

"But Daisy is the prey, Miss Wildflower, as you were with Johnny Monroe. Children must never be prey."

Horatio reminds me of Daddy sometimes. An honorable man.

"I'll talk to Victor," I say.

I stand to leave, and June hugs me. "Daisy is fortunate to have you," she says.

"Is she?" I ask, already wishing I had done more when I first noticed how she had changed.

"She is fortunate," June repeats. She holds me by both shoulders, looking into my eyes like she did when I was a young mother and overwhelmed. I take a deep breath.

"Do not underestimate how important this is," she says. "What you do at this moment will affect seven generations forward, and seven generations back. Actions taken today will heal old wounds and prevent new wounds."

"You're scaring me," I say with an uneasy smile.

June laughs a short laugh. "Well, I don't mean to. It's just that people don't realize how one choice can change everything."

I tell her that I understand.

When I arrive at Victor's, it is nine o'clock, and he is finishing breakfast. He invites me in and asks if he can fix me something to eat. I decline but join him at the table.

"I didn't expect to see you so soon," he says. "Everything okay?"

"I need your help, Victor."

"Of course," he says, sitting forward in his chair.

I tell him that what I am about to say to him must be kept in confidence. He assures me that Mary Jane is still asleep in the guest room. We carry our two coffees and sit on his porch in two large wicker chairs for further privacy.

I tell him why I'm there.

"You can count me in," he says. "We can take Mary Jane's Caddy. It's big enough to carry all of us."

"But don't tell her why," I say, thinking of the Katy's Ridge grapevine.

He agrees.

As expected, Daisy is still asleep when I return. I let her sleep. Despite my fatigue, I pull together the plan, calling everyone to arrange that we meet at eleven A.M. tomorrow so we can be in Nashville after lunch.

By early afternoon, Daisy is up and pretending that what she said last night never happened. After she eats, she disappears into the backyard. Physical exertion is probably the best thing for her right now. Meanwhile, I am preoccupied with my plan.

My sister Amy knocks on the front door and follows me into the kitchen. I am surprised to see her. Amy isn't the type to just drop by to chat; that would be more like Meg. She makes herself a glass of iced tea and sits at the table.

"Word's gotten around about what you intend to do," she says. Her thin lips form an almost perfect line.

Within seconds I realize that I have underestimated the Katy's Ridge grapevine.

"Who told you about this?" I ask, hands on my hips, standing at the kitchen sink. Victor would never tell someone about our plan. Nor would Daniel or Horatio.

"What does it matter," she says with a huff.

"It matters to me," I say. "This is about Daisy, my granddaughter, your great-niece."

"I haven't told anyone else," she says, and I wonder if this is true.

"Who told you?" I ask a second time.

She hesitates before confirming that it was Mary Jane who overheard Victor and me on the front porch.

"She must have been hiding in the bushes to overhear us," I say.

Amy scoffs. "You're so naïve, Louisa May."

I know she is using my old name on purpose to irritate me. I wonder what she means about me being naïve. Not that I have any inclination to invite her thoughts.

"You need to keep your nose out of it," she says, sounding just like Mama. "This is none of your business."

"My granddaughter is none of my business?" I stand taller, feeling the full measure of my feistiness. "I am not in the mood for your holier-than-thou act, Amy." An act that seems to increase in intensity the older she gets.

"How do you know she's even telling the truth?" Amy taps her foot, but I refuse to be blindsided again. "Girls her age are prone to exaggeration, you know. You don't want to go accusing an innocent man."

My temper rises like the first tiny bubbles in a pot that promises to build to a rolling boil.

"I believe her," I say, my voice just above a seethe.

"You could get in a lot of trouble for this," she says with another toe tap.

"What do you propose I do?" I ask, wondering what caused Amy to turn into this person. Even Mama could be open-minded if an occasion called for it.

"Let sleeping dogs lie," she says.

"Well, that mangy dog in Nashville isn't sleeping. He's got his paws on Daisy."

We stare at each other. I remember how guilty Amy felt after Johnny because she didn't say anything about what he had done to her.

"If you had told me about Johnny, I might not have been hurt," I say to her.

She narrows her eyes and then crosses her arms.

"It will sort itself out without your help," her words clipped.

I wonder if my other sisters feel the same as Amy about confronting Jerry. Not Jo; she is more like Daniel. As for Meg, unless the news story has made it to Hollywood, I doubt she has an opinion about it.

Amy stands as if to reason with me, not knowing that her argument is making me even firmer in my position. She repeats what she has already said. It's all I can do not to slap her.

"If women don't protect girls, Amy, what hope do we have?"

"You won't be able to go back and undo this," she says. "Jerry is a prominent man. He has a lot of power. He could do things to you."

I slam the dish towel on the counter, refusing to say aloud the words I want to say. Words guaranteed to hurt her. Words telling her it's a good thing she never had children if she were going to turn a blind eye.

"Just stay out of it," I tell her. Disappointment undergirds my anger. "And don't spread this around. Tell Mary Jane not to spread it around, either." I pause, thinking how odd it is that Amy is the one Mary Jane told. "By the way, since when are you and Mary Jane friends?"

"She came into my shop this morning," Amy says, looking away.

"Well, this is none of her business, and it's none of yours, either."

She turns to leave. "This is a mistake," she says. "Just wait and see."

Her threat sounds like a curse and gets the desired effect. Within seconds, doubts creep into my resolve. Doubts that warn me that I am doing the wrong thing. Doubts that insist that it won't matter anyway and that somehow Daisy will be the one to pay for it.

CHAPTER TWENTY-SIX

Daisy

When I hide my shovel under the back porch, I hear voices coming from the kitchen. Who is talking to Gran? I wash my hands at the outdoor spigot, proud of the territory I covered today. I have mapped out the area in front of the boulder as a grid. Every day I dig a foot down before covering it back up if I don't find anything. Joseph McAllister wouldn't have buried something deeper than that, considering he was telling his wife to dig it up if anything happened to him.

When I go into the kitchen, Gran's sister Amy is leaving. Gran's cheeks are red like she just ran a sprint.

"I need to talk to you about something," she says. Gran sits at the table, and I join her.

I remember my confession the night before, and my face warms. I wish now I'd kept my mouth shut.

"I need you to trust me," Gran says.

My shoulders edge toward my ears. "Trust you about what?"

"With what I'm about to tell you."

My heart races toward the door, but the rest of me stays put.

"We're going to Nashville tomorrow," Gran says.

"Why?"

"At no time will you be in any danger," she says. "I promise you. This is all about getting you safe again."

"What have you done, Gran?" I ask, even though I don't really want to know. My right knee jiggles the way it does whenever I have a big test at school.

"We will only be in Nashville for the afternoon," Gran says, "and then we'll come straight back here."

"What are we doing there?" I ask.

"Let me worry about that," Gran says.

My insides get as jittery as my leg.

"I'll make a deal with you," she says thoughtfully. "If you trust me and go along with my plan, I'll let you drive the pickup every day for the next two weeks."

My knee stops shaking. My insides calm. Turns out I am a sucker for a carrot dangling in front of me, if the carrot is learning how to drive.

"Agreed," I say.

THE NEXT MORNING Gran and I get into the pickup. As part of trusting her, I am not to ask questions. All I know is that we are going to Nashville. To my surprise, we go back to where we had dinner a couple of nights ago. The Jeep and the giant Cadillac are still in the driveway. It feels like a hundred years have passed since we were here, even though it was just the other night.

Victor comes out and gives us a wave. Gran thanks him for helping us, and I don't even know what he is helping us with. We get into the massive Cadillac the color of the filling of a chocolate eclair. It reeks of heavy perfume. Instantly, the three of us lower the windows to let in the fresh air.

Gran makes me sit between her and Victor, saying we have more people to pick up.

"More people?" I ask.

She nods. Gran has put her hair up in a French braid like she does when she wants to look good. She wears a flowery blouse with her best jeans.

I remind myself that trusting her means I get to drive the pickup every day for the next two weeks. I would rob a bank for that, maybe even embezzle money, if I even knew what that meant.

Victor smells of aftershave and coffee. His aftershave competes with the perfume in the car. The perfume wins. Less than a minute later, we pull up in my Great-Uncle Daniel's driveway. He comes out and gets in the back seat. Nellie waves from the porch. Something is up, and nobody is talking.

Victor drives to the Sectors' place. Gran's friend Horatio gets in the back seat with Daniel. I am relieved Adam isn't coming, too.

We drive out of Katy's Ridge and through the dying small town of Rocky Bluff and then get on the interstate. Windows go up, but the perfume smell has barely faded. The others talk. I listen to determine our destination. When I feel uneasy, I focus on the dangling carrot with car keys at the end.

We take the main exit to downtown Nashville. It is busy, but we manage to find a parking place on the street. I recognize where we are now. We are close to where my father works. My back stiffens. I turn to Gran with a look that says, *Surely we are not going to see my father.*

"Trust me," she says.

The five of us get out of the car and walk past my father's Mercedes in the parking lot. I haven't been to my father's office in years. Inside the grand foyer, I realize how important he is. He is a record producer in Nashville. I've been to Mom's agent's office, and it is nothing like this. In the lobby, my father's name is in gold

lettering. His office is on the top floor of the building—the entire top floor. Gran pushes the button to call the elevator.

A fluttering starts in my chest that reminds me of the hummingbirds flitting around Aunt Sadie's wildflowers in the front of her house. But the hummingbird in my chest isn't seeking nectar; it's trapped in a building and desperately trying to get out.

"Wait," I say to Gran. "We can't do this. You need to call this whole thing off."

"Trust me," Gran repeats. Her look is one of pure determination.

An army of old men, along with my grandmother, steps into the elevator. They hold the door open for me, but my legs won't move. I am frozen in the lobby. Gran steps out of the elevator and takes my hand, guiding me inside. Daniel pushes the elevator button. The elevator dings with each floor, my fear rising to new heights. We are going to my father's office.

On the sixth ding, the door opens, and we enter a large hallway leading to an office. My father's name is painted on the glass door. Once we get inside, we approach a woman sitting at a desk. She reminds me of a younger version of my latest stepmom, who was also his secretary before they got married.

"We're here to see Jerry," Gran says to her, checking her pocket watch as if we have an appointment.

The woman rolls her desk chair back to get the full view of us. "What is this about?" she asks.

"Tell him his daughter, Daisy, is here to see him," Gran says.

"He's in a meeting." The secretary looks down at her desk as though she is not a very good liar.

"We're not leaving until we see him," Victor says, now standing next to Gran. Daniel and Horatio step forward, too. It never occurred to me that someday, a quartet of senior citizens would have my back. I stand straighter, realizing I am not alone.

The secretary pauses and then looks at me. "Is it important?" she asks.

I tell her it is. She picks up the phone and tells my father that I am waiting to see him.

When he opens the door, his smile fades as soon as he sees Gran.

"What's going on?" he asks me. "Are you okay? Who are these people?" He and Gran exchange looks. I almost expect them to hiss or growl at each other.

"We need to talk to you, Jerry," Gran says.

"What about?" my father asks.

"You'll probably want some privacy," Daniel says, motioning for us to go into his office.

My father hesitates but then tells his secretary to hold his calls. We follow him inside, and he closes the door. When I walk past him, he narrows his eyes at me as if I will live to regret inconveniencing him.

Gold records grace the walls, framed and mounted, most of them my mom's. He sits behind his large wooden desk in a black leather chair. My mouth feels like I've been chewing cotton balls, and my right leg is gearing up for a rumba. The only thing that comforts me is that Gran is here, along with her geriatric posse.

"I'm busy. You need to tell me what this is about and then leave," my father says to me.

"I never liked you, Jerry," Gran begins. "I never understood what Lily saw in you, though I think you took advantage of her innocence when she was first starting out."

"You collected a bunch of country rednecks in my office to tell me this?" My father sits taller in his chair.

Gran walks behind his desk, causing him to swivel.

Even though Gran is tiny compared to him, he lets her speak. Maybe because he thinks this is the quickest way to get her out of his office.

I sit back in my chair, my mouth opening with the revelation that my gran has become a superhero. She tells him that she knows what he is doing and that he has to stop, and that if he doesn't, she will contact the authorities. Meanwhile, my father's threats echo in my mind. Threats that I would break my mom's heart. Threats that if I ever told I would pay. I can't help but wonder what this moment will cost me.

"I see you've been caught up in one of Daisy's lies." He sounds calm. "Don't be embarrassed, Lou. I've been caught up in them, too. Haven't I, Daisy?" He looks at me, and the hummingbirds inside my chest threaten to throw up all over his desk.

"I've been fooled by her just like you have," he begins again, his voice smooth. "Too bad you got these men involved, too. All of you are wasting a perfectly good day for no reason." He pauses and clears his throat, glancing at me to make sure I'm watching. "You see, Daisy has been a pathological liar since she was a young girl. Lily and I even got her into therapy at one point."

"That's not true," Gran says. "Daisy is one of the most truthful people I have ever known."

My father accuses Gran of being gullible. "Didn't Lily tell you about the counseling sessions?"

"Well, yes, she did, but they weren't about Daisy lying."

Lowering my head, I think back to the therapy sessions I was made to attend when I was in third grade. Therapy sessions that were supposed to make me more sociable. As far as I knew, they had nothing to do with lying. At one point, the therapist had me drawing turtles and talking about what it would be like to come out of my shell. Did I have a lying problem, too? Like all kids, I told white lies to keep myself out of trouble. But was it more than that? The room blurs with the beginnings of tears.

Horatio stands. I realize again how tall he is, even taller than my father. He dwarfs Gran, who is still standing by the desk. When

he speaks, his voice is deep and resonates like a bass line walking alongside a melody.

"I know a liar when I see one, and it's not Daisy." Horatio looks straight at my father.

Then Daniel stands, too, as well as Victor.

"It will take a while for the authorities to investigate," Daniel says. "But we are going to make sure that Daisy is safe."

Victor speaks next: "I've done business in Nashville, and I know a couple of judges," he says. "By the time we're finished with you, you'll be ruined. Now tell your daughter that you're sorry for calling her a liar."

Gran and the old men stand around me like giant oaks. I tell myself not to cry.

Daniel reinforces Victor's request: "You need to apologize to your daughter for calling her a liar."

Horatio crosses his arms, looking even more intimidating. No one would ever know this gentleman carves statues of mother bears with her cubs.

"Bee has already called social services," Gran says.

My father laughs. "You're the pervert, not me," he says to Gran with a smile. "You think they'll believe *you*?"

At this moment, I hate my father even more.

"Besides," he begins, "even if what Daisy says is true, you've got no proof. It's her word against mine."

"But I do have proof," I say.

Everyone turns to look at me, including my father. His gaze warns me to keep my mouth shut or else. But what is the *or else*? *Or else* everything will change? *Or else* my mother will realize again that she made a mistake by marrying him? *Or else* he will finally have to admit he did something wrong? Even I know that he will never do that.

"How do you have proof, Daisy?" Gran asks.

"I kept all the dates in a notebook," I begin. It was Karana, in

Island of the Blue Dolphins, who gave me this idea. She marked all the days that she was deserted on the island on a rock. "I also made tape recordings with the tape recorder I got two Christmases ago. I have at least a dozen recordings of him saying things to me that he shouldn't have been saying."

The air in the room shifts, as though all the permanently sealed windows in the high-rise have opened, and a mountain breeze has been let in. My father stands, saying that he will no longer tolerate my lies. But the air has left his balloon. He shoves his way past Victor and Horatio. When he leaves his office, I exhale, not even realizing I had been holding my breath. Gran applauds and walks over and puts an arm around me.

"Do you really have proof?" she asks.

I tell her I do.

"I'm so proud of you," she says. "You were brilliant to make recordings."

"I'm proud of you, too," I say. "And I didn't lie."

"I never doubted that you were telling the truth," she says.

Daniel, Horatio, and Victor agree.

With my father gone, the confrontation over, I sit and lower my head. Tears come like an unexpected afternoon thunderstorm. Gran pulls a chair close and holds my hands, telling me how brave I am. However, I don't feel brave at all. It wouldn't be like my father to let this go so easily. The war has just begun.

CHAPTER TWENTY-SEVEN

Wildflower

Lily returns to the States after her tour. She telephones to tell Daisy and me that her plane has just landed and she is driving back to Katy's Ridge. I decided not to tell her anything about Jerry until her return, and I worry about how she will take the news.

Meanwhile, in the ten days since we confronted Daisy's father, I am getting glimpses of the real Daisy. She is talking more, and I even heard her laughing with Nellie yesterday.

Mama's American flag hangs from the front porch in honor of the Fourth of July. Earlier we picked up Aunt Sadie and brought her back to Mama's house. Keeping my promise, I let Daisy drive us to and from. Now, we all sit on the front porch waiting for Lily.

Sadie sits in Mama's rocker, staring out into the distance, as though deep in thought. Old Rufus, as always, sits at her feet. With so much going on with Daisy, I sometimes forget how much Aunt Sadie might be grieving Mama, and how much I am grieving her

as well. Two huge events have marked the summer of 1982: Mama's death and Daisy's secret coming to light.

A car pulls into the gravel driveway, and Daisy runs down the hill to meet Lily. They emerge in the distance, both smiling. A few years ago, Lily's career took off like a runaway train. A train I am not so sure she knows how to exit. With Lily and Daisy, time together is the issue, not an absence of love and caring. However, I have no idea how Lily is going to react to what Daisy and I need to tell her. According to Bee, many children are not believed, and this can be incredibly damaging, even worse than the abuse.

Daisy carries Lily's overnight bag into the house, while Aunt Sadie and I hug our world traveler, welcoming her home. When she removes her sunglasses, I take note of the dark circles under her eyes. *Be careful what you wish for*, Mama used to say, meaning dreams have their dark side just like everything else.

With Lily's arrival, we sit on the porch. Later, we will walk across the street to Daniel's house for a family barbecue. But right now, it is just the four of us. Mama's broom stands next to the door, reminding us of her absence.

Daisy comes outside carrying a glass of iced tea for her mom. She lets the screen door slap at her heels like I used to do as a girl, an act that drove Mama crazy. Nostalgia floats in on the warm summer breeze, honoring all those arrivals and departures. Thresholds crossed.

Lily and Daisy sit on the porch swing as I lean against one of the posts. I told Lily yesterday on the phone that we had something to talk about when she got here. *Nothing terrible*, I said, which was a lie, but it made no sense for her to worry in advance.

"Okay, I'm here. Tell me what's going on," Lily says.

Sadie, Daisy, and I exchange a look as though wondering who will do the talking. When we got home from Nashville that day, I went over to Aunt Sadie's and told her all about it. That evening, she delivered bottles from a special batch of her prized blackberry

spirits to Daniel, Victor, and Horatio. Sadie seemed to think that a man like Jerry wouldn't admit defeat so readily and predicted that more was coming. I hope she is wrong.

Lily's long earrings sparkle in the early-afternoon sun. Even in jeans, she seems somehow more glamorous than the rest of us. I still remember her on this porch as a girl, singing Daddy's favorite songs, the whole family teary-eyed with wonder. Lily has a gift. A gift that she has put out into the world. Not many people honor their gifts, though some do, and those are usually people I admire. Yet from observing Lily, I know that being admired isn't easy, either.

Meanwhile, Aunt Sadie is quieter than usual, and I wonder if she is spending too much time alone. We exchange looks, but the silent message she sends is that it is Daisy who needs our attention, not her. Daisy and Aunt Sadie have been spending more time together, and that may be part of the change in Daisy. If I had to call it something, I would call it a blossoming.

"Are you the spokesperson for this little meeting?" Lily asks me.

I tell her I am. Daisy sends me a grateful look.

"Then tell me," Lily says.

"First of all, there's nothing to worry about," I begin. "Nobody has died. Nobody is hurt or sick."

"Well, that's good." Her laugh dies quickly when we don't join in.

"My friends and I took care of it," I begin. "But I need to tell you what happened."

"Something happened?" she says. "You said it wasn't anything bad."

"We didn't want to disturb you on your tour," Sadie says.

Last night I lost sleep deciding how we might tell Lily, and now those thoughts have flown out of my head.

"Are you in trouble?" Lily looks at Daisy, who lowers her eyes,

as though courage is needed and she can't seem to find where she last put it.

"No, Daisy isn't in trouble," I say. "But Jerry is."

"Jerry?" Her voice makes a crescendo.

I take a deep breath, asking God for courage, and I wonder if this means that we are on speaking terms again. Then I tell Lily everything, including how I rounded up three good men to go with me to Nashville and confront Jerry. I tell her about Jerry calling Daisy a liar, and how Daisy kept a record and recordings of the incidents.

Lily's eyes widen as the story unfolds and then fill with tears. When I finish, she wraps her arms around Daisy. The two of them hold each other and cry. Lily says over and over how sorry she is, that she had no idea. Within seconds, my fear that Lily might not believe Daisy evaporates. She has done the right thing, the essential thing, which is to believe.

Instead of mother and daughter, they look like sisters sitting there, their heads touching and tears falling. At this moment, it feels like what happened with Johnny was a disguised blessing if this many years later, we can be here for Daisy. Aunt Sadie nods and rocks as though she is in the midst of a prayer meeting and the Holy Spirit is visiting. I find myself getting teary-eyed, too, but then realize the story is far from finished.

"We need to decide what to do next," I say.

Lily turns to me, as though just now realizing this song has another verse.

"Bee spent an entire afternoon on the phone with an attorney," I begin. "Even though Daisy has proof, the lawyer didn't think it was wise to take it to court because of the damage the exposure might do to Daisy. Even more damage than a custody case might do. So we were basically left with no good answers," I conclude.

Daisy wipes tears with the bottom of her shirt, and Lily puts her arm around her.

"We'll get through this," she says to Daisy.

Meanwhile, I hold on to the promise of healing seven generations forward and seven generations back that June told me about. I want to believe that as a family, we can recover.

"The McAllister women have always made the best of the hand life dealt us, as have most women," Aunt Sadie says.

I think of Mama again, and her hard life of always plowing to the end of the row. We need time to grieve before continuing to plow.

"Never underestimate the McAllister women," I say. "We're sturdy stock." Although at this moment I don't feel sturdy at all.

"I'm going to take some time off," Lily says. "Nashville can live without me for a few weeks. Okay if I stay here with you?" she asks Daisy.

Daisy smiles, though I imagine we're both wondering if this will really happen.

June spoke of it as a pattern repeating from the past until someone dares to break it. Like putting a stick in the spoke of a moving bicycle tire. Daisy survived the crash. Now, these mountains can help her heal.

CHAPTER TWENTY-EIGHT

Daisy

My mom keeps looking at me as if I am a baby bird that has prematurely fallen from its nest, and she is somehow responsible. I tell her I am going for a walk. She offers to go with me, but I tell her I need to be alone.

"Are you sure?" she asks.

I tell her that I am sure.

The truth is, I need a break from all the attention. I want to dig for treasure, and this is one secret I want to keep to myself. Pretending to take a walk, I descend the hill and turn right at the mailboxes. Then I circle back through the woods, the house in sight the entire time.

Gran and Mom are on the front porch having a second cup of coffee. They are talking, probably about me, but I can't hear them. I imagine they won't go into the backyard for anything. At least, this is my hope. Later this afternoon the family is gathering for the Fourth of July at Nellie's, which promises to be overwhelming. Gran says it will be my chance to meet all my cousins, firsts and

seconds. I wonder if I should take paper and pencil and take notes on my abundance of family. This is the opposite of living on an island alone like Karana, and I suddenly understand what a loss this was for her.

In the back is the large boulder that is bigger than the chicken coop. I use a smaller rock as a stepping-stone and climb up from behind. From the kitchen window, only the top half of the boulder can be seen, as well as the forest up above. While I'm digging, no one will even know I am there unless they walk around the side of the house.

For now, I sit on top of the rock overlooking the small barn to my left and the chicken coop to my right. In front of me is the back of Granny McAllister's house. Within seconds I hear the voice of a young Wildflower talking to her friend Mary Jane about Wild-flower's father. I am relieved when the voices fade.

Welcoming the quiet, I take a deep breath, suddenly realizing how worried I was that Mom might not believe me. Or that she might blame me or be angry at me. But my mom has been none of those. If anything, she seems to blame herself. I don't want that, either. I just want this whole thing to be over.

I've been digging for days, and so far I haven't found anything except an old kitchen fork and a quarter. It's not like I have a trea-sure map with a big *X* marking the spot. All that Joseph McAllister said was that he had buried some important things near the boul-der. It's big, and that's a lot of space.

It rained last night, and the boulder has a small puddle in one of its crevices that a bee is drinking from. From here I can see where I've already dug. Sections stretch out below me like hopscotch squares. Five of them, for five different digs. The moss helps me hide what I have done. It comes up in sheets, and I return it once I finish, like a rug in a movie covering a secret trapdoor. I didn't realize I was strong enough to dig a hole. I'm not that

athletic. But there is something about doing it that feels good. I am getting stronger.

I think of Joseph McAllister, my great-grandfather, and ask his spirit to tell me where he hid the metal box with the McAllister treasure. I wait for a response and get nothing. I wonder again why Granny McAllister didn't dig up the gold coins and make her life more comfortable. I guess there is a chance she did and just didn't tell anyone, and that all this digging will be for nothing. Yet, somehow, I am okay with that, too.

There is little proof of a windfall, given the state of things before Mom paid for the renovation of the place. I overheard her on the telephone, talking to contractors. They were surprised that the old house hadn't fallen down around Granny McAllister. You wouldn't know that by looking at it now, though. It seems almost totally new.

After climbing off the boulder, I go and get the shovel under the porch, along with the old pair of thick garden gloves I found in the back of Gran's pickup. I imagine Gran digs holes all the time working for the plant nursery. She is strong for an old woman. I pull up the big pieces of moss and lay them to the side and cut out a new square, marking the space. Then I dig around the roots and rocks and loosen the soil. After a few minutes, I am sweating like crazy. I am about six inches down, not deep enough to even bury a baby bird. With big stabs, I let the tip of the shovel explore, listening for anything that sounds like metal hitting metal. Nothing. I go down another six inches then finally give up on this square of the grid.

"What are you doing?"

Nellie's voice makes me jump. She carries a basket to gather eggs and walks over to me. She looks down at my hopscotch squares, and at the hole.

"You digging your way to China?" She laughs.

My brain rushes for a reasonable explanation of why I'm digging holes in Granny McAllister's backyard.

"I just needed some exercise," I tell her. "Gran says I don't get outside enough." Neither statement is true.

"So, you're digging holes just to have something to do?"

I nod and smile as though waiting for her to recognize my brilliance. She rolls her eyes instead.

"You're weird sometimes, Daisy." She walks toward the coop. "I've got to see what the chickens have left. Mama wants to make deviled eggs for the picnic, and our chickens had a lackluster performance today. They don't like the heat. You like deviled eggs? I love them."

I imagine a permanently perky Nellie married to Adam Sector and rustling up eggs from her own chickens someday. Eggs she will feed several children of different ages who all look like Adam.

"Hey, do you mind not telling anybody about what I'm doing?" I lean against the shovel, trying to downplay the importance of my request.

"Sure," she says, as if she can understand why I might want to keep my digging a secret.

Nellie isn't really the type to go digging for treasure, not unless a river runs through it. Her biggest secret is probably a *Brides* magazine buried underneath the sweaters in her sweater drawer.

While waiting on Nellie to gather eggs, I look up into the trees, sunlight sparkling among the limbs. Until now, I never noticed that places could be this beautiful. Seconds later, a banjo picks out a slow song, its melody as pretty as the place. I imagine my great-grandfather sitting on the back porch playing for me while I dig.

Nellie waves before leaving, and I hope she doesn't tell Mom and Gran that she just saw me in the backyard. This might prompt them to come see what I am doing.

With Nellie gone, I scatter the dirt back over the hole, spread it out and then stamp it down, and cover it again with moss. I

think of the grid I have mapped out in my mind. If I do one square a day, I will have the entire area covered in ten more days. That will take more sneaking around, but I think it is doable.

"Daisy?" I hear my mom call from the front porch. "You need to come get ready for the picnic."

I can't remember her ever calling me to come home before. In Nashville, I am seldom outside. I don't yell back because I don't want her to be able to track me down. I hide the shovel and gloves under the porch again. An orange cat sits on an old wooden chair nearby. Did he hear the banjo, too?

I pet him. "Are you missing Granny McAllister?" I ask.

He leans into my touch.

"The humans get all the attention when someone dies, and the pets go unnoticed," I say.

He purrs.

"My mom is calling me, but I'll be back later." His meow sounds sad, as though resigned to being alone.

"I promise." I rub his ears to seal the promise.

Mom calls again.

Making as little noise as possible, I set off through the woods again. I arrive at the bottom of the driveway and then come up the hill huffing and puffing from all the running. It feels good to run, though. The only running I ever do at home is during PE, and I never get to enjoy it because I'm trying not to look stupid.

"Where have you been?" Mom asks.

"Just around," I say.

"Why are your knees covered in mud?"

I look down, the evidence of my treasure hunting in full view.

"I fell, but I'm okay." I seem to be setting a record for lying today.

Mom tells me to wash up, that we are about to go over to Daniel's for the Fourth of July picnic. I answer with a "yes ma'am"

that causes her to smile. My newfound manners have surprised even me and have accidentally drawn more attention to myself.

In the meantime, I imagine finding the metal box full of McAllister treasure and presenting it to her. She will laugh about how well I hid my secret from her. Then, since Mom is always searching for new song ideas, she will probably write one about digging for buried treasure and the surprises that come. I can almost hear it now.

My hands ache from digging, and I go inside to take a shower and put on clean clothes. When I am in the backyard, I feel like a detective, or maybe an explorer. This is precisely something Karana might do if she was trapped in Katy's Ridge instead of on the island with the blue dolphins. When we read the book in my English class last spring, my teacher, Miss Nelson, asked us what we thought that Karana learned about herself during her time on the deserted island. Maybe that is a good question for me, too.

The digging isn't only about unearthing the treasure, but something more profound. Maybe I am discovering things I never knew about myself. Like how sneaky I can be, and also how much I enjoy being outside and putting my hands in the dirt, even if it is just to dig a hole and then cover it up again. I never thought about what I might learn from all the digging. It seems related to all this family I never knew I had. Treasure of a different sort.

CHAPTER TWENTY-NINE

Wildflower

The Fourth of July barbecue is at Daniel and Jo's, as it is every year, though I haven't attended in ages. My sisters are here, as well as their spouses, kids, and grandkids. I estimate forty people, maybe more. All my family is together again, this time without Mama.

Aunt Sadie goes into the house to help Jo, and Lily introduces Daisy to her different cousins. It is good to see Lily in Katy's Ridge again, and even better to see her with Daisy. I see resilience in Daisy I never knew she had. She is taking off more on her own. Exploring the woods, learning the roads. I wonder if all that digging out by the boulder has anything to do with it. She doesn't know I know about that, but I like to see her occupied in a physical activity instead of with a book. Not that I have a problem with books. But there is something to be said for fresh air, too.

As a girl, I dug all kinds of holes, created forts, climbed trees, and built treehouses, mostly with my boy cousins. Mama was none

the wiser. Or maybe she knew all along, too. It occurs to me that I may not have known Mama at all.

It is warm and humid. A typical summer day in the south. Daniel stands in the backyard at the barbecue pit under the shade of the maple trees. He waves when he sees me. His three-year-old grandson, Matthew, hugs his knees, looking up as if Daniel is one of those giant redwoods in California I've seen pictures of. When I approach, Daniel asks me how Daisy is.

"We told Lily an hour or so ago," I say.

His eyebrows lift. "How'd she take it?"

"Better than I thought, though I suspect her anger is coming in on a slow train like mine did. At first the news is sobering and tragic, but then you get mad."

He nods. "I invited Victor, Horatio, and June to the cookout, too."

"I'm glad," I say. In truth, they feel like family, too.

Danny, Jo and Daniel's son, approaches with his younger wife, Louise. It is hard to believe he is middle-aged. She keeps a protective arm on her enormous pregnant belly, and a smile doesn't leave her face. The three-year-old belongs to her, too. What must it be like to be pregnant and happy about it? Even my overzealous imagination has trouble envisioning that.

June and Horatio walk up the hill, having just arrived. June carries a casserole dish and juggles it as we hug.

"How did your talk go with Lily?" she asks.

"So far, so good," I say. "Lily said all the right things."

"I bet Daisy is glad that's over," she says. "At least the telling part. As you know, this is a dragon with a long tail. Many parts to slay."

Horatio stands nearby and nods. June is right. It has taken me decades to get over the long tail of what Johnny did to me. I wonder if I am fully over it now. I think of Matt Monroe, from the same family of dragons. I feel a twist in my gut.

"Thank you again for coming with us," I say to Horatio.

"You're welcome, Miss Wildflower. If you need me again, just let me know."

They walk over to the picnic tables to put down June's casserole dish. We will have time to visit later. Grabbing a soda from the ice-filled cooler, I find a lawn chair and sit, family and friends gathered around me. We speak of simple things. The weather. The kids. The jobs. It is a relief from the seriousness of the earlier conversation with Lily and Daisy. Yet life has a way of becoming serious for all of us, whether we speak of it at a family picnic or not.

My nephew Bolt, Jo and Daniel's oldest son, was named after Daddy, but the nickname given to him as a boy has stuck with him forever. Bolt is here with his wife and three teenage sons and their various girlfriends. Nellie stands on the porch, along with Adam Sector and Daisy. Of the three, Nellie is the only one talking.

Nat, my sister Amy's son and my favorite nephew, comes over to say hello. He looks just like his father, Nathan, who is celebrating the Fourth of July in the cemetery with Daddy. Nat is an English teacher at Rocky Bluff High School. His wife, Sally, is in the house with Jo, and his four kids—ranging in age from five to fifteen—are scattered among the crowd.

Amy's daughter Lizzie, who was obnoxious as a child, is in a cluster of the family standing near the picnic tables, a dog at her side. Unmarried, Lizzie works as a dental hygienist in Harriman. Every year I receive a Christmas card that includes an Olan Mills photograph of her with her current dog.

My sister Meg waves from the steps of the house. She is there with Janie, Cecil's daughter from his previous marriage, who is still as nondescript as ever.

Tired of sitting, I walk to the back of Daniel's property near his old barn. In the distance, Daniel, Victor, and Horatio stand under a giant maple tree. Heroes, in my mind. I wonder if they are talking

about our Nashville trip. For all we know, we have disturbed a hornet's nest.

Victor salutes me with a bottle of beer. I bow my head in his direction. Sometimes I wish I was attracted to him. It would make life easier, for sure. But it is our friendship that I hope to develop from here on if he is willing.

As evening falls, a bonfire is lit near the barn—our version of fireworks. Music plays from a distant radio. Laughter erupts at different times from different groupings, but within minutes, everyone has gathered to watch the fire. Lily and Daisy pull up lawn chairs next to mine. It is so unusual to have us all in one place, I find myself trying to memorize the scene. I didn't think to bring my camera with me when Mama took ill and certainly didn't mean to stay longer than a day or two.

I catch Daisy studying me, and with a glance, I ask her how she is. She shrugs, followed by the faintest of smiles. But even her shrug seems somehow lighter. Sitting by the fire, Lily appears to relax, though her attention has not left Daisy. Behind the smile, I imagine she is thinking about what to do next.

Meanwhile, Meg escorts Aunt Sadie to a chair in front of the fire. Our eyes meet, and she offers a reassuring smile.

All is well, she tells me, *even though it may not seem that way for a while.*

I want to believe her.

The fire crackles, the smoke rising to the heavens like prayers. For centuries, our ancestors have gathered in front of mesmerizing fires. We are simply the latest. Shadows of flames illuminate the barn, dancing across the old boards like the first black-and-white films without sound—the human story dancing across the screen.

I think again of that night, so many years ago, when Jo was giving birth to Bolt, and I was pregnant and next in line. Terrified, I went into that barn to escape Jo's cries. Mama noticed I was gone

and came and found me. When she walked into that barn with her lantern fully lit, shadows flickered against the inside boards. The light played tricks, and I thought Mama was the gold Mary. In times of trouble, everyone needs an angel to call on. Real or imagined.

I look over at Daisy, who stares into the fire. History repeats itself until we break the patterns, June said. I wonder what pattern I need to break now. Then I think of Mama gone to be with Daddy and wonder if they are watching. Life is brief and full of loss. But I am convinced that we are observed from the shadows by those who came before.

"I think I'll go home," I say to Lily and Daisy. "It's been a big day." I stand. They say they understand. Earlier, we told the truth to one another about hard things. We survived. A quiet revolution ensued.

After several goodbyes, I walk down the hill, letting go of the warmth of the fire, the warmth of family. The world gets quiet again. My eyes adjust to the new darkness. I have walked this path thousands of times. My heart has memorized each step. As the moon reaches toward fullness, I appreciate the light it provides. I also thank the gold Mary for not deserting me.

Crossing the road, I continue up the driveway and the dirt path beyond. The Redbud Sisters gather to my left in the dark. I wave. I imagine them waving back. When I smell jasmine, I know exactly where I am. It was afternoon when we left, and I wish I'd thought to leave a light on in the house. If Mama had been here, she would have remembered, but the house will be filled with light soon enough.

The moon winks at me through the trees. When your parents are gone, it is easy to feel next in line. I stop on the path, my secret sense giving me a nudge. I listen for footsteps. I hear nothing except night sounds. Night sounds that Daddy taught us never to fear.

Then I get a whiff of Daddy's pipe tobacco. I tell myself that I should have skipped Aunt Sadie's blackberry spirits when toasting our country's independence. But as I begin to walk again, footsteps join mine. Mama always chided me for my overactive imagination, and while Daddy believed in spirits, it wouldn't be like him to haunt a place, but here he is.

"Daddy?" My voice sounds small like I am a girl again.

"Wildflower?" Daddy says from the darkness.

Tears fill my eyes. Stranger things have happened in these mountains, I tell myself. Aunt Sadie has been talking to spirits for years.

"Are you in heaven?" I ask him.

"Something like," he says.

"Something like?"

He chuckles. "You were always so full of questions."

I always thought it was Lily who was that way, but maybe she got it from me. Then I remember all those questions I used to ask Daddy to ask God when I would sit on his grave. Questions like, *Why does lightning strike old dead trees?*

Daddy chuckles. "Because they call the lightning to them to help them go," he says.

"They call it? Like they ask for the lightning's help?"

Silence follows. Perhaps it is a daydream instead of a night one. But I have felt Daddy's presence more than once since I've been back in Katy's Ridge.

"Let me see you," I whisper.

For nearly forty years, the one thing I've wished for when I've blown out a birthday candle is to see Daddy again. I can't believe it has been that long.

"I can't do that," he says, sounding as disappointed as I feel.

"I still miss you," I say.

"I know you do," he says softly. "But I'm right here. I've been here the whole time."

My tears fall in earnest.

Nearing the house, I feel his presence walk away from me in the night. "Is Mama with you?" I call after him.

He begins to whistle, and the tune fades with each step.

Moonlight sprinkles across the porch steps to light my way. I open the door and walk inside, announcing to the old house that I am home.

CHAPTER THIRTY

Daisy

At the barbecue, Nellie hovered around Adam, but it was me he kept looking at around the edges of the conversation. Nellie isn't clueless, but she possesses a stubborn version of hope. I can't imagine being that way. Not that it matters. Adam is much older than me—seventeen—and I'll be leaving soon to go back to school in Nashville.

Mom announced at the picnic yesterday that she plans to stay in Katy's Ridge for a few days. Last night I overheard her talking to her agent on the phone. Her last words to him were: *I'm doing it. Figure it out.* We haven't talked about my father, but I can tell she's thinking about it by the way she looks at me.

We stayed at Sadie's house last night, and when Gran picked me up this morning for my driving lesson, Mom was still sleeping. Gran says Mom's been overdoing it for years and to let her sleep. But I wonder how long it will last before Mom feels like she has to get back to work and not upset her fans.

I question if I will ever see my father again and if I even want

to. I've gone over what happened in his office a hundred times. The memory causes me to cringe, and also feel proud. People stood up for me and told my father his behavior was unacceptable. I can't imagine what will happen now.

I park the pickup at Granny McAllister's house, and Gran congratulates me on a good job.

"I'm not ready to go inside just yet, you want to take a walk?" she asks.

I tell her yes, even though I planned to dig at the boulder in the back when Gran got busy doing other things. Lately, she's been making lots of phone calls to get Granny McAllister's affairs in order.

Gran pulls out her pocket watch to note the time, and I remember the owner of the watch playing his banjo for Granny McAllister before she died. After the funeral, when Gran showed me some photographs she found, I had proof that I didn't imagine Joseph. It was him.

We walk along the road at first, but then we stop in front of a small boulder and a twisted tree.

"When I was a girl, I was the only one who used this path," she says. "Nobody in my family even knew it was here."

"What kind of tree is that?" I ask.

"It's a dogwood," Gran says. "Its branches are twisted like that because all its life it's been reaching for sunlight."

When I look up, I see other trees, all with branches reaching toward the sky, worshipping the sun.

"This is the secret path that I told you about. It leads to the back of the cemetery," Gran says. "I used to go and visit Daddy up there every other day, sometimes more."

I follow her into the thick forest. The path she follows disappears in places, but she keeps going as if she could find her way blindfolded. Gran is quieter than usual. The deeper we go into the woods, the deeper she appears to go into her thoughts.

We stop at a little bridge. I get out the rabbit's foot she gave me, and it makes her smile.

"Daniel and Nathan built this new footbridge the year your mama was born," Gran says.

Voices from the past confirm her statement. Two men talk about a third, and I hear Wildflower's voice, too.

Where could he be hiding? a man asks.

Then Wildflower evidently sees something shiny in the ravine, and they take off to find it. I hear their breathing deepen as they work their way down to the stream, and then I hear Wildflower scream. The voices from the past fade. I return to the present day without Gran even knowing I was gone.

"For a time, you could hear whispers coming from down there," Gran says, looking into the ravine.

"Whispers?" I look where she is looking. Of all I have heard already, there were no whispers.

Dizziness forces me to clutch the railing. I didn't realize how high up we are.

"You okay?" Gran asks. She places her hand on mine, and I feel instantly better.

"What were the whispers about?" I ask.

"It was after Johnny died," she says. "You could hear them here on the footbridge. It was creepy. Of course, it could have just been the wind and the water talking to each other," she continues. "But Lily heard it very strongly, and Johnny's sister could hear it, too."

"Mom could hear the whispers?"

For the first time I wonder if Mom might hear voices, too. I think again of buried treasure. What is hidden inside me that is like my mom that I never realized I had?

"For years Lily wanted desperately to know who her father was," Gran continues. "In a way, I guess he was telling her."

Goosebumps come. Something that seems to happen often here in the mountains.

"I think those whispers drove Johnny's sister mad," Gran says. "Melody fell and died here, too. It was strange. And sad," she concludes.

"For a small mountain community, it sure seems a lot of people die here under suspicious circumstances," I say.

"Well, only those two."

"But your father?"

"That was an accident," she says. "Well, all of them were accidents, I guess."

I begin to take notes in my mind again. Johnny Monroe was my mother's father, my grandfather. He was not a nice guy and died from a fall before my mom was born. He fell from this bridge. His sister fell from here, too, after hearing whispers coming from below. I clutch the rail harder, looking into the ravine. Death is everywhere, it seems, but also life.

"It's called the secret sense, by the way," Gran says.

"What?"

"That thing you have where you can see and hear things that nobody else can. Sadie calls that the secret sense."

"It has a name?"

Gran nods. "It's a gift. Believe it or not, you're lucky to have it."

"Lucky?" Not once have I thought it was lucky to hear voices.

"I have it a little bit if only I'd listen to it," Gran continues. "Other than hearing those whispers, I'm not sure about Lily. My mama didn't have it, either. But Sadie does. You two should talk."

I nod, thinking maybe we should.

"What I wanted to show you is just over here," Gran says.

Ahead is an open area filled with wildflowers. Gran sits on a bench that looks like something Horatio made for her. I sit next to Gran. Here in the mountains, she is different. Here in the mountains, I can see why her father nicknamed her Wildflower. She blooms.

For the longest time, we sit in silence, like we're in church and

the mountains are ministering to us. Inside the silence is more silence. I think about how hearing voices from the past has a name. It is called the secret sense, though the secret sense is also more than voices. But the secret sense can actually be something good. Something that other people in my family have and that passed down to me as an inheritance.

"I brought you here for a reason," Gran says. "I consider this place sacred because this is where my life changed forever."

I look around, trying to imagine anything bad happening here.

"I dug up wildflowers all over the mountain and replanted them here, and collected seeds from others," Gran says. "Tiger lilies mainly. Hundreds of them. I set up those cairns, too, and Horatio made the bench for me."

In one area of the wildflower beds are rock statues placed in a circle.

"At first I created this as a way to not let Johnny win," Gran begins. "He made me afraid to be here in the forest by myself, so I decided to make something beautiful out of something ugly." She pauses, and her voice softens. "But I also think I created this place because this is where I first saw the gold Mary."

"The gold Mary?"

Gran pauses again.

"She was hovering in that tree over there," Gran says, her voice softer still. "She was the most beautiful thing I've ever seen. Like an angel surrounded by sunlight, and the look on her face was pure love."

Gran pauses again, and her eyes glisten with new tears. "In those moments with her, I felt totally safe and loved."

I try to imagine what I might have done. Maybe I would have planted hundreds of flowers, too. Then I remember one of Mom's early songs.

"Mom wrote a song with a gold Mary in it," I say.

Gran's surprise opens, and she blooms even more.

"The second album," I say.

"Do you remember the words?" she asks.

I think back to the lyrics. "It's something about coming home, and a gold angel watching from a giant oak on a moonlit night."

Gran lowers her head. "She *did* remember."

A new breeze sweeps through the tops of the trees.

"Mom told me once that she can only write songs about things that have touched her heart in some way."

Gran stays quiet for so long I ask if she's okay. She says she is, and I believe her. What surprises me, even more, is that I feel okay, too. How is it possible that my life is a total mess, and I feel okay?

"Can I confess something to you?" Gran asks. She looks at me as if she's been holding back saying this for days and even now wonders if she should speak it. I know what it's like to confess. I tell her to tell me.

"Lately, I've wished that I'd handled what happened with Johnny better. If I had, maybe this wouldn't have happened to you."

I pause. "I don't think that's how things work, Gran."

"How do you know?" she asks.

I shrug. I don't know.

Another long silence follows.

"People didn't talk about things back when I was a girl," Gran says.

"People don't talk about things *now*," I say.

She looks at me like I could be right. "For the longest time, I thought Mama blamed me for what happened. You know you're not to blame, don't you?"

I try on the words like a brand-new outfit, testing to see if they fit: *You are not to blame.* But deep down, I don't believe it. I must have done something wrong. I must have asked for it somehow.

Gran turns to me as if she's heard my thoughts.

"Daisy McAllister, you did nothing to deserve what happened to you. You didn't do anything wrong. Do you hear me?"

I close my eyes, finding Gran's belief in me almost unbearable. For once, I wish the voices from the past would come and rescue me from the present. But I hear nothing other than the soft sounds of the forest.

"Can I tell you another secret?" Gran asks.

I tell her she can.

"I've often wondered if the gold Mary comes for us when we die," Gran begins again. "Not the grim reaper, like those awful cartoons, but a loving mother, full of light."

"I think other people who love us might come, too," I say. "When I was sitting in Granny McAllister's bedroom before she died, I saw Joseph."

"You saw Daddy?" She turns to me, smiling.

"Clear as day."

"Did he say anything to you?" Gran asks.

"He didn't, but he looked right at me. He knew I was there."

Gran looks up into the trees, crying and smiling at the same time. "Did he say anything to Mama?"

"He sang to her," I say.

"What did he sing?" She stands as though she might float into the top of the trees herself.

"'Goodnight, Irene,'" I say.

She laughs. "Mama always loved that song."

Gran starts to sing. Her voice is not anything like my mom's. It isn't bad or good, and when she invites me to join in, I do. While we sing, two butterflies circle our heads as if enjoying the tune.

After we finish, she sits on the bench again and takes my hand.

"Thank you for telling me about Daddy," she says.

"Thank you for showing me this place," I say.

At this moment, I feel safe and loved. My shoulders relax, followed by an unexpected rush of fear.

CHAPTER THIRTY-ONE

Wildflower

On the way home, I breathe deeply, feeling cleansed by the tears I shed in the forest. It's not like me to cry so freely. But tears don't scare Daisy as they do me. She also doesn't mind silence, though it's fertile ground for me to wonder what she's thinking. Considering all the secrets that have come to light lately, she seems remarkably fine. Resilient.

A faint whistle rides the breeze.

"You hear that?" I ask.

Daisy nods.

"Daddy used to whistle everywhere he went," I say.

"Maybe you're conjuring him up."

"Then why would you hear him, too?" I ask, amazed that neither of us is spooked. Here in the mountains, spirits roam the hills freely. Or at least it seems that way.

Daisy is smart like Lily was at thirteen. Yet it's a different kind of smart. The secret sense is awakening in her. A tea bag dropped into hot water, the flavor just now releasing.

We pass the gnarled dogwood and the big stone that mark the entrance to the path. A man steps out of the briars wearing a straw hat and carrying a bucket. He startles us, and I say my favorite cuss word. It is Melody Monroe's son, Matt. He smiles and holds up his pail.

"Blackberries," he says. "There's a huge patch in that clearing over there."

I nod, not returning the smile. I wonder if Matt has any idea how close he is to the last place I saw his mother alive. Or how close he is to the ravine she fell into and died.

He tips his hat to Daisy. I realize they have no idea that they are cousins. Hiding my fluster, I tell Daisy that we need to get going and wish Matt good luck with his blackberries. I can't seem to shake my distrust.

Daisy and I walk along the road and then turn at the mailboxes to go up the hill. Mary Jane's Cadillac is in the driveway next to my pickup. She is listening to an oldies station on the radio, her hand out the window holding a cigarette and moving to the rhythm of the Bee Gees who are *Stayin' Alive*.

"I've been waiting for you." The music drops, as does the cigarette to the ground as she gets out of the car.

I tell Daisy I'll meet her at the house and she goes on ahead.

Mary Jane crushes the cigarette under her shoe, releasing a smoldering, bitter smell. She looks up the hill as if to make sure Daisy is not within hearing distance.

"I can't believe that stunt you pulled in Nashville," she says, her words smoldering and bitter as well.

"Victor told you?" I ask, finding the possibility hard to believe.

"No, Victor didn't say a word. It's getting around the grapevine."

It occurs to me that Mary Jane is the one who started this particular vine, based on what my sister Amy said when she huffed her way up this hill to confront me. I find it interesting as well as

alarming that it's the women who come to put me in my place, not the men. Men have actually been helpful.

I begin telling her that it is none of her business until she interrupts.

"It is definitely my business if you involve my brother in it."

"Victor is old enough to make his own decisions," I say.

"Victor doesn't have a clear mind where you're concerned." She crosses her arms.

"When I saw him the other night he seemed clear-minded," I say, fighting the temptation to cross my arms, too.

"Wake up, Louisa May," she says, spitting out the words as if they are meant to hurt me. "He's been in love with you since we were kids."

Mary Jane straightens the collar of her blouse, as though briefly remembering decorum.

"You're like a magnet when it comes to trouble," she begins again, putting her hands on her hefty hips. "Mama told me that a long time ago." She pauses long enough to point her finger at me. "You need to leave Victor alone. Don't encourage him. You'll bring his life down to your level."

"Victor is a grown man," I say. "What he does with his life isn't your concern."

"Are you forgetting what you are?" Her lips purse as if she's eaten something bitter. "You ruined Bee's life, and now you want to ruin Victor's?"

My face warms, and I unwittingly make a fist. "Well, at least I don't have to wonder what you think anymore," I say.

Mary Jane huffs. She returns to her car and turns on the engine, the fumes from her exhaust adding to the toxic mix. "Stay away from Victor," she warns out the window.

As she backs down the hill, I narrow my eyes at her and then spit in the dirt. For years I looked up to Mary Jane and her sophisticated family. They were everything the McAllisters were not. But

nothing is ever what it seems. I always knew that Victor was in love with me, but why is that my fault? And why am I to blame for Bee and me falling in love? Most importantly, who appointed Mary Jane judge and jury? Certainly not me.

Daisy and Aunt Sadie wait for me on the porch. With each step, I am more convinced that we were right to confront Jerry. If our family and friends don't take a stand for us, what hope do any of us have?

"Everything okay?" Aunt Sadie asks.

"Not really," I say, climbing the steps to the porch.

The phone rings in the kitchen, and I go to answer it. I assume it is Lily, but it's actually Bee. After I tell her about the earful Mary Jane gave me, she sighs.

"People disappoint me sometimes," she says.

"Me, too," I say.

"The good news is, I found an attorney in Nashville who will take our case," Bee says. "The bad news is, she doesn't think we will get very far. It seems Jerry has friends in high places."

"Why doesn't that surprise me?" I twist the telephone cord between my fingers until it starts to cut off my circulation and they begin to tingle.

"How's Daisy?" she asks.

"Surprisingly fine," I say.

"Maybe confronting Jerry was a good thing," Bee says. "At least she knows she doesn't have to go through this alone."

I tell her about seeing Matt Monroe on the trail, and how unnerved I was. A thought occurs to me, and I say to her that I plan to visit him. She asks why.

"To lay old ghosts to rest, I guess."

"Well, be careful," Bee says.

On most days, she is more cautious than I am. Although after what happened with Johnny, I've had a watchfulness that can be

exhausting at times, as though predators lurk behind every rock. I find myself hoping that this isn't the case for Daisy, too.

Like Amy, Bee prefers to let sleeping dogs lie. Or at the very least, to avoid any conflict that might arise.

WHEN I RETURN to the front porch, Aunt Sadie is sewing quilt pieces while Daisy sits on the swing. It is strange to see Sadie sew by herself. Yet again, I am reminded that Mama is gone.

"That was Bee," I say to them. "She sends her love."

Daisy smiles, and Aunt Sadie excuses herself to go take a nap. With Sadie inside, I ask Daisy if she wants to drive over to see her mom. She answers with another smile. Although I have always known that Bee is Daisy's favorite, my status seems to be on the rise. Maybe teaching her to drive has something to do with that— or confronting her father. Either way, I am grateful for it.

Daisy is getting better at changing gears; her bucking bronco days are over. When we arrive at Sadie's, Lily is still in her summer nightgown and sitting on the porch swing having a cup of coffee. She hugs Daisy, who settles in next to her, and gives me a look telling me that we'll talk later about me teaching Daisy to drive. After we visit for a while, I kiss them both on the cheek and tell them I have somewhere to be. Not letting the moss grow on my idea, I get back in my pickup and head toward the Monroes' place and a date with history that a week ago I would have never antici-pated. No time better than now, I think, to give myself courage. Waiting might only change my mind.

CHAPTER THIRTY-TWO

Daisy

G ran is barely out of sight when the telephone rings inside. I tell Mom that I will answer it, and she thanks me. On the fifth ring, I pick up.

When I hear my father's voice, my insides freeze.

"I can't believe you talked your grandmother into showing up at my office." He sounds angry.

My palms turn into a sweating mess, and I wish the phone cord would stretch to the front door, so I could tell Mom who it is.

"I didn't talk anybody into doing anything," I say to him.

"Oh, come on. You know what you did." Street noises fill the background. Is he calling from a phone booth?

"That queer grandmother of yours had better leave me the hell alone."

My wrist throbs from holding on to the phone so tightly. Paralyzed, I can't seem to stop listening or hang up.

"You need to tell everybody that you lied. Tell those people that you were mad at me and made it all up. You hear me?"

Unable to speak, I try to swallow the fear choking me.

"You're going to regret crossing me, Daisy," he says. "I warned you."

All the hopeful feelings I've had since being in Katy's Ridge vanish. My cheeks burn.

When my arm finally moves, I slam the kitchen phone on its cradle with enough force to make the picture hanging on the wall swing on its nail. Seconds later, I run out of the house. I follow the road toward the lake. Mom calls after me, asking what's wrong. But I don't stop. Something about running feels necessary. I want to run away from my father's call. Run from everything that's happened.

At the sparkling lake, with nowhere else to go, I stop, and my tears begin. In the next moment my mom catches up with me, out of breath, and still in her nightgown and slippers. I never knew she could run so fast.

Her breathing labored, she asks what happened. Through tears, I tell her, and she pulls me into her arms again.

"I'm so sorry, Daisy." Her body is warm from running. Her embrace is everything I need. At a moment when everything feels wrong, she reassures me that everything will be all right. I want to believe her.

CHAPTER THIRTY-THREE

Wildflower

A newly paved driveway points the way to the Monroe place. Years ago, I slogged through mud up to my ankles to talk to Melody Monroe when she was living in that dilapidated old cabin. A large metal mailbox stands near where I park, the red flag up as though waving a danger sign. I promised never to return to this place. However, something is drawing me here.

Walking from here gives me time to prepare, though I'm not sure what I'm preparing for. I think of what Bee said about Jerry having friends in high places and that he will more than likely get away with his treatment of Daisy. Jerry won't be the first man to escape responsibility, nor will he be the last, and I have no idea what this has to do with Matt Monroe.

At the end of the road, a new cabin stands where the old one used to be and is triple the size. Trees cleared from around the cabin allow sunlight to break through where there used to be darkness. Landscaping surrounds the cabin. Robust native plants sit in rustic beds with large stones placed to get the most natural

setting. To be honest, it looks like something I might have created.

The old outhouse is gone, as well as the oak tree where Ruby Monroe took her own life at the age of twelve. I remember coming here as a girl with Daniel after Johnny talked dirty to Mary Jane and me. Kudzu vines had swallowed the place. That first visit, a young, barefooted Melody opened the door, her eyes revealing a deep sadness. What would she say if she saw this place now? Does Matt Monroe feel all the ghosts around him?

For the longest time, I stand in front of the cabin and take in the transformation.

"Welcome," a voice says, coming out of the woods.

Startled, I give a short, flustered wave.

Matt Monroe places several pieces of fresh-cut wood to the left of the house on the evenly stacked woodpile.

"Cup of coffee?" He could be Johnny's twin, though an older, well-kept version. The resemblance resides most in the way he stands and holds his head.

"Sure," I say, suddenly questioning why I am here.

Matt takes off leather gloves and walks over to shake my hand. His hand is warm and soft, no calluses.

"It's hard to believe this is the same place," I say.

He smiles, and I think how lucky he was not to get Johnny's teeth in the rolling of the genetic dice.

"When I first got here, I thought I was crazy even to consider building something here, but I think it turned out okay."

"Better than okay," I say, which elicits another smile from him.

Katy's Ridge is changing. People who defected have come back. At least Victor has. And although Matt never lived here, he has come back, too, in a way, to claim the family homestead. He seems friendly enough, yet why do I feel like I am sweet-talking a snake into not biting me? And is my distrust in my imagination or based on fact? The resemblance helps to confuse me.

Matt leads the way up to the sturdy porch, where a small wooden table sits with one chair. I imagine this is where he eats his meals in the summertime, overlooking a view of the mountains provided by a chainsaw.

"I had no idea the Monroe property was sitting on such a beautiful piece of land," I say.

"It was a diamond in the rough, for sure," he says. "I've got instant coffee, is that okay?" Matt asks.

I nod. He invites me to sit, saying that he will be right back. He enters the house, easing the screen door closed so it doesn't slam. It is unusual to see a man living alone who isn't a widower. Although maybe he is. I know nothing about Matt Monroe and must admit I am curious.

Does he feel the pull of history here, too?

It occurs to me that maybe we are part of a reconciliation party, pulled together to heal the past.

You're beginning to sound like June, I tell myself, but there are worse things, of course.

Matt returns with two cups of steaming coffee on a wooden tray, along with two bowls of blackberry cobbler, complete with a scoop of vanilla on the top. He apologizes for not asking first, making it impossible for me to refuse. For a Monroe, he is polite, as well as cultured, perhaps fifteen years younger than me, maybe more. And his cobbler is fabulous.

"Did you know my mother very well?" he asks after we finish our desserts.

"Not well," I say. "Melody didn't come that often."

"The coroner's report in Rocky Bluff says that she died from an accident. A fall. And that her blood alcohol level was off the charts." He takes a sip of coffee as though noting a change in the weather.

"Twenty years ago, when she came back to Katy's Ridge, she

was having a rough time and drinking a lot," I say. "That was right before she died."

"I mostly lived with my father," he says. "I saw her only a few times a year. I knew she drank a lot and had some rough stuff in her past. I never knew exactly what."

I think of Daisy, and how determined I am to help her work through anything rough.

In the silence that follows, it seems we are both questioning why I am here. I wish I had an answer for that. My imagination produces the ghosts of Johnny, Ruby, and Melody standing below the porch, watching us talk and wondering the same thing. How is it that we humans are supposed to finish up unfinished business? Does just talking about it solve it?

"I heard you live in Nashville. Do you like it there?" he asks.

"It's a great city," I say, already tiring of the small talk.

"But?"

"I guess I'm just a country girl."

He smiles, and I see who Melody might have been if life hadn't defeated her.

"Why did you leave Louisville?" I ask.

"Too many ghosts," he says.

I catch myself smiling. "It's not easy to get away from ghosts," I say.

"Do you ever think of moving back to Katy's Ridge?" he asks.

"Not really," I say, and wonder if this is true.

"Isn't your daughter that famous singer?"

"Yes, Lily McAllister is my daughter."

"Cool," he says, suddenly sounding younger.

I don't mention Lily is down the road at Sadie's place, or that she and Matt are actually cousins.

"So Lily and I are related?" he asks.

"You're cousins, I guess," I say, not revealing my surprise. As

much as I have tried to bury the past, it keeps popping up. Unearthed. Exhumed by the latest Monroe.

"My mother mentioned when I was a boy that I still had family here."

Does Matt think his Uncle Johnny and I were sweethearts? Nothing could be further from the truth. I sit straighter, my feistiness warming up for the day.

I debate whether to be truthful. "For the record, I had no choice in the matter," I say, as the truth wins out.

Matt pauses, a pained expression on his face. He reaches for my hand, but I manage to pull it away. I suddenly don't want to be here.

"I should tell you something." He pauses as though putting order to his thoughts. "I've been researching my family tree, and you might find some of it interesting."

I wait. Matt's eyes find mine. "You mentioned not having a choice?"

I nod, already regretting my latest admission.

"Well, that kind of makes sense," he begins. "On the Monroe side of the family, I had a great-grandfather who evidently got his young teenage daughter pregnant and was run out of West Virginia by the sheriff. He ended up in Katy's Ridge with his son. That son was my mother's father."

I think of Arthur Monroe, his creepiness evident when Daniel confronted him about his son, Johnny. He was a drinker, too.

A heaviness sits on my chest. "So you're telling me that history was repeating itself when Johnny Monroe attacked me on a trail to the cemetery when I was thirteen, because Johnny came from a family of predators?"

Matt nods. "Sins of the father," he says. "Thankfully, I've never married or sired children."

For several seconds we sit in silence. It appears the gravity of the situation has not been lost on either of us.

"After I moved here, I went to a local fortune-teller," Matt says.

"June Sector?"

"Yes. You know her, of course. Everybody knows everybody around here."

I agree.

"She said something about generations repeating themselves until someone breaks the pattern."

"That's interesting," I say. "June said the same thing to me."

"How do you suppose we do that?" he asks.

"I have no idea," I say.

We exchange a smile.

"I've been giving the family graves a face-lift," Matt says, "and putting flowers on them, and telling different family members to rest in peace. But other than that, I'm not sure what else to do."

I tell him I'm not sure, either. But at the same time, it seems that sitting here together and talking about these characters from the past is somehow part of the solution, too.

After another long silence, I tell him I need to get back to Lily and Daisy.

"Can we talk about this again?" he asks.

I tell him that I would like that. After our handshake, I leave the porch and start to walk back to my pickup. When I turn around at the edge of the clearing, he is still watching me. We exchange a short wave.

As I get back to the road, I wonder if I have misjudged him. Simply because he is a Monroe doesn't make him a bad person. My secret sense was right to guide me here.

CHAPTER THIRTY-FOUR

Daisy

While I pretend to read, my mom and Sadie spend the afternoon together. After their talk, Sadie suggests that the two of us take a walk to the lake. We leave Mom and saunter down the dirt road.

"Wildflower thought it would be good if we talked," she says.

I nod. Aunt Sadie is eighty-three years older than me, but she isn't wobbly or anything. She is my great-great-aunt. Until we came to Katy's Ridge this summer, I never gave family trees a thought, or whether a cousin was a first, second, or third. It all seemed too complicated—not that I knew I had any, anyway. But just like my body is getting stronger every day that I dig, now my awareness of family is getting stronger, too.

"A lot has happened lately," Sadie says. "How are you doing with that?"

Grown-ups tell kids what to do and don't ask questions. I try to say to her that even though my life is falling apart, I finally feel like I belong someplace.

Our walk is slow but has a rhythm to it, like one of Mom's slow songs that makes a hush fall over the crowd. Is this what Gran calls a "mosey"? She has been saying I need to learn how to do this. If so, Sadie has mastered the art. I match her rhythm, letting it settle into my bones. We get to the small dock at the lake and sit on a bench under the pines. Instead of wading into the conversation, she jumps right in.

"Wildflower says you have a different kind of secret sense, where you hear voices from the past?"

I thought I was all out of secrets except digging for treasure, but hearing voices is a secret, too. If anyone can understand, it would be Sadie.

"It's more like conversations," I say. "Like watching a scene on television between two actors, except I can't see them, I can only hear them."

The beginnings of a smile come to her wrinkled face.

"What do these people say?" she asks.

I think about how to answer her question. "Well, they talk about things that seem important in some way," I begin. "It's usually a conversation that somehow changes things, and it's not always for the good."

"Is it the same people that talk to you?" she asks.

"Different people, depending on who I'm with, and it doesn't happen all the time, just every now and again."

"Do the people in these conversations ever talk just to you?"

I pause again to think. "Sometimes, I have the feeling the voices want me to tell someone something. Or they want me to tell whoever I'm with what I've heard and maybe give them a message."

"A message?" Sadie looks at me as if peering through an opening into another time and place. "Can you give me an example?" she asks.

Sadie's face reveals no judgment, and she is taking me seri-

ously. I tilt my head slightly to the left and my chin downward. "Sometimes I can tune the voices in," I tell her. "It doesn't always work, but I might as well try." I close my eyes to listen as we sit in comfortable silence. Tiny waves lap the shore as I open to the past.

A few seconds later, old-timey music begins to play, featuring a fiddle and a pennywhistle like Mom used once on a song. Several people talk at a gathering. The volume turns up on two of the people, and the other voices fade into the background. From the sound of their voices, I decide it is an older man and a young woman. By some means, I know that Sadie is the young woman.

"An old man is speaking in English, but it sounds funny," I say. "He's trying to talk you out of going somewhere. He calls you headstrong, and says you don't know what you're getting into."

"That's my Da," she says, her voice sounding like the young woman from the past. "He used those exact words when I told him I was coming to America."

"Well, he wants you to know that he was wrong, and that he is very proud of you, and that he loves you."

The music fades, and the airwaves close. Aunt Sadie's eyes turn red and tears pool.

"I'm sorry," I say, thinking I've done the wrong thing.

"No, no, no," Aunt Sadie says. "These are good tears." Sadie sniffs and pulls a red bandana out of her pants pocket and blows her nose. She takes in a deep breath. "For all these years I've been sad that Da and I didn't end things well. Now I can finally lay it to rest."

I study the tight places that have formed on my hands from shoveling. It never occurred to me that the voices could be a good thing.

"My grandmother had the same gift," Sadie says, putting her bandana away. "She was known throughout the village as someone who could give and receive messages."

"Give and receive?"

Sadie nods.

"I didn't know it worked the other way, that I could give messages to the dead, too."

"Most things work both ways," she says. "With that in mind, please tell Da that I love him and that I think about him every day."

I do as she asks.

Sadie says things that I never hear anyone else say, except for Gran sometimes. But with Aunt Sadie, it's like her mountain medicine isn't just about plants, but words, too. Words that heal the broken places inside.

For a long time we sit in silence, as if we've found a treasure of a different sort and thanks must be given.

"Tell me what to do with it," I say finally.

"Listen to it," Sadie says. "And if it makes sense, pass on the message."

"If it makes sense?"

"Yes, well, you have to be careful, of course. For the most part, you will keep this gift to yourself unless you trust the person to receive the information."

"So, it's nothing bad?" I ask.

"No, child. It's nothing bad," she begins. "In fact, it's a perfect thing. You gave me a message from my Da that will comfort me for the rest of my days."

She squeezes my hand, and I let the medicine of her words sink into me.

"The thing about gifts, though, is that you need to protect them and use them wisely," she says.

"I'm not sure how to do that," I say.

"I'll help," she says. "We can talk about it more while you're here. I can tell you stories of my grandmother, so you don't feel strange and different."

"Do you hear voices, too?" I ask.

"No, not voices, but I have a sense when someone from the

other world is near. For instance, I know you met my brother, Joseph, at the house the night you arrived. I didn't see him, but my secret sense told me that you did."

"It's true," I say. "It was one of the rare times when I got more than voices. I could see him, too. He was right there with her."

Sadie smiles. "You have no idea how glad I am to hear that."

"Does Gran have the secret sense, too?"

"She would have it more if she trusted it and actually used it."

"What about Mom?"

"She had it a little when she was a girl, but now I think she uses it to write songs."

I nod, believing this to be true.

"You, however, have received an extra helping." Sadie smiles. "I guess we were due."

In the meantime, the sun sparkles and dances along the top of the lake. For the first time in hours I haven't thought about my father and how angry he is. Spending time with Sadie feels more important than worrying. I don't begin to understand how the invisible world works, but I feel as though I've glimpsed the real McAllister family treasure.

CHAPTER THIRTY-FIVE

Wildflower

On my way home, I go by Aunt Sadie's house to pick up Daisy. Lily is taking a nap, and when she wakes up, I will tell her that a new Monroe relative lives nearby who is different from the others, and that she may want to meet him. Aunt Sadie and Daisy are gone, but I can guess where they are on such a beautiful summer day. I walk down the dirt road toward the lake and think about Matt Monroe. I can't help but feel that our meeting was an excellent beginning to reconciling the past.

When I see Sadie and Daisy sitting on the bench at the edge of the lake, my secret sense confirms the importance of their friendship. Long ago, Aunt Sadie helped me heal, too. To have Sadie help Daisy is not only fortunate but feels like an act of grace.

Sadie turns as though she senses me coming. Looking back over my life, I cannot remember a time when Sadie didn't appear happy to see me. I breathe in the pine-scented air and think how unusual it is to see young and old sitting together. I join them.

For several seconds we don't speak, but settle in with one

another as we watch the lake. Like the river that flows through Katy's Ridge, the lake also ebbs and flows, little waves lapping gently against the shore, their rhythms seemingly linked.

"We've been having a good talk," Aunt Sadie says to me.

"I figured you would," I say. "What have you been talking about?"

"Family inheritance," Aunt Sadie says, giving Daisy a wink.

Daisy offers a rare smile and seems more at peace with herself.

Aunt Sadie takes my hand, and I take Daisy's, the McAllisters united. My shoulders relax, and I let myself believe that everything is going to be all right.

Moments later, we decide that we are all hungry, and we rise from the bench and walk back up the dirt road to Sadie's house. A note sits on the kitchen table from Lily saying that she is running to the A&P in Rocky Bluff for groceries and will be back shortly.

From the kitchen, we hear a car drive up and a door slam. Is Lily already back from the store? Daisy runs to greet her. We wait for them to return to the kitchen. Instead we hear a man's voice.

Sadie and I walk toward the front door, where we find Daisy wide-eyed and still. On the other side of the screen door is Jerry.

"I've been looking all over for you," Jerry says to Daisy. "Get in the car."

"No!" I tell him. "Daisy is certainly not getting in your car."

Daisy steps back as though inching away from a copperhead.

Jerry steps inside. He is several inches taller than me, and my attempt to block him from Daisy only makes him smile.

"Get your things," he says to her.

"I'll telephone the sheriff," Sadie says to me, turning toward the kitchen.

"I wouldn't advise that, old lady," Jerry says.

"I can do whatever I like," Sadie says, her tone as serious as I've ever heard her.

"The sheriff already knows I'm here to pick up my daughter. I stopped by his office on my way here."

Sadie looks at him as if confronted with the same copperhead.

"Go get your things," Jerry repeats to Daisy.

Daisy suddenly looks younger. At thirteen, she is still a girl in many ways.

"Her things aren't here," I say to Jerry.

"Where are they?"

"Mama's house."

He looks at Daisy and points toward the car. "We'll go by there before we leave."

Daisy's eyes are filled with desperation and tears.

"Jerry, what are you doing here?" I ask, trying to sound reasonable.

"My daughter has fallen under a bad influence and is making up stories. My lawyer says I can get a court order to keep her away from you if I have to. He's already talked to a judge in Nashville."

My head throbs. Jerry looks like a lawyer himself, with his suit, tie, and shiny shoes, and he seems to enjoy intimidating three females of various ages in their casual summertime clothes.

I realize Jerry's car is still running out in front of Sadie's house. He has no intention of talking or doing anything except making a quick escape.

"Daisy is staying here with Lily," I say.

"Lily's here?" He looks down the hallway as though waiting for her to appear.

"Well, she will be here soon. She had to run to the store."

"Right," he says, as though I've just given his leg a good pull.

"She has a lawyer, too, Jerry."

"I'm sure she does," he says, his teeth almost gritted. "Have her lawyer talk to my lawyer." He motions for Daisy to come with him.

Stepping next to Daisy, I put an arm around her shoulder to anchor her in place. At this moment, I wish I had Mama's shotgun.

Physically, Jerry has at least sixty pounds on me and is six feet tall, to my five feet, two inches.

"Let's just wait until Lily gets back," I say, remembering how he softened earlier when her name was mentioned.

He narrows his eyes as if seeing a trap. "Daisy will be at my house. Lily knows where to find me."

I still can't believe Lily married this jerk, after a sweetheart like Crow. Meanwhile, Sadie and I exchange a look that reveals how helpless we feel.

"Sadie, call Daniel," I say.

Sadie disappears into the kitchen.

"I don't want anyone to get hurt," Daisy says. "Mom can come to get me later."

"But Daisy—"

"Mom will know what to do," she says.

Will she? I wonder. It seems the world is not set up for justice.

"Get in the car," Jerry says again. Daisy walks past me and out of the house.

"You leave Daisy alone, Jerry. You hear me?" The full force of my hatred comes out in a single look. It has no impact. He returns to his car, Daisy already inside.

As soon as he drives away, I scream my frustration. Never in my life have I wanted to kill somebody more. Not even Johnny, who left me for dead on the trail. In the kitchen, Sadie is hanging up the phone.

"What do we do?" I ask, sounding frantic.

"Daniel will be at the house when they pick up Daisy's things. He'll try to talk some sense into him."

I suddenly fear for Daniel. "I've got to do something," I say to her. My walk has fury in it, my fists clenched. "Daisy will not spend one more night in that man's house," I say aloud.

I get into my pickup. It starts with a gasp and a sputter, not up for a high-speed chase.

CHAPTER THIRTY-SIX

Daisy

"That grandmother of yours is a piece of work." My father wears leather driving gloves to hold his leather steering wheel. "I'm going to make sure you never stay with her again."

"But I like to stay with Gran." I hate how wimpy my voice sounds.

"It doesn't matter what you like." He drives faster on the narrow curves than is safe.

My father has never been overly nice, but he's never been too mean, either, not like now.

Compared to Gran's old pickup, my father's new Mercedes purrs. It is automatic, so the only challenge is staying on the road. We pull up into the driveway, and I wonder if he even knows that Gran's mom died. Standing in the shade of the Redbud Sisters is my Great-Uncle Daniel. His arms are crossed in front of his chest, his chin firm. But compared to my father, he seems old.

"Go gather your things," my father tells me. "And don't waste

any time." I want to ask him what he will do if I do, but not enough to actually voice it.

I head up the hill while my father walks over to Daniel.

As I pass, Daniel asks if I'm okay.

I shrug. *Okay* is not the word I would use. I am determined. Determined to keep everyone safe and not make my father angrier than he already is.

By the time I get to the porch, I hear angry words exchanged between Daniel and my father, and I want to cover my ears. I hope Nellie doesn't hear them fighting or she might get frightened.

Inside the house, I put my things in my backpack. I hear the faint strains of a banjo and think of Grandaddy McAllister, who is of little help as a ghost except to serenade my exit. When I return to my father's car, Gran has pulled up and is standing next to Daniel, who tries to reason with my father. My father appears to get angrier with every second. Gran challenges him, and his voice gets louder. I realize I am trembling, but also frozen in place.

A man walks up the driveway at a quick pace. I recognize him. He was picking blackberries on the secret path to the cemetery. I try to recall his name. Matt something.

"Are you all right?" he says to Gran while looking at my father. "I was passing by and heard yelling."

He nods to Daniel and then looks at Gran again.

"This is Daisy's father, Matt," Gran says. "We're having a disagreement."

"You and your goddamn disagreements," my father says to Gran. "Daisy's mine. She goes wherever I say."

My stomach lurches, and I get a sudden taste of the oatmeal I had for breakfast.

"But she doesn't want to go with you." Gran stands firm. If she is as terrified as I am, she isn't showing it. But she is also at least six inches shorter than him, and I don't want her to get hurt.

Daniel asks my father to calm down so that they can talk, but this makes him even more aggravated.

"This is none of your business, old man. Or yours," he says to Gran.

My father pulls me toward the car. I forget to breathe. Gran tells him to stop, her voice frantic.

"You're the one who needs to stop!" my father yells. He then calls her a degenerate and looks at Gran with pure hatred.

I don't even know what that word means, but it must be bad. My father releases me and then lunges toward Gran. Daniel and Matt step in to prevent my father from reaching her. It is Matt who grabs my father and pins his right arm behind his back in some kind of karate hold. I gasp, and my heart races even faster.

"It's you who needs to be stopped," Matt says to him. "This ends here!"

After several seconds of nonstop cussing, my father squirms free. His face is red, his eyes full of anger. He mumbles something about calling his lawyer, but he has lost his bluster. He tells me to get into the car. Still frozen, I stay where I am. He tells me again, this time louder. The others try reasoning with him again. He reminds them that he is my father and has the right to take me wherever he wants.

Finally I unfreeze and get into his car. He gets inside, too, and locks all the doors with the push of a button. He grins at Daniel, Gran, and Matt as though he has outsmarted them.

With a look, Gran tells me to trust her, that she will figure something out. I nod and tell her not to worry. But this is the most worried I have ever been. Driving away, the redness leaves my father's face, but I imagine he is still seething. My heartbeat stops racing.

As we leave Katy's Ridge, we pass places that are now familiar. The river where my cousin Nellie and I talked. The house that Bee

used to live in. The road that leads to the school. Another road leading to the Sectors' place.

When June Sector told my fortune, she saw something in the cards that scared her. I wonder if the incident that just played out was it.

On the drive back to Nashville, my father and I do not speak. The silence feels almost as dangerous as his anger. I stare at my hands, thinking that I won't get to finish digging for the McAllister buried treasure. If I see Gran again, I will tell her about it so she can finish the job.

By two o'clock, we enter the ritzy neighborhood where my father lives. He pulls in front of his house and pushes the button that unlocks all the car doors.

"Go inside. I have to go back to the office." He doesn't look at me.

I hesitate.

"We'll talk later." The angry look on his face pushes me out the door.

I think of the fox Nellie and I watched when we were at the river. The rabbit sat unmoving to be invisible to the fox. In this scenario, I am the rabbit.

My father appears oblivious to the dynamics of foxes and rabbits. I doubt he has ever been a rabbit in his life.

"Louise is there, just knock on the door," he says before I close the car door.

Louise is their housekeeper. A black woman who lives on the other side of Nashville. She makes their meals, does their laundry, and reads *People* magazine when she eats her lunch apart from the rest of the family. I suddenly realize how hungry I am. If I ask, Louise will make me a peanut butter and banana sandwich. I like Louise.

My father drives away. I shiver despite the oppressive summer heat.

Once inside, I will call Gran so she won't be worried. Days ago, she made me write the phone number at Granny McAllister's house in my diary. It comforts me to know that when I call, the phone will ring in the kitchen, and I will be able to picture Gran standing there weaving the long red cord between her fingers as she talks.

When I knock, Louise opens the door, looking surprised to see me. "Well, hello, Miss Daisy. I thought you were staying at your grandma's house."

"Change of plans," I tell her, stepping inside the massive foyer.

"Is she home?" I ask, motioning upstairs.

"Getting her hair done," Louise says.

We exchange a look of mutual relief.

"You want a sandwich?" she asks, as though she has picked up on my hunger.

"Yes, thank you," I say. "But first I need to call my Gran and let her know that I made it okay."

She nods. "Just put your things in your room and come back down. I'll fix you something."

Grateful for Louise's easiness, I climb the stairs and remember how just hours ago I was terrified that Gran or Daniel might get hurt. Before that, I was sitting at the lake with Gran and Sadie. Even with all that McAllister secret sense in one place, none of us saw this coming.

When I call Gran, she answers on the first ring. "Are you okay?" she asks.

"He dropped me off at his house and went to his office."

"Are you there alone?" she asks.

"The housekeeper is here. The wife isn't. Tell Mom not to worry," I say.

"I will. But we're all worried, Daisy."

"I know," I say. "I'm worried, too."

Gran asks for my number there, and I give it to her. She tells

me not to hesitate to call the police "if anything happens." I hate that she even has to say those words. But I already know that calling the police won't do any good. The police chief has had dinner over here more than once, and my father is generous with their charities. He also knows lawyers and judges in Nashville. Some of them live in this neighborhood. Even at thirteen, I have figured out that a wealthy fox can get away with things.

"Once Lily and I talk, we'll call you back," Gran says.

"Mom's not back yet? She's been gone for hours."

"I know," Gran says. "She must have gotten waylaid."

I nod, forgetting she can't see me.

"Daisy, are you all right?" Gran asks.

"Yes," I say, not feeling the least bit all right.

"We're going to get you out of there," Gran says.

"Okay," I answer, but I don't believe it. My father has won. He is someone who always wins.

After I hang up the upstairs phone, I go to my bedroom and put my backpack on my bed. When I go downstairs again, my father's wife comes through the front door.

"What are you doing here?" She doesn't look glad to see me.

"My father dropped me off." I wonder if he told her about us showing up at his office. I doubt it. They barely talk at dinner. I can't imagine them having a heart-to-heart about something important. According to my father, wives are to be clueless and attractive. A Mercedes for the home. Something that purrs and doesn't talk back. It makes no sense that he and my mom were together. Except I heard her tell one of her friends once that he was a father figure, since she'd never had a dad.

"He never tells me anything," the new wife says, more to herself than to me. "Louise?" she calls toward the kitchen. She smells of expensive perfume and cheap hair spray.

Louise arrives in the front hallway. She stands at attention like a soldier in a war except with her eyes lowered.

"One more for dinner, it seems." She brushes past me like she is a faster car passing me on the interstate. I have never known what to call her. Her name is Kathleen, and my father calls her Kathy when he is in a good mood. Kathleen is not someone I would ever call *Mom*, and I can't imagine that she would want that anyway.

"Just keep quiet, okay?" Our eyes meet.

I nod, knowing that, to her, this means to stay out of sight—except for dinner, where we pose as a real family. If he has anything to say at all, I imagine my father will come up with some excuse for why he had to retrieve me from Gran's house. But for now, I will keep quiet and go into the kitchen to hang out with Louise.

While I eat a sandwich, I invite Louise to join me in the breakfast nook. At first she says she can't, but then she sits to drink a cup of coffee while keeping an eye on the kitchen door for Kathleen. She pulls a *People* magazine from under a cushion. Lady Diana is on the cover.

While she clucks at an article, my mind wanders to Katy's Ridge. How could I possibly miss a place I have only been for three weeks? But it seems something monumental happened while I was there. At the Fourth of July celebration at Daniel's house, I realized for the first time that I was part of something bigger. I belonged to a family tree with deep roots. The proof of my family ties filled several picnic tables.

Meanwhile, I regret telling Gran my secret. If I had kept my mouth shut, my father wouldn't be threatening to get a restraining order against her. And Mom wouldn't be all worried and guilt-ridden. Now, the only way to get through this is to forget. Forget about digging for buried treasure. Forget about finally feeling like I belong somewhere. Forget about Katy's Ridge.

CHAPTER THIRTY-SEVEN

Wildflower

S adie and I sit on the front porch waiting anxiously for Lily to return from the A&P. She must have had other errands, because she is long overdue. We anticipate her coming here since she planned to make dinner for us. I think of Mama, who would be having a conniption right about now. The grief is still new. Raw.

Then I remember how Matt Monroe stepped in to help me, putting Jerry in an armlock. If he hadn't stepped in, Jerry might have shoved me down the hill or even worse. My gratitude feels as strong as the grief. A Monroe stepped in to save me from harm. I think of patterns breaking. Sticks in the spokes of bicycle tires. Good apples not falling far from the tree instead of bad ones. At this moment, I wonder if Matt and I could become friends. But first I must save Daisy.

I haven't told Sadie how heated the exchange became or how Jerry tried to come after me. I don't want her to worry more than she already is.

"I wish I'd told Daisy to lock her bedroom door tonight," I say to Sadie. "But surely she knows to do that, right?"

Sadie puts a hand to her chest as though to keep her heart from breaking open. "Surely," she says.

We hear the car, and then eventually the sound of someone walking up the hill. Lily steps into the porch light's reach. Carrying a bag of groceries in each hand, she smiles. She has no idea what has happened while she has been gone. I stand to greet her, telling myself to stay calm.

"I forget how steep this hill is," she says. "But it's good exercise."

"For sure," I say, wondering how to tell her.

Lily puts the bags on the bottom step. "I ended up driving to Harriman to get a decent bottle of wine," she says. "Where's Daisy?"

"I tried to call you at the A&P," I say. "I couldn't find you anywhere."

Lily drops her purse off her shoulder onto the bottom step, too, as though realizing something heavy is coming. "Mama, what's happened?" The concern is written across her face.

"Jerry came and got her, honey. We were over at Aunt Sadie's, and he just drove up and told her to get in the car."

"And you didn't stop him?" Her voice crescendos.

My attempt at staying calm crumbles. "That man is twice my size, Lily. He pushed me aside like I was nothing. Not to mention he told the sheriff in Rocky Bluff that he was coming to get his child," she continues, "and that we were a bad influence. I didn't have much choice."

Tears rush to greet her anger. "Mama, what are we going to do?"

"Did you call your lawyer today?" I ask. "You mentioned you might."

She pauses. "He thought that any kind of restraining order would antagonize Jerry into trying to get sole custody again."

"Jerry tried to get sole custody? You didn't tell me anything about that."

Lily looks at Sadie, and I wonder if Sadie knows something I don't.

"I didn't want to worry you," Lily says.

"Why did he want sole custody?" I ask again.

"He said I was an unfit mother because I was on the road all the time."

My fists clench to keep my teeth company. "But as your record producer, he wants you on the road all the time."

"I know," Lily says.

"Besides, being on the road doesn't make you an unfit mother. Daisy stays with me. It's not like she stays alone and sleeps on a park bench."

Lily hesitates again. Even when she was a girl, I could tell when she was keeping something from me, and this is one of those times.

"Lily McAllister, what aren't you telling me?" I look at Lily and then Sadie, who lowers her eyes as if the two of them are in cahoots. I've never known Sadie to keep anything from me.

"Mama, leave it alone," Lily says. Now she is the one reaching for calmness.

I put my hands on my hips as we stand eye to eye. "Tell me," I say. Rufus looks up at me as if I might start growling any second.

Lily and Sadie exchange a look, and suddenly I realize what's going on. Instead of conniving something, they are protecting me. I see now that this secret has love wrapped around it. Until now, I didn't realize secrets could work that way.

My defenses drop. "I appreciate what you're trying to do," I say to them. "But it's best that you tell me the truth."

"Jerry told his lawyer about Bee," Lily says.

It takes me a few moments to realize what she's saying.

"So Bee and I are unsavory characters? Is that what you're telling me?"

"Mama, I'm so sorry. People are so stupid sometimes."

I let out a scream that sounds more like a groan. I want to pace out in the yard like an angry rooster, stir up some dirt, and peck Jerry's eyes out.

"I know, Mama. It's awful."

"Has he always felt that way about me?" I ask.

"He's always been jealous of how much power you have over me."

"Me? Power over you?" I let out a gritty laugh. "Since when do I have power?"

"Oh, Mama. You do. You just don't see it."

We sit together on the bottom step, putting our best thinking caps on, as Bee used to say.

Aunt Sadie has been a silent witness to all that's going on. She sits above us now in Mama's rocker. I turn to look at her and notice a weariness I haven't seen before. Drama is harder to bear as you age. I know this for a fact.

"What do you think we should do?" I ask Sadie.

She looks thoughtful. "I think you and Lily should go get her."

"Go get her?" I say.

Lily and I exchange a look as though in disbelief that we didn't think of this ourselves.

"If we do that, we need a strategy," Lily says.

"Do you need to call your lawyer again?" I ask.

"He's useless," she says, appearing deep in thought.

A lone lightning bug sparkles in the white oak nearby as though carrying a message of hope. Later this evening, hundreds will glitter in the trees like Christmas lights. Every night we've been here Daisy and I have watched their magical display from the porch.

"No one gets to tell me whether or not I can spend time with my granddaughter," I say.

Sadie and Lily look at me, their surprise turning to smiles.

"Do you want to drive, or shall I?" I say to Lily. "We'll come up with a plan on the way."

"Let's go get her," Lily says.

We stand and take the groceries into the kitchen, where Lily prepares roast beef sandwiches to take with us, and Aunt Sadie makes us a thermos of coffee. It is nine o'clock on a Saturday night, and we are about to drive to Nashville. I could call Daisy and tell her the plan, but if Jerry answers, he may figure out that something is up.

We're coming, Daisy, I tell her. *We'll be there in a couple of hours.*

Earlier, I told Bee about Jerry coming to get Daisy. I call her again, since I promised to keep her informed. She gets quiet when I say that Lily and I are driving to Nashville to rescue Daisy.

"What is it?" I ask her.

"This feels dangerous, Lou."

Now it is my turn to get quiet. "We've got to do something, Bee. Listen, I need to go."

"Wait," she says. "What can I do to help? I feel powerless over here."

I pause. I don't tell her that Jerry has used us as a reason for Lily to lose custody. That would break Bee's heart.

"Why don't you go and sit in front of Jerry's house in case we need you," I say. Lily tells me the address, and I give it to Bee.

"I wish I could get Daisy a message that I'll be right outside," Bee says.

I give her the phone number, too, but tell her not to use it unless there is an emergency. We don't want Jerry to catch on.

She agrees that this makes sense. "Even if I just go over there, it's better than sitting here doing nothing," Bee says.

"Exactly," I say, "and if we need reinforcements, you'll be there."

She agrees.

TWO HOURS LATER, we enter Jerry's upscale neighborhood. Lily pulls in front of a sizeable red-brick mansion surrounded by a brick wall. A gate stretches across the front, but luckily, it is open. On the street, Bee waits in her car. Lily stops behind her and flashes her lights as though we are in a scene of a Hollywood thriller. Are the good guys here in time? Will the bad guy escape?

Bee gets out of her car and appears to be traveling incognito. She wears a sweatshirt, jeans, and a ball cap pulled low, her hair pulled back in a rubber band. We exchange hugs, sealing a conspirators' bond, despite the dismal reality that we are rescuing Daisy from a predator, her father.

"Let's do this," Lily says.

"Do what?" Bee asks.

We both look at Lily.

"I'm just going to reason with him," she says, "and if that doesn't work, I'll threaten him."

Bee and I exchange a look, maybe both thinking that this is the worst plan in history.

"Don't worry," she says. "I've got tricks up my sleeve."

"Tricks up your sleeve?" Bee asks.

"Tricks up my sleeve," she repeats.

The three of us get in Lily's car and drive through the large black iron gate. The drive is circular, allowing for people to be dropped off in front. Lily parks the car just beyond the door and turns off the engine.

"No lugging groceries up a hill here," I say, imagining that the kitchen is all of fifty feet away.

"I doubt they even go shopping for themselves," Bee says. "The housekeeper probably does it."

"He's done quite well, it seems," I say.

"Because of me," Lily says. "I'm his biggest client."

I suddenly fear for her, but we've got to get Daisy out of there. "You ready?" I ask her.

"Almost," she says.

She pulls down the visor and looks into the mirror. After applying fresh lipstick, she fixes her hair. It is eleven thirty. However, the lights are still on downstairs. My insides flutter, as though my secret sense is waking up from a long sleep and sensing danger. I remind myself that this isn't a drug den in a poor neighborhood but the home of a wealthy music producer. An executive who unfortunately has a lot of powerful friends who look out for one another.

My second thoughts give birth to third ones. Every few seconds, I look into the rearview mirror expecting Jerry to walk up and ask us why we're loitering in his driveway.

"Maybe this is a bad idea," I say.

"Too late now," Lily says. "I'm going in." She steps outside. Before closing the door, she leans down and asks: "How do I look?"

"Like a million bucks," I say.

"Good. Jerry likes money." She winks at me, but her smile is laced with jitters.

The doorbell echoes through the large house. I look to the upstairs windows, wondering which bedroom is Daisy's.

Help is on the way, I tell her.

The door opens, and Jerry's surprise is evident. Thankfully, he invites Lily in.

CHAPTER THIRTY-EIGHT

Daisy

At my father's house, I can stay up until midnight if I want to. It is his wife who goes to bed early, nine thirty, as though it is always a school night. It is almost eleven thirty. For the last hour I have written in my diary everything that happened today. I never miss Nashville when I leave, so it is odd how much I miss Katy's Ridge.

The house is quiet. The door opens, and my father steps inside. The suddenness of his appearance sends a shudder through me. I didn't lock my door, and I chastise myself for not thinking. In the daytime, it is easy to forget nighttime happenings.

It is my father who locks the door behind him. A clear, distinct click. He steps into the room and stops at the end of my bed. I sit against the bed frame, a pillow behind me. My breathing grows shallow, jagged, and I don't look up from my diary. Maybe if I don't look up, he will go away.

For a solid minute, he doesn't speak. He isn't angry like he was in Katy's Ridge, but I know he is here for a reason. He sits on the

bed next to me, the mattress lowering with his weight. My body stiffens. I hold my breath. I feel upside down. Unclear which way is the sky and which is earth. I keep writing. If I keep writing, maybe I will be able to right myself.

Seconds later, the doorbell rings. I exhale. The spell suddenly broken, my father leaves my room. As soon as I hear his footsteps on the stairs, I jump out of bed and lock the door. My heart beats as though it is running all the way to Katy's Ridge, where life is more simple and safe.

Voices drift up the stairs. I try to make out who it is, grateful that they broke the spell. I go to my front window and open it, gasping my surprise. Gran and Bee are below my window. They look up. Bee waves, and Gran smiles despite the worry etched onto her forehead.

My fear vanishes. I smile. "What are you two doing here?" I ask in a loud whisper.

"We've come to rescue you," Gran says.

She isn't your typical knight on a white horse, but I'll take it. Unfortunately, my bedroom doesn't have any trees to shimmy down.

I ask who is talking to my father, and they say it is my mom.

"Mom's here?"

Gran nods.

I narrow my eyes to hear the voices better. But I can't make out what my mom is saying. My father raises his voice to get my mom to back down. I can't make out his words, either, but he is the type to threaten if he doesn't get his way. All of a sudden, there is another female voice, and I realize that Kathleen has joined them in the living room.

This should be interesting, I say to myself.

"What's happening?" Gran says from below.

I shrug, thinking that this is maybe one time when the gesture is appropriate.

"Pack your bags," Gran says.

"Why?" I say.

"If our plan works, you'll be going back with us."

I wonder if this is possible. I can't imagine how my mom will talk my father into letting me go back to Katy's Ridge. The one thing he told me on the drive here was that he wasn't going to let my mom win. Ever.

With a sudden shudder, I flash on him coming into my room. I've got to get out of here tonight. No matter what.

Following Gran's suggestion, I grab my things, putting them in my backpack for the second time today. A feeling of hope comes over me. I smile at the girl in the bathroom mirror, her fate still unknown.

The voices downstairs get loud again. Three voices.

When I go back to the window, Gran suggests I sneak downstairs.

I tell her I will try. Bee holds up crossed fingers, wishing me luck.

Earlier today Sadie, Gran, and I sat on the bench by the lake. Three generations of McAllisters together. A tribe of strong women. Sturdy stock. I remind myself that I am a McAllister, too. A thought that suddenly means something to me. I stand straighter and sling my backpack over my left shoulder.

When I open the door, the voices get louder. I freeze like a rabbit seeing the fox. Unable to move, I tell the rabbit part of myself that everything will be okay and that I will be safe soon. I think of Gran and Bee outside waiting for me. With renewed courage, I inch my way downstairs.

"Who do you think you are?" my father says to my mom.

"I'm Daisy's mother, that's who I am, and don't you forget it." Mom sounds strong.

Halfway down the stairs, no one has noticed me.

"Get out of my house," Kathleen says to my mom. Kathleen

stands closest to the door, her arms folded across her chest. She is wearing a fancy bathrobe covering her equally elegant nightgown and matching gold slippers. I hug the rail so she won't see me. She looks younger than my mom, even though my mom isn't that old.

"I'm not leaving until I have my daughter," my mom says from the living room.

"We'll see what the police have to say about that." My father walks over to the telephone.

I stop mid-step, wondering if my father would try to stop me if I started running. I need to get closer to the door.

"Jerry, if you call the police I swear to God you will live to regret it," my mom says.

He chuckles and picks up the phone anyway.

"I can ruin you in this town, Jerry, simply by telling the truth. If it's me against you, I have more people who will believe me than you do."

He laughs. "You exaggerate your importance."

Mom pauses, and I can almost feel her desperation. "Does Kathleen know about your latest girlfriend?" she asks.

Putting down the phone, my father looks at his wife, whose expression appears to sour like a glass of milk out in the full-day sun.

"She's lying," my father says to Kathleen. But Kathleen's expression sours even more.

Whether truth or lie, Mom's warning has the effect she intended. My father has weakened. At least momentarily.

"We also have proof of what you did to Daisy," my mom says.

"Daisy?" Kathleen's eyes narrow.

"This is none of your business," my father says to her.

Kathleen turns to go to her bedroom upstairs. She sees me. I expect her to tattle that I've been listening. Instead we exchange a look that holds more kinship than hatred. When she passes me on the stairs, she lowers her head, as though she knows more than she

is saying. Was she aware of my father coming into my room at night? Moments later, she slams her bedroom door, clearly for my father's benefit, given the forcefulness of the slam.

Aware that I have forgotten something, I make my way back upstairs to get the four cassette tapes hidden in the top of my closet. Proof. They will do me no good if my father is the one who finds them. I quickly put the tapes in the top of my backpack, as well as the small notepad with the list of dates that document the cassettes.

It would have never occurred to me to make tapes if I had not been recording myself reading sections from *Island of the Blue Dolphins* for an oral book report. The recorder was right there in the top drawer of my nightstand, the microphone easy to hide.

I sneak downstairs again, out of sight of my parents still arguing in the living room. My father accuses my mom of blackmail.

"I'll be finding another record producer, too," my mom says.

He laughs at her again, but something is underneath his laughter that wasn't there before. Does he know that she has won?

Focused on the front door, I walk briskly downstairs.

"I'll be out in the car," I say to Mom, catching a glimpse of my father's surprise as I close the door behind me.

Once outside, I run to Gran and Bee. All smiles, they give me hugs. We wait on Mom, practically holding our breath. She finally steps outside with a thumbs-up, and we hurriedly get into the car. We drive through the gate and stop long enough for Bee to get into her car and leave. Mom drives, with Gran in the passenger seat and me in the back seat. My fast breathing finally slows.

Above the Nashville skyline, a full moon watches. I imagine the moonlight sparkling on top of the lake next to Aunt Sadie's house. When I ask where we are going, Gran says, "Home," and within minutes, we are on the interstate heading toward Katy's Ridge.

CHAPTER THIRTY-NINE

Forty Years Later

Wildflower

At ninety-four, my two great childhood fears have long been outgrown: dying young and Johnny Monroe. Johnny has been dead now for almost three-quarters of a century, and I did not die young. Far from it. My only regret is that I wasted so much precious time worrying that I might.

After Mama's death, I moved back to Katy's Ridge and lived in the old house. Aunt Sadie lived with me in the last years of her life. A more natural death, I cannot imagine. One evening she was laughing and celebrating her ninety-ninth birthday with family, and the next morning she simply didn't wake up. A smile graced her face as though all her questions were answered in that moment of passage.

"Mama, you need anything?" Lily stands by the bedroom door, a cup of steaming tea in her hand.

It is hard to believe Lily is eighty-one now, and Daisy is fifty-three. I still remember them so clearly as girls.

I chuckle.

"What's so funny?" she asks, handing me the tea.

"I was thinking about how we pretend to be all grown up, but at the same time, we are still the girls we used to be."

She smiles. "Well, that's a good thing, isn't it?"

"I hope so."

To my continued surprise, once Lily had her fill with traveling, she came back to Katy's Ridge to settle, opting for a simpler life, if there is such a thing these days. Lily now lives at Sadie's place by the lake and has a few horses and a small recording studio.

Lily admires the hummingbird quilt that I recently returned to my bed. After Mama died, I took it off and preserved it until now. Every night the past tucks me in and warms me. In my imagination, I can still see Mama and Aunt Sadie sitting together at the kitchen table, collecting piece after piece and sewing the squares. Somehow, it seems they stitched me together in the process.

I am not a person who stays in bed, but more and more I feel like lingering. Some mornings I find myself wanting to stay with my dreams instead of getting on with regular life. Not because I dream of flying or exploring the fantastical, but because, more often than not, they deliver scenes from when I was younger. Things I had forgotten. Things like the smile on Daddy's face when he opened one of my homemade presents as if I had given him jewels from Buckingham Palace. Other times, I remember the rhythm of Mama's broom sweeping the front porch. Or the smell of an apple pie baking in the oven, the juices bubbling with cinnamon. Last night I dreamed I was looking down at Lily as an infant in her crib as she slept, my love for her practically busting me wide open.

"Daisy will be here later this afternoon," Lily tells me. "She's bringing the girls."

Saturdays are for family time. Lily always comes over and makes my breakfast. Most Saturdays, she makes biscuits just like Mama used to make. Sometimes we'll have them with eggs and bacon and strawberry preserves from the pantry. Preserves that Sadie made herself the last year of her life. Other times we'll eat biscuits hot out of the oven with real butter and honey from the Sectors' beehives.

While I was lingering this morning, I remembered Aunt Sadie's call to me that long-ago morning when I was still living in Nashville. Daisy was staying with me for the summer. Life changed after that. Life does that sometimes. Changes in an instant, or over a single summer. That summer, I remembered what was truly important: family and a sense of place.

"You need some help getting up, Mama?" Lily asks.

"I'm not *that* old," I say to her, even though sometimes I feel like I am.

When one arm refuses to find its sleeve, she helps me put on my robe. Then she follows me to the bathroom, the old wooden floors singing their song to us along the way. I stand in front of the mirror over the sink and look at the wrinkled face looking back at me. I smile at the old girl that is now me, standing alongside my gracefully aging daughter.

"You're beautiful, Mama," Lily says.

"So are you, sweetheart." I take a mental snapshot, not wanting to forget us standing here together side by side. Mother and daughter. I wonder if she is doing the same.

"You ready for breakfast?" Lily asks.

My eyes widen for her benefit, though my appetite isn't what it used to be. We walk arm in arm to the kitchen, and I sit at the oak table, which is nicked with memories, some of which are older than I am.

Lily puts a plate of breakfast in front of me and then sits at the table. She always eats earlier than me.

"I'm feeling nostalgic this morning," I say to her.

"Are you?"

My white hair, captured in a loose braid, crosses over my shoulder, reminding me that while I wasn't looking, I became an elder.

"Eat, Mama." Lily pushes my plate closer.

"You were a good cook even as a girl," I say. "Not to mention, you could run like the wind, and had a singing voice that brought tears to the eyes of anyone who listened."

"Thanks, Mama." She kisses me on the cheek.

Lily's singing career was still going strong when she walked away from it a decade ago. But she continues to write songs. Every now and again, she attends an awards show, and I'll watch it on the television in the living room.

"You longed to travel back then," I begin again, "and you were in love with Crow Sector. Secretly, of course."

Lily looks past me as though remembering. "I never thought for an instant that we would end up back here in tiny Katy's Ridge," she says.

"Neither did I," I say. "But *never say never*, as the saying goes."

"Do you ever wish we hadn't left in the first place?" she asks.

"Not at all," I say. "We needed to get you to Nashville so important people could hear you sing. You might still be unknown if we had stayed in Katy's Ridge."

I think of Bee, who died four years ago. We talked on the telephone every day, and I was with her when she died, our friendship as strong as ever. After Mama's funeral, Bee never returned to Katy's Ridge. But all those people who rejected us are dead and gone now. Dead people are easier to forgive. If I've learned anything after living so long, it is that we're all, in our own way, doing the best we can. Of course, that's sad in some cases. The other thing I've learned is that frightened, closed-minded people

are everywhere—north, south, east, and west—not just in the Appalachian Mountains.

"If we hadn't moved to Nashville, I probably would have married Crow and had six kids and a bunch of grandkids by now," Lily says.

"Hard to imagine," I say.

One child was enough for Lily, as it was for me. Of everyone in our family, Daisy is the most maternal, loving every age and stage. Her two daughters are teenagers now.

"Mama, can I ask you a serious question?"

"Of course," I say, taking a bite of biscuit for her benefit.

"Do you have any regrets?"

"Oh my, plenty of them," I say, without even thinking.

"Really?" Lily's surprise surprises me.

"Of course," I say. "I'm not sure how you avoid regrets in this day and time."

"Like what?" she says, looking genuinely curious.

I ponder my answer. "Well, I wish I hadn't stayed in Nashville as long as I did after your career got underway. I could have had more time with Mama before she died."

"But that's hindsight, right?"

"I guess."

"Anything else?" she asks.

"There's about a thousand times I wish I'd listened to my secret sense when it gave me a nudge," I begin. "But the truth is, we have very little control over what happens. It has taken me a lifetime to realize that. Although I do believe that we can choose to love life instead of fear it."

I think of Daisy and that dramatic summer when the truth came out about her father. She spent every summer with me afterward and came back for numerous holidays. When it came time, she went to Vanderbilt and got a master's degree and finally a PhD in counseling. She married Adam Sector, and they built a house at

the edge of June and Horatio's property. Adam and Daisy have the best marriage I have ever witnessed. Daisy has a private practice in downtown Rocky Bluff, and she also has clients who drive all the way from Nashville to see her. Thankfully, Rocky Bluff has come alive again and has the cutest little downtown area that even tourists want to visit.

Everything rises, and everything falls, I think. *And then it rises again.*

"Lovely breakfast," I tell Lily, though I've left half of it on my plate.

Turning my attention to my morning chores, I rise to put cat food in the bowl by the back door for the latest orange tabby to grace our kitchen. Her name is Pumpkin Spice, and I am convinced that she is a distant descendant of the original Pumpkin from when I was a girl.

With the breakfast dishes washed and put away, Lily helps me gather eggs from the chicken coop. Then we fill the two bird feeders in the back before sweeping the front porch like Mama always did. Finally Lily and I walk to the mailbox and back to get my exercise for the day.

Saturday rituals with Lily are something I look forward to.

"The day I can no longer walk this hill to my house is the day I'll be ready to die," I tell her.

"You say that every Saturday, Mama."

"Well, it's true."

"I know," she says with a smile.

When we return to the house, it is time for a nap. I take two short naps a day now, one after breakfast and my chores, and one after lunch.

"My naps are rehearsals for the final curtain," I tell Lily.

She laughs. "You're getting lots of practice then."

The hardest part of being this old is all the people who get off the stage before you. I think of all those original characters in the

play that is my family drama. For those of us lucky enough to go three acts, it seems an unusually long touring engagement at times. I still miss Mama, and of course Daddy, and Aunt Sadie. Jo is my only sister left. After Daniel died, she moved in with Nellie, who lives in downtown Memphis. Nellie is a marine biologist who studies rivers and is currently unmarried.

"Wake me up if I'm asleep when the girls get here," I say to Lily.

She says she will and pulls the hummingbird quilt over me, tucking in the corners. Daisy had her girls late. She was almost forty and had trouble getting pregnant, so it's hard not to think of them as miracles.

As soon as I close my eyes, sleep comes, as well as the dreams. Daddy plays a song on the banjo that makes Mama smile, and she leans back on the sofa, her face relaxing into a happy life. Daddy's rich voice fills the room, his fingers softly picking a tune on his banjo.

"I'm very proud of you, Wildflower," he says to me in the dream. I let his words and music fill me.

When I wake up, Daisy is sitting in Mama's old rocker by my bed.

"Hello, sweetheart," I say.

"Hi, Gran." She smiles.

"You know, I still remember when you were thirteen and sitting up with Mama in that old rocking chair."

"Being thirteen is something I try to forget." Daisy laughs a short laugh, sounding just like her mom.

"Where are the girls?" I ask.

"They took a walk up the old cemetery trail, but they'll be back soon," Daisy says. "How are you feeling, Gran?"

A person can tell when they are cherished. The feeling is mutual. After that summer, when she told me her secret, we became close and remained close.

"Any day aboveground is a good day," I say, thinking of Victor.

This was his saying before it was mine, and it always made us laugh.

Victor is the latest of my friends to go. He died six months ago. I put a roll of peppermint lifesavers in his coffin. We spent many evenings together playing Scrabble and talking about old times— one of the things old-timers do best. I saw his sister, Mary Jane, at his funeral. We barely spoke, our friendship needing more than forgiveness to revive it.

Often, Matt Monroe joined Victor and me in the evenings. The three of us became close friends over the years. I would like to think that Matt and I did our part to heal the past. Matt and Lily have become friends as well. Sadie taught them how to make her blackberry spirits before she died, and they have continued the tradition out behind Lily's recording studio.

Lily enters my bedroom. "Are you ready to move outside, Mama?"

I climb out from under the covers, my body voicing its complaints. "I wonder if when we die we toss off these old bodies like hummingbird quilts."

Daisy and Lily look at me.

"I may use that in a song someday," Lily says. She starts to hum as if already creating the song. Daisy and I exchange a look that says, *There she goes again.*

"I remember this quilt," Daisy says, straightening it on my bed.

"It made sense to bring it out again," I say.

"It's beautiful." She studies the stitching, admiring the skill put into it. One of Sadie's quilts ended up at the Smithsonian, donated by a wealthy woman in Nashville who had bought it from Sadie in the 1950s.

Meanwhile, Lily tries to tame my hair and then gives up, pronouncing me beautiful despite my imperfections.

The three of us make our way to the porch. It is a glorious summer day in the Tennessee mountains. One of those days when

you realize why you live here. The honeysuckle is in bloom, along with the wild roses, their scents competing as though in a contest to see which is the sweetest. The morning fog is a distant memory, and the day is crisp and clear.

Heather and Holly walk up the hill carrying two bunches of wildflowers, freshly picked. Youth is an elixir to me these days. It's hard to believe I used to be as young and vibrant as the twins are at thirteen, the age their mother was when everything changed.

When they give me the flowers, I am overcome by the beauty. Orange tiger lilies mix with purple irises, sprigs of lavender, and white wild roses. Like their mom, they call me Gran, though I am actually their great-gran. To keep things straight, Lily is called Nana.

The girls exchange a look, pleased with themselves. Heather has hair to her waist, and Holly's is short. Heather is much more outgoing than Holly, whose shyness is infamous in the family.

"Can I re-braid your hair?" Holly asks.

I nod. It is another Saturday ritual that sustains me.

With a gentle touch, Holly releases the old braid, shakes my hair out and brushes it, and then begins anew. She weaves together the strands.

"Did you bring your instruments?" I ask.

"Of course," Heather says. "We know how you love it when we play."

From the time they could walk, Heather and Holly have played musical instruments. We found Daddy's banjo in the attic, and Lily had it restrung and restored so Heather could play it. Holly plays the fiddle or violin, depending on where you're from. Their father is very devoted and has taken them all over these mountains to learn folk tunes from the elders in the tradition, and they have become quite good.

Heather finishes my hair and takes a photograph with her phone to post on the World Wide Web. My ancient brain refuses

to take in these newfangled electronics. We didn't have a telephone until I was grown, nor did we have indoor plumbing. A distant banjo plays in my memory. It would be just like Daddy to show up for our Saturday concert.

The eighty-second anniversary of Daddy's death is in three months. Even this many years later, I never forget the anniversary. We all have signposts in our lives of painful and celebratory things. It is the price we pay for living.

No one can escape it, I hear Aunt Sadie say.

I smile.

"I heard that, too," Daisy says, rocking in the chair that Mama always sat in when she stopped long enough to rest.

"You heard that?" I say.

She nods.

I sometimes forget that Daisy hears voices from the past.

Heather and Holly tune their banjo and fiddle. They sit on the top step of the porch, instruments in hand. Like their grandmother Lily, they don't have a moment's hesitation about sharing their gifts.

Heather starts first, picking out a tune, and Holly joins in. Pumpkin Spice jumps in my lap, and I pet her, closing my eyes and letting myself drift away on the music. Lily sings along, a melody without words, and at this moment, an emotion fills me that must be joy. I picture the fullness of the river and the expansiveness of the forest around me. Every note is alive, just like every inch of this mountain is alive.

When I open my eyes, Daisy is watching me. I wonder what she's listening to besides the music. But then I instantly know. My secret sense has been generous lately, having forgiven me for all those years I didn't pay attention. Together, we remember the day she found the treasure.

. . .

I SIT at the kitchen table, listening to the faint sounds of Daisy's shovel breaking ground. It has been a week since we returned from picking her up at her father's house. Then the shoveling stops. Seconds later, the kitchen door opens, and Daisy rushes in, her eyes alive with excitement.

"I found it!" she says.

She drops a metal box onto the table, leaving a nick on the table to remind us for years to come. It never occurred to me that she might actually find something as a result of all that digging.

"What is it?" I say. The box is rusty and covered with dirt, the size of two large cigar boxes. It has a latch, but no lock.

"It's your daddy's," she says. "Before Granny McAllister died he came to her bedside and reminded her of the metal box he buried out in the backyard. I think he wanted me to hear him so that I could unbury it."

"Daddy told you?"

Daisy nods, not taking her eyes from the box. "Should I open it?" She looks up to get my response.

"Well, I sure wouldn't do all that digging and then not *open it," I say with a smile.*

Daisy pauses, biting her lip.

"I don't think I ever told you how Daddy loved to send us girls on scavenger hunts," I begin. "Sometimes he would spend an entire Saturday afternoon hiding things all over this mountain for my sisters and me to find. As the youngest, I rarely won, but I had a great time scavenging for things."

We look at the box.

"In a way, it makes sense that Daddy would bury something for us to find years later," I say. "It also makes sense that he would save something for a rainy day even when it was already pouring outside."

Daisy nods.

"Well, open it," I say.

She wipes her hands on her jeans. At first the lid refuses to budge, but Daisy gets a butter knife from the kitchen drawer and runs it along the edges of the dirty latch.

"Got it," she says, slowly lifting the lid.

The contents are carefully wrapped in a piece of waxed cotton. Her eyes widen again, taking it all in. I step closer to see. She carefully lifts each item from the box, looks at each one, and then hands it to me.

Inside is a stack of letters between Mama and Daddy, from when they were courting and newly married. A red ribbon is tied around the collection that is in incredibly good shape given it has been buried underground for decades. Only the very edges of the pages have tattered.

Next Daisy hands me a small bag of gold coins. The coins are from Scotland, marked with a symbol of some kind. We giggle and note the heaviness of the leather pouch, marveling at its contents. Underneath the coins is an old deed for a piece of property in Glasgow. We open it and study the signature and date. It is signed by Daddy's father and is dated August 2, 1856.

"What do you think these things are worth?" Daisy asks.

I tell her I have no idea, but that we can find out.

From the bottom of the box, she pulls out more letters, written to me and my sisters on our twelfth birthdays. Handwritten notes from Daddy. Daisy hands me mine. As I read the letter, tears blur the words before me.

~

TO MY DEAR WILDFLOWER, on the occasion of your twelfth birthday.

I am watching you bloom into a young woman, and I am so pleased by what I see. You are a kind and thoughtful person, full of curiosity and wit. Sometimes, I can't believe you are my daughter, because you are so much more than I deserve. Watching you grow up has meant the world to me. I remember your first steps as you held your mama's hand, and I remember watching you recite "I Wandered Lonely as a Cloud" from memory and with such feeling in front of your entire school.

I have always been so proud of you. My beautiful, courageous Wildflower, I have no doubt that you will do great things with your life, and

you will do them with great enthusiasm and love. The world is so lucky to
have you, as I have been.
    Love,
    Daddy

DAISY and I exchange another look as we return from our journey to the past. The treasure amounted to enough to build a small library in Katy's Ridge, where Sweeney's Country Store used to be. The treasure to me that summer was Daddy's letter. But I am convinced the real fortune Daisy found in the summer of 1982 was herself, and her family.

In many ways, Daisy's fortune has been my fortune, too. If we hadn't come back to Katy's Ridge that summer, and if she hadn't found the courage to tell me her secret, I might never have left Nashville and come home.

Nodding to the melody, deep contentment settles over me. The old tune mingles with birdsong, as sunlight and shadows dance in the trees. Someday, I will toss off this old body like a hummingbird quilt. My spirit will walk outside and be greeted by all those who have gone before me. I imagine Daddy as a young man, and Mama, too, and my sisters and Daniel and Nathan and Aunt Sadie along with all her beloved dogs, as well as Pumpkin the cat, and his orange tabby descendants that we came to love. Reunited, it will be as if everything that happened on this old porch has been heaven, after all.